THE COMPLETE EMILY BERNAL TRILOGY

A WHAT DOESN'T KILL YOU TEXAS-TO-NEW MEXICO ROMANTIC MYSTERY SET

PAMELA FAGAN HUTCHINS

SKIPJACK PUBLISHING

FREE PFH EBOOKS

HEAVEN TO BETSY (EMILY BERNAL #1)

A WHAT DOESN'T KILL YOU TEXAS-TO-NEW MEXICO ROMANTIC MYSTERY

ONE

I wedged myself up to the bar between an urban cowboy and a sequined octogenarian with a cigarette dangling from her lips. *Is that a gun in your holster or are you just glad to see me?* I shied away from Little Joe Cartwright or Brett Maverick or whoever the heck he thought he was while also trying to avoid the business end of Grandma's cancer stick. I looked up at myself in the mirror behind the premium liquor bottles, a head shorter than the cowboy and a head taller than the little old lady—and a damn sight more harried looking than either of them.

Why did everything have to be so hard? All I wanted was one teensy-tiny little drink. Well, that wasn't completely true. I also wanted as far away from my mother as I could get. Siberia-far, or maybe even Pluto-far. Oklahoma City-far would do in a pinch. Across the lobby from her in a hotel—which now called itself a Wyndham but which everyone in Amarillo would forever know as the Ambassador—wasn't nearly far enough. Especially since we were there for the wedding reception of my high school boyfriend, Scott, to his third wife—who was nineteen and pregnant.

I raised a finger and leaned across the wooden bar, trying to catch the attention of the bartender. Too late, I felt the wetness. I looked down. I'd plopped my breasts into someone else's spilled drink. Great. Just then, the bartender's blue-shadowed eyes swept over me.

"Virgin mojito, please," I said.

All I got was the back of her orange hair, teased so high it looked like cotton candy, Halloween-style. I grabbed a fistful of napkins from a dispenser and mopped up Lake Titicaca—the bar top and the underside of my rack. At least I'd worn a simple black dress tonight, so it wouldn't show. Much.

"Need some help, Blondie?" Little Joe asked. His voice had a rumbly drawl to it—not quite Texan but close—which I might have found pleasant if he hadn't called me by my hair color.

I studied him. He was tall, well over six feet—at least with his boots on —and a good ten years older than me, judging by his crow's feet. Age, or was it weathering? My eyes slipped down to his boots. The leather was worn, but cared-for, with a few dark lines of oil tracking scratch marks and scuffs. I flicked my eyes quickly back up, but not so fast that they didn't take in his narrow hips circled by a brown leather belt and his flat stomach behind the silver and turquoise buckle, the deep chest, and the wide set of his shoulders. His upper lip looked lighter than the rest of his face, like he normally wore a mustache and had just recently shaved it off, and what-ever had weathered his face didn't hide his great cheekbones or the lone dimple to the left of his half-smiling mouth. Maybe Little Joe wasn't a city slicker after all.

Willie Nelson crooned in the background. He was a regular artist on the soundtrack to my life—my heroes have always been cowboys. Yeah, Willie, mine too, until they weren't. Back in another life, I'd had a weak-ness for Little Joe's type. I couldn't help it, really. I was the daughter of a steer-wrestling father. And now it wasn't just cowboys that had let me down, but the male species in general. So, did I need some help, from *this cowboy*?

"I don't think—"

"What're ya drinkin', sir?" the bartender asked.

Steam whistled from my ears like I was some fancy-schmancy espresso machine. Oh sure, ignore the woman and bring the guy another round. I wheeled toward the cowboy, ready to let fly a string of invectives about him and the barmaid and my whole miserable life in general, but I saw no drinks in front of him. Maybe it wasn't another round. I clamped down on my ire.

He looked me in the eye for a split second—long enough for an unwel-come frisson of pure animal response to unleash itself in my lady parts—then turned back to her.

"Bourbon neat. And a virgin mojito."

Spit in a well bucket, as my father used to say, before he left us for the circuit rodeos one year and never came back. Hell, maybe he was still saying it, somewhere else, wherever it was he'd gotten off to.

"That's really not necessary," I said.

Little Joe flexed his jaw and his lips twitched. "You looked like you had your hands full."

I wanted to tell him to keep his eyes further north, but thought better of it. Instead, I ignored his words and retrieved five dollars from my clutch. Holding one end of the bill, I wafted it toward him.

"Thank you for ordering my drink," I said in my most saccharine voice.

He nodded and took the money. As he straightened it and slid it into his battered, brown leather wallet, he said, "Name's Jack. Jack Holden."

"Emily Bernal." I scrubbed the dry bar with my pile of napkins until the bartender handed me my mojito. No fresh mint, so basically just a lemonade. I sighed. "Well, thanks again, and have a nice night."

He touched the brim of his gray felt cowboy hat.

Before I'd turned away from Jack, my mother's voice trilled in my ear like three-inch acrylic nails scratching across a chalkboard.

"There you are, Emily."

I tried to hide my shudder. "Yes, but I was just headed to the ladies' room."

She beamed at me, reflecting a vision of what I would look like in twenty-five years, if genetics trumped will: Indecently long legs made even longer by stilettos, better-than-medium height, round blue eyes, and dewy, Mary Kay-slathered skin going crepe-y at the edges. She'd fit her trim body—thicker through the middle—in a snug dress slightly less long than was proper for her age, and was wearing the best blonde that money could buy from the shelves of Walmart. Trailer park meets the Southern church lady—that was my mother.

She opened her mouth to torture me. "I was just telling Doug Munroe what a wonderful paralegal you are," she said, "and he wants to meet you. His law firm is really the best in town, and—"

"I'm not even sure if I'm staying," I said. "And I have a job." *And the beginnings of a killer headache*, I thought.

"A job in *Dallas*. If Rich isn't going to do conversion therapy, then you've really got to—"

I pushed back from the bar and flashed her a megawatt smile. Before I could answer, though, Jack's voice interrupted. "Agatha Phelps, always good to see you."

My mother took notice of Jack, tilting her head to the side, and shaking it.

"Oh my, if it isn't the infamous Jack Holden," she said. "What trouble are you causing tonight?"

He wiped a smile from his face. "I have a question for you."

She twinkled. "What is it?"

Jack's voice dropped lower, and Mother leaned in. I tried not to. "What's the difference between erotic and kinky?"

"I'm sure I don't know." She raised her brows. "And I can't think why any decent man should." She leaned closer, twinkled brighter.

"Erotic uses a feather and kinky uses the whole chicken." He smiled on the dimpled side of his face only. "And you know it's only part of my job."

My mother giggled like a tween girl. "That's the only reason I'll forgive your manners."

I shook my head. "I'll come find you later, Mother." They both looked at me, my mother's eyes wide like she'd forgotten I was there.

I studied my gap-toothed smile in the bathroom mirror, it and me in a gilded frame, and fluffed my bangs. They needed a spray of dry shampoo and blast of Aqua Net, neither of which I had with me. I turned to the side and smoothed my hand over my stomach. At least there was no baby bump, yet, and my dress was nearly dry. I lifted my chest and shoulders. "Put 'em on a shelf, ladies," my pageant coach used to remind us before we went onstage. That was more than twelve years ago, though, and my shelf was a little lower than it used to be.

A woman's voice from behind a stall door crowed, "Did you see Emily Phelps? I can't believe she showed her face tonight."

A second voice snarked from the stall next to her. "I hear she's not woman enough to keep her man."

They both laughed like she was Melissa-flippin'-McCarthy or something.

I picked my drink up from the counter and tossed it at the ground outside the two stalls. Overpriced lemonade splashed its target, eliciting a squeal.

"Woops," I said. "I guess I'm not woman enough to hold my drink either."

Damn, that felt good. I tucked my five-pound clutch under my arm, pushed out the door, and headed for the pool area as fast as I could wobble on my heels. I'd look for my mother later. For now, I just wanted to stand outside the fence around the little pool at the center of the atrium and imagine myself 3000 miles away from all of this pettiness. I wouldn't have a care in the world, and I'd gaze peacefully into the aquamarine ocean off of St. Marcos, the island home of my best friend, Katie. She used to be an attorney at Hailey & Hart, the law firm I probably still worked for in Dallas. Thinking of her in the same breath as I thought of my woes made me feel guilty, though. She'd emailed that morning asking if I'd heard from her husband, Nick, who hadn't come home last night. I hoped Nick was only a big douchebag like my husband, Rich, and not truly missing. I needed to call her. Well, why not now? Or when I got to the pool, anyway. It's not like I wanted to talk to anyone else.

But I had to make it past the happy couple's receiving line—which I'd already been through, thank you very much—before I could stare at the swimming pool. That is, I had to get through the throng of people who probably thought that I regretted giving Scott back his promise ring when I left for Texas Tech—a throng of very familiar faces, all of them reacting visibly at the sight of mine. A former neighbor, from back when we lived in town. A classmate I hadn't seen since graduation from AHS. Some kid I'd babysat when I was twelve. I fended off each greeting as I braved the gauntlet to the pool, repeating myself into a mantra.

"Oh my goodness!" Lean in, hug without touching bodies. One-handed shoulder-pat three times. "So great to see you. I'm meeting someone, can we catch up later?" Air kiss. "You, too. Bye-bye now!" Keep walking.

Was I as conspicuous as I felt? I tried not to imagine the inevitable whispers in my wake, because, sure as shooting, everyone here knew my business as well as if it had been front-page headline news—above the fold. I tested my face for the confident half-smile I was determined to wear and adjusted the corners of my mouth up ever so slightly.

The chlorine smell of the pool cut through to my cerebral cortex and I sharpened—in a good way. I placed my hands on the black metal top rail of the fence and looked over at the people gathered around the pool at patio tables. It wasn't as crowded as the bar area, but that wasn't saying much. My ex had married another local *and* they'd sprung for an open bar, so almost everyone in town had shown up. But I didn't care if I was alone in the crowd. I didn't care if I was standing in the stripper heels that I'd been forced to borrow from my mother who thought they were high-class. I didn't care if my life was in shambles and my marriage was history. I only cared about the next few good breaths. My eyes found the water, and I sucked in the chemically poisoned air like it was a magic potion. If I could just have about two minutes of this to shock my senses, I might survive the night.

Still breathing deeply, I pulled out my phone, scrolled through my favorites page, and pressed Katie's name. As it rang, I worried about the time difference. I could never remember which time of the year she was two hours later, versus the regular one hour later than me in Texas. Either way, it was only eight thirty here. It would be okay. After three rings, she picked up.

"Emily?"

"Katie! Has Nick shown up? I haven't heard from him at all."

"No, and his plane is missing and the police are no help." Her voice sounded brittle and shrill.

"Are you, um, holding up okay?" She used to have a problem with alcohol. I'd nearly added "sober," but she didn't sound drunk. Just scared.

"I'm not sure. But my in-laws are here—you remember Kurt and Julie?—and our nanny, Ruth. Kurt and I think Nick headed to the Dominican Republic on a case he's working. We're headed there in the morning."

Nick worked as a private investigator, so this didn't sound totally implausible. "I'm praying for you guys."

"Thank you. I was about to try to sleep, not that I'll be able to. How are things with you? Everything good?"

Now was not the time to weigh her down with my problems. I crossed my fingers. "Fine. I'm great, other than worried about you."

"Yeah, you and me both. Thanks for calling."

"I love you."

"I love you, too."

We hung up, and I stood staring at the water, my phone still in my hand. It sounded serious. Nick and Katie had twin baby girls and a preschool-age boy. I closed my eyes and said a short, silent prayer for Nick's safe return, then added, *And help me maintain just a little dignity as I go through all my . . . stuff. Amen.*

A throat cleared beside me, and I jumped.

"So, you're looking for a job?" a man's voice asked.

My eyes, the traitorous little magnets, tracked to the right, following the pull of the sound that I already knew was the voice of Jack, the man formerly known as Little Joe.

"You following me?" I asked.

The dimple twitched. "I do believe I staked my claim here first."

Oh. I didn't have a response to that. I just tried another breath of bleachy air.

"Agatha Phelps is your mother."

I pursed my lips, then answered. "I take it the two of you know each other."

"She roped me into teaching a class on Apache religion and its Mountain Spirits a few weeks ago in an 'Understanding our Neighbor' series on different religions at her church."

I snorted. "I didn't think the Panhandle Believers congregation was into comparative religions."

"Let's just say it felt more like they were gathering information to convert the last of the heathens."

"So why do you go there?"

"I don't." Jack raised an eyebrow at me—the one on the dimple side. "Your mother practically runs the place."

"Tell me about it."

"She talks about you."

The muscles around my eyes and across my forehead tightened up.

Someday, I'd owe half my wrinkles to my mother and the other half to Rich. "That's great."

He cleared his throat. "I'm looking for a legal assistant at my law firm."

I reevaluated his cowboy authenticity again and decided he was still the real thing, just urbanized. I opened my mouth to say I wasn't looking for a job, but what came out was, "What type of law?"

His nice, rumbly voice said, "Criminal defense, mostly."

I shook my head. "No offense, but yuck. I do employment law."

The dimple again, but not so much that it pulled the side of his mouth up.

"Based on your taste in jokes, you'd probably enjoy the sexual harassment cases."

"My clients make your CEO harassment defendants look like they're still wearing training pants."

I remembered flipping through the paper that morning, over dry white bread and black coffee, because that's how we roll at my mother's house. What I recalled was a big criminal case, and quotes from the attorney. What was the name? Had it been Jack Holden? Yes. Yes it had.

"You're that attorney who got the super pimp acquitted last week, aren't you?" I said. "Whose client was the guy who ran the prostitution ring cleverly disguised as hot women delivering pizza in tap pants and bustiers? What do they call guys like him? Marketing geniuses? Or sleazeballs?"

He turned to me and dipped his head, speaking only after an uncomfortably intense and lengthy pause.

"You're that woman whose husband took all her money and left her for a man who pretends to be a woman, aren't you? What do they call that, experimentation? Or a fetish for transvestites?" He asked, sipping his Bourbon.

Boom! A sound like a cannon shook me to my pointy toes, followed by a nanosecond of stunned silence. A woman's scream pierced the air just as a loud, slapping sound reverberated from the surface of the pool. Water splashed up on my dress and I gasped. Jack pushed himself in front of me. There was another moment of profound silence, then noise exploded all around us. I was tucked behind Jack, his arms extended low behind him, on either side of me. I stepped around him to get a view of the pool. A cloud of red was growing in the water around what looked to be a man's torso.

"Well, that's something you don't see every day," Jack said.

I looked up from the grisly scene. The man had fallen from above the pool. My eyes climbed, searching each floor of balconies, moving like one of my grandmother's old Selectric typeballs across a blank page. There! I saw her, three floors up, a gun dangling in her two hands, her black hair pulled back, her white apron tied over her burgundy maid's dress. The shooter.

I leaned in toward Jack and pointed at the woman. "Better hurry, she looks like she needs a lawyer."

TWO

The aroma of fresh-baked cookies and brewing coffee filled the air of the Panhandle Believers Church Sunday school wing the next morning. Watercolor renditions of Jesus with lambs, Jesus handing out loaves, and other well-known biblical scenes (featuring Jesus) adorned the pale blue walls. I walked down the hallway searching for Mother, trying to keep my footsteps quiet. Despite the fact that I was possibly the whitest girl in the Texas Panhandle, I liked to pretend I was an American Indian when I was a child, dressing up like one at Halloween, and hanging on Dad's every word as he taught me to move like an Indian scout. I tiptoed over linoleum floors like Sacajawea now, through unfamiliar territory.

I heard a female voice coming from the room ahead on my left. "Any prayer requests today?"

The respondent stopped me in my tracks. "You all know my daughter is home. Her husband has strayed, in a . . . most unnatural way. I need prayers for Jesus to heal his heart and convert him back to . . . relationships with women . . . with Emily."

The silence after her proclamation didn't last. I heard tsks and hmphs and oh mys.

I ground my teeth, but I didn't make a sound. Thank God I'd decided not to tell my mother my really big secret yet—that Rich had knocked me up before I'd found out about his other life. Never mind that it was practically the Immaculate Conception. Or maybe even a toilet seat conception. Our sex life had died off long before he'd met his boyfriend, except for an occasional drunken grope in the dark. But pregnant by your gay soon-to-be-ex-husband? Yeah, the Sunday school class would have had a field day with that little nugget of information.

"Thank you, Agatha. Anyone else?"

A different woman spoke. "My niece got married last night. Thank you all for coming."

A collective coo rippled through the room.

"Some Mexican woman murdered a man in the middle of the wedding. His body fell in the pool. Sue was standing there when it happened, and bloody water splashed on her shoes and dress."

The women in the room gasped, and the woman lowered her voice.

"She was so traumatized she went home with her mama and didn't leave for her honeymoon this morning. She thinks it's a sign that God doesn't favor her marriage. Please pray for Jesus to heal her heart and return her to her husband. And for that woman who ruined her wedding to be brought to justice."

Someone near the door spoke softly. "In Mexico."

And a voice near her said, "Uh huh."

Several more women asked for prayers for their ill family or relatives in the military, and a few others asked for praise for healing and babies and good fortune. The voice of the woman who had asked for the requests then led them in prayer. I turned to walk away before she got to me, and as I did so, I felt something catch on the floor. I looked down. The loose heel on my favorite brown leather riding boots had caught in a tear in the linoleum. I knew I should have glued it down this morning before I left Mother's house. It had ripped clean off.

"Great," I mumbled before I picked it up and stuffed it in my bulging handbag.

"Hi, Emily," said a male voice, grating and familiar.

I looked up into the face of my high school American history teacher. It was a good thing I'd recognized the voice, because I wouldn't have recognized him by sight. The formerly fastidious and slim man had tripled in size, and his hair had all fallen out on top, leaving a ring of muskrat brown on the sides and back.

"Hello, Mr. Walsh. You look well!" I ignored the fact that he had stopped walking, as if wanting to chat with me. "So sorry," I said. "I have to run."

I walked off, my gait uneven in my heel-less boot. I had to get out of here. This time I didn't employ stealth. I'd promised Mother when I dropped her off earlier that I'd join her for church after I finished my errands—I'd wanted to, even. The faith of my youth had deserted me in my twenties, and I yearned to return to it now that I was in crisis, to take sanctuary in it. To be the twelve-year-old who was baptized during vacation Bible school. The girl who felt real joy in her heart. But Mother had made me seem salacious to her friends here, and it didn't sit well with me. Their whole interaction didn't, really.

"Emily!"

I wasn't surprised to hear my mother's voice behind me. I waited for her to catch up. She had a bright smile on her face, but there was worry in her eyes.

"Yes?"

"Aren't you still joining me for church?"

I looked at the ceiling then back at her. "I don't think so."

"But I told all my friends—"

"Yes, I heard."

She lowered her voice and fussed with the lapel of her sunflower-yellow suit dress. "Where are you going?"

"I don't really know."

"What's wrong?" She grasped my wrist. "Emily, don't be ashamed because of what Rich has done. God loves you."

I pulled my wrist away. "Ashamed? Why would I be ashamed?"

Rich had cheated on me and humiliated me, but, when I got really quiet inside, I ached for the Rich I used to know. I hated that he felt he had to live a lie. Not bad enough that I forgave him for ruining my life, but still, it was sad that he'd spent years pretending. I didn't cause Rich to be Rich, and I sure didn't feel he could take a pill or go through "therapy" and be cured of being himself.

A sharp noise came from my throat. "It isn't God I have the problem with."

I pushed open the front door of the church and burst into the blinding sunlight. I turned back to look at the building. Brown brick. White trim and cross. Sprawling two-stories surrounded by black asphalt parking lots. It was a normal-enough-looking church. So what was wrong with it? As much as I needed solace right now, why couldn't I find it here? Was it the church, or was it me? The words of the women in the Sunday school room rang through my head again. If those were the people in a normal church, then maybe the congregation I was looking for wasn't normal at all. I headed for the car.

Five minutes later, I slipped into a booth at Whataburger with a copy of the Sunday paper and a small coffee. I took out my phone and pulled up my bank app to look at my account balances. I had seven hundred thirteen dollars in my checking account, down from the one thousand I'd had the last time I checked. Spit, I'd forgotten about using my debit card for my plane ticket here. This was all I had left from my last paycheck, and Rich had drained our joint accounts dry. I'd used up my paid time off with my law firm, and I wasn't sure how much more unpaid time they'd grant me. It was time to either find a job here or go back to Dallas—immediately.

I put my phone down and turned to the paper. A picture of the body in the pool last night filled the top half of the front page. Yellow crime scene tape circled the pool area. I flipped pages, barely reading the words. Sports section. No rodeo articles, but a picture of a small contingent of Kona Ironman Triathlon contestants from the area headed to Hawaii. I shook my head. Exercise for me was riding a horse, thank you very much. I'd leave the swimming, pedaling, and running to the masochists. I took a slug of lukewarm coffee. I took a bigger sip, then a gulp. I flipped more pages, reached the Classified Ads. One more sip of coffee in my cup. I raised it as I turned to the Jobs section, saw the ad for Litigation Paralegal Wanted, and stopped with my coffee cup halfway to my mouth.

Polk Street in downtown Amarillo on a Wednesday morning made a Sunday evening in the 'burbs of Dallas look gridlocked. Score one for West Texas. I'd spent many a Saturday night cruising Polk when I was in high school, and it didn't look markedly different than it had twelve plus years ago—except for the late model cars, and the Courtyard by Marriott in the old Fisk Building. Even the iconic art deco Paramount Theater façade and signage had been restored to its original glory. It was amazing how time seemed to stand still here. I turned down Fourth, parked, and walked the half-block back toward Polk.

I was heading to the Williams & Associates law firm, having responded to their ad for a litigation legal assistant in the paper and landing an interview. A few days ago, I would have sworn I'd be back in my Uptown condo in Dallas by now, handing divorce papers to Rich in person along with a piece of my mind. Something inside me, though, just couldn't return to the scene of his crime, and of my pain. Plus, my holdout in the condo would be short-lived. Rich and I hadn't saved much for rainy days. He had a premarital trust fund to turn to, thanks to his wealthy family, but I had no claim to it. I didn't have the money to pay for the place, not on my salary alone. Might as well let Rich move in Stormy—that was her name—or have the hassle of selling the place fall on his shoulders. So, here I was, interviewing for a job all the way up in Amarillo, while some anonymous process server was delivering my divorce petition in Dallas.

"Emily Phelps? Is that you?"

The heavy drawl stopped me as much as hearing my name did. I turned around. Melinda Stafford. My high school arch nemesis. She had teeth so white I wished I hadn't left my sunglasses in the car. Her helmet of chestnut hair gleamed above and around her face. As big as her hair was, her body was as tiny, compacted and sculpted like a yoga master. But instead of yoga pants, she had on a tailored brown jacket and a short, black pencil skirt with chunky leather pumps.

I feigned enthusiasm and choked some perky into my voice. People had plenty of reasons to talk about me without adding snob to the list.

"Hello, Melinda. How are you?"

She dug in the pricey red, orange, and pink Fossil purse hanging from her shoulder. No Target clothes or accessories for her—but then she always had been as shallow as a Texas river in August.

She said, "Fabulous. Just on my way in to work. I'm an ADA here. You know, Assistant District Attorney. Always lots to do."

Of course I knew what an ADA was—I didn't live in a shoebox. However, I hadn't heard she was one.

She pulled her hand out of her bag, producing a business card, which she extended toward me, then held onto it when I reached out and grasped it. She lowered her voice just enough to let me know we were girl-friends discussing something scandalous.

"My mom said she saw you at church yesterday. She's in your mother's Sunday school class, so I've heard all about what you've been up to, and I just can't wait to catch up over coffee. Call me." She released the card.

When Hell freezes over, I thought. I screwed my face up into its brightest smile. "Well, I won't keep you then," I said. "So nice to see you."

Off she went in one direction, and off I went in the other, seething. I should have been used to these excruciating reunions by now, but I wasn't. I needed to rise above them. That, or scat back to Dallas. Neither option set my wick afire, to be honest, but I'd just do the job interview, and later I could reevaluate my life for the millionth time.

It was only half a block to the Maxor Building, site of the Williams & Associates offices. The ten-story tan structure looked so native that it made me imagine it was once a Panhandle sandstorm that had blown itself out and stayed put. We had a lot of windstorms, but most of them blew through. The conditions in these parts were so rugged that many folks gave up and moved on like the storms. Only the toughest stuck around. The ones that left complained that all the cattle feedlots stunk—but that was just the smell of money, my dad had always said—and that the barren terrain was ugly. But not me. It was just different, in a vast way that was big on cloudless sky and Technicolor sunsets. It shouted of freedom and wide-open spaces. You could loosen your belt here, lean your head back, and draw a full breath. You could see a storm coming from a hundred miles away, and you could gallop a horse at full speed forever without stopping or turning unless you darn well wanted to. Those were the kinds of things you didn't realize you missed when beauty closed in on you. Or on me, rather. When it closed in on me, in Dallas. I'd only left this place all those years ago because it was time for me to go, not because I hated it.

I pushed the Maxor's glass doors open and walked to the elevators. I got off on the sixth floor and set my chin as I scanned the hallway for the Williams & Associates offices. I found them, just to my right. My appointment was at nine a.m., and it was five minutes till.

This was it. My first job interview in eight years. "You've got this," I whispered to myself. I ticked off my qualifications in my head. I'd worked as a legal assistant at a top-notch Dallas firm. The Texas Board of Legal Specialization had board-certified me as a paralegal in civil trial law. I had a magna cum laude degree in political science from Texas Tech that would have led to a law degree if I hadn't decided it was more important to marry my beautiful Colombian boyfriend. Ah, regrets. Well, despite my questionable personal choice, I was more than qualified for the job.

A text buzzed on my phone. I fumbled for it and read the message. It was from my friend Katie's brother, Collin: *Nick home safe. Katie asked me to let you know.*

I texted back quickly: *Thank God! Great news! How are you?*

I wanted to call Katie to tell her, too, but I held back. I didn't know where the heck Nick had been. And, if he'd done something bad, I didn't know what to say. I was partly responsible for getting the two of them together, and I didn't believe he had it in him to hurt her. But that's what I'd thought about Rich and me. I'd email her later, after I'd had more time to think about it.

Honestly, though, just seeing Collin's name pop up on my phone gave me a little buzz of excitement. Collin was a state cop in New Mexico, and he'd always had a crush on me, according to Katie. He was about as different from Rich as a man could be, which really appealed to me right now. I could do with someone who would make me feel good. Who was I kidding, though? Collin had *always* appealed to me. I just didn't meet him until after I married Rich. I waited a second to see if he'd text again, but then looked at my watch. Four minutes till nine. Time to get a move on.

I entered the offices and sat on a nubby tweed couch in a lobby that was empty except for a desk with nothing on it but a newspaper and a small handbell in the center. The newspaper sat face-up and fully assembled, like no one had read it. Of course, the top story was still the assisted topple of New Mexican Spike Howard into a hotel swimming pool, midwedding revelry, courtesy of the sexy señorita with the smoking gun.

I walked over to the desk and smoothed my hand over the picture of her standing on the balcony, then left the paper to peruse the rest of the lobby. Remington-like prints of cattle drives and buffalo hunts adorned the two full-sized walls, and a black iron, cursive Williams & Associates sculpture hung behind the desk. I listened carefully for a few moments, but only heard the ticking of a clock somewhere out of sight. My foot scrubbed against the Berber carpet. It was brand new, and very nice.

"Excuse me," I called out. "I'm Emily Bernal. Here to interview for the legal assistant position."

A clinking noise sounded from the interior of the offices, moving closer at a rapid clip. A tiny fluff of white dog bounded down the hall. Pomeranian. When it reached me, it stood on its hind legs and placed its front paws against my shins. It couldn't have weighed more than five pounds.

"Hello, you little sweetie pie. What's your name?" I set my handbag on the desk and reached down for the pink rhinestone collar and shuffled through the tags that had given away her approach. "Snowflake. That fits." I crouched down lower and massaged behind her ears. "Where's your owner, Snowflake? Or am I interviewing with you?"

"No, that would be my job," a familiar voice said.

"You're not Williams," I accused.

I tamped down the flicker of humiliation I felt at seeing Jack Holden and his damn dimple. This man knew all about my trials and tribulations and wasn't afraid to mention them in a less-than-complimentary way. Though maybe I'd deserved the way he'd said them to me. I wasn't at my best that night. I stood up, sucking in my stomach and straightening my posture until I reached my full height of five-foot-nine-and-five-eighths in my modest two-inch pumps.

"I'm 'and Associate.' Williams retired. I run the place for him."

I shook my head. "Did you do this on purpose?"

"Do what?"

"Lure me in here under false pretenses?"

His dimple puckered and the left side of his mouth rose. His jacket was gone, and so was his hat, revealing what appeared to be sun streaks in his dark hair. Otherwise, he looked about the same as he had on Saturday night. Pressed Wranglers, lived-in boots, and a vintage, red plaid Larry Mahan shirt.

"I'm pretty sure I placed an ad in the Sunday edition of the *Amarillo Globe News*. Not in a special message sent only to you."

I tapped the paper on the desk with my forefinger. "But the ad said litigation paralegal."

"Yes, we spend a lot of time in court."

"You left out the criminal part."

"Look, I didn't force you to come in today. If you don't want to interview, no hard feelings." He shrugged.

I realized I'd lost my manners, as my dear mother liked to say. "No, no, of course not. I'm glad to be here." I gestured toward the empty chair behind the desk. "I think I must have spoken with your secretary to set up this interview. Is she out or something?"

He nodded. "Yes."

The skin around my eyes tightened in confusion. Was that an answer to my question? It didn't feel like it.

He beckoned me with a wave of his hand. Snowflake fell in behind him and I followed the two of them down a long hall lined with wainscoting and more Western art. We passed a door on the right. He gestured toward it, turning and walking backwards for a few steps. "Kitchen. Bathrooms are back past the elevator." He reversed course again and we kept going, entering a door on the left. "Williams's old office. Mine now."

I drew in a ragged breath. The rectangular room we entered was easily a thousand square feet with windows all along the outside wall. The other walls were paneled, as were the floor and the ceiling. A picture gallery hung on the long interior wall beside me, with what looked shockingly like a real Remington in the center. Around it, lesser—but still magnificent —photographic pieces were carefully interspersed with framed diplomas and certificates. A large, arresting black and white of an old, abandoned mine stood out. Above the mine entrance, a lopsided sign read Sacramento Silver Mine. In the bottom right, the photographer had scrawled *Old Dreams at the Wrong Turn Ranch – Lena Holden*. A relative of Jack's? A framed photo of an old Indian hung there, too—one I couldn't fail to recognize, what with my Indian infatuation in my younger years: Geronimo. Below his picture was a quote of some kind, but I wasn't close enough to read the small print.

A round conference table with six cushioned leather chairs on casters stood in the near side of the room. In the center was a giant desk, and its natural wood beauty was marred only by a maelstrom of papers. Picture frames lined up on the near edge of the desk, their backs to the door. The far side of the room featured built-ins: cabinetry on the outside edges and shelving in the interior. Beautiful volumes of the South Western Reporter in tan, red, and black stood back to front to back along the shelves. A piece of fabric stuck out from the left side of the cabinets, like toilet paper on a shoe. Otherwise, the room was perfect.

"Have a seat at the table."

I lowered myself into the sumptuous dark brown leather and let my hand run across it. "Wow."

Jack sat in the chair across from me and Snowflake settled at his feet. "Williams spared no expense. I got it for pennies on the dollar. What he cared about most was that I carry on his legacy. He did a helluva job preserving human dignity and constitutional rights for decades, from right in this office."

"So his practice was . . ."

"Criminal law."

"Criminal defense?"

"Absolutely. Somebody has to make sure our rights are protected. Mr. Williams had a passion for due process—for privacy, for innocent until proven guilty, and for liberty."

A flicker of something patriotic stirred within me. When put like that, criminal defense sounded like a noble calling. "Is that why you do it?"

"I agree with him."

My flicker died in a wave of irritation. Jack had a way with not answering a question. Well, I wasn't going to beg for it. I pulled a pen from my handbag and a yellow pad from my briefcase.

"Can you tell me more about the job?" I asked.

"I have far too much work, and I need help, but help that doesn't require a law degree. We do a lot of legwork for our clients, and we've got a bunch of them." He chuckled. "Oh, and you were right about the woman in the hotel, by the way. Her name is Sofia Perez, and she did need a lawyer—the court-appointed one. Me."

I blushed. Ms. Diplomatic, that was me. But to think he now represented the killer I'd seen Saturday night, the perpetrator of the murder that was the talk of the town, was a little bit titillating, in a smarmy, reality-TV kind of way. And I wasn't above watching an occasional episode of *The Real Housewives of Orange County.*

"Holy cow, really?"

"Really. And she's an illegal immigrant, and the sole parent of a six-year-old girl no one can find. Sofia is a bit . . . distressed. Can't figure out heads from tails with her."

My heart lurched. I felt something in my gut and realized it was empathy. For the missing child, of course, but also for the killer, which surprised me. Maybe Jack was piping some brainwashing chemicals in through the vents. I tried to refocus on what he was saying.

"And besides all of our existing clients and their cases, we've got some high roller who wants to set me up on a retainer to defend his employees and associates. Could be a lot of work, because they're in a line of business that often puts them at risk for misunderstandings with the law."

"What, the mafia?"

"Night clubs and importing from Mexico. Anyway, I need help. I need it immediately. You told me everything I needed to know about you in the application you sent in with your resume. I assume that if I match your old salary at Hailey & Hart that would be sufficient? Plus, I have a little benefit program for my employees—standard stuff, medical, 401k, paid time off. I can give you a copy of all that paperwork."

Employees? What employees? I hadn't seen or heard a peep from anyone but him. The benefits and his offer didn't make sense, but it was far more generous than I'd expected in Amarillo where the cost of living was so much lower than in Dallas. And, boy, did I need the benefits, with a baby on the way.

"I'm, that's, I mean, thank you," I said. "That gives me a lot to think about."

He bounced his pen tip against the glass table and it made a sharp *clack* noise. "So that's a no?"

"It's a maybe. But I do have a question, if you don't mind."

"What's that?"

"Is Snowflake your dog?"

It had bugged me since I walked in. A big cowboy and a little white dog in a pink collar?

His face grew very still. "I'm responsible for her." He put down his pen and stood up, walking over to his desk.

Another non-answer. Had I touched a nerve? Ex-girlfriend? Ex-wife? Did Snowflake come with the office? God, this recalcitrant man was enough to drive a woman mad-cow crazy.

"Alrighty then." I stood up and wiped my sweaty hands on my skirt.

Jack returned and thrust a business card at me. I was accumulating quite a collection today.

"When can you give me an answer?" he asked.

I read the card. R. Jackson Holden. "Um, tomorrow morning?"

"How about by the end of today? I could really use your help with the Sofia Perez case tomorrow."

My throat felt constricted. The thought of working on Sofia's case excited me, but this was all really fast to make a decision so much bigger than he realized. I couldn't just say yes. A few things about Jack rang alarm bells with me. The office with no employees, the overly generous offer without asking me any questions. And the way he made my palms sweat. Especially that.

"I'll try."

I stuck my semi-dry hand out toward him. As his fingers touched mine, tiny shocks rocketed up my arm. We shook, his yellow topaz eyes boring into me as we did. I looked down at our clasped hands. No wedding ring.

The rest of my morning was busier than you'd expect for a woman with no life. I'd brought my walking clothes and made two laps around the minilakes of the Medi Park loop on the northwest side of town, enjoying the fall air and pondering my options. None of them seemed good, and my mind returned to Sofia's plight: a young mother far from home, facing possible life in prison, whose child had disappeared. I didn't know which was worse. And why had she shot that guy anyway? How could Sofia—or any mother—risk a life without her daughter unless she had no other choice? If she was here illegally, that probably meant she didn't have much support either.

I had always turned up my nose at criminal law, but this woman tugged at my heartstrings. Surely the police were looking for the little girl. I sighed. I really shouldn't let myself get caught up in this case when it was unlikely I'd take the job, but thinking about it calmed me in a strange way, in a "You think you've got it bad, Sister—what about her?" way. Because I didn't, even if I *was* about to become a single mom. Not compared to Sofia.

Or to my friend Katie, although at least Nick had returned home safely. Time to suck it up and write that email to her. I typed as I walked, my eyes darting back and forth from the path in front of me to my screen, like I was in REM sleep.

Katie – SOOOO happy to hear Nick is safe. When you have a chance, let me know what happened, and I'll fill you in on a few developments around here.

What I really wished was that I had the money to jet off to paradise to visit her. That I could cry on *her* shoulder for a change. Lord knew she owed me. She'd cried mine soggy for years before she and Nick got together, before she quit drinking. Looking back, it was an odd dynamic. She'd sort of been my boss, and was seven years older than me, but I'd been the one who was married and centered. Now the roles had reversed, only she didn't know it yet. I hit send.

When I'd finished walking the loops, I was queasy and craving veggie curry. Better than craving pickles or fried jalapeños, but it called for an emergency lunch stop at nearby My Thai. I hid in a corner in the back and ate quickly, hoping not to be recognized.

"Ma'am, are you ready for your check?"

I looked up at a waitress too old for her jet-black dyed hair and nose ring. She wasn't the waiter who'd taken care of me so far, but maybe they'd had a shift change. She wore a short-sleeved top, and her arms were covered in tattoos from wrist to elbow. Really, I thanked God regularly that I had resisted extra piercings and tattoos.

"Yes, thank you."

"I know you." She nodded and my shoulders stiffened. Not again. "You're the one who ran your car through the Taco Villa when we were in high school, right?"

I exhaled the tension away with breath I hadn't realized I'd held. "Guilty."

Her words took me back to my Oldsmobile Toronado, which I'd inherited when my father never came back to claim it. The thing was huge, truly defining the "full" in "full-sized," so I'd called it The Boat. The Boat ejected oil like Spindletop and only turned to the left. What it lacked in drivability it made up for in space, though. One time I crammed eleven of my closest friends in it for the drive to Dick Bivins Stadium for the homecoming football game. Memories. And, yes, I had accidentally left it on and in drive when I dashed into the Taco Villa for a bean burrito (mild, extra sour cream) over lunch during school one day. It had ended up marooned on a pile of demolished bricks that used to be the front wall, engine revving.

"I was there. I'd just finished with a dentist's appointment and was ordering at the counter with my mom. Scared me to death."

"I'm so sorry."

"Oh no, it's okay. You got me out of fifth period."

We both laughed. I stuck out my hand. "I'm Emily."

We shook. "Nadine. I was a few years behind you at AHS."

"Well, it's been a pleasure running into you, Nadine."

"Do you live here?"

I paused. "Just moved back."

"Things are pretty much the same. If you ever need help settling in, though, I could reintroduce you to the Hummers crowd."

Hummers had been the hot hangout before I moved away, and still was.

I liked this woman, and not just because she didn't seem to know a thing about my recently sordid past.

"Thanks. That would be great," I said.

We traded phone numbers, then she held out the check, and I slipped in a twenty and handed it back to her. She smiled and moved on to another table.

My phone notified me of an incoming text. I didn't recognize the number. I opened it to find a picture of Stormy modeling one of my red silk nightgowns at my condo. And looking better than I did in it. My blood simmered. Another text followed it: *This is mine, too.* The simmer escalated to a rolling boil.

I attacked my iPhone with angry finger darts as I forwarded the photo to Rich and said: *Your boyfriend is a witch. While he's invading my privacy, tell him to make himself useful and box up my things and ship them to me.*

I stared at the phone, waiting. Seconds passed, minutes passed.

I felt Nadine's eyes on me and she mouthed, "Do you need anything?"

I pretended to smile, and shook my head no. I stared at my phone again. Still, no reply. Well, in the decision of whether to return to Dallas or stay here, this dropped a few lead weights on the staying here side of the scales. I'd liked my condo and job, but the only thing I'd truly miss in Dallas, besides anonymity, would be Goldie, the horse I rode a few weekends a month. She'd feel abandoned. Maybe someone could show her this picture of Stormy so she'd understand.

I saved the photo in case I needed it for the divorce, or as a reminder of why I was really, really pissed off at my soon-to-be-ex-husband.

Feeling like I deserved a good spoiling after that little nasty, I headed straight for a mani-pedi splurge at Top Ten Nails, which I put on my rapidly expanding credit card tab. I settled into the pedi chair with hot water bubbling over my feet and shoved my sunglasses on. I stuck my headphones in my phone jack and turned on some old No Doubt, then laid back and closed my eyes. One hour quieted the voices of the nosy noo-noos and their ilk in the bathroom at the wedding, and banished the memory of Stormy's picture—somewhat. When I was done, I left my sunglasses and headphones on while I made a trip to Natural Grocers for me, and the Walmart Supercenter for Mother. By the time I'd loaded the last of the bags in the car, I'd churned through my life and job options again and decided to hold out for a better fit on a job, with a less dangerous boss than the mysterious Jack. I just didn't need any more problems. Sofia's or his.

I pointed Mother's 2002 Honda Civic west on old Route 66—better known these days as I-40—and headed for home, passing the ten upended and graffiti-covered cars at the world-famous Cadillac Ranch. Technically, I'd grown up mostly in Bushland, a whopping fifteen miles from downtown Amarillo. Now it was barely on the outskirts of the city sprawl. Yes, at nearly 200,000 people, Amarillo was considered a city, thank you very much, but my dad had wanted a place for livestock. Our little white three-bedroom/two-bath house had fifteen acres and a barn, which he'd deemed just right. The barn had fallen into disrepair, after he left when I was sixteen, and the entire property screamed neglect. He'd taken the horses with him, and Mother had sold the three cows to a chop shop, one by one —much to my dismay—long ago, including even Sir Loin, whom I'd helped bottle-feed when he was an orphaned calf. Other houses, nicer houses, had sprung up around us.

I wished she'd let go and move closer to Panhandle Believers, where she worshiped and also worked as a church secretary, but she was stalwart. She had never divorced Dad, and she wasn't going to leave their home, either. She just lived her life here like it was Madame Tussauds and she was a wax figure, refusing to mention him. It killed me.

An ancient, multicolored Jeep Wrangler with a lift kit was parked in front when I got to the house. It was a vehicle I hadn't seen before. I loaded my arms with grocery bags and headed in. The sound of my mother's laughter from the den greeted me. She had Wednesdays off.

"Mother? I'm home. I have your groceries."

"Thanks, dear. When you're through, join us in the den."

Join us? Who was *us*? "Okay."

The inside of the house/Madame Tussauds had last been updated in my early teens. Red cedar paneling—Dad's stylistic input—made me feel like I was in a cheap ski lodge. The kitchen cabinets were also red cedar, clashing violently with busy floral wallpaper in blue and purple hues. Those had been Mother's contribution. All of this and gold Formica, too, which they'd chosen as a joint project. No wonder I had issues. I dropped the bags on the counter and made a second trip in from the car.

Mother's bright voice burbled one wall away, along with the occasional resonance of a deep male voice. A gentleman caller? When Hell froze over. Maybe it was church business. I put the groceries away, washed my hands, and went to the den. Mother sat on the red brick hearth with an array of photo albums at her feet. Beside her perched my omnipresent new friend Jack with one of the albums splayed across his knees. They both looked up when I came in.

I didn't bother to sit, just stood in the doorway. "What are you doing here?" I asked.

"Background check."

"I didn't say I'd take the job."

He shrugged. "Formalities."

"And you don't need to do it in person. With my mother." I glared at her, to make sure she knew this was not okay with me.

"Mother knows best," he said. Mine beamed. "Besides, when I saw you lived halfway to Heaven, I couldn't resist."

"Halfway to Heaven?"

"Nearer to the Land of Enchantment anyway."

I gaped, still uncomprehending.

"New Mexico," he continued. "My home state."

Heaven. Well, it kind of fit this place, in a completely opposite way.

He tapped his index finger against a page. "And look what I learned: Miss Rodeo Texas. I couldn't have gotten that by calling to verify your employment."

My jaw dropped.

"And you still have that cute little thing with your teeth." He pointed at his mouth, his lips curled back showing his teeth and altering his voice. Then he made an up and down motion above the crown of his head. "Your hair was even . . ." he trailed off, blinking, then said, "taller."

I stepped in front of him, hand out. "Give that to me."

My mother sighed and clasped her hands in front of her. "My baby girl has always been so beautiful."

An urge to throttle my mother came over me. I turned to face her, then stopped and sighed. It was undeniably my past.

"First runner-up," I corrected.

"Very impressive. It's sure to come in handy in our line of work."

I didn't want to imagine how. "Our?"

"I'm being optimistic."

"Sounds more like presumptuous."

He didn't comment, and flipped a page backward in time.

"Sit down, dear." Mother patted the hearth.

I lowered myself to the bricks. I hadn't looked at this album in years. I didn't want to now, with Jack, but I did want easy access to snatch the offending memory book away if necessary.

Jack held up a picture of a masked and caped woman riding a black horse around the track at Texas Tech's Jones Stadium in Lubbock, her long blonde hair trailing behind her in the wind. "What were you doing here?" he asked.

"I was the Masked Rider."

"Ah." His dimple appeared, digging deep in his cheek. "The Masked Rider of the Red Raiders. At New Mexico State we called you guys the Red Rodents."

I couldn't help laughing, a little.

My mother chirped in. "You should have seen her flying around that stadium, Jack. I was so proud of her."

He winked at Mother and flipped back another page. His face cracked into a lopsided smile. The page was filled with pictures of me riding an Appaloosa. Balancing my weight as she turned around a barrel, low over her neck with my hands on the reins as I yah'ed in her ear, rubbing her behind her ears with her nostrils wide as she heaved for air after a race. I wanted to trace my finger over every spot on her rump. I'd loved Flibberti-gibbet, or Jib, as I'd called her, more than I'd loved any other horse, before or since. We were Southwest Region champs my senior year.

"You really did *do* rodeo," Jack said. "Not just the pageants, I mean."

"Scholarshipped and all."

He looked at me, past my mother. "Now I'm *really* impressed. Why barrel racing?"

I smiled wide. I loved it when I got this question. "Because girls weren't allowed to compete in bull riding. But I did goat tying, and I was a heeler and breakaway roper, too."

Mother grabbed my hand and squeezed it. "And she was a rodeo clown. You know, the ones who protect the riders from the bulls."

Gordon, one of the bull riders on the rodeo team at Tech—a guy who was a real mentor and friend to me—had been gored by a bull and died when I was a sophomore. It hit me harder than anything had in my life since my dad left. Gordon was the reason I had taken up rodeo clowning. But that was personal, so I kept quiet.

"That's something I never would have guessed." Jack made an exaggerated stretchy face with his eyebrows high, then nodded and flipped back a few more pages.

One photo took up the entire left-facing page. Me, with braces and two long braids tied off with little pink bows, only fourteen years old, holding an enormous trophy. Class IV All Around Champ, XIT Rodeo. Standing beside me, looking every inch the rodeo cowboy and proud papa, was my father. Incandescent in my eyes, at least back then. His big, scratchy hand had gripped my shoulder, and I could still remember its warmth through my pink snap-front Western shirt.

I reached past my mother, pulled the album to my knees, and shut it firmly. "Enough about me."

Mother put her hand on my arm. "We hadn't gotten to your kindergarten album yet."

Jack stood. "Another time, Agatha." I gave him a few Brownie points for letting the subject of my Wonder Years drop, for now at least. And then he said, "Emily, we have a meeting at the Potter County Detention Center at nine with Sofia. Can you be in the office by eight tomorrow so we can ride out there together?"

I shot a glance at the wall clock. It was four. Nearly end of the day. I pressed my palm against my abdomen, fingers splayed slightly over the cranberry bean-sized embryo inside. I'd told myself I wasn't going to work with Jack. I didn't like criminal law. But something about him knocked me off balance. And the thought of that woman and her child, the promise of getting out of my mother's cloying house each day, and the possibility of distracting myself from my messed up life? All good stuff, and I could keep looking and snag a more suitable job when it came along, if I wasn't so obviously pregnant by then that no one would hire me. Besides, beggars couldn't afford to be choosers and, as Jack had pointed out when we met, I was flat ass broke.

"See you then," I said.

THREE

Snowflake greeted me as soon as I entered the office the next morning. I reached down to let her lick my hand and she jumped on her hind legs around me, dancing like a circus poodle.

"Good girl," I said. "Tomorrow I'll bring you a treat." My abdomen cramped and I pressed a hand into it, then stood back up. "Jack?"

I started walking down the hall toward his office. He appeared in the doorway, his dark brown hair wet, tucking a dress shirt into a pair of slacks. He held his hand up to stop me.

"Let's meet in the kitchen." He said. Then he disappeared.

I spoke under my breath and made a sharp right-hand turn. "Okay . . ."

Jack joined me moments later. We sat in hard-backed chairs at opposite sides of the rectangular wood-topped table. The smell of something cheesy and spicy hung in the air. Chorizo? I'd loved the Mexican sausage until I gave up meat five years earlier. My traitorous stomach growled, then lurched toward morning sickness. Clearly white toast with Mother wasn't going to cut it if I had to face the aroma of Jack's *desayuno* every morning.

Jack buttoned the cuffs on his shirt. "How was the drive in from Heaven?"

It took me only a split second to get his meaning. "It will be much nicer when I have my car here and don't have to ride with Mother."

"Ah, so it's like being dropped off in front of school."

"Yeah, pretty much." Only worse.

Jack tugged on his shirtfront with both hands then used them to smooth it. "So if you don't mind, I'm going to have you work at the desk out front. I set a computer up on it last night, and it's networked with my server."

I hadn't noticed. "And your secretary?"

"Works offsite."

"Uh huh." I wasn't in love with the idea, but this was basically a temp job. And it was better than officing in the kitchen, I supposed, since I hadn't noticed any other rooms in the office space.

"Also, when you come in each morning, if you could ring the bell on the front desk before you come down the hall, that would be great."

I stared at him a few beats then burst into laughter. Obviously he was kidding. I winked. "Okay."

"Thanks, and, really, do it any time you come down the hallway. Just give it a few good rings."

"You're serious? Why?"

"Why what?"

My mouth worked a little, but no words came out.

He threw his hands up. "I like my privacy. Just ring the bell, okay?"

I opened my eyes wide and raised my brows. "If you think that will be sufficient to save you from a sexual harassment lawsuit when you're back there doing," I waved my hand in the air, "you know, pervy stuff, it won't."

He rolled his eyes at me. "If that's all the commentary you have, it's time to leave for the jail."

He unfolded his long body, and I tried not to imagine the kinds of things I wasn't supposed to catch him doing in his office.

"I'll meet you at your desk in five," he said. "It's booted up. Username is Emily. Password is RodeoQueen, no space."

I performed the mother of all eye rolls back at him, but he'd already left.

The Potter County Detention Center was a twenty-minute drive from the office out to the middle of nowhere on Highway 60, past the International Airport, near the defunct Air Force Base, and halfway to the metropolis of Panhandle, as in the town of Panhandle, and not the general geographic area. Today was my first visit to the jail, despite my mother's warnings of delinquency and nights in the pokey when I'd come home tipsy three or four times in high school. A spooky, abandoned building loomed on the left side of the highway.

"That's the old jail," Jack said.

It looked like a set for *The Walking Dead*. Gunshots echoed, and I gripped the armrests as cramps hit me again.

Jack saw me tense up. "Shooting range."

We were passing a huge earthen berm. I relaxed, a little. How vulnerable Sofia must have felt on this long, scary drive. Not only was she caught dead-to-rights shooting some guy, but she wasn't even a citizen of this country. If I'd been her I'd have died of a coronary before ever reaching the jail.

Finally, on our right, we approached a large brown sheet-metal building that could have been a warehouse, or a furniture store, or a church—but was none of those. It was the jail. Jack pulled into the parking lot. The building was new-ish, and from the outside it looked like a giant cow poop had fallen from the sky and gone splat. Around it stood nothing but prairie, tumbleweeds, railroad tracks, boxcars, and cattle.

Jack led me through the glass doors into a foyer with linoleum tile squares, brown walls, and a plastic brown "rope" about eight feet long that separated a walkway along one side of the room from chairs on the other. At the end of the walkway was a brown-uniformed deputy behind glass. Jack moved to a line of tape on the floor in front of the deputy. Ahead of us was a sign on the glass that read "Wait behind the line until called."

I shivered and wrapped my arms around myself. The county was paying to keep this place subarctic, but they weren't wasting any money on air fresheners. It smelled like sweat, body odor, and overfull Pampers.

The deputy waved us forward. Jack put his driver's license in a drive-up bank teller drawer. I added mine, and the deputy slid them in.

Without looking up, she said, "What's the purpose of your visit?"

Jack cleared his throat and adjusted his tie, because that's what he had on. A tie. And a sports coat with his slacks. He still rocked his lived-in boots, but otherwise, he looked ready to go to church.

"I'm an attorney," he said, then pointed his thumb at me. "She's my paralegal, and we're here to see a client."

The woman squinted at him under her gray hair, so short it was practically a crew cut. Her eyes were lost in a maze of squinty wrinkles. She nodded. "Yeah, I recognize you. You represented me and my husband when they repo'd our mobile home."

This wasn't the reception I was used to getting when going to meet a client, after years in my shishi Dallas firm.

"Of course. I thought you looked familiar. How are you?" Gone was his almost-Texas accent, and in its place was a sho'nuff Amarillo drawl.

"Yeah, well, not so good. After you lost our case, my husband left me."

"I'm sorry to hear that."

She made a noise somewhere between a snort and a raspberry, picked up a pen, and looked down again. "Bar number?"

He leaned in and lowered his voice. "Double-oh-seven, 855198, license to litigate."

I held my breath for her response, cringing, but laughing on the inside. She looked up so slowly that I almost turned blue.

Her voice dripped acid as she said, "Client name?"

Jack gave it to her, and she typed a few keys before directing us to Attorney Room A3. We left the foyer and walked past some lockers and a bank of visitation phones where another deputy met us. Behind him yet another deputy escorted an officious-looking man with a clipboard. That deputy spoke into his radio, and, a few seconds later, there was a loud buzzing noise as the cage clanked open, literally shaking the floor and sending vibrations through my body. The deputy and clipboard guy entered the cage, and it clanked shut behind them. Another loud buzz sounded, followed by a clank of the interior door. More vibrations. They disappeared into the bowels of the prison, and the inner door clanked again, but not before a loud scream from within pierced my eardrums. More vibrations from the floor coursed through my body.

I started to sweat. All I had on under my jacket was a white tank that looked much more boobalicious than it had two months ago. I hadn't planned to take my jacket off, but the sudden surge of heat made it imperative. I slipped the jacket from my shoulders quickly and crossed my arms over my chest.

Our deputy, a heavyset fifty-something man with a gray buzz cut, introduced himself as Walker. He immediately noted what I was hiding behind my crossed arms with a nod and a smirk, and I scooched my arms further up. As he walked, his keys swung and jangled in counterpoint to his oddly graceful steps. He reached overhead to slap the hallway door-frame as we went through it—for God knew what reason—exposing the lower quarter of his gut, which wobbled like he was an overweight belly dancer. Or one of the hippos in Fantasia. I was transfixed.

"Emily." Jack spoke under his breath.

"What?"

"Keep your eyes in your head. He's married."

I sputtered.

He half-grinned.

The guard stopped at the first of two heavy blue doors that had A3 stenciled in white on them. "Here you go," he said. "The good room. You must be royalty or something."

"Thank you, Deputy Walker." Jack reached for the handle on the door nearest us, twisted it and opened the door. He gestured for me to enter first and whispered, "I think he likes you."

I accidentally whacked him with my handbag as I passed through.

Jack shut the door behind us, and we were alone. A single table dominated the attorney end of the room, running its full length from the doors on either side of it to the chain link fence separating us from the inmate area. There were two chairs on our side of the table, luckily, because I couldn't have gotten to the other side of it unless I went out and entered through the separate door.

"This is—"

"Twice as big as the other rooms," Jack said, interrupting my thought and turning it on its head. "It's bigger because it doubles as the Parole Hearing Room. In the other rooms, we're separated from the clients by plexiglass and have to talk with them on one of those visitation phones. It's a Hepatitis C nightmare waiting to happen."

"That's awful!"

Jack took the chair nearest the chain link barrier and I sat beside him, putting my yellow legal pad on the table in front of me, and my pen to its right.

"It has its upsides," Jack said. "The graffiti on the walls in there is pretty entertaining." He shook his head. "They call it an Attorney Room, but I can't imagine the attorneys are the ones writing 'Railroaded by dirty cop' on the walls."

"Yeah, they'd be more like '4th Amendment rocks,'" I said.

He laughed. "I called ahead to reserve this room so we could bond a little with Sofia. That's hard to do on one of those phones through plexi-glass. We need her to open up to us. The only downside is that after we're done talking, she'll be strip-searched." He gestured at the chain link fence. "Since we could pass her a shank or drugs or anything we wanted to for that matter."

"How inhumane!"

"It's a jail, Emily."

"So Sofia will be searched . . . everywhere?"

"If by that you mean anal and vaginal, then yes, everywhere."

Poor Sofia! "And us?"

"Us, what?"

"Are we searched?"

He grinned. Before he could answer, a door opened in the area behind the chain link fence. Jack stood up and I followed suit. Deputy Walker led Sofia in. The tiny woman shuffled toward us in her leg shackles and enormous orange jumpsuit. Her wrists were handcuffed in front of her, and her heavy, dark hair was pulled into a low ponytail. A few wisps had fallen into her eyes and across her swollen, scabbed lips. She sat, eyes downcast, doing nothing about the strands of hair that would have driven me around the bend. She smelled like sweat and fear. The whole room did. I smiled at her, but she didn't so much as blink a bloodshot eye.

"I'll be right here if you need me. Knock twice," Deputy Walker said, pausing to demonstrate the rap-rap he was looking for, "when you're ready to leave or if she gets out of hand. You shouldn't have a problem with her, though." He winked at me, and my blood curdled. "She ain't but a little bitty ol' thing, and she's real quiet."

He exited and the door closed behind him with a heavy thud. We sat down.

Jack spoke first. "Hello again, Sofia. We met at your arraignment Monday. I'm your attorney, Jack Holden."

Her lips moved, and a whistley, Mexican-accented voice came out. "I remember you," she said. "Hello, Jack."

Her accent made the words sound like "Ell-oh, Jock."

"This is my assistant, Emily," Jack said.

"Mucho gusto, Sofia," I said. I'd minored in Spanish at Tech.

"Mucho gusto."

Jack put both his hands on the table in front of him. His thumbs did a quick dance on its surface. "So, Sofia, you understand you've been charged with the murder of Spike Howard, and that I entered a plea of not guilty on your behalf."

She nodded. "And you help me find my daughter."

A scream reverberated through our room. I jumped. It wasn't Sofia, but it sounded and felt like it was in there with us. What in God's name made someone scream like that?

Jack sucked his top lip in, and his forehead wrinkled. "Remember, we talked about that. Child Protective Services and the police are looking for her. Did CPS send an investigator out to meet with you yet?"

Her clasped hands writhed in their metal bracelets. "Si, yes, but they no find her."

"They're very good at what they do. I'm sure they'll find her soon."

"She's only six. We just move here, we have nobody," she said, her voice rising an octave across the words. "Please, you must help her." Her distress was so palpable that my own pulse sped up in response.

"My job is to help you. To defend you. If I am successful, we get you out of here, and you can take care of your daughter. That's what we need to talk about today."

"But I am guilty."

Clank. Buzz. Clank. The loud noises sounded like the ones I'd heard earlier when the door to the central prison was opened.

Jack pursed his lips. "What do you mean by that?"

"I pick up the gun from the table by the bed and I walk toward him, and I shoot him."

He shook his head, even though he said, "Right, you told me that before, but I need to know everything about what happened, so I can figure out how to defend you."

"What do you mean?"

"Well, we can say you were insane—crazy, loco en la cabeza—or temporarily insane." He drew the crazy circles in the air by his head.

"But I not crazy."

"I know you're not that kind of crazy, but the court says that if you don't know right from wrong, even just at that moment when you shot him, that's crazy."

She shook her head slowly as she spoke. "I know it is wrong to kill him, but I have no choice."

Clank. Buzz. Clank.

Jack drew a deep breath. "Why did you shoot him, Sofia? *Why* didn't you have a choice? Tell us that."

Sofia looked down and chewed her lip. We waited. She didn't answer.

"I can't defend you if you don't help me understand."

She looked up and I saw huge tears in the corners of her eyes threatening to spill into the tear tracks already cut through her cheeks. She shook her head, fast and hard this time, then stopped.

Jack glanced at me and gave the tiniest of nods. I shrugged my shoulders and lifted my eyebrows. He glared at me, his eyes throwing daggers. What did he want? I couldn't read his mind. He dug his boot heel into the bridge of my unbooted foot.

"Ow!" I snapped under my breath. Sofia looked at me. I looked at Jack.

Jack mouthed, "You talk to her."

We had a guilty murder defendant and Jack wanted me to take over the interview without any prep whatsoever on my first day of work ever as a criminal paralegal. This wasn't exactly how we did things at my firm in Dallas. Fine. I pushed one hand against my crampy abdomen as I gathered my thoughts. I spoke in my most gentle voice. "Sofia, what's wrong? What's making you quiet?"

She sniffed then wiped her nose with her forearm, causing her cuffs to rattle as she did, but she didn't answer.

If I were her, I would want to protect myself, unless I was protecting someone else. Like a child. "Tell me about your daughter."

She swallowed, hard. "She such a good girl."

Clank. Buzz. Clank. I felt my shoulders tense in response to the sounds.

"Does she go to school?"

Another scream, this one echoing in my cranium and vibrating through my body.

"No."

"What does she like to do?"

More screams. They were giving me a headache behind my right eye. I had to block them out.

A tear dripped down Sofia's cheek. "She color."

"Does she get that from you?"

Sofia shook her head. "When she scared, she sings." She smiled. "I teach her that."

"Does she have a favorite song?"

"'*Tengo una Muneca.*' It mean *I have* . . ."

"*A doll,*" I finished for her, then recited its lyrics, in English. "Dressed in blue with her little shirt and her lace shawl."

"Yes." Her smile widened. "She have a doll like that, too."

Her words reminded me of something I hadn't thought of in years. My mother, tucking my doll in with me, and singing "Hush Little Baby" to us both. Warmth spread through me.

"She must be wonderful," I said. "And you sound like a great mother. Does she look like you?"

She nodded and wiped her nose.

"What about her father? Could he have her?"

"No. We have no one. We are alone."

"Is he deceased? *Muerto?*"

Her head fell forward and she cast her eyes down. This time the tear fell on the surface of the table.

I leaned around Jack, toward her. "Sofia, what is it?"

Her head came back up, and both eyes bored into mine. "I am guilty. They will send me back to Mexico, no?"

Jack stepped back in. "If they find you guilty, yes. Or if you make a deal, probably."

"What is 'make a deal?'"

"Where the State of Texas offers you fewer years in jail if you plead guilty, and you agree. Then there's no trial."

She nodded, slowly, her eyes sharp and smart through her bruises.

He went on, taking his time. "The rule isn't one hundred percent clear, but the INS would hold a deportation hearing, and if they decide you committed a violent offense, and if you have been sentenced to a year or more of jail time, they usually send you back. Do you understand?"

Again, those intelligent eyes took it in, and she nodded.

"But if we get a not guilty verdict at a trial, then no deportation hearing. You stay."

"How long would that take, to be not guilty?"

"We would have to go to trial, and that would be several months from now."

"And I stay in here?"

"Yes." Jack turned to me. "Her bail was set at one million dollars. The way it works is that the defendant or someone on her behalf has to come up with at least ten percent of that amount to meet bail. And they don't get it back. Sofia wasn't able to make bail. But if she had, they would have just transferred her to a federal facility to await a deportation hearing, so not ideal either way."

"Oh," I said to him—clank, buzz, clank—and then to Sofia, "*Lo siento.*"

"And my daughter? What about her?"

Jack stood up and leaned on the wall. "It all depends on what happens with you."

Their predicament made my mouth dry and I fought down nausea. I couldn't imagine how she felt. But then I couldn't imagine why she'd killed Spike Howard either, or why she was avoiding talking about her reasons with the only people who could help her.

Again, Sofia shook her head, even more violently this time. "I am guilty. I go back to Mexico. Soon is better than trial. Now. You tell the judge that."

The pregnancy hormones were wreaking havoc on my self-restraint, and I blurted out, "I don't understand. Why won't you let us help you?"

Sofia sat back in her chair. "It's for the best. You just help my daughter."

Jack said, "Sofia, if they deport you, they'll deport Valentina, too. Is that what you want?"

Sofia leaned forward and her voice grew strident. "Please help her. She is little. She is alone. You must find her. We have no family, not here, not in Mexico. She needs a family. She needs to stay here, in the U.S."

Clank. Buzz. Clank. Scream.

Jack stood up straight. "CPS is going to find her—the police will help them—and they will take care of her. She'll have her own attorney and the court will appoint someone special just to make sure she's doing okay. Our job is to help you. Do you really want to spend your life in a Mexican prison?"

Sofia looked at me. "Please, you must find my daughter. Protect her from the bad men. Please don't let them take her away."

Clank. Buzz. Clank. Scream.

Jack's eyes met mine, and both our brows rose. He didn't speak, so I answered her. "What bad men? Has someone tried to hurt her?"

Sofia started rubbing her fingers together and whispering in Spanish. I wasn't a Catholic, nor still fluent by any means, but I recognized Hail Marys when I heard them. She rocked back and forth, rubbing and touching her fingertips and continuing her frantic whispering. I heard a lot of *Dios*, and something about an "Elizabet" but that was all I could make out. She closed her eyes and prayed louder.

A sense of urgency was building in me, like a hot air balloon filling in my chest.

"What aren't you telling us?" I said. "You need to talk. Please, let us help you."

But Sofia didn't say another word.

My phone rang almost the second Sofia left. I looked at my screen. It was Rich.

"Do you mind if I take this real quick?" I asked Jack.

"No problem. You want me to wait outside?"

"If you don't mind."

Afraid that it would roll to voice mail because it was taking me so long to answer, I pressed to accept the call, but didn't say anything.

Jack grabbed his briefcase and sidled out the door.

From the phone I heard, "Hello? Is anyone there? This is Rich Bernal calling for Emily."

His Colombian English was stiff and formal, even after twelve years in the U.S.

I put the phone to my ear. "Hello, Rich Bernal, this is your green card speaking."

"Emily, please, you know that is not true." His Rs still rolled ever so slightly. His sexy voice was the second thing I'd noticed about him—after his mesmerizing eyes. Well, neither worked on me anymore.

"I wanted you to know that I received your text," he said, "and that I apologize on behalf of Stormy and myself."

"I've got a way you can make it all better."

"What is that?"

"I need my car, ASAP. Can you have someone deliver it to me?"

"Will you not be coming back to move your things?"

"You can throw stuff in the trunk—anything you haven't pawned or that Stormy hasn't already tried on, too, if you have time. I'll send a mover for the rest, later. Right now, I just need my wheels."

"That isn't fair, Emily. You must know I am no thief."

"Well, your boyfriend is."

He sat in silence for a long moment, and I could picture him pushing back the cuticles on his nails, or smoothing the hair back from his brow. "We must talk."

"About?"

"There are things you don't understand."

"Really? And here I thought you wanted to apologize."

"That, as well. But also how we manage the dissolution of our marriage. What we tell other people."

"I'm going with the truth. We can talk about the rest of it some other time. Right now, I need to get back to work."

"Emily, please wait."

I sighed. "What?"

"Truly, I care deeply about you, and the pain I have caused you pains me as well. I am sorry. You were not my green card. You are the finest woman I have ever met. I was raised under the expectation that I would marry and provide an heir for my father, as he did for his before me, and as my ancestors have done for hundreds of years."

"You know what?" I said. "I care about you, too, and I want you to be happy, despite your family. I just didn't want it to be at my expense. Good-bye, Rich."

I ended the call and set my phone down on the table—hard. My forehead followed it. It was a consolation of sorts that Rich would get more grief from his family than me, but one that made me feel strangely guilty. And I hadn't done a thing wrong. I wanted to hate Rich. I was certainly angry with him. He just wasn't very hateable. Visions of good times passed flitted through my head: breakfast in bed with crossword puzzles, Rich spooning chicken soup into my mouth while I was sick, seeing his car approach when I had a flat, his face in the crowd when I was racing through a rodeo arena. No, he wasn't hateable. And that made me even madder at him.

I couldn't keep Jack waiting. I gathered my things and went into the hall, where I almost didn't notice Deputy Walker escort us out. I loped to keep up with them, which wasn't easy because I really didn't feel so hot, even though I was relieved to discover that there was no strip search on our way out of the secured area.

My mind was spinning from the weird meeting. I still had no idea why Sofia had killed Spike. I had some guesses—maybe he'd attacked her in her hotel room. But she was the only one who could support that theory. And what about her daughter? Where was she? The practical side of me that had worked in law firms for eight years had other issues, too. Like a criminal attorney being so accommodating with advice on her non-criminal issues.

I exited into the parking lot, trailing behind my boss. Well, I couldn't get answers from Sofia, but I could try to get some from Jack.

"So, do you practice immigration and family law, too?" I asked.

"I grew up on the border. Practiced law there."

I felt too crappy to put up with more of his evasiveness, so I half-growled at him, "That's not an answer."

"Every lawyer on the border does a little immigration."

He walked to his side of the Jeep. I followed him. "And family law?" I asked.

"If I need to, yes." He opened his door and got in. I stood there. He lowered the window. "Are you coming?"

"So does the court pay you for all of that?" I asked.

His lips twitched and his eyes twinkled. "I hired a law practice manager, huh?"

I could play this game all day if he wanted to. I put a hand on my cocked hip and tapped my toe.

The stupid dimple appeared, but I refused to let it soften me. He said, "No, the court won't pay us for helping Sofia with her other problems. But she can't afford to pay for anyone else, and she needs help. So, I answer her questions."

"So her daughter? Can we help find her?"

"I answer her questions, but I don't take on free work. I'm not a private detective. The police are looking for the girl. CPS is looking for her. They'll find her. We can't lose focus. Sofia is a criminal defendant. She's our client —her daughter isn't."

His answer didn't sit well with me. I walked around to my side, trying to digest his words, and got in. As I did, a wave of nausea hit me. Ugh. I crossed my arms around my middle and leaned forward.

"You okay?" He braced his hand against my seat back and turned his head to look behind us, then started backing out of the parking space, old school.

"Uh huh. So what's next for her?"

I touched my forehead and felt a thin, cool layer of sweat. This felt like more than morning sickness. It felt like I'd eaten something spoiled, or had the stomach flu. I tightened my gut and stared out the front window.

Jack put the Jeep in drive and it lurched forward, which didn't help my situation.

"We've got to get her talking to us. Find out why she killed this guy and what kind of defense we can put on."

"But she said she wants to make a deal."

He turned on his blinker and the Jeep's engine raced as he transitioned from brake to gas pedal and rolled onto Highway 60. A metallic horn blared. Jack slammed on the brakes, and my body continued forward until it stopped with a painful jerk from the seat belt. I put my hand over my mouth to keep from throwing up and watched a little sky-blue Nissan LEAF drive away, the middle finger of its hunched male driver high in the air.

"Tree-hugging asshole," Jack yelled, saluting him back. He lowered his voice, and his hand. "Sorry. Those bastards make me sorry when I vote Democrat."

He pulled into our lane and accelerated hard.

"Yes," he said. "She says she wants a deal, and I'll make one for her—if she doesn't change her mind first. In the meantime, we need to see if we can find out anything about Sofia's life before last Saturday night, which is going to be hard. Most people who live in the U.S. illegally try not to leave tracks."

His last words hung in the air and chilled me. If Sofia was here illegally, so was Valentina. And, if what Jack said was true, how would anyone ever find that little girl?

FOUR

My nausea continued on and off that night and into the morning, but the cramps let up. I'd looked up nausea and cramps in first trimester online, and was relieved to learn it was normal. Just not fun. For about two seconds I considered calling in sick, but it was only my second day, and I'd woken up with an image in my mind of a black-haired waif with huge eyes that begged me to find her and keep her safe. I couldn't very well do that lying in bed. Besides, cowgirls aren't crybabies—that's what my dad had told me—and I had a feeling Jack ascribed to this point of view as well. It was Friday. I would call a doctor if I didn't feel better by lunch; I could lick my wounds over the weekend.

I crawled out of the twin bed I'd slept in for most of my childhood. It was lumpy, thin, and saggy. I also didn't love the western-themed matching bedspread and curtains as much as I had when mother had made them for me as an eleventh birthday present. I missed my California King back in Dallas, with the silver silk sheets and the black satin comforter. Come to think of it, though, I didn't love them all that much, either. They were Rich, through and through. My next bedroom would be all about me, the grown-up Emily—whenever I could figure her the heck out—and nobody else.

I stood at the closet door and surveyed my limited choices. I hadn't been thinking career wear when I'd bolted for home the day after Stormy had, well, stormed in on our romantic dinner—the one I'd made for Rich to celebrate sharing my great news with him. "The rabbit's died" took on a whole new meaning when Rich's scary secret lover showed up in our candlelit dining room, before I'd a chance to even tell him about the baby.

Also, because of that dead rabbit, my clothes would soon be snug. I'd have to get Rich to ship my things. And I'd need to shop . . . and tell Mother. The thought of admitting to her that I'd somehow gotten pregnant just before my husband revealed his double life as a cheating bisexual burned my biscuits. Almost as much as the dread of Rich learning about his baby, and the possibility of sharing custody with Rich and Stormy.

All kvetching about Stormy aside, it wasn't even that Rich preferred a man. It was just that I'd chosen heterosexual marriage, and I thought Rich had, too. If I'd been thrown over for a genetic female, I'd probably be as crazy mad as I was now. But it wouldn't be such a hot topic of hometown gossip. So, yeah, fact: Stormy being a he who dressed as a she was probably never going to make my life easier. I put my palm over my abdomen. My little peanut and I would be delaying our announcement chat with Grandma as long as possible. Rich? Twice that long. I pulled out a stretchy navy pantsuit and held it in front of me. I would just wear this every day for the next two months and pretend I was stress-eating. Or not.

When I'd finished showering and dressing, I slipped into the kitchen to grab a quick breakfast. Not much appealed to me but, after dealing with the smell of Jack's food yesterday, I knew I had to have more than toast. I tiptoed to the refrigerator in the semi-darkness and opened the door and retrieved a plastic jug of OJ.

"I made coffee and toast," my mother said in her sparkly morning voice.

I startled, and the OJ jug hit the porcelain tile floor, cracking open. An orange lake formed in front of me and I jumped back. "Spit!"

"Sorry, dear."

Muttering under my breath, I crouched to the floor and started wiping up the mess.

"Good morning, Mother."

"How was your first day?"

Church activities the night before had kept Mother out late. I was asleep by the time she came home, so she hadn't had a chance to grill me about my job then.

"Peachy."

I threw the wet, orange paper towels in the trash under the sink.

"Did you enjoy working with Jack?" Mother asked. "He's such a gentleman, and so handsome."

Gentleman was not the word I'd have chosen to describe the man who told the chicken and the feather joke, but whatever.

"He was fine," I said.

I sat across from her at the ancient kitchen table. Art Deco green Formica on a round top perched on chrome legs. It went about as well as you'd expect with the rest of the kitchen.

"You know, you're thirty years old with only one Fallopian tube. If you're really splitting up with Rich, you could do worse than Jack."

She just had to bring up my Fallopian tube. Not what I wanted to talk about at breakfast. Part of me could understand—she'd yearned for grand-kids since the day Rich and I got engaged. I reached over and squeezed her hand.

"It'll be okay, Mother. Really. Let's let that go for now."

She sat in silence for a moment. "Any interesting cases?"

I appreciated the change of subject. "Jack's representing the woman who killed the guy who fell into the pool at the wedding."

"No," my mother breathed.

Without her war paint, she looked closer to her age of fifty-five. Lines radiated from her mouth and eyes. Her white-blonde hair hung limp and thin. But her eyes flashed with interest.

"She's not even in this country legally," she said. "How can she afford Jack?"

I nibbled a corner of toast experimentally and swallowed. It went down okay, so I kept going, talking between bites.

"The court appointed the case to him. He has to take it. That's how it works."

She harrumphed. "So that woman doesn't pay a cent in taxes while the rest of us work to pay the bills for her defense when she murders a U.S. citizen in cold blood."

What she said was the truth, or at least part of it. I knew well how Mother felt about this issue. Things hadn't been easy for her, especially after Dad left, and she resented anyone she perceived as getting assistance that she didn't or couldn't get. It was harder for me to decide exactly where I stood on it. Especially after meeting Sofia yesterday.

"Well, she's our client, so you're going to have to make the best of it. Besides, her daughter is missing. She's only six."

She shook her head, pulling her pink, flowered housedress together at the collar. "What will my friends think when they hear you're working on her case?"

"Hear? Why would they even need to?"

"Well, you know. They're all very *interested* in what's going on with you."

I munched my toast and closed my eyes. I wondered if Jack would represent *me* pro bono if I accidentally committed a violent felony against my mother.

Right on time I walked through the door of the Williams & Associates offices. Snowflake was waiting for me. I hefted my purse onto the desk and pulled out a baggie. In it, I'd saved a toast crust for her.

"Sit." The dog sat her tiny bottom on the floor immediately. "Good girl." She took the snack I offered her and smacked it with gusto. "Where's the resident despot?" She swallowed but didn't answer.

As expected, the remaining odors of Jack's spicy breakfast lingered in the air. I activated my emergency plan, snatching a baggie of saltines from my purse and popping one in my mouth. I sucked lightly on it, absorbing the salt into my tongue and softening the cracker before chewing slowly. Ah.

I took a seat at my desk. The computer was already on and I wiggled the mouse to wake it up. Shaking my head, I typed in my username and the RodeoQueen password. The computer logged me in and pulled up my home screen. The background was rodeo me, in a crown and sash. I growled, long and low. Jack knew not what he was doing, messing with a pregnant woman first thing in the morning. I opened my settings and clicked through options until I was able to change the offending image. I replaced it with a nice, soothing beach scene and exhaled.

Time to beard the lion in his den. I rang the bell with vigor.

Silence.

Picking the bell up, I started walking down the hall, ringing it for all I was worth.

"Ready or not, here I come."

No answer.

From inside Jack's office, I heard a creak and a thump. Rustling and clacking noises. Then a smack. I made it to the doorway. I sucked in a breath for courage, and breached the ramparts.

Jack sat at his desk, laptop open in front of him. From this view, without his hat on, I could see gray woven into his hair.

He looked up. "Yes?"

I scanned the room suspiciously, looking for signs of the twenty or so people it would have taken to make all that racket. Or possibly a herd of runaway steers. The room was empty, though, except for him. Empty and normal looking. God knew what he'd been doing in here, and I sure as heck didn't want to know myself, but somehow I couldn't keep from asking anyway.

Walking to his desk, I said, "What was all that noise?"

"What noise?"

"It sounded like you were having a party. Or a bomb went off."

He shook his head. "I dropped some books."

"Huh." Maybe. "Well, whatever it was, I just wanted to tell you, you're a thief."

He raised one eyebrow, framing the amber eye below it perfectly. For a second, I stood there, mesmerized. My super-irritating boss really did have arrestingly beautiful eyes. I gave myself a mental slap. And *I* was pregnant and not-yet-officially divorced and *he* had posted my Miss Rodeo Amarillo picture on my computer.

"The picture of me? My computer background?"

"Ah, yes. No, not a thief."

I waited several long seconds for him to elaborate, but of course he didn't. I threw up my hands and let them fall back against my thighs. It was only 8:05 in the morning and already he had me discombobulated. I'd have to learn not to let this man get my goat.

"Well, I'm here. What would you like me to work on?"

He lifted a file from his desk into the air. "Here's Sofia's file. Find out everything there is to know about her."

"Not a problem. I've tracked down enough people in my years as a paralegal—if Sofia's information can be found, I'll find it."

I reached out for the file but he held onto it. I put my hand down.

"And call Judith," he said. "Tell her we'll be there by noon tomorrow and can meet with Paul Johnson after lunch. Ask her to make all the arrangements."

"Who's Judith?"

"My secretary."

Ah, the missing secretary. "Can I get a phone number?"

He offered the file and I grabbed it. He scribbled something on a piece of paper. I grabbed that, too, and read the number. The area code was 575. I held the paper up.

"Where's 575?"

"Tularosa."

"Tula-huh?"

He cocked his head at me. "New Mexico. Near Alamogordo."

I still drew a blank.

He shook his head. "Southwest of Ruidoso, Albuquerque, Santa Fe?"

"Oh. Never heard of it. Why do I call her there?"

"Because that's where she is."

My hand itched. Did I really want to slap my boss? I'd never been a violent person before my pregnancy. I clenched my fist and used my most patient voice: "Why is she there?"

"Because that's where my office is."

"I thought this was your office?"

"This is my office, too."

"You realize you're about as clear as a mud puddle right now, don't you?"

He spoke very slowly and distinctly. "I have offices in Amarillo *and* in Tularosa. We are going to New Mexico tomorrow. Do you hear me now?"

"We, Kemosabe? I don't recall you asking me if I could travel. And for how long?"

He raised his left brow, the dimple side. The man had a lot of left-centric talent, I'd give him that.

"You have other plans?" He asked, sounding shocked at the thought.

Forget slapping. I wanted to strangle him, which made him the second person I'd imagined inflicting injury upon in the span of an hour. Was it them or was it me?

Them. Definitely them.

By noon my nausea had abated enough that I decided I didn't need to see a doctor. There was almost nothing I hated more than doctors, even at the best of times. I'd been in Amarillo for two weeks now and *still* hadn't set up an appointment with an obstetrician. It was pretty much a guarantee that, once I did, my cat would be out of the bag. No point in rushing to get to someplace I wasn't ready to go. Plus, I'd seen a doc in Dallas after I'd first peed on a stick. He'd said everything looked fine. I wasn't the first pregnant woman in the history of the world, and I'd survive.

Working diligently through the morning, Snowflake and I learned all there was to learn about Sofia Cristiana Perez of Amarillo via Mexico: nada. As in not a darn thing. Although the file on Sofia that Jack had given me was anorexically thin, I already knew from it that she had no prior criminal record, or any other kind of official record for that matter. Still, I double-checked everything imaginable. I also knew most of the information she'd given us was bogus. She'd submitted the Social Security number of a woman named Maria Delgado to her employers at the Wyndham/Ambassador. In fact, that's the name they knew her by. The phone number she'd given them was a throwaway. The address matched a mailbox storefront. When she was arrested, she'd given the police a different address, one for a very sketchy apartment complex that didn't have a name, in an even sketchier part of town. That's also when she'd told them about Valentina. The police and CPS had gone to pick the girl up, but she was gone.

That was about all we knew.

I sighed. What now? Snowflake sighed, circled three times, and curled up in a ball under my desk. I rubbed the little ball of fluff with my toes. Jack had left for the courthouse two hours ago, so I was on my own for additional ideas. I found a notepad in the desk drawer that said Williams & Associates at the top in the same stylized text as the wall hanging behind my desk. I co-opted it and started a list.

1. Call apartment's office.
2. Find the real Maria Delgado.
3. Call CPS to find out what they know from looking for Valentina.

I chewed on the capped end of my pen, then added

4. Find out more about Spike Howard.

No phone number was listed online for the nameless apartments. I pulled up the property records for their address. A Michael Q. Scott owned them, though what possible middle name started with a Q, I couldn't imagine. I did a white pages search. Found him and his phone number. Dialed it. When he answered, I explained why I was calling.

His voice was high-pitched, and very loud. "Lady, I don't give out no information on my renters without a court order. They got as much a right to privacy as anybody."

"But—"

"I already told the police and that CPS fairy. Ain't nobody named Sofia Perez rent from me. That apartment's rented by a totally different feller. He's all paid up through December. That's all I care about."

"Could you ask him to call me, Mr. Scott?"

"What, are you deaf? I don't give out no information on my renters."

I thought hard. What did I have left? An appeal to his humanity? "I'm not asking you to give me information, just to have him call me. A little girl's life could depend on it—a little girl that lived in that apartment."

"Yeah, well, I don't know no little girl that lives there neither. So bring me a court order or leave me alone."

He hung up.

Well, I knew more than I had before I'd called, but still nothing about Sofia. I would just have to visit the apartments on Monday. Not something to look forward to, so I prayed I'd find leads that would point me in a different direction. That meant back to my list. I put a star by the apartments' address and moved on to the next item. Find Maria Delgado. Nah. That one would be hard. I skipped to the third one. Call CPS. Much easier.

I dialed the number for the CPS investigator listed in the file: Wallace Gray. An automated voice answered and asked me to leave a message. I said my piece and ended the call. Crap. I looked at the fourth item. Find out who Spike Howard is. That was no easier than "find Maria Delgado," so I skipped back to item two.

I started by hunting for the Maria Delgado that matched the Social Security number Sofia had used for her job. I plugged the name and number into a couple of different databases. On the tenth one, People-Finders—voila—I found a phone number with an 806 area code. I dialed and someone picked up on the first ring.

"*Hola?*"

"Is this Maria Delgado?"

"*Yo soy* Maria."

I whipped out my stumbling college Spanish on her, and I managed to glean that a) she had no idea who Sofia Perez was, b) she had no idea how Sofia Perez had gotten her Social Security number, and c) she didn't know nothing 'bout nobody. Not that I believed her, I just had no leverage to get her to talk. I asked for her address, but she refused to give it to me.

That's okay. I had it from the Internet. I read it to her. "*Si?*"

She hung up.

I put a big star by her address. More fun follow-up for Monday.

Spike Howard was next. According to the *Amarillo Globe News* articles about the shooting, he worked for an import business and was visiting Amarillo on behalf of his employer. I Googled him and found a mother lode of information. I clicked, shuddered, scrolled, grimaced, and printed screens. Mr. Howard was from Roswell, New Mexico. All I knew about Roswell was that some spaceship supposedly crashed there and was covered up by the feds. That, and it was the location for the supernatural show we in Lubbock followed with cult-like glee while I was in college, since Roswell was only about a few hours away.

But where Spike Howard lived wasn't the most interesting part of what I found—though maybe interesting was the wrong word for it. More like the most disturbing part. Spike boasted a criminal record with assault charges going back to his teens in Dona Ana County, which was pretty far south from Roswell. In fact, it was on the border. Those crimes were bad enough, but it got worse. He'd done time under the "sexual conduct with a minor" section of the New Mexico criminal statutes. My stomach roiled as I read an article from the *Roswell Daily Record* that said he and an accomplice—an Amarillo man named Harvey Dulles—had exposed themselves to the ten-year-old daughter of Howard's live-in girlfriend in Roswell, then had taken turns making her touch them down *there*.

"An Amarillo connection?" I breathed. Snowflake snorted and rolled over in her sleep. Yes, Spike's friend Harvey was from Amarillo.

My phone chimed, interrupting me, and I jumped a little, bouncing my chair and jarring Snowflake. She yipped and rearranged herself.

Collin: *Sorry slow response. Traveling. I'm good. How are you?*

I smiled. It's always nice to hear from good-looking men who like you. I couldn't revel in it long, though. I was onto something with my research, no matter how oogie it was.

Neither Spike nor Harvey spent more than five years inside prison, which shocked me. How could child molesters get out so fast? Wouldn't they be the same people with the same tendencies doing the same thing, just to new victims? God, I hoped Jack didn't represent *that* type of defendant. I wanted no part of defending child molesters.

I started running Harvey Dulles through all my favorite databases. After his release, he'd returned to Amarillo—according to his voter's registration information—and he owned a house here, per the property records, which it appeared he'd inherited from his mother. Spike's connection to Harvey was too significant to ignore. Was Spike really in Amarillo on business, or was he hanging out with his old buddy? Or both? I printed out pictures of each man and put them in my file. Neither one was going to win any beauty contests, but Harvey was especially ugly with a smashed-in nose and shaved head.

A thought chilled me. What if Sofia had taken her daughter to work with her? What if this child molester, Spike, had exposed himself to Valentina, or worse? That would be enough to make a mother grab a gun and blow a man's head off.

My phone rang. Another number I didn't recognize. I answered. "Emily speaking."

The male voice that answered transported me back to Oak Lawn in Dallas. "This is Wallace Gray. I'm the CPS investigator working on the case of Valentina Perez. You called about her."

I straightened my posture. Excellent! "Hi, Wallace. Yes, I did. I'm Emily Bernal, the legal assistant for Jack Holden. He's representing Sofia Perez, Valentina's mother. We met with Sofia yesterday, and she was really worried about her daughter. I was hoping you had some good news about her that you could share with me."

"Nooooo, I wish I did." His voice dropped. "You're not tape recording me, are you?"

That got my attention. "No, why?"

"Because I am not granting permission to be recorded, and I don't want what I say on the news. So, this is all off the record."

"I'm not a reporter. I'm just a paralegal looking for our client's daughter."

"Good." Now he flat out whispered. "Then may I speak frankly?"

I tucked my phone tighter toward my shoulder and dropped my voice, too. "Yes, please." I almost laughed at myself. We were acting like two kids telling secrets on the playground.

"We can't find anyone that has ever seen or heard of Valentina."

I stood up, accidentally knocking my chair back, its rollers not responding on the carpeted floor. Snowflake raised her head. She looked like she was starting to get annoyed with me.

"No one?" I asked.

"No one. Not neighbors, not your client's co-workers. She's not

enrolled in school or day care. The police haven't found anything, either."
He pitched his voice even lower and softer.

I cupped my hand over my non-phone ear to block out other sounds as
he spoke.

"Is it possible your client's, you know, nuts?" He asked.

Was it? I thought about the woman I'd talked to the day before.
"Hmmm. I've only met her once. She didn't seem crazy."

Nausea came over me again, and I slipped the last saltine from my
baggie and nibbled it silently. Snowflake smacked her lips. I fished some
broken pieces out of the bag and tossed them to her. She licked them daintily, then swallowed them whole.

"There was no evidence whatsoever that a child lived in that apartment. None. Not clothes, a toothbrush, toys, nothing. Wait, I take that
back. There was one picture on the refrigerator—an odd drawing of a
brown person in a skirt. But that was it."

"That sounds promising, at least as evidence of a child. Did you get
anything else from it?"

Snack completed, Snowflake stood up and stretched, then whined. I
shot her a look. What did the whine mean?

"Yeah, it was interesting. The guy in the picture wore a skirt and no
shirt, and he had a big thing on his head—feathers or horns or something.
He was dancing or hopping, too. There were two letters in the bottom
right corner, an E and a P."

"Where little artists usually sign their pictures. Those aren't her initials,
though."

The P could be for Perez, but the E didn't fit Sofia or Valentina.
Snowflake's whines had increased in the last minute and now she walked
to the door and started howling.

"Nope. But it did look like it was drawn by a child, a young child,
although I can't say whether it was a boy or a girl, if that would even mean
anything. But there were no pictures of a girl in the apartment. The police
said there were none in Sofia's purse or on her phone either."

I shook my head. "That's just odd. What kind of mother doesn't have
pictures of her kid?"

"The kind that doesn't have one, maybe." He clucked.

Snowflake's howls changed to glass-shattering yips.

"What's that noise?"

"The office mascot, Jack's dog."

I decided Snowflake must be asking for a potty break, which wasn't a
bad idea for me, either. Yesterday afternoon Jack had set me up to take her
out every few hours. I snapped my fingers and she leapt over to me as I

pulled her leash from my left hand drawer. I clipped it on, then grabbed a doody bag before returning to the subject at hand.

"But Sofia was genuinely upset, to the extent she wasn't acting in her own best interests. She seemed sincere to me."

I opened the door and Snowflake lunged against the leash like a five-pound sled dog.

"As she would, if she was delusional."

"She said she wasn't crazy. Of course, she could be delusional about being sane."

Delusions of sanity. I could relate to that. I pressed the elevator call button.

"Have you *ever* had a murder defendant that didn't want to claim they were crazy?" Wallace asked. "That's crazy right there, to say you're not crazy."

I laughed. "Would you believe this is my first murder defendant? My first criminal case, even. I just started yesterday. I've been a civil litigation paralegal for nearly ten years. In Dallas."

Ding. We entered the elevator and Snowflake paced and whined. I prayed the call wouldn't drop and that the dog could hold it until we got outside. The doors closed and we descended.

The connection held up, and Wallace continued. "So you don't know the first thing about anything, do you, girl? Of course not. You just moved to Amarillo. The real question is why do a damn fool thing like that?"

The elevator doors opened at the ground floor, and we exited—me calmly, and Snowflake like the place was on fire.

"I can't say I didn't know better. I grew up here." Snowflake all but came unhinged as we walked outside to the Maxor courtyard. A huge outdoor kitchen area on the far side of a stone patio dominated the space, but the whole square area was surrounded by grass and mature oak trees nestled against the building's L-shape. Outside a black metal fence, down-town buzzed by us on two sides.

Wallace laughed once, loud, like a bark. "I'm so sorry."

I unclipped Snowflake. Her tags jingled as she bounded into the grass and got down to her business. Atta girl. She looked at me with something like relief on her little features.

"Yeah, I know, but waddaya gonna do?"

"Tell me about it. I got transferred here from Houston. Well, I'd be happy to help you in any way I can. You just say the word and Wallace is on the way."

"I'll take you up on it, and soon. But let me just ask you: Are the police and CPS still actively looking for Valentina?"

His tone darkened. "Absolutely. This mama may be crazy as a June bug, but if there's even the slightest chance some little six-year-old girl is out there alone with all the predators there are in this world, I simply will not give up until I find her."

His words filled me like helium, and it was so real I imagined I'd sound like Minnie Mouse when I spoke. He was one of the *truly* good guys. I bagged up Snowflake's leave-behind and tossed it in the trash before we reentered the building. The dog pranced like she owned the place now.

"Good. Did Sofia tell you anything about bad men she was afraid of?" I asked. "Afraid would get Valentina? She hinted at this with us and then clammed up."

"Huh-uh," he said. "And that would be weird, since she told me she just let the girl stay at home with the door locked while she was at work."

That felt wrong. Sofia didn't seem like the kind of mother to leave her six-year-old at home alone, especially if she was scared of bad men. We hopped an elevator going up.

"Nothing about the father?" I asked.

"She said he was dead."

"Okay, she didn't give you much more than she gave us, then."

The doors parted at our floor. Snowflake lunged against the leash, panting and straining toward the office. I tugged her gently in the other direction and she looked up at me, confused.

"Well, your bad guy angle is new to me," Wallace said. "Listen, the police are still going door-to-door and talking to informants, checking in with homeless shelters, and rousting people in all the usual types of places kids go in that area. We'll keep looking for her. And you let me know if you guys learn anything, okay?"

I pushed the bathroom door open and let Snowflake walk in first.

"I will," I said.

Then I had a thought—I didn't want to go alone to the shady areas I'd have to visit as I searched for information on Sofia.

"I'm going to visit witnesses that may have information about Valentina on Monday," I said. "Some you may have already talked to, but sometimes people decide to open up when you circle back to them. One of them you didn't mention, though. The woman whose identity Sofia used to get a job."

I'd positioned myself in a stall.

"Could you hang on a second?" I pressed mute.

"Sure."

Snowflake stood in front of me, staring. It gave me stage fright. I closed my eyes. Better.

When I was done, I ended mute and said, "I'm back. I was telling you about going to talk to witnesses. If you'd like to come with me, to any or all of them, you're welcome to. Strength in numbers."

"Would I ever. Who's driving?"

I washed my hands at the creamy tan marble sink. I wasn't sure when Rich would have my car delivered.

"I don't have a car here. Yet." Yeah, that made me sound like a loser. "I'm getting mine shipped to me soon," I added quickly.

I turned to look for a blower. None. I eyed the towel dispenser. Empty. Okay. I fanned my hands, which basically did nothing. I wiped them on my navy pants.

"How about I pick you up at nine thirty? If we have time, I can take you to lunch at the GoldenLight Café. Great burgers and, *Lord*, the Frito pie! You'll probably go into cardiac arrest after your first bite, but it'll be worth it."

I pulled the door open to Williams & Associates, unclipping Snowflake to let her run free. She sprinted back to Jack's office like white lightning. I decided not to tell Wallace that I was a vegetarian—yet. I lowered myself into my chair and leaned my head back.

"Perfect," I said, before giving him the address.

I ended the call smiling. Not that I wasn't going to worry about that little girl—whether she was real or not—but at least Wallace was on the case.

The door swung inward, and my boss followed. My heart did a little acrobatic number in my chest, which annoyed the pee-waddlin'-squat out of me. He had a longer list of bad qualities than Rich, and I went through them in my mind: eccentric, annoying, cryptic, and pushy. Snowflake careened down the hall and launched herself at him full speed. He crouched and caught her in one arm, mid-flight. She set upon him with kisses and yips.

"Well? Did you break Sofia's case wide open yet?" Jack asked. He set the dog down and she ran circles around the office, jumping on and off the couch during each loop.

"I keep learning less instead of more," I said. "But the police and CPS think she's dreaming up the daughter. They're still looking, but—"

"What?"

He put one arm over his head and one at his waist and did a little mariachi dance. Snowflake stood on her hind legs in front of him then started hopping and spinning.

"We'll plead insanity," he said. "And the APD and CPS will testify on our behalf. That's the best news I've heard all day!"

I raised my brows as my mouth fell open. I didn't know about *Sofia's* mental health, but I was pretty sure my boss was nuts.

FIVE

When Jack told me we were going to New Mexico on Saturday, I assumed he meant on Southwest Airlines. I knew things were amiss when he directed me to meet him at the Tradewind Airport. I hadn't ever heard of it, and I was pretty sure that Southwest hadn't either. It turned out that the little airport was only ten minutes south of downtown. Emphasis on the *little* part. It had a convenient location going for it, but nothing else that I could see. Mother drove me, and she pulled into the tree-lined lot, right up behind Jack's car. He emerged from the driver's seat, and I waved at him. He waved back.

I got out and pulled my luggage from the backseat.

Jack, with Snowflake on a pink leash at his heels, came around to stand beside me, facing my mother and her open window.

"Agatha, I hope you're having a blessed Saturday," he said.

I heard the teasing note in his voice, but it didn't seem she did.

"You too, Jack."

Then she bit her lip and my heart sank to my stomach. *Here we go.*

"This trip doesn't have anything to do with that illegal alien client of yours, does it?" my mother asked.

I cringed. I could only thank God that she hadn't added "or her little brown girl" like she had with me last night, as she explained how messed up it was that not only were we paying for that woman's defense but for the girl's schooling and health care. Maybe she'd forgotten I'd married a brown man (notwithstanding that it didn't end well)? My God, if she was that upset about Valentina, I'd hate to see how she'd act if she learned I was pro-choice.

Jack ignored the implications of her comment. I realized I didn't know how he felt about these issues himself.

"No, nothing at all," he said. "We're on a different case entirely."

Which I wished we weren't. I had ended yesterday energized, engaged, and determined. I would have rather visited the witnesses in Sofia's case today, and maybe I could have turned up some leads on Valentina's whereabouts. A cloudy vision of the little girl I'd never seen had haunted my dreams again last night. In them, we were at a rodeo. I had on my bright red-and-yellow clown uniform and was in the ring, protecting the cowboys when she ran in, a tiny wisp of girl in pink Barbie pajamas. A bull charged toward her and, before I could distract it, I woke up. I wasn't sure it was Valentina, but who else would it be after a day of researching her mother and her?

"Oh good. Well, take good care of Emily. She's been through a lot lately, what with—"

I stepped up to her window, blocking her access to Jack. I leaned in and kissed her cheek. "Goodbye, Mother."

She took the hint and rolled up her window. When I was sure I'd seen the last of her taillights, I turned and started wheeling my suitcase toward a pint-sized terminal. My little bag bounced and hopped across the pock-marked parking lot. It appeared it had last been resurfaced after the Second World War. Jack—and the ever-jingly Snowflake—caught up to me.

He tugged on the sleeve of my turquoise tunic and said, "This way."

He pointed toward a large sheet-metal hangar—not unlike the county jail where we'd met with Sofia—then took off at breakneck speed. Snowflake's legs churned to keep up with him. All she needed was a little buggy behind her and she'd look just like a thimble-sized harness racing horse.

After a few minutes, I'd fallen a hundred feet behind them. A white-hot feeling rose up in my insides and I thought about chucking a rock at him to remind him I was back here. Dear God, what was it with me and all of these felonious urges lately? I scowled, at myself and at my boss.

"'Scuse me, Jack, hold up."

Jack turned back. The morning sun made him look like a young John Wayne on the big screen. "Sorry."

He waited for me, then slowed down enough that I could trot beside him. That worked for about fifteen seconds. The weather was crisp and football-ready, but I was sweaty and lightheaded. I fell behind again, so I reached out to grasp his arm.

"Stop, please."

He did, turning quite abruptly, and my forward momentum plowed me (and my suitcase) into him. He caught me by an elbow on one side and my waist on the other. Even in his grasp I kept going until my face landed against his chest. Somehow, Jack managed to keep us both upright. The impact sent shockwaves of sex-starved pregnancy hormones rushing through my body. With only my knit tunic and leggings separating me from him and his cowboy wear, he felt good. Darn good. Snowflake yelped at our feet, but I tried to block her out and linger in the unexpectedly nice moment.

"Whoa, Bessie," Jack said in my ear.

I bristled. That solved my hormonal problem. "Are you calling me a bovine?"

I wrenched my arm away and stood back on my own two feet.

He squinted at me, looking a little spooked. Then his mouth made an O.

"Uh," he said, "just an expression."

Pausing for emphasis between the words, I said, "Jack. Ass."

His jaw fell. "What?"

"Just an expression."

I raked a murderous glare across his face, daring him to cross me, but instead he grinned ear to ear.

"Jack. Ass." He said it just like I had. "I like it."

"Argh!"

I didn't care that I was yelling as I started marching toward the hangar again, dragging my bag, which by now had a rock caught in one of its wheels, which stopped spinning. I hated that he'd driven me to cursing, and hated it even more that he liked it. He caught up easily and fell in stride with me.

Well, the horse was out of the barn, so I might as well ride it. "Do you mind telling me what the travel arrangements are, Mr. Ass?"

Was it my imagination, or was that a twinkle in the eyes that didn't meet mine? "Sure. I have a Cessna 172—er, Skyhawk. It's very comfortable. Snowflake rides shotgun, so you'll be in back. You can even nap. It'll take about three and a half hours to get there."

This didn't sound right. This sounded really quite wrong, in fact. I swallowed, hard.

"A Skyhawk? Is that a jet?"

He laughed, too loud. "No, it's, um, a single engine, and, uh, it has high wings and a propeller."

Suddenly I saw spots. I didn't look at him, just tried to breathe evenly and get through this spell of lightheadedness. As my vision cleared, I spied a totem-pole-like sign ahead. White arrows pointed from it in all directions. Big blue letters on each arrow identified different destinations and mileage to them from here. Albuquerque was about halfway down: 285.

I gulped a big breath and spoke in a rush: "You didn't think it might be worth mentioning to me that we're flying in a toy-sized airplane? And where's the pilot of this thing anyway?" My voice wobbled like I was singing opera.

He turned to me, and his whole body radiated his grin. "Emily, you aren't scared of small planes, are you?"

Four hours and three barf bags later, Jack hollered back to me that we were making our final descent. Snowflake peered out the side of her kennel from where it was buckled into the seatbelt in the front passenger seat.

I shot a feeble bird toward the front seat and muttered, "Not you, Snowflake."

I kept my head in bag number four, my body slumped against the side of the plane, and my head vibrating along with the frame. The engine, prop, and wind noises were unbelievably loud, and I was now attuned to every change in the sounds—and even more so to every bounce and wobble. I already knew we were going down. The only question was whether it was by design or not; I was past caring much.

I decided to sit back up. I loved Albuquerque, and if we were going to die, I wanted the last thing I saw to be the city and the Sandia Mountains, not the inside of the airplane. All I had left was the dry heaves, anyway. I couldn't believe how sick I'd been. I'd never gotten airsick before. It was probably my little bean. I kept the bag right where it was, just in case, and peered out the window.

What I saw cleared my head and dried my mouth instantly. No city. No mountains. Just desert right below, coming at us, fast.

"Jack, we're going to crash!" I screamed, lurching forward and dropping my barf bag to the floor.

I put my head between my knees and my hands over the back of my head. The barf bag had fallen on its side between my feet and the last of my stomach bile trickled out and pooled in a foamy mess that managed to reach both of my soles. At least I hadn't worn sandals.

No answer from Jack. Just then the plane hit the ground with a wrenching jolt. I tensed, ready for us to cartwheel into broken bits and flames. The plane roared, then slowed so fast it was like the wheels had hit a sandbar. My body weight strained forward against my seat belt, and my head bounced on my knees as we careened over rough earth.

And then the pressure eased and we slowed, almost to a stop, and made a tight left turn. The plane rolled forward almost casually, jostling me again, but more gently this time. Slowly, I sat up. No carnage. No inferno. We had landed, and I wasn't dead.

The plane was taxiing down what looked like a little dirt road to a tan metal barn with a silver roof. Beside it was a pole with an orange flag—no, an orange bag or sock of some kind—blowing horizontally in the strong wind. Next to it was some kind of big white tank on thin metal legs. I could now see mountains behind us to my left, which I was very glad I hadn't seen before landing. They were way too close. Where were we?

A vintage blue Suburban was parked near the barn. As I watched, a woman of medium height with long, dark gray hair got out of the driver's side. She was clad in blue jeans and a boxy shirt that, even from a distance, had a New Mexican vibe to it. Earthen colors. Something long hanging in the neck area. As we got closer, I could see that she wore moccasins on her feet, and that she had dark skin, sharp features, and broad cheekbones. She walked to the barn and raised its door. Jack pulled the plane to the entrance, turned it around facing back where we'd come from, then shut it off.

The instant quiet was deafening.

He opened his door and hopped out, then leaned back in, saying, "Welcome to New Mexico."

I thought very seriously for a moment about punching him in the throat. But he was the only criminal attorney I knew, and it was pretty clear I was going to need him to represent me sooner rather than later at the rate my hormones were going. I kept silent and gritted my teeth.

Jack moved his seat forward and stepped out of my line of vision. Outside, I heard the woman greeting him and his friendly reply. I had to pull myself together. I unbuckled my seat belt and carefully gathered up my three full puke bags. Stepping gingerly over the mess in the floorboard, I followed him out, then reached back in for bag four on the floor. I held them up to show Jack, cocked my head, and lifted my shoulders.

He pointed to a barrel inside the barn. "You okay? Need a bottle of water?"

I tilted my chin higher and nodded.

"There's a case of bottled water just on the other side of the hangar from the barrel."

"Thank you."

I disposed of my mess and grabbed a water, sucking saliva like mouthwash through the insides of my mouth to try to make it a little less vile. I uncapped the bottle, took a slug, swished and spit away from Jack and the woman, then greedily sucked down half the contents. Only then did I walk back toward them, smoothing my hair into place.

Jack put his hand on the woman's shoulder. "Judith, this is Emily. Emily, Judith."

His secretary. The one I'd talked to on the phone. I dipped my head. "Hello, Judith. Very nice to meet you. I'd shake your hand, but it was a rough flight and I'm . . ."

She nodded as I trailed off, but didn't say a word to me. To Jack she said, "I had Mickey drop me off, Boss. I thought I'd make sure everything here was all right and ride back to the office with you."

I wondered how much there really was to take care of here, in the middle of a pasture, but she went on.

"I mowed the runway and ran off some pronghorns," she said. "We've got some prairie dogs that have set up down near the end. I don't think they'll be a problem, but you might want to take a look."

Wow. If that was the kind of work his secretary did, I was really glad I was the paralegal.

Jack treated it like her mowing the runway was no big deal. "Thanks. Sounds good."

He got Snowflake out and grabbed our bags while I retrieved my purse. We took our things to the Suburban, and Snowflake and I got in, but Jack walked back to the plane with Judith. They positioned themselves on either side of the fuselage, leaning over at the waist and placing their hands on the struts. Together they rolled the plane a few feet to the tank I'd seen earlier. Jack lifted a nozzle and stuck it into the wing of the plane. Fuel, I surmised. While this was going on, Jack went into the barn and came out with a spray can of Lysol. He leaned into the backseat and appeared to spray it, for a very long time, then brought the bottle back and tossed it in the trash barrel. I burned with mortification. A few minutes later, he and Judith pushed the Skyhawk backwards into the barn. Then they came back out, Jack pulling the door down shut behind him. He fastened a padlock, then followed Judith to the Suburban. He clambered into the driver's seat and she went to the front passenger side.

"Next stop, the office," Jack said, starting the Suburban down a dirt road leading away from the barn and the runway.

The land was dotted with clusters of green yucca (with tall stalks of dried blossoms) and other high desert plants, like tufts of cascading bear grass. There were some whitish-pink and some bright yellow flowered shrubs, neither of which I recognized. The nearby foothills were treed, although we were too far away for me to tell with what. There were no trees out here on the desert plain. It looked so desolate, with no people or buildings in sight—save the hangar behind us. More desolate even than the Panhandle.

The Panhandle might not have trees, but it had grassland—not desert

—and there weren't many spots that were as devoid of civilization as this. Heck, as devoid of all forms of life. I felt like I was on the surface of the moon, a million miles away from my own life. Not just from my life in Dallas, but from my reestablished life in Amarillo. From Sofia, who was doing God knew what in a prison, and from Valentina, the little girl I'd never seen but couldn't get out of my mind. I hoped they were all right. There was nothing I could do from here.

My phone chimed. "Sorry," I said. I turned off the ringer and read the text.

Collin: *Emily, you there?*

Me: *If by "there" you mean New Mexico, the answer is yes.*

I hit send. The answer came back immediately.

Collin: *No way! Where?*

Me: *Tularosa.*

I thought I was in Tularosa, anyway. I definitely wasn't in Albuquerque. We could have been anywhere, though.

Collin: *"So you're near Alamogordo?"*

I remembered Jack's explanation.

Me: *Yes.*

Collin: *That's where I am this weekend. How long are you there? Any chance of getting together?*

Collin lived in Taos and was based out of Santa Fe. What was he doing here? And wanting to get together, now, when I was pregnant? He didn't even know I was getting a divorce.

I typed: *I would love it. I'm here for work, just for the weekend. I'll let you know my plans as soon as I talk to my boss. So . . . maybe.*

We crossed a cattle guard and turned right onto a paved highway. I looked back at the entrance, marked with a metal sign suspended above the gate: Wrong Turn Ranch. Wind tossed it to and fro. The name sounded familiar.

"Where are we?" I asked.

Jack turned until I saw his profile and said, "Highway 70. Halfway between Bent and Tularosa. The Sacramento Mountains and Lincoln National Forest are behind us, the Sierra Blancas behind you to your right. We'll be at my office in about ten minutes."

I laid my head back against the seat and let my eyes close. It had been a rough few hours. Judith and Jack talked while I remembered Collin and his 501 jeans, looking as much like Tom Cruise in *Top Gun* as Tom Cruise ever had. I strolled into the dream as the Kelly McGillis character, the instructor in the leather jacket, only I had a baby bump, and Tom Cruise didn't give me a second glance.

I must have dozed off, because when the Suburban jolted to a stop (typical Jack), it woke me up abruptly. I looked around us. We were on a broad, small-town street in a residential neighborhood. Scrubby trees and patchy yards stretched in front of stucco houses—or adobe, I guess they called it here. Jack had parked in front of a small, red adobe house with a Columbia blue door and a metal Kokopelli bear totem painted in the same color hanging beside it. The front yard was grassless and covered in small, red landscaping rocks. An aged bronze sign hung like a flag off a pole. It read Law Office.

Jack put the Suburban in park and said, "Home sweet home."

SIX

Judith ushered me inside. "Lobby," she said as we walked through what once was a den. It now housed an old leather couch and side chair, a coffee table with a Johnny Football-covered Sports Illustrated on top of a stack of magazines. A deer antler lamp sat on an end table between the couch and chair. Black and white photos of mountain and desert scenes adorned the walls.

"Kitchen." She pointed to her left as we walked down a central hall. The small room had white cabinets and appliances on three sides with a wooden table and chairs in the center.

She swung to the right. "Conference room." A large, weathered, round wooden table anchored the room. Burgundy leather rolling chairs surrounded it. A corner table held a phone. Again, landscape photography hung on the walls, these in color.

Judith took a few steps, then stopped and turned to me. "Here's the bathroom," she said, indicating the door on the right side of the hall. "Jack's office." The left. "Mine." The right again. "He had me set an extra desk up for you," she said. "You have your laptop?"

"Yes, I brought it." I patted my shoulder bag. I'd even stashed my clutch in it, since I'd prepped it for airport security. It was nearly two pounds lighter and a few inches slimmer than usual. I flashed her a big smile. Her face remained still. I noticed that, for a woman of her age in such a dry climate, she sure didn't have many smile wrinkles or laugh lines.

She stood in the doorway to her office and pointed at a bare table. "The network cable's underneath."

"Thanks."

She walked in soundlessly, not so much as flinching to show she'd heard me.

Jack came up behind me, his boots noisier than Judith's. "Everything good?"

I nodded. Judith's cold welcome wasn't something I would unload on him.

"What's our plan?" I asked.

"Judith ordered in lunch for our meeting with Paul Johnson. He'll be here at one. That's . . ." he glanced at his watch, "in half an hour."

I had time to brush my teeth and take a French shower, at least. "Is the car unlocked? I need to grab my overnight bag."

He tossed me the keys—a horrible throw—and my left hand shot up and caught them as they went past my ear.

"Why don't you come to my office when you're done and I'll bring you up to speed."

"Thanks. One more thing." I inhaled and my breath hit a wall, stopping shallow. "I have a friend in Alamogordo. Do we have time for me to go out for breakfast tomorrow?"

His eyes narrowed slightly. "We'll leave about ten a.m. Can you be back and ready by then?"

"Yes, thank you."

I rushed through my ablutions in the ancient bathroom. It was so small that my elbow hit the rubber ducky shower curtain while I washed my face. I rubbed my face with a tear away paper towel from a kitchen-style roll, then put on some nude lipstick and mascara. *Still too pale,* I thought. I swiped the lipstick over my cheekbones and lightly rubbed it in. Better. In the mirror, I saw a photograph behind me. The photographer had captured four Native American dancers with elaborate headdresses, their bare torsos painted with white symbols, skirts hanging almost to their knees over moccasin boots. I turned to study it. It was really beautiful. The photographer had signed it in the bottom right corner. I leaned in close to read the name: *Mountain Spirits. Lena Holden.*

I thought about the name for a moment. I recognized it—and not just because of the obvious last name—but I couldn't place it. Damn pregnancy hormones. Besides turning me into a rage monster, they'd siphoned off a fair portion of my brain function.

I took a moment to text Collin before I left the bathroom: *I can meet for an early breakfast if you can come up my way.*

I packed up my bathroom bag and returned it to the car, then went to Jack's office.

His Tularosa digs were nothing much compared to the ones in Amarillo, but it was still a nice, warm space. A rug that looked to be a Native design graced one wall, a bookcase covered another, and UNM Law and NMSU diplomas hung on either side of a large, bare window. The desk here looked much like the one in Amarillo: messy, with picture frames turned to face Jack. Two armchairs with cowhide upholstery sat in front of his desk; I took the one nearest the door. Jack had his back to me, a book in his lap. Snowflake snoozed in a bed by the door, looking awfully at home.

I cleared my throat.

Jack swiveled around and set the book on his desk and closed it. I read the title: *Spider Woman's Daughter*. Anne Hillerman.

"New client," he said. "Paul Johnson. Native New Mexican. Grew up in Las Cruces. Made his money in nightclubs, in New Mexico and West Texas. Started importing cheap art from Mexico. You know, like the metal chickens and geckos. Made more money. Has a ranch just east of here—gorgeous place, near Bent."

He said this like the location would mean something to me. It rang a little bell, but I couldn't place it.

"Not far from where we flew in this morning," he said.

Ah. The bell rang louder. "What are we doing for him?" I asked.

"Nothing yet. He asked me for this meeting so he could explain what he's looking for. He wants me on retainer."

"You mentioned that his employees tend to attract negative legal attention?"

"Yep," Jack said. "Bouncers. Truck drivers. Warehouse guards. Rough types."

"What do you want me to do during the meeting?" I asked.

"Listen. Ask questions. Then, next week, I want you to find out everything there is to know about him."

"That's all?"

"And eat. I have a feeling your stomach is kind of empty."

"Hello?" a girl's voice called from the front of the office.

Judith was in the kitchen working on lunch, so I walked out to the lobby. A tall, thin teenage girl in knee-high buckskin moccasins stood there. Freckles covered her cheeks and a large, distinctive nose, but elsewhere her skin was so white it was almost blue. It was her hair that captured my attention. Somehow she'd fashioned her kinky black hair into individual locks, almost like ringlets, except that it radiated from her head, no strand longer than what appeared to be shoulder length. It was part

Afro, part dreadlocks, and part finger-in-a-light-socket. I couldn't have made a single hair on my head defy gravity like hers.

"Hell-*lo*." She snapped me out of my trance.

I adjusted my tunic, and cleared my throat. "How may I help you?"

"My father sent me in to find out if this is Jack Holden's office. He has a meeting with him." She dragged out the "fa" in father and dropped an octave on "ther." The girl didn't like her dad much.

"Yes, this is the place."

"He said to tell him he's on the phone and will be in as quickly as he can." She rolled her eyes ever so slightly. "That means don't hold your breath."

"Great. Thank you."

The girl made a show of giving the place a once-over, then walked out without another word on whisper-soft footsteps that put my scouting skills to shame.

Twenty minutes later, Paul Johnson joined us in the conference room. Jack and I made small talk with him as we got situated. He didn't look like any businessman I'd ever known. He looked like a bouncer gone to seed—with a grizzled chin and hooded eyes—who'd stolen himself some fancy cowboy clothes. He stood six foot six in his boots, and he had to be at least three hundred pounds. His buttocks and thighs strained against Cinch jeans, and his girth tested the snaps on his shirt. Despite all of that, he had a ready smile and booming laugh, so I ignored the seediness as best I could and concentrated on the fact that he wanted to bring a lot of business to the firm I worked for, however temporarily.

Judith rolled in a cart and arranged three place settings in front of us. Addressing Jack, she said, "It's from Casa de Suenos."

"Thanks. Good call. Best New Mexican food in Southern New Mexico." Jack smiled at her.

"In all of New Mexico." Paul reached for one of the two plates of enchiladas. There was red chili and green chili—he chose red.

I wondered if any of the entrees were meatless. "Thank you." I reached for a platter of fried things. Fried appetizers were usually veggie. And anything fried was my favorite food group these days. I pushed two onto my plate.

Judith nodded at me. "Avocados Borrachos. Beer battered fried avocados. They're good with that jalapeño ranch dressing."

This was as friendly as she'd been to me so far, and I was so shocked I couldn't think of a response before she turned and disappeared, leaving the door open.

I scooped some of the ranch onto my plate, then added generous helpings of rice and beans. I looked up at Jack, and he nodded at my plate and raised his left eyebrow. It rehabilitated some of the sexiness he'd lost by flying me in a small plane to a dirt runway in the middle of nowhere. I grabbed another avocado and wiggled my eyebrows back. He hadn't put a thing on his plate. I dipped the avocado in ranch, then bit into it. I groaned, and both men looked over at me.

"Excuse me." I coughed into my napkin. "Something stuck in my throat."

Jack's dimple appeared quick as a heartbeat and disappeared just as fast. "Are you okay?"

I felt my checks heat. "Yes, thank you."

Paul dug back into his food, but he was the next one to break the silence anyway, speaking through a big mouthful as he chewed. *Raised in a barn*, I thought.

"Thanks for having me over to talk, and for the lunch," Paul said. "I just bought some property on the south side of 70. I guess that makes us practically neighbors, Jack."

I caught a glimpse of a half-masticated bite of red enchilada in Paul's mouth. My gag response hovered near the surface these days, and that triggered it. I covered my mouth with my hand and pretended to cough again, averting my eyes. I saw the twinkle in Jack's.

"You said on the phone you wanted to talk to me about putting my firm on retainer to help you when there are criminal matters impacting your business dealings." Jack said, not acknowledging Paul's comment about neighbors.

Paul said, "That's right."

This time, he showed us green enchilada, but I was able to suppress my gag. I put my fork down.

"May I ask how you found us?"

Paul popped a whole fried avocado in his mouth and said, "I read about you in the Alamogordo paper, a few years back—when you were still with the DA's office. Then I heard on the news that you were representing that woman up in Amarillo, the one that murdered the Roswell guy, and that you had an office here, too. I said, 'That's the attorney I need to call.'"

Jack stuck to the subject, still talking over an empty plate. "You have employees that have been charged with murder?"

Paul shook his head and held up his hand, still chewing. Too much food crammed in his maw for even him to talk through it? That must be some mouthful. He opened his mouth and sprayed some rice on the table in front of him. I looked away.

"No," he said, "but assault and battery. New Mexico and West Texas. You never know when a man will have to defend himself with deadly force in the kinds of work I have them doing, though." He paused, looked at his food, then back up at Jack. "Is that what that woman in Amarillo was doing? Defending herself?"

I'd known Jack just long enough to see the change that came over him. His jaw flexed, barely perceptibly, and his pupils dilated. His nostrils flared ever so slightly. And he thumped his pen once, hard on the tabletop.

"Run me through your businesses and where you operate. Then we'll need to go over your past legal troubles, and what you're facing now. See if I can help, and how."

I pushed my sadly full plate back, opened my laptop, and started taking notes.

SEVEN

After our meeting concluded, I devoted the rest of the afternoon to researching the names of businesses Paul had given us. I wouldn't have thought it in the first ten minutes, but after spending two hours with Paul, I liked the guy. I think he'd even won Jack over. He had a self-deprecating sense of humor and told funny stories about the nightclub business and the escapades of drunken patrons.

As I worked, I kept flashing back on the signed photo of the Mountain Spirits in the bathroom. I went and studied it again and perused the other photos in the lobby. Lena Holden's name appeared in the bottom right corner of all of them. Who was she? I returned to my laptop and resumed work. Finally, I broke down.

"Judith?"

The woman hadn't said a word since I'd returned to our shared space after the meeting, hadn't even glanced my way. In a flat voice, she answered without looking away from her computer screen.

"Yes."

I rolled my chair in her direction—not too close, but close enough that I could talk in a voice that Jack couldn't hear. "The photographs in the office are so beautiful. They're signed by Lena Holden. Is she related to Jack?"

Two eyes sharp as flint slowly rose to meet mine. The hair I'd thought was gray earlier was really more salt-and-pepper. She wore it pulled back into one long braid, and the black strands running through it matched her eyes. Her nose dominated her face, but she was beautiful, nonetheless.

Without changing expression, she stared at me until I almost said, "Never mind."

Then she looked back at her screen. "Jack's wife."

"Oh, okay. Thank you. I, um, didn't know her name," I lied, heart pounding.

Jack's wife. I rolled back to my desk, flummoxed. Well, he must have been one of those guys who didn't wear a wedding band. I should have guessed it, given that he never gave a straight answer to a question, but I couldn't help feeling misled.

It took all I had to focus on my work. I'd made it only about halfway through my list when Jack asked me to brief him on what I'd found so far. My research was as happy as the hair on a mangy dog at that point, so I stalled him for ten more minutes and scurried to pull something together.

When I had myself somewhat organized, I joined him in his office. I gave him the quick run-down on Johnson, looking at my yellow pad instead of up at him. In a nutshell, it was too soon to tell much about his new client but, so far, I'd found nothing that contradicted what Johnson had told us.

"I'll finish the rest when we get back to Amarillo," I said. "Especially the stuff about Mr. Johnson, personally."

"Sounds good," Jack said. "I have a stack of other clients I need to get you started on soon, too."

That made me think about Sofia. And Valentina. "Have you heard anything about Sofia?" I asked.

I snuck a glance down at the phone in my lap to see if I had any notifications from Wallace, but I didn't. Other than him texting to confirm that he was picking me up at nine thirty on Monday, I hadn't heard from him, but it wasn't as if I'd expected to—it's just that I'd hoped for good news.

Jack looked at me funny, like *I* was funny. "The guards don't exactly call me with updates on my clients," he said.

"Yeah, well, I—never mind."

I wanted to pop off at him, but I was tired. Belatedly, I realized that, once again, he hadn't even answered what I'd asked.

From the lobby area of the office, Judith called out goodbye. The front door shut behind her and Jack and I were left alone.

"Time for us to pack up." He stood and grabbed his briefcase.

I stood, too, and asked, "Where am I staying?"

Tularosa didn't seem like it had a lot of hotels, and I had left everything up to Judith, at his request.

"The guest suite at Wrong Turn Ranch," he said as he closed his laptop and disconnected his power cord.

"Where we landed today?"

"Um hmm." He stuck his laptop in his bag. The Anne Hillerman book followed it.

I hadn't seen signs for a bed and breakfast at the entrance. Oh well. It must be a nice place, if it had a landing strip. I felt a flicker of hopeful excitement that sent tingles through my body, reenergizing me, enough that my bad mood started to fade away.

"Okay," I said.

I gathered all my things, then stopped. Even if this job with Jack was just short term, it didn't hurt to try to win Judith over. Plus, maybe I had unknowingly offended her somehow. She'd taken care of everything for me, after all, whether she'd wanted to or not. I would try harder. I jotted a quick thank-you note to her and left it in her chair.

Jack, Snowflake, and I got in the Suburban and drove out of town, toward the mountains. The setting sun cast a red glow across their slopes, and the desert in front of us looked almost golden in the evening light. A pronghorn antelope with large horns grazed off the highway to our right and, in the distance, the rugged desert topography morphed rapidly into foothills.

I snuck a glance at Jack's profile and asked, "Did you grow up here?"

He nodded—and kept nodding for a few seconds. "My dad bred race horses."

My jaw dropped. "You're kidding me. That's awesome!"

The last of my hurt feelings gave way. I could be upset later. This topic was too alluring to resist.

The way his face moved, I knew his left side was smiling and dimpled, even though the part I could see remained basically the same.

"Yeah, it wasn't bad. He and Mom retired to the RV touring life. They stop in a few times a year."

"What happened to the horses?"

"They're still around. There's a full staff and a ranch manager who profit-shares, so it runs like a top."

"I'd love to see it, if we have time."

He shot me a funny look. "I think we can fit it in."

He turned on his left blinker, and we turned into the Wrong Turn Ranch gate.

"That's a funny name," I said.

We drove fifteen feet further and Jack braked at a small sign. I read "If you're here, you've made a wrong turn. Highway 70 is behind you."

I laughed. "I love it."

He was looking at me, so I got an eyeful of the dimple and lopsided smile this time. His wife must love those. Irritation flickered in me, but it wasn't enough to overcome the good feelings that had taken over. Jack drove on, and the road split in two in front of us. The left fork was less traveled. He stayed to the right.

"Airstrip that way." He pointed left.

How convenient that the ranch had an airstrip on their property for visitors. I wondered how many people really flew themselves around, though. It made for a unique marketing angle for a remote B&B, I supposed. It could help to differentiate them for an upscale clientele. Maybe that's why they didn't have a sign for the B&B on the road. Privacy for the rich and famous. I hugged myself.

The road wound to the right, toward the mountains. "We came right over these mountains when we landed?" I asked.

"Yep."

I couldn't believe I'd been completely oblivious to them, but then I *had* been otherwise occupied. Ahead of us I saw the B&B. It was a large, two-story log house set against the foothills of the mountains. It had what looked like a guest house way off in the distance behind it, and multiple ranch-type outbuildings closer-in of various sizes in tan metal with silver roofs. The main house looked well-kept, but like it had seen a lot of history —the good kind.

I sighed. "It's beautiful."

"And really warm for this time of year. Some of the trees haven't even dropped their leaves yet." Jack said. He gestured toward the mountains, and I saw flashes of yellow and red in the treetops, deciduous outposts in a vast expanse of evergreen.

I turned my attention back toward the B&B. Beyond the buildings I saw something even better. I drew a reverent breath. Horses. *Lots* of horses. As we drew closer, I could see that they were quarter horses— really amazing ones—in blacks and rich browns. A truck pulled up to their gate and a black horse with one white sock ran toward it, tail and head both high in the air.

"They even have horses," I said. "What a great place."

"Yeah, I think it is."

Jack pulled to a stop in the circle in front of the house. I got out with my purse and laptop bag and went to the rear to get my suitcase. Jack set Snowflake on the ground and waved me off. I almost scampered up the steps to the front porch, my heart thumping with excitement. What a fantastic getaway this was turning out to be, small planes and barf bags aside. When I reached the door, I stopped. Snowflake sat and looked up at me questioningly. I wasn't sure of my B&B etiquette. Knock, or go on in?

Jack solved it for me. He shouted, "It should be unlocked."

I held my breath, pulled the lever on the front door, and pushed it open. The front entry opened onto a trussed great room. A stone chimney was centered on one wall, stretching to the high ceiling. The stones were enormous, some at least a few hundred pounds. Leather furniture and Southwestern rugs and blankets filled the space. My heart caught in my throat. Most women dreamed of mansions on grand estates or in exotic cities. Not me. I dreamed of a ranch house and horses and mountains and . . . I faltered, the emotion of my true situation catching up with me: broke, almost single, pregnant, living with her mother in Amarillo, and about to be co-parenting with an ex and his cross-dressing lover. Well, this was still what I dreamed of, even if I only had it for tonight.

Jack set my bag down behind me. I turned to him, and I could barely contain myself.

"This place is perfect," I said. "Thank you so much!" And then I launched myself at him and hugged him so tight, I heard a little oomph as I squeezed the wind out of him. I let him go. "Oh God, I'm so sorry. I just, well, thank you. This is a real treat for me."

His eyes were wide, but he was laughing. "I'll show you to your room."

"Are you staying here, too?"

"Yes, I am. And if you hurry up and grab a jacket in case it cools off, I'll take you to see the horses."

I grabbed my suitcase and yelled, "Let's go!"

Ten minutes later, I was chewing Jack's already minimal posterior down to a nub.

"You could have just told me," I said. "You know, like used words, and said 'Emily, Wrong Turn Ranch is my place.' And then you could have given me a choice whether I was even comfortable staying at the house of my boss, whom I've known less than a week."

He listened attentively and calmly, not batting an eye. When I had finished my tirade, he pursed his lips.

"So you don't want to go for a ride?" he asked.

"ARGH!" I said, almost shouting. "I *do* want to go for a ride. But that's beside the point."

"Well, my point is that we're going to have to hurry." He lifted his head and slung it back toward the east. "Sun's setting."

"Fine."

He nodded. "Fine." He started walking toward the barn again.

"Howdy, Jack," a man's voice said as we approached the largest of the tan structures.

Sliding doors opened to a wide interior corridor. Ah, horse stable—not barn. A sacred place.

"Hey, Mickey. This is Emily, and we want to get in a quick ride before sunset. She's an old hand. Can I grab Jarhead for her?"

A large man with a low black ponytail fastened with a long silver-studded leather strap was halfway down a ladder extending up into a loft area. When he reached the ground, he dusted his hands on his loose jeans, then lifted off a straw cowboy hat and mopped his forehead with his arm. "Evening, Emily."

"Hello, Mickey."

He put his hands on the back of his hips and leaned back, stretching. "Jarhead's fine. He's at the end down there on the left. You want me to saddle him up?"

"No, but do you mind bringing a saddle to fit Emily? Sun's sinking. And how's the big boy?"

"Hopper's good. We brought him in this morning and got him ready for you."

Jack strode down the center corridor, and Mickey fell in beside him. Instead, I lingered at each stall. The horses stuck their heads out. They were beautiful quarter horses and my heart ached with memories and affection. A mare heavy with foal. A stallion, bellowing. A yearling with a bandage on its face. I loved the tough little quarter horses. They were the horses of my youth, bred for power and sturdy like a tank—the mount of choice for cowhands because their sprinting, spinning, stopping, and backing prowess make them ideal for working cattle. And for racing. In fact, quarter horses got their name because they are the fastest animals in the world at the quarter mile.

Then I came to a thoroughbred, which stopped me short.

"You raise thoroughbreds, too?" I asked.

Thoroughbreds are also racers, but over longer distances. They are taller and leaner than the muscle-bound quarter horses, and also more flighty. You don't often see them on ranches out West because they don't have the power, skills, durability, or temperament to make themselves valuable.

Both men turned to me where I was standing in front of the stall of a pawing, snorting black horse. He bobbed his head up and down, then reared on his hind legs. Jack walked back to stand with me and Mickey disappeared through a doorway.

"That's Hopper," Jack said.

The horse calmed down and stuck his head out of the stall like the others, reaching toward Jack, who moved forward and placed his hands on the sides of the animal's head and scratched in long strokes up to his ears and down to underneath his muzzle.

Puzzling. The name, the thoroughbred amongst all the quarter horses.

"He's yours then?" I asked.

"He's a jumper." Jack released the animal and walked to the end of the barn. "This is Jarhead. He's a retired racer."

I went over to say hello to the deep red horse. His hindquarters were massive, and, as he shifted his hooves in the stall, his muscles flexed and rippled.

"Hey, Jarhead," I said, holding my hand out for him to sniff.

Mickey returned with saddles, blankets, bridles, and brushes. "Here you go."

Jack slapped Mickey on the back and turned to me. "You good saddling him?"

I smiled and reached for a brush.

"We pasture the yearlings along here." Jack held his hand out, pointing, and swept it to his right, indicating several enclosures. Hopper pranced underneath him, moving forward in a sideways trot that was mostly in place. Jack swung around and indicated additional enclosures. "Mares and foals, newly pregnant mares, and those over there are some more retired racers."

"This is quite an operation."

Jack pushed Hopper into a canter, and Jarhead bounced under me, eager to catch him, but waiting, just barely, for my okay. I clucked and squeezed my heels in gently. The power as he surged forward sent adrenaline racing through my veins. Jib, my Tech barrel racer, had exploded like that at the start of a race. Well, almost. Jarhead was in a whole different class of racer. I reined him in.

"Settle down," I said. "We're just out for a Sunday drive, old boy."

The horse made impatient panting noises in rhythm with his steps. We pulled alongside Jack and Hopper.

"Jarhead placed in the All American Futurity ten years ago. He lives to sprint. Don't be afraid to remind him who's in charge."

At his words, I literally couldn't catch my breath for a few seconds. Jack had me on equine royalty. The world famous All American Futurity had a purse of over two million dollars. It was the richest horse race in the world, and I sat astride a horse who had come in second.

"Holy cow." A smile spread uncontrollably all across my face. "No worries, I'm good."

The left side of Jack's features crinkled and lifted.

We came to a corner in the fences. I recognized two side-by-side posts as a gate. Jack got down and handed me Hopper's reins. He walked to the two posts and pulled them closer together, slipping a wire loop off the top of one, and then lifting that post out of a wire loop near its base. He carried the post and short section of barbed wire fence forward, and I walked Jarhead through, leading Hopper as he danced with high knees like a show horse. Jack left the gate on the ground and remounted Hopper. The horses loped along, and I drank in the arid high country. Highway 70 sloped in front of us to the right, and across it was the entrance to another ranch.

I pointed. "What's over there?"

"Our new client."

Well, Paul hadn't been kidding when he said he and Jack were neighbors. Like, across the street.

We continued uphill and parallel to the road. When we got to the top of a treed rise, Jack pulled Hopper up. We let the horses walk and catch their breath.

Jack waved his hand at the crown of his head.

"What?"

"Your hair." He poofed his palm upward from his crown. "It's got that *Something About Mary* look to it."

I reached up, and, sure enough, my bangs stood spiky and pointed north. Aqua Net and wind weren't a great combination. I tried to smash them down and looked at Jack.

"Uh uh, not yet."

I pressed my palm down to hold them against my head and said, "You may just have to call me Cameron the rest of the night." Hand still holding my hair, I looked into the distance over to Johnson's place. I saw something tall and metallic sticking up in the air against a hillside. "That's a crane!"

"Lots of construction going on."

"Does he live out there?"

Jack pointed further to the east. "See the roofs?"

"Yes."

"That's his house, and headquarters." He turned Hopper back the way we'd come. "Sun's almost set. Time to get back. When we have more time, remind me to show you the cemetery, and the silver mine ruins."

He urged the thoroughbred into a full gallop, and I gave Jarhead a loud "yah" and let the racer feel the old thrill of leaving another horse behind to eat his dust.

EIGHT

Clods of dirt flew around me. I was standing in the middle of a rodeo ring. My scalp itched, and I reached up to scratch it under my fright wig, but I had no wig. I patted my head. Something sprouted from each side of the top. Hairy things. Wide at the base and tapering to a point. Hollow in the front. Were they ears? But I wasn't an animal. I brought my hand down, touching my face as I went, and bumped into some kind of mask over my nose. A protrusion. Hairy again, and ending in a smooth button.

Dust settled. I saw a little girl. Dark skinned. A short pink nightgown and fuzzy pink slippers. Long black hair in a ponytail. Her back was to me, and I looked beyond her, toward the chutes. I heard the snort of a bull, an unmistakable sound, a sound of pure testosterone and bad temper. The metal railings of the chute clanged as he threw his body against them, and dust filled my nostrils along with the musky odor of the bull. Metal crashed hard—so hard I could feel the vibrations in my feet—and then the enormous bull was out. Two thousand pounds of writhing, twisting, jumping, thrashing, stomping black fur on the hoof barreled at me, one sharp horn jutting from each side of his head. The little girl turned to me and screamed, catching the bull's attention. A cowboy still clung to the bull's back, one arm raised per the rules, but the bull pivoted his body as he jumped, literally bending his front half in the opposite direction midair, and the cowboy flew off, landing inches from the metal rails. The bull bucked wildly toward the girl.

It was my job to get between the bull and the other people in the ring, but how could I? I'd been out of position when he entered it. My heart hammered in my chest, and I lifted my arms to wave at him, ready to lure him away from her. He

*swung his muzzle around, slinging snot and saliva, and his eyes locked onto mine.
He thundered past the girl and straight toward me.*

I gasped and sat up. Heaving breaths, I placed a hand over my chest.
My heart pounded inside like Jarhead's galloping hooves. *It was just a
dream*, I told myself, as I sucked in air. Slowly, I became aware of my
surroundings. Something smelled good. Bacon. How many years had it
been since I'd had any? My hungry stomach lurched.

I flopped into the pillows and pulled the fluffy, white duvet back to my
chin. Through half-closed eyes I took in the mountain springtime colors of
the room and concentrated on breathing in slowly through my mouth.
Bright lavender, yellow, and green accents made the room look like a field
of wildflowers. Tall pine furniture brought in the high desert forest. It
soothed me. And, truly, it even beat the honeymoon suite I'd shared with
Rich in Belize for luxury.

Ugh, I didn't need my ex in my mind spoiling this for me. It made me
remember that he still hadn't signed the divorce papers. I wanted them
done before he found out about my pregnancy. I'd thought he'd have
signed and returned them on the day he got them. What was he waiting
for? He'd moved on to his new life already. It was time to let me move on
to mine.

I tossed the covers to the foot of the bed and swung my feet over the
side. My phone sat on the bedside table, and I snatched it up to see the
time. I read the digital display, but in my mind I heard my father's version:
The little hand is almost to the seven and the big hand is two freckles past
a hair. Collin would arrive to pick me up any minute. I scrambled to the
bathroom and broke my own personal record for speed showering and
throwing on makeup—without even barfing. My abdomen cramped up a
few times, but I told it to cut it out, and it seemed to listen. I gave my nails
a once-over. They were rounded and smooth and the clear coat of polish
would have to do. Pregnancy had strengthened them. I donned a clean
pair of leggings and a red and black tunic with my boots, pulled my ponytail back in place, and dashed down the log-hewn staircase, only fifteen
minutes late.

The stairs landed between the kitchen area and the great room. Along
with the bacon smells I'd noticed earlier, several voices wafted toward me
from the kitchen side on my left—male and female voices, chatting and
laughing. In fact, it sounded like a party.

I burst into the slate gray and blue kitchen, but nobody even looked up
to greet me.

Jack stood sideways at the stainless steel range, stirring something in a
skillet and talking to a man and a woman who were seated in tall, wooden

stools at the bar. Jack picked something from the skillet and tossed it downward.

He said, "There you go, girl."

Snowflake.

The vent pulled an aromatic cloud upwards, and its noise masked my arrival. The man seated on one of the stools was definitely Collin—from his dark blonde, military-style hair cut to his twinkling eyes and the permanent smirk that varied from unrestrained to its current, barely visible quotation marks on either side of his closed mouth. He turned and whispered to the woman seated next to him—a woman I didn't recognize. Jack's wife, maybe? She had straight brown hair, hanging shoulder length. In profile, her blue eyes looked enormous while her small nose tilted up just a smidge. She seemed tiny, but muscular, and her voice sounded rough, like a mini food processor.

I realized I was gaping, and I gave myself a mental smack. I was invited to this party, too. I walked up to Collin and said, "Hey, Stranger!"

He stood up and hugged me off my feet. "Hey, you!"

"I see you've already met my boss."

"Yeah, somebody slept in, and we've gotten a tour of the whole 1500 acres. Haven't seen you in over a year, but that's fine, Em, you go ahead and get your beauty rest."

"Hey now!" I socked him in his upper arm. Solid.

Collin didn't even pretend my punch had hurt. "Jack made us mimosas and Irish coffees, and we've decided this is the best breakfast spot in Otero County, so pull up a stool. I'm buying."

"And I'm Tamara." The beautiful little brunette dragged my attention away from Collin and stuck out her hand.

I shook it. "Emily."

Tamara? Not Lena, Jack's wife? So, was Tamara here to see Jack or was she with Collin? Was I supposed to recognize her name?

Jack waved a spatula to get my attention, interrupting my musings. I lifted my eyes to him. His hair looked damp at the ends, and longish. No hat. A white tee with his jeans.

"Want to set the table for me?" he asked.

"Sure."

I scrutinized my boss harder. Host *and* short-order cook. This I hadn't expected.

"Silverware in the drawer to the right of the dishwasher. Plates above to the left, glasses above to the right, napkins in the dispenser closest to the table."

I set to work on the silverware, counting to four each for spoons, forks, and knives.

"So, Collin, fill me in," I said. "What've you been up to?"

"Just got back from St. Marcos. And Puerto Rico. And the Dominican Republic."

"What?" I stopped halfway to the table, silverware in hand.

"Yeah, I joined on the hunt for Nick," he said. "Long story short: Bad guys sabotaged his plane and it crashed flying out of the DR. Tamara helped us figure out where he went down, and we—Katie, Nick's dad, and me—plucked him off a rock he'd drifted to west of Puerto Rico, then cruised back to St. Marcos on a luxury yacht where we ran into more bad guys and had a shoot-out in a south shore harbor." He took a sip of coffee. "All's well that ends well."

I set the silverware on the table with a thump. "Oh my God," I said. "I knew he was missing and that he'd made it home safely. That's it. I had no idea of the rest. No wonder Katie hasn't answered my email."

I went back for the plates.

Tamara leaned over and kissed Collin long and hard on the lips. "You try to get yourself shot up wherever you go."

I tried to keep my eyebrows from shooting up. Well, that answered the question of who Tamara had come with—and pretty much ruled out an admiring Collin rehabilitating my bruised ego.

"You're no slouch in that department, either." Collin cleared his throat, pressing the side of his closed fist against his mouth. "Tamara flies Black Hawks for the good old U.S. Army. Why she agreed to marry a lowly state cop, the world will never know."

Collin had proposed to a military pilot. It defied imagination. The fact that he was engaged was mindboggling, but to a military pilot? Times two. A stripper would have made more sense, given his past. Tamara held out her left hand, and a big, fat sparkler caught the light from the fixture above. Except the light wasn't even on. The square diamond sparkled all on its own.

I put the plates on the table and flashed a lot of teeth as I said, "Congratulations."

My words came out sort of squealy, and I realized I was a little jealous. I'd thought I was the only woman with class Collin had ever noticed. I looked up to find Jack's eyes on me. Collin's engagement was disappointing, but Jack being married, I realized, had hit me far harder. I looked away from my boss and lifted Tamara's hand to inspect the rock. Snowflake had joined me and gazed up as if to see it, too.

"Gorgeous," I said. "And shocking that a lunkhead like Collin could pick it out."

"Isn't it? And I had no idea he was going to propose, either, so I didn't have any input. But it's perfect. Makes up for most of his other faults."

I looked away from Tamara and the ring, up and across the kitchen island, and found Jack's eyes still on me, assessing me like I'd assessed the diamond.

A fifth voice, a male one, pulled me away from Jack's gaze. "Somebody making breakfast?"

We all turned and Snowflake sprinted across the room. I saw Mickey standing in the doorway, his long hair loose, his jeans clean and pressed. He leaned down and ruffled the little dog's fur.

"I am." Jack said as he turned off the gas under the skillet and pulled it away from the burner. "Everyone, this is Mickey, the pride of Mescalero, New Mexico, and the Wrong Turn Ranch Manager for the last ten years. We're both Aggies, but he got his degree from the Texas institution and played linebacker while doing it." Mickey held up a thumb, the gesture known throughout the Southwest as "Gig 'em," which told us that Mickey had gone to Texas A&M.

The words "Ranch Manager" sunk in. I didn't know why I had assumed Mickey was a stable hand. Heat crept over my face. I felt petty. I'd just been caught in the act of stereotyping, even if no one knew it but me.

Mickey introduced himself to Tamara and Collin then turned to me. "Morning, Emily. How was Jarhead?"

I rallied. "Amazing. I think he wants to move to Texas with me."

Mickey threw his head back and laughed. "Oh no. He's the one horse here we can't afford to let go. His stud fees keep this place running. But he loves attention and needs a lot of exercise, so come back and see him anytime."

"I will."

Jack broke in. "Grub's almost ready. You staying?"

"My wife made me one of those green smoothie things this morning." Everyone else groaned, but it sounded good to me. "But if there's enough, I can help you make sure nothing goes to waste, before we head out to church."

"More than enough."

"Okay, but it's got to be our little secret."

I grabbed one more plate and laid a setting of silverware on it before passing it to Mickey, who turned and put it on the table.

Collin stood up and stretched his arms over his head, exposing a little ab in the process. He'd bulked up some since I'd seen him a year ago. Like he'd worked out more, lifted more.

"Okay, Em," Collin said. "I spilled, now it's your turn. What have you been up to?"

Where to begin? I shot a quick glance at Jack, who stood frozen at the refrigerator door, his eyebrow in a high peak as he watched to see how I'd handle this one.

"Gee, let's see," I said. And without thinking it through, I blurted out, "Well, a lot, like at the romantic dinner I had staged to tell Rich we were having a baby, his lover, a cross-dressing man named Stormy, pulled a Glenn Close, so I moved back in with my mother in Amarillo—which Jack calls Heaven only it's anything but—where I listen to her go on and on about the sanctity of marriage and the wonderful results of conversion therapy. So I filed for a divorce, took a job with Jack, and here I am."

Too late, I remembered Jack hadn't known the baby part. I looked at my feet. Well, he was going to figure it out soon enough anyway.

"Holy shit." Collin sat back down.

"That's what I said. Sort of."

I leaned my weight on the countertop through my hands and babbled to fill the Grand Canyon-sized silence that had fallen over the room. I didn't dare look at Jack again.

"So Jack has me working on all kinds of great distracting stuff," I said. "Like trying to figure out why his undocumented client killed a Roswell man before our very eyes at my high school boyfriend's wedding and whether or not Jack's new across-the-highway neighbor is guilty of anything worse than horrible table manners."

"Nice summary," Jack said.

My eyes cut to Jack, but Mickey pulled them to him as he spoke. "Tell your mother, with all due respect, that Native American history does not shine a righteous light on reparative therapy. I can't condone cheating, but I have some empathy for your husband with the conversion issue." He pointed to his head of long hair. "Some Christians in the Americas thought our long hair made us heathens, once upon a time, and tried to force us to change who we were, culturally."

"I don't think modern medicine shines a righteous light on reparative therapy either," Jack added.

Collin said, "I think the military's version of it was 'beat that shit out of 'em.'"

"Which no one shines a righteous light on these days, even the military," his fiancée said.

"Well, my mother is nuts, and she doesn't listen anyway. I've decided to ignore her. I hope Rich does, too." I surveyed the room starting with Collin. "But, honestly, even with my, um, messy personal life, what's keeping me awake at night is a work thing. The six-year-old daughter of our client has gone missing, and Jack won't let me go find her."

Jack set a container of sour cream out on the island, then waggled his finger. "A girl who is not our client."

My shoulders bowed up. "But maybe if we found her we'd figure out why *our client* shot the guy, and we could defend her."

Jack grabbed a set of tall wooden salt and pepper shakers from the kitchen countertop and deposited them on the table.

"We can," he said, "when CPS or the police find her, because that's *their* job."

We glared at each other for a few seconds, until Mickey interrupted us.

"A missing little girl, huh?" Mickey cleared his throat. "You probably could tell by looking at me that I'm Native American. Apache. So is Jack, by the way, if he hasn't told you already, although only one quarter, courtesy of his grandmother, who is also mine, a fact he forgot to mention earlier. We're first cousins." He slapped Jack on the back, and Jack bowed his head and grinned. "So here's what the old ones taught us, and maybe this will help you sleep better, Emily."

He turned to the group, and his voice took on a storytelling tone, and I could picture him in front of a fire, the eager faces of young Apache kids gazing up at him.

"The Mountain Spirits ensure the well-being of the Apache people. From the earliest I can remember, we would gather to watch the dancers, who danced to summon the Mountain Spirits. One of the dancers was always dressed as a clown. The Clown was greatly feared by all of us children, because our parents told us that if we were bad, the Clown would take us away."

Collin pounded a fist on the counter. "I knew it. Those fuckers always terrified me."

Tamara hooted and Mickey and Jack hee-hawed. Not me. I remained silent, transfixed by Mickey's words. "Go on," I urged him, when the others had settled down.

Mickey went to the cabinet and retrieved a coffee mug. It had the Wrong Turn Ranch's *WTR* on it, as if it had been burned into the cream-colored mug with a red-hot branding iron.

Mickey poured coffee as he continued. "They did this to teach us discipline, to make us listen to the lessons of the Mountain Spirit Dancers, lessons that would teach us how to survive. As we grew older, we realized that the Clown was there as our teacher, to save us from the evil in the world. So, Emily, whenever I hear about a child that is lost, I think about the Mountain Spirit Dancers and especially the Clown, and I hope they taught their lessons well to her."

I had a troubling thought. "She's not Apache, though. She's Mexican."

He stirred milk into his coffee mug. "Geronimo is arguably the most famous Apache. Perhaps you've heard this quote from him? 'There is one God looking down on us all. We are all the children of one God.' Our God extends past the boundaries of a reservation, or a tribe, or a country. My personal belief tells me that you should have faith that spirits are working to cast out the evil, and you will find her."

Collin raised his mimosa. "That sounds good to me. Followed up with a little honest detective work and a can of whoop-ass."

Laughter rang in the kitchen again, echoing in my skull, rattling loose the dream I'd woken to that morning. Only now, in the dream, I was the clown fighting evil. Or at least a big, evil-looking bull.

Jack held a platter in each hand. Eggs and bacon on one, skillet potatoes and tortillas on the other. "Ghost stories over," he said. "Buffet style breakfast tacos. Grab a plate and get after it."

The others gathered to eat, but I sat lost in my thoughts.

Jack ferried Snowflake and me to the little airstrip in the Suburban.

I broke the silence first. "Thanks for that."

He drove with one hand on the wheel, the other hanging out the open window. "For what?" he asked.

"Breakfast. It was nice."

I looked out the side window. A black mare loped in the pasture to the right, tail high in the air. A glossy colt ran beside her on impossibly long legs.

"I was going to tell you about the baby thing," I said. "I hadn't found the right time."

He nodded. "Anything else you need to tell me?"

"Like what?"

"Like the story between you and your friend Collin?"

"No story. You now know all my dirty little secrets." Even the ones I didn't owe a married boss.

His face twitched in a way that told me his left side was smiling. "You do keep it interesting."

He parked the Suburban outside the hangar, and we both exited the vehicle. This time, I helped him pull the plane out. He used some kind of pusher-lever-thingamajiggy attached to the front wheel, and the whole operation was easier than it looked. I pulled the Suburban into the hangar for him and closed and locked the pull-down door.

I was a little nervous about getting sick again, but I tried to block it from my mind. Instead, I watched Jack's preflight ritual.

He noticed, and when we got in the plane he said, "You were kinda mad at me on the way here. I skipped my normal safety talk because you didn't seem in a receptive mood."

"That's an understatement."

He grinned. "Just remember it's highly preferable to enter and exit the cabin when the propeller isn't spinning. But even if it's off, always approach from the backside of the plane. It could get turned on suddenly. And stranger things have happened than propellers flying off or people tripping and falling into them. Just give them a wide berth, whether they're on or off, okay?"

"No problem." I didn't want to lose my head like Marie Antoinette.

He reached into a large case in between the front seats and pulled out a folded brown paper grocery sack. "I thought you might need this for the trip back."

He handed it to me. It was lined with a Hefty trash bag. Written in black Sharpie on the side were the words *Emily's Barf Bag*.

I took it from him. "Thanks, Jack Ass." And then I held it in front of my face so he couldn't see my huge grin.

NINE

Monday morning I arrived at Williams & Associates to see Snowflake's nose pressed against the glass panel to the side of the entry door. When she saw me, she started spinning and leaping. She looked especially feminine and shiny. And damp. Very, very damp. How could I not smile, seeing her? So I did, and then gave her the crusts I'd saved her from my breakfast toast.

The first thing I did upon entering was start ringing the bell. I put some elbow grease into it. Wallace would pick me up in forty-five minutes. I needed a tête-a-tête with the inscrutable one before I left.

He surprised me with an immediate response. "Come on back, Emily. I have someone I want you to meet."

I furrowed my brow. "Snowflake, what did you put in his breakfast taco this morning?" She followed me into Jack's office.

There I saw a sallow, wizened man. Strands of silvery hair swept across the crown of his head. His suit hung from his frame, three sizes too large, but it was dapper and immaculate. He was sitting behind Jack's desk like he owned the place. Jack sat in one of the chairs in front of it.

I felt like I needed to push my lower jaw back up. "Yes, boss?"

Jack stood and raised his voice, over-enunciating his words. "I want you to meet Clyde Williams, the name partner of Williams & Associates. We were just going over our files. Clyde, this is our new paralegal, Emily, the one I was telling you we stole from a top-notch Dallas firm."

I choked and covered it by clearing my throat. Stepping briskly forward, I leaned across the desk and extended my hand. Clyde took it and bowed his head to me. He kissed the top of my hand, and I nearly giggled. Old guys rule.

I emulated Jack's speaking voice. "An honor to meet you, sir." I gestured to my baggy jeans and sweater. "I apologize for my attire. I'm interviewing witnesses today, and they might find traditional office attire off-putting."

His voice rasped and broke as he spoke. "Not a problem, young lady. A treat to meet you. Welcome to my little firm. I've been under the weather of late and Jack has graciously stepped in to cover the caseload while I'm out. Good man, Jack. Glad we were able to trade favors in each of our times of need."

I shot Jack a look. What the heck did Clyde mean, and which man had told me the real story of their alliance? My money was on Clyde. I didn't dwell on it, though, not while Clyde was turning on the charm.

"Jack has told me we're very lucky to have you."

"Oh—"

Jack cut my moment short. "Emily is working primarily on the two new matters we discussed: Perez and Johnson. I'm integrating her into some of the other clients this week. I could really use her help on Freeman and Escalante. Freeman, you'll recall, is charged with a bogus resisting arrest and assault of a police officer, and Escalante with burglary when he turned the tables on a militant religious group that was harassing him. They're good cases."

I didn't want to work on anything but Valentina, but I kept my lips zipped.

Clyde clasped his hands together. His knobby knuckles dwarfed the rest of his fingers.

"I wish I could say I've recovered enough to dig in and help on the day-to-day caseload, but not yet. I'll just have to stick with an advice and counsel role until the quacks clear me for duty." He sighed. "Damn far sight from back when your dad and I fought in Korea together, son. Old age isn't for sissies."

He unclasped his hands and placed them on the arms of his chair. He pushed down and his rickety body slowly rose. I wanted to leap around the desk and help him, but Jack didn't move, so I held my breath and waited. Ten seconds later, Clyde stood to his full height—five feet, two inches, or thereabouts. He grabbed the cane he'd hooked over the chair arm and started toward the door.

The walk to the lobby took another five minutes.

I whispered to Jack as we trailed Clyde: "I'm following up in person with witnesses that may be able to shed some light on Sofia. The CPS investigator wants to tag along."

"Focus on Sofia, not Valentina," Jack hissed at me.

I hissed back, "I know. Anyway, the CPS guy is picking me up in half an hour. Unless you have something else for me, I plan to use any other time I have left today to work on the Johnson background information. Okay?"

He scowled. "I have an evidentiary hearing on Freeman, so I'll be in court this morning, and Johnson has already called twice today. My plate is full through Wednesday, so let's sit down soon and talk about the other cases I need you working on."

That sounded as close to a yes as I could expect him to choke out, having known him for a week. Well, I'd just have to find Valentina fast then.

"Okay," I said.

We reached the exit and Clyde turned. "Nice carpet, Jack. Is it new?"

Jack wiped the scowl from his face. "Yes, sir, it is." The left side of his face twitched up. "Steve Rogan couldn't pay his bill."

Clyde beamed. "Service in kind. Gives a man his dignity. Nicely done."

I felt like the only one in the room that spoke English. What the heck were they talking about?

Clyde reached for my hand again. "Young lady, you seem like a sensible sort."

If only he knew, but I wasn't going to burst his bubble.

"Take care of Jack," Clyde said. "He's one of the best, and he's had a rough go of it."

I wanted to pump Clyde for more information, but with Jack glowering at me, I refrained.

"Yes, sir. Absolutely."

Remembering what he'd said about his military service, I saluted, then felt silly, but he cackled and squeezed my arm.

He nodded at my stony boss, seemingly oblivious to Jack's ill humor. "She'll do."

Wallace had texted me to meet him at the curb, and our timing was perfect. He pulled up in a silver Nissan Altima, and I didn't even have to break stride as I exited the building. The car's shiny, spotless exterior shot an intense glare into my eyes, and I shielded them with my hand as I walked toward it.

I set my purse on a floor so clean that I almost lifted my feet. As I swung my eyes to the driver, I couldn't help but notice that the entire inside shone like the outside, without a scratch, stain, or other blight in sight. Wallace inspected me with neon blue eyes as he eased off the brake.

"I really hope you're Wallace." I said, smiling at him. He had a lovely cherub's face under a head of thick, sandy hair.

He nodded, then eased away from the curb so gently it felt like we were riding in a bubble. The car purred.

"I am. Nice to meet you, Miss Emily. Where are we headed?"

We passed between the two fiberglass quarter horse statues at Third and Polk. On the left, a buckskin painted with a mountain stream scene on one side. On the right, a palomino decorated with paintings of Marilyn Monroe. The quarter horse statues were all over the city, and I loved them.

"Fifteenth and Adams." I recited a street number.

His face spasmed, Jim Carrey style. "That's an ick part of town."

"Yeah. Maria Delgado isn't living the glamorous life."

Wallace shook his head. "One-third of the Hispanic population in Amarillo is living below poverty level," he said. "Poverty drives a lot of our removals, although I have to give props to the Rainbow Room. They help a lot of impoverished families keep their kids, by outfitting them with the basic necessities: car seats, clothing, diapers." He shook his head again. "But they can't help when the desperation of poverty leads to violence or substance abuse."

"How do you deal with all that? Worrying about Valentina alone is eating me up."

He tossed his head, sending his wavy, highlighted bangs back in place, and said, "Jäger shots and group sex." I must have gasped aloud because he laughed and added, "Just kidding. We're in Amarillo, remember? I work out like a fiend. Triathlon."

"You bicycle in the winds out here? That's impressive."

"Not all that impressive. I know someone who did the Kona Ironman this weekend. *That's* impressive."

I'd flipped through the coverage the night before and had quite a surprise. A woman I met when I went as Katie's plus-one to a Baylor Law School reunion was being interviewed on TV. Michele Lopez Hanson had done the Ironman as a tribute to her pro-triathlete husband, who'd been murdered a few months earlier. He'd been a great guy, and I felt tremendously sad for her—and a little in awe, as well. Another reminder that I didn't have a corner on the "going through tough stuff" market.

"I had a friend who did it, too," I said. "I need to find something to help me with the stress, but I don't think it'll be endurance athletics. Or Jäger shots and group sex."

He decelerated the Altima gently as we approached the dilapidated white box of a house that appeared to be our destination. The car stopped so gradually that I couldn't be sure when it happened. A text came in on my phone. I read it quickly, and my cheeks flamed.

Collin: *You look great, even knocked up.*

Collin was fun and funny and magnetic and easy on the eyes, but I wasn't sure how to take his text. He was engaged, and I liked Tamara. I knew how to respect commitments, even if Rich and Stormy didn't. Well, Collin had always been a kidder. He was probably playing with me now. I just wouldn't play back.

"Game plan?" Wallace asked.

I turned off my screen and put away my phone. "I'll ask her how Sofia got her information, and then maybe some follow-up questions. When I'm done, she's all yours."

"Got it."

We climbed out and picked our way through tufts of grass and broken glass in all different colors. A dark brown piece had a scrap of red and silver label on it and the letters *ECAT*. I steered clear of it. If there was a sidewalk, the yard had long since consumed it. The house sat on cinder blocks, and I saw yellow eyes peering at us from underneath it. I hesitated, but there was no growl, just a fetid odor, like something rotten. Or dead. I kept going, wobbling on the first wooden step, and Wallace grabbed my arm. He was several inches taller than me. Lean, but toned.

"Thanks," I said

"Can't have you getting injured before we even question a witness."

My eyes swept from his brown tasseled loafers and up over his long-legged khakis-with-a-white-button-down-shirt kind of outfit.

"A fashion conservative." I actually said that, didn't just think it. Spit.

"Camouflage." He looked at me seriously, eyes twinkling. "Sometimes I go crazy and wear a blue shirt, though."

I chuckled and knocked on the door. It felt insubstantial against my knuckles. I thought I heard movement inside the house, and I leaned close and listened. If there had been a noise, it had stopped. We stood and waited for another thirty seconds. I knocked again and walked over to the lone front window to the right of the door. The boards sagged under my weight. I stuck my nose close to the glass and framed my eyes with my hands. The dust on the window partially obscured my vision. I made out a couch, a TV with a protruding pre-LCD backside, and a low coffee table with a peeling wood-veneer surface.

I gave up. "I don't see anyone, but I could have sworn I heard people in the back of the house."

"We can come back later," Wallace said. "If we stand here much longer, we might get shot."

I clutched my handbag tighter. "That wouldn't be pleasant."

As we walked back toward the Altima, Wallace said, "So, you work for the infamous Jack Holden."

"I do. But why is he infamous?"

"Maybe more enigmatic than infamous. Nobody knows a thing about him other than that he's a great attorney. And hot. The cowboy thing really isn't in right now . . . but on him? It's classic."

I couldn't argue with any of that. I had a thought. "Have you ever seen his wife?"

"Nope. Didn't know he was married." Wallace unlocked the Altima with his clicker. "Check your shoes before you get in, please."

I twisted to see the heel of my kicked back foot. It looked good. I repeated it for the other and decided it needed a scraping to get the grass off, but there was no curb. I scrubbed the bottom of my foot against the asphalt street. That would have to do.

I lowered myself into the car beside Wallace. He pulled out a Handi Wipe and cleaned his hands before putting them on the steering wheel, then dropped it in a car-sized trash can on the back of my seat.

I suppressed a smile. "Can we try the hotel formerly known as the Ambassador next?"

"The hotel formerly known as the Ambassador. I like that. We could do a symbol for them, like Prince."

"A Ghostbusters type of thing, only with a dead body in the circle."

He laughed. "Let's head there now. What are you wanting to get out of it?"

"I'm hoping some of Sofia's coworkers can tell me about her. Something. Anything."

"Well, they didn't tell me diddly squat," Wallace said. "But maybe they'll like you better than me. Shucks, I already like you better than me."

I laughed. Wallace made a precise three-point turn, and we drove back to Adams and then south to I-40. He stayed on the access road until we approached the Ambassador, and he pulled in and parked.

"Since I talked to the manager once before, why don't you let me lead?" He asked. "He might be more cooperative with me than with someone from a defense law firm."

"Good idea."

Wallace hurried off. A text came in for me.

Mom: *I'll pick you up at 5:15, okay, honey?*

God, I wished Rich would hurry up with my car.

Me: *Yep. Thanks, Mother.*

The hotel formerly known as the Ambassador had a Monday morning busy-ness to it, but without the big crowd from Scott's wedding, or the black comedy vibe that Spike's tumble into the pool had given it. I wondered if the murder had helped or hurt their business. It wouldn't have made me want to stay here, but the marketing gurus always say that there's no such thing as bad press.

I walked over to the tables at the pool. Clear water rocked gently as a woman with a white swim cap breaststroked its length. She moved so slowly she nearly sank.

The steady thump-thump of footsteps alerted me to Wallace's approach. "We're in," he said. "Or, I am. I told him you were my colleague, so don't mention your law firm."

"Slick move," I said. I got up and followed him toward the managers' offices.

"He's going to bring them to us one by one, and the HR woman will sit in on the interviews. We're to check in with her first."

Wallace seemed to know his way around, and we ended up outside an office that said *Linda Grace* on a nameplate to the right of the door. He knocked on the wall beside it.

"Linda? CPS here for the follow-up interviews."

Industrial-grade neutral paint covered the bare walls—and it smelled fresh. The woman behind the modular, L-shaped desk pointed to the two chairs in front of it.

"Have a seat," she said.

Sitting in her own chair, she looked round, like a Weeble, with a very squat neck. And short like a Weeble, too. I wondered if her feet even reached the floor. She didn't help matters by wearing a red and purple horizontally striped dress. A silver-accented frame decorated with a cross showed Linda standing with an older man (whose stringy beard gave me the icks) and two children who seemed about six years old—a boy and a girl. From their size, they looked like they must be either twins or very close in age.

"This is my colleague Emily," Wallace said.

I smiled and said, "Nice to meet you, Linda."

She nodded and typed something at her keyboard.

We sat. Wallace leaned to me and whispered, "She's a real people person, puts the human in human resources."

I stifled the laugh that tried to sneak out.

Wallace shifted in his seat and leaned forward. The voice he used dripped honey. "Linda, we just have a few short questions for you before the first witness arrives."

Linda made a bitter beer face. "I already talked to the police."

"Yes, but we're trying to find Valentina, Sofia's daughter."

Without the facial contortions, Linda's features looked porcine. Her skin was pale, and she had dark circles under her eyes.

"We knew her as Maria." Linda said. She tilted her head as she studied me. "Say, don't I know you?"

I struggled to place her face. "I'm not sure. I grew up here. Went to Amarillo High. Graduated twelve years ago."

She crossed her arms. Her bosom created such a protrusion that it looked like she was dancing an Irish jig. "Yes, we're the same age," she said. "I went to Tascosa. I heard you just moved back to town."

This wasn't going anywhere good. "Yes, I did."

Her piggy eyes squinted, and, for the first time, she smiled. "You're the one whose husband—"

I broke in. "So about Maria." I felt Wallace's eyes boring into me, but I ignored him. "As we try to help her daughter, anything we can learn about her as a mother and who she associated with is incredibly helpful. We're trying to figure out how Sofia found the Maria Delgado identity. It's possible that whoever helped her get it has Valentina. Or maybe she wrote something on her application that would lead us to Valentina. I was hoping you'd let us look at her employee file, or, even better, give us a copy."

Pink spread across Linda's face. "Those are confidential employee documents."

"Of course," I said.

I licked my lips. Linda would feel defensive about being tricked by an applicant. She had to report new hires to the INS, and the hotel could get in a load of trouble if she'd half-assed the hiring process. I tried to sound empathetic.

"It must be very frustrating that she submitted fraudulent papers," I said. "But Sofia isn't still your employee, is she? If you'd like, we could get a waiver from her. It's just hard, since she's in prison, and it might take us a week." I pointed at her framed picture. "Meanwhile, there's a little girl, just about your daughter's age in that picture, missing. I can only imagine how frightened she must be. I hope Valentina can make it a week. I hope she's not being molested or tortured, that she has food—"

Linda held up her hand. "Stop. I know she's missing, but the police already have the documents."

Wallace broke in. "Nobody wants to find her more than CPS, not even the city police, and we're a *state* agency. Your cooperation would be much appreciated, and I wouldn't ask if we didn't believe it was the Christian thing to do, ma'am."

I wanted to applaud. Wallace might not be from around here, but he'd figured out how to work within the system. I gave him a silent *woot*.

Linda lumbered to her feet. She pushed her chair back with her body and headed for the door. As she walked, the heavy brush of her thighs against each other made a grating pantyhose sound. Wallace and I looked at each other and I slapped my hand over my mouth. He licked his index finger and tapped it in the air as if touching it to a hot stove. God would smite us for sure now. Wallace had used the Lord's name to pressure a witness, and then we'd been uncharitable toward the woman helping us. Her attitude sure made it hard to be nice, though. I resolved to try harder anyway.

Linda returned, panting. She handed me a stack of papers, without a word.

I thumbed through them. An application, the results of a background check, some new hire paperwork, and copies of Maria Delgado's Social Security card and green card.

"Thank you very much," I said.

Linda grunted.

Wallace perused the documents as I did, and I pointed to the list of references on her application, then at the emergency contact in her new hire papers. My hands felt tingly with excitement. Leads.

A stiff, male voice behind us interrupted my thoughts. "If you and your colleague would be so kind as to join us, Mr. Gray, I have arranged for the coworkers of the woman we knew as Ms. Delgado to take turns speaking to you. You, too, Linda."

By the time I'd hefted my handbag and turned around, all I saw was the retreating backside of an African American man. I moved quickly with Wallace behind me and Linda trailing us. The man stopped at a doorway and turned. He had incredibly good posture—God, how my pageant coach would have loved him—and hazel eyes that were almost green. He wore a white dress shirt with the Wyndham logo on the collar and a name badge above it that read Russell Grant.

"Thank you, sir."

Wallace echoed me. "Thank you, Mr. Grant."

We entered to find a white woman waiting for us in a room identical to Linda's office except that it held a round, faux cherry table with four chairs instead of a modular desk. There was nothing on the walls in there, either. Maybe the hotel just hadn't rehung the decorations yet after painting.

Wallace and I both greeted the woman and took our seats. Without lifting her eyes from the table, she mumbled a reply in the voice of a three-pack-a-day smoker. She wore a burgundy service dress and had mostly gray hair and a stocky frame. Linda joined us a minute later, moving in a side-to-side rocking motion and breathing harder than before. She was definitely on a path to cut to the front of the line on the heart transplant list.

The manager stepped inside. "You'll be speaking to Cindy here first," he said. "Then I'll bring Aracelli in fifteen minutes, and you'll finish up with Roberto in another fifteen. They're the only ones available."

He left, closing the door behind him.

The meeting with Cindy yielded nothing. She kept her eyes on the table and spoke in a detached voice. She knew "Maria" only at work, they didn't talk, she'd never seen her daughter, and she didn't know anyone who was friendly with her. Aracelli had nothing for us either, but her voice strained and cracked when she spoke—once I thought I even saw tears. But, no matter how hard I tried, I couldn't get her to talk about Sofia.

Roberto was a different story.

The slight man wore a male version of the same burgundy service clothes the women wore. He looked into my eyes as he talked, and his tone was urgent.

"I work in the big rooms, the ballrooms, and I fix little things in the guest rooms," he said. "Leaky sinks. Shower curtain rods. Things like that." He looked straight at Linda. "I been here six months, I work hard." He turned back to us. "Maria work hard, too. She very serious about work and about her daughter. Two times she bring a little girl here and hide her while she work." He looked down. "I sorry I no tell you, Mrs. Linda."

I kicked Wallace under the table. This contradicted what Roberto's coworkers had told both of us, so far, about Sofia.

Before Linda could speak, I asked him, "Valentina?"

"Yes, she call her Valentina. The girl pretty, like her mama. She don't talk. She just sleep and color pictures. She color pictures for me."

"Where did Valentina sleep and color pictures?"

"She little, and she ride on her mama's cart, hide behind the curtain."

"Did she ever go into the rooms?"

"Yes, I see her once."

Linda sniffed. "We can talk about this later, Roberto."

His voice came out very soft. "Yes, Mrs. Linda."

I wanted to whack Linda for casting a pall on our conversation, but I forged ahead.

"Roberto, this is very helpful. Just a few more questions. Did Sofia—Maria—tell you about any friends?"

"No one."

"Anybody Valentina stayed with?"

"No."

"A man, her husband, or Valentina's father, perhaps?"

"Never."

"Nothing about bad men, or men wanting to hurt or take her or Valentina?"

"No, Miss." Roberto's shoulders heaved and he put his face in both hands and rubbed it. When he looked back up and dropped his hands, he shook his head. "I wish she did. I wish I could help that little girl."

I started to thank him, but he sat up straight again and said, "Wait. You ask about bad men, and I saw a man that might do something maybe bad.

He have a bald head, shaved"—he rubbed his scalp—"and he run out of the hotel that night. The night Maria, I mean Sofia, shoot that other man." He raised his hands palms up. "I think, why he in a hurry? But then I forget and never see him again."

I wanted to pound the table and shout, "Yes!" But I settled with asking him follow-ups. "Was he white?"

"Yes?"

"How old?"

"Not so young, not so old."

"Did he have anyone with him?"

"I don't think so." He shook his head. "No."

"Did you see where he went, or if he left in a vehicle?" I asked.

"No," he said. "Sorry."

I reached across the table and patted his hand. "Don't be sorry. This is great. Thank you, Roberto. Thank you."

"Is that all?"

"It is. Adios."

"Adios." He rose to leave and Linda went with him.

Valentina had been here, and Spike might have seen her. Remembering Spike's past and his connection to his old partner in crime—Harvey—here in Amarillo, it wasn't out of the question that Harvey had been here, too. If Harvey and Spike were together, they could have been up to their old tricks with Valentina. Sofia might have caught them in the act, and, as a mother, she would have had to stop them. They might be the "bad men" she told Jack and me about. Heck, Harvey might even be the guy Roberto had seen running from the hotel. His description fit. Too late, I realized I should have shown the picture of Harvey to Roberto.

It was possible. It was more than possible. I whispered a prayer that I was wrong, that a convicted child molester did not have Valentina, then turned to Wallace.

"I think I know where to find her. And we need to hurry."

TEN

Wallace punched it through the yellow light on the access road at Georgia Street.

"So you think this Harvey and Spike molested Valentina, and Harvey has her?" he said.

"Maybe," I said, "and it's terrifying."

"I need to call it in."

I ignored his comment, and he kept driving. Harvey's address was in the file I'd brought with me, and I entered it into the Maps app on my phone. He lived southeast of downtown, in the home he'd inherited from his mother before he'd done time. Siri called out the directions in her mezzo staccato voice: "Continue on Interstate 40 for 3.4 miles."

Wallace had the Altima up to ninety-five miles per hour. He whipped around slower traffic like Jeff Gordon as he continued to accelerate. Siri had us exit at Ross-Osage, and Wallace took the corner with wheels screeching. He made another hard right on Twenty-seventh.

"We're almost there," he said.

We came to an intersection. One of Stanley Marsh's many fake traffic signs throughout the city was planted in the yard of the house on the corner. This one read Undead End. Cryptic Texas kitsch, but this time it was eerie as well. We made our last left at the corner onto Olive Street and Wallace slowed down.

"It's up on the right, nearly to the end of the block." Wallace pointed. The street dead-ended a few hundred feet after Harvey's house.

"What is that, where the street ends? It looks like . . ."

"Llano Cemetery."

It was creepy—made creepier by the undead sign. Not that I believed in the undead; live people were way scarier than zombies anyway. Wallace executed a perfect U-turn again and parked facing Twenty-seventh across from the gloomy gray house belonging to Harvey. There were no other cars in front of it. It looked better than Maria Delgado's, but that wasn't saying much. It had a front sidewalk and a shuttered window left of the front door. A garage jutted off of the right front of the house in an L—an obvious afterthought added by someone with little or no construction skills. The yard was even worse than Delgado's, though, and the paint was cracked and peeling on the garage and window frames. Missing shingles on the roof formed a crazy quilt pattern.

I opened the car door and jumped out. My heart hammered harder than it had the time Jib had stumbled at full gallop and I'd watched, helpless, as the ground came at me in slow motion. Jib had rolled over me, but we'd both come out of it okay. I said a little prayer for Valentina, for Wallace, and for me—that we all would be okay now, too.

I spoke into the car: "Wallace, we need a plan."

"Yeah, here's a plan," he said. "We call my office and the cops. By the book."

"I can't stand the thought of leaving her in there another second," I said.

I pulled my hair off my face and behind my head in one hand. The wind had picked up quite a bit in the last two hours.

"If she's in there," Wallace said.

"And if she's not, we look like idiots for running off to the police and accusing this guy half-cocked," I said.

"There is that."

I made a decision. "I'm going in," I said.

"You're going to get me arrested," Wallace replied.

"Nah, it will be fine."

"I hope this means you thought of something."

It didn't. I refrained from saying so.

He climbed out and locked his car. "Fine," he said. "But I have 911 punched into my phone, and I'm dialing if we see any sign of her."

I ran to the front garage and peeked in through one of the dirty windows. No vehicles, but a tire sat in the middle of the floor beside a large oil stain. A rake and shovel hung on the wall.

"Come on." I motioned for Wallace to follow me around back.

"Don't you want to start with the doorbell?" he asked in a hiss louder than his speaking voice.

I ignored him. Moving quickly, I opened the side gate to the back yard and slipped through. The first window we came to had battered shades covering it from the inside. The next window was high, small, and opaque. I moved on and peered in the last side window. No lights. No people. A mattress on the floor. A bedroom?

I ran into the deserted, treeless back yard. It made the front look pampered. Someone had burned a pile of garbage on the concrete patio, leaving behind a can of Wolf Brand Chili with a half-burned label and a pile of ash. The wind sifted the ash and scattered some in our direction.

The window on the near side of the back door had a black trash bag over a missing pane with duct tape that was starting to lose its adhesive at the edges. This window looked in on the other side of the same empty bedroom I'd just seen.

On the opposite side of the back door, we found the window to the kitchen. Again, no people. A large cardboard box sat upturned in the tiny eating area. A rat was scavenging on a plate and fork sitting on the box. The sink below the window had another garbage bag in it, and roaches scurried in and out. The refrigerator door hung open.

I tried the back door and, to my surprise and horror, the handle turned. I pushed the door inward as softly as I could, and it swung open. I arrested its progress before it hit the cabinets inside and leaned in after it.

Wallace stumbled backward. "Oh no. No no no. No trespassing."

"But it's open," I said.

"It's still trespassing. I could get fired."

Would Jack fire me if I got arrested for trespassing? Probably not. And if he did, wasn't my job with him temporary anyway? I felt an odd pang in my chest at the thought, but I refused to consider what it meant. I didn't have time to get sappy. I lifted my chin and stepped over the threshold.

"Oh shit, Emily. Come on now, don't go in there."

"I'll be right back. You just keep a lookout."

I tiptoed into the kitchen. If Valentina was in here, she was leaving with me.

The stench in the house hit me with the force of a one-ton bull. Rotting garbage. Urine and feces. The rat looked up at me from its perch on the box, its front paws to its face, its tiny jaws working on its prize. The roaches ignored me. I pulled out my phone and activated a low-beam flashlight app, forcing myself to walk through the kitchen and the dark doorway beyond it.

The kitchen emptied into a den that had access to the front door. There was a bedroll on the carpet—carpet that crunched under my feet. Beside the bedroll was a backpack in a bluish color, flat and empty. A pair of men's tube socks partially inside out, bunched up in sweaty, dirt-caked folds hung from the backpack's open zipper. No people in here, at least not now. Because there obviously *was* a person living here—a gross person who preferred life in the dark away from prying eyes.

Another doorway on the far side of the room beckoned, darker than the one from the kitchen. Sweat trickled down my back and I stood frozen in place. Someone had to do this. Someone had to care about this little girl enough to do this; the only someone here was me. I crept across the living room. My mouth and eyes watered, and something large pushed my heartbeat up into the base of my throat, nearly gagging me. I stopped, swallowing over and over until the nausea passed and I could slink forward again.

The doorway entered a short hall with a bathroom in the middle and doorways to my right and left. I knew there was a bedroom to the left—I'd seen it through the window. It had looked empty, but what about the clos-ets? Or what if the person living here had fled to this bedroom after I'd peeked in earlier? I couldn't skip it. I had to be thorough. So I stepped into the tiny room—it was empty, thank God—passed the mattress, and faced the closet. Its door was ajar. It was empty, too. I hadn't known I was holding my breath until I realized I was lightheaded; I exhaled in a gush, trying desperately to quiet my breath.

A text chimed. I froze. If someone was in here, they now knew for sure that I was, too. It could be Wallace warning me of something, so I glanced at it.

Rich: *When can we finish our talk?*

Sheesh. Ex-husband. If I ended up dead because that text alerted the boogie man, it would be his fault. It figured that he'd continue to mess things up for me. But no boogie man jumped out. I stayed motionless for several seconds, then moved on.

The bathroom was next. I poked my head out the bedroom door. The hall was still empty. Belatedly, it occurred to me that a weapon would have been a smart idea. I'd left my handbag in the car, though, so if I came upon someone who wasn't glad to see me, I'd get to practice my rusty self-defense skills. I rolled my neck, and it cracked. Thanks to years of goat tying and classes at the YMCA in Dallas, I'd learned that my strength was in getting an attacker flipped and on the ground. Then I could drive my palm up through the bridge of his nose or jab my fingers in his eyes. If I had to. I shuddered, swallowing down more nausea. For the first time since I'd entered the house, I remembered that I was preg-nant. A pregnant woman had no business in here. But then, neither did Valentina.

I made my way silently into the bathroom. It was peppered with little spotlights from where the crushed blinds gapped. Dark stains streaked the sink and curtainless tub. The laminate had detached from the countertop and broken away in patches. But there was nothing and no one in the room.

Again, I leaned out slowly to check the hall before entering it. All clear. On to the last room. Its door was three-quarters of the way shut. I didn't like that at all. I held my phone's flashlight in my left hand and pushed the door back until it met the wall with a thud. No doorstop. No sound in the room. A sharp pain ripped through my abdomen and I dropped to my knees in shock, a strangled cry escaping my lips before I could hold it in. My phone bounced once helplessly on the carpet, landing flashlight down.

"Emily!" Wallace's voice echoed through the silent house, and his footsteps followed it. In seconds he was on the ground behind me, his hands on my shoulders. "What happened? Are you okay?"

"I think . . . yeah, I'm fine. I don't know what happened. A cramp or something."

This baby seemed to want me to always know it was there. I didn't think this cramp was normal, though. When we finished today, I'd make a "first available" obstetrician appointment. I'd vomited up my news in New Mexico yesterday and lived through it. I'd survive the onslaught of Amarillo gossip that my condition would unleash, too.

Wallace slipped his arm under my shoulder and around my back. He hefted me up, grunting at first until I helped him.

"I'm sorry to scare you," I said. "Really, I'm fine. Thank you."

"I thought you'd been stabbed or something," he said.

It had felt like it. "Yeah, I overreacted." I took several deep breaths and waited for the pain. None came. "Just one more room and we're done."

Having Wallace with me gave me courage. I stepped into the room, avoiding another mattress and a pile of crap (literal crap, the origins of which I didn't want to consider) and faced the closed closet door. I yanked it open, and screamed my fool head off.

I wasn't the only one. The two teenagers huddled in the closet joined in with me. I backpedaled and fell onto the mattress. Wallace, who had remained in the doorway, leapt into the room, arms raised in a judo posture, knees flexed, on his toes.

The screaming stopped.

"Don't hurt us," one of the teenagers said in a high-pitched voice.

The other added in a slightly deeper one, "I know we're not supposed to be here. We'll move out, I swear."

"What in hell? How old are you?" Wallace reached a hand out and pulled me to my feet. "Emily, give me some light."

I pointed my phone at their torsos so as not to blind them. They were filthy. Two gangly waifs in blue jeans and sweatshirts, ridiculous, dark knit caps on their heads. Girls? I looked closer. One a girl, one a boy. The girl had one green eye and one brown eye, and the boy had a nasty scar on his neck—long since healed, but brutal looking.

The boy spoke. "Eighteen."

Wallace put his hands on his hips. "Don't try to bullshit me."

They looked at each other, and the girl whimpered softly.

The boy repeated, "Eighteen. So you can't call our parents."

Wallace shook his head. "Show me some ID."

The boy stood up and helped the girl stand, too. "We don't have to show you nothing. You're not the cops."

Wallace pulled out his wallet and flipped it open to an ID, which he pointed at them. "Better. Child Protective Services."

I put my hand on his arm. He looked at me, and I mouthed, "My turn, please?"

He swept his hand at me and gave a slight bow.

I turned to the kids. "We're looking for a man named Harvey Dulles. This is his house. Have you seen him?"

Two head shakes. Still, it was the boy who answered. "The skinhead that lived here left last week."

Last week? That was around the time Sofia killed Spike. "How do you know?"

The girl piped in. "Because we've been camping out in the cemetery for a while now, and we watch the neighborhood. He packed up his truck like he wasn't coming back. We waited a few days, and when nobody came, we moved in." She looked down. "It was starting to get cold at night."

"Have you seen a little Hispanic girl, about six years old?"

They both shook their heads. I wrestled with the information. So Harvey had moved out. Why would he abandon a home he owned free and clear? That was suspicious behavior. Irrational and suspicious. I wanted to cry, to flail, to scream. I didn't.

I turned to Wallace. "All yours."

His voice softened. "Here's the deal. I can't pretend I don't see two kids who are fifteen at the oldest standing in front of me without enough to eat, not going to school, and with no one to keep them safe. I promise I'm going to help you guys, but you're going to have to come with us."

The boy bristled. "Yeah, like CPS ever helped us before? That's why we're here. We got stuck in a house where we were raped and beaten. We made a run for it. Bet CPS doesn't even know we're gone and those foster assholes are still cashing the checks."

Wallace swallowed hard; I heard his throat catch. "It's not supposed to be like that. If I'd known that was happening, I'd have taken you away from them and turned them over to the cops. Which is what I'm going to do now." He pointed at the door. "Let's go."

They stood there.

"When was the last time you two ate?" Wallace asked. "I'm buying you a quick lunch before we do anything else."

The boy stepped forward, pulling the girl with him. They headed toward the door, and Wallace followed them out. I fell in behind them. When we reached the back door to the house, the boy suddenly pushed the girl through the door and pulled it shut behind him. The two teens sprinted across the yard, catapulting themselves up and over the fence around the cemetery. By the time Wallace wrestled the door open and the two of us were outside, they'd disappeared from sight, back into their secret world.

I thought back to the sign at the end of the block: *Undead End*. Well, yes, in a way it was undead. As in two real live kids living feral in a cemetery. It hurt to think about it.

"Dammit." Wallace snapped his head forward and then back, punctuating his frustration. He pulled out his cell phone and typed rapidly, then put the phone to his ear. "Marsha, hi, this is Wallace. I'm at Twenty-seventh and Olive, by Llano Cemetery. I saw two youth, a boy and a girl about fifteen years old, who came out of an abandoned house. They were filthy and malnourished. When I tried to talk to them, they claimed to have escaped an abusive foster home and bolted into the cemetery. I didn't get their names, but the boy had a big scar on his neck and the girl had different colored eyes. They were both white, I think." He paused. "Yes, thank you." He hung up and put his phone in his pocket.

I pressed my hand into my aching abdomen and said, "Wow."

"Yeah. It breaks my heart to see kids like that, to hear what they've been through."

"What do we do now?" I asked.

"Nothing we can do. The cops will try to pick them up for us, and we'll move them. I'll see if I can figure out who they are, what family they were placed with, and arrange for a little visit with the foster parents."

We walked back around to the front of the house. My thoughts ricocheted between the two waifs we'd just seen and Valentina, whose situation was even more dire.

"Do you see stuff like this a lot?" I asked.

"Too much. There are so many good foster parents, but there are some who are in it to milk the system, or to take advantage of the helpless. Sometimes I hate people."

I walked through the gate first, and he shut it behind us. I put my hand on his arm. "I had no idea it was so bad. I mean, you read about this stuff, but it's never touched my life before. What you do, well, Wallace, you're one of my heroes."

He started to smile and then his face collapsed into trembling lips and blinking eyes. He pulled me to him in a long hug.

"Thank you." He held me back out again. "What about you, Ms. Asskicker? Charging into that house alone with nothing but your good looks to protect you? You're *my* hero."

He slung an arm around my shoulder, and we walked back to the car together.

ELEVEN

It turned out that "quick" to Wallace did not mean eating in the car. But by now that didn't surprise me. Because we were running behind, we skipped the GoldenLight Restaurant in favor of a counter order at Wiener-schnitzel. Wallace: chili cheese dogs. Me: two orders of large fries.

I got a text from Jack: *Back at office. Status?*

Had it only been that morning that I'd talked to Jack and met Clyde? I tried to remember if I'd told him when I'd return. I knew how badly he wanted me to move on to other clients. I glanced at my phone. One-thirty p.m. Well, Wallace and I only had one more stop. I could be in my chair and working on Johnson by three p.m., at the latest. How mad could Jack be? Pretty mad, probably. That called for emergency measures.

Me: *On the road to last witness. Stopping by office in 15.*

I added on two chili cheese dogs and a large fry for Jack.

"Wanna meet the hot enigma that is my boss before our next stop?" I asked.

Wallace wiggled his eyebrows. "Do bears wear fur?"

We planted ourselves in a yellow and red laminate booth where I scarfed down my fries as my stomach did happy cartwheels.

Wallace gave me the stink eye. "You don't do mystery meat?"

"I don't do meat at all."

He pulled his mouth into a moue. "Vegetarian?"

"Yep."

"Huh. And I thought it was hard to be gay in Amarillo."

I pulled a skinny, yellow highlighter from my handbag to mark the names of Sofia's references for her work persona: Sofia Perez—using herself as a reference for her fictitious work identity, that made me snort—and Liliana Diaz. Both numbers looked familiar, and I rifled through the big Redrope file I'd brought with me from the office, an almost-red accordion file that was simply known in legal circles as a Redrope. The phone number for "Sofia" matched the number of the phone the police found on her at the time of her arrest. Well, she was certain to get a good reference there. More interesting, the phone number given for Liliana Diaz turned out to be the number I'd called to speak to the real Maria Delgado on Friday.

I lifted my eyes from the page and grinned. "Like hell Maria knows nothing."

"Oh yeah." He shimmied his shoulders and torso in a chair dance as he bobbed his head. "She can run, but she can't hide."

I recalled that Sofia had given one more name in her paperwork. I'd seen it in there somewhere, earlier. I flipped past the application to the new hire paperwork. Bingo.

"Emergency contact: Victoria. No last name given," I said. "Wanna call it?"

"Sure."

Wallace punched in the digits as I read them aloud. He held the phone to his ear, eyebrows raised at me while he waited.

"What do you want to bet it's out of service?" He said. Then his expression changed. "Yes, hello, my name is Wallace Gray, and I'm calling about Maria Delgado—" His mouth dropped into an O. "Hello?" He shook his head at me as he lowered his phone. "A woman answered and then she hung up on me."

"Let me try." I dialed from my own phone. Three rings. Five. Ten. No answer, and no voice mail. "Well, that sucks." I stuck my wadded up napkin into my empty, nested fry holders and drained the last of my iced tea. "I'm ready when you are."

We threw away our trash and pushed the doors open into the bright midday sun. After we got back out to the Altima, Wallace handed me a Handi Wipe and we repeated our cleaning ritual like raccoons. We drove downtown with the bag of food for Jack after we had everything to Wallace's satisfaction.

When we reached the office, I rang the bell on my desk immediately.

Wallace dropped his head and looked at me under furrowed brows. "What in God's name are you doing?"

"Jack likes his privacy."

Wallace gasped, a hand over his chest. "OMG, he's naked back there, isn't he?"

"I sure as heck hope not." I rang again. "Jack, it's Emily. I have Wallace from CPS with me."

Heavy boot steps sounded in the hall. Wallace adjusted his posture. And damn me to Hades, I adjusted my girls, too. I would have been ashamed of us both, if I'd had time.

Jack sauntered into the lobby, his hand extended. "Wallace from CPS, nice to meet you. I'm Jack Holden."

Wallace's voice came out deeper than it had with me. "A pleasure. I've heard your name many times. And, of course, our interests overlap now with your client Sofia Perez, and CPS looking for her missing daughter, Valentina."

I held up the bag. "I brought you food. In case you hadn't eaten."

Jack shifted his eyes from my face to the bag and back again. "A peace offering? Do I even want to know why?"

Wallace busted out a gut laugh, and I hurried to speak before he finished. Jack didn't need to know *everything*.

"Just being considerate," I said. "Agatha's training."

Jack took the bag and rustled through it as he said, "My new paralegal is trying to expand her duties to law practice manager—not that I don't need the help—but she has her heart set on working the family law angle, Wallace. I keep trying to tell her that our focus is the criminal defendant, that we can count on CPS, the police, and the ad litem."

He snared a chili cheese dog, wrapped it in a napkin, and peeled back the paper wrapper.

"I can attest that she had a laser focus on Sofia today."

Jack took a bite and chewed, eyes twinkling in a way that said he wasn't convinced Wallace was telling the whole truth. He got a little chili on the left side of his mouth, so when he half-smiled around his mouthful, the chili rose toward the dimple. My stomach fluttered, and an urge to lick it off came out of nowhere. I never had thoughts like that, especially not about married men. It had to be the pregnancy hormones. It had to be. Well, surely it was okay just to *look*. I forced a dry-mouth swallow.

"Laser focus," I said.

Jack finished his bite. "When do you think you'll be finished with the interviews?"

"I should be back around two-thirty," I said. "Three at the latest."

"Okay, then," he said.

"Nice to meet you, Mr. Holden." Wallace nodded.

"Jack, please. You, too."

We exited the office, and, as we walked to the elevator, Wallace fanned his face with his hand. "The chili on his mouth," he said. "Oh, honey, to be that napkin."

"Tell me about it."

A few minutes later, we headed north toward Sofia's little, nameless apartment, which appeared to be three blocks west of Maria Delgado's place, according to Siri.

"This is it," Wallace said, as we approached a dumpy block of buildings. "Help me find the manager's office. Last time I was here, the guy was already at Sofia's place with the police."

"I've got my eyes peeled," I said.

Wallace drove slowly around the block. Two-story four-plexes with white siding squatted on scraggly turf, one after another. Gaps in the siding revealed black liner, making the complex look like a mouth full of bad teeth. There were no balconies or patios. No grassy lawns or playgrounds. No parking lots. A worried cat slunk between two of the buildings with an underfed dog hot on its tail. Cars in a rainbow of colors—but similar in their states of dilapidation—lined the streets.

"There it is." I pointed to a ground floor unit with a sign in its window that said Manager.

Unfortunately, there was no parking space near his unit, so we circled again and parked along the street on the opposite side of the complex.

"We're right by their apartment. I saw it last week. Want to go there first?"

I nodded. "Sure." I kept my Redrope and handbag under my arm and followed Wallace between the buildings, placing my feet carefully amidst piles of dog poop. "Nice place."

He snorted. "It's worse than you think. Most of these units house multiple families. It's like little Mexico City."

Residents had strung clotheslines from window to window between buildings and their clothes and linens waved like flags.

I pointed to them. "No laundry room."

"No nothing." Wallace stopped in front of unit 1C, an interior ground floor apartment. "This is where Sofia lived." He knocked. "I wouldn't be surprised if the manager has already moved in another family. It appears to be a high-turnover business."

There was no answer.

"Want to try some neighbors?" Wallace looked around at the nearest ground floor units.

I smiled and jiggled the doorknob. The lock felt flimsy, like interior doorknob locks. I used to unlock the door to my parents' bedroom when I was a kid, using just my mother's hairpins. I'd put my hair up over lunch, securing the runaway strands with bobby pins, so I pulled one out. I slipped it in the lock and wiggled it gently until I heard a click. I pushed the door open and walked in.

Wallace shook his head. "She graduates to breaking and entering."

"Does that mean you're the lookout again?"

He sighed and followed me, closing the door and relocking it behind him. "You're an incredibly bad influence."

"You should have known me in high school."

"Were you one of those wild Amarillo girls who drank Boone's Farm wine and snuck out to spy on the devil worshippers at the Marsh estate?"

I winked at him. "Don't make me lie to you." I walked into the kitchen. A crayon drawing hung from the refrigerator by a magnet. "Is this the drawing you told me about?"

"Yeah. I guess the cops didn't consider this evidence."

I snatched it down and slipped it in my file. "Good. I do."

"Lord, woman. Do all paralegals act like you?"

"It seems criminal law has already had an impact on me." I reached for a drawer.

Wallace stopped me. "At least use a towel to keep your fingerprints off stuff, okay?"

"Good idea." A dishrag hung over the kitchen faucet. I picked it up, then started opening drawers and cabinets with that hand. I found a few pieces of silverware, some plates with daisies in the center, and a stack of plastic tumblers. The only food to speak of was a bag of rice and one of beans.

"Not much here," I said.

Wallace shook his head, his face soft. "Yeah, a pretty meager existence."

I walked the confines of the apartment with Wallace watching me. I checked under the couch, between and behind cushions, in closets, cabinets, and every other nook and cranny. No jacks, candy, or colors. No nothing.

"You were right," I said. "No sign of a child living here, except for that drawing."

Still, though I didn't know how to explain it, I felt Valentina's presence. I sat down on the worn, silvery blue sofa, pulled the drawing back out, and studied it. A lone man stood in front of a hill. The man had on shorts, or maybe it was a short skirt. The artist had scribbled all over his brown body in white crayon. On his head were big ears, sort of like animal ears. His nose was big, too, but more like a snout. Brown scribble over the face. Black for the hair. The man smiled back at me, and in the crude drawing, I thought I saw affection on his face. The man wasn't scary, but he wasn't familiar either. I put the drawing away and stood up.

Wallace was sitting at the kitchen table checking his phone.

"Onward," I said.

He jumped to his feet. "Manager's office?"

I shook my head. "Let's chat with the neighbors while we're over here." I pried a space between the slats of the plastic white blinds. "Coast's clear."

I opened the door for Wallace and he exited. I relocked the doorknob and headed to unit 1B, adjacent to Sofia's place. I heard children's giggles and a happy squeal.

"*Niños, parada*," a woman said, which I translated automatically to "Children, stop" in my head. I knocked.

Silence.

I sensed a presence on the other side of the door. Possibly the woman who I had heard talking to the kids?

"Hello, ma'am. I'm from Sofia's attorney's office. She sent me to talk to you."

Silence.

Going on a hunch, I added, "Victoria, please?"

Silence.

I said all of it again, in Spanish. This time I heard the sound of a hand lock turning, and the door opened three inches. Narrowed black eyes regarded me from the slit behind a security chain.

I smiled. "*Tu hables ingles?*"

"*Si*. Yes."

"Good. Hello, Victoria. I'm from the office of Jack Holden. He is the attorney who represents Sofia. We're trying to help her. Could I talk to you for just a minute? Maybe we could walk outside, or my colleague Wallace —" I gestured back at him, "and I could come in for a minute?"

She stared at me.

I saw movement behind her, and one little hand appeared around her knee. Then a face. Then above it, another face. And by her waist, a third one. Three little girls.

"Not him. I talk to you *solamente*. Five minutes. You come in."

I turned to Wallace and whispered, "Maybe you could knock on a few more doors?"

He nodded and left.

I turned back to her. "Thank you."

She opened the door, revealing a small woman with long, dark hair in a low bun. She tugged at her purple velour shorts. Her T-shirt said Amarillo Sox on it.

"Beautiful little girls," I said.

I smiled at them, and the cuties giggled and ran to the couch—a threadbare number in a silvery blue, like Sofia's. The fibers were so synthetic looking that if I'd thrown a match on it I wasn't sure if it would melt or catch fire. Each of the girls held a doll, and the littlest girl's doll looked homemade, with long, brown yarn hair, a blue dress, and a piece of ivory-colored lace over her shoulders. I winked at her, and she held the doll up for me to see, grinning so wide my heart melted.

"Thank you," Victoria said.

She pointed at her wooden kitchen table, and we took seats adjacent to each other. My chair wobbled at its joints, so I held very still. There were no lights on in the apartment, and I struggled to adjust to the dim atmosphere.

"Victoria, what is your last name?"

She paused. "Jones."

I nearly laughed at the obvious lie, but instead I nodded with a serious expression on my face. I didn't want to spook her or insult her.

"Thank you, Ms. Jones," I said. "Now, you know that Sofia is in jail, for shooting a man, right?"

Victoria nodded, eyes steady and wide.

"Had you ever met the man she shot—Spike Howard?"

She shook her head no.

I grabbed the file and retrieved a picture of Spike. "But you've seen his picture in the paper and know who I'm talking about, right? This man?"

She nodded. "I never see him before."

"Did you see any other men around Sofia's place?"

"No."

I pulled out the picture I'd printed of Harvey. "How about him?"

She shook her head.

"Have you known Sofia long?"

She put her hands on either side of the seat of her chair, and slid them under her thighs. "Since she move in. One month, maybe two."

"How do you know her?"

"Her daughter play with mine."

"Ah, so you know Valentina."

The girls giggled again, and Victoria shushed them. "*Si*, yes."

"Sofia is very worried about her. Have you seen Valentina since Sofia was arrested?"

Victoria's eyes shot over to the girls, then upwards, then down at her feet. "No."

"Do you ever babysit her, keep her when Sofia is at work?"

Victoria moved her hands and squeezed them between her knees. "No."

"Never? Not even when she goes to the grocery store?"

She studied the tabletop in front of her. "No. *Nunca*."

Never. "Okay." I thought for a moment. "What about Maria Delgado?"

Victoria moved her head back and forth in tiny shakes. "I don't know her."

I leaned closer to whisper, "Did Sofia ever talk about where she came from or—"

"No." Victoria sat up in her chair, leaning against the backrest ramrod straight.

I continued: "Her husband—"

"No." She rocked back and forth just a little.

"Or why they came? Maybe some bad men?"

"No." She wrapped her arms around herself and continued the rocking.

"No?"

"*Nada,*" she whispered, still rocking.

Nothing. Which is what she had told me. Nothing. She was lying. I was sure of it. But why? What was she scared of? I needed time to think. I rummaged through the papers in my Redrope to buy myself time. An idea came to me, and I looked at the black-haired little girls again. All three had a high single ponytail and wore pink Barbie pj's. One appeared to be about five years old, and the others were maybe seven and eight. Close to Valentina's age.

"You were friends with Valentina, right?" I asked them.

Victoria jumped up, knocking into the table as she shushed the girls. "I answer your questions," she said. "You go now."

I nodded, and slowly put the pictures of Spike and Harvey back in my file.

I walked to the door, Victoria on my heels.

"Thank you, Victoria."

She was already closing the door behind me as I crossed its threshold. I heard her engage the doorknob lock and slide the security chain until it dropped into position with a tiny but final plink.

TWELVE

Five minutes later, Wallace and I walked to the manager's office, comparing notes along the way. He hadn't been able to get anyone to open the door. I hadn't been able to get a straight answer out of Victoria. Together, we added up to a goose egg on our efforts.

"At least we figured out who the woman with the incredibly bad phone manners was," Wallace pointed out.

"It's the little things," I agreed. But even I realized that my voice sounded flat.

Wallace put his hand on my shoulder. "You know, most of the time the people here illegally are too scared to talk. If they get involved, they could be discovered, and that could lead to deportation. So don't feel bad that Victoria didn't open up to you. Remember, you got her to open that door, so now we know who she is. That really *is* something."

Wallace knocked on the door of the manager's unit, 8A. The door flew open and an emaciated white man wearing a wife-beater T-shirt stepped out, an army tattoo on his left arm and a challenging look on his face. His B.O. backed me up two steps, and I put a fist under my nose.

He trained his flashing eyes on Wallace. "You again."

Wallace cleared his throat. "This is Emily Bernal from the law firm representing Sofia—"

The man turned on me, blasting me with halitosis. "I already talked to you on the phone, lady."

He fished a pack of Camels and a lighter with a suggestive female silhouette on it from the rear pocket of his jeans.

Hello to you, too, Mr. Michael Q. Scott, I thought.

"I was hoping you might be able to tell me if you'd ever seen either of these men." I pulled out the photos of Spike and Harvey and splayed them in one hand in front of him.

Very deliberately, Scott picked a cigarette out of the pack, shoved it between his lips, returned the pack to his back pocket, clicked his lighter until it flamed, lit his cigarette, and puffed three times. He didn't so much as glance at the photos. "Nope."

My blood started simmering. "I assume that means no you *won't* since you didn't look. However, I am asking you, as nicely as I can, to just look at these photos one time. Have you ever seen either of these men?"

He sucked his cig and then blew out smoke. He shifted his eyes to the pictures and stuck the lighter in his pocket. "Yeah."

"Both of them?"

"Nah. I seen the dead one on the news. Never seen the other guy."

The simmer in my blood sped up. "Mr. Scott, Sofia is very worried about her daughter. Have you seen her anywhere?"

"God, lady, I already told you. I didn't even know she had a daughter."

I felt pressure building under the lid of my simmering pot. "Funny. Her next-door neighbor, Victoria, did. She said her three daughters used to play with Valentina."

He snorted. "You're lying."

I came to a full, rolling boil. "I most certainly am not."

"You want to know how I know you're lying?" He pointed his cigarette at me, and I fantasized briefly about smashing it back into his face. He continued: "Because Victoria Nunez in 1B only has two kids. She brings 'em with her everywhere."

I stood motionless. If she only had two daughters, why had she told me all three girls were hers?

But before I'd even finished the thought a woman's unearthly screams rent the air from the interior of the complex.

I turned and sprinted back to Victoria's apartment.

Cramps ripped through my abdomen as I rounded the last corner, panting and grimacing. I ignored the pain. Victoria and two of the little girls stood huddled and screaming outside their apartment. Victoria clutched the cloth doll I'd last seen in the arms of the smallest of the three girls. She wasn't there with them now.

I reached Victoria and leaned on my knees. Between ragged breaths I asked, "What is it? Are you okay?"

Victoria shook her head and her screams turned to sobs. "He took her. A bad man took her."

"Took who?"

"V-V-V-Valentina!"

Now I screamed. "No!"

I looked at the doll with new eyes and realized what a fool I'd been. The doll had a blue shirt with a lace shawl, just as Sofia had told me—a doll to match the lyrics of her daughter's favorite song.

Wallace arrived seconds after me. He grabbed Victoria by both arms. His voice was preternaturally calm. "Who took her, Victoria?"

"No lo sé. Algún hombre la tomó de esa manera." She pointed through the building.

Wallace opened his mouth, then looked at me.

I translated. "She said, 'I don't know. Some man took her that way.' To the street."

I took off again, toward the street we'd parked on. Wallace's Altima stuck out from the clunkers lining the curb, but no cars were moving and there were no empty spaces. I ran to the right down the block, peering in windows, searching between cars. Nothing. I ran back, scanning the cars and the buildings across the street. I met Wallace where I'd started as he ran back from checking the street in the other direction.

"Did you see anything?" I asked him.

"Not a damn thing."

"We've got to talk to Victoria."

"First I have to call 911, and my office."

"But I have to talk to her first," I insisted.

"Then talk fast. I can lose my job—or get thrown in jail—if I don't follow protocol."

He pressed a button on his phone and put it to his ears, and I ran back to the apartment.

When I reached Victoria and her daughters, she'd gathered both girls into her arms where they cried together on the small scrap of concrete outside the door to their home.

"Victoria, I need you to talk to me. I need you to tell me everything. *Pronto.*"

"You not find her?"

I shook my head and pointed to her apartment. She set the girls down and headed inside, holding tight to two little hands. She sat at her kitchen table, and pulled her children up onto either side of her lap.

I didn't have time to be warm and fuzzy. The cops would be here soon, and I needed answers. "Start from the beginning, Victoria Nunez."

I pulled a yellow pad and pen from my Redrope.

Victoria wiped her eyes and nodded. "I keep Valentina while Sofia working. I watch TV and see news that the *policia* arrest Sofia. Sofia tell me that if anything happen to her, hide Valentina, so I-I-I . . ." She put both her hands over her face and sobbed momentarily, then gathered herself and continued. "So I tell people Valentina mine."

I nodded. "Good. Now, have you ever seen the men whose pictures I showed you, or any other men around here?"

"No, never, but Valentina talk about her papa. Say he tell her and her mama to come here on the train that goes underground. Only, when they get there, it's a bus with a dog on it. She say he's coming, that he come soon. That he stay and work so the mean cowboy who's scared of Indians can make pretty jewelry." She threw up her hands and shrugged. "I do not understand her, but she say it."

None of it made sense to me, either. I scribbled notes verbatim, frantically, and prayed I'd be able to decipher them later.

"Did she tell you where her father worked?" I asked.

Wallace walked in and took one of the seats.

"She say Mexico."

"What did Sofia say about him?"

"She never say nothing." Victoria nuzzled the side of the head of the sobbing older girl and squeezed her little one.

"What did Valentina have when the man took her? What was she wearing?"

"She still in Barbie clothes, pink, and the man have a gun. Valentina's brave, she grab her backpack and try to run away, but he catch her." Victoria choked on a sob, then spoke again. "She drop her doll. She love her doll."

"What did the backpack look like?"

"Pink Barbie. Valentina like everything pink Barbie."

"What did she have in it?"

Victoria's eyes widened. "She never lets anyone touch it. I don't know."

That was weird. I wasn't an expert on little girls, but from what I'd seen and what I remembered from my own childhood, a little girl showed off her treasures, got them out and took a loving daily inventory, caressed them and sang to them. I heard sirens outside, and my racing heart sped up even faster. I had to hurry.

"Tell me about the man who took her," I said. "What did he look like?"

"Big man, white, no hair on his head, and a tattoo here—" she pointed to the inside of her left upper arm, "that say E-S-L." She pronounced it Ay-Essay-Ellay. "But the E's funny."

I swung the paper around to her. "Can you draw it?"

She nodded, and did, drawing the Greek letter sigma: Σ.

I heard footsteps outside. "Do you have a picture of Valentina?"

Victoria reached in her pocket and got her phone, nodding. "I text you one, yes?"

"Yes." I said my number and she typed it and hit send.

A loud knock sounded at the door. "Police."

"We've gotta let them in," Wallace said under his breath.

I shoved the paper and pen into my folder. "Thank you, Victoria. You've helped Sofia and Valentina a lot. I will tell Sofia. The police will want to talk to you now."

I placed my hand on hers and gripped it. I squeezed, and she flipped hers and squeezed mine back.

Tears rolled down her cheeks again. She whispered, more to herself than to me, "*Lo siento. Lo siento.*"

Wallace opened the door and let the cops in.

THIRTEEN

A big-bellied, uni-browed police officer with basset-hound eyes and a bad attitude questioned both of us. Officer Samson. I made a mental note not to get in his way in the future, but he let Wallace and me go an hour after he arrived.

I'd texted Jack moments after the police got there: *Must talk ASAP. Where are you?*

I hoped he wasn't mad that three o'clock had long since passed. I kept sneaking peeks at my phone, but heard nothing until we were walking away to the car.

Jack: *Driving to PCCB.*

PCCB, PCCB, PCCB? I realized I had stopped and was tapping my foot. Relax girl, I told myself. I didn't do my best thinking when I let myself get all jacked up. I took several deep breaths and tried again. PCCB . . . Potter County Courts Building. I nodded.

I texted: *Meet you there.*

I climbed into the Altima. Wallace pulled four wipes out and handed me two. I sanitized like the Energizer Bunny, my adrenaline still pumping.

"Can you drop me at the Potter County Courts Building?" I asked. "I have to meet Jack." I dropped my wipes in the little trashcan and buckled in.

"On my way." He peeled rubber. "You're good at this, you know?"

I blew air through my pressed lips. "I don't know about that, but I really, really want to find this little girl."

He nodded. "Me, too. Hey, can I get a copy of your notes from your interviews with Victoria?"

"Absolutely. I'll scan them for you now. Just call or text later if you have questions."

I used Tiny Scan on my phone to text them to him while he drove, holding myself upright as he took all the corners too fast, like he'd done on the way to Harvey's place. He had some legit driving skills. I hit send on my text to him and looked up. He had pulled into the parking lot behind a familiar building that looked a heck of a lot like *2001: A Space Odyssey*'s version of a courthouse. I'd never had reason to go to the PCCB in my youth, but I had been in the old art deco Potter County Court*house*. The Courts Building was nothing like that one.

I turned to Wallace. "It's my first time here, and—"

He smiled and pointed. "Through the back door there. Security's just inside it."

Security. "Oh no."

"Huh?"

"I forgot about going through a metal detector."

He frowned. "You're packing?"

"Yeah."

He guffawed and slapped his knee. "You really are an 'Amarilla' girl, aren't you?" He said, aping the local accent like a native.

"Guilty. And yet I forgot my handbag in the car when we were at Harvey's house. How smart was that?"

He opened his glove compartment. "Stash it in there, Annie Oakley. They probably won't even make you go through the metal detectors—I'll bet every attorney in that building's carrying—but better safe than sorry. And you're going to have to come bail me out if I get thrown in jail for possessing it without a license."

I put my treasured gun in the glove box and grinned. "Of course. Thank you. For everything."

"You, too. We did good today."

"Yes, we did." I put my hand on the door handle and tucked the Redrope folder and handbag under my arm, then stopped. "We're going to find her, aren't we? I mean, she's got to be okay."

Wallace leaned toward me and snagged me in a hug. "I sure hope so. I'll be on my knees praying we do, morning and night."

I twisted and put my arm around him, squeezing tight for a long few seconds. I loved that Wallace was a man of faith. Did he manage to find a church here where he felt at home? I made a mental note to ask him later. Mother's church was a no-go, but I was pretty sure I'd go to Hell if I didn't expose my baby to religion, starting in utero. I almost laughed at the thought. This was more a sign I was an "Amarilla" girl than even my concealed handgun permit or the lessons at the shooting range along with the engraved baby Glock 26 (now in Wallace's glove box) that my father had given me on my fifteenth birthday. "Wrong girl," it said around the mouth of the barrel.

We released each other and I bounded out of the car.

"Wait," he hollered, and I stopped. "For your safety, take the ramp, on the left."

"What?"

He pointed toward the building. "When it's dry, always use the ramp. When it's wet, always use the stairs. It's maintained by the county." He rolled his eyes. "Just trust me."

I laughed and waved goodbye and took off for the courthouse. My feet pounded a quick drumbeat on the sidewalk. Jack had just reached the top of the ramp, so I called out to him. He looked my way, saw me, and waited. He didn't appear pissed, but he didn't look warm and fuzzy either.

I picked up my pace for the last few steps up the tiled incline and over an oddly painted metal bridge of some sort.

"Thanks," I said. "So glad I caught you."

"I'm in a hurry," he said. "We'll talk inside."

"Okay."

We entered, and he gestured toward the security station. The PCCB was shaped like an L inside from this direction, with security jammed into the corner at its base with a corridor to the right as its horizontal line, and a corridor in front of us as its vertical line.

"What is that odor?" I asked Jack. The whole place smelled musty and vaguely unhealthy.

"Vanity, plus precipitation."

"Jack, seriously, what is it?"

"This place leaks like a sieve."

"Ah."

I plopped my now-two-pounds-lighter handbag onto the conveyor belt and walked slowly through the scanner.

"Hello, Mr. Holden." The Potter County Deputy manning the scanner looked at Jack like a long-lost friend, his white teeth gleaming except for the missing left eyetooth.

"How's your sciatica?" Jack walked around the security station while he chatted.

"Pains me something fierce when it rains, but, other than that, I can't complain."

"Take care, Lucius."

"You too, Mr. Holden."

Lucius waved me through the metal detector, and I collected my handbag on the other side.

Just then, I heard a commotion. I turned to see a female deputy handcuffing the man behind me in the line. A Leatherman tool lay out on the conveyor belt, but that didn't seem to be the problem.

The woman—a dead ringer for my mother—held a baggie in front of the man's face and said, "Sir, you are under arrest for possession of an illegal controlled substance."

Jack pulled me along by my upper arm. "Happens all the time."

"What?"

"Some poor sap surrenders his knife only to have his dope fall out right in front of the deputies."

I laughed. "Another potential client."

"Somebody has to protect their rights, and it keeps me from digging ditches."

We headed to the elevators. There were two, but one had a piece of white copier paper taped to it. In large, black print it read OUT OF ODER. While I started telling Jack about the day's discoveries, Jack pressed the up button, then pulled a pen from his briefcase.

"I found out a lot more about Sofia, but something even bigger happened."

Jack drew an R below and between the O and D with an upward pointing arrow. Then he wrote (-1 Sp) at the top of the paper. The elevator doors opened, revealing a floor that looked like the top of a bunch of blue Legos and walls plastered with sheets of wood-grained paper. I stopped speaking. Two men in business suits stepped out, one looking like any ol' attorney in Dallas, and the other in boots, a felt Cowboy hat, and a Western-cut suit with snazzy lapel stitching. We got on, and before we turned around, I saw a flier for "Birthday Cake! Cheryl is turning the big 5-0! Join us in the District Clerk's Office for Cake and Fun!" taped to the back of the elevator. Jack pressed the button for the fifth floor.

"Go on," he said.

"We found Valentina. I mean, we found where she'd been staying."

He raised his eyebrows.

I took that as, "Great job. Please continue." So I did. "She was with the neighbor who babysat her, Victoria, who was also Sofia's emergency contact at work, but that's beside the point. Sofia had made Victoria promise to hide Valentina if anything ever happened to her. And, at first, Victoria lied to us and said she didn't know where Valentina was. But then the apartment manager said Victoria just had two daughters, and there were three girls there when I interviewed her. As we were talking to Mr. Slum Lord, Victoria and her girls started screaming their heads off, so we ran back." I stopped to breathe.

The elevator doors opened on the fifth floor. A woman with a cane and long silver hair got on before we could get off. Jack pressed the Open Doors button and we waited for her to situate herself.

"First floor, please," she said in a voice that didn't waver.

He pressed the 1 button, with his index finger this time, and we slipped out before the doors closed, in front of two soft drink machines covered in more fliers.

"Keep talking." He pointed to our right and we walked into a large foyer, then he turned left toward the doors of the DA's office.

"And one of the little girls was gone. A man had just kidnapped Valentina. We ran after him, but we didn't get a look at him."

"Did you see his car, get a license plate?"

"No, nothing."

"Jiminy Christmas."

He pulled open the door to the DA's office and I walked ahead of him into a very small foyer.

I lowered my voice. "I know. Then Wallace called 911, so I hurried in to talk to Victoria before the cops could get there. And that's when she told me everything, only it made no sense, and we still have no idea where Valentina is, or who took her. But Victoria sent me a picture."

I pulled it up and put my phone in front of his face. He stopped, gazing for a second with me at Sofia, sans bruises and swelling with her pink-clad little angel. Then he broke away and nodded to the large blonde woman who was looking at us from behind a glass panel. She was surrounded at her desk by framed inspirational religious quotes, pictures of horses (my kind of woman), and photos of her with two look-alike girls.

"Jack Holden. I have an appointment with ADA—"

The woman interrupted him, her voice thick with small-town Panhandle twang. "Oh yes. Just a moment. You can wait over in the lobby."

Jack's brows furrowed and we walked back into the small waiting area behind us. He lowered his voice, a little, and said, "I hate it when these prima donna ADAs make me wait. I never made a defense attorney sit out here like a kid outside the principal's office when I was an ADA."

Just as we were about to take seats, a new woman's voice said, "Jack." It was a voice that raised the hairs on the back of my neck.

Both of us whirled. It was Melinda, tucked into a black pencil skirt and starched, white, tailored blouse that fit like a leotard. I fought the urge to lick my thumb and scrub the dirty spots off my jeans from my earlier tumbles. Instead, I fluffed my bangs and smoothed the sides of my ponytail.

She did a double take. "Emily. What are you doing here?"

Before I could answer, Jack did. "Emily's my paralegal. I assume she's welcome at our meeting?"

"Um, yeah. Sure. Right this way."

Was it my imagination, or did her pressed lips mean my presence irritated her? Or maybe it disappointed her? She'd looked at Jack a moment ago like a red-tailed hawk I'd once seen lock eyes on a rabbit seconds before snatching it into the sky, twenty feet from where I sat daydreaming in summer grass. I'd had nightmares about hawks for a week after that. Oddly enough, I'd had nightmares about Melinda for twenty years.

The door past the receptionist's area buzzed, and we followed Melinda's sashaying hips through it and down a hall to an open door on our left. She gestured for us to go in.

Right before we entered what looked like a small conference room, I whispered to Jack. "I just don't know how we're going to tell Sofia."

He looked me in the eyes, and something in them caught me off guard and sent my heart lurching into my throat. I stopped, and he did, too. He smiled at me. Automatically, idiotically, I smiled back, and I felt myself go all gooey. He had the most amazing tawny eyes, especially when they looked at me like that.

Long seconds later, he finally turned to Melinda and said, "So, what's this emergency summons about anyway?"

We walked in and she shut the door with a heavy thud. I put my hands to my cheeks to see if they were as hot as they felt. They were. Melinda and I both took seats—her at the head of the table, and me on the far side—but Jack stood by the chair nearest the door. He'd missed a loop with his belt, and I found myself wanting to fix it for him, which was his wife's job. That made my cheeks even hotter. How was it that Jack could distract me like this when, seconds ago, I'd been so upset about Valentina's kidnapping?

Melinda clasped her hands in front of her on the table. "I wanted to tell you in person, before you heard about it on the news. There's been an incident at the jail."

Jack stopped short, his hand on the back of a chair. "What kind of incident?"

"The kind where your client Sofia Perez was killed, unfortunately."

It took a moment for the shock of her words to break through the haze Jack's eyes had put me in, and I gasped aloud. Sofia, dead? I'd only met her once, but my entire life had revolved around her and her daughter for the last week. Valentina, missing . . . and no longer with a mother, or even a father (that we knew about). Well, I guess we wouldn't have to worry about how to break the news to Sofia about Valentina after all.

To my horror, I burst into tears.

FOURTEEN

I paced in front of Jack's desk.

"But we could file a wrongful death suit on Valentina's behalf, as Sofia's survivor. Or on behalf of Sofia's estate. Or something!"

That last part came out a little louder than I'd intended. Jack didn't yell back, but Snowflake shivered in her sheepskin doggy bed beside his desk. "It's called a survival action, but Valentina isn't our client."

"Sofia is."

"Emily, finding Valentina has nothing to do with filing a survival action."

"But our client was murdered in cold blood. Melinda may call it a gang fight, but that's a crock and you know it. How come Sofia was the only one hurt, much less killed? And on the same day Valentina gets snatched? Something more is going on here, Jack. Something much, much more. And the DA's office is covering it up. It's total bull honky!"

A big grin spread across his face ear to ear. "Bull what?"

I crossed my arms and glared at him. "You heard me."

Jack stood up and started pacing back and forth behind his desk, which made Snowflake sit up and whine.

Too late, I realized it was probably bad form to yell at the top of your lungs at your boss of one week. But, really, Jack could drive anyone into a frenzy. The man was infuriating. One minute he was confusing me with inappropriate goo-goo eyes in the DA's office, and the next he was shutting me down about Valentina. When she needed my help more than ever.

"You're right," he said. "The circumstances suck, and a survival action isn't out of the question. But not until we're caught up on some other things. Then, and only then, I very well may support your request to expand the practice into civil litigation and ask you to help look into it. In the meantime, you did an amazing job today and really broke things open for the police. They're going to find Valentina, and you'll have made that possible. But, Emily, that's their job, not yours." His voice softened. "You certainly have a passion for managing my practice, and I'm not complaining about it. Passion is good."

I stared at the floor, thinking for a moment. "I haven't told you everything."

Jack leaned back against one of his tall cabinets. "Oh, shit."

"What? No, I didn't do anything. Well, I mean, I didn't get caught doing anything." I held up my hand as Jack started to interrupt. "Just listen. We know Sofia shot Spike, but she wouldn't say why. I looked into Spike's background, and he did time for molesting a child with another guy—a Harvey Dulles from Amarillo. I gave you a copy of my research, remember?"

"Right."

"Well, today I learned Sofia used to bring Valentina to work and hide her there, where she'd sleep or read or color or whatever."

"So?"

I crouched beside the shivering Snowflake and started massaging her neck. Poor girl didn't like high emotion. She still shook, but she seemed to relax some into my hand. "So, Spike has a record for doing bad stuff with kids. Sofia shot him. What if those two things are related? I got to thinking: what about the possibility that his old buddy Harvey was there, too? One of the hotel employees said he saw a man running away from the hotel the night Sofia shot Spike, a man that fits the description for Harvey. Harvey could be a witness for us. Or, he might even be the one who has Valentina."

Jack rubbed his jaw. "Okay. I'm still listening."

I stood back up and leaned my tush against the edge of Jack's desk, facing him. "Wallace and I went to Harvey's house before we went to see Victoria," I said. "Before I knew she had Valentina. Harvey wasn't there. Two homeless teenagers told us he moved out in a hurry last week. I haven't checked with his employer yet to see if he's still working, but he could have her, Jack."

He shook his head. "Did you tell the police about Harvey? Because Valentina—"

"I know. Isn't our client. And yes, I told the officer that questioned me at Victoria's my theory. I got a few nods, but he wasn't won over."

"Is that all?"

I thought about trespassing at Harvey's house and my B&E at Sofia's apartment.

"Yeah, that's all," I said. "I just wanted you to know everything, plus, it could be a lead for a survival suit."

"Which we aren't going to look into yet."

I crouched and resumed stroking Snowflake, as much to soothe myself now as her.

"I know, but just keep it in mind," I said. "We've got one known creep living in Amarillo, and his creepy buddy shows up here. Sofia kills the buddy, so isn't it possible creep number one knows people that know people in PCDC? He could be behind Sofia's death, too."

"Noted. For the future. For now, just finish Johnson. Then I need to unleash your passion and brilliance on my other cases."

I crossed my fingers behind my back and said, "No problem."

Mother picked me up at the curb forty-five minutes later for the ride back to Heaven. Suddenly, a heavy tiredness coursed through me so hard that I could barely lift my hand to open the door. I flopped into the seat like a lead weight.

"Hi, Mother," I said.

When she didn't reply, I turned to her. She was biting her lip—always a bad sign. Today had already been a long, hard day. I closed my eyes. *Lord, give me strength.*

I tried again. "What's wrong?"

She tilted her head back, the better to raise her nose in the air. "Imagine my disappointment to have to hear through the grapevine that my own daughter is having my first grandbaby, instead of hearing it from her."

Well, this wasn't good. Surely the news of my just-booked-half-an-hour-ago OB appointment for Wednesday hadn't spread that fast.

"Who told you that?"

"So you aren't denying it?" She braked at a green light and the car behind her honked. She pressed the accelerator.

I let my weary head fall back against the front seat cushion as we shot forward. "Um, congratulations, Grandmother."

She cleared her throat, then went silent.

"Mother, I'm only eight weeks along." Well, nearly nine, but who was counting? "I just found out myself. I had planned to tell you tonight anyway." I hoped the crossed fingers I'd used with Jack earlier had a lasting effect. "So, who told you?"

"Katie emailed me. One of those online cards from Jacquie Lawson." She sniffed. "It was just lovely. A little bear with balloons."

I choked back a groan. Collin. I hadn't mentioned "mum's the word" when I'd told my story in New Mexico. Especially in relation to *my* mum.

"How sweet of her," I said.

"She's very kind. And so I called Rich—"

"You *what*?!" I sat forward so hard and fast the seat belt pinched me. "No, Mother, no, tell me you didn't."

"What? He didn't pick up so I just left him a voice mail."

Oh God, oh no, oh, my mother. "WHAT DID YOU SAY?"

"Don't use that tone with me, young lady. I told him congratulations on the baby and how excited I was to be a grandmother."

I put my head in my hands and then a giggle started that seemed to ricochet back at me as it bounced off the insides of the car, escalating and multiplying until it was a symphony of inharmonious cackles. I giggled so hard I needed to change my panties. I laughed, literally, until I cried, and by the time it stopped, I was choking on little sobs.

"You called Rich instead of me."

Now it was her turn for the hot seat, and she squirmed.

"Well, I—your new job, and, because I just—so, yes, and I knew I'd see you soon anyway." She clamped her mouth shut.

I blubbered a little as I spoke. "Mother, that man's lover crashed my baby announcement dinner, and Rich chose *him* over me. So, guess what? I hadn't told him yet. He doesn't get to share this part. It was supposed to be my little secret. My baby. Mine. Not his, and not Stormy's."

"Emily Josephine Phelps Bernal, you cannot mean to tell me you aren't going back to Dallas to raise this child with him."

She put on her blinker and turned onto the I-40 access road.

"I most certainly can."

"You can't divorce Rich now. The baby is proof he's not gay."

I hooted. I couldn't help it. "Were you not listening to the part where he doesn't want to be married to me, the part where he chose Stormy, who is a man? I'm sorry, Mother, but the ability to make a baby does not determine your sexual orientation."

She huffed. "Still, I cannot for the life of me see how you, a girl whose own father left you, would deny your child a father?"

She accelerated up the entrance ramp and merged into what passed for rush hour traffic in Amarillo. My pulse accelerated with the car. I held my tongue, fuming, working it out in my mind. What was this about? How could she say these things to me? Dad left when I was nearly grown. And it *had* hurt. It *still* hurt. Yet I knew it probably hurt her more. Lord knows she was the one who had to face the humiliation when other people whispered. I was beginning to understand what that must have been like. Plus, for years he'd sent postcards and letters and gifts and checks to me. He'd called on my birthdays. He'd begged my forgiveness and tried to explain, in his own way, that he wasn't the kind of man to live in one place, with one woman, and that he couldn't come back anymore.

So, yeah, it had hurt, but I hadn't felt as "left" as she had. That was until I was a senior in college, anyway, when all his cards and letters just stopped, and he never called me again. I had Rich who told me he wanted to be my husband, so I didn't need a father, and I moved on, too. An arrow sliced through my heart and out my back. Now I'd moved on from being left by a father to being left by a husband.

I softened my tone. "Mother, it is in part because I had a father at home and lost him that I fully understand the difference between what I went through and what it means that my child's father won't ever live in our house. This baby will always have a father, but won't have to know the hurt of a father leaving."

"But what will I tell my friends?" she shrieked, turning to me, and swerving into the lane to our right.

A horn blared and Mother jumped in her seat, overcorrecting to her left, earning her another honk. She straightened her wheel and squeezed her lips together. I grabbed the armrest on the door. She wasn't going to have to worry about this if she killed us both. I bit my lip hard, holding it in. I'd grown up believing in honoring and respecting my parents. I didn't always practice it, but I tried. Right now, I tried really, really hard.

I turned the radio on as a distraction. "A murder suspect was killed today in a prison riot at the Potter County Detention Center—"

I snapped the dial off.

Mother made a *hrmph* sound. "At least the rest of us won't have to pay to keep another criminal fed and clothed for the rest of their life."

"Enough!" My yell was so loud and high-pitched it hurt my own ears, and Mother ducked. "Enough with your comments. If you so much as open your mouth the rest of the way home, I'll . . . I'll . . ." I stopped. I had no idea what I'd do, I just knew neither of us was going to like it. I exhaled and dialed down my volume. "Just enough, okay?"

She bit her lip, again. It was white, as were her knuckles. I felt a little bit guilty, but not so much that I wasn't able to appreciate the blessed silence on the rest of the drive.

FIFTEEN

I stalked from the elevator to the office the next morning an hour early in a hailstorm of text messages from my soon-to-be ex-husband. I hit the front door like a battering ram.

Rich: *Why didn't you tell me?*

Rich: *We must talk!*

Rich: *I deserve a reply!*

Those were the three latest I'd received. Oh, I had a reply for him. Boy, did I have a reply. I grabbed the door and threw my whole body into slamming it. The door swung closed on its hydraulic brake to a whispery soft landing behind me.

Snowflake met me, but she slunk away when she saw the mood I was in. No toast crusts for her today. I slammed my handbag down on my desk. I hadn't slept worth a dang last night. Dreams of Valentina tormented me, her screams, her sweet face and her adorable little Barbie pj's, a large bald tattooed man dragging her by the arm away from the rodeo arena while I watched, helpless, standing directly in the path of a charging bull. Hours later, I was struggling to keep my toast down and reeling from bickering with my mother the entire drive to work. Rich's text barrage was just piling on at this point.

A note lay on my chair. *Johnson and only Johnson until you're done.* Oh, not Jack, too. The yellow-bellied sapsucker didn't have the guts to tell me to my face. He had to leave me a little note. I wanted to scream at him. *I know, I know, already. I know what you are ordering me to do, to ignore an inno-*

cent little girl who needs someone to care what happens to her so that I can go to work for clients who have done bad things.

The bell on my desk beckoned me, not to ring it, no, but rather to ignore it. It beckoned me down the hall on sneaky feet. It beckoned me to Jack's luxurious and oh-so-private office. So I led with my chin and sailed down the hall, holding the clacker of the bell still as I moved soundlessly toward my boss.

Once at the door to his office, I stopped at the precipice, teetering on a doubt. He had asked me to ring the bell to give him his privacy.

The devil on my shoulder whispered in my ear. *Well, wouldn't a little privacy be nice? You sure don't have any, though, so why should he?*

Nah, bell shmell. It was a stupid, chauvinistic rule, and it shouldn't be okay to hold me hostage in the lobby so he could hide behind his "privacy."

I took a deep breath and barged in, bell clanging. "Screw your bell rule, Mr. Holden, I'm not playing your little power game anymore."

The first words came out as a bellow, the last few words came out a whisper, as I took in what I saw.

Jack's tall built-in cabinet on the left side of the office was open, revealing an enormous photographic portrait of a family in what looked like hiking clothes, in a mountain setting with tall pine trees and a glistening stream. In the middle stood a striking woman with flawless skin the color of toasted caramel. Her long black hair was thick and lustrous, parted on the side and swept back as if with her fingers. The camera had caught her smile midlaugh. It lit her eyes like sparklers. She had one arm around two grinning kids: a little girl—maybe eight years old?—who was lucky enough to look just like her mother and a little boy who shared their looks and appeared to be slightly younger than his sister. On the other side of the boy, his arm around the two children, too, stood Jack. But that Jack had hair down to his shoulders and looked fifteen years younger than the short-haired man standing beside the portrait now, glaring at me like a bull does at the rodeo clown just before he tosses her over the rail.

"Is there a problem, Emily?" he said, nostrils flared, fists balled.

I now took in the easel and paper in front of him, and the unfinished charcoal drawing of the little girl from the portrait on a spotted pony. A hideaway bed extended from the left built-in cabinet, Snowflake huddled in terror on a pillow. I took in the man in his white tee and his jeans, a Fender shirt on a hanger looking ready for wear on the table. I smelled spices and cheese and, on his desk, I saw his breakfast taco.

Suddenly I knew the answer to all his mysterious morning noises, and, worse, knew what a horrible person I was.

I tried to answer him. "No." No sound except a wheezy crackling noise came out, and I repeated myself, louder. "No." I backed up, my hand behind me on the doorframe. "I'm sorry."

I fled back to the lobby and on to the bathroom down the hall, face in my hands, tears leaking through my fingers. What a dumbass I was. A total dumbass. A total clueless dumbass. I shook my head, cringing, as I remembered Jack's face, and the picture of his daughter that he'd drawn from that beautiful, beautiful portrait of his family. A total clueless, selfish dumbass.

I leaned against the closed door inside a bathroom stall. Still, what was he doing living on a pullout bed in his Amarillo office if he had a family like that somewhere? They sure weren't living at Wrong Turn Ranch in New Mexico either. And then it hit me. He wouldn't have a shrine like that to his family if they were still with him. So, had Jack's wife left him, and taken the kids? Was he in the middle of a divorce? It was possible, but it didn't change my invasion of his privacy, or how upset he was with me, or how upset I was with myself. It could mean he hadn't misled me about his marital status, and that my anger about it had been unjust, though.

Five snuffling minutes later, I washed my face and slunk to my desk. I booted up my laptop. Typing the words RodeoQueen somehow brought the rain down from my eyes again. I mopped them with my light peach sweater. Bangs and thuds resounded from Jack's office, and I flinched at each sound. I opened my Johnson file and tried to find my place.

Footsteps approached along with the tinkle of Snowflake's tags. I tensed, not ready to face him.

"Here are the other client files with instructions for your next few projects when you're done with Johnson. I'll be in court today." His voice sounded tight and echo-y.

I tried to make myself sound neutral, even though tears threatened to fall again. "Okay, thanks."

He opened the door and disappeared down the hall with Snowflake and me staring at the space he left behind.

I spent the morning on a variety of tasks, most of them not work related. Of course, there was my ongoing text war with Rich. Luckily, he'd disappeared about an hour ago. I needed the breather—from him and from a persistent ache in my abdomen, which I hoped was just stress.

I had emailed a few prospective employers about jobs I found in the *Globe News*. One as a legal secretary, another as a receptionist. Unfortunately, there weren't any ads for paralegals. I hated to take a job outside my field, especially for less money, but I'd blown it this morning, and I needed a backup plan—fast. I hoped Jack didn't fire me before I found something else. My heart lurched and made a liar out of me— it knew I hoped he didn't fire me at all.

I checked my personal email, something I only did every few days. In it was an email from Katie, dated yesterday.

Emily: Congratulations on the baby! Collin told me the fantastic news, and also a lot of other not-so-great things, but I want to hear it from you. Call me, and I promise I won't make it all about me for a change. <3 Tell your mother hello for me, and take your prenatal vitamins.

I would call her, for sure, but not when Jack could walk in. I flagged the message.

On a whim, I had texted Nadine, the waitress from My Thai: *It's Emily. We bonded the other day over my crash landing into Taco Villa back in the day, and we talked about getting together. Want to grab dinner?*

Despite all the nonwork stuff, I had uncovered a wealth of juicy nuggets for Jack on Paul Johnson, so I felt virtuous about that, at least. I eyed the new client files. My stomach growled. Which to deal with first? Neither.

I grabbed my phone and texted Wallace. Again: *Any news on Valentina? Do you know if the police found Maria Delgado or Harvey?*

When neither Wallace nor Nadine answered me, the new project work seemed to glow like a bright light, refusing to be ignored. I grabbed the first file.

My phone rang. Thank God. "Hello?"

Crackle. "—Ily Ber—" Crackle.

"Our reception is terrible. This is Emily Bernal speaking."

"I have your—" Crackle-crackle.

I stood up. "I can't hear you."

Crackle-crackle-crackle. "—car."

I climbed up on the couch, trying to get my phone higher, to reach better coverage. "Can you repeat that?"

The call dropped.

The door opened. Wallace stood in the doorway in pressed khakis, work boots, and some Paul Bunyan-like plaid shirt. His eyebrows shot up.

I tried for a graceful dismount. "Um, bad cell reception."

"That's what I'd say if I was caught doing a Tom Cruise on the couch."

I laughed and he held up a bag. 575 Pizzeria. "I got a red pie and a white one," he said. "Both meatless, since I learned you were a rebel yesterday. Hungry?"

My mouth watered. "You went all the way to 575 Pizzeria?"

"I'd have gone twice that far for their pizza."

We walked to the kitchen. Was my tongue hanging out like a dog's, or did it just feel like it? I grabbed plates and napkins and set them out while Wallace extracted the boxes from the bag. When he opened the first lid and that cheesy, doughy goodness wafted my way, I nearly cried.

"I've had a really bad day. Pizza is about the only thing in the world that could make it better. You're psychic."

He grinned, mouth full of a piece of the basil, garlic, and pine nuts red pie.

I put a piece of each pie on my plate. "And today? Let's just say today can bite me."

I chomped into the white pie and exhaled to cool the cheesy part that stuck to the roof of my mouth. It was wonderful, and I admired it in my hand, covered in stripes of white cheese and green chiles.

He laughed, half-choking. "You're not much of a cusser."

I brandished a slice. "I may not cuss tough, but I fight tough."

"I believe that after yesterday."

"Hey, you didn't happen to bring my gun with you, did you?"

"No way in hell I'm carrying that thing without a license," Wallace said. "Do you know what happens to men as gorgeous as me in the slammer? I like to choose my dates, thank you very much."

I snorted, then laughed. "Did you find those teenagers we saw yesterday?"

Wallace held a hand up until he finished chewing a bite. "The police did. The kids' names are Greg Easley and Farrah Farud. Their case worker —Byron, you'd like him, good guy—took them back to a group home until we investigate the abuse allegations."

"That's good, I guess."

He waggled his hand and nodded. "It's a start."

We ate in silence a few moments until I had enough food in me to return to my favorite topic. "You brought me an update on Valentina, didn't you?"

"Now who's psychic?" He grinned.

"Psycho, more like it."

A voice in the lobby interrupted. "Excuse me, anyone here?"

I took a gulp of my tea through a bite of red pie before saying, "Yes, just a moment!" I jumped to my feet, chewing frantically and mopping sauce from my face and hands.

"Expecting someone?"

I headed to the door, looking back at him. "Nope."

The man in the lobby/my office looked about my age, ordinary in a white skin, brown hair, brown eyes kind of way, in clean blue jeans and a long-sleeved blue tee with the words Professional Drivers, Inc. across the chest. He held a clipboard and a ring of keys. He had a pleasant smell that I couldn't place.

"Hello, may I help you?"

"I'm looking for Emily Bernal." His voice had a weary undertone to its friendliness.

"That's me."

He nodded. "I called earlier. I have your car for you. I'll just need a credit card and to take you downstairs so you can check it out and sign for it."

Rich had failed to mention when I should expect my car, since baby talk had dominated the last fifteen hours of our interactions. I took the bill and recoiled. Gas, delivery fee, and money for a taxi to the airport and a plane ticket back to Dallas. It was more than I had left in my checking account. I retrieved my Visa card and handed it to him.

"Thanks," I said.

He swiped the card in his phone reader and typed on his screen.

Wallace had joined us by now. "Looks like you can drive this afternoon," he said.

I scribbled my name with my fingertip on the phone extended toward me. "Where are we going this afternoon?" I asked Wallace.

"Well, no one's tracked down Maria Delgado yet. Obviously the job calls for our Scooby Doo investigator team skills."

I laughed again. Thank God Wallace had come. "A team on which I am clearly Velma. Can we look for Harvey when we've corralled Maria?"

"Yep. And then, later, you might want to play around on the Internet. With the name Antonio Rosa."

"Why's that?"

"The gay-hating manager of the apartments finally coughed up a name to the cops. Antonio is the guy who paid for Sofia and Valentina's apartment."

"Heck yeah." Before I could stop myself, I did a fist pump, and even went a little airborne. It wasn't pretty.

Wallace burst out laughing at my feeble curse and leap, and I laughed, too, loud and real, heart hammering. The bad morning receded a little. We were going to find Valentina—I just knew it.

The driver interrupted. I'd forgotten he was there. "If you don't mind, I've got a plane to catch."

"Of course," I said.

Wallace added, "Pick me up at my office."

Jack wasn't here to ask permission, so I pretended that if he had been, he would have said yes.

SIXTEEN

The light green Mustang I'd given myself as a landing-my-first-job reward eight years ago still ran like a top, but it was looking rode hard and put up wet. I didn't even think about cleaning it until two blocks from the CPS building when it hit me how far it was below Wallace's standards. The delivery driver had used paper mats, but those had only covered dirty mats and carpet underneath. Residue of lattes past clung to the drink holders. A gym bag with used clothing glared at me from behind the passenger seat. Trash of spurious origins littered the back floor mats. I searched the glove compartment and console at a red light. No Handi Wipes. No miniature trash can. Oh well. Too late to do anything about it.

Wallace stood on the sidewalk in front of a nondescript building (amongst other nondescript buildings and large surface parking lots) fiddling with his phone. I tapped my horn lightly, and he looked up. My car withered under his scrutiny, and he hadn't even gotten in yet.

He slammed the door and then gasped. "Emily. No."

"It's not like you're going to get Ebola from it or something."

Wallace cocked his head, eyebrows up but eyes soft. "I'm not so sure. That's why Uncle Wallace is going to treat you to the most divine car wash ever." I sputtered but he shook his head. "This little baby is borderline vintage, and she deserves preservation."

Wallace directed me to the The Works car wash, and, once there, paraded around like a VIP. Talk about a place where everybody knows your name. He must have practically lived there, or owned stock. The trip to The Works for auto detailing set us back forty-five minutes. I decided not to let it bother me that we'd spent the time on my car. I'd left Jack a note that I'd be back in by midafternoon, and we were just making one stop at Maria's. It shouldn't take that long, and even I had to admit that the Mustang looked fabulous, with a little prance in her step after the detailing. Just in time to hang out in a neighborhood where she would have blended better in her previous condition.

Wallace made no secret of studying me as we drove away from The Works. "Okay, so I've held back as long as I can. Who peed in your Post Toasties today?"

I shook my head. "Who didn't?" Then, because there was nothing else I could do, I laughed. "After the quality time we've spent together, I feel it's time to share."

"Sharing time, yes!"

I laughed harder, startled by his shout. "So, I'm back in Amarillo because a gay transgender man named Stormy who was dressed like a woman crashed my 'Surprise, honey, I'm pregnant' party to stake his claim to my husband, Rich, who had in the meantime drained our finances Sahara dry."

Wallace stared at me for a moment. I looked at his face. Expressionless. I was afraid I'd offended him somehow, but then he said, "Wow, that's some major-league sharing. I hope you don't expect me to top that."

I shook my head. "Oh, and that's not even all. My girlfriend Katie found out from her brother Collin that I was preggers, so she congratulated my mother, who ripped me a new one for keeping her in the dark and took it upon herself to inform my ex, whom I hadn't told yet either and who's basically been strafing me with text fire all day. Oh, and I got in a snit at Jack and barged in on him half-dressed and in the midst of drawing a lovely charcoal picture of his daughter in front of his shrine to the family I didn't know he had, and he's not speaking to me."

"Jesus, Emily, I hope you've got your therapist on speed dial."

"I can't afford one, thanks to Rich."

"And here you are back in Amarillo."

"Where everybody is a little too interested in my business. 'There goes poor Emily who wasn't enough woman to hold onto her man.'"

He shook his head. "Honey, it doesn't sound like any woman was woman enough for your man."

"Ironic, isn't it?"

He reached over and patted my knee. "Don't worry. I'm sure you'll be old news by Christmas."

I snorted.

"And Emily? I think the term you're looking for about Stormy is transvestite."

"Good to know for when I tell the police why I slapped the bitch." I clapped my hand over my mouth. "Sorry."

He whooped. "Don't be sorry. That's the spirit." He smacked me a high five. "Okay, you're allowed one more hour to pout and be the center of attention. After that it's my turn."

"Deal."

"In the meantime, take me back to the part about Jack and half-naked."

The conversation lightened. It felt good to get all of it out, and my mood improved. I turned into Maria's neighborhood and decided to swing around the block first.

"I don't think she can park in back, but let's take a look," I said.

All we saw on the next street was more houses, and there was no alley between the two streets.

"Yeah, and she doesn't have a front garage either," Wallace said. "She's going to have to park on the street."

"I wish we knew what she drove."

"Or if she has a car at all."

"True. I didn't find anything registered to her."

I parked the Mustang three houses down. We walked to her door. I heard a giggle, and the sound of feet. I rang the front bell, then knocked. No answer. No lights. No more sounds.

"Someone doesn't want us to know they're here," I said. "But the laugh sounded like a child." I chewed my top lip. "Valentina?"

"It sounded more like a little boy to me."

"You're right. Let's watch the house for a while. Unless you can think of something else?"

"No, sounds good."

We hadn't been in the car five minutes when I pointed out a slight Hispanic woman in jeans and a black jack-o'-lantern sweatshirt headed toward us, from beyond Maria's house. She carried white plastic grocery bags with a red and blue logo on them looped over her arms.

Wallace leaned in her direction. "That could be her."

"She looks about the right age."

We knew to expect a fifty-ish woman from the information I'd found on her.

I tucked my handbag under my arm and put my hand on the door latch. The woman cut across the yard of the house next door at an angle toward Maria's. Wallace and I looked at each other and nodded, and we slipped out of the car. We walked toward Maria's house, moving quickly. The woman noticed us, and she started running, groceries spilling all across the grass. Oranges, avocados, a quart carton of milk, tortillas.

I shouted but my words were punctuated by gasping breaths as I ran to intercept her. "Maria, wait, someone kidnapped Valentina Perez. We're not with INS, we just want to help the little girl."

She didn't slow down. Wallace surprised me with a burst of speed and he made it to the door before she did. She stopped short, and I hit the front steps full tilt.

Crack! My foot exploded through the old wood and my momentum threw the rest of me forward into the steps: knees first, then gut and hands. All of the air came out of my lungs in a "woof." And then I yelled bloody murder, rattling the windows.

"Mother Goose!"

"Emily!" Wallace had a panicked look on his face.

The woman looked at me, then at her front door and moved toward it.

"No! I'm fine." I pushed myself up with my right hand, and I waved my left at her. "Don't let her get past you."

Wallace stayed put. "Maria, please. We don't care what you're doing, or who the little boy is inside that house."

She drew a shaky breath.

Wallace continued. "Some white guy, big, with a shaved head, took Valentina. You know who Valentina is, right? Sofia's daughter? Sofia, the one who used your ID to get a job, the one on the news who killed a guy at a hotel last week?"

I had meanwhile gingerly pulled my foot out of the splintery hole in the bottom step. My navy shoe stayed behind, so I reached in and got it. I sighed and put it back on. The wood had torn my knit pants, but the pants had protected my skin. I'd have an ugly bruise and I had splinters in both hands, but I wasn't really hurt that badly. I rubbed my stomach. The cramps that I'd endured off and on the last few days were still there, but no worse than before. *Sorry, baby.*

Maria took a step back, shaking her head.

I stood up. "I'm Emily and we talked about all of that on the phone last Friday. You're Maria, aren't you?"

She shook her head again.

"A six-year-old little girl. And you could help her, couldn't you?" She didn't react at all. I softened my voice, pleading. "Please. The man had a tattoo, an ESL, a weird E, here, on his arm." I pointed to the inside of my left upper arm.

Finally she spoke. "You not cops?"

I definitely recognized her voice from our phone conversation. "No, we're not."

"Not INS?"

"No."

"Then go. You trespass, and I defend myself."

"What?"

She pulled a handgun out of her purse. I raised my eyebrows and Wallace put his hands in front of him, palms forward, and said, "We were just leaving."

Back at the office, I took Snowflake out to do her business and then settled in at my desk. I was disappointed—and sore—from the visit to Maria's. I felt virtuous for the Johnson report I'd left Jack in his chair that morning and it didn't appear he'd been back to the office while I was gone. That meant my brownie points were already in the bank, so I allotted myself fifteen more minutes to sleuth online. I'd still have two hours left in the day to work on the new client projects afterward.

A text came in, Nadine answering mine from earlier: *I'm working tonight. Coffee tomorrow?*

I could go before my OB appointment at eleven. I texted back: *9:30 at Roaster's on Georgia?*

She agreed. I had a girlfriend date. I typed it into my calendar, then started Googling ESL and ΣSL. ESL had common usage as "English as a second language," resulting in a crushing load of hits about adult education programs. No way would some thug tattoo English as a second language on his arm. ΣSL brought up concepts only an engineer or mathematician could understand. I added Mexico to each term, but that didn't help.

The door in front of me opened, and I rapidly closed my browser. I swallowed and looked up to try to make amends with my boss, but it wasn't him.

"Hello, Emily."

It was Rich.

The Colombian man standing in front of my desk didn't look much older than he had when I'd met him in my freshman English class at Tech. He was slight of frame in his skinny jeans, thin black sweater, and overly stylish ankle boots. Dark and sexy in an Enrique Iglesias sort of way. But I didn't feel the rush I used to with his intense, beautiful eyes locked on me —just a sadness, a regret that made my shoulders sag, a panic that stole my breath. What the heck was he doing here?

"How did you know where to find me?" Like I didn't know. But I wanted to hear him say it.

"Your mother. We must talk."

"I'm at work." I stomped toward the kitchen, away from him, but he followed.

"I understand, and I promise we will converse in a civil manner."

"Speak for yourself." I moved around to the far side of the kitchen table.

He stood in the doorway. "Emily, I'm so sorry. I do not deserve your forgiveness, but I'm asking for it."

I rolled my eyes. Three weeks without his private school South American English made it foreign to me again, and irritating.

"Yeah, but not so sorry that you can't cheat on me and leave me broke. Give me a break, Rich. This isn't about me. You're here because of the baby, so just get on with it."

"Come back to Dallas. I want us to be a family and raise this baby together."

I cackled like a deranged hen. "That's priceless. You, me, baby, and Stormy. We'll have to get a California King. I call dibs on the side of the bed closest to the bathroom."

"If you come back, I give you my word I will not continue with Stormy. I will take the reparative therapy classes your mother has suggested I sign up for. The conversion."

"No."

"No, you don't want me to take the conversion?"

"No, I won't come back to Dallas; I won't stay married to you. You are the baby's father, and we can work out what that will look like, and I won't try to keep you out of the baby's life. But I don't want you in my town, or in my office, or in my house. I will not see you anymore while you're here. And if you show up again, I will call the police and tell them you're harassing me."

"You don't mean these things, surely?"

I stood up, put both hands on the table and yelled louder than I had when I fell through Maria's porch step earlier. "Get out. Get out, get out, get out!"

Rich stood for several moments, his mouth working but no sound coming out. I crossed my arms, but then a horrible pain tore through my abdomen. I grimaced and put my hands back on the table. Rich didn't notice, or if he did, he must have thought it was about him, because he put his hands up in defeat, took two steps back, and then turned, stopping at the door. "As you wish. Goodbye, Emily." Then he left.

As soon as he disappeared from sight, I gasped and clutched my stomach. I half-turned and put my hip on the table, then stood up again. Blood. Blood on the table. Panic gripped me. I heard the office door open and shut.

"Are you okay?"

Jack's voice. He was standing in the kitchen doorway, and his warm, golden eyes looked concerned, not angry. Had he heard everything? Probably. But that was the least of my problems now.

I shook my head no. "I think I need to go to the emergency room."

SEVENTEEN

The Southwest ER nurse squeaked away on white hospital shoes. He'd taken my blood, my temperature, and my pulse and pressure. Now the waiting for a doctor began. The light pink and white curtained space didn't give much privacy, and not only could I hear the moaning woman to my right, but I could see skinny ankles and bare feet under the curtain to my left. Liquid dripped to the floor by the bare feet and I averted my eyes, adjusting myself on the absorbent pad the nurse had placed under me. Jack sat in an armchair with a pleather seat, to the right of the bed.

I trained my eyes on my cold bluish toes. "You don't have to stay," I said.

"I'm not leaving you alone." He folded his arms across his chest and leaned against his seat back.

For the last hour, I'd tried to stay calm and keep my fears at bay. I didn't really want him here. At the same time, I did. I didn't know what I wanted about a lot of things. But one thing was for sure: I wanted to think about something other than why I was here.

Work. We could talk about work. "I left you a report on Johnson."

"Thanks. Did you get started on Freeman?"

Words fizzed behind my lips, then died. Did I get started on Freeman? *Of course not,* I wanted to shout. *I was looking for that little girl you don't care about.* But I didn't have the moral high ground here. I had been a giant horse's rear end to him.

"No. I'm sorry." I took a sip of water through a straw and felt calmer.

"Johnson may have atrocious manners and business deals on the fringe of polite society, but he hosts the biggest annual charity event in Las Cruces."

"Really?"

"Yep. It's a whole weekend of activities anchored by a three-day golf tournament that raises money for after-school shelters and programs. A keep 'em off the streets initiative."

"Huh."

"He's never done time, although most people suspect he gets away with breaking the barrier before the flag is tripped, if you know what I mean." He didn't answer, so I quickly added, "You know, when a horse starts early, before the steer breaks the barrier—"

"No, no. I know what you mean. I was just thinking."

I nodded, but he didn't elaborate, so I continued. "I can't make up my mind about him. He has a bad reputation with women, but I read that he's a good father. I met his daughter at your office last weekend, and she doesn't seem to like him, but it could just be a teenager thing."

Jack nodded.

"People hint that he's shady with his businesses," I continued, "but he raises money for kids. He may just be someone rough around the edges who's risen above his past."

Jack rubbed his forehead. "Which could make him a great client. He sent us our first case this week. An assault and battery charge against one of his employees."

"That's good." He didn't respond, so I added, "Right?"

He ignored my question. "This weekend he's having a housewarming party. Out at his ranch. We're all invited, and I think we should go. I mean, if you're feeling up to it and you don't have other plans."

I thought of spending time with my mother giving me the silent treatment, versus out at Wrong Turn Ranch with Jarhead, where I could possibly sneak over to Roswell and see what I could find out about Spike and Harvey.

"Okay," I said. "Sounds good."

He cleared his throat and looked down. "About this morning."

Oh, spit. I closed my eyes. I didn't want to think about it. I shouldn't have to deal with something that big and humiliating while I lay bleeding in an ER, should I? I could change the subject. Yet I didn't want it to linger on.

"Yes?"

He took a pen out of his pocket and thumped it on his leg, one time. "It's okay."

I swallowed hard, and then tears came. I tried to speak, failed, then tried again. "No, it's not, and I know it. You asked me to give you privacy, and I violated your space, and your, your—"

He sighed, cutting me off. "Memories. But it's not like you took them from me. I still have them."

His words sunk in, and I realized that my earlier suspicion had been right. His wife and kids were gone. It was sad, but a tiny place in me felt a flicker of hope.

"I'm so sorry."

He rubbed his chin, and I saw he hadn't shaved today. "Hey, guess what? I bunk in my office."

"Yeah, I kinda saw that."

He laughed, and I gave him a watery smile, but inside I hurt for him, and, I admit it, I wondered what had happened. The wife must've left him for someone else, I decided, because he sure didn't act like a guy who'd quit her of his own accord. I'll bet they were the reason he'd come to Amarillo, maybe following them here. I wondered about the little girl and her pony in the charcoal drawing. About her brother. I hoped his kids knew how much he missed them.

"So don't sneak back there outside of work hours—you might catch me snoring."

"I'll ring the bell."

He smiled. My heart did a crazy flip and I cursed it. How could I go from so frustrated to feeling like this, while I was working for this man and pregnant with someone else's baby? Meanwhile he was hung up on his ex-wife and kept a shrine to her in his office, or apartment, or whatever it was when you lived where you worked.

Just then, the curtains to our space parted, and a tall, thin woman with pale skin, freckles, and light auburn hair stepped in. She looked a little like Katie, only not as pretty. She read from the notebook in her hand. "Mr. and Mrs. Bernal?"

Jack stood up. "No, we're not married. I'm Mr. Holden and she's Ms. Bernal."

The doctor looked up. "Okay, no judgment here. I'm Dr. Marshall."

I jumped in. "He's not the father."

My mother's voice shredded the uncomfortable silence following my words. "Oh, my baby, I'm here."

Jack put his hand on my mother's shoulder and said, "Agatha, I'm leaving her in your good hands. And Dr. Marshall's, of course."

I shot a frantic glance at him. He started backing up and nodded at me. "Emily."

My mother grabbed my hand and wrung it in hers.

"I'm sorry to have to tell you this, but you've lost the baby."

Dr. Marshall's cool voice an hour later made the words sound innocuous. But they weren't. I'd expected them, but still they gouged a black, empty hole inside me. She turned to include my mother.

"I'm not sure if you know the stats, but one in five pregnancies end in miscarriage, so this is fairly common."

"Oh my God," I said. "I had cramps for a few days. I spotted. I should have come in sooner."

I felt sick with guilt, certain that my baby would have lived if I'd come in the first time I'd spotted, if I hadn't been running around all over Amarillo trying to find Valentina, if I hadn't fallen through Maria's steps, if Rich hadn't cornered me, if I hadn't galloped Jarhead at top speed across the New Mexico highland desert last weekend. So many ifs. So many possibilities, all pointing back at me. I hadn't kept my baby safe. I hadn't protected the life entrusted to me.

I had let my child down.

Mother wailed. "Oh no. I did this. I did. I'm responsible." Her words sounded hollow to me. She couldn't be. I was.

The doctor shook her head. "Really, miscarriages around the eighth week aren't unusual, and—"

"But emotional distress . . . and upsetting her . . ."

"No, no. Our ultrasound shows bleeding from her right Fallopian tube. She had a tubal pregnancy. It was never viable."

Dr. Marshall's words rang in my ears: Never viable. Never viable. *Never* viable.

So I hadn't done this to myself, to the baby. Instead of making me feel better, it made me feel worse in an incredibly empty way. The prospect of this baby was never viable. Never *real*. I stared at the speckled white ceiling tiles over my bed. Square after square marched across the room in a military-style cadence, chanting, "Never real. Never real. Never real." Like being a man's beloved daughter. Or wife. Never real. Never real.

"Oh, my poor darling girl!" Mother pushed my hair back from my forehead.

Dr. Marshall touched my mother's arm. "She's doing great, Mom. Pregnant ladies are tougher than you'd think." She turned to me. "We need to get you into your regular obstetrician as soon as possible for follow-up. They'll decide whether you need surgery."

Surgery. Well, who cared? If the baby wasn't real, nothing was at risk, and surgery was just a bother, a nuisance. "I have an OB appointment tomorrow," I said.

My mother grabbed my hand in a grip as strong as a man's. "What kind of surgery?"

"In a low percentage of the cases after a tubal pregnancy hemorrhages, part or all of the Fallopian tube has to be removed. But it's a very low percentage."

The blood drained from my face. I know this because I could feel every drop.

"But I only have the one Fallopian tube," I said. "On the right. I had the other removed years ago. Tumors. Noncancerous. But they were bad, and, well, I can't lose the right tube or I can't ever have children."

My mother pulled my hand to her chest.

"We saw that on the ultrasound, and it's something to discuss with your obstetrician, of course. But, again, removal isn't required very often, and even then it's usually only partial. You can still get pregnant with only part of one tube."

My free hand pressed into my mouth, holding in my heart.

"I'm surprised your doctor didn't see this earlier, actually. While it wasn't viable, a tubal pregnancy can be ended before it causes damage to you."

One time, when I'd been coming to get Jib from the pasture, she'd startled and ran into me headfirst. The crack of our skulls had knocked me out, and I still remembered the impact. I felt that skull crashing again now from Dr. Marshall's words against my brain.

"I just moved here. I was between doctors."

"Ah, I understand. That's too bad. But your chances of losing that tube are so slim. You have to try not to worry about it. Now, I'm going to release you because we were able to stop the bleeding. But I'd like you to stay off your feet until you get to the doctor. Come right back here if you start bleeding again before then."

Dr. Marshall rattled off some more instructions, and I saw Mother nodding, but I just stared at the doctor's bouncing lips.

Oh God, I thought. *Please forgive me for being a careless, selfish, vain woman.*

Numbness spread over me, everywhere but my chest where a heavy weight crushed down on my heart. My baby had never been real. And now I might never get another chance to have one.

EIGHTEEN

Two Tylenol PMs and a few large glasses of Mother's boxed white zinfandel had silenced the voices in my head last night, but I'd awoken three times, screaming. Each time, it was Valentina's face I saw. Once, the girl was calling my name. She was dressed in an odd skirt with white markings on her face and a funny hat that stuck up around her head like the rays from the sun—the way a child would draw them. Once, she was bloody and lifeless. The last time, around six a.m., she lay in a coffin.

I knew further sleep was futile. The scent of coffee already filled the house, so I rose.

I padded on bare feet to the kitchen. "Mother?"

She looked like a ghost in her long white gown, standing at the sink. She turned to me. "You should be in bed."

"I couldn't sleep." I poured myself coffee into an extra-large, blue ceramic mug and added some powdered hazelnut creamer. Stirring, I said, "Nightmares. No cramping or bleeding, though. I think the worst has passed."

She turned back to the sink, and I saw that she was staring out the window into the predawn darkness. Her coffee cup sat full beside her on the counter.

"I'm sorry, you know," she said.

"About what?" I asked.

"Being rough on you. Pushing you about Rich."

I absorbed her apology. My response didn't come easily to my lips.

"Thank you," I said, finally. "And I'm sorry I didn't tell you sooner. I'm sorry that you won't be having a grandbaby yet."

At my words, her shoulders heaved. I went to her, put my hand on her shoulder as she sobbed, "I've been so lonely for so long."

I pulled her into a hug and rubbed between her shoulder blades, hushing her. "Shhh. It's going to be okay."

"After you, I had miscarriages, you know. Tubal pregnancies."

My stomach twisted, hurting for us both. "I didn't know."

"Finally, I just gave up. And your father . . ." She took a few deep breaths and pulled back until she held my eyes with her own, wounded. "I don't want to drive you away, too, Emily."

I stood frozen in her gaze, immobilized in the minefield of our shattered memories, losses, and fears. When I spoke, I tiptoed through them, half-expecting an explosion with every syllable. "You are my mother, and I am your daughter. That's forever."

She tightened her hold on me, her hug fierce and desperate, and I hugged her back just as hard. Behind me, the kitchen clock tick-tocked its witness to my promise. Then she released me.

She didn't bother to wipe her tears, just grabbed her coffee and asked, "Toast?"

"That would be perfect."

We ate together in silence, taking turns with the sections of the newspaper. My hands shook as I held the sports section, and I laid it on the table to read.

After breakfast I showered and retreated to my room. I closed the door and leaned back against it, exhaling slowly. Long minutes passed while I just breathed. When my shaking stopped, I stood and tried to figure out what to do with myself. Not long term, just for the next few hours. All I had to do was figure out right now, nothing else.

My coffee with Nadine was at nine thirty and my doctor's appointment wasn't until eleven, so I had an hour and a half to fill; I didn't want to spend it thinking about a legacy of never-to-be-real babies. I booted up the desktop computer Mother kept in there on a little table. I checked my personal email. I had responses from both of the jobs I'd inquired about yesterday. I drummed three fingers on my desk and decided that I didn't want to pursue them. Not now anyway. But I didn't want to close any doors either, just in case. I moved them to my "saved" folder.

I texted Jack: *I'll be out today.*

I figured he could guess why. I started to type more, but I couldn't decide what to say, so I stopped and hit send.

Then I wrote a quick email to Rich, whom I prayed had flown home last night: *Went straight to ER after your visit. Lost baby. I'm sorry. Appreciate no further correspondence.*

I hit send, and then a new email appeared in my inbox. I didn't recognize the address: AmarilloMama@gmail.com. I opened it.

Sofia mentioned a man she called Antonio.

That was it, and there was no name at the bottom.

Antonio. The same first name as the man who had rented the apartment Sofia and Valentina lived in, per Wallace. Could this Antonio be the same person? It seemed highly unlikely he wouldn't be. I hit reply.

Thank you for contacting me. Who are you? Can we talk?

I clicked on send.

I sat stock-still, hand on the mouse, thinking. Who could have sent the email? It had to be someone who was involved with Sofia or Valentina and knew that I was, too. Maria Delgado. Michael Q. Scott. Victoria. The employees I'd interviewed at the hotel. For that matter, Wallace, Melinda, Jack, or someone from the jail. Any of them could have sent it.

Who would have my personal email, though? Or who could have found it? But then I remembered something. I pulled up Google and typed in my own name. Several entries came up. My LinkedIn profile. My Facebook profile. And my old blog, *Just Emily*. I hadn't posted on it in over a year. I clicked through to the "About" page. I read my bio:

Wife, daughter, legal professional, and rodeo enthusiast. I'm many things to many people, but underneath it all, I'm really just me, just Emily.

Wow, that needed an update. Beneath the bio, my email address. The one I'd just heard from AmarilloMama on. So it could be anyone. Truly, anyone.

My insides churned. For twelve hours, I'd thought of nothing but myself, and nothing of Valentina, while she was out there somewhere, captive, or, God forbid, victim. If nothing else in my life had been real, I knew this little girl and her plight were. My heart pounded a call to action. Someone had contacted me, because they believed I was the right person for this information. That I was the one Valentina could count on. Not the police. Not CPS. Me.

If I'd wanted to find Valentina before, now I was consumed by the need —like a terrible thirst. Well, I wasn't at work today. Jack couldn't tell me no. I pulled a piece of paper out of the printer and started making two lists: 1) Facts and 2) Questions. The list of my questions was twice as long as the facts.

It was past time to get serious about finding this girl.

I was hard at work when Nadine spotted me, making up for lost time on volume consumption of caffeine. The round Roaster's logo haloed her head as she walked up to my table, and she neatly blocked out its picture of a bright red mug. It made her look a little angelic, except for her facial piercings and dark arm tattoos. Well, those, the Harley outside, the pack of Pall Malls in her shirt pocket and her biker boots and chains. But, still, more angelic than it probably sounds. She was right on time, and I was early. I'd camped out in Roaster's Coffee two hours ago, sitting with my back facing the window and my front toward the counter service and its blonde wood veneers, and a great view from my seat of the trophy prong-horn antelope mounted on the wall.

"Emily?"

"Hi, Nadine."

"Hey," she said. "I'm just going to grab a coffee and be right back."

"Sounds good."

She joined the long line at the counter. I looked for a stopping place on my research and made a few quick notes. I'd spent the last two hours trying to find Antonio Rosa and Harvey Dulles. So far, I didn't have much to show for my effort, especially with Antonio. Sure, I'd found some people with the name, but no mention of any in Amarillo in the last ten years—except from the mouth of Michael Q. Scott and the email of Amaril-loMama. There was no reason the Antonio I was looking for couldn't be from elsewhere, though. I found one in Lubbock: deceased. One in prison in Oklahoma: not promising. One in Houston: long shot. One in Billings, Montana: also deceased. I tried looking for an Antonio in conjunction with the names Sofia and Valentina, and that didn't add a single thing to my results. I even tried him with ESL and ΣSL. Zero, zip, nada.

I did a little better with Harvey. All I had to do was call the probation department for Potter County and ask to be connected with his probation officer. Two transfers later, I verified Harvey's address and employment. Only I knew he wasn't living at the address the crotchety old male voice had barked at me, which I wasn't able to share with him because he hung up on me so fast. But I hadn't known Harvey worked road maintenance for the Texas Department of Transportation, so the call had been worth it.

So I phoned TxDOT and learned that Mr. Dulles no longer worked there, a fact over which I expressed deep dismay, because poor Mr. Dulles's father had died and I couldn't find him to let him know. The very young-sounding woman with the high-pitched voice on the other end of the line told me that I should try the Polo Club, because that's where his supervisor had found him when he hadn't shown up for work.

"Leering at strippers," she added. "And drinking al-co-hol."

I had years of practice adapting to this line of conversation, in my own home, no less. "Oh no. It seems Mr. Dulles has strayed from the path."

She dropped her voice. "I don't mean to sound un-Christian, ma'am, but I'm not sure he was ever on it."

We ended our call, and I pulled the Polo Club up online.

The interesting thing (to me) about this fine entertainment and libation establishment—besides that a strip club called themselves a Polo Club—was that they were mere blocks from my old high school, in a nice area of town, right next to the city Girl Scouts of America offices. Anyway, they didn't open until four-thirty, but I would definitely be checking them out later.

A text came in from Jack, and it made me happy to see his name on my phone: *Take care. Let me know how you are.*

I wondered if it was a good idea that I was developing a crush on my impossible boss who was still hung up on his ex-wife. Probably not. And probably a rebound crush anyway. I needed to get over my divorce before I started thinking about other men. And then I needed to focus on some-thing—someone—real.

I thumb-typed quickly: *Headed to doctor now. I'll let you know if I need to be out after today. Thanks for rescuing me yesterday.*

Nadine set a foamy mug down on the table, the clack of the cup pulling me out of my work. She bounced into the seat at my three o'clock, bobbing and wriggling a few times to get comfortable. The small chairs weren't quite enough for her ample curves, and her thighs and bottom spilled over the sides.

I slid my papers aside. "I am so glad you could come. I've kind of had a poopy last day or two, and this is a high spot."

She peered across the table at me, a serious look on her face. "Whoa, if coffee with me is the high spot, then we need to get you laid or something, fast."

If I'd had coffee in my mouth, she'd've been wearing it. "I think I need to hold off on that until we get my female medical issues straightened out."

"Girly problems? Yuck." She pulled the cigarettes out of her pocket and started rotating the packet in her fingers.

"Miscarriage. Headed to the doctor after this."

"Mary, mother of Jesus!" she said. "I'm so sorry. And, of course, ignore me on the getting laid part. Nadine opens mouth and inserts her big, fat freakin' foot."

"Nah, you're fine," I said.

She put the cigarette pack on the table. "I had a miscarriage before I had my first son." She inhaled, nodded, exhaled, like she was toking weed or something, which I had never done, but had witnessed Rich do repeat-edly enough back at Tech. Maybe I had tried it, courtesy of secondhand smoke. "It happens. It's awful. But I'm sure you'll be pregnant again in no time."

I hoped not soon, but someday. I changed the subject. "So, you worked at My Thai last night?"

"No, My Thai is my part-time day job. I take some late shifts as a bartender now and then."

"I'll bet there's more money in bartending."

"Especially where I work. I have to put up with a high douche-baggery-to-IQ ratio, but other than that it's fine."

Again she would have made me spew out my drink in shock. "Sounds interesting. Which bar?"

She grinned. "It is. The Polo Club. And no, I don't dance. I just push the booze."

My mouth dropped.

She saw my expression and said, "I know, I know. Objectification of women. Exploitation via the sex industry. Even working there perpetuates it. I've heard it before. But I prefer to think of it as a smart woman taking advantage of the weakness of men."

I grinned. "No, I was thinking I had planned to go to there this afternoon, to track down a witness in a case."

"Are you a cop?"

"Legal assistant. My boss is a criminal defense attorney."

"You should give me a stack of his business cards. I could keep him busy from here to eternity."

Business cards—something I should probably get ahold of. If I was going to stick with this job, I needed cards of my own, too.

"I'll bring you some," I said. Then I reached into my bag and shuffled through papers for the picture of Harvey Dulles. I held it up and asked, "Does he look familiar?"

"Harvey? He lives there. Literally, for the last few weeks, he's there every time I am. Sits at the bar and drinks Crown and Coke, slow and easy. Drinks and stares."

I half-jumped to my feet in excitement. My abdomen chided me, and I sat back down very gently. "That's who I'm looking for!"

She smiled, and it pulled one corner of her mouth up, like Jack, but without the dimple, and plus one nose ring. "Fun. Can I be of any help?"

I grabbed Spike's picture and slapped it in front of her. "Have you ever seen him with this guy?"

A man's voice spoke before Nadine could answer. "Emily?"

Inwardly, I shouted, *Can't you see we're having a conversation here?* Outwardly, I hit the tape mark on the stage, tilted my head, and flashed my pearly whites. Which reminded me that I really needed to pick up a pack of whitening strips at the store. Coffee, tea, and soda were not a friend to sparkly teeth. I greeted my mother's boss.

"Pastor Robb. How are you?"

"Good, although worried about you. Your mother sent around a prayer request for you again last night." He pulled at the collar of his sweater. His face was so florid I wanted to fan him with Spike's picture.

"She must get a volume discount. Pastor Robb, this is my friend Nadine. Nadine, Pastor Robb."

Nadine beamed. "Oh, we've met. Great seeing you, Eugene."

His tomato-red face drained of all color in an instant. "Nadine, you said? Um, hello, yes, well—" he pulled up his sleeve and looked at his watch, "—so sorry, church business, and I'm running late." He scrambled like a dog on a tile floor toward the exit.

Nadine turned to me. "Eugene is a big fan of dancing." She winked. "Now, where were we?"

I laughed and slid the picture of Spike an inch closer to her. "I love your job. Have you seen Harvey with this guy?"

She tapped the picture four times with her middle finger. "That's the guy that got blasted off the balcony at the Ambassador, or whatever they're calling it now. He came in with Harvey the day before it happened. Freaked me out when I saw him on the news."

"Has Harvey talked about it?"

"No, but I asked him. And he said he didn't know the guy. I wasn't sure why he lied, but most of the slimeballs in the Polo Club do."

"Did you hear Harvey and this guy, or Harvey and anyone, talking about a woman named Sofia, or hear of a little girl named Valentina?"

I handed her a printout of Victoria's picture of Sofia and Valentina.

"I've seen the woman," Nadine said. "But only on the news. She's the one that popped Spike, right?"

"Right," I said.

"No one mentioned their names around me." She handed the photo back.

"Okay, how about someone named Maria?"

"There's a dancer named Maria. Harvey talks to her sometimes."

My Maria was definitely not a Polo Club dancer. "What about a tall white guy, shaved head, a tattoo like this?" I fished Victoria's drawing from the papers and placed it over Spike's picture. "On his arm, maybe the upper arm, or the inside of his arm."

She moved closer to the table, which started her bobbing and wriggling again. "You mean other than Harvey?"

I couldn't believe my ears. "Really? Harvey has this tattoo? Are you sure?"

"Not a hundred percent, because he's been wearing long sleeves now that it's getting colder. But he came in a few times this summer, and I saw a tattoo like this. I'm ninety-five percent sure, and I know I haven't seen anyone else with it. As for tall white guys with shaved heads, I see a lot of them, in addition to Harvey."

My pulse accelerated and I wanted to get up and break into the Cotton-Eyed Joe, my equivalent of a touchdown dance. My instincts had been right all along. Harvey was involved. And now I had an inside source.

Hold on, Valentina, hold on.

"How about you text me whenever he comes in, and I'll come check him out myself?" Maybe I could find out where he lived. And who was keeping him in Crown and Coke.

"Yeah, sure. I'm working again tonight. He's always there."

"Awesome. Either I'll come in, or my friend will. He's a CPS investigator, Wallace—"

"Oh, I know Wallace. I volunteer for the Rainbow Room. He's my favorite investigator."

I should have expected she'd know him, in a town where everyone knew everybody. "Yeah, he's great. And you—two jobs, kids, *and* a volunteer gig? You're like Wonder Woman."

"You know it." She flexed an arm, then leaned toward me. "Seriously, the Rainbow Room helped me, once upon a time. I owe 'em."

I stood up. "I'm going to refill my coffee. Need anything?"

"I'm good."

I filled my cup, dumped in a packet of yellow stuff and a splash of Half & Half, and returned to the table.

After I sat down, Nadine spoke in a soft voice. "Um, Emily, I think you're bleeding."

"Oh my, where?"

"It's on your pants. And a little on your chair. I saw it when you walked over to the coffee. It's not like really bad or anything. But, with the miscarriage and all, I figure it's not your monthly visitor."

No, please God, no. I didn't need more of this stuff now, not when the trail to Valentina was getting hot. I stood up and craned my neck to see the back of my pants, but all I saw was stars as I slumped back into my chair.

NINETEEN

Nadine's discovery put an abrupt end to our coffee. She insisted on helping me to the bathroom, even though I was sure I'd only gotten light-headed because I stood up too fast. I assessed my bleeding problem from the stall and found that I'd forgotten to put a maxi pad on before I left home. Not smart. Definitely, I was bleeding, but I was also only an hour away from seeing my doctor, and I wasn't bleeding *profusely*. Not enough to run to the emergency room. I'd just go to the doctor's office a little early and maybe they could work me in.

We exited Roaster's into a twenty-five mile per hour grit-filled wind—double the speed I'd found unpleasant earlier. Nadine mother-henned me all the way to my car. I opened the door to the Mustang and the wind caught it, pushing it to its furthest point. I got in and had to use both arms to pull it closed again, even with Nadine pushing from the outside. The sky had turned to the color of dust, and trash tumbled across the parking lot—not just the paper and bags of a normal windy day, but cardboard boxes and glass bottles. I waved goodbye to Nadine and headed quickly toward my obstetrician's office, careful to dodge the projectiles that whirled past one of Stanley Marsh's signs (Road Does Not End) across the street in front of me. It seemed all the Marsh signs I saw followed a similar, creepy theme. Gusts pushed my car in and out of my lane.

While driving, I realized that it wasn't too terribly out of the way to drive past Maria's again. I tried to assume the best of people and, right now, that theory told me that there was always a chance Maria had soft-ened. That if I could just look her in the eye as I held up a picture of

Harvey and ran the name Antonio Rosa past her, I'd at least see a flicker that would tell me whether she knew something—anything at all. Heck, I could show her Valentina's drawing. Yeah, it was a long shot, but something about it seemed right. Plus, I didn't feel bad and I wasn't really bleeding very much and it was way too early to show up at my doctor.

Thinking of Valentina's drawing reminded me of something I'd dreamed. I tried to pull it back into my consciousness, but all I could remember was that I'd seen Valentina over and over, not where or when or what she was doing and with whom. But there was a similarity between my dream and her drawing, just out of sight, just out of reach, like the fireflies that I would try to catch each summer when they'd light up, only to grasp at nothing as they darkened and buzzed away.

I didn't bother hiding my Mustang down the street this time. I parked in front of Maria's house and opened the door only to have it ripped from my hands by the wind. It had gotten even stronger in the last ten minutes. The sky around me was in full-blown brownout. I strode to the door, leaning so far against the wind that if it had died suddenly, I would have fallen face-first to the ground. I used one hand for my purse and the other to hold my hair out of my mucous membranes. That left none to cover my mouth and protect it from grit, so I breathed through my nose with my head tucked down, trying not to suck too much dirt down my windpipe, and feeling really glad I hadn't worn a full skirt or flimsy blouse. When I got close to the house, its bulk somewhat blocked the gale. I straightened up and pulled errant hairs away from my eyes and mouth. Nothing like a windstorm to strip a woman of her dignity and professionalism.

I walked the outside edge of the steps where I knew the treads had maximum structural support, giving the unrepaired hole I'd left the day before a wide berth. I rapped smartly on the door, and it fell away under my knuckles.

I tightened my grip on my handbag. An unlocked door didn't seem very Maria-like.

"Maria? Are you home?"

No answer.

"Is anyone here?" I called.

I hesitated. If the door was open, I was invited in, which seemed to be a trend for me lately. I glanced at my watch. I had fifteen minutes before I needed to leave for my doctor's appointment. Plenty of time to run through and scan for information. Or to find and question the little boy and possibly other people that didn't like to answer Maria's door. I just wouldn't touch anything, I'd be silent as Sacajawea, and I'd hurry.

I stepped into the first room, remembering my father's lessons from long ago. I imagined leaves and twigs and rocks under my feet, and I placed each foot down light as air, and did it again. And again. And again. If I was less than silent, the sound of the wind muffled my indiscretions. I tiptoed around the living room. It was a dump, with ratty, dirty furniture that smelled as bad as it looked. The walls were bare except for stains and pockmarks.

My silent feet moved on to the kitchen. White linoleum, white counters, white cabinets, white sink, white refrigerator, white microwave, black oven, and a silver range top crowded the box-like space. Dirty dishes teetered in the sink, far too many for one woman, or even a woman with a family. These were dishes for a party of ten. The trash bulged up on its lid as well.

I stepped out of the kitchen. The little house couldn't have many more rooms. Two bedrooms and a bathroom, I'd guess. Suddenly a loud thrumming interrupted the silence, and I reached in my handbag, groping for my Glock. Frantically I searched the small purse then remembered. I'd left it in the glove compartment of Wallace's car, and wherever it was now, it didn't do me a lick of good. I listened more carefully to the thumping thrum, and then almost laughed aloud. The sound wasn't coming from the house. I was frightened of my heartbeat and a ringing in my own ears.

I moved quietly to the back of the house and stepped into the left bedroom. Sleeping bags were rolled and stashed against the walls. One, two, three, four, *five* of them in a rainbow of colors. A double bed sat in the middle of the room, but it was stripped bare, its sheets nowhere to be seen. The only other furniture was a desktop and a funny little machine in the back corner, like a printer, sort of, but smaller. I walked closer to it. It said Zebra ZXP Series 3 on top. Some ID cards lay by the desktop—Hispanic faces and names—and I compared the output hole in the Zebra thingy to the cards. They matched.

I scanned the room again. The closet accordion door was closed. I opened it. It was crammed full of clothes arranged by men's, women's, and children's wear in descending sizes. Holy crap, was Maria helping out the entire undocumented community? Food, bedrolls, clothes, IDs? Excited now, I resumed my search, but the dense silence was shattered with a terrifying ringing noise. Not my ears this time. Spit. My phone. I fumbled in my handbag. My display read Wallace. I pressed accept.

"Wallace," I whispered, "Meet me at Maria's ASAP. She left her house open, and I've found—"

Something incredibly, unpleasantly hard cracked into the back of my head. I felt myself crumpling, my phone tumbling, and my cheek landing on the carpet as the lights went out.

I returned to the conscious world with another loud ringing in my ears and two blurry faces peering down at me in front of a white background that hurt my eyes. "Where am I? What happened?"

The two faces turned to my left. A third face appeared, this one above a police-blue uniform. It said, "Emily Bernal?" It sounded like a he.

"Yes?" Each word, his and mine, was an anvil strike on the wedge that was cracking open my skull.

"I'm Officer Wilson. Do you know a Maria Delgado?"

A light brown mustache floated above his upper lip, bobbing up and down like a prairie dog from its hole. My eyes locked onto it.

I spoke carefully, trying not to hammer the wedge. "Sort of."

Talking hurt so much. I lowered my voice, and he leaned the mustache further toward me. It smelled like garlic and onions.

"This is her house," I said. "I, um, I was meeting her here." I hoped he could see how painful this was for me and would stop.

But the mustache kept bobbing. "Did you see her?"

"No." Ouch.

"How'd you get inside?" The mustache did a hippety-hop. It almost made me giggle, but even the thought of giggling hurt.

"Door was open. I called her name and came in. And, sir, my head really hurts."

"Sorry." The mustache didn't stop, though. "What happened next?"

"My phone rang. Something hit my head." I gestured at him and behind him at the other faces. "Then, this." My voice faded on the last word.

His eyes narrowed into slits that further emphasized the furry creature on his upper lip. Maybe not a prairie dog. A mole? No. Possibly a rat? Yes, I'd seen plenty of rats in the barn behind our house, and they jumped around like this thing did.

"Did you ever see Ms. Delgado?"

"No."

I winced. I reached up to touch my head but missed and got nothing but air. I put my hand back on my leg.

The rat loomed over my face, blocking out the glare behind his head. "Did you see anyone else?"

"No." I closed my eyes. No more rat.

"So Ms. Delgado was alive last time you saw her?"

"Yeah, yesterday. What, she isn't now?"

"Ms. Delgado is dead."

My eyes flew back open. "What happened? Where is she?"

"Blunt force trauma to the head, like you, but apparently you got lucky. She's across the hall." He wrote something on a notepad he had in his left hand. "I'll let the paramedics get back to you." And he and the rat disappeared.

I felt a little irritated. I was a victim, but he had pumped me for information as if I were a suspect. But then my bleary brain got smarter. I *was* a suspect. I'd never been one before. How weird, in a not-good way.

The two faces I'd first seen moved back into the tunnel of my vision, a white man with longish brown hair and a black woman with short dark hair. Behind them, a third face appeared. Things darkened and took shape. A popcorn-textured ceiling with water stains. The open closet full of clothes. The edge of a mattress. Floppy sand-colored hair streaked with highlights.

"Wallace . . ." I reached a hand toward him.

He couldn't get past the paramedics, and I let my hand drop.

"Way to scare me to death, Emily," he said. "I nearly had a heart attack trying to get here, worried about you, only to find Maria dead and you *looking* dead."

"You called the ambulance?"

"911 the second I saw you."

I tried to smile. "Thank you."

The woman spoke. "Excuse me, ma'am, we need to ask you some questions, and then we can let you speak to your friend." Her voice flowed like warm honey. Alabama? Mississippi?

Wallace shot me a thumbs up.

The woman resumed. "You appear to have been struck in the head with a heavy blunt object. You lost consciousness, and you have a concussion, which is why your head hurts. You probably feel a little foggy and nauseous, too?"

"Yes."

"You'll feel like that for a while. Anyway, we just got here right before you woke up, and, because your vitals were steady, we let the officer go first, before we could do a complete exam on you. There's a fair amount of blood around your torso." She put her palms on my abdomen and probed gently in a search pattern. "Do you recall why?"

I looked at her blankly.

"Do you remember being shot, or stabbed, or sexually assaulted?"

Oh God. My girly parts. "I was about to go to my doctor's. I had a tubal pregnancy and hemorrhaged and lost the baby yesterday. I'd just started bleeding again, right when I got here, before I got knocked out." To my dismay, I started to cry, which made my head hurt worse. "And they said if this happened they might have to remove my tube and I can't lose this tube or I can never have a baby because this is the only tube I've got."

Wallace crouched beside me, and a shocked expression flitted across his face. He grabbed my hand. "I didn't know you'd lost the baby. Why didn't I know? You poor thing." He turned to glare at the woman. "She needs to be in the ER, not laying here with her reproductive organs spilling out. Or do you want to be responsible for the babies this gorgeous creature will never have?" He jumped to his feet, clapping. "Come on, people!"

And unbelievably, the paramedics snapped to attention. Wallace hovered nearby. I beckoned him closer. He put his ear near my mouth, and I spoke in a rush.

"Harvey Dulles has the tattoo Victoria described and my friend Nadine says he's at the Polo Club daily. I got an anonymous email telling me Sofia talked about a man named Antonio. I couldn't find anything on him, but that must be critical. And, of course, I'm sure you noticed Maria is running some kind of underground house here and—"

"Shh. I've got it, and I'll fill in the police. You've done good. Worry about you for a change." He kissed my cheek. "I'll be right behind the ambulance."

A swell of emotion surged up through my chest and lodged in my throat. "Don't tell anyone else about me though, okay?"

He saluted me crisply.

Five minutes later, I was in the ambulance, speeding toward the ER with the sound of a siren battering my skull.

TWENTY

I awoke to a familiar, white-tiled ceiling and pink curtains around my bed. Even as my eyes opened and took in the room, vivid images remained in my mind, and their resonance shot white-hot panic through me. A slim, short Native American in a clunky headdress and tall buckskin moccasins stood pointing after a bald man running with Valentina under his tattooed arm. Tall evergreen trees loomed behind them.

"Go after her," the Indian said, the words a little cloud of fog in the air.

I stopped to look at the Indian again. I couldn't help it. It was just so odd. The Indian's body was painted white and he wore a mask that looked like it was made of real animal hide, down to the animal ears protruding in front of the headdress.

"Go," the Indian shouted, and this time I ran, but it was too late. A bull thundered between us and barreled straight at me.

"Valentina!" My voice came out hoarse and thin. I tried to sit up.

A hand pushed my shoulder down. "Emily, you're in the recovery room, at the hospital. It's okay." I knew the voice, but its words made things worse.

"Wallace, the Indian tried to send me after Valentina, but now I can't see her. Where is she? Where did she go?"

"You're dreaming. You need to be still so you don't hurt yourself."

I rolled my head to face him, pleading. "But it was real. She was here. She was . . ."

My voice trailed off as I tried to explain to Wallace where I'd seen her, but the images had slipped away. I didn't know where she was anymore. Valentina was gone. I dropped my head to the pillow.

He lifted my hand and squeezed it, then held on. "It was a nightmare," he said. "It's okay. You've just woken up in the hospital from surgery."

I didn't want to be in a hospital. I didn't want surgery. I nodded and tried not to cry. It had been so real. I wanted it to be real.

A very short man with coarse salt and pepper hair on either side of a smooth cranium and face appeared behind Wallace. He looked Indian, as in from-the-country-of, and he had just the slightest hint of curry on him, like he'd lunched at My Thai. It cleared some of my haze.

"Ms. Bernal, you're awake," he said. "Good. I'm Dr. Patel, and I performed your surgery today."

His cheerful voice and distinctly Indian accent seemed surreal in Southwest Hospital in Amarillo. "Thank you."

"Well, I am pleased to report the operation was a complete success. Your hemorrhaging was getting much worse, quite dangerous to you, actually, and we were able to stop the bleeding."

"My tube?"

His head bobbled right to left to right almost imperceptibly. "Yes, well, unfortunately we had to take out most of the tube to secure your recovery. There's still a bit left, possibly enough that you might be able to become pregnant later, possibly not. I wish I could provide you with a more precise prognosis, but I can't. There is reason for optimism, however, and I urge you to embrace it."

Wallace squeezed my hand again. "This is good news, Emily," he said. "The most important thing is that you will be fine." He repeated himself, emphasizing the words: "The most important thing."

I nodded, and I thought I heard myself say "Thank you" to the perky-voiced doctor as I stared at his blue scrubs. But, inside, I saw myself standing with my back to the edge of a swimming pool in a hotel where I'd seen a dead man sinking. I felt my body fall backward and hit the water. It was so soft and warm slipping over my skin. I sank below the surface and realized I couldn't breathe, but I wasn't scared.

As I sank, I whispered, "My baby and Valentina, both lost. And now I can never have another one. Just like my mother. Everything, lost."

Dr. Patel's singsong voice pulled me up, up, and out of the water. "Ms. Bernal, I need to verify that you understand what I just told you?"

I wanted to slip back under, and it irritated me that he interrupted. I spoke in a short voice. "Yes, yes, I understand."

"You'll need to see your own obstetrician in two weeks. The name was in your file, so we alerted her office about your situation and told them to expect your call."

"Thank you."

"You should stay here perhaps another half hour, then our staff will check you out to whoever will be driving you home."

Wallace raised his hand. "That's me."

Heaven, I thought. *Home is Heaven. Do you hear that, God? I'm going to Heaven.*

"Very good. I'll be sending you with a prescription for pain medication, if you need it. Please rest for twenty-four hours. After that, you may resume your normal activities, but please refrain from strenuous ones, including sexual intercourse, for several days." He perched a pair of wire spectacles low on his nose and lifted an electronic tablet, his finger poised above it. "Do you have any other questions for me, Ms. Bernal?"

Water lapped against my chin again.

"No," I whispered, before I let myself sink to the bottom.

I sat in the front seat of Wallace's Altima and counted the Vicodin he'd picked up for me at the Target Pharmacy on Soncy Road. Six pills. I had enough to stay zonked for two days if I wanted to. Which I did. I looked at the clock on the dash: Five p.m.

Wallace buckled his seat belt. "It's too soon for one now."

"I know." My phone dinged, so I checked my texts.

Nadine: *Harvey is here. Thought you should know.*

Spit! And I was basically an invalid, unable to do anything about it. But not without a friend, one who was completely mobile.

"Wallace," I said, "remember how I told you that my friend Nadine said Harvey Dulles is a regular at the Polo Club?"

"Vaguely. There's been a lot going on."

I watched him watch me out of my peripheral vision. Had I only met this amazing human a few days ago? Here he sat with his best Salvage jeans covered in my blood, driving me to Heaven through a brownout, halfway to New Mexico. And with me about to ask him for another favor.

A knock on the window startled me. I turned and saw the person craning for a clear view into the car.

"Gah," I yelped. Out of the corner of my mouth, I gave Wallace the scoop. "ADA Melinda Stafford, who's been a burr under my blanket since we were kids." My voice dripped pique.

"Oh God, I hate that bitch," Wallace said.

"Well, put on your happy face, because I know from excruciating experience that she's not going anywhere." I pressed the button to lower the window. Nothing happened.

"Let me turn the key."

He did, and I tried again. The window slipped into the door.

Melinda wrapped her French manicured claws around the doorframe and leaned so far in she was almost in my lap. The wind and dirt followed her.

"Emily, I thought that was you," she said. "How are you?"

"Fine. How are you Melinda?"

"I'm fantastic. I heard about you on the news just now. You're famous."

"I guess." I conceded.

The Maria Delgado murder would be topping the hour tonight on the local stations. Jack had texted me that a camera crew and reporter had shown up at the offices. He hadn't asked any questions other than if I was all right, for which I was grateful. And thank God I'd missed the reporters. Wallace and I had heard some coverage on the radio when we'd driven from the hospital to Target. They'd pronounced my name wrong—then again, everyone around here said BUR-nal instead of Bare-NAHL.

"So, that's interesting that you're working with Jack Holden."

My headache was coming back. "Yep."

She flicked lint I couldn't see from the sleeve of her charcoal gray suit jacket. "Is he dating anyone? I've got this campaign fundraiser for my boss, black tie, and I need a date. I'll bet Jack looks yummy in a tux."

I heard a noise like a strangled cat from the driver's seat. Melinda did, too, and she finally seemed to notice Wallace.

"Oh. Hello, Wallace." She gestured back and forth between us. "I guess it makes sense that the two of you are friends."

He put his hand over mine and pinched it, hard. "Hello, Melinda. And why is that?"

"Well, you know, Emily's ex-husband, and, um, stuff."

I lightly smacked Wallace's hand and tried to block out her last words. Before I could think of a way to redirect her, she went on. "My goodness, Wallace, you are just covered in blood." Her eyes gleamed with excitement, and she turned an eye for crime scenes on the inside of his car. "And you are, too, Emily. "

She reached in and snatched my prescription bottle from my hand. I wrested it back from her, but not quick enough to keep her from grasping the essentials.

"Yes, Dr. Patel, the surgeon, I've used him as an expert witness. Are you okay, Emily? Vicodin, that's heavy stuff. What was it, were you injured at the scene where that woman was murdered? Or was it a car wreck?" She stood back and worked the car over with her eyes, looking for evidence.

I stuffed the pills in my handbag. "Female problems."

Melinda put her hands back on the door, arms straight, shoulders high, face leaning in. She studied me like a chemistry experiment gone awry.

"You didn't, Emily, surely you didn't—I mean, I can hardly bear to say it, but you didn't abort your baby, did you?"

My lips moved, but nothing came out. My hands flexed and closed into fists.

Wallace grabbed both of my wrists and leaned over me to yell at Melinda. "What in the world would make you think it's okay to ask that question? Emily had a miscarriage yesterday and emergency surgery today. She could have died, and you march up here like the Morality Police? Who do you think you are?"

Melinda didn't appear to realize she was getting her rear chewed, or at least she didn't care if she did. She put a hand over her chest.

"Oh, I am so glad to hear you didn't do that, Emily." She patted my shoulder. "A miscarriage, huh? It's for the best, I'm sure."

I jerked my wrists away from Wallace, and with a quick twist to my right, I made room to draw my arm back. Then, in one diving lunge, I punched Melinda in the jaw, landing halfway out the window, with my sore gut across the door. It hurt my hand, my head, and my abdomen, but it made the rest of me feel so much better. I pulled myself back in, wincing.

Melinda squealed like a stuck pig and covered the side of her face.

Wallace banged the steering wheel with both hands. "Holy shit, holy shit, holy shit."

Over her histrionics and Wallace's hysteria, I said, "It's my legal right to choose, but I wanted this baby, and I'm heartbroken to have lost it."

Melinda's words came out muffled by her hand. "I think you broke my jaw!"

"Impossible. I had a terrible angle."

She pointed at me. "I'm going to call the cops and have you charged for assault."

I gave her my mother's address. "Be sure you tell them how much Vicodin I'm on. I've only been in criminal law for a week, but from what I've learned, I'm pretty sure they'll find I lacked the capacity to know right from wrong at the time my fist met your face." I rolled up the window.

Wallace put the car in gear. "Holy shit," he said again. "You just punched an ADA in the face."

I smiled weakly. "I've wanted to do that since fourth grade."

Dr. Patel hadn't said a word about abstaining from alcohol, so I'd raided Mother's box of white zinfandel again that night. Really, I hated the stuff and could barely get the first glass down without gagging, but the second was easier. I heard the door open, close, and lock when Mother got home. Wednesday nights are big church nights, but she was home early.

"Emily?" She whispered from outside my door. "Pastor Robb said he ran into you today, with the wrong kind of person. And then I heard about you on the news." She increased her volume. "Emily? Are you okay, honey?"

Pastor Robb was one to talk. My light was out, so I stayed very still and didn't answer. I didn't have to tell her my news. If I did, she'd have it in the inbox of every member of Believers Church in seconds. I'd be mostly normal by tomorrow, anyway, so it wasn't something she needed to worry about. Or worry *me* over.

I made my voice sound half asleep, which wasn't hard. "Fine. Sleeping. Love you. Talk to you tomorrow."

Silence. She stood outside my door for a long time, then said. "Well, goodnight, then. I love you, too."

I listened to her footsteps down the hall. I waited through the sounds of water in her bathroom and the click of her bedroom door closing. Then I tiptoed to the kitchen for a wine refill. When I was safely back in bed, I turned on the lamp and got out my phone.

A text message had come in while I was in the kitchen.

Wallace: *I can't believe I skipped church tonight to come to The Polo Club.*

Wallace: *I bought a drink for Harvey, using my gaydar-blocking super powers. Got him to talk about Spike's death. Tried to bait him about Sofia. He didn't bite.*

Pfffffft. I typed fast: *Keep me posted. Hate feeling helpless.*

Wallace: *Helpless? WTF, when I'm on the case? Go to sleep.*

Fat chance I'd sleep, not with Western décor assaulting me from the outside and the ravages of my messed up life assaulting me from the inside. I took a slug of white zin. Another text came in, but it wasn't Wallace. I swiped over to my Messages homepage.

It was Jack: *Worried about you.*

It was crazy, because I'd swung up and down and through every emotion in my repertoire in the last day and a half, but this was the moment that made me sob like a child. My shoulders heaved, but I muffled my cries, scared of attracting Mother. Tears overflowed my eyes. Why did Jack have to go and turn out to be so damn kind? As many people as I had run into here that reminded me of the things I didn't like about this place, I'd met that many more that gave me hope, like Jack, Wallace, and Nadine. The problem with hope, though, is that it sometimes reminds you of the reality that keeps you from feeling hopeful in the first place.

So here was my reality: I couldn't have a baby. I tilted my wine glass up and drained the last drops from it.

Sure, the doctor had said I had a slim chance. What that really meant was that I had barely any chance at all, almost none, which always ended up meaning none. No hope of a father coming back. No hope of my husband wanting me. No hope of babies. Tears pooled below my nose. I was thirty years old, alone, broke, and barren, a cautionary tale to every rodeo queen who'd ever worn the sash.

I pulled out my phone and hit a number in my favorites.

"Emily?" Katie's voice was a happy squeal.

I cut her off fast before she could congratulate me and said, "Something bad has happened."

A pause. The sound of a small child's laughter. "Hang on," Katie said. "Let me ask my mother-in-law to put Taylor in bed, and I'll go where I can hear you better."

"Okay."

I heard jostling and muted voices for thirty seconds or so. Then she came back on. "I'm here. Tell me."

I started talking, fast, trying to beat the blubbery tears I knew would come. I almost made it. "I lost the baby today. Miscarriage. And I lost Rich, I lost the condo and our savings, and I've lost the baby, too. And now, and now . . ."

"Shhh. It's okay, I'm so sorry. Shhh now." Her beautiful soothing voice harmonized with my sobs until I got myself under control.

"I may not be able to have a baby now."

Katie knew my background, so I filled her in only on the new development.

"I lost most of my only fallopian tube."

I downed the rest of my wine in one swallow.

"I'm sorry, honey. Very sorry." She paused. "You sound a little slurry."

I barked a laugh. "Yeah, I've been nipping at Mother's stash of box wine."

"Do they have you on pain meds?"

"Some."

"Go easy on the booze. Take it from a semi-pro. It's not going to make it better."

Maybe not later, but it would now. "You know what else?"

"What?"

"I'm working for a criminal attorney, and his client's little girl disappeared, and it's like I'm the only one who really, really cares. How messed up do you think that is?"

"I think what's messed up right now is my sweet friend Emily. I think you need to stop thinking and go to sleep. Things will look better in the morning. You can start working on all this then."

"I'm not sweet," I said. "I haven't been sweet since Stormy came to dinner."

Shows how little she knew. Why had I called her again? What I needed was another glass of wine.

"I gotta go, Katie."

"I love you, Emily," she said. "Call me tomorrow—or any time."

"Love you."

I ended the call and snuck to the kitchen for another refill. I left the lights off, opened the refrigerator and pulled the box out. It felt almost empty. I shook it and the meager remains sloshed around. I knew that this was at least my third glass, but certainly no more than my fourth. And they were very small glasses. It sure wasn't my mother who'd drained the box. She drank thimblefuls every Friday night and then apologized for it. If she were Catholic she'd probably even confess it—though, to her, Catholicism was a sin in and of itself. My head spun. Religion was just too dang confusing for me.

I lifted the hem of the red flannel nightgown I'd borrowed from Mother and wiped the tears from my face, then lost my balance just a little bit. I caught myself against the doorway to the kitchen. I sipped my wine. I couldn't end up like my mother. I didn't want to be a bitter church secretary living alone in a house as far past its prime as me, judging and begrudging everyone else. I loved her. She was my mother. But that didn't make these things untrue. I weaved down the hall, trying to be Sacajawea again and running headfirst into the door to my room instead.

"Ouch," I whispered.

"Is that you, Emily?" Mother called.

I shook my head and put a finger over my lips. "Just using the bathroom. G'night."

"Goodnight."

I opened my door. Maybe this was my fourth glass after all. I crawled back in bed, leaned against the wall, and pulled the cowgirl-covered bedspread up to my chin. So, yeah, I couldn't have hope, and that included about Jack. Still, I couldn't *not* answer the man's nice text. He was worried about me. I stared at my phone on the bedside table until my eyes closed. Opened them and stared at it some more. Thought about Jack's half smile and dimple and twinkling eyes and great boots. I really did love his boots. And his jeans. Yes, I loved those Wranglers. My eyes closed again.

The phone rang, waking me. I had listed over and drooled on my pillow. I reached for the phone and turned it to face me. Wallace. Adrenaline coursed through my veins, and I sat up straight again. It could be about Valentina.

I answered. "Hello?"

"Hey, I'm driving Nadine home, so I decided to call instead of text and die."

"Good choice." Choice came out like "choyse." I touched my lips, but they felt okay.

"Your voice sounds funny. Did you take too many pain pills?"

I spoke carefully, enunciating brightly. "Nope. I only took one."

"Emily?"

"I've had a little . . . wine."'

He sighed. "Stop it. You're going to make yourself sick mixing booze and painkillers. And I need you to sober up so I can tell you about Harvey. I'm putting you on speaker, okay?"

I stretched my jaw and eyelids, trying for sober. "I'm good. Tell me."

"Hi, Emily." Nadine's voice.

"Hi," I said. "Thanks for your help."

"No problem. This is fun."

Wallace took over. "Okay, so here's the scoop. We followed Harvey home, and—"

"Noooo, Wallace, that's dangerous." As hard as I'd tried, dangerous came out "dangerush."

"Look who's talking—or trying to," he said.

I nodded to myself. True on both counts. "Whaddya find?"

"We know where he's shacking up—with one of the Polo Club dancers. Not one of the better-looking ones, if you ask me, but my opinion may not count for much."

Nadine said, "You have a keen eye for beauty, Wallace."

"Thank you, Nadine."

I made a gagging sound. "Not important. What about Valentina?"

"I couldn't exactly barge in after him, or knock on the door in the middle of the night. But I can tell the cops about him now, and we can check it out, later."

I tried to sound like I was in charge. "Tomorrow morning."

"You're on bed rest through tomorrow," Wallace said. "And you're about to have a wicked hangover."

"But the cops won't do spit."

He laughed. Nadine did, too. She asked, "Did you just say spit?"

"What?" I asked. "What's wrong with spit?"

They both laughed harder, and Wallace clucked. "Go to sleep, Emily."

I hadn't said anything funny, at least I didn't think I had. Plus, I needed to know something. "Wallace, wait."

"What?"

"Do you think any man will ever want to marry me now that I'm thirty and barren?"

He yelled in my ear. "What? A) You're gorgeous. Maybe even more gorgeous than I am, thanks to that perfectly precious gap between your teeth, although it's still a very close contest. B) You're not barren, and no one uses that word anymore. C) Stop choosing gay men and you'll find plenty who want to marry you. Shit, you've almost got *me* wanting to propose."

Did I choose gay men? I counted back. Rich. That was one. Now Wallace. That was two. Hardly a trend. Then I remembered. Gordon, my rodeo team mentor, had come out his sophomore year. Okay, that made three.

Nadine chimed in. "I'd marry you."

This confused me. "I thought you were straight, Nadine? You have kids."

"I'm just jumping on the bandwagon."

I held my hand up in the stop gesture, then dropped it because I realized they couldn't see. "But even if some straight man does want to marry me," I said, "if I do turn out to be barren, he'll leave me then. Or he might even leave me anyway, regardless."

Both of them yelled "No" at the same time. Then Wallace said, "No shit, Emily, stop drinking right now. Pour the wine out. You've poisoned your brain."

"I'm serious."

"I know you are, but you're also wrong."

"So I should text Jack back?"

Wallace sort of shouted at me and I pulled the phone away from my ear, staring at it in surprise. I could still hear him, though. "What? Where did that come from? Oh my God, woman, you make no sense. Yes, if Jack texted you, answer him, after you sober up. Right now, pour out the wine, and when you're done with that, go to bed. And don't get up until tomorrow night. You hear me?"

I put the phone back to my ear. "I hear you." I started to hang up. "Wait!"

Wallace sighed. "I'm pulling up in front of Nadine's place. Make it snappy. I want to get home and go to bed."

"You said you skipped church. What church do you go to?"

"Unitarian."

Nadine said, "Agnostic here."

"I'm not sure what I am." I stopped, thinking hard. I wasn't one hundred percent sure what agnostic was either and how it was different from atheist, but now probably wasn't the time to ask. I knew, though, that the three of us, we were like refugees from the Island of Misfit Toys. Thinking that made me smile. "Wallace, I need a church. Can I visit with you?"

"Yes, you can. Now, goodnight."

"Goodnight."

I pressed end and stared at Jack's text again, trying to think of what to say to him, this time holding my phone by my head on the pillow. I typed: *Had minor procedure, I'm fine. Thanks for checking on me. I've been thinking about you all day, and I was really happy to get your text.*

That sounded ridiculous and schoolgirl-ish. I changed it to: *Had minor procedure, I'm fine. Thanks for checking on me. See you Friday.*

It still sucked, I knew, but I couldn't send the first one, and I couldn't come up with anything better than the second. I sent it, then stared at the ceiling, thinking about Jack in his boots and babies and lost little girls until I fell asleep.

When I walked into work Friday morning, I had the wicked two-day Vicodin and box wine hangover Wallace had predicted. I also had a bad case of the blues over my single remaining Fallopian tube—a sliver so tiny it was about as useful as teats on a boar hog. I thrust the door to the Williams & Associates office open. Lost in my own thoughts, I nearly ran over the man kneeling to lay tile in the lobby/my office. It was beautiful tile—a large, beigey-rusty-streaky tile. The brand new carpet that had been removed to make room for the tile was now in a roll leaning against the wall. If the lobby had needed remodeling, this tile would've been a great choice. But it hadn't, unless something drastic had happened since I'd last seen it on Tuesday.

Snowflake danced back and forth between the tile guy and me. I reached into my handbag and tossed her some toast crusts. She gobbled them and returned her full attention to the tile guy.

"Good morning," I said.

"Mornin'," he replied.

He didn't stop his work. He was kneeling on the concrete subfloor in dirty white kneepads over baggy blue jeans. He had just finished smoothing and cutting lines into gray grout, wielding his hand trowel like a paintbrush. Now he placed one of the tiles on the grout, perfectly aligned with the one beside it. When he'd finished securing it, he wiped his forehead with the sleeve of his New Orleans Saints sweatshirt, knocking his LSU Tigers cap loose and revealing his shaved black head.

I walked around him to my desk and sat down. It was going to be hard to concentrate with a construction project going on in my personal space, not to mention with the shrill whir of the tile saw and the chalky smell of fresh cut tile. I rested my head in my arms for a moment, trying to pull myself together. I'd slept until five p.m. yesterday, and my days and nights were all mashed and mixed up. I breathed in and out slowly. All I had to do was manage to get through today. After that, I could take my last few

Vicodin and put my brain to sleep for the weekend, with my door shut, and the world at bay.

"You okay?" The tile guy had stopped working and was staring at me with eyes of deep black ink.

"Oh, yes, sorry. I just need some coffee."

He grunted and went back to work. I grasped the bell on my desk and rang it, then walked down the hall, stopping by the door to the kitchen.

"Jack?"

He appeared at his office door and said, "Good morning." He pulled out his half smile-dimpled-raised eyebrow magic.

It made my heart sing, but today it was a sad song. "Teardrops on My Guitar."

I avoided eye contact and said. "Thank you for the flowers."

I'd discovered the arrangement on the porch when Wallace and Nadine woke me the previous afternoon to let me know the police had found no sign of Valentina at Harvey's. Mother had come home while they were there. Her discombobulation over my obviously gay and biker chick friends was the brightest part of my last few days, other than punching Melinda Stafford.

"You're welcome."

I ducked into the kitchen and took a seat.

"How are you?" He sat down, but at a sideways angle. Our knees were inches apart.

"Fine." Physically, anyway, but I kept the rest to myself. "What's going on in the lobby?"

"New tile."

"No, I mean *why*? Was there a water leak or something?"

He jerked his head toward the door, speaking softly as he did. "That's Freeman, our client. He does tile. So he's doing ours."

I clenched my fists. Five minutes after I got to work and Jack already had my eyes crossed. I just wanted to know why we were getting new tile. It didn't seem like a complex question. Could the man ever answer me straight? I opened my mouth to snap at him, but snapped it shut instead. Jack and Clyde had talked earlier in the week about the new carpet. A client that couldn't pay his bill. Services in kind. Okay, it took me a while, but I got it. My eyes grew moist and my hands relaxed. Something about crying most of the last few days had loosened my on-off switch. I swallowed the tears back.

Jack filled the silence. "I read your Johnson report. I think we're good to go there."

I gave him a leaky smile. "Thanks. And it appears he can afford to pay in cash."

Jack leaned back in his chair, which scooched his knees forward. They bumped mine, and I jerked my legs away by reflex. Jack didn't appear to notice.

"I had a very entertaining call from ADA Stafford yesterday," he said. "She claims to have suffered physical injury and mental anguish at the hands of one Emily Phelps Bernal."

I slouched back down, which bumped our knees again. "I'm sorry. I can explain."

He put his hands behind his head, his elbows out to the side and tipped his chair back just so far that the front legs lifted from the ground. He'd rolled his sleeves up this morning, enough that I could see the smooth, tan underside of his forearms. I'd assumed Jack had a suntan on his face and neck, but instead it appeared to be his natural skin tone.

"I can only imagine," he said.

"Seriously, she's evil. When we were eight she sat behind me in class and cut my ponytail off one day. Short."

His chair came down with a thunk, and he brought his hands back to his knees. "I messaged over a check to cover her doctor's bills."

"I'll pay you back."

"No need. I'd have paid more than that just to have seen it."

A horrible thought occurred to me. "Are you going to the fundraiser with her?"

"She did ask."

"But are you going?"

After a long pause, he said, "Conflict of interest. And lack of."

I hadn't realized I'd held my breath until he answered and I started breathing again. He clasped his hands between his legs. Today he was wearing a pair of jeans so old the knees were white, with a flannel shirt. Flannel and faded jeans meant he didn't have court today.

"If you're up to it, I need you to help me on Freeman," Jack said. "We could be going to trial before Christmas, and I've got a long way to go with it."

I nodded. Maybe if I worked really, really hard on Freeman and Jack's other clients, he'd let me get started on a wrongful death survivor case, which would mean we would have to find Valentina.

"We'll leave for Tularosa after lunch."

My throat tightened. I'd forgotten about New Mexico this weekend. "I don't have my bag with me," I said.

And I'd planned to do my own reconnaissance at Harvey's stripper-girlfriend abode later that day. I'd lost twenty-four hours—more, really—on finding Valentina, and no one seemed to have made any progress in my absence.

"We can swing by Heaven on the way." He levered himself out of the chair and started walking out.

My emotions went to war, over Valentina, and wanting to stay here to look for her. My lost baby, and desire to hibernate. My job, and needing to keep it. Jack, and my attraction to him. New Mexico, and the possibility of a sleuthing side trip to Roswell.

"Jack, wait," I said. He stopped, and I continued. "I don't think I'm very good company right now. I might not be at my best for Johnson's housewarming. I'm . . . recovering."

At least the parts of me that could recover. The part of me that wanted to be a whole woman and a mother someday wasn't even near the path yet.

He puckered his lip up to the left, and I fell for it. With that one little expression my emotional resistance crumbled like dry sod. How could the left side of his face do such interesting things? He was right-handed, after all. I'd checked.

"Noted. Now, let's get to work," he said.

TWENTY-ONE

The next eight hours passed in a blur and ended with the wheels of Jack's plane thudding to earth at Wrong Turn Ranch. I still wasn't a fan of small planes, but last time I'd puked my guts out in the little Skyhawk, and this week I didn't use a single barf bag. It wasn't lost on me that Jack had replenished the stash in the seat pocket to overflowing. Amazing what the absence of a fetus could do for a woman's queasy tummy. Even more amazing what its absence did to her heart. The rest of me didn't feel that bad, and I hoped I could put away everything sucky about my life for a weekend. Some things I couldn't change anyway, and I needed to learn not to dwell on my new reality. Mountains, horses, and green chiles might be just what I needed to try to get my head right.

As we bounced down the runway, I checked my phone. Jack had practically hog-tied me to his side the entire morning as we put together a work list and game plan for Freeman and Escalante and the new Johnson case. We'd barely finished in time to grab lunch at Taco Villa on the way to Heaven. A bean burrito with sour cream usually cheered me up, but it didn't today. Besides my sadness about the lost baby (babies?), I hadn't managed to sneak away to Harvey's crash pad, and I knew I had to entrust it to Wallace. I loved Wallace, and Lord knew he meant well, but he was a rule follower, at least in his professional life. I'd texted Nadine on my way to the airport, asking her to go with him. She was someone who knew that there was more than one way to skin a cat, and she'd texted back a *Yes* five seconds later.

That was over four hours ago, and it was six o'clock in Texas. I'd hoped to hear how it went from them by now. But I had no messages.

I sent them a group text: *Update?*

Jack pulled the plane to a stop in front of his little barn-hangar, then spun the Skyhawk. He turned off the engine and the propeller slowed gradually, *thwum, thwum, thwum,* until it stopped. The silence screeched in my ears, but I was getting used to it after several flights.

Jack leaned around his seat. "You okay back there?"

I nodded and pulled the corners of my mouth up. My face felt like it would crack.

He opened his door and pushed his seat forward. Brisk air hit me in the face—cold air, really. I noticed the sky for the first time. Black clouds to the west veiled the falling sun. I shivered and hopped out. Then something strange happened. The temperature and the dry scent of sage and pine acted like shock paddles to my emotional system. I drew in a full breath and let it out. I looked around me, and it was like someone had adjusted the focus on my lens. Emily lives on, even if just barely.

Jack's eyes sparkled. "Brr. Let's gas her up quick, then get her inside before we unload."

"Good idea."

This time there was no Judith to meet us, but I knew the drill. He opened the roll-up door and I moved the Suburban outside. When I returned, he had fastened the tow bar to the nose wheel. We maneuvered the small plane to the gas tank.

"Why do you gas it up when we land?" I asked as the fuel pumped.

He pointed at the sky. "Sometimes the weather or other circumstances dictate a rapid departure in less favorable conditions."

"Oh. Okay."

I rubbed my arms. When the plane was full, we pushed it inside. He chocked the wheels and chained the plane in place. Wind gusted into the hangar and rattled the walls and roof. We grabbed the dog and the bags and made it into the Suburban in one trip. By the time Jack started the engine, snow was falling and the sky all around us had turned dark gray.

I rolled down the window and let the flakes fall against my hand as we drove. "It's beautiful."

"Yeah, I love these early-season storms."

"Not great horseback weather." Not that I should ride anyway.

He took a left, toward the ranch house. I don't know why it surprised me, since it was after the workday, but it did. Something about heading straight to the house felt more like a date than a work weekend. But, of course, it wasn't a date. And if it had been, what a horrible date I'd be. The weather and high desert smells had helped rejuvenate me, but I had a long way to go before I was good company. I wanted to slap my cheeks to perk myself up and put some color back into my face, but held back.

Jack rolled his window down, too. "Yeah, but the weather will change five times this weekend."

The house appeared out of the dark skies, sudden and large, and no less impressive than last time. Jack swung the Suburban around to the far side and parked in a three-car garage. Even in there, the snow and cold wind followed. He closed the garage behind us.

Just before he opened the door to the house, Jack turned back to me. "Your friend Collin contacted me this week. I told him we'd be back tonight for a Saturday work function. He asked if he and Tamara could take us to dinner. And I . . . uh . . . I told them we needed an early start so that it would be better if they came out here."

Did I mind? I wasn't sure. "So you *didn't* tell them about my miscarriage?"

Jack opened the door and motioned me through. "They said they're bringing dinner. All we have to do is sit and eat."

I wanted to throttle Jack for forcing me into this. My mood had improved, but only enough for a soak in the claw-footed tub I'd discovered in the guest bath last weekend. I wasn't going to give that up.

"How long do I have?"

"They'll be here at six-thirty. Oh, and Mickey and his wife will be here, too."

Ten minutes from now. A regular dinner party. "No promises. I'm really not feeling all that well, but I'll try to come down."

He looked at his feet, then opened the door. "Yeah, I understand."

I escaped up the stairs, each step ponderous. How could walking up one flight make me this dizzy? I knew I was out of shape, but maybe the surgery had weakened me more than I'd realized. I dropped my handbag on the bed and my suitcase in the corner and headed straight for the bathroom. The white porcelain tub stood regally in the corner on its pewter feet. I turned both spigots on full blast and started opening cabinets and doors as fast as I could, searching for bath salts. I found cucumber bubble bath and dumped in half a cup. The water steamed, so I eased off on the hot, tested it with my hand, and eased it back further. I let my clothes fall to the floor. I took out my clip, twisted my hair high on my head, and refastened it.

Two bottles of water stood by the sinks, and I grabbed one, uncapped it, and slugged it down. Then I looked at the counter again: a bottle of Dancing Bull merlot, an old school corkscrew, and a plastic wine tumbler. This was a giant step up from boxed white zinfandel. Naked, I sunk the corkscrew deep in the cork, my hands shaking. I twisted, twisted, twisted, then flipped one end down to make purchase on the bottle's lip and depressed the other end, easing the cork out slowly until it made a soft popping noise. The velvety, red liquid splashed into the glass, *glug, glug, glug*. I filled it the proper two thirds, then, after a pause, I filled it to millimeters below the rim.

The aroma called to me and I buried my nose in the top of the glass, inhaled, then inhaled again, deeper. I sipped, holding it in my mouth, the liquid gliding over my tongue, the different notes of the wine playing out their symphony, and I closed my eyes while I savored the sweet music until it crescendoed, then I swallowed.

A deep sigh broke from my lips. I set the wine glass on the small wooden table at the head of the tub, dialed the timer to fifteen minutes, and sunk eyeball deep into the bubbles and water.

When I climbed out of the tub an hour later, waterlogged and wrinkly, I was a little unsteady on my feet. Only one glass had made me tipsy? Well, that little lunch burrito had been hours ago. I needed food, and the only place I could get it was downstairs. I didn't want to waste the wine, though. I poured another full glass emptying the bottle.

I padded to my suitcase and put on a mossy green velour dress with my boots. The fabric whispered over my skin. A chorus of laughter erupted below. Male and female voices. Happy, normal people. The scent of something tangy. My stomach growled, long and echo-y. I held my hand to my belly, feeling its emptiness, its deep pit of nothingness. Food wouldn't fill that void.

I applied burnt sienna lip-gloss and ran a brush through my hair, still undecided about whether to join the group. While I wavered between stay or go, I teased my bangs back into shape and sprayed them with Aqua Net. I opened the door without crossing the threshold, just to test the air outside my room. More laughter. Voices. Collin's. Tamara's. Jack's. Mickey's. Others I didn't recognize. I smelled that tangy aroma again, plus something spicy, and my stomach rumbled. Darn it, I had to go down there. My hand reached up of its own volition and did one last touch test on my bangs. They were fine. Vanity even in the depths of a blue funk. I ventured out, and down the stairs.

I entered the kitchen with my half-full glass in hand. Faces swam before me. At the kitchen table, Jack and Mickey sat with a woman I didn't recognize, who had her hand on Mickey's knee. To my surprise, Paul Johnson sat with them, too. What was he doing here? Tamara and Collin manned the business end of the kitchen, busily arranging a platter of pizza slices.

I waved. "Hello, all."

My name echoed in the air. *Hello Emily-ly-ly-ly-ly-ly*. I blinked. Snowflake bounded to me. I reached down and ruffled her ears.

The woman I hadn't met stood and grasped my hand. Hers was cold and tiny, but she had an iron grip. "Laura Begay," she said.

We shook. She was so short I could see the top of her head, the side part of her sleek, brown bob. She probably weighed half what I did, max.

"Emily."

She sat back down and patted Mickey's knee. "Wife of this character."

Mickey's eyes reflected her, and in them you could see how lovely she was. "She left out 'jockey of international reputation.'"

"Wow," I managed. Normally, I would have clung to her every word, dying to hear about such a fascinating job. Maybe she'd give me another chance some other time.

Paul did better than me. "Hey, I knew I'd heard of you."

She smiled at her husband and then at Paul. "It's a job."

Conversation resumed, and I sidled over to Jack and spoke under my breath. "What's Paul doing here?"

He tilted his head toward mine. "Paperwork."

Which explained why he'd come, but not why he'd stayed. I waited, but Jack didn't elaborate.

Collin removed the foil off some buffalo wings he'd pulled from the oven. "Voilà." He gestured his hand in the air with a flourish, throwing his hip as he did it.

Tamara golf clapped then went back to work uncorking a bottle of white wine on her hip—3 Blind Moose pinot grigio—while Jack set out glasses, seven of them.

"Fill 'em up, people. You can't eat anything Collin cooks sober, I promise," she said.

No one needed further prodding. I poured pinot grigio in a fresh glass, feeling conspicuous, but no one even glanced at me, which confirmed my suspicion that Jack had clued everyone in on the change in my maternity status. Somehow I'd become unable to keep anything about my life private, like I was a walking Match.com billboard, a constantly updating Facebook status. Maybe my blurting everything out last weekend had something to do with it, as did my mother and her friends. Even Collin.

Voices pulsed and throbbed around me. People teased and laughed. I stayed quiet. My wine buzz had me a little queasy, until I polished off two pieces of the chile-enhanced New Mexican pizza that Tamara and Collin had made, after I picked off all the chicken, anyway, as best I could. The queasy went away, as long as I kept my eyes off the food in Paul's mouth. It gave way to mellow, and I watched Snowflake successfully beg for food from everyone assembled until she collapsed in a food coma on her pillow in the corner. I tried to follow the conversations around me, and more than once I felt my lips curve upward, until finally I laughed.

I glanced up into Jack's eyes. He looked away quickly, but the aftereffect remained, a wake lapping against my skin.

Laura shushed everyone. "I want to play a game."

Mickey splayed his hands around her waist and pulled her back onto his lap. "Me, too."

She slapped at one of his hands. "Not that game. I brought Boxers or Briefs."

"Which one are you wearing now?" Collin asked, his eyebrows peaked high.

Tamara punched his bicep. "It's the name of a game, dipshit."

"I should go," Paul said. "I've already overstayed my welcome after barging in on your party."

"Noooo," a chorus of voices shouted back at him, although I wasn't one of them.

"How would your life ever go on if you missed Boxers or Briefs?" Mickey asked, and Paul laughed.

He stayed. Five minutes later we sat at the large wooden kitchen table. I cast my eyes on its scarred wood surface. There was a purposeful scar in front of me, a crude, childlike etching. I leaned down. *Jackson.* I looked to my left. No others there. I looked to my right. *Julia.* A shiver ran through me. Were these the names of Jack's kids? I sipped my wine and caught Jack watching me again from across the table.

Laura explained the rules. "We're playing to six. Mickey, you're going first. Roll the die, baby."

He did. The die had statements on it instead of numbers. It landed on *I have.* "Now what?" he asked.

Laura said, "Everybody reads the 'I have' lines on their cards and picks the one that best fits Mickey, either because it's true, or because it's funny. Then we'll vote on the most funny and the most true, and each of the winners get a token." She pointed at the box, which held the round blue token disks. "Then we move on clockwise, so Jack will roll next."

We studied our cards. I picked, "I have fun in the dark," and slapped it down on the stack the others had piled in front of Mickey.

He cleared his throat and read the lines from each card in a serious tone. Soon we were all whooping and hollering, even me. I won for "true." Tamara won "funny" for "I have zits the size of Sweden."

Jack rolled the die, which landed on "I like." We all piled our cards and he read them. "I like mullets" won for true and for funniest.

Jack said, "I refuse to give a token to that one for truth."

"Whoa, cousin, is your Apache name Cheating Bull now?" Mickey said, straight-faced. "In high school he won a special award from the cheerleaders. 'The tight end with the tight ass and the nice hair.'"

This caused an uproar. Snowflake opened one eye, but closed it again quickly.

"It's nice to know my attorney has two advantages to use in my favor every time he enters the courtroom," Paul said.

Jack smiled and touched the ends of his hair. Mickey leaned around Paul and patted Jack on the bottom, and we all just laughed harder.

Tamara set two fresh bottles of wine in front of us. "Now that everyone is drunk, we're breaking out the cheap shit."

I chose the Chateau Ste. Michelle Riesling. As I took a slow swallow, Jack's eyes again sought me out. When I pulled mine away, I stumbled across Collin's gaze.

He didn't pretend he wasn't looking. "You hanging in there, beautiful?"

A silence fell over the group. I lifted my glass in the air. "Recovery by grape." As I set the glass down, I saw Tamara glare at Collin.

"Here, here," Paul said, and lifted his glass toward me.

I smiled, grateful to him.

"Your turn, Standing Hair," Mickey said.

I looked up and saw he was speaking to me. "Huh?"

Everyone laughed so hard they spewed wine. Jack pretended to pat his bangs. Snowflake stood up and turned around once before lying down again, but not without shooting us a disapproving glance first.

Oh. Standing Hair. I reached up to mine. My bangs felt all right to me. A little stiff, possibly, and fluffy, but standing? "Hardly," I said.

I rolled the die and got "I don't think." Five heads bent to their cards followed by five cards hitting the table in front of me. I picked them up and starting reading them aloud. When I got to, "I don't think those pictures on the Internet were of me," I felt heat in my face.

Collin rubbed his hand across his mouth, leaving a straight face behind. "Sure they were. I'd know that sweet ass anywhere."

The laughter from four people hurt my ears, and I pretended to laugh with them, but I couldn't. I was too conscious of the fact that Tamara wasn't laughing. I liked her, and Collin was going to make her hate me when I hadn't done a thing.

We voted, and Laura got her sixth token and won. Game over, thank goodness. I started to say I was headed up to bed, but Laura beat me to it.

She waved an almost empty wine glass in the air. "Girl time. Boys go smoke cigars and drink boy stuff."

"Yay!" Tamara shouted. She plunked another bottle of wine in front of us. My bleary eyes couldn't read the label. It was white, and I was drinking white, so I topped mine off.

Jack rose. "Let's take a walk, gentlemen."

Paul, Collin, and Mickey got up, grumbling but good-natured.

As he stood, Mickey asked, "Hey, Standing Hair, did you ever find that little girl you were looking for?"

Heavy silence fell. Everyone turned toward me.

I swallowed. "Not yet. Her mother was murdered in jail, so now the girl's an orphan. I will find her though, if only Jack Ass will let me look for her."

Howls around the table. "Jack *Ass?*" Mickey asked.

I sniffed. "I always assumed that was what Jack was short for."

More peals of laughter. I locked eyes with Jack, and his surprised me. They weren't angry, they were something like proud. Of me? He was laughing as hard as everyone else.

Mickey nodded. "It was supposed to be a family secret. Seriously, though, about that little girl, you'll find her, I believe it. Last week, I felt it. That you're the one."

Paul said, "So, do you have any leads?"

I looked over at him. I couldn't read his eyes, but I thought he looked amused. *Don't write me off as a piece of fluff,* I thought. Others have before, and they learned better.

"I do," I said.

"Oh?" Mickey raised his eyebrows.

The room around me seemed to shrink, wood-framed windows and backsplashes of rectangular slate moved toward me, butcher block island and Shaker-style cabinets loomed closer, and the waves of gold, rusty brown, blue-gray, and tan in the granite crashed forward. Everything blurred at the edges.

"Ask me when I've recovered from this hangover," I said.

Laura brandished her wine glass. "But we've only just started."

I shook my head and held up four fingers. "This is day three for me." I looked at my hand and pulled a finger down, amidst snorts and more raucous laughs.

Laura sat down at the head of the table. "Okay, enough of this serious stuff. Y'all go away." She waved her hand at the guys.

Snowflake followed them, trotting with head and tail up. Someone had her second wind, and believed she was a boy.

"So, Emily," Laura said. "Tell me more about you. Jack said you work for him?"

"I'm his paralegal in Amarillo."

"How long have you guys been dating?"

I shook my head vigorously, which was a mistake. The closed-in room listed a little. "Oh no, we're not together. I just started working for him a week or two ago. I'm here for a client event tomorrow. At Paul's house."

Tamara and Laura looked at each other, and Laura's eyebrow height told me she didn't believe me while the set of Tamara's lips suggested I'd answered wrong. Was the boy-girl grouping designed for Laura and Tamara to interrogate me?

"I swear. In fact, I pissed him off so bad earlier this week I thought he was going to fire me. The only reason he didn't is because he felt sorry for me about what happened, you know, my, um, miscarriage."

Both women made sympathetic big-eyed faces and tsking noises. Laura reached across the table and put both her hands on mine. "I'm so sorry, honey."

"Thank you." I needed a new subject. I blurted, "So, Laura, a jockey? What do you ride?"

"Quarter horses."

"Did you ride Jarhead?"

She grinned. "I sure did. He's my favorite."

This interested Tamara, and the conversation took off between her and Laura. I watched the two of them for a little while. They both had on silver and turquoise earrings, and it made me wish I'd worn mine. They would have looked great with my dress. I picked up a pencil from the center of the table and started doodling on a napkin.

Tamara snatched the napkin. "What are you drawing here, Standing Hair?"

My face burned. "Um, I don't really know. "

She held it up in front of her. "You like the bad boys?"

"What?"

"You're doodling the gang sign for the East Side Lobos."

I pointed at the ΣSL I'd drawn. "You know that symbol?"

"Sure, I grew up in Las Cruces, and they were big there."

"I've seen it around here, too," Laura said.

Tamara cocked her head at me. "How do you know them?"

"The man who took the little girl I'm looking for has a tattoo like this."

Tamara patted the inside of her left upper arm with her right hand. "Here?"

"Yes."

"Then I'd be willing to bet he's a Lobo."

"You're the first people who've recognized it," I said. "Can I ask you a few more questions?"

"Sure."

I stood up, unsteady on my feet. I held up my index finger and tried to speak clearly. "One minute. Let me grab the file."

Five minutes later, after I'd finished visiting the potty in my room, I pawed through my laptop bag in the dark, feeling for the Redrope file that my fingers knew by heart. When I found it, I ripped it out, letting the bag fall to the floor at the foot of the bed. I spun around, quick like a cutting horse, in a hurry to get the file back to my new best source of information, Tamara, but I bumped into something very solid in the doorway. Big hands wrapped around my shoulders.

"Whoa there, Em, where're you off to in such a hurry?"

Collin, too close, blasting booze in my face. The lights in the hallway weren't on, so I couldn't see him well, but I'd know him anywhere. He wasn't all that tall, five foot nine or so, but he made up for it in muscle mass, which I couldn't miss, as close as he was to me. I wanted to run, but he'd been a friend for years, and I couldn't duck him. It was rude. I brandished my file.

"Taking this file downstairs to show Tamara," I said.

"Well, I was taking this upstairs," he said, slurring his words, thumping his chest, and tilting his head back. The downstairs light was just bright enough to illuminate that wide Collin grin. His eyes were half-mast. "I was looking for you."

"Me? Why?"

"I can't quit thinking about how you went and got yourself unhitched. You've known I've been in love with you since I met you, haven't you?"

I closed my eyes, mortified. "No, I mean, I kind of thought maybe, but not for sure, and not—"

He wrapped his hand around the back of my head and pulled my forehead against his. I pulled back, to no avail. "You knew. And here you are, and I'm engaged, and . . ." His words dwindled off and his lips landed on mine. I stumbled backwards. My mind was screaming, *No!* but my lips were trapped by his.

Before I could twist away from him, I heard a shriek from the stairway.

"*Pendejo!*" Tamara stood on the top stair, Paul one below her, but towering over her. She snarled, but Paul grinned.

Collin released me and jumped back. I fell on my bottom against the doorframe in the entrance to my room. As I did, I saw Jack from my peripheral vision at the opposite end of the hall. I turned. His lips were set in a hard line. I wanted to run to him.

"Hey, baby," Collin said.

"Don't 'hey baby' me. I saw you sneak up here after her. "She wrestled something off her left hand, then threw it at Collin. Metal hit the wall and I heard what I knew was her ring fall to the carpet. "I hope you've got a ride, asshole. And a place to stay."

She whirled and ran into Paul, who turned sideways to let her by. Collin took off after Tamara without looking back at me crumpled on the floor.

"Tamara, baby! Tamara, it's not what you think—" His protests echoed through the house.

Paul stood there, sipping from a cocktail glass, watching them go.

I sat where I'd fallen and put my head on my knees. The file lay on the floor beside me. I scooted it to me, protecting it from God knew what, and wrapped my arms around my legs. Jack's footsteps thudded in the hall as he walked toward me, and I didn't look up. I could feel the heat from my face on my thighs, even through my skirt. I sucked in a breath and held it until Jack passed.

Except he didn't. The boots stopped by my feet. He leaned against the wall and slid down the length of it until he was sitting on the ground beside me.

"You and Collin, are you . . . ?"

"No, never. That whole thing was quite . . . disturbing."

He grunted and I heard a slosh and a swallow. "So, you okay?" he asked. His voice sounded different than before, and not just because he slurred even worse than Collin. It was gentle. No fending me off. No teasing. Just caring. Warm.

I nodded then realized he couldn't see me in the dark. "Not really." I lifted my head just enough to wipe my nose, and when I rubbed my sleeve under it my hands brushed against wet cheeks. I hadn't even known I was crying again. I swallowed, determined not to let Jack know. "What were you guys drinking, anyway? Collin's wasted and you sound drunker than him. Not that I'm exactly sober."

"Mescal tequila shots." His arm went up and I heard the slosh again. "Mickey's downstairs puking."

"Nice."

Jack scooted his butt closer to mine and put his arm around me. I stiffened, nervous, but that was all he did and I relaxed into him.

I heard the slosh again. "Want some?" he asked.

I guffawed, half laugh, half sob. I lifted my head and reached out. My hand met a bottle. I leaned against the wall, arching my back slightly so I could tilt my head. It tasted like drinking a bottle of my face astringent, not that I had ever tried it, but what I imagined it would taste like. I gasped, and some of the tequila sprayed from my mouth. I giggled. My eyes had adjusted to the light and I looked at my boss's profile. He had nice lips. A perfect nose. I didn't know many men who had perfect noses.

"Good stuff," Jack said.

"Yeah." I tipped the bottle back again, and this time I did better. The liquid burned my throat and warmed my insides.

"Better stop." Jack reached for the bottle.

"One more." I tilted it back and managed another big swallow. Warmth settled over me, and I passed it back to Jack.

We sat side by side for a few minutes. From downstairs we heard the front door slam, heavy footsteps, then Collin's voice called up the stairs. "Jack?"

"Yeah?"

"Can I crash on your couch?"

Jack groaned softly. "All right."

"Thanks, man."

I giggled again, and Jack leaned his face toward mine. I drew a quick breath and held it, my heart hammering. Then I burst out with giggles again. "I think I'm drunk."

"I think I should tuck you in," Jack said.

He leaned forward and got up onto his knees with an *oomph*, then turned and used the wall to stand all the way up. He held a hand out to me and pulled me up. I fell into him, giggling again.

I whispered, "Tamara is so mad at Collin," and laughed more. "He tried to kiss me." I held up a finger and waggled it in the half-dark. "That was not a very smart move."

Jack gave a rumbly snort. "Not at all."

Movement caught my eye. The teenage girl I'd met last weekend at Jack's office appeared in the stairwell beside Paul, who had never left, it seemed. With the light behind them, the girl's hairdo was even more impressively large than last time.

"Come *on*, Dad." She grabbed his arm.

"Stella, you're such a good girl to give your old man a ride home," Paul said.

She muttered, but loud enough I could hear her. "Like I ever have a choice."

I watched the back of Paul's head as he descended the stairs. I shivered and threw both arms around Jack's neck. Then I laughed again, nestling there until my mirth tapered off. I kept one arm around his neck and removed the other, standing up straight. "Kay, where's my bed?" I whispered.

"Over here," Jack whispered back.

We lurched to it like two kids in a three-legged race, and fell face first into it.

I mumbled into the covers. "Jack?"

"Hmm?"

I turned to him. "Thank you for tucking me in."

He rolled to face me, and that's when it happened. I wasn't sure which one of us started it, but the next thing I knew we were wrestling in a ferocious lip lock that was just about the best kiss I'd ever had. Shoot, it probably was *the* best, but I was too drunk to be sure. His big, rough, cowboy hands grabbed both sides of my face and his mouth consumed me, like my lips were the only thing between him and certain death. He kissed me like I was the first place belt buckle at the county fair. Like I was the prize at the bottom of the Cracker Jacks box. Like it was the Olympics and I was the gold medal.

And I kissed him back, my hands tearing at his shirt and shimmying up his tight stomach and sculpted chest. His breath hissed at my touch, and I wriggled closer. My bare foot slid and hooked around the back of his knee, pulling him into me.

He groaned. "Emily."

I kissed him harder, panting. "Jack."

"Emily," he said again. "I have my boots on."

I rubbed my foot up and down his leg, definitely feeling boot. "You doooo."

He sat up on one elbow and stared down at me. He reached his free hand behind my neck and grasped me at the nape of it, pulling me up to him for one last kiss. My lips clung to his even as he released me. "Wait," he said.

I watched him as he stood and stumbled around, yanking at his boots, hopping, cussing, and finally falling on his rump. My eyelids fluttered. I let them close for just one second, and I murmured his name as I thought about how good his lips felt on mine. I sighed, smiling. The last thing I remembered before I fell asleep was the hard contours of his body pressed into me, and then nothing at all.

TWENTY-TWO

When I woke up, I had a face full of warm skin, but the bed was spinning too fast for me to enjoy it. I mumbled, "Sorry," and rolled onto the floor with a thud, then ran into the bathroom. I splashed cold water on my face and swished it in my mouth and groaned. My clothes were mussed but all in place, and I sighed in relief. I had a vague memory of a make-out session, and that was mortifying enough without the horror of waking up naked. Jack was my boss, and I was a not-yet-divorced woman who had just lost a baby, for God's sake. One who didn't want to put herself in a position where she had to figure out how to tell a man she was probably not the one he wanted to take home to mama, because she was a bust as a baby-maker.

Oh God, that reminded me. What if I hadn't fallen asleep and had done . . . more? Dr. Patel had told me not to have intimate relations for some period of time, but I couldn't remember how long he'd said. I hadn't really listened because I didn't think there was even the tiniest of chances that it was relevant. Who knew?

I paced in a wavering line back and forth in the bathroom. What was the right thing to do? Should I go sleep somewhere else? No, that was even worse. I had to get back in my own bed, I just couldn't plaster myself all over my boss, that's all. A memory of his hands tangled in my hair, my body pretzeled around his washed over me in a haze of lust. It was undignified, somewhat slutty, even, no matter how good he felt.

The clock on the bedside table read five a.m. I crept back to the bed in the dark, tripping over my shoes. I held myself motionless, not breathing.

The bulk in my bed shifted and the mattress creaked. I stole around to the other side and tried to alight with the weight of a feather, outside of the covers. Once in place, I held myself frozen, listening to be sure he was asleep.

His body flipped over, and I tensed.

"Good morning, Standing Hair."

I felt a giggle wave starting and I bit my lip, trapping it inside. "Good morning to you, Cheating Bull."

"You sure do fall asleep fast."

I moaned. "I know, I'm sorry."

"Me, too."

He reached for me, sliding his arm under me and around my waist with the covers still between us. He pulled me to him in a strong and possessive way that made my pulse pound in a place that was supposed to be recovering from its recent medical procedure.

"Jack," I said.

I'd intended my voice to sound like I was holding up a stop sign, but it came out more flashing green light, and then nothing came out at all because Jack had his mouth on mine. A knock on the door broke us apart, and Jack growled.

"Just a minute," I called.

Jack's hand around my waist drifted south. "If that's Collin, I'm going to beat his ass."

I grabbed his bottom lip between my teeth and sucked once, hard. "Just a second."

After cupping my bottom and pulling me into him once more, Jack released me. I crawled out of bed and walked to the door. "Who is it?"

"Mickey. I need Jack."

"I haven't seen him."

"Well, if you do, tell him that one of the hands just called in to tell me that he found a dead body in our southeastern pasture."

"I'll find him and tell—"

Behind me, Jack jumped to his feet and pulled the door open. Mickey stood outside, wearing last night's clothes, Snowflake at his feet. From the bags under his droopy, bloodshot eyes, and the yellow tint to his skin, it looked like he'd had a rough time.

Jack turned back to me and said, "I'm sorry." He pulled my face to his by the nape of my neck. I had a sense of déjà vu, then he kissed my socks off, almost literally, since when he grabbed me, the carpet dragged one of them down to my toes. He released me and reached back inside the door and grabbed his boots, Snowflake leaping at his face to steal a kiss as he did.

I stood open-mouthed, my lips burning, as the two men and the dog walked away. Then I gave myself a shake and scrambled after them.

Jack stopped long enough to step into one of his boots, and I caught up with them.

"Tell me everything you know," Jack said to Mickey.

"Kenny was doing rounds and he found a dead guy in the middle of the southeastern pasture, right off the highway. He said there was no identification on him, and he didn't recognize him, but the guy looked Mexican, really skinny, and like he'd been beaten pretty badly. No signs of anyone else out there, or any kind of altercation, either."

Jack hopped into the other boot. "Have you called the police?"

"Waiting on you, cousin-man."

They walked down the stairs, with me still hanging on their every word.

"Call 'em," Jack said. "I'll get coffee and we can drive out together when you're off the phone."

Mickey had his cell phone out by the time Jack finished speaking, and he walked over to the mountain-facing windows in the great room. I followed my boss into the kitchen and leaned forward against the breakfast bar. He put the dog out and poured her some food and water.

"I'll make coffee if you want to change or anything."

He smiled at me, and it was strange to see this new, open Jack in the full light of the kitchen.

"You should sleep," he said. "Save up your energy for Johnson's party later, and maybe a ride with me, if we can squeeze it in."

In light of our shenanigans last night, it seemed odd to think, but I probably shouldn't ride. I hadn't really told him anything about my surgery, but I would just have to deal with it later, if it came up.

"A dead body?" I said. "I can't sleep now. Is this a normal thing around here?"

Jack turned on his automatic coffee maker after filling it with grounds from a canister that smelled spicy and delicious.

"Nope," Jack said. He set out two travel mugs. "Want one?"

"Sure."

He placed a WTR porcelain mug beside the others. Snowflake yipped, and I walked to the door and let her in. She went straight for the food bowl.

Mickey joined us in the kitchen. "Tularosa is on the way, and it sounds like we should expect Alamogordo to show up, too. If they decide there's a chance he came from the reservation, they'll get the res police involved as well. Gonna be a long day."

Jack poured each of us black coffee while Mickey talked. Mickey claimed his mug and headed out the door to the garage. Jack hung back. He opened a cabinet by the refrigerator and retrieved keys, handing them to me.

"I'll be riding with Mickey," Jack said. "The Suburban is yours. Go into town, get yourself food, go shopping, whatever you want. We'll leave here for Johnson's at about four-thirty, so I'll see you sometime before then. Call if you need me."

He leaned in and kissed me hard, and a smile broke out across my face. He grinned back, his face an inch from mine. "What are you smiling about?" he asked.

I shook my head. "I can't help it."

I watched his Wrangler-clad butt as he walked out, and covered my mouth to keep my smile from coming out aloud.

Collin's voice behind me on the stairs broke me out of my trance some minutes later. "What's going on?" He yawned.

As I turned away from my view of the mountains, I caught sight of most of his midsection as his morning stretch lifted his shirt. I averted my eyes. I didn't feel ready to talk to him, but it seemed I didn't have a choice.

"Dead man down out in a pasture. Cops converging." I stifled a yawn. "Too early."

"Too early for me to comprehend a word you just said," Collin said. "Other than it sounded too much like my day job."

Motioning at the mug in my hand, Collin walked toward the kitchen. "Coffee?"

"Should be some left. Jack just made it."

I moved to the base of the stairs, halfway into the kitchen, halfway in the great room.

Collin tilted the carafe all the way over until the last few drops ran out. "My head tells me we partied like rock stars," he said.

"Something like that."

He dug in his pocket. "I crawled around in the hall last night for half an hour and finally found this." He held up Tamara's ring. "She didn't come back for me."

"Do you blame her?"

He sighed. "No."

"Have you checked on her? She shouldn't have been driving."

"Yeah. She called me when she got home, to chew my ass again."

I nodded. "Good."

Snowflake sidled up to me and rubbed against my ankles.

"Yeah, um, Em, about what happened between us—"

I crossed my arms. "Whoa, Collin. There was no us. There was you, wasted, and there was me, blindsided."

"Well, yeah, that. I'm sorry. I really messed things up."

"Yes, you did."

He sipped coffee. "But I spoke the truth, even if I shouldn't have. I fell in love with you the first time Katie brought you around. Life never works out like I expect it will. I always thought someday you'd dump that putz husband of yours for me and we'd be together. I didn't ever imagine you'd go through what you have, or that I'd find Tamara in the meantime."

"Thank you, I think."

"Don't be like that. You know I don't mean anything bad. I may be a dumbass, but I'm a dumbass that has been in love exactly twice. You're the first, Tamara's the second. I should have told you years ago, but my pride never let me. Which doesn't matter now, because I'm going to make up with Tamara, even if it takes me a decade after pulling an asshat stunt like I did last night."

I smiled. "Well, if I had to tell the truth, it would be that I was pretty convinced you'd be around if I ever needed you, and that I was disappointed when I found out you were engaged."

Collin strutted around the kitchen but then clutched his head, like the cock of the walk with a tequila headache that he was. "Ha. I knew it."

"For about two minutes."

"Don't ruin my moment."

"A minute and a half."

"Hey, let me take you to breakfast, make it up to you."

"Don't you need to make it up to Tamara instead?"

He shook his head. "She flew out this morning. Doesn't get back until tonight. Military shit. I'm stranded and starving."

I looked at the clock. Six a.m. I'd have to drive him home anyway, since I suspected we were a little outside of Yellow Cab's range, and I needed food. He was behaving, so, why not?

"Okay, but let's wait for a civilized hour. I'm going to shower. I'll be back down here at seven-thirty." I retreated up the stairs with Snowflake right behind me.

I shoveled in a bite of huevos rancheros, minus the huevos. *More like frijoles rancheros*, I thought. Refried beans stuck in a mass of heat to the roof of my mouth. I opened my lips a smidge to suck in air. After a few cooling breaths, I chewed happily. Our surly waiter had made no apologies for the forty-five minute wait for our food, but the chow was so good that I forgave him.

Collin had ordered steak and eggs, and he dug into his rib eye, extra rare. Blood oozed onto the plate, and he sopped it up with his tortilla in one hand and his meat on the tines of his fork in the other. He waved the beef bite as he talked, and its delicious aroma wafted toward me, teasing me. Sometimes I missed meat, especially now that I didn't live with Rich the vegan.

Collin talked while he chewed. "This place is an institution. Tamara introduced me to it the first time I came to visit her."

"This place" was the Old Road House in Mescalero, a joint so local it had no sign out front. The red adobe restaurant was one-story on the parking side, and two-story in back, with wooden rafters, red tile floors, and a casual crowd of locals who seemed to find us slightly repellant, if fascinating. Green and red chiles hung in bunches on the inside walls alongside an elaborate papoose board, a feathered headdress, and a magnificent Apache bow.

"You come down a lot?"

"I do. She can't get away as easily as me."

I half-listened as Collin continued talking. The other half of me concentrated on my food . . . and eavesdropping on the two guys at the table behind me. They'd come in after us, and, when I'd turned to look at them, it was clear they were from a branch of Mickey's family tree. From the sound of their hushed voices, something had them excited. Or maybe agitated was a better word for it. I resisted the urge to turn and watch them.

The first man's voice said, "Well, I heard somebody's been selling silver, a lot of it, and they found it near here. Sure wasn't you or me or anyone else we know working a claim."

A higher voice, still male, answered him. "Ain't nobody been spending money that I can see. It's probably just rumors, man. There's always rumors."

The first voice spoke again. "Yeah, probably. But still, keep your ear to the ground and your eyes wide open. I want in on it if it's real."

Collin snapped his fingers in front of my eyes. "Earth to Emily."

I jumped. "Sorry. I'm in a hungover daze." I cut another bite of frijoles rancheros and scooped it up. Delicious. It was the perfect eating temperature now.

"So, you said you were taking a file to show Tamara last night. Want to run it past me? I've been told I'm a fairly competent investigator."

"I can't believe you even remember." Last night was a blur, but I took myself back and recalled the conversation I'd had with Laura and Tamara. "Tamara identified a tattoo for me, one on the arm of a guy that kidnapped that little girl that's missing, Valentina. She's the daughter of our client, who died in Amarillo."

"Show me."

I drew the ΣSL on a napkin like I'd done the night before and slid it over to him.

"And what did Tamara say about it?"

"That it was the sign of the East Side Lobos, a gang that runs in Las Cruces."

"Interesting. And Jack?"

I sat, blinking, as I realized that I hadn't told Jack about the tattoo. My mind retread the day Valentina had been taken, rushing to PCCB, telling Jack the story but cutting it short to meet with Melinda, her news about Sofia, and then nothing. I'd never given him this piece of information. I felt like an idiot, a greenhorn.

"I don't know," I said.

Collin squinted at me, but I shook my head. He shrugged. "Okay, what else do you know about the guy?"

"White skinned. Bald head."

"Like a skinhead?"

"The witness didn't give me that impression. But maybe."

"I'd be surprised. Not many skinheads in the Las Cruces gang community. They're usually up northwest. I deal with gangs all over the state in my job, even though I'm based in Santa Fe. Them and every other low-life scumbag within five hundred miles."

"Well, honestly, I'd thought the kidnapper was an Amarillo-based scumbag, this guy who's a known pedophile with jailhouse ties to the man Valentina's mother murdered."

"Did he grow up in Las Cruces?"

"I guess he could have. He's done time in New Mexico."

"Yeah. So maybe this doesn't rule your guy out."

I pondered it for a moment, then shivered. "I've been focused on someone in Amarillo, but whoever has her could have taken her anywhere. Even here, I guess."

"It's easy to hide someone in this area."

A cold dread seeped through me. I'd seen how desolate it was around here. "I don't get it though. Why take Valentina in the first place? And there's more. Her mother was murdered in jail the same day Valentina was taken. The ADA said it was an accident, but how is Sofia the only one hurt in a jail fight? I don't buy it. It feels connected to Valentina's kidnapping, to me. And now we're talking about the kidnapping being potentially tied somehow to southern New Mexico. But how? Maybe if I could figure out the tie, I could find her."

"Didn't you say they were undocumented?"

"Yes. Why?"

"Lots of illegals come through here from Mexico. Their community is very tight, very closed. They help each other out. It's also big business, though, and some less scrupulous types traffic folks illegally across the border. Usually the same type of assholes smuggling drugs, so I'm involved with more of these immigrations gone wrong than you'd imagine."

"Well, even if she entered the U.S. here, I still think it's more likely we'll find her somewhere in West Texas. I mean, why would someone go out of their way to kidnap a six-year-old child in Amarillo and bring her all the way back to southern New Mexico?"

He took another bite of bloody steak and talked through it. "Not for anything good, I can promise you that."

His words put the exclamation point on my fears, and I felt nauseous. The events since last night had been distracting, to say the least, but the full weight of Valentina's disappearance was bearing down on me again.

"Emily?" a woman called from the side of me nearest the dining room.

I turned. It was Laura. "Hey, good morning." I pulled a chair out. "Would you like to join us?"

She looked from me to Collin and back to me again, and her voice grew chilly. "No, thank you. I saw Jack's Suburban outside. What a surprise to see you with Collin."

I felt my brow crease. What was the matter with her? "Um, Jack left with Mickey hours ago, and he told me to take the Suburban for breakfast."

"Yes, I'm picking up food to take out to them."

I realized that Laura had every patron in the restaurant hanging on her words. I asked, "Is everything okay?"

She shrugged. "About what you'd expect."

A male voice called out from the cash register. "To-go order's ready for you, Laura."

She looked at me again, then pointedly at Collin. "See you later, Emily."

"Bye," I called after her.

"Brrrr," Collin said. "Is it just me or is it freezing in here?"

I ignored him, my stomach churning. Laura hadn't liked seeing me here with Collin, and it was her version of the tale that was headed straight back to Jack.

TWENTY-THREE

I dropped Collin off at Tamara's place in Alamogordo and navigated my way back to Wrong Turn Ranch by noon. I'd canned my hopes for a quick trip to Roswell to see what I could find out about Harvey and Spike. Laura's censorious face had worried me since she'd left the Old Road House. I'd all but jackhammered Collin out of his seat when he'd wanted to linger over coffee and reminisce about the old days in Dallas. I tried not to panic. I hadn't done anything wrong, even if, apparently, it had looked bad to Laura. It was still okay to feel hopeful. I parked the Suburban out front and hurried into the house.

Sucking in a deep breath for courage, I opened the tall, wooden front door. "Hello? Anyone home?"

No answer except the sprinting feet and jingling tags of a little white dog.

I stepped inside and pulled the door shut behind me. Snowflake appeared, acting as excited to see me as if we'd been parted for years. I knelt and rubbed her ears, then straightened. Since Jack wasn't there, I decided to snag some apples or carrots or whatever I could find and head down to the stables. I was in the kitchen filling a brown paper bag with horse treats when I heard someone on the stairs. My heart pounded, and I watched the foot until a man appeared. He was a dark-haired man, but darker than Jack. Mickey, not looking any fresher than when I'd seen him that morning.

"Hello," I said to let him know I was there.

He looked at me in a way that said Laura had given him an earful.

Mouth set, eyes flat and cold. His voice matched. "Emily. You've had a busy time since you got here."

His words cut me like razor wire, and I wanted to lash out. He didn't have to be so presumptuous. But Jack was his cousin; I was just some woman Mickey hardly knew.

I nodded. "Yes, it's been a busy morning. I had to run Collin home, and we grabbed breakfast on the way."

As I spoke, the apples started rolling off the cabinet and dropping to the floor, one by one. Bounce, thud, roll. Bounce, thud, roll. I crouched and grabbed one in each hand, but still they kept rolling away in all directions.

"Mickey, Collin is my best friend's brother, and—"

He held up a hand. "I don't need the details. There's only one thing I need, and that's for you not to fuck with Jack. He's had a really bad time of it, and you're the first smile I've seen on his face in five years."

I stood up in the middle of the green mess at my feet. "I promise, I didn't. I'm not. I won't." I spluttered in my protestations.

Before I could ask Mickey to enlighten me, he grunted and broke in.

"Make sure it stays that way."

He continued on the path I'd interrupted—his exit. The door to the garage slammed behind him, and the kitchen windows in the kitchen rattled with the force.

"Hey," I yelled after him, remembering too late that I had no idea what had happened with the dead man they'd found, or where Jack was. But Mickey was gone.

I crawled around on the kitchen floor, picking up the rest of the apples. I finished filling my bag with produce and started toward the barn. It felt crisp and clean outside. Jack had been right about the weather changes over the weekend. Last night's snow had already melted, and the temperature had soared. The sun shone directly overhead, warming me even more than the air did.

I needed that sun, I needed to overcome the cold water lapping waist-high around me again. Laura's and Mickey's reactions to me had knocked me back, and that precarious hold I had on a hope for happiness seemed to be slipping from my grasp. As the water rose, I felt vulnerable, to thoughts of losing my baby, of losing my chance at any babies, ever, of losing Valentina. A drowning Emily was no good to anyone, not to Valentina, who was still out there (I hoped) and not to Jack, who—it appeared—faced his own troubles, ones I knew little to nothing about. Which was a problem, too. He knew my problems, or most of them, and I knew none of his. So I turned my face up to the sun and soaked it in, greedy and desperate for its warmth.

It was a short walk to the horse barn. The huge doors on either end stood wide open, creating a tunnel down the center. A strong breeze bordering on a wind whisked through it. It blew much of the sweet odor of bedding, feed, and horse away, but I still got a whiff, and it comforted me some. I walked from stall to stall, stroking necks and scratching heads. I wanted to find Jarhead, to see if he remembered me, and let him have first dibs at the treats, as was the due of a champion. He was near the end on the left, as he'd been the weekend before.

Just past his stall I noticed something I hadn't last time. A half glass interior door. I walked past Jarhead to take a look. A sign on the door read Mickey Begay, Ranch Manager. Inside was a large, modern office. What I wouldn't give for an office in a barn full of horses. I admired it for a few moments, then walked back to Jarhead.

"Hi, boy." I held my hand out, palm up, to let him get a good sniff of me. He did, and he snorted and tossed his head. "Hey." I rubbed his neck, giving his muscles a quick massage. He nuzzled my arm roughly, as if asking me to take him out to play. I laughed and dug into my bag for a carrot.

"What do you think you're doing?" Jack snapped.

His voice jolted me like an electric cattle prod, and I jumped back, the bag dropping to the ground, the same apples rolling around the barn as had rolled across the kitchen floor. There was no sign of a dimple on Jack's glowering face; I ignored the spilled fruit.

I bumbled my words. "Carrot . . . Jarhead . . . looking for you . . ."

"We have him off food and water. He has colic." He had his hands on his hips, but he was looking at the horse, not me.

"I'm sorry. I didn't know. I could walk him for you, if you'd like."

"I've got him." Jack snapped a lead line onto Jarhead's halter.

"Okay." My eyes strayed to the apples, some of them still rolling. "How did it go with the police and the dead guy this morning?"

"We're done." His voice clipped the word.

"Thank you for letting me borrow your car. I took Collin home. We stopped for breakfast first and I saw Laura."

"I heard." He led Jarhead from the stall and shut it.

"Jack, whatever you heard, whatever is making you act this way toward me, I just want you to know I didn't do anything, and nothing has changed. About me, I mean about me and you. How I feel about you, about last night."

"Good to know." He started walking Jarhead away from me.

"Jack."

He kept walking.

I'd tried as hard as I could. I didn't know what else to do, so I raised my voice. "JACK ASS. Listen to me, please."

He stopped, shook his head, and looked back at me. "Too much, too soon, for both of us. Let's rewind. Start over where we were yesterday, before last night."

I stood there, slack-jawed.

Jack and Jarhead walked out of the barn into the sunshine together. I sank onto a bale of hay, apples at my feet in the half-light of the barn, by myself.

My black skirt for the Johnson housewarming cut into my waist, giving me a muffin top where I'd tucked in my red silk blouse. I'd packed without considering the lingering impact of my former pregnancy on my midsection. I'd only gained a few pounds, but apparently they were all around my middle. Luckily I'd brought a black fleecy vest, so I put it on, and checked in the bathroom mirror. It hid the bulge, but did nothing for the bags under my eyes. A crying binge in the bathtub had seemed like a good idea two hours ago. Now, not so much. Good grief, my moods these days were as up and down as the Dallas Cowboys. I did one more pass under my eyes with concealer.

"Get it together," I told the woman in the mirror, then headed downstairs.

Jack and Snowflake waited for me in the great room. He was staring out the picture window and didn't seem to notice that I'd entered. It gave me a chance to study him.

When Mickey told me that Jack was part Apache, I hadn't seen it. But with him standing in the natural light beside a wall of family photographs, I did. His Apache grandmother wasn't hard to identify, not just because she looked Apache, but because in one black and white picture she was dressed traditionally, in a flowing hide skirt, a blouse with metal work at the neckline, and beads around her neck. Her features foreshadowed those on Jack's face: the stony set of his jaw, his thick dark hair, the intensity of his expression. All of these he got from her. But where did his tawny eyes come from?

My own eyes skipped from face to face in the photographs until I found the source. A tall, blonde woman whose light eyes glowed like a cat's, holding the hand of a light-eyed young Jack on one side and the hand of a Jack-lookalike husband with dark eyes on the other, a man with Jack's same lopsided grin punctuated by the same killer dimple. My eyes traveled further, to a picture of Jack with his wife and kids on horseback— Lena on Hopper, it looked like, and his daughter on the spotted pony— and further still to his daughter holding a tiny Snowflake with a giant red bow around the puppy's neck. I stood silently and breathed until I had myself under control.

"I'm ready when you are," I said.

He faced me, and it took a few seconds for his eyes to refocus from wherever they'd been. "Let's go then." He sent Snowflake to her bed, and she snorted and huffed to show her displeasure at being left, but settled into it anyway.

In the car, I broke the long, tense silence first. "Are things all finished up with the dead guy?"

Jack turned onto the highway and the tires hummed against the pavement as pine trees rushed past us on both sides. "The police haven't been able to identify him."

"Do they know how he died?"

"He looked Mexican."

Asking Jack questions was like a game of tetherball, with only one person hitting it. Me. I tried one last time. "No tattoos, nothing at all to identify him?"

"Brown from Alamogordo PD told me they're going to run prints." He added in a mutter, "After he made himself at home in my living room and drank a pot of my coffee."

I wanted to scream, "Give a straight answer to just one goddamned question, Jack Ass," but it wouldn't do any good. Plus, I'd go to Hell for taking the Lord's name in vain. If Jack was trying to irritate me into being happy that he'd dumped me before we'd ever gotten started, his non-answers were a good way to do it.

I stared out the window for a while until I had calmed down. Without turning back to Jack, I said, "He's like a ghost."

"He's like an illegal."

How had I lived so isolated from the desperate world of undocumented immigrants for so long? I'd known that people of Mexican heritage came from Mexico, that there were immigration laws and that employers had to follow them. I watched the news and the vitriolic debate on the issue. I heard my mother's complaints about it from time to time. Yet, somehow, it had existed separate and apart from my real life. I hadn't known the people that risked their lives to get here. I hadn't imagined what was worse than living here, poor, on the fringes. I'd never bothered to think past how awful I believed it was to be the teenage daughter of a sad, penniless mother and a runaway cowboy.

We drove in silence, and my thoughts focused not on the irritatingly sexy man beside me, but on the dead man with no identity and maybe no country, about Sofia and what she had done—why she might have done it—and Valentina alone, or worse. It put my troubles in perspective. I had lost a baby that was never born and a percentage of a chance of a future baby that God might never have intended for me anyway. Sofia and Valentina were together for six years, and had lost each other. Valentina hadn't just lost her mama—she was without a father, too. What would happen if no one found her? Would she die? Would she be sold by Harvey —or whoever had her—to the highest bidder? Or simply used up by whoever was around? Hell, what would happen if she *was* found? She could be sent back to Mexico where she didn't know a soul—something her mother had gambled and lost her own life to prevent.

I chuffed and put my hand to my mouth. Jack glanced at me, then back at the road. My mind zeroed in on those huge brown eyes and pigtails, the threadbare jammies with pink pills of fabric and a giant Barbie smile across a tummy. The blue-shirted doll with the lace shawl, just one more thing the girl had lost. It was time for me to quit feeling sorry for me. I was letting myself get jammed up with an emotionally unavailable man that I didn't need, risking a job I did, and focusing on things that I couldn't have, while forgetting about what was real and right in front of me. Suddenly, I felt the scratch of flint deep inside, once, twice, three times, and then a flame that spread like wildfire.

I didn't know how, but I knew that I had to find her, that we were each other's second chance. Here I was giving up on myself, like some nag ready for the glue factory when Valentina needed me. I had more than enough clues pointing me to information in southern New Mexico, and I was here. I would figure out what those clues meant, one way or the other.

A sick feeling came over me, and I realized I had to speak to Jack.

"I forgot to tell you something important," I said.

His jaw flexed. "What?"

"When I was looking for information about Sofia, and I found Valentina, only I didn't know it, and then she was taken by the bald guy, there was something I learned about the kidnapper from Victoria, something I forgot to tell you because we were cut short by Melinda telling us Sofia had died."

He shot a glance at me. "Go on."

I searched my handbag for paper and a pen. No paper, but I found a pen, so I drew the ΣSL on my hand.

"He had a tattoo on the inside of his upper arm. His left arm. Like this one." I held my hand out beside the steering wheel. "Victoria saw it. Harvey has one. Last night Tamara told me it stands for East Side Lobos in Las Cruces. Have you seen it before?"

He turned his eyes to it, and they widened. He looked back at the road, then again at my hand. "Yes. Yesterday. On Spike Howard's autopsy photos."

TWENTY-FOUR

"You look beautiful, as always." Paul kissed my hand and then tugged me through the front door into a hug. His sheer size made me feel Lilliputian. "And how's my attorney?" He released me and clasped Jack's hand in a bro shake to his chest, clapping him on the back at the same time. "Can't tell you how glad I am to have the two of you here. The bar's out on the back patio." He winked. "A little hair of the dog."

"Thanks, Paul," I said.

I moved far enough away to keep him out of my personal space. His effusive greeting was just too familiar for me, especially after the weird last twenty-four hours.

Galvanized by the newly rekindled fire to find Valentina, I decided I was done feeling guilty. I saw Jack's stern jaw from the corner of my eye. He looked like a man who'd eaten a mess of bad eggs. Well, good. He deserved to feel bad. He'd overreacted and shut me out when I'd tried to explain. I ignored him and turned for the bar.

The entry hall emptied into a room with an amazing ceiling that pulled my eyes upward, and I marveled at the octagonal cupola lined with rafters across intricate tongue-in-groove boarding. Inset windows alternated levels on each of the cupola's sides. Below it was a sitting area of oversized leather and cowhide couches and armchairs. An enormous rug in caramel brown and white spots with darker brown sections every few feet anchored the furniture. It was one of the most uniquely beautiful floor coverings I had ever seen. The chandelier of two metal hoops, one suspended three feet above and within the circumference of the other, hung from fifteen-foot chains. An immense stone fireplace dominated one wall and its opposite wall opened onto a bustling kitchen. Huge wood-framed glass doors and windows covered the back wall and opened onto a patio. The doors were propped open, and a brisk breeze coursed through the space carrying the dry smell of pine and sage.

I wanted to find a quiet place where Jack and I could continue our conversation about Spike's tattoo. I walked ahead of Jack through the room toward the back patio, where a few on-time guests like us milled about. When I got outside, I stopped, mesmerized by the view. Paul's backyard ended in a high, rock-faced hillside with trees hugging the edge of its summit, their coniferous branches bouncing and swaying in the wind. It was pure, rugged drama, and I stared at it for long seconds before I turned back to Jack, but he'd disappeared.

I started to look for him, but was interrupted by a teenage boy.

"Drink, ma'am?"

A tattoo of a snake wound around his neck, but his real attention grabber was a nose ring. Where I came from, you used those things to clip a lead to an animal that needed a little extra motivation to behave. And the tattoo? I wanted to tell him that he didn't need to brand himself like a steer, but I held my tongue.

I almost ordered wine, but last night had left me tired and dehydrated, which more alcohol would only make worse. "Sparkling water with lime, please."

"No problem."

Round metal tables and chairs dotted the patio with centerpieces of stone and cactus weighting down each table. Movement to my right caught my eye, and I saw Paul's daughter Stella leaning against the far back edge of the house smoking a cigarette. She looked angry, and incredibly alone.

"Thanks for your note," a woman's voice said, from my left.

I followed the voice and saw Jack's secretary, Judith. With makeup on, she was strikingly beautiful. Jack had told me all of his employees were invited, and I'd hoped she'd be here, that I'd get another chance with her.

"Hi, Judith," I said. "Isn't this house amazing?"

"Yes. Big. And very expensive," she said. "Lots of people from the reservation have worked on it."

Something about Judith whispered to me of ancient things, of traditions that lived on in more than photographs. She looked timeless in turquoise and silver dangling earrings and a matching neck cuff that looked as old as the land around us. Her low, thick ponytail was fastened with a large clip, and it, too, was silver, with round pieces of turquoise set within etched scrolls.

"Did you know Paul before he became a client?" I asked her.

"No, he's not from around here—the Mescalero reservation, I mean, or Tularosa. But my brother worked construction here. At this house."

"Oh really? What does your brother do?"

"He's an electrician."

The teenage cocktail waiter returned with my drink. "Here you go, one club soda with lime. And for you, ma'am?"

My phone chimed. While Judith gave her order, I checked the text. Wallace, in a group text to Nadine and me: *Nadine and I visited Harvey today.*

I typed a quick reply: *Any sign of Valentina?*

Wallace: *No. He swears he's never met Sofia or her, and that he lost track of Spike when they got out of prison.*

Me: *Impossible. He was seen running away from the hotel the night Sofia shot Spike.*

Harvey's denial made me want to dig deeper with Wallace. What did you ask him? What did you see? How did he explain that tattoo? But I reminded myself that I could count on Wallace and Nadine to handle it. I had to.

Wallace: *We'll take another pass at him.*

Me: *Thank you, guys.*

I needed to stay off the phone at a work function. I slipped it in my pocket and returned my attention to Judith, who stood gazing up at the rock face. Without turning toward me, she started talking again.

"I used to come out here with my friends when I was a girl," she said. "There were fences, but we didn't care." The wind blew a wisp of hair from her clip and it fluttered to the side of her sharp cheekbones. She pointed to the top of the rocks. "When I first came out here, we convinced ourselves we'd seen Mountain Spirits dancing up there. Who knows, maybe we did."

She tucked the hair behind her ear. The sun reflected off her earring. "It became our place. We started to dance when we came here, like them, facing the Sacred Mountain." She pointed north to the white-capped Sierra Blanca Peak in the distance. She turned to me and smiled for the first time since I'd met her, then returned her gaze to the rocks.

You know of the Mountain Spirit dancers?" Judith asked.

"Yes. Mickey told me about them," I said.

She nodded. "I was always the clown, painting myself white, wearing the nose and the ears. I liked scaring the little ones."

How to say this nicely? "I'll bet you were good at it."

"I was."

"I was a clown, too. A rodeo clown."

As I looked at her profile, images ran through my head, of my recent dreams of the Clown Dancer, and of something else. A crude drawing in Crayola, a man in a skirt, an oversized crown of sticks on his head, his skin crayoned white. Animal ears and nose. Was Valentina's drawing of the Mountain Spirit Dancer's clown? If she had come to the U.S. through southern New Mexico, it could be. That brought up interesting possibilities. But maybe I was just projecting my thoughts onto her picture.

"We have that in common." She sighed. "I worked for Jack when he was with the DA in Las Cruces, did you know that?"

"I didn't."

"Yeah. I moved to the city when I was younger, but I always wanted to come back here."

"I can see why. It's magical, spectacular."

"That day when the bomb went off, I was there. Before it happened, I saw the Dancers, I saw the Clown. They were in front of the building, by the flags."

She'd lost me, lost me in a way so profound I didn't know how to ask what she was talking about. She wasn't making sense. Was she crazy, or was I missing something? It felt important, game-changing even, so I didn't dare interrupt.

"The Clown took the Dancers to the parking lot, to Jack's car," Judith said. "And I followed them. Then he cried, the Clown did. I didn't know what he meant, so I looked around, to ask someone else, but I was the only one there."

I held my breath, literally. Judith's eyes had teared up, and I didn't think it was from the wind. I stayed silent.

"Nobody else saw them. And later, when it happened, I knew they had been real, and what the Clown had been trying to tell me."

She turned to me again, tears now streaming down her face. "Being here, it forces me to remember. I still feel guilty—I didn't understand what the Clown meant, and I should have. I could have saved Mrs. Holden and the children from the bomb. I could have kept them out of Jack's car. They would be alive today."

A chill ran through me, and my mouth hung open uselessly. Jack's wife hadn't left him and taken the kids. They were dead. *Dead.* Judith looked into my eyes, and I realized that she needed me to respond.

"I'm so sorry," I said.

She backed away. "Please tell Jack I was here," she said. "I just don't think I can stay. Because of the memories."

In the wake of Judith's revelations, I couldn't stay either. My mind reeled, sifting through her words for the facts. A car bomb at the court-house? Jack's wife and kids *dead*? It was so much worse than anything I'd imagined about Jack's past. Losing your whole family to a car bomb—one I had to assume was meant for him since it was in his car at his workplace —how did you ever recover from that? I choked on a sob and took off from the patio toward some outbuildings in the distance. I needed a place to hide, a place to think, a place to mourn Jack's family. My rapid walk morphed into a slow, blind jog.

Loss was everywhere. My loss. Sofia's. Valentina's. And now Jack's loss —his loss swallowing mine up whole in its immensity. Mickey had mentioned Jack not smiling for five years. I wondered if Jack fled to Amar-illo after the bomb, had lived in his office shrine for this whole time, hiding from everything but his memories, only for me to come along and defile his sanctuary. My jog sped into a blind run, until I planted my booted foot on a rock, stumbled, and went down on my hands and knees.

"Oomph."

I lifted my palms. Dirt and rocks and blood. I rose and lifted my skirt. More rocks, dirt, and blood. There was a gaping hole in my black stockings on my right knee, but my long, black skirt would cover it. I brushed off my knees and let go of the fabric. Hair fell around my face, and I probed for the bobby pins that held my back-teased strands in place. I pulled one out and re-secured it. That would have to do. The fall had sobered me a little, and I started walking again, aimless but still generally toward the three green metal buildings now only a hundred feet away.

When I reached them, I walked to the back of the first one, out of sight of Paul's party. I crouched with my back against it. *Breathe. You can't make sense of this unless you breathe, and think.* Maybe it was time to ask for help, too. Like from the Big Guy. But I was really rusty. Sure, I muttered pithy little prayers now and then, but when was the last time I'd truly meant it? I didn't really need to ask myself that, though. I knew exactly when. My senior year at Tech. When Christmas and my birthday passed without hearing from my father, I quit religion cold turkey. In retrospect, I could admit that God probably wasn't the one to blame, but it was easier at the time. In the ensuing years, my problem was more organized religion than Him, but the result was the same either way.

Ever since then—and especially lately—I'd done a little too much of the *why me* and the *not fair* instead of just being thankful for what I did have. I probably didn't deserve to ask for help now, but I was going to give it my best shot anyway. I pressed my hands together and closed my eyes, but all that came out of me was *why me, why this, why anyone, you have to make it better.* I tried again, softly, under my breath.

"God, I don't understand all this."

Long moments passed, silent except for my deliberate breaths. In. Out. In. Out. The rhythm hypnotized me, and underneath my closed lids, my eyes fluttered. Just as I faded out, I realized with a sudden clarity, a certainty, that things in my life were as they should be, that I was where I should be. I closed my eyes again.

"Thank you for bringing me home and to a new career and new friends, and a chance to help make a difference in things that really matter. And I promise I am going to find a church, just not that Believers one or any church that Melinda Stafford would consider attending. Amen."

Men's voices interrupted me, close and moving my way. I looked harder at the outside of the building where I'd taken refuge. It appeared to be a warehouse of sorts. To my right was a huge roll-up door, open about halfway. The voices came from inside the building. Instinct took over; I stood and crept to the edge of the door, craning to hear.

A deep voice spoke. "Mr. Johnson said the police don't have a clue that's Alejandro they found dead at Wrong Turn Ranch. And I haven't heard any talk about the stupid bastard taking his silver mine story to the Apaches. You may have dodged a bullet, this time. But we need to make an example out of him to the others, because this can't ever happen again. Or next time we'll be making an example of you."

A higher, thinner voice answered. "Alejandro was our only problem. The rest of 'em are scared shitless. Once they see we got the girl back—and what we do to the little brat—they'll be back down in that mine diggin' Apache silver for all they're worth—with their mouths shut."

Their words had frozen me in place, once again forcing me to decipher the truth from half the story. While I didn't have enough to get the full picture, I got the gist. Making examples out of people, problems with a terrorized labor force, silver belonging to the Apaches, a recovered little girl, them knowing who the dead guy was at Jack's place: trouble that all added up to bad, bad stuff here on Paul's ranch.

I had to get out of there, and I had to get to Jack. I gathered my skirt in one hand and placed my feet one in front of the other gently and carefully, but quickly. As I crested the side of the building back toward the house, I broke into a run. An arm snaked out and grabbed mine, jerking me to a stop.

"Whoa, whoa, whoa now," the higher-pitched man said.

I yelped and clawed at the hand cuffed around my arm, at the fingers biting into my flesh. I couldn't get the hand to budge, so I turned to face the body at the end of the arm.

Two white men stood beside an open side entrance that I hadn't noticed on my blind flight out here. They both grinned, but not in a friendly way. The man holding my arm was tall and thin, with dusty clothes and limp hair that bore the imprint of a hat brim.

The other man—the man with the deeper voice—was thicker and paler and he had a shaved head. He wore pressed jeans and a checkered shirt and spoke first. "Sorry, miss. You scared us. We aren't used to strangers out here where they aren't invited. You here for the party?"

I swallowed hard and nodded. "Yes."

Tall guy loosened his grip on me some but didn't let go.

"Didn't you see the 'no trespassing' signs?" He pointed back toward the house. A metal pole with a rectangular sign jutted up from the ground. It did say No Trespassing in black letters against a white background.

My heart galloped in my ears. I struggled for composure, for the bravado that had always sustained me, like when I faced down a drunken two-hundred-pound Neanderthal from the Tarleton rodeo team who had mistaken my decision not to knee him in the balls the first time he'd groped me as weakness. He didn't get a third chance.

I straightened my shoulders. "No, I didn't. I'm so sorry. I was looking for a private place to make a call." I held up my phone.

Tall guy snatched it from me. "Let's see." After a few swipes and taps, he said, "Huh. Nothing here."

I had to convince them I was harmless. "I know. I've got man troubles. I got out here and lost my nerve." I lifted my shoulders in a "silly little me" gesture.

"What's your name?" tall guy asked.

"Emily. I'm a friend of Paul's."

"Ah, shit, Tanner, she's that nosey Texas woman he told us about. The one that works for the lawyer."

Tanner, the thicker, paler man, narrowed his eyes.

I forced out a hollow laugh. "That's me! See, I'm his friend. I'm sorry I came out here, guys, really. I won't do it again."

Inside, my heart twisted. Paul was dirty, and he was talking about me to his henchman—and not in a nice way.

Tanner thwacked my phone against his palm a couple of times. And then I heard a child's scream, high-pitched, soul wrenching. My face reacted before I could steel my features, and I knew how I looked. Scared. Horrified. Concerned.

Dangerous.

"Fuck," Tanner said.

He ripped off his snap front shirt, revealing a plain white T underneath it. He whipped the shirt over my mouth, muffling me, as he reached into his pocket and pulled something oblong out and jammed a sharp point at one end of it into my arm, all in a series of deft motions.

"Whaaa—"

I felt myself crumpling to the ground, but not before my eyes locked on Tanner's left arm. At his tattoo.

"East Side . . ." I whispered. But before I finished my thought, the world went black.

TWENTY-FIVE

I opened my eyes but saw nothing. The smell of dust filled my nose. My eyes adjusted to the darkness, but still I could barely see. Everything looked so indistinct. I shook my head, trying to fix my vision, but all it did was make me nauseous and create blurry after-images of the things I couldn't make out anyway. Where was I?

"Lady?"

A little girl's voice, clear and close. I turned my face toward the sound and saw a darker blob near what seemed to be the floor.

"Yes, hello."

"You okay?"

I tried to reach toward her, but couldn't move my hands. I pulled harder and realized they were fastened together with something rough. "I'm okay, but I can't see you very well. And I'm tied up." I closed my eyes again.

"I see you, but the mans tie my hands. When I first here, I no can see. The bad man stick me. It make me sleepy and sick."

Her voice was heavily accented with the sounds of Mexican Spanish.

"Yeah, me, too."

I closed my eyes for a moment and focused on calming down. I needed to be in the moment, be aware. To think things through. Like, how does a blind idiot who's gotten herself knocked out for the second time in a week free herself and a little girl out of hand bindings? I shifted my feet and groaned. And foot bindings.

"Sweetie? Are you okay?" I asked.

"Yes." She stopped speaking then said, "I'm scared."

"Me, too, but that's okay. My name is Emily. What's yours?"

There was a long pause.

"Sweetie, are you there?"

"I call myself Betsy."

Her English grammar came out as a literal translation of the way it would be said in Spanish. How formal, how cute, how painfully sincere. My heart leaned toward her and I wished I could hug her. Heck, I wished she could hug me.

"Betsy. Okay, well I'm starting to feel a little bit better, and I'm going to need your help getting us out of here. Can you help me?"

"I try. How?"

"I'm figuring that out right now. Are your feet tied up?"

"Yes."

"Can you roll over to me long ways?"

"Roll like log?"

"Exactly, like a log."

"I can!"

I heard the sound of a little body rolling across the floor to me, and I smiled, despite our circumstances. The kid was charming. I opened my eyes again and realized my vision was clearing. I saw her small body and long black hair.

"I'm here!"

"Very good. I want to untie your hands. Can you roll behind me and put your hands against mine, so I can feel the knot in the rope they tied yours with?"

"I try."

Her bright little voice sounded so can-do. I smiled. She pushed the rope around her wrists into my hands.

My fingers worked it as I talked to her. "So, Betsy, tell me about how you got here and where you're from."

I found the end of the tough twine and worked my fingers to the knot. I needed to loosen the piece across the top into a loop, then push the stiff twine back through.

"From Mexico with Mama and Papa. We hide in a truck with chickens and lizards."

The twine was so tight that I couldn't get it to budge, and I had no leverage. I pushed and pushed and was finally able to wedge my thumbnail between the strands. I wiggled my thumb back and forth, up and down, back and forth, up and down. The twine strands gripped each other as if with pinchers. Was it loosening? I couldn't tell. Back and forth, up and down. Finally, I felt the tiniest of gives and gave a little gasp.

"What?"

"Hold really still. I think I'm getting it."

Back and forth, up and down. Another tiny slip. Back and forth, up and down.

"How you get here?"

"By being really dumb."

Back and forth, up and down. I now had the whole tip of my thumb in the loop, thank God, because I couldn't keep doing this much longer. My thumbnail was about to come off. I put my wrist into the movement as I answered her.

Now I worked the end of the twine through my hard-won loop. I felt the knot. At least two more. I ignored the pain in my thumbnail and started wedging my nail in again.

"You pretty, Miss."

I grunted. "Thank you, sweetie. I can't wait to see you once we are both untied. My eyes have started working again."

And were adjusting to the dark of the room, lit only by waning light from two high windows, too high, I saw, for me to reach.

Five minutes later I got my thumb tip through, and gritted my teeth in agony. I didn't want to see my poor thumb. I could feel the shredded skin on either side of my nail with my forefinger. It felt like hamburger. After another three minutes, I had one loop left to go. I switched to my left hand. It was slower, but at least I had the hang of it.

"Done."

"You did it!" Betsy said. I heard rustling behind me. "My hands hurt."

"I'll bet they do. Can you undo mine now, please?" Urgency strained my voice. The process had taken far longer than I'd hoped, and now that I could see the door, I expected it to burst open any moment with Tanner and Skinny Guy. All this would be for nothing.

I felt her fingers go to work. "Too tight. I can't."

Of course. Her little fingers weren't as strong as mine. I scanned the empty room, looking for some kind of tool. But it was just us, four walls, and a concrete floor. I frowned, concentrating as I took inventory, then I smiled. I did have something. Saved by my own vanity and how oblivious men are to all it takes to make a woman a goddess.

"Reach up into my hair and pull out one of my bobby pins. You can slide one into the knot to help you loosen it."

"Bobby pins?"

"Hair pins. Pins in my hair."

Small hands picked through my hair. Even in these circumstances, it was a lovely feeling. I felt a pin pull free.

"Got it."

"Great. See if you can stick the whole thing between the edges of the top knot."

She made little grunts and I felt pressure, this way and that. "I did it! I got it!"

"Good girl. Okay, wiggle it and move it around to make the knot looser. You can keep doing it until it's big enough to pull open."

More pressure. I listened for footsteps outside our door, my mouth dry as wood shavings. The pressure on my wrists changed and I felt grating as one strand of twine slid its way out of the first knot.

"I do it again."

"You're awesome. Thank you." The tension of listening was making it hard to breath. Faster, I prayed. Faster.

"One more."

Dear Heavenly Father, thank you for bringing Betsy and me together. Help me to help her. Amen.

The rough twine abraded my wrist as Betsy pulled it off altogether.

"You did it! Now I'm going to have to give you a big hug."

I wheeled around and saw for the first time the girl I'd been working with and talking to. Pink Barbie pj's, big black eyes, and long black hair. One of the three little girls I had watched giggle on a couch in Amarillo, the one who had shown me her favorite doll, a child whose picture Victoria sent me and I kept on my phone. Valentina Perez, who it seemed was calling herself Betsy. My heart roared.

She threw her arms around me. "You the lady who knows my mommy, right?"

There was no time for questions now. I hugged her tightly for a brief second, my emotions raw and swollen, then let her go. "I am, and I've been looking for you. I'm so glad to see you! Now, we need to hurry, so let's untie our own feet."

I grabbed one of my bobby pins to help me with the knots this time, because, as I had suspected, my thumb was pulp. I made fast work of them.

Valentina aka Betsy had made good progress on her own knots.

"Want me to finish that?"

She nodded and I quickly freed her legs.

"Okay, now, stay close behind me, and don't make a sound."

I palmed the bobby pins and dropped them in my skirt pocket for later, just in case. We stood and faced the door. I held my breath as I tried the handle. Locked. Time for the bobby pin after all? I eyed the door handle but there was no lock in it. I looked closely at the jamb and just made out the dark presence of a thrown deadbolt, from the other side. No bobby pin was going to solve this problem. I stood staring, thinking, despairing, when the lock snapped back and the handle turned. I clapped one hand over my mouth to stifle my scream and threw the other in front of Betsy as the door opened slowly toward us.

A ghostly figure stood in the doorway, light behind it, a finger across its lips. Male or female, I couldn't tell, but it was slight and tall for a woman or short for a man, with some kind of enormous thing on its head. Its body was clad in a white mesh suit, with a black skirt nearly to the top of knee-high buckskin moccasins. Its face was ghostly white with an animal hide mask over the nose. The drawing, I realized. It was like the figure from Valentina's—or Betsy's—crayon drawing in the apartment back in Amarillo.

Behind me, Betsy clung to my skirt, her head against my hip. My arm slipped around her shoulders like I'd been protecting her all her life.

"It's okay," Betsy said. She stepped around me. "She's my friend."

The figure nodded. It pointed down the hall and whispered in a low voice, "Go, quickly, out and left to the stable. There's a horse ready for you there."

"Thank you," I whispered.

"My backpack?" Betsy asked.

"Do you know where it is?"

She shook her head.

"We'll look for it later. Now, we have to go."

Betsy ran to the figure and hugged it hard. "Bye, friend."

I snatched her hand before she'd removed her arms from the apparition. "Let's run."

But as I stood close to the figure, I suddenly realized I knew her, and as our eyes met she knew it, too. Stella. Paul's daughter. I didn't have time to analyze the hows and whys. I nodded at her, and we ran.

I pulled Betsy behind me so hard that she was practically aloft. I tried to run silently in my high-heeled cowboy boots on the concrete floor, but they clomped alarmingly. I fought through the cobwebs in my brain, trying to shake off the lethargy of Tanner's drug. It felt like I'd spent days as a captive in that room, but I realized only hours had passed. Lights still twinkled from the back patio of Paul's house, and party sounds floated toward us .We raced through the dark out of the office building and to our left.

"Hey! Stop right there!" a deep male voice yelled.

It sounded like Tanner, but I wasn't turning around to verify. My boots were so loud I couldn't hear his steps, but he had to be closing in on us. I couldn't go faster than Betsy was able. Suddenly, the stable loomed ahead, close, its opening a black cutout in green metal sides. We burst in, and a startled nicker to my right stopped me short. A saddled horse. I pulled the reins from a hitching post and jumped on. I held out my hand to Betsy.

"I'm scared," she cried.

"I've got you," I said. "I promise."

She grasped my hand and I pulled her up with strength I didn't know I had. The horse snorted and hopped as Betsy's small body landed belly first across the saddle horn in front of me. She cried out, and I pulled her upright and slung her leg across the horse. A figure grew larger in front of the backlights from the ranch house. I would have to rush him with the horse, but I knew he'd go for help after we got away. I scanned the barn frantically for a club or a whip or, or, or . . . but all I saw was a lasso hanging from a peg on the wall. Well, it would have to do. I wheeled the horse, grabbed the rope, wrapped its end around the saddle horn feverishly, whacking poor Betsy over and over in the process, but the brave little girl didn't make a sound. I gave the horse a sharp kick.

"Yah!"

The horse bolted from the barn, straight at Tanner. I held onto the reins and Betsy with my left arm and swung a loop around and around over my head with my right. I guided the horse with knee pressure and my body weight as I leaned to the left, and Tanner scrambled away from us. The horse responded, moving in unison with me. I could thank God later for a well-trained quarter horse, but for now we were nearly upon Tanner. He ducked, reaching for his hip.

Gun.

I let my loop fly, the hiss of rope gliding off my fingers. In slow motion, it sailed through the dark and over the unsuspecting Tanner. I gave it a jerk as it settled over him, and wrapped the lasso around the saddle horn.

"Back, back," I ordered, throwing my weight against the back of the saddle, pulling firmly with the reins.

The horse all but sat on its rump as it stopped, then began backing quickly. Tanner hit the dirt, his arms immobilized. He grunted, loudly, then cussed me at the top of his lungs as the horse dragged him through the dust and gravel.

"Betsy, sit here, and hold on to this horn. I have to tie him up so he won't follow us."

I could see the huge round whites of her eyes. She nodded, speechless. I ripped the tie-down rope from where it was fastened. Later, I'd have to thank God for well-outfitted tack. I ran to Tanner, who was still slowly being dragged by my new favorite horse.

"You bitch," he said.

I lashed his feet together, then dragged them up behind his rump and caught his hands in the same tie-down, rendering him helpless. When I'd finished, I jumped up and threw both hands in the air automatically, to signal I was done, but there was no official dropping the flag and timing my efforts, and this was no rodeo. I pulled my arms down and pretended I hadn't just done that.

I looked down at Tanner. "Looks like you're the bitch to me."

I searched the ground behind him for the gun I'd seen him draw. I caught a glint of light ten yards back. I trotted out and grabbed the six-shot pistol. 357 Magnum. I checked that the safety was on and then stuck it in the tight waistband of my skirt. I took the horse by the bridle and guided him as he dragged Tanner into the barn. That was better, but still, the man could squeal for help. I needed something to use to gag him. I took off a boot and hooked two fingers through the tear in the knee of my tights and ripped until I had the whole lower section off. I jammed my foot back into the boot then leaned over and pinched Tanner's nose shut until he had to open his mouth to breathe, and I shoved my stocking in, moving fast to avoid his teeth. Then I unfastened the lasso from the saddle horn, tied it to a post, and pulled the barn door shut as I led the horse out with Betsy astride him.

I remounted behind Betsy and gave her a squeeze. "Let's get out of here."

TWENTY-SIX

It was getting out of there that presented the next problem. I couldn't go barging in on Paul's house party, since I no longer had any idea who was friend or foe. Except for Judith, who had long since left, and Jack, who might not be there anymore, either. I didn't have my phone so I couldn't call them. A really hideous possibility occurred to me: Paul knew about the Collin fiasco last night. Who was I kidding? He probably knew about this morning, too. All Paul had to do was tell Jack I'd left with Collin. When I didn't show up at Wrong Turn Ranch, Jack wouldn't worry about me. He'd make the natural assumption. *Spit.*

Well, I knew the way home, and I had a good horse and a gun that I wasn't afraid to use, so I'd just ride. The only problem with this plan was that when Tanner was discovered where I'd left him hog-tied and gagged, he'd tell them I'd fled via horseback, and they wouldn't have any trouble guessing which way I'd gone. Okay, so that meant I'd have to move quickly, and maybe even be a little bit sneakily.

I leaned down toward Betsy's ear and whispered, "You ready to go real fast?"

Betsy nodded, her silky hair rubbing under my chin. "What's the horse's name?"

"I don't know. Why don't you give him a name?"

Again the silky caress of her nod. "Thunder."

"Yah, Thunder," I shouted into the night as I smacked him lightly on his shoulder with the reins.

He responded by leaping forward in a quarter-mile sprint that would have earned Jarhead's approval, then settled into a ground-eating gallop. I steered us wide of the house, down the dark side of the entrance, the only way I knew to get off of Paul's land.

True to his name, our mount's hooves thundered on the ground beside the road. I caught sight of the highway ahead, but as we neared it, headlights swept across the pasture in front of us to our left. It was a vehicle, behind us, and it would catch us in its beams when the curves of the road aligned in its favor. There was nowhere to hide.

"Yah, Thunder, yah."

"Yah, Thunder," Betsy echoed.

The horse ran faster, panting but eager and fleet. The pavement ahead would be slick and treacherous under his hooves. I had to pull him up and let him trot across, but not too soon. I tried to judge the distance in the dark as the headlights swept across our backs and to our right. If they'd seen us, we were goners no matter what I did. We had almost reached the highway, and I pulled Thunder up short. He whinnied, but obeyed, and I urged him into a trot to cross the road at an angle away from Jack's place, trying to get far enough east that a vehicle turning toward Wrong Turn Ranch wouldn't see us. When we reached the grass on the other side of the highway, I guided Thunder to the right and gave him his head. He galloped easily. I turned back to look at the vehicle exiting Paul's ranch. Thunder's tail flew high behind him. *Turn left*, I willed the car. *Turn left.*

And it did. As soon as its taillights disappeared, I slowed Thunder and wheeled him back around.

"Where we go?" Betsy asked.

"To my friend Jack's house."

"How far?"

"A little far. We're looking for a gate so we can turn off this road onto his ranch. Can you help me look for a place on the fence where two posts are close together?"

She pointed ahead of us. "There?"

Her young eyes were far better in the dark than mine, and I strained to see two posts close together. I found them; she was right.

"Yes, good job. You hold onto the saddle horn and stay on Thunder while I open the gate."

Again, we were exposed to any vehicles leaving Paul's ranch. I hopped down and pulled on the tight wire with all my might. My arms shook, but I was able to get it just clear enough that I could slip the top loop off and pull the post out of the bottom loop. I threw the gate aside and led Betsy and Thunder through. I hated to take the time to close the gate behind us but, if I left it open, it would be an easy clue for anyone following us.

I pushed us faster again now, following the eastern fence line to the north, straight away from Paul's ranch and the highway traffic. I kept a hand on the saddle horn with Betsy's, fearful that Thunder would lodge his hoof in a prairie dog hole in the dark, but he ran on at a three-quarters pace without faltering.

Betsy shouted, "Fence."

Again, she was right. The quarter moon gave her just enough light to be our eyes. *Another thing to be thankful for*, I noted. We cut left along the fence and soon came upon a west-facing gate. I stopped, wavering. As much as I wanted to cut farther north, we could go west here, then north at our next opportunity. I wavered, then chose. West and north it would be. We hurried through and resumed our journey northward along the eastern fence. I slowed Thunder to a lope and his breathing settled with it. He nickered. His hooves drummed the ground rhythmically. We spooked some horses as we ran past their sleeping figures, and they jumped to their feet, snorts and whinnies following us. Betsy's head began to sag against my arm until she slumped in a dead weight. With my adrenaline ebbing, drowsiness sank over me, too. It wasn't so long ago I'd been unconscious and drugged. I shook my head vigorously. I had to stay alert.

As I rode I started thinking through all I'd learned and what might lie ahead. Assuming Paul and his buddies were looking for me, they'd go to Jack's. They could be there now, passing the mescal bottle around, waiting for me. That meant I needed to come from the direction opposite the entrance—north to south—and find a phone to call Jack from, to let him know what was up.

I came upon a north-facing gate. "Wake up, sleeping beauty," I said to Betsy.

She rubbed her eyes and grabbed the saddle horn. I opened the gate and let us through. We rode north again. I tried to think of where I could find a phone. I pictured the barn and fixed my mind's eye on the closed door at the end of the stalls. It had a sign on it. Mickey Begay, Ranch Manager. A business office. It had to have a phone, or a fax, or a computer. Well, it didn't *have* to. Everyone carried cell phones these days. But it might.

Thunder must have sensed the ranch headquarters with all its stabled horses before I did because he tossed his head and sped up again. A few minutes later, I saw the lights and the dark shadows of the Wrong Turn Ranch buildings on my left.

I bobbed my head. "Heck yeah."

We'd managed to end up on the north side, in the dark and everything. I patted Thunder's flank. He was sweaty and warm and magnificent. A final gate was just ahead— an iron one with a latch, which was far easier for me. I roused Betsy for the last time and told her our plan, then pointed Thunder toward the stock tank for some long overdue sips of water.

Once we were through the gate, I held Thunder to a walk and we picked our way to the back entrance to the barn. I hopped down, and this time I set Betsy on the ground beside me. "Hold Thunder's reins for me, okay?"

"Okay."

There were two doors: the big one to the center aisle between the stalls, and a small one into a room with a window. The one with the window was the office. I pulled at that door, but it didn't budge. Locked. I had tools though: bobby pins and a gun. The gun was too loud and too much tool for the job, so I pulled out the bobby pin and set to work. The lock didn't yield.

I put the bobby pin away. Guns were good for more than shooting bullets. I pulled it from my waistband and held it by its barrel. I gave the windowpane nearest the door a thwack with the butt of the handle. The glass emitted a high-pitched crack as it splintered inward. I stuck my hand through and tried to reach the doorknob. It was too far away, and the opening was too small for me to crawl through.

But I had one more tool at my disposal. A slim little girl. "Betsy, I'm going to help you crawl through that window, okay? When you get inside, you need to unlock the door. But don't turn on the light."

She nodded, her eyes silver dollars.

I used the gun handle to whack out the rest of the glass, the bits clinging to the window frame. Betsy gave me Thunder's reins, and I dropped them, securing them under my boot. I picked her up and boosted her through the window, shaking with strain as I held her in the center, away from any shards I might have missed.

"Is there somewhere for you to land? Just with your shoes, though. I don't want you to cut your hands."

"Yeah. A table."

I grunted as she swung her legs down, then her weight eased off of me as she stood up. I heard her knocking over God knew what as she climbed down. I stuck my face in after her.

"The door is right there." I pointed to my right.

She turned the knob and it stopped.

"Okay, is there a button you can turn in the door knob? Or is there a latch you can turn above it?"

She peered close. "In the knob." She twisted something.

"Okay, try the door again."

She did, and smiled so brightly it nearly lit up the darkness. The door swung open.

"Great job! Now, can you hold Thunder?"

While she held the horse, I went in the office. On the far side was the open door to the interior of the barn, and on the adjacent wall, a desk. I searched the small room for a phone. Buried under Friday's newspaper on the desk, I found one. I picked it up. It had a dial tone, thank goodness, but I realized I had no idea what Jack's number was. I had his cell phone number programmed into mine, but Tanner and his skinny sidekick had taken that hours ago. I lifted the phone's base and looked for speed dial buttons. Nothing. But there was one that held promise: Redial. I pushed it and held the receiver to my ear.

"Hello?" It was Jack.

I hadn't expected to cry, but a sob broke from my throat.

"Mickey? Is that you?"

"No, Jack, it's Emily, but don't say my name. Say, hey, okay, Mickey."

There was a pause. "Hey, okay, Mickey."

"I'm in the barn office. Some of Paul's men drugged me and locked me in one of their outbuildings, with a little girl. Jack, it's Valentina. I have her. We escaped, and I have so much to tell you, later. But I was scared that they would be there with you."

"Yeah, that's great, but you're right about that," Jack said.

"I can't let them find us. I'm going to take Valentina to the hangar and we'll hide there until you can come for us." I heard voices in the background, voices I recognized. Paul. Tanner. The tall, skinny guy. My hands trembled around the receiver.

"Sounds like the only thing you can do about it," he said.

"Are you okay? Should I call for help?" I asked.

"Yeah, but I'll call the vet myself in the morning. Meet me there?"

"Yes, thank you, Jack, thank you!"

"Be sure to keep an eye on the other horses though. It might be catching."

A breath caught in my throat. "I will."

"See you then."

"Yes, see you then."

As I hung up the phone, I heard the sound of the stall entrance opening in the far end of the barn. I tiptoed out of the office and shut the exterior door as quietly as I could. I sure didn't feel groggy anymore.

"Someone's coming. We have to go." I put my finger to my lips.

Betsy put her finger to hers.

I lifted her onto Thunder's saddle, and heard a noise right behind me. Glass crunching underfoot in the office. I looked from Betsy to the exterior door and grimaced, hesitating, then got the gun from my waistband again and stood by the door with it raised over my head in both hands. When the door opened, a man's head poked out, and I lowered the butt of the pistol with all my strength on the base of his skull.

"Ugh phuh." He landed on his face in the dirt.

"Good enough." I said.

I slipped the pistol home in my skirt and hoisted myself up quickly behind Betsy. So much for avoiding strenuous physical activity for a few days after my surgery. Between riding, roping, and whatever you'd call what I'd just done, I'd be lucky if my uterus didn't fall out on the desert floor before the night was over.

"Is he dead?" Betsy whispered.

"No, sweetie, he'll just sleep for a while," I said into her ear, my voice barely more than a vibration.

I squeezed my heels into Thunder's flanks, and turned him north again. Behind me, I heard the bolt throw in the near end center stall entrance and the doors creak open. There was more than one of them. Spit. I dug my heels into Thunder's flanks and he flew over the ground in the dark.

"Son of a bitch," I heard a voice say. But if he said anything else, we were too far away by then to hear.

The echoes of the gunshot shattered the silence of the night, and the cry of an owl followed them. I'd hated to use the gun, but it was the only way I could think of to get past the padlock on the hangar door. I'd just have to count on the wind to cover—or at least disguise—the location of the sound. Luckily, Thunder appeared to be used to guns, because he hadn't even flinched. I slipped the lock off. I pantomimed for Betsy to take her fingers out of her ears, and she did.

"In here, sleepy girl." I pulled the door up and motioned Betsy inside.

Betsy hesitated. "It's dark."

"Yes, but Thunder and I will be with you. Here, you hold his reins. I have to get the airplane outside, all right?"

I'd decided that if we needed to make a run for it, I'd have the plane ready. If all was well, putting it back in the hangar was no big deal for an old hand like me. And I was sure all would be well, and that we'd just sit here and wait in the dark for a little while, because, by now, Jack would have called the cops and Mickey and who knew whom else. The cavalry would be on the way.

Giving Betsy the job of holding Thunder's reins seemed to help her. The calming impact the horse had on her was amazing, and I sensed a budding horsewoman. She led Thunder in and his hooves clopped on the concrete floor. I heard her whisper to him. "It's okay, Thunder. I'm not scared of the dark, are you?"

I nudged along the base of the wall with my foot looking for the tow bar. My boot clanked metal. I reached down and lifted it. The darn thing wasn't as light as Jack had made it look. I remembered that he'd somehow attached it to one of the plane's three legs. After a few false starts I clamped it around the front one. I crouched down, leaned back, and heaved on the bar. The plane crept forward, inches at a time, but gathered speed. I did it again, over and over, until I had it clear of the building, where I removed the bar and tossed it into the brush.

In the distance, a pair of headlights bounced. Jack. My heart seized. At least I hoped it was Jack. I had no way of knowing if it wasn't. I needed to act fast now, but I didn't know what to do. My thoughts tumbled for slow, agonizing moments, then I pulled them together.

"Okay, Betsy, can you bring Thunder back out? We're going to take one more ride."

Girl and horse appeared in seconds. She was solemn, seeming proud to be in charge of the gorgeous creature.

Now two sets of headlights shot through the darkness toward us, bouncing up and down as both vehicles hit the bumps on the one-lane dirt road out to the airstrip. Two wasn't necessarily bad news. If the first car hadn't been Jack, then the second one surely was. A girl could hope, anyway.

"We're going to ride out to the runway so we can have a good view of my friend Jack as he drives up." I threw Betsy up onto the saddle and checked my waistband for the gun. It was still there. I jammed my foot in the stirrup and threw my leg over. "One more time, Thunder. Yah!"

The powerful hindquarters bunched and Thunder shot forward, down the worn grass leading to the airstrip. I wanted out of gun range in case one of those vehicles or both were the bad guys, but close enough to see what happened at the hangar. I had to gamble that the bad guys were packing shotguns or pistols— there was no way I could get out of range if they'd brought rifles with scopes. I shivered at the thought of night vision capability. However, even if they *did* bring the long-range guns, I had a really quick ride. I patted the horse's neck as he ran.

I pulled Thunder up halfway down the runway and turned us back around. A Suburban was lurching to a stop at the hangar. Jack. Thank God. He looked around, not finding us, so I pulled the pistol out and shot it in the air. He turned toward the sound.

"Jack! Meet me here!" I yelled, as loud as I could.

He must have heard me or sensed me or just flat out guessed right, because he jumped into the plane in three strides. I heard the engine and propeller roar to life. The vehicle on the dirt road was only a few hundred yards away from the hangar. The Skyhawk started out to the runway, and I urged Thunder toward it at full gallop, his hooves pounding faster than the racing heartbeat crashing in my ears. When we were ten yards from the plane, I pulled back on the reins.

"Whoa, boy." I jumped off, pulling Betsy with me, and slapped the horse on the rump. That's when I noticed the brand on his flank: ΣSL. "Get, yah, get."

He took off toward the ranch house at a dead sprint, the stirrups bouncing on his sides. As he ran from the runway, he passed a tall Indian in a gigantic headdress made of wooden stakes, his whole white-painted body naked except for his tall moccasins and black skirt. This was not Stella, no mere girl playing dress-up. A chill ran through me, and the Indian raised a hand in the air. "Mountain Spirit Dancer," I whispered. I closed my eyes and reopened them, and he was gone.

I scooped Betsy into my arms, shaking off the ghostly vision. "You've been very brave, and I need you to do it one more time. Okay? Can you trust me?"

"Yes," she yelled, over the roar of the propeller.

I stood off to the side of the runway. The plane lurched to a stop beside us. Jack threw the door open and I approached it from the rear of the plane —his warning before about the propeller in my mind—and handed Betsy to him, scrambling in after her. I strained to see back the way Jack had come. The chase vehicle careened into the hangar area and barely slowed down as it turned toward the runway. I slammed the door.

"Hold on, this will get rough," Jack said.

I put Betsy in my lap and pulled the seat belt over us both as the little plane gathered speed and leaped and bucked down the runway.

"Do we have enough runway left for takeoff?" I shouted over the engine noise.

Jack didn't answer. He pulled back on the yoke, hard, as I heard shots ping off the skin of the plane.

"Spit!" I screamed.

The front wheels of the plane lifted, dropped back to the sod, and lifted again as headlights bore down on the wing outside my window.

With a final jolting lunge, the Skyhawk lifted off the ground, perilously low, wings dipping from side to side. Betsy turned in my lap and buried her face in my chest with both her arms tight around my neck. She made a noise like an inward scream. I hugged her hard, my face buried in her hair. Three more bullets shook the plane in rapid succession. I held my breath —*please God, please God, please*—and the Skyhawk shucked them off and climbed, up, up, up into the night sky.

Jack leveled the plane off and leaned toward me. "Did you really just scream 'spit?'"

TWENTY-SEVEN

"But I not understand. Why I can't stay with Miss Emily?"

The words came from the sweet voice I'd grown to love like no other in one short day. We were sitting around the kitchen table at my mother's house: Betsy, Jack, Nadine, Wallace, and me. I looked at my mother standing by the refrigerator, and she walked over to Betsy, crouched before the child, and reached for one of her hands before I even knew what she was doing.

"We wish you could, Betsy. You are welcome in our house anytime." She looked at my friends one by one. "All of you are."

I nearly dropped my eyeteeth over that one, and I reached out and grabbed my mother's hand for a squeeze, then said to Betsy, "Wallace is going to find you a family with a mommy and a daddy. A really nice family, maybe with brothers and sisters for you to play with."

So much had come to light in the last twenty-four hours. Not just that this little girl's real name was Elizabet, changed to Valentina when her father had broken the girl and her mother free from Paul's human trafficking operation. Not just that he'd put them on a bus to Amarillo via an Underground Railroad of sorts for illegal immigrants. Not just that this child with no country had Americanized her name to Betsy all by herself. But also that the man who died on Wrong Turn Ranch was her father, Alejandro, beaten by Paul's men.

The police had pieced that together when they rescued the small army of immigrants that Paul had smuggled over the border with his import business. Paul had put the illegals straight to work in the tunnels from his property to a lucrative vein of silver he'd discovered under Mescalero Apache land. At least it was lucrative if the labor was free. Some of the immigrants—the kids and the young women—had a higher value when sold to the kind of people that liked their sex toys untraceable and disposable. A task force was at work now, hunting for the ones they knew about. All we could do for the others was pray.

By the time we figured out that Antonio Rosa was just a pseudonym for Alejandro, we weren't even surprised anymore. How the man had scraped together the money to get his wife and daughter to safety, no one quite knew. We did know the ending though: Spike Howard—Paul's private bounty hunter—floating face up in a hotel swimming pool in Amarillo. Sofia's arrest and murder contracted by Paul. Tanner, suspected (at least by me) of murdering Maria Delgado, who police confirmed to be the person who sent me the AmarilloMama email with information that she might have learned while helping Sofia and her daughter. Paul, it seemed, had hired Jack so he could keep tabs on what we were learning. And then there was Betsy, now an orphan in a country that wouldn't claim her as one of their own.

And it was that last part that I was leaving out in explaining things to her. That the U.S. government would have to decide whether Betsy stayed here or went back to Mexico. That I was no shoo-in to keep her, even if the INS let her remain in the U.S.: single, no kids, living with my mother, and months away at best from being approved by the foster care much less the adoption system. I kept my face smooth and smiling, though, because Betsy didn't need to know any of this yet. And she might never know.

She stared at the tabletop. "Will you come see me?"

"Of course I will!" I said. I ignored the pain shooting through my abdomen from overdoing things so dramatically in the previous twenty-four hours and scooted my chair nearer to hers. She launched herself into my arms. I breathed in her sweet smell and let her hair dry my tears.

After a few minutes, Wallace stood and cleared his throat. "Okay, Betsy. Time to go."

"I'm taking you to the Rainbow Room so you can pick out some clothes and a toy. Would you like that?" Nadine took Betsy's hands and pulled her up.

"But I have clothes." I had bought her a new set of Barbie pj's at Walmart on our way here.

Nadine smiled. "So you do. But this will be fun."

I stood up, too, and patted Betsy on the shoulder. "A girl can never have too many clothes."

Betsy turned to me. "But I lost my backpack."

I squatted, eye level to her. "I'm so sorry."

"Mama said never lose it."

"You can get a new one, honey."

She shook her head. "I can't."

"Would you like me to see if I can find it for you?"

She nodded at me, round-eyed. "Yes, please."

I stood up and let Wallace and Nadine lead her away.

Jack and I waved goodbye to them from the front door, not stopping until the Altima taking Betsy away had disappeared from sight. When it had, I broke down completely. Sobs tore through me, and I buried my face in my hands. How could I lose another child in less than a week? I couldn't be thankful that she might go to someone else, maybe even someone in Mexico. Everything in me screamed that she was meant for me, and me for her. God meant this to be, didn't he? Wasn't that why he'd thrown us together, her when she'd lost both her parents, and me when I'd lost everything else? Wasn't it?

Jack put his hand on my shoulder, guiding me down the sidewalk toward his Jeep. I didn't resist, but my body stiffened at his touch. Besides pushing me away, he kept secrets so large that they crowded all the air out of a room, and I had kept one of my own from him, too, that my procedure hadn't been minor, and that it had serious consequences. I could go along with him now, but I knew better than to let him in.

"Come on," he said.

He turned and raised his hand to my mother, who was watching from the living room window.

Mother gave him a thumbs up through the glass.

"Where are we going?"

"You'll see."

We drove in silence from Bushland to downtown Amarillo. He parked on the street outside the Maxor Building.

"You're taking me to work?"

"To the office."

We got out, and I followed him to the elevators. We rode up together in silence and got off on the fifth floor. He unlocked the office and motioned me inside first. The silence bothered me. Something was missing. My heart lurched. Snowflake. In our frenzied escape, we'd left her in New Mexico.

"Snowflake—"

He smiled. "Is just fine. She's having a fun vacation with Uncle Mickey and Aunt Laura."

I nodded, relieved, but then asked the important question. "Why are we here?"

He took me by the arm. "Come on."

We walked back to his office. He positioned me facing the wall of diplomas and pictures.

"What?"

He pointed to the photograph of Geronimo. "Read that."

I stepped forward. He did, too, and put a hand on my shoulder. At first I shrugged and tried to move away from him. He was part of my loss, after all, by his own choice. But he just held on. I quit fighting him.

Then I read the engraved quote aloud. "There is one God looking down on us all. We are all the children of one God."

I couldn't breathe. I had told Jack of the Mountain Spirit Dancer on the runway, of Stella's impersonating one to help the people her dad had enslaved, of Judith's childhood story, of my dreams, and of Betsy's drawing. He hadn't said much at the time, but I realized now that this was his response, and it was, well, the most perfect answer ever, secrets or no secrets between us.

"Jack—"

He pulled me around to face him and wrapped both his arms around me, my arms and hands the only barrier between us. Tears slid down my face again. Faster and faster they came until I gave in to the sobs and let the anguish pour out of me.

They slowed and I found my voice. "They have to let her stay. She doesn't have anyone." I hiccupped and wiped my face with one of my hands. "I want her. I want to adopt her. What do you think, Jack? Do you think I'd be a good mother to her?"

Jack leaned back and held me in front of him with one hand on each of my shoulders. That dangerous dimple pulled the left corner of his mouth into his even more dangerous half smile, and his eyebrow lifted along with them. "Why wouldn't they let you give a little Heaven to Betsy when you're represented by the best family and immigration lawyer in a two-state area?"

For once, I didn't mind that Jack hadn't really answered my question.

I smiled and lifted my chin three degrees, forcing the river of tears into a new tributary across my face. "With the best criminal law practice manager on the fifth floor of the Maxor Building."

He lifted the picture from the wall and handed it to me, and something like hope flickered in my chest.

EARTH TO EMILY (EMILY BERNAL #2)

A WHAT DOESN'T KILL YOU TEXAS-TO-
NEW MEXICO ROMANTIC MYSTERY

CHAPTER 1

Multicolored strands of lights twinkled from every surface around the dining room of the Big Texan Steak Ranch, even from the antlers of mounted deer heads and the ears of one embarrassed-looking coyote. Only the buffalo head maintained its dignity. Well, he and the giant fiberglass Santa guarding the exit door. I'd wanted to come here ever since my rodeo-cowboy father ran off before my promised seventeenth-birthday dinner, but, in light of the news I'd just received, all of the decorations were suddenly a little too much. I cradled my iPhone between my ear and shoulder, one hand clutching the neck of my poncho and the other slinging my purse straps over my other shoulder.

"Come on," I whispered to Jack, my boss—a man who can't figure out if he's a southern New Mexico rancher or a West Texas criminal defense attorney. Throw in the fact that he is mysterious, wounded, and part Apache, and you can probably see why half the women and nearly that many men in both locales had him starring in their own dreamland versions of *Fifty Shades of Grey*. Not me, though. In my dreams, he starred with me in *The Notebook*.

One eyebrow shot toward his hairline, and he answered at a normal decibel. "But we're celebrating, and our food hasn't come yet." The celebration was for my graduation from the foster-parenting classes I'd been taking for the last two months. "And I really need to talk to you about something."

In my ear, Child Protective Services investigator Wallace Gray answered. "Hello, Emily. I'd almost given up on you."

"I just saw your texts."

They'd come in a flurry, so by the time I'd read them, the whole story scrolled before my eyes. Two teens living in a CPS group home, Greg and Farrah, had run away and were reported as soliciting rides at Love's Travel Stop, not ten minutes from where I now stood glaring at Jack. Love's was a cross-country trucker mecca, situated right off I-40 outside Amarillo. The kids were likely to get more than the kind of ride they intended from the type of person who'd pick up runaways.

"I thought you'd want to know," he said. Wallace and I had taken a special interest in the pair recently when we accidentally rousted them from an abandoned house while looking for a missing girl. They'd run away from us then, too.

"Definitely. Thanks."

"Their caseworker is picking me up in ten minutes."

"Who is it?"

"Byron Philly. I don't think you've met him."

"Uh-uh."

"I need help. We can't get there for half an hour. Any chance you can get there sooner, see if you could find them?"

I didn't like the thought of Greg and Farrah out there in the cold. "We can be there in ten."

"We?"

"I'm with Jack."

"I hope you mean *with* Jack, and not just with him, if you know what I mean."

I knew, but after one incredible-if-tipsy make-out session that seemed to be going somewhere, I had blown it with Jack, who didn't seem big on second chances. As for me, my oops-I-prefer-men-who-dress-as-women husband, Rich, wasn't officially an ex yet. Any day now, though.

A waitress sashayed up to our table. From her diminutive size, she couldn't possibly eat here much, at least not the famous 72-ounce steak dinner. She popped a tray stand into place with her hip in a strangely provocative way, then balanced a load of food on it. Jack pretended to be staring at his phone instead of her tush. Her hands now free, she tossed a long braid behind her shoulder and turned to us with an electric smile, flashing a mouthful of metal.

"Who's rare and who's"—she glanced back at the tray again and frowned, as if still in disbelief—"grilled beefsteak tomatoes?"

Being a vegetarian in the cattle capital of the universe isn't easy. I put my hand over the mouthpiece of my iPhone. "To go. Check, please." Then, into the phone: "See you soon." I hung up.

Her brown eyes made **O**s, but she pulled out a handheld waiter pad and tapped a few keystrokes. "Your bill will be here in a moment." She smiled again. "Y'all come back, now, when you've got more time to enjoy your dinner."

Jack sighed, long and vibrato, and pulled out his wallet.

The trip in the dark along the I-40 access road to Love's only took us five minutes because I had stuck out my hand for Jack's keys when we got to his Jeep Wrangler—a monstrosity of patchworked panels in colors neither nature nor the automobile industry had designed to be used together—and Jack had obliged. I turned the Jeep into the yellow, red, and orange rainbow of the Love's compound, and it jounced and splashed in brown melted snow from earlier in the day. New flakes were beginning to fall, though, and it would soon be a blanket of white once again. I eased the Jeep across the apron of concrete past the noncommercial pumps and store, and onward toward the big-rig pumps and acres of overnight truck parking.

I glided to a stop. "Where do you think we should look?" I asked.

"I wasn't aware you cared what I thought. You know, since you basically kidnapped me from my dinner."

I threw him a side-eye look, but I smiled. "Can you please help me find the kids?"

"It takes a little longer than a quarter of an hour for a prisoner to develop Stockholm syndrome." From my peripheral vision, I saw his one dimple indent for a nanosecond.

The man had a quick wit, I'd give him that, even if he rarely answered a question head on. "Thank you for the psychology lesson, Patty Hearst." I let off the brake and we crept forward, salt crunching under the Jeep's slow-rolling tires. "Okay, they're trying to hitch a ride out of town, so they'll be watching the truckers, but they won't want to be seen." I scanned the three sides I could see of the store. Nada. Not even Christmas decorations. Maybe Love's didn't celebrate the season.

"A lot of activity here for a Wednesday night." Jack was referring to the fact that Amarillo basically shut down on Wednesday nights for midweek church services.

"I doubt that long-haul truckers go to Wednesday night church on the road."

Big rigs were lined up at the pumps and covered all of the lot I could see. Engines rumbled, and dark gray diesel exhaust escaped the dual chrome pipes on each side of one truck's cab, like puffs of smoke rings from the end of a cigarette. The sooty heaviness of it made me feel dirty.

Searching for the two teenagers catapulted me back to my own childhood for a moment. When I was young, my father had encouraged my obsessive love of all things Native American by teaching me to scout like an Indian. "A real scout gets close to the land," he would say, as we'd get out of the car. "He tests for scents." We'd sniff together. "He touches the earth." Together, we'd lean down and run our fingers across dirt or grass. "That's it, my little Sacajawea," he'd say, and throw me up onto his shoulders for a ride.

Twenty-plus years later, I rolled my window down, and my hand itched to open the door, to get close to the earth, sniff it, and touch it, but I didn't do it. Cold air bit my exposed skin. I pinched my poncho together high on my neck as a tight popping noise resounded from somewhere in the truck lot. Jack and I met eyes during a long silence, then three more pops blasted through the air in rapid succession.

"Backfiring truck?" I asked, even though I didn't think it was.

"Possibly yes, but probably gunshots."

And Greg and Farrah were out there somewhere. "We'd better check it out."

I accelerated past the truck pumps and into the relative darkness of the parking area. I skirted the outside edge, and we peered down the rows. One after another revealed nothing but cabs with blackout curtains and hulking trailers with personality mud flaps—Dallas Cowboys, Yosemite Sam, the ubiquitous posing nude woman. I turned down the side of the lot farthest from I-40. Shadowy figures darted from between two rows halfway across the lot and into the field on the other side. One looked taller than the other, and they appeared to be holding hands.

"There they are!" I floored the Jeep, and we rocketed over the lot, gaining speed rapidly.

A tire hit a pothole and jarred us so hard I worried we'd broken an axle, but the Jeep kept charging forward. When we reached the spot where the two people had disappeared, I turned sharply to the left. Lighted asphalt gave way to dark field, and we bounced over clumps of prairie grass and God knew what else. Jack braced himself with one hand on the ceiling and one on his door's armrest. The snow hadn't melted out here, but it wasn't deep, and the Jeep smashed through its half-icy crust.

"I can't see anything. Can you pan the headlights?" Jack said.

I slowed and turned first to the left for twenty yards, then drove in a huge circle. When I judged that we'd completed a loop back roughly to where we'd started, I turned to the right to continue across the field.

Wham—crunch! The Jeep slammed into something immoveable. My head bounced off the steering wheel, and I bit my tongue, hard. Warm, coppery fluid oozed into my mouth.

"Mother Goose!" I yelled. "Are you okay?"

An enormous deflating airbag muffled Jack's response.

"What?"

The bag fell away. "I said, 'Other than I can't breathe.'"

"Oh." I pounded the steering wheel with one fist. "We lost them, and I wrecked your Jeep." I turned to him. "I'm so sorry."

He pushed the limp airbag off his legs. "I'm sorry your airbag didn't deploy." He turned to me and covered up what sounded suspiciously like a laugh with a cough. "You look like Count Chocula."

I turned the rearview mirror to me and saw the blood trickles out of each corner of my mouth. I almost laughed, too. He reached over and wiped the blood from beside my lip, and the heat from his thumb seared my skin. I gasped, and he jumped back.

The inside of the Jeep sizzled and popped with electricity as we stared at each other. Then he broke eye contact and fumbled for a flashlight from the glove box and opened his door. I put my fingers to my throat. They bore witness to the slowing of my jackrabbit heartbeat.

"I'll go assess the damage." Jack jumped out, leaving his door ajar.

I shivered, cold from more than his sudden absence. It was snowing harder now, and—this being the coldest and snowiest winter in one hundred years in Amarillo—of course the wind was blowing it straight sideways at what felt like a bajillion miles per hour, right through Jack's open door. Flakes dappled his empty seat, closer and closer together. People had died of hypothermia in warmer conditions than this. The heater was already on high. I leaned over and shut his door, or slammed it, rather, then put my cheek on the steering wheel and looked out the side window into the night, shivering.

A white face under a black knit cap appeared like a specter outside the window. I screamed before I could stop myself. It was the young man we'd been chasing. Greg. I rolled down my window.

"Hey," he said. "I know you."

"Yes, you do, Greg. I'm Emily. We met when you were squatting in that deserted house by Llano Cemetery. Where's Farrah?"

A female face with one brown and one green eye framed by pixie-short black hair materialized from the darkness behind him, her body blending with the night. "Are you hurt?" The girl pointed at my bloody face.

I used the back of my hand to wipe some of it away. I glanced at my hand. Now I had smears of blood across it. "No, I'm fine. My friend is seeing if our Jeep is, though."

"It's not," she said.

"Your front end is, like, wasted," he said.

Ugh. And here I was trying to scrounge up enough money to get a place of my own—as in, not with my mother. "You guys have created a bit of excitement tonight."

Greg harrumphed. "Maybe."

"How would you describe it, then?"

"I'm not going to let the same thing happen to Farrah twice."

"What do you mean?"

Farrah put her hand on Greg's upper arm. "It's okay."

He shook his head. "It's not. No one believes us about what that, that" —he threw up his hands—"monster did to you." He glared at me. "He should be in jail. Why do they take his word against hers?"

I knew that Farrah claimed she'd been sexually abused, that CPS was investigating the father—although it didn't feel right to think of him that way—in their last foster home, but that they hadn't reached a conclusion yet. "I'm sorry—"

Farrah stepped between Greg and me. "There's an older boy in the group home. It was about to happen again. I'm not stupid. So Greg said we had to go."

I heard clanging from the front end of the car. "I can understand that." Better than she knew, thanks to a drunken lout from the Tarleton rodeo team. He got a feel of my breasts and a knee to the balls. I was maybe thirty pounds heavier than her, though, and seven inches taller. Suddenly, I understood her vulnerability in a way that I hadn't when I'd heard her story third person from Wallace. "But where will you go?"

Greg moved forward, too. Both of them were so close I could have touched their cheeks. "We'll be fine. I can take care of her."

A sharpness rent my chest. "Let me help you."

"You can't. No one can."

"I can try."

Farrah smiled with her mouth only. "Thank you. Really. It's . . ." She trailed off.

I gestured toward the backseat. "Hop in, where it's warm."

Both kids took a step back, then another, as the boy shook his head. "We wanted to see if you were okay. We have to get out of here."

"Wait! At least take my card. It has my office number and my cell number. Call me if you need anything, *please*."

I pulled a card from the outer side pocket of my handbag, where I'd learned to stash them for easy access. People in need of a criminal attorney were often in a hurry to get someplace else, it seemed. The card had the addresses for both the Amarillo and New Mexico offices for Jack's firm. I stuck it out the window. Snow fell and melted on my bare hand. The wind flapped the edge of my wrap, and I held on to the flimsy cardstock with a tight grip between thumb and forefinger.

Greg leapt forward and snatched the card, then retreated just as quickly. The two kids took another step back and the snow and the night swallowed them whole.

Jack hopped back in the car, letting in a gust of icy air and swath of falling snow with him. "You hit some kind of concrete stanchion."

"I'm so sorry. I'll pay for the repairs."

"No need." His lip twitched. "It didn't even dent the bumper."

For a moment, his words didn't make sense. Greg said the front end was "wasted" and I'd heard a clanging. Then a warm glow spread from my chest outward as I realized that Jack was pretending I hadn't caused any damage, and I could only guess it was to keep me from paying for repairs. A truly kind gesture, given the state of my finances, which he knew all about. I played along. "Really? Wow. We hit the concrete so hard."

He stomped his boots on the floorboard. "Lucky break."

The glow spread further, grew hotter. "Did you see the kids?"

"No, sorry."

"No, I mean, they were right here, at my window. Didn't you hear me scream?"

"I didn't hear a thing except the wind." He craned to see out my side. "I don't see anyone now."

As hard as I stared into the darkness and swirling snow after them, I didn't either.

CHAPTER 2

I parked the Jeep at the edge of the truck lot near where a crowd had gathered. Blue and red lights flashed in all directions. Curiosity clawed at me, and I took a few steps closer to the throng. It parted for two EMTs and a gurney, and through the gap I saw someone big and black on the ground, his head in a pool of blood. He wasn't moving, and the people around him had the hushed mien I'd come to associate with tragedy. I shuddered. Behind his body, a woman peered between the curtains of what looked like the sleeping compartment above a tractor cab whose license plate read TUCK69.

"Crime scene, ma'am, you need to step back," a female officer said. She was bundled to her eyeballs with a thick scarf, and she shouted through it to be heard. A roll of yellow tape hung in her hand.

"What happened?"

"A man's been shot."

So the noises we heard had been gunshots. "Is he dead?"

"Afraid so. Now, move along. Give us room to do our jobs."

I backed away, still mesmerized by the blood on the new layer of snow in the parking lot.

"Isn't that Wallace?" Jack asked, reclaiming my attention.

I turned, and he pointed back toward the Love's store. Another crowd had formed there under the shelter of the big-rig gas bay. A tall, lean man with sandy-blond hair stood out among them.

"It is."

Wallace lifted a hand to us as we started walking toward him, then put it on one hip and shook his head, his highlighted hair swinging perfectly over his eyelid. How could he always look so put together, even in the cold and blowing snow, when I looked like the Abominable Snowwoman? I fluffed my bangs, hoping for presentable, and snow fell from them to my face.

Wallace said, "What took you so long?"

"We were following the kids," I told him.

"You found them?"

"We did. And lost them again. They're gone."

Something about my words tore at me. I'd lost a baby of my own in October. A miscarriage, and I'd lost my one Fallopian tube, or most of it anyway, at the same time, meaning I was probably barren. Babies. Children. Loss. Thinking about it made time slow down, and as I watched the snow fall I could see every individual flake in the sky around me, suspended almost to the point of not moving. I had to shake it off; I was nearly over it, and I couldn't let everyone see it still leveled me. I huffed a deep breath, and let it out slowly through my mouth.

Jack had been standing beside me like a wooden drugstore Indian, but he ended his silence. "She wrecked my Jeep."

Wallace turned to him now. "She's hell on wheels, but I hear she's much better on horseback."

Jack made some kind of noise halfway between a snort and a laugh.

Wallace introduced a chunky guy with acne and lank hair who had materialized beside him. "This is Byron Philly, you guys. Despite the fact that he looks like a bad episode of 21 Jump Street, he's actually a married father of three and a responsible adult."

"Nice to meet you, Byron. I'm Emily Bernal, paralegal at Williams and Associates. I work for him." I hooked my thumb at my boss.

"Jack Holden." Jack shook Byron's hand.

"Byron Philly. Sorry." He shook his head, like he was trying to clear it. "We have a newborn at our house and no one is getting to shower or sleep. Nice to meet y'all. Now, which direction did my kids go?"

I gestured behind us. "Way out across the field." The snow fell faster, and I could feel the flakes landing on my nose.

"Could you tell if they were dressed for the weather?"

I thought back, eyes closed. I'd gotten a good look at Greg. Black watch cap. Faux leather lined aviator jacket. Gloves? I wasn't sure. As for Farrah, I couldn't say. She'd blended against the darkness, and by the time she'd appeared, it was her words I had focused on, not her clothes. But even hats, coats, and gloves wouldn't do much good on a night like this. "Coats and hats. Other than that, I couldn't say. The weather looks like it's getting pretty bad."

He grimaced. "I'll update the cops." Byron walked toward the Love's entrance and a congregation of men and one woman in blue uniforms.

I turned to Wallace, who was admiring Jack while Jack picked at a fingernail, which of course he made look smolderingly hot. Wallace waggled his eyebrows in Jack's direction for my benefit. Bless his heart. Wallace never quit trying to promote a match between us, and I had to admit I hoped he'd succeed. I rolled my eyes at him anyway, though.

Wallace said, "Well, you guys missed some excitement. One of the truckers was shot and killed out in the lot."

"Yeah, I saw the scene. Gruesome."

Jack dipped his chin once. "Yep. I think we heard the shots, too."

To Wallace I said, "I'd guess we almost drove up on it, but then the kids came sprinting by, and we forgot about the shots."

A tiny woman approached from the direction of the truck lot. She strolled slowly, almost casually, but her eyes darted left-right, left-right, left-right as she picked her way across the snowy ground cover in sky-high wedge-heeled boots. Fake leather extended all the way up to her thighs where it almost met a zebra-print tube skirt. The one inch of exposed leg was covered by nothing except fishnet. On her upper half she wore a waist-length jacket with black strands of something that wasn't fur. Her eyeliner, fingernails, and long, straight hair were as black as the coat.

She zeroed in on Wallace, calling to him. "Hey, I know you, right?"

As she got closer, I saw that her makeup didn't hide the testaments to hard living that time had etched around her eyes and mouth. Thirty-five or more years of time, if I had to guess.

Wallace evaluated her for a few seconds. "Yeah, I think so, but I can't remember where."

"Well, I'm a dancer. Do you ever go to any clubs?"

"Do you by any chance dance at the Polo Club?"

"I do."

"That must be it. I was in there not too long ago on an investigation."

Her eyes opened so wide I was afraid they'd get stuck that way. "Are you a cop?"

"Not that kind of investigation. I work for Child Protective Services."

She exhaled. "Whew! Well, thank God." She whispered in his ear and his eyes widened. Goose pimples rose on the back of my neck. I didn't like secrets unless they included me.

After a good thirty seconds of furtive back-and-forth whispers, Wallace reincluded Jack and me in the conversation. "I'm going to walk Ms.—"

"You can call me Ivanka."

An eastern European name with that drawl? I didn't think so.

"—Ivanka over to my car, and give her a ride home."

"Good night, then," I said.

"Ivanka" shot a last furtive glance over her shoulder at the Love's then took his arm, pulling him along. It was hard to say which of them had the better swing to their walk, but I gave Wallace the edge.

I looked at Jack and he arched his left brow.

I frowned. "I wonder what that's all about."

Byron walked in our direction with a uniformed officer. As they neared us, though, Byron peeled off after Wallace and the woman. The policeman kept coming. He had on an Amarillo Police Department coat, and it looked warm, as did his blue knit cap with a white owl's head on it, the Rice University mascot logo. I envied him that coat and hat. I was freezing to death. My toes had started losing feeling. I'd worn thin socks under my boots, not expecting to spend the evening out in the weather. I stamped my feet one after another to warm them.

The officer stopped in front of us. "Emily Bernal and Jack Holden?"

The guy looked familiar. Jack caught my eye and raised the same eyebrow he had a moment before. He recognized him, too?

"I'm Emily. Have we met?"

The officer got out a small spiral flip notebook and a pen without looking at me. "Possibly. I'm Officer Samson, and I need to ask you a few questions about Greg Easley and Farrah Farud."

"Okay." I stared at him, my mind flipping through a card catalogue of faces.

White male. Puffy, dark-circled eyes. Uni-brow. Dishwater hair shot through with gray. He was Jack's height, maybe six foot one, not lean like Jack, though. But the guy I pictured in my mind's eye had a good six inches of Wonder Bread protruding over his belt and skinny legs. Right now this one looked thin under his jacket. Still, I knew it was the same guy.

So I recognized him, but from where? I cross-referenced places, looking for a match, and got one. He'd questioned Wallace and me at a witness's apartment when the little girl we were searching for had been abducted. Not just any little girl. Betsy, the one I would adopt as soon as the great state of Texas approved me, if all went as planned. Jack—who I could tell definitely knew the officer, too—didn't say anything about it, so I didn't say any more either.

"I hear the two of you saw Greg and Farrah tonight, the runaway teenagers?" Officer Samson stood with pen poised.

Jack gestured at me. "I saw two figures running from the truck lot. She saw more than me."

I nodded and pointed toward the field we'd plowed up with the Jeep.

"I talked to them, about ten minutes ago, out in the middle of that field. They took off from there."

Samson squinted at me. "What did you talk about?"

"I ran our vehicle into some concrete thing, and they came up and asked if we were all right. I said yes, and then they took off."

"To where?"

"I have no idea."

"Which direction?"

"I'm sorry, it was so dark and snowy that I couldn't tell."

He frowned and wrote something. "Where did you first see them, when they ran from the lot?"

"On the back side, about halfway down."

"And you were where?"

"Also on the back side, but we were pretty far away. We'd made the turn to the back."

Two women hurried past us, dressed not unlike Ivanka, but one was bonier than Ivanka and the other had horrible teeth. They cut their eyes down and veered away from Samson.

He scowled after them. "Damn lot lizards. They're half the problem out here."

I hadn't heard that expression. I looked at Jack, and he mouthed, "Hookers." Oh. *Oh.*

Samson was talking again. "Did you hear any gunshots here tonight?"

I nodded. "Yes, several. Right before the kids came running out."

He looked up quickly. "Did they have any weapons on them?"

"No, not that I saw. They just looked scared and young and cold when I talked to them in the field."

"Did you see anyone else when they ran from the parking lot?"

"No."

He turned to Jack. "And you?"

"No."

"Did you happen to see the shooting"—he pointed toward the murder scene—"or anyone with a weapon?"

We answered almost at the same time. "No."

Officer Samson chewed the end of his pen. "All right. Call me if you think of anything else." He handed each of us a card.

We agreed, and Samson walked back toward the Love's. There was nothing left for us to do there, and Jack and I walked toward the rear of the Jeep. I was frozen through and through by that time, and Ivanka, Wallace, and Byron had disappeared, and I still didn't know what my best guy friend had learned from the dancer.

My stomach growled. "You know, I'm really cold, but even more, I'm strangely hungry."

Jack snorted. "No one to blame but yourself for that."

"Yeah, well, I'm eating my dinner the second I close the door to the Jeep." Then I leaned toward him, my voice low in case the friendly Officer Samson could still hear me. "Say, had you met that police officer before? I met him once, at Victoria's apartment, when we were searching for Betsy."

"He was one of the cops at the scene when they charged our client with assault, one of the state's witnesses against Alan Freeman."

Alan Freeman was our client. I'd first met Alan a few months ago, when he was retiling our office floor to pay his bill. I didn't know which I loved more, the fact that Jack let his clients pay in whatever form they could swing, or that Freeman was the kind of guy who lived up to his responsibilities.

"I thought it was a former cop, Jason somebody or other, who Freeman supposedly assaulted?"

Jack walked me to the passenger side and opened the door. I climbed in, and he leaned in a little after me. My pulse accelerated and my brain function decelerated in response. "Wu, yes."

"Woo what?" As I spoke, I realized he meant "Wu," as in Jason's last name, and not "woo," as in seek the affection, love, or support of another. My cheeks started heating.

He raised his left eyebrow, and it was all I could do not to bridge the last few inches of gap between our lips. The dimple puckered. Flames climbed my face. "Woo-hoo." He slammed the door, and I caught a glimpse of his lopsided smile.

I exhaled. "Whew," I said, and put my cold hands to my flaming hot cheeks.

CHAPTER 3

On a self-declared break from Freeman trial prep the next morning, I parked my aging green Mustang on Wentworth alongside the almost tree-less playground at Windsor Elementary. Someone had hung red and green tinsel garlands around the one scraggly evergreen near the school build-ing. The previous night's snow still clung to the ground around the tree and across the playground, but the precipitation had stopped. Not a great day to pretend to power walk through the neighborhood. Usually I parked farther away—it made me less conspicuous—but today the temperature hovered below freezing, and with the wind-chill factor it felt like fifteen degrees. No way was I walking any farther than I had to, even to see Betsy.

If I could see Betsy, that is. I glanced at the time on my phone. It was still two minutes until recess time.

When I found the orphaned girl and Jack and I brought her back from New Mexico, I'd handed her over to CPS via Wallace. She had become the most important person in my life by then, and I was desperate to make her my forever daughter. Wallace showed me how to work within the bureau-cracy of the state system, and urged me to trust it. I'd signed up on the foster-care and adoption lists. I'd taken the classes. I was saving up to move out of my mother's and into my own place, at which time I could schedule a home study. I scrolled back to an email I'd sent myself with the link to a listing for a duplex off Soncy Road that sounded perfect. I needed to book a time to see it. Meanwhile, CPS had placed Betsy with a large foster family with a good record. The Hodges. Trevon and Mary Alice.

The Hodges had fostered, all told, twenty-three kids, per Wallace. They specialized in noninfant and nonwhite kids, and kids with disabilities; in other words, they took the kids who were hard to place. Wallace said they had a history of keeping them long-term, until someone else adopted them or they graduated from the foster system, whichever came first. I initially found this admirable—astounding even. How difficult it must be to raise so many children, some of whom required extra care.

Then jealousy crept in. They had Betsy. I didn't. I'd stalked them a little. On Facebook. While grocery shopping. At their church. Okay, I admit it, the Hodges were an impressive sight with their line of multicolored ducklings in all shapes and sizes following behind them. I'd finally decided maybe Betsy had drawn a lucky card from the deck with them. All those siblings. A family with values, with morals.

But the Hodges wouldn't allow me to visit Betsy. It was their right, but I didn't like it, and it made me even more determined to maintain a relationship with her, not less. I checked the playground again. Still no kids. It was time for them to be outside.

I'd begun these clandestine visits to her school as soon as she'd started the first grade, which was the first time she'd attended a school of any kind. Betsy and her parents had entered the U.S. courtesy of a scurrilous human trafficker named Paul Johnson. When other kids her age were discovering the joys of recess and snack time in kindergarten, she was captive in southern New Mexico on Johnson's Ranch where her undocumented parents were enslaved in a silver mine. When other kids her age started first grade, Betsy was hiding under her mother's housekeeping cart at the Wyndham/Ambassador Hotel, coloring pictures and singing to her doll, after her mother had escaped from the ranch. So, she hadn't had a chance to go to school before now. The girl was smart, though, and I knew she would catch up with her classmates fast.

A text came in on my phone from Wallace: *No word from Greg and Farrah. Getting really worried.*

I shot a quick text back: *Me, too.* Then I remembered the thing that was still bugging me from the night before. *Why'd you leave so fast with "Ivanka"?*

Wallace: *She was looking for a sympathetic person to help her make an escape before she got busted.*

Me: *For what?* I could make a good guess since I'd heard Samson call the two skanky women lot lizards.

Wallace: *She's a lady of the night, honey.*

Me: *Oh. Okay.* She'd picked the right person for empathy. *You're such a nice guy.*

Wallace: *Outcasts are my kind.*

We ended our text conversation, and my mind flashed on Sunday school past, of stories of Jesus washing dirty feet and hanging out with prostitutes. Wallace could try to pretend it was just solidarity, but the man had the biggest heart I'd ever seen.

The bright voices of children floated across one hundred yards of open playground to my ears as they charged out a side door. *Bravo, Windsor Elementary,* I thought, *for not letting a little inclement weather throw you off your game plan.* The kids were wrapped like mummies, and I realized that they were probably running late because of the extra time needed to get them all bundled up.

Knuckles rapped on the window by my left ear, and I jumped, spilling my Roasters large breve with sugar-free hazelnut—my favorite coffee drink—on the black Red Raiders sweatshirt I was wearing over a long-john top.

"Spit in a well bucket!" I shouted. It was an expression I'd picked up from my father, before he'd split.

Mother hated cursing, but she didn't mind the work-around expressions favored by Dad and me. So spit, heck, darn, and Mother Goose made the cut. Any variants of damn, shit, crap, hell, ass, and—gasp—the f-word did not. Nor expressions she considered vulgar, like douche or vagina. I tried not to even think them, even in the direst of circumstances, let alone say them.

I glanced out the window and recognized the woman standing there in a gray wool dress that cascaded from the bottom of a white jacket. A white wool cap covered her head, and she'd crammed long, curly brown hair under it, given away by the messy strands that had escaped. She'd knocked with bare knuckles, and I watched as she pulled an insulated ski-type mitten back onto her hand.

"She" was Mary Alice Hodges, with a runny-nosed, snowsuited toddler of indeterminate gender on one hip. We hadn't met, but I'd seen her, of course, when gathering information on her and her family. Not that I was going to disclose that I recognized her, or how. I hit the down button on my window with one hand and scrounged with the other in my purse for something to sop up the spilled coffee. Jackpot: a fistful of napkins from Taco Villa. I pressed them to the spill site like it was a bullet wound as cold air violated my warm, cozy space.

"May I help you?"

"Ms. Bernal?" She pronounced my Colombian (married) surname Burr-NAL, like most every other non-Hispanic person north of the Mexican border. But I had to wonder how she even knew who I was.

"I'm Emily Bernal." I stressed the correct pronunciation: Bare-NAHL. "What can I do for you?"

"I'm Mary Alice Hodges, Betsy's mother, and—"

The word *mother* tore at my gut, and I couldn't let that slide. "*Foster* mother, isn't it? I've been trying to reach you through CPS about bringing a Christmas present over for her. You may recall hearing my name. I'm the person who rescued her when she was kidnapped."

I knew Betsy would love my gift, too. She had lost her treasured pink backpack when she'd been held captive, and I'd bought her a new one like the one she described—since I hadn't found the one she'd lost, despite repeated calls to the task force of federal, state, and Alamogordo officers and the trustee for Johnson's Ranch.

"I'm sorry, but that won't be possible. We don't allow Christmas presents in our home. That's our special time to praise God for the birth of the Christ child."

I could feel my jaw drop, and I stared at her. I had no response to that. Poor Betsy. Presents rocked. I'd considered the Hodges top tier because of siblings and morality, but I also hoped for fun and happiness. Maybe they were a loving family who made up for it in other ways, though. I knew how much worse it could be—neglect or abuse was a whole 'nother level of Hell from unhappy—but it wasn't what I wanted for this sweet little girl who had stolen my heart.

Mary Alice switched the child to the other hip. "Betsy said she's seen you here."

I didn't doubt that she had. Betsy and I had talked on one of my many visits, until a teacher put the kibosh on it. After that, I would wave to her as I walked laps around the school block, soaking in the sight of her and her nearness.

My pulse sped up, throbbing in my ears. "Yes, and . . . ?"

"I thought my husband made it clear that we don't welcome outside interference with the young people we bring into our home."

The child in her arms suddenly threw its head back and wailed, flailing and kicking. I stared at the toddler, distracted. The hood came off its head, revealing short locks of wavy cotton-candy hair. The haircut looked very male, even though still babyish, and I decided to run with that gender classification. The little boy lifted his face again, still squalling, and I took a closer look. He didn't look like your normal everyday kid. Something about the eyes. Down syndrome, I realized.

"Ms. Burr-NAL?"

"Um, yes, well, I've never spoken to your husband, but Wallace Gray with CPS did let me know you've turned down my requests to see Betsy. I wasn't given a reason."

She bounced the boy up and down and made shushing noises for a few seconds, then turned her attention back to me as she continued to bounce him. "We keep tight control over the type of people our children associate with."

My face grew hot. "All righty then. You have a nice day." I reached for the button to raise my window.

She put her free hand out as if to stop me. "You need to stop bothering her here."

I recoiled and released pressure on the button. "Bothering her? I'm in a parked car a football field away."

"You know what I mean."

A roaring started in my head. "I'm not really sure that I do."

Her eyes narrowed and I saw her arms tighten around the child. He squealed. "Don't make me take this further, Ms. Burr-NAL."

The roaring intensified. "Further? Should I be scared of something?"

She leaned away from the child, toward me. "The wrath of God," she whispered. "You should always be fearful of the wrath of God."

I laughed aloud. "Okay, gotcha. Thanks for stopping by." I rolled up my window.

She took three steps backward, then whirled, almost falling on the packed snow along the gutter. I watched in my rearview mirror as she strapped the boy into a car seat in her oversized army-green van, then went around and climbed in on the driver's side. She started the engine, but she didn't leave. Instead, she looked at me—or the back of my head, at least—then lifted a phone and spoke, waving a fist in what looked like punctuation to her words. Her eyes fell. She nodded. She set the phone down and stared toward me again, a half smile on her lips. Finally, she grabbed something at the height of a steering wheel gearshift and her vehicle engaged. She accelerated away from the curb, her van fishtailing for a moment as she passed me, snow spitting up behind her tires as they caught.

"Well." I said it aloud, even though I was by myself. "She's a whack-job." I chuckled, but it wasn't a laugh of mirth. If that woman had been holding up a cross instead of a baby, I would have sworn she was attempting to exorcise demons from my soul in her last moments at my window. I wouldn't have been completely surprised if the archangel Saint Michael had swooped from the sky to assist. But now I was the one thinking crazy. I breathed out through my pursed lips, very slowly and deliberately.

Clearly, the Hodges were ultrareligious, in a way that made my church-lady mother look like a trifler. Still, I didn't understand Mary Alice's behavior. Wallace said he had informed the Hodges that I intended to seek adoption of Betsy as soon as I could gain state approval. They'd known that when they first got Betsy, just like they'd known that I'd saved the girl's life and forged a strong bond with her. So why forbid me to see her in the first place, and why the fuss now? Maybe they considered me to be an unsuitable kind of person. Yes, I'd been the talk of Amarillo for a few months after I moved back from Dallas, pregnant and humiliated by my cheating husband's sexuality and paramour. But that was him, not me. Surely I was not such a threat to a child that I had to be warned off.

I peered through my passenger-side window, looking for Betsy in the playground full of shouting kids. My eyes sorted through them. Too tall. Hair too light. Hair too short. Skin too dark. Skin too white. When I'd narrowed them down to short brown girls with long dark hair peeking out from under their winter caps, I found her. Tiny and adorable. She saw me looking at her, and she waved at me, using her whole body.

I raised my hand, waving back. She looked around and I saw her eyes lock on the back of a teacher, and then she took off, a tiny pink dynamo hurtling in my direction. I jerked open my car door without hesitation, cutting the engine and pulling the keys out as I did, and ran toward her, coatless. Betsy made it twenty-five yards and I covered the other seventy-five. She slammed into me and I lifted her into a huge swinging-around hug.

"Hi, Emily!" Her high-pitched voice sang out, as she pressed her cold face against mine. It felt wonderful.

"Hi, sweetie-pie! How are you?" I set her down. Her long hair hung in braids fastened with pink scrunchies on each side of her head. She had lost a front tooth.

She frowned, very serious and adult suddenly. "I'm good, but I miss you and Thunder." Thunder was the horse we'd escaped on together.

I laughed. "I miss you, and I'm sure Thunder does, too."

Her face lit up. "Have you found my backpack? Mama would be so mad I lost it."

I stuck out my bottom lip. Per Mary Alice Hodges, I couldn't give her the new one, so I didn't mention it. "No, no one has seen it. I'll ask them to keep looking, okay?"

A whistle blew.

Betsy looked back toward her teacher, who was walking toward us, fast, head shaking back and forth, whistle in hand near her lips. "Uh-oh."

"Yeah, uh-oh." I hugged her one last time, and she ran back to the teacher.

I walked toward my car. At the last second, I turned. Betsy was walking backwards, waving to me, and I pulled out my phone and quickly snapped a picture. I got in the Mustang, restarted it, and blew on my cold hands as I watched her.

She rejoined her friends in what looked like a game of tag, a good way to stay warm out there. Watching her kept my face stretched in an ear-to-ear smile. Even though she'd lost both parents and now lived with the killjoy Hodges, I hoped she took some comfort in knowing she had me, and that I truly wanted her. I thought of my parents. Until I was sixteen, I'd felt wanted and loved by them both. After my dad left, especially after he cut off contact when I was a senior at Texas Tech, I still had my mother. It's not that losing my father's love didn't hurt me, because it did, but I knew I wasn't alone. Of course, it was possible the Hodges were loving people and made Betsy feel wanted, too. It just seemed highly unlikely to me after meeting Mary Alice.

My phone rang. I answered it without looking, my eyes still on Betsy. "This is Emily."

"This Ava," a lilting, cheery voice said. "You know, Katie's Ava in St. Marcos."

My best girlfriend and former boss at Hailey & Hart in Dallas, Katie Kovacs, had left the practice of law to live in the Caribbean, where she had reinvented herself as a singer and keyboardist with her new friend Ava Butler. I'd gotten to see Katie and Ava perform several times. They were the real deal. They'd almost landed a New York recording contract but Katie got cold feet when she became a mother. I remembered that Katie said Ava had a little girl now, too.

"Hi! Wow, what a nice surprise to hear from you."

I watched Betsy, half-listening to Ava. Betsy got tagged and was "it." Her friends dispersed, and she began to chase them.

"I got a manager book me a bunch a stateside gigs. I gonna be up your way soon."

"That's great. You realize it's winter here, right?" Ava was an island girl. I couldn't imagine her here in the waterless, palm-treeless Panhandle anytime on purpose, much less in this freezing cold weather. And if Ava was coming all the way to Texas for gigs, motherhood must not be slowing her down as much as it did Katie.

She laughed. "Yah mon. I asking for double rates."

Another rap on my window. This one sounded like it was shattering it. I gasped and wheeled, dropping my phone and ducking toward the center of the car as I did so. No glass fell in on me, and I regained my composure quickly, ready to shout at Mary Alice, only it wasn't her.

CHAPTER 4

From the console where my phone had fallen, I heard, "Emily? You okay, Emily?"

An officer waited outside my car, one hand clutching a baton that he had tucked under his elbow. He was young. And short. Red haired. Full faced and thick bodied. Behind him stood Officer Samson. I rolled my window down again.

Before I could speak, the new officer said, "I'm Officer Burrows. Step out of the car, please, ma'am."

"Certainly, Officer Burrows." I held up one finger. He shook his head, so I made it fast before he could object further. I grabbed my phone and said to Ava, "Sorry, gotta go—police."

Ava's voice sounded concerned, but I was already hanging up the phone. "Oh, bad news. Okay, I call you."

I set my phone on the passenger seat. "Do you need my license and registration, sir?"

The officer's voice grew louder. "Step out of the car, ma'am. Don't make me say it again."

Officer Samson echoed, in a more gentle voice, "Ms. Bernal, if you could please do what Officer Burrows asks you to do."

My throat constricted. I unbuckled my seat belt and grabbed my winter coat. I opened the door and got out, then started to put it on.

Burrows snatched it away from me. "Hands on the hood of the car, feet shoulder width apart."

My mouth went dry and it took a second for his words to register. He gave me a shove on the shoulder, spinning me around. It jarred me out of my confusion, and I did as he said. Behind my car I saw not one but two squad cars parked at an angle, blocking me in like a dangerous criminal.

I moistened my lips. "What's the problem, sir?"

He didn't answer, just patted me down everywhere, and I do mean everywhere. It was the first time anyone other than my OB/GYN had touched me *there* in four months, and this wasn't exactly the way to break that unwelcome streak.

"You're going to wait in the back of my car while we search your vehicle."

"Why do you need to search it?"

He took me by the upper arm—his fingers biting into it even through fleecy sweatshirt material and long johns—and led me to the cruiser, my coat still in his other hand.

"Officer Burrows, am I under arrest?"

He said nothing.

Thinking back to the advice I'd heard Jack give clients, I said, "I do *not* consent to a search of my car. Nor do I consent to being locked in your vehicle, unless I am under arrest."

Burrows opened the back door to the cruiser and dropped my coat to the ground. Without warning, I felt a cuff snap around my right wrist and my arm pulled behind me. My first reaction was to struggle, but I stopped myself. My father had always told me to respect authority, even when it didn't deserve it. Might made right, in the moment, because dead couldn't be undone. Jack could help me sort this out later.

I looked up at Officer Samson, but his eyes were hidden behind aviator sunglasses. Burrows grabbed my left arm and jerked it behind my back to join the other. The second cuff snapped closed. I wanted to shrink into invisibility. Betsy's recess bell hadn't rung yet. She was still outside. If she was looking, she could see all of this, with no one to explain it to her, to tell her I would be fine. Her mother had died in prison, and her father had died escaping Johnson's Ranch. Watching me, powerless, could be incredibly traumatic for her, and I prayed she was playing with friends and didn't see what was happening one hundred yards away.

Burrows put a hand on top of my head and shoved me down enough to topple me into the backseat of the car. The whole scene was surreal for me. My only brush with the law had been a few traffic tickets. A vision flashed through my mind of a tie-down roper's lariat sailing over the head of a calf. The rope jerked tight as the quarter horse stopped and threw its weight in reverse. The calf thrown on its side by the cowboy, who then wrapped three of its ankles with a piggin' string and threw his own arms into the air to signal he was done. Now I knew how the calf felt.

"We're searching your car because a citizen called in a pervert taking pictures of kids. We were given a license plate number and vehicle description same as yours, and you match the description of the photographer." Burrows leaned over and picked my coat off the ground and threw it in after me, then slammed the door.

Mary Alice Hodges and her wrath of God. It had to be. My heart beat like a hummingbird's wings against the inside of my chest, and I struggled to think of what Burrows and Samson would find in my car that could get me into trouble, or give them reason to give me trouble. My purse was there with my "baby" Glock 26 inside, and my license to carry in the wallet inside the same purse. I had nothing else in the Mustang except my dry cleaning and the half-spilled cup of coffee.

Well, nothing except for my iPhone on the front passenger seat. I had never taken a dirty picture in my straitlaced life, certainly not of any children. My mind raced through its contents. There was a photo of my husband's girlfriend—a man named Stormy who lived as a woman, although he kept his junk, if you know what I mean—wearing my red negligee. The tramp had texted it to me, and I'd saved it for the divorce, just in case. That one was embarrassing and inappropriate. But did I have any pictures of kids?

I had saved one on there of Betsy with her mother, which I'd used for identification purposes when I was searching for her. Then there were a few I'd snapped of her on the playground, innocent stuff, because it made me feel better to be able to look at them, like the one I'd taken today. Pictures any mother would take, and while I wasn't her mother, I was going through the process of trying to *become* her mother, after all. But I'd password protected my phone with the ultra-secure "1111." I figured it was so obvious no one would ever guess it. Hopefully that included the police, so they wouldn't be able to look at my photos. Then all of this would be moot, and it would get straightened out quickly enough. It had to. I hadn't done anything wrong.

I strained to see what the officers were doing, my view obscured in part by the metal barrier between the front and back seats of the police vehicle. I could see that they had popped open my trunk. Geez. I knew it was empty except for my spare tire, but months of working with Jack kicked in and my brain moved past what they might find to whether they even had a right to search my trunk in the first place. Burrows was treating this like I was Public Enemy Number One, and I was pretty sure Jack would tell me it was an illegal search.

I heard the trunk slam. Footsteps crunched on the snow, coming closer to where I sat trapped in the backseat cage. The driver's side door opened in front and a body landed on the seat. Air whooshed out in protest. The door slammed. In the confined space, I smelled garlic and cheap after-shave. My nose and forehead wrinkled. Burrows put my purse and phone on the seat. He spoke into the radio, holding it with his left hand while he continued to mess with something I couldn't see in the front seat with his right.

"I need a tow into impound on a Ford Mustang, green, on Wentworth Drive across from Windsor Elementary." He read off my license plate number. "I've arrested a suspected child molester, an Emily P. Burr-NAL—B-E-R-N-A-L. I'll be bringing her in. Also, she was in possession of a handgun."

"I have a license to carry! It's in my wallet."

I wanted to scream. How did we jump from the bogus improper photos to the inflammatory and even more screwed-up child-molester accusation? And then the bit added on about my gun to make it sound like some kind of huge deal, like I was a dangerous felon, when it wasn't and I wasn't either. I knew it wouldn't do me any good to argue with him about the semantics, no matter how damaging, but I couldn't believe his gall.

Burrows holstered the radio and turned to me, unloading my Glock as he did. When he had it empty, he inspected it. I saw him read the words engraved around the mouth of the barrel. "So, you think I'm messing with the 'Wrong Girl'?"

"My dad thought so, at least." The gun, and the words, were a fifteenth-birthday gift from my Wild West-throwback father. "I only know *I* didn't do anything wrong, and I don't understand what's going on."

Burrows lowered the gun and shoved it into something I couldn't see from the backseat. Still facing the center of the front seat, he said, "Emily Bernal, we take sex crimes very seriously in this town, and you're under arrest for taking improper photos of a child."

A klaxon horn sounded in my head, and white-hot panic seared me from the inside. Burrows turned his head forward in the driver's seat, and all I could see was his red hair and fuzzy neck that needed a shave.

"Arrested? Improper photos? That's ridiculous. I didn't do any such thing."

He switched on the ignition. "If you haven't done anything wrong, Ms. Bernal, then I'm sure we'll get it all straightened out at the station."

He spoke by rote. "You have the right to remain silent. Anything you say can and will be held against you in a court of law. You have the right to the presence of an attorney before and during any questioning. If you cannot afford an attorney, one will be appointed for you free of charge before any questioning. Do you understand these rights as I've explained them to you?"

He turned back to me again. This couldn't be real. I shook my head.

"You don't understand them?"

"I understand them." I shook my head again. "When do I get my phone call?"

Burrows snorted, and we accelerated into the street with a jerk that snapped my head back against the seat.

CHAPTER 5

Utilitarian gunmetal-gray steel and dirty industrial-white paint filled my view of the storage area before me. Odds and ends of paraphernalia littered the inside of evidence cages. Phones. Wallets. Jackets. Belts. Caps and hats. A motorcycle helmet covered in Arizona Cardinals bumper stickers.

Jack stood behind me while I signed for return of the personal items that I had been required to check in earlier. The officer behind the desk—young, freckled, and open-mouthed, with a nameplate on her chest that read TINSLEY—couldn't tear her eyes away from Jack. *Get in line, sister*, I thought.

I pawed through the tray of my belongings. My purse was there, with my wallet, gun license, and gun (unloaded), as was my coat, but there was something missing. "My phone?"

Without looking away from Jack, she said, "Huh?"

"Officer Burrows took my phone. I need my phone back." I looked at the voucher, which listed my personal property. The phone wasn't on the list. "This voucher's wrong, too."

"Is that your signature on it?"

"It looks like it, but the one I signed listed my phone."

"Well, now, isn't that strange." She smiled at Jack. "Let me check with the officers." She picked up a desk phone and punched a few numbers. "We're missing the inappropriate-photo suspect's phone. Burrows brought her in; Samson was with him. Yeah, Rin Tin Tin." She put her hand over the mouthpiece and whispered, "They call Burrows the drug-sniffing dog because he's so good at busting kids smoking pot." She winked at Jack and spoke into the phone again. "Burr-NAL—B-E-R-N-A-L. Okay. Thanks." She hung up. "Someone's gonna ask him. You can wait over there." She nodded her head at a bench against the wall.

Jack and I looked at each other. He shrugged and we sat. From our side of the room we had a view of the balding strings of silver tinsel strands tucked above the window to the evidence room. Above it, cut-out red letters that hooked together and hung crookedly spelled MERRY CHRISTMA. I wondered if anyone would replace the S.

Jack's phone beeped, but he didn't look at it. "You're sure they checked your phone in earlier?"

"Positive. Why do you think Burrows would keep it? He knows I didn't take any dirty pictures. This whole arrest was just harassment."

Jack pulled his bottom lip. "Is your phone password protected?"

"Yes."

"Did you give the password to them?"

"No. Why?"

"Do you get work email on your phone?"

"Yeah, but—"

"It's the thin blue line."

The Dallas Area Rapid Transit Light Rail Blue Line went from downtown out past White Rock Lake. I had ridden it occasionally when I worked for the Hailey & Hart law firm in Dallas. "I'm confused. How did we get on the subject of trains in Dallas?"

His left eyebrow drew toward his hairline. "I'm talking about how police officers stick together. They call it the thin blue line."

"Oh." I picked some imaginary lint off my sleeve.

His dimple sunk in and out like it was in spasm, and his eyes twinkled. "We have a case against Wu. The police stick together. Maybe someone is trying to see if you have anything on your phone about the Freeman case."

I considered it. Could Jack be right? "Really? Would they even know I work for you?"

Jack said. ""Hmm. Dunno. Probably. It's a small town."

Jack and I had been together the night before when we talked to Samson at Love's, but we weren't working a case. We could have been two people out on a normal date, albeit a really lame one at Love's Travel Stop. I thought back through the last two months. Had my name appeared on anything related to Freeman's case? Paralegals didn't sign pleadings. I hadn't been with Jack when he deposed the officers, either. That was before I came to work at Williams & Associates.

But it hadn't been the first time I'd met Samson. Honestly, I couldn't remember my conversation with Samson two months before when Betsy had been kidnapped. Oh well, like Jack said, it was a small town.

"That'd be too convenient, right after Mary Alice rousted me. I saw her make a phone call, then, bam, ten minutes later, Burrows shows up. He's harassing me for her."

"Maybe."

"That woman terrifies me."

"Hodges? Why?"

"I told you. She *threatened* me with the wrath of God. It was creepy. And then this." I gestured around the room. "What did she do that could make them do this to me?"

"If she did." Jack's phone beeped. He ignored it.

"She did." I snorted. "How'd you get me out, anyway?"

"After a discussion with your attorney, the assistant district attorney decided not to book you."

My voice came out at a higher pitch than I would have liked. "Thank you, but how—"

He pretended to pop his knuckles. "You have the best criminal law attorney in two states."

"No, seriously."

"I'd at least put me in the top five."

"Jack."

"The charges were BS. Plus this was a new ADA, and I told him you worked for me."

Which was good. If it had been my archnemesis, ADA Melinda Stafford, my butt would still be planted on a bench behind bars.

"That was smart."

"I promised him you wouldn't go anywhere near Betsy again without supervision."

"But that's impossible."

He looked at me slant-eyed. "Emily, I'm not sure if you understand the seriousness of your situation. This is a felony involving a child. You can't afford to be charged in the first place, even if I get you off five minutes later. Period."

"I know." The implication of the type of charge I was facing wasn't lost on me. "Even the suggestion of this could ruin my chance of adopting Betsy."

"We won't let that happen."

Ugly truth smacked me in the forehead, a few hours too late. "She knew. Mary Alice Hodges knew what this would do to my adoption chances, and she did it on purpose."

Jack's phone beeped again, and he didn't even glance at it.

"Check your darn phone already," I snapped.

His left eyebrow lifted, pulling the dimple in and mouth up. "It's going to be okay, Emily." He typed a few keystrokes on his phone and swished through text messages. "Wallace. The Hodges called him, and so did Burrows. You're not answering your texts. He's a tad concerned."

"Do you think I need to call him?"

He held his left hand up in the "stop" gesture and a scar caught my attention. I'd seen Jack's hands plenty of times, even felt them on me in ways that made my cheeks flame to remember, but I'd never noticed the scar on his left palm before. And it wasn't insignificant. It was round, like a cigarette burn, but bigger. And puckered. I stared at it as he spoke.

"Let's focus on what's on your plate here, for now."

"Where'd you get that scar on your hand?" I pointed at his left hand, which was now on his leg.

Jack's yellow-brown eyes flicked to mine and then down, and butterflies went crazy in my tummy. How could he irritate me so much, then calm me, intrigue me, and excite me all in less than a minute?

Officer Tinsley called my name from behind the counter. "Ms. Bernal?"

I jumped up and hurried over, Jack moving in long, lazy strides beside me. "Yes?"

"The officers didn't see a phone in your car. They're real sorry and hope you find it."

"But I saw Burrows put it in the front seat of the cruiser, and Samson was right there."

"I'm sorry, ma'am, but that's not how he remembers it."

"He?"

"Burrows."

"Don't all cops have those body camera thingies after Ferguson? Those would prove I'm telling the truth."

"Um, no, sorry, ma'am, our department doesn't have body cams. We do have the dash cams, but they're only triggered in certain situations, or when an officer turns them on."

"So was the camera on when I was arrested?"

She stared at me, slack-jawed.

Jack put his hand on my shoulder. I looked up into his eyes. They were warm, and he nodded at me. I took a small step back and he moved into the gap I'd left.

"Officer Tinsley, thank you for checking for us. Could you let Burrows and the other officer—Samson, was it?—know to expect me to file an official complaint of misconduct with the department, on behalf of Ms. Bernal, for excessive force, falsifying paperwork, and refusing to return her phone? We'll be seeking the dash cam footage then."

"Um—"

"Thank you. Now, let's talk about getting Ms. Bernal's vehicle back."

CHAPTER 6

After Jack took me to pick up my Mustang from impound, we had enough time left in the day to squeeze in one more productive task. We headed toward the office, and I drove behind Jack, caressing the leather by my thigh in a soothing way. My Mustang was closing in on nine years old, but she was still beautiful, and she'd suffered a violation at Burrows's hands every bit as much as I had. At eight, though, she was still only half the age of Jack's vehicle.

The Jeep still bore the ignominy of the previous night's crunch into concrete. Jack had tucked the deployed airbag back into the dash and duct-taped it up. As he backed the Jeep into his parking space in the garage, I saw that the front bumper hung askew with a big fat crease where the chrome had flaked away in the center. The grille had also caved in partway and the left front quarter panel had buckled.

He ducked into the passenger side of the Mustang as I turned on the radio to a country station.

I tightened my lips so I wouldn't smile. "I thought you said there was no damage to your Jeep last night?"

Jack didn't look at me. "There wasn't."

"But the bumper is all messed up, Jack. However did *that* happen?"

"It was already like that."

I shook my head. "I don't remember it looking like that before."

"I did it last week."

"You didn't mention a fender bender." I let my smile out, and he realized I was onto him and grinned with a sheepish look on his face. "Hey, is your Jeep even street legal now without the airbags?"

He nodded. "But the whole system has to be replaced and reset. On both sides."

"Yeah. Since one side tried to kill me, I think that's a good idea." A song I loved came on, and I turned it up. "As long as I'm rockin' with you, girl, you know I'm Cool Whip—"

"Cool with," Jack interrupted.

I turned the radio down. "What?"

"The song. 'As long as I'm rockin' with you, girl, you know I'm cool *with*.' You said 'Cool *Whip*.'"

My cheeks heated just a little. "That's what I said." I put my hand on my signal switch. "Which way?"

Jack had only told me we needed to run an errand, not where or for what reason.

"ABC Half-Price Resale."

I turned my trusty steed north. ABC Half-Price Resale—which was as much a discount clearing house as a resale store—belonged to our client Alan Freeman. "Why for?"

"Continuance until mid-January."

Alan's trial had been set in two weeks, right after New Year's.

"Since this morning?"

The Second Baptist Church flashed by on our left. In temporary letters, an announcement blazed across a white sign out front: LOW SELF-ESTEEM SUPPORT GROUP WILL MEET THURSDAY AT 7:00 PM. PLEASE USE THE BACK DOOR. It made me smile.

Jack said, "Got a call while you were, um, detained."

I pumped my fist in the air. "Woo-hoo!"

A continuance wasn't a surprise. In fact, the real surprise would have been if it hadn't been continued. But we'd prepped only enough to stave off emergency, and we would have had some serious scrambling to do these next two weeks if the post-New Year's schedule had stayed firm.

The case wasn't a shoo-in, but we expected to win it. It was Freeman's word against Wu's. Wu claimed he'd caught Alan soliciting sex from an unidentified woman who had run off in the alley behind the resale store. Wu said when he approached Alan's vehicle, Alan leapt from his car to make a run for it. Wu claimed he gave chase, and that when he caught him, Alan assaulted him with a beer bottle.

Alan's version was completely different. He said he'd gotten out of the car at Wu's request, there was no prostitute, and that Wu had tackled him, and both men fell to the ground. Wu had hit his head on a broken bottle when he landed.

And that was it, as far as evidence would go. No dash cam. No *real* witnesses. Wu had been a rookie in training, and Samson was riding with him, but Samson said he'd run after the supposed prostitute. Alan wasn't charged for solicitation, and he didn't have a history of priors. Wu had since left the force. It looked and smelled like something from the back end of a cow. The recent high-profile cases of police violence and false statements against black men didn't hurt us at all.

I cruised down historic Route 66, now known as Amarillo Boulevard, heading east from downtown toward Alan's shop. Alan worked two jobs: one laying tile for his own little one-man tile company—he did that nights and Sundays and holidays—the other running the resale shop his parents had left to him early that year. The shop was in the part of town you'd expect for resale: stubby strip malls, barred windows, homemade signage, and shallow parking lots. Cars with snazzy rims riding low to the ground. Small storage units. Fast food restaurants on every corner. Everyone talking on brand new mobile phones.

Which made me think of something. "I have an idea."

I glanced at Jack, and he raised the eyebrow on my side. He wasn't the world's most verbose human, so I took that as, "Please, Emily, do continue."

"There's some app that is supposed to find your lost iPhone. Maybe we can see who has my phone that way, since the police are insisting I lost it."

"Doesn't it have to be turned on for that to work?"

"Maybe. Why?"

"Whoever has it has long since copied all the data, removed the SIM card, and deactivated it."

"But they're cops!"

"Cops know every bad-guy trick in the book."

"Bastards."

"Some of them."

I turned into the cramped parking lot for ABC Half-Price Resale, Joe's Barber Shop, Broughton's Shoe Repair, and Cisneros Automotive. Despite Jack's pessimism, I was still planning to try the app. Maybe the cops had misplaced my phone. Or been sidetracked. Or were stupid. I pulled the Mustang into the one tiny parking space available, and we walked toward the storefront.

A man had just left Alan's store, and I nearly ran into him on the sidewalk. He smiled down on me with a weathered face, then tipped his gray felt cowboy hat. "Emily Phelps. Merry Christmas to you."

It only took a second and it all came back to me. Heavy equipment whirring near my head. A mouth filled with plaster of Paris. Giant needles.

Saliva running down my chin. Numb cheeks. My childhood orthodontist, Dr. Parks.

I was able to smile, barely. "Hello, sir, and Merry Christmas to you."

His face drooped. "Oh no." He leaned closer. "Smile again." I obeyed without thinking. He shook his head. "You haven't been wearing your retainer, have you?"

Jack snorted, and I shot him a look.

"Um, well, I did sometimes, for a while"—by which I meant for two to three weeks and never again—"and then I moved, and I couldn't find it."

Dr. Parks opened his wool overcoat and reached into a shirt pocket. He handed me his card. "Make an appointment, please. You'll regret it for the rest of your life if you don't. Headaches. Painful chewing. Mouth breathing. Alteration in the shape of your face. Speech problems."

I gaped at him. "Are you serious?"

He nodded, gravely. "Come see me."

"Thank you." I felt dazed for a moment, then regained my manners. "Nice seeing you."

He waved and walked into the parking lot.

I touched a fingertip to the gap between my two top front teeth.

Jack pulled the door open, and the bell jangled. "After you, Snaggletooth."

I kept my eyes to the front, trying to pretend I hadn't heard him. We walked into the scent of a Christmasy cinnamon-apple pie that had to be coming from a room deodorizer, as I knew there was no kitchen onsite. Alan saw us and waved. His shaved head wasn't covered by his usual LSU Tigers cap. At six foot two, he towered over the woman peering into the glass-counter display of jewelry in front of him. He was one of those muscular guys you knew just from looking at him could outwrestle a grizzly bear. I'd first met him when he was tiling the office lobby—which doubled as *my* office—and he'd been kind and respectful of my space on a particularly bad day for me. I had warmed to him instantly, and I didn't believe for a second he had tried to pick up a prostitute. Or assaulted a cop.

"Be with you in a few minutes," he called.

I smiled at him. To Jack, I said, "You can do your Christmas shopping while we wait."

My boss made a sound like *Great idea* or *Bah humbug*. It was hard to tell which. Actually, I knew Jack never left this place empty-handed, and I didn't either.

Alan worked the shop alone, mostly, while his wife cared for their children, and he had an eye for display. The tile artist in him, I supposed. He'd used for-sale items to create a cozy Christmas scene: a tall, skinny wooden

Santa attended by a legion of "elves"—garden gnomes in Santa hats—and surrounded by beribboned "gifts" like books and jewelry. I picked one up. *Owl Babies*. I thumbed the pages, but it was too young for Betsy. I returned it to its spot in the display. I surveyed the music section, looking for something small and piano related for my friend Katie. Most of the items here were too big to ship to her in the Virgin Islands, though, so I moved on. Electronics, then electrical equipment. I hefted a well-cleaned chainsaw. Not much call for it in country as thin on trees as the Texas Panhandle.

In the household items, I came upon an exquisite toy horse, a black stallion with a silky tail and mane, posed mid-prance. I'd had one very similar to it when I was a girl, and it reminded me somewhat of Thunder. If I were buying a present for Betsy to go in her new pink backpack, this would be the one. I knew I shouldn't let myself think about her, but I couldn't help it. The price tag read seventy-five dollars. It seemed steep, but the item was probably vintage, and it was in pristine condition. I could always give it to her later, when the Hodges didn't have her anymore. When I adopted her. A lump formed in my throat. If that ever happened, after today. I tucked the horse under my arm. I was buying it, darn it.

"Son of a bitch." Jack's voice wasn't exactly a shout, but it carried enough that Alan and his customer looked away from their discussion toward him.

I looked at him. "What's up?"

"Goddammit."

It wasn't like him to use the Lord's name in vain. He cussed, but rarely in a profane or vulgar way. I hurried over to him. He didn't look like he'd thrown a shoe.

"Jack?"

"Take a look at this."

He was standing in front of a sawhorse on which was mounted a gorgeous men's Western saddle. The leather gleamed and the black suede seat begged to be stroked. The same black material adorned the silver corner plates, which were accented with inset turquoise. I'd never ridden on anything so beautiful, in all my years of rodeos and pageants.

I set the toy horse down on a shelf, then ran my finger over the seat. "Wow. What is that gorgeous material?"

"Ostrich. And it's mine."

"You're buying it?"

"No. I already did, in a manner of speaking. Fifteen years ago."

I scrutinized my boss. He didn't look crazy, unless you counted crazy mad. His lips were pressed and his pupils dilated. I knew if he had a pen in his hand he would whack a desk with it right now, something he did whenever he was royally pissed. The bell jingled and Alan's customer left carrying a small bag.

He walked over to us. "Hey, guys. Jack, is something wrong?"

Jack stuck out his hand and Alan shook it. "This saddle. Tell me about it."

Alan rubbed his chin between thumb and forefinger. "I got it in last week. I'm told it's by Harris, a fancy saddlemaker out of Carolina."

"It is."

Alan's eyebrows rose. "You know your saddles."

"You could say that."

"So anyway, again, from what I'm told, the seat is made of ostrich hide and the accents are sterling silver and turquoise. New, a saddle like this goes for about thirteen thousand on their website."

"That's only a little more than my wife paid for it."

In the months I'd known Jack, he had never once mentioned that he had previously been married, that he had a wife and two children until a car bomb meant for him took their lives in Alamogordo, New Mexico. I only knew about them from other people. Hearing him mention his wife now froze the blood in my veins. This was big.

Alan squinted at Jack. "What?"

"When she had it made for me, as a wedding present."

"You're telling me this used to be yours? What are the odds?" He grinned.

"No, I'm telling you it's still mine. It was stolen two weeks ago."

CHAPTER 7

I've always found it difficult to tell when the blood drains from a black person's face. It's not like they go pale. I lose all color; literally, I look like bleached flour. Alan looked ill now.

"Seriously?" he asked.

"I'm afraid so. But don't take my word for it." Jack pointed at the saddle. "Underneath the left stirrup, way up high, you'll find my initials, JPH, and a date. June 7, 1996. Then hers: LTH."

LTH. Lena Talbert Holden. I knew this because I had resorted to Google to fill in the blanks about Jack's past.

Alan lifted the stirrup, turning it for us to see as well. JPH 6-7-96 LTH. "I don't know what to say."

"Tell me about the person who brought it in."

Alan's eyes closed. "Oh man." He walked to the shop door and turned the OPEN sign to CLOSED.

I whispered to Jack, "I didn't know there'd been a robbery at the ranch."

"Greg and Farrah interrupted us."

My brain whirled trying to understand what he meant. Jack was often unclear to the point of obtuse. I hadn't been able to decide if it was his greatest skill or greatest curse. Greg and Farrah had come up to the Jeep when I crashed it into the concrete, but they hadn't interrupted anything. Then I realized he meant that the issue with Greg and Farrah had interrupted our conversation at dinner the night before, when he'd told me we needed to talk. Probably. That, or he was speaking in tongues.

Alan's voice and shoulders sagged. "We need to talk." He trudged back from the front door to us, instantly twenty years older. "Follow me."

He took us behind the U-shaped display counter of guns, jewelry, and coins and on through a heavy closed door in the center of the back wall. Alan flipped on light switches as we walked down a short hall. There were three doors at the end of it. One stood open, to a bathroom on the left. Another closed door on the same side had a plaque that read OFFICE. The last one, on the right, was closed as well. Alan opened the door on the right, again switching on a light. We entered a room filled with cardboard boxes, office supplies, and merchandise.

Alan stopped but didn't turn around. "I keep most everything sellable out front, but if things aren't moving, or if a customer puts something on layaway, I put 'em here. Also, stuff I haven't gotten around to pricing and preparing for display is back here, and a few other things. Things that don't feel right, sometimes."

He crouched down and reached for a box under a table and dragged it out. He opened the flaps. Inside was a cigar box.

He lifted it out and flipped the lid, handing it to Jack. "Does any of this look familiar?"

Jack sucked in a breath. He lifted a currycomb from the box, sterling silver with inset turquoise and something engraved on it. I peered over his shoulder. Jarhead. The date. All American Futurity. Second Place. I put my hand on Jack's shoulder. He sifted his hands through the box and his eyes glazed and drifted far, far away.

I turned to Alan. "Jarhead, the name that's engraved there, is Jack's horse. A very famous racehorse. These are keepsakes, or really more like treasures."

Alan sank into a crouch, his head in his hands. "Shit. It's bad."

"What? What is it?"

He stood back up and began to pace. "When Mama and Daddy died, it messed me up. A gas leak. Who has gas leaks anymore? At least they didn't know what was happening to them; they didn't suffer." He wiped his eyes. "I didn't want this place. I was real happy doing tile. Man, it's like therapy to me. I get in a zone, and when I'm done it's the most satisfying thing in the world."

"You're very good at it."

He smiled, but it was a sad smile. "Thank you. There's so much more to this place than I'd realized. The first week I was here, an eighteen-wheeler pulls up out back. The guy unloads boxes and wheels them in on hand trucks like he owns the place. 'Where do you want your merchandise?' he asks me. 'What's going on?' I say. 'You Edward Freeman?' 'Hell no, that's my daddy and he's dead.' 'Well, I was told to drop this off for him and let you know that payment will be collected in the usual manner.' I'm like, 'What is this shit?' And all he tells me is, 'Special merchandise. Hot sellers, if you know what I mean.'"

Alan stopped and mopped his brow, and I squeezed his arm. It looked like he was about to have a heart attack. Jack had put the box down and was listening, arms crossed.

"I tell him to get that stolen shit out of my store. He does, but not before he warns me that this isn't going to go well for me or him. He practically begs me to take it. Says he'll pay for it, only don't make him put it back on the truck. It was some good shit, too. Jewelry, high class. Phones. Laptops. The kinda stuff that sells, I've learned, and sells for top dollar." He took a deep breath. "They sent an enforcer to see me three weeks later."

"Oh no," I breathed.

"The guy says I owe him some money, that my father had paid him once a month, that it is the price of doing business. Man, I didn't know what to do. By then I'd dug into the books, and our income had been down in the last few weeks. Now I understand why, even though I didn't then. Daddy was getting hot inventory at a reduced price, and that's how he was making enough money to share it with the likes of this guy. He was burying the payments back in Cost of Goods Sold for the merchandise. But I hadn't figured any of that out then. So I told him to get stuffed."

"What did he do?"

"Nothing then. But he comes back the next month. Asks if I'd gotten any smarter. I hadn't. He beat the shit out of me right then and there and said next time it's gonna be my family." Alan and his wife had three daughters, five, eight, and twelve.

"Jesus," I said. "That's scary."

He nodded. "Yeah, and I still didn't get any smarter the next month. I figured he was bluffing. Somebody burned a cross in my yard the next night. My girls still cry when they talk about it."

"I'm so sorry." And I was. Alan was breaking the law. He was hurting other people by his involvement in this scheme. But I wasn't sure what I would have done in his place.

"I'd been mad at my pops until then, but suddenly I felt sad for him. Sick, even. A month later the guy came back. I paid him. A truck showed up the next week and dropped off merchandise, and they've been coming like clockwork ever since. The trucks, and the collections."

Finally, Jack chimed in. "How's that going for you so far?"

"Not so good."

"Are you ready to take it to the cops?"

Alan closed his eyes and licked his lips. The silence in the room was shattered by a loud noise from right behind the back wall, the distinctive almost-train-like sound of the horn of a big rig.

"I'm too damn scared of 'em to cross 'em. Plus, I'm on trial for beating up a cop. You think the police are gonna believe my black ass if I take this story to them? No. No way. And at the end of the day, I can't let anything happen to my wife and girls." Alan shuddered, then opened his eyes. "That's probably a delivery outside. I gotta go see."

Jack nodded but said, "If it's them, don't let them know we're onto you guys."

Alan snorted. "No way in hell." He reached up with both hands and rubbed his cheeks, hard. "I can't take a chance you'll be seen, but you can listen from the hallway if you want."

Jack nodded and motioned to the doorway at me with his head. We went inside, one of us on either side of the door.

"We should get his license plate number," I whispered.

Jack shook his head no.

"I could walk out the front door and around the back."

"In an alley in a bad part of town. No one has a good reason to be back there, certainly no former Miss Rodeo Texas."

I growled. *First runner-up.* "You're letting this go? Chances like this are about as rare as . . . as . . . as . . . as wings on a cat." As soon as I said it, my cheeks heated. Whatever I'd meant to say, that wasn't it. Well, surely Jack would get the point.

His left eyebrow shot sky-high.

I lifted my chin to match it. "In my experience, anyway."

He grinned and put a finger over his mouth. "Shhhh."

The horn honked again. I heard a roll-up door ascending, and then Alan's voice. "You're early."

"So sue me."

"I have customers. If I'm not expecting you, I haven't cleared my schedule. Chill, man. You're drawing attention back here blasting your horn."

"Fuck you."

"Where's Chuck?"

"How the hell should I know? Are you going to help me unload or not?"

Alan didn't answer, but moments later we heard the two men grunt and something heavy land with a thump. A squeaking that sounded like wheels turning came closer, then more grunting, louder, and another thump. More squeaking. Clanking. A resounding clang followed by lesser similar noises.

272 PAMELA FAGAN HUTCHINS

"I won't be here next week. Christmas."

Alan answered, "Good."

"Yeah? Well, fuck you, too."

The rolling door descended noisily and a scraping sound and click followed. The thud of rubberized footsteps approached.

Alan came around the corner. "He's gone."

Jack nodded. "That's a pickle you've got yourself in."

"Man, you have no idea."

"You gonna let this continue?"

My eyes swung to Alan. He said, "I don't know what else to do. My family . . ."

"We could offer this information in return for the DA dropping the assault and resistance charges."

Alan backed up, his foot hitting the wall behind him. "No way, man. No damn way. I'd rather do time than mess with these people."

Jack held his hand in the air. "Okay. I don't want to see you end up in worse trouble later."

Using my least nosey and most winning voice, I asked, "You don't happen to have that driver's name or license plate number, do you?"

Jack took a giant step over to me and stepped on my foot.

"Ow," I said.

Alan shook his head. "What? No." He walked quickly into the storage room again and came out with the cigar box. "Take these, and your saddle. Please. I'm sorry as hell about 'em. And if you can send me a list of what else you have missing, I can see whether it ended up here."

"Thank you." Jack took the box. "Oh, before all of this, we had come by to tell you that your trial is continued until mid-January."

Alan's shoulders slumped farther. "I don't know which is worse. The trial sooner, or worrying about it longer and having it later."

Jack smiled, but it didn't reach his dimple, or his eyes. "I'll send you that list." He stuck out his hand and Alan shook it. "We'll talk to you the first week in January for sure, if not earlier."

"Jack, um—" I wanted to buy the toy horse for Betsy, but as soon as I started to speak I thought better of it. Now wasn't the time.

Jack cocked his head as he waited for me to continue.

"Never mind. Merry Christmas, Alan."

Jack went and got his saddle. I followed him back out into the store and to the front door. The door was locked by a keyed deadbolt. Alan had come with us, and he pulled keys on a metal hoop from his jeans pocket and let us out.

"Merry Christmas to you both." Alan locked the door behind us.

I glanced back and saw that he'd left the sign as CLOSED. I pulled my own key ring out and walked to my Mustang.

As I clicked to unlock its doors, Jack looked at me and shook his head. "He's not telling us something. Something big."

CHAPTER 8

Jack still had the *Amarillo Globe News* delivered to Williams & Associates every morning, and I grabbed the paper from the floor outside the door as I walked into the office. Snowflake spun in circles as she waited to see what I'd brought her. The four-pound Pomeranian ruled the place. Not that Jack told me this himself, but she'd belonged to Jack's young daughter. I'd seen the picture of her holding the dog as a pup with a red bow around her little white neck out at Jack's family's place, a racehorse breeding facility in southern New Mexico called Wrong Turn Ranch.

"Hi, girl." I offered the dog one of the buttery toast crusts I brought her from my own breakfast each day, and she gobbled it up.

Setting my purse down on the desk in my lobby office, I shook the paper open and laid it beside my keyboard. Standing, I read the highlights. The murder at Love's grabbed the headline below the fold. "No Leads on Truck Stop Murder." I scanned it. Charlie Tucker—that had been the guy's name—from Oklahoma. No mention of a suspect, or even witnesses. The article mentioned that this was the first murder at that Love's Travel Stop, but that the police had been called out on multiple occasions before for "public indecency." My nose wrinkled. Public indecency could be a whole lot of different things—child sex crimes, pimping, prostitution, obscenity— none of them something I wanted to think about this early in the morning. Officer Samson's lot lizard remark sprang to mind.

The right-hand article below the fold caught my eye, too. "Phil Samson Named APD Officer of the Quarter." A picture of Samson accompanied the article.

"Speak of the devil," I said aloud.

I sat down in my chair. I scanned the article while my computer booted up. Apparently Samson crawled in through the sunroof of a car that had been hit by a drunk driver. He discovered a boy who had stopped breathing. The story described how he'd dragged the child out and saved him with CPR, amongst other acts of heroism.

Someone shoved the door open, rattling the walls.

Wallace's voice shredded the silence. "What the hell, Emily?"

Snowflake sprinted over to dance around Wallace's size-twelve feet, the tags on her collar jingling and her toenails clicking on the beige and rust-colored tile floor.

"In a minute, Princess," he said to her, as he balanced a tray holding two coffees.

A tall woman in biker clothes with jet-black hair, sleeve tattoos on her pale arms, and a nose ring followed closely behind him, holding a coffee of her own. Our mutual friend Nadine, a Thai waitress by day and a drink slinger by night at the Polo Club, one of Amarillo's finest stripping establishments.

"Good morning, Nadine."

"Morning," she mumbled. Her bloodshot eyes suggested she'd worked the late shift.

I addressed Wallace. "I'm fine, thank you, Mr. Gray, and how are you?" I tilted my head. "Oh, is that coffee for me?"

He handed me a tall Roasters cup and pulled the other out and set it on the corner of my desk. Then he leaned over and ruffled Snowflake's hair.

"Breve?" I asked.

"Do bears relieve themselves in the woods?"

Wallace had memorized how I took my coffee even though I secretly kept my Roasters order on a page in my iPhone's note app. Some things just didn't stick in my gray matter. Coffee orders, phone numbers, whether or not it was okay to wear white shoes before Memorial Day.

"Ah, you're so sweet. Thank you."

Wallace air-kissed at me, then put his grim-lipped face back on. "You're making my life difficult, you know that? This situation with Betsy is *tres* tricky. You can't go around stalking the kid behind my back when I'm trying to help you adopt her."

Nadine took a seat on the tweed couch underneath a Remington knock-off of a cattle drive, but Wallace remained standing in front of me with his hands on his hips. Wallace was over six feet tall, but today his hair poof gave him an extra inch of height.

"Hardly stalking. I've tried to be patient, but those people are impossible." I sat down and jarred my desk with my knee, almost knocking over the framed picture of Geronimo that Jack had given me, along with one of his most famous quotes: *"There is one God looking down on us all. We are all the children of one God."*

I continued my rant: "They won't even let me take her a Christmas present. I don't think they're allowing Christmas presents at all, for that matter."

Wallace frowned and pondered the Christmas tree Jack had let me buy for the corner of my office area. Instead of putting a star on top, I'd crowned it with a berobed Lady Justice with her blindfold, sword, and scales, who I'd glued to a Popsicle stick before attaching it to the tree with pipe cleaners. Christmas rocked. What was wrong with those people?

Nadine swallowed her coffee too fast and coughed, then said, "That's nucking futs."

"I know! Please, Wallace, can you get permission for me to take Betsy a gift? Please?"

He looked back at me from the tree. "I'll do my best, but I can't make you any promises."

"Or at least deliver it to her." I pulled the new pink backpack from where I'd stashed it a few days ago under my desk.

Nadine pointed at it. "I could get that to her, tell them it's from the Rainbow Room." In addition to her two part-time jobs and raising two kids as a single mom, Nadine volunteered a few hours a month at the Rainbow Room, helping outfit less fortunate kids and families with the bare necessities. They worked hand in hand with CPS, which is how she and Wallace had come to be friends.

Wallace nodded. "That could work."

"Thank you, Nadine." I handed the empty backpack to her. "I'm not exaggerating, Wallace. They're freaky—and scary."

"What do you mean by 'scary'?" He pulled a blue upholstered armchair from beside my desk that had been displaced by the Christmas tree. He plopped down into it.

"Babbling about the wrath of God, siccing the cops on me. She gave me nightmares. If she can do that to me, how must those kids she fosters feel around her?"

"They have nothing but nice things to say about her."

"Because she'd threaten them with the wrath of God if they didn't, I'll bet."

"You're serious, aren't you?"

"I am."

Nadine chimed in. "I think there's such a thing as too religious."

He laughed. "Coming from an agnostic, that isn't surprising."

I said, "History is full of horrible things done by zealots in the name of religion."

"As are current events. I'm not sure the Hodges are zealots, though. They *are* definitely very religious, and they're strict. But the kids do well under their watch, so far. And it's a blessing to me to have someone eager to take the special needs kids."

I frowned. "But Betsy isn't special needs."

"She is in the foster system. It's different than in the medical and educational worlds, where *special needs* means autism spectrum or learning disabilities or cystic fibrosis or something like that. Foster-care special needs includes all that, but it also means kids that are older, and thus hard to place, or part of a sibling group, and thus hard to place, or a minority over the age of two, and you get the picture." He'd described the line of ducklings I'd seen with Hodges to a T.

"And Betsy falls in the last category."

"Six-year-old Mexican girl? Definitely."

"But she wouldn't be hard to place. I want her."

"I know you do. And I know you're getting set up to foster and adopt as fast as you can. I am so proud of you, honey, really, I am, but where are you on the house hunting?"

"I'm going to look at a duplex today." I held up three fingers in the Scout's honor gesture.

"Okay, keep me posted. Meanwhile, a stable family has taken her in. Try to think of that as a good thing."

I shuddered. "Stable except that they keep expanding. Exponentially, practically. How many do they have right now?"

"Including their own? Twelve."

Nadine's eyes popped wide. "No way. Twelve?"

I shook my head. "Holy guacamole. How can they take care of that many?"

"How have people ever? My best friend at SMU was a Mormon. Ninth of twelve. The older ones help by taking care of the younger ones."

I hadn't known he'd gone to SMU, but somehow I wasn't surprised, even though he was from Houston. "I was one of one. And my mother barely held it together."

Wallace smacked his palm to his forehead. "'Things not to say in your foster and adoption home study interviews,' by Emily Bernal. Closely followed by 'I was arrested for taking improper photographs of children.'"

"Noted." I sipped coffee. Wallace pointed at me then pantomimed wiping his lip. I ignored him and took another sip. "I guess the bigger question is why anyone would want twelve or however many temporary kids. Besides being a do-gooder, I mean."

His eyebrows shot up. "Really?"

"What, is that a dumb question?"

"Not from a former beauty queen, I suppose." He changed his voice to a southern drawl. "Some people out there in our nation don't have maps."

"Huh?" Nadine said.

You'd either caught the famously clueless answer to a pageant question by Miss South Carolina in the Miss Teen USA pageant back in 2007 or you hadn't. Or maybe I watched too many beauty pageants.

"Very funny, wise guy." To Nadine I said, "Beauty pageant joke."

Wallace flipped his hand over, dismissing me. "They're Christians. They believe it's their duty, plus they get to save all those souls."

Nadine shook her head. "They want the kids because of money. They get seven hundred dollars apiece, monthly. Do that math."

"In my head? I wasn't a math major." I punched it into the calculator on my computer.

"It was sort of a rhetorical question."

"Except that it wasn't a question." I looked up. "Eight thousand four hundred smackers a month. One hundred thousand and change a year. Wow."

"And if you're frugal, you can live on that, even with twelve kids. No outside income required."

"So it's Mary Alice's job."

Nadine snorted. "Proving I'm in the wrong line of work."

Wallace said, "And her husband's job, too, what's-his-name."

He hadn't asked, but I filled in the blank anyway. "Trevon." I had their dossier memorized.

"Yep. Well, enough of that." Wallace jumped to his feet and grabbed a bronze bell with a black handle off my desk. Jack kept it there so I could let him know when I was coming down the hall, since his office doubled as his condo, complete with a Murphy bed cleverly hidden in some built-ins. Wallace rang it vigorously. "I have to see Jack."

I winked at Nadine. "He's still straight, Wallace."

"Details." He kept ringing. "I need an update on Betsy's petition."

Wallace was referring to a Special Immigrant Juvenile status petition that Jack was putting together, pro bono, for Betsy. On top of that, Jack was preparing to file a survivor action on her behalf for the wrongful death of her mother, Sofia, who was murdered while incarcerated in the Potter County Detention Center. First we had to exhaust the completely unhelpful grievance process with PCDC, though, however long that took.

"Don't mind us," Nadine said.

Wallace kept ringing.

"He's probably on the phone and gonna come down the hall and kick your butt for making that racket." I pointed at the still-ringing bell.

Wallace set it down. In a thick accent and girly voice he said, "You think Jack's gonna 'kick my butt'? Well, spit."

"Mock my ladylike manners if you must, but we'll see who gets to move to the front of the line at the Pearly Gates."

Heavy footsteps stomped down the hall toward us before we saw Jack.

"What in hell is so important?" He stalked into the lobby, the hem of his jeans halfway in his boot tops, his shirttail untucked. His hair was mussed and pupils wide. A spider web of creases marred his cheek, and he had a little wet smudge by the corner of his lips.

I tried not to laugh but felt my lips compress.

Wallace put a hand on one hip. "I thought this office could use a little more cowbell."

Jack rubbed his eyes and looked blank, but Wallace, Nadine, and I laughed.

"Hi, Jack," Nadine said.

"Morning, Nadine."

Wallace reached his hand out, and Jack shook it. "Seriously, I want an update on Betsy."

The office phone rang, which only happened during business hours when Jack's secretary, Judith, transferred calls directly to us from his office in Tularosa, New Mexico. Otherwise, she handled it, or it went to voice mail. I looked down at the phone. A red light by my extension indicated the call was for me, not Jack.

I picked it up. "Williams and Associates, Emily Bernal speaking."

I heard deep breathing on the other end. Jack and Wallace continued talking without me.

"May I help you?"

Click.

Weird. I hung up and tried to rejoin the conversation, but it didn't take long to get lost when the subject was immigration. I was a litigation paralegal—board certified in civil litigation, in fact—recently converted to criminal law, where I had far to go before I achieved mastery, as it was. Now I was tackling immigration, and I'd learned a lot about this foreign-to-me (no pun intended) area of the law in the past two months, more than I'd ever aspired to. My head swam with acronyms: DACA, DAPA, DHS, USCIS, ICE. Family law, too. Fewer acronyms there, but lots of new concepts around guardianship, foster care, and adoption. And I'd even picked up some estate/probate where it crossed over with family law. Throw the immigration, family, and estate laws in on top of the criminal, and I had one overfull cranium.

One thing I did understand clearly: Betsy needed permanent legal resident status, and the only way she could get that was if the Department of Homeland Security, the aforementioned DHS, granted her Special Immigrant Juvenile status and issued her a J visa. Which they might do if we could produce her birth certificate, prove that she was a ward of the state of Texas, and show that it was in her best interests to remain in the U.S.

We had jumped through some of those hoops already. CPS was administering her temporary living arrangements and issuing checks to the Hodges for her care. The probate court that handled Sofia Perez's estate—which included virtually nothing except guardianship of Betsy—had signed an order making Betsy a state ward. Jack had received it the day before.

"This is my first J-visa case," Wallace was saying.

Jack leaned against the wall and crossed his arms over his chest. "Mine, too."

"The CPS attorney—Ralph Hanson, do you know him?"

"Of him. Haven't met him."

"Ralph gave me some forms to fill out for the application." Wallace pulled some documents from a black leather briefcase. He handed them to Jack.

Jack scanned them quickly. "Looks like the two we need. Filling them out should be easy enough. The tough part is that we need a copy of her birth certificate."

"Yeah, and I've been trying to find hers practically since the day we found her. It's like looking for a needle in a field of haystacks. She doesn't know where she was born, and we don't know if Perez is really her last name."

"Can't you get a birth certificate at the Mexican consulate offices now?"

"Yeah, but you have to be from an area that isn't so rural that their records aren't computerized, and appear in person with an ID. Betsy is six. She has no ID."

My throat tightened, and I felt my pulse in its hollow. The phone rang again. I snatched it up. "Williams and Associates, Emily Bernal speaking."

Breathing again.

"May I *help* you?" My tone was curt, I knew, but the prank caller was interrupting me at a seriously bad time.

More breathing, then a throat clearing. Nadine looked up at me from playing with her phone.

"Listen, whoever you are, either speak up, or don't call again." I hung up the phone, and winced at the sharp sound it made as it hit the cradle.

Jack and Wallace both turned to me. Jack's left brow lifted.

"Prank caller," I said.

Jack's forehead creased in a frown that didn't reach his lips. "Okay."

His face relaxed, and he turned back to Wallace. "So until you find it, we're dead in the water."

"Find what?" I asked.

"We're still talking about Betsy's birth certificate," Wallace said, then, "If ICE shows up and takes her before we find it and file, they can deport her." He was referring to Immigration Customs and Enforcement, better known as ICE.

My hand flew to my throat over my drumming heartbeat. "They wouldn't do that to an innocent little girl, though, would they?"

The phone rang again. I yelled, "Spit!"

Wallace and Jack shared a look. Nadine laughed.

I tried to sound pleasant. "Williams and Associates. This is—"

"Um, Emily, I think you know me and my friend, and we're in trouble. You offered to help and we think you're the only one that maybe can. But we can't talk to you unless we know you'll keep it between us."

I recognized Greg Easley, even though we'd only met twice. I didn't know many boys his age, for starters, and his voice had a raspy quality to it that was unforgettable. My eyes flicked up to Jack, then Wallace, then Nadine. All three watched me, the conversation about Betsy at a standstill.

I smiled at them and used my brightest voice. "Hi, Katie, great to hear your voice. Sorry, I thought you were a prank caller. I'm in a meeting right now with my boss and my friends Wallace and Nadine. Can we talk later, like in fifteen minutes?" My friend Katie and I talked a lot, and my watchers all knew her by name. They relaxed and looked away; Jack and Wallace resumed their conversation about Betsy. I strained to hear them in one ear and Greg in the other.

"That CPS guy is there? You can't tell him it's us. Please."

"I won't."

He exhaled loudly, like a horse almost. "You want us to call back in half an hour?"

"Yes. We should be done by then."

"This number?"

"Yes, please."

"Okay, yeah, that's fine."

"Great. Talk to you then."

"Yeah, um, thanks. Bye-bye."

"Bye."

Six eyes settled on me again, and I prayed they couldn't read my emotional state from my face, because inside my stomach was doing flip-flops about Greg and Farrah.

I picked up a stack of papers on my desk and tapped their bottom edges against my blotter, straightening them. "So, where were we?"

CHAPTER 9

Jack walked Nadine and Wallace to the door ten minutes later, and the phone rang as it shut. I prayed it wasn't Greg again and lifted the receiver to my ear.

"Williams and Associates, Emily Bernal speaking. May I help you?" I needed my greeting on a recorder at the rate I was using it today.

"Hello, Emily. This is Mickey. May I speak to Jack?" Jack's cousin Mickey Begay worked as the ranch manager at Wrong Turn Ranch. His wife, Laura, raced their quarter horses as a jockey. A good one.

"Of course, Mickey." I pressed hold. "Mickey for you, Jack."

Jack dropped his lanky frame into the chair in front of my desk. My skin tingled at his nearness. "Can you put it on speaker?"

I pursed my lips in a questioning way, but he didn't react. I pressed speakerphone and nodded toward him.

"Hey, Mickey. What's up?" he said.

"Hey, Jack. You still coming out tomorrow?"

"Weather permitting."

"I need to bring you in on something."

"Shoot."

"Laura's had a miscarriage. Another girl."

My eyes shot to Jack's. I hadn't known they were trying to have kids.

Jack's voice softened. "I'm sorry, man."

"Yeah, me, too." Mickey sighed. "She's taking it even harder this time. You know her doctor told her the reason she's having so much trouble getting pregnant is her body weight?" Laura kept her weight way, way down as a jockey.

"I remember."

"There's also like a seventy percent higher risk of miscarriage for women who are underweight. After the first miscarriage, he said she has to be serious about iron and folate and fresh fruits and vegetables when she *does* get pregnant."

My mind went back to my own miscarriage and surgery. I closed my eyes, sad for Laura. I knew obesity was a risk factor for miscarriage, but I hadn't known that being underweight was, too.

"I'm sorry," Jack said again.

"Yeah, she didn't even know she was pregnant this time, so she didn't realize it was time to supplement and change her diet." Mickey cleared his throat. "She's decided to retire so she can gain some weight."

"Wow, that's big."

I nodded, agreeing with Jack even if I couldn't speak and let Mickey know I was on the phone, too.

"Yeah. So I wanted to give you a heads up that she's having a tough time right now."

In the background, I heard Laura's voice. "I'm home." Then, "Who are you talking to?"

Mickey said, "Jack."

"Okay."

"You all right?"

"I'm going to lie down."

"I'll be in there in a minute, hon."

Silence for a few seconds. Mickey whispered, "Okay, I think she's gone."

Jack had rested his forehead in one hand, elbow on my desk, but he lifted it now. "Let me know if there's anything I can do."

"I will."

"For you, too."

"Thanks, Jack."

They said good-bye and hung up. Jack and I stared at each other. His eyes were soft and warm and golden and kind, and I rested there in them for a moment.

"You okay?" he finally asked.

I nodded, still looking into his beautiful eyes. He reached a hand across my desk, palm up, and I placed mine in his. Electricity shot up my arm as his fingers closed around mine.

A loud, long whine interrupted us. Jack looked down. We both knew who it was.

"Need to go, Snowflake?" The tags jingled madly, and he reached down to pet her. "I've got to take her out," he said to me.

"Do you need me to do it?"

"No. Some cold air will do me good."

I pulled my hand away from his, grabbing the leash from my desk drawer and handing it to him. He snapped it on and they walked to the door.

"Don't you need a coat?" I asked.

He turned to me one last time and grinned big, all on the left. "Coats are for sissies." Man and tiny dog exited, and I caught one last glimpse of them through the sidelight window before they disappeared down the hallway.

The phone rang again immediately. I snatched it up, repeating my standard greeting by rote at twice its normal speed.

Greg's voice said, "Emily? I called earlier. Can you talk?"

"Hi, Greg. Yes, I can."

"Are you alone?"

"Yes, but only for a few minutes."

"Okay." I heard whispering in the background.

"What is it?"

"Remember how last night we said we didn't need help?"

"Yes."

"Well, we've changed our minds. We, um, saw something. Last night."

I reached for my Roasters cup. Cold, half-full. "What was it?" I took a sip. Still delicious.

"We saw someone shoot a man."

A chill settled over my face. The gunshots. The black trucker's red blood against white snow. "At Love's?" I put the cup down.

"Yeah. And now today we saw on TV the person that got shot died."

"Yes, he did. But I don't see how that changes things. Not that I don't think you need help. I do. But what's the problem?"

"We didn't just see it. We were really close, and the person saw us, too."

That did change things. They were witnesses to a murder, to a murderer. "Oh my gosh, that is scary. But it was dark. I'm sure you weren't recognizable. Please try not to worry." Like my words would stop them from it. Poor kids. I would worry in their shoes. But then I had an idea—they could help the police bring the killer to justice. I stood up, wireless receiver to my ear, and walked to the door. "I know it would be upsetting, but do you think you would be able to look at suspect photos or work with a police sketch artist, maybe? To help them ID the person? The paper said they don't have any leads." I leaned until I got a look down the hallway in the glass. No Jack and Snowflake. I walked back to my desk and sat.

His voice was firm. "No. We're not safe. Before, we only had to find a place to stay, find jobs. Now, no matter where we go or what we do, they'll always be out there."

I jiggled my mouse and my background picture of Betsy popped up, one I had taken outside the school a month before. She had pigtails high on either side of her head, and she was laughing so hard her face had scrunched. I touched an index finger to the screen on her button nose. A pang of longing shot through me.

I turned my full attention back to Greg. "I understand. But CPS and the police can protect you. Why don't you let me come get you, and I can take you in to talk to Byron and—"

"No. We can't. We won't. It has to stay a secret, or you'll never hear from us again."

I felt the wrinkles between my eyebrows furrow. "I don't get it, Greg."

"You don't have to." His voice grew shrill. "But Farrah is never going back where someone can hurt her, never. I won't let her. If you won't help us, fine. Just say so."

I used my most gentle tone. "That's not what I'm saying. But there are things I'm scared of, too." I touched Betsy's nose on the screen again. "I'm trying to adopt a little girl right now. I can get in big trouble if I help you guys and don't report it to CPS." I ran through what little family law I knew from my years as a paralegal and from my CPS training. I was pretty sure harboring a runaway was a criminal offense. "I could even go to jail or be fined a lot of money."

"Not if no one finds out."

"But people *do* find out things."

"We won't let them."

Ah, to be invincible and in control, or at least to be young and convinced you are. "What exactly is it you guys are asking me to do?"

"Help us find a way out of Amarillo so we can be safe."

My gut clenched. Even though I'd told him the consequences, he didn't know how much they were asking of me. Of course they didn't. They couldn't. They were young, and in trouble. "Where are you now?"

"Are you going to help us?"

"I'm going to think about it." And pray about it.

"We'll decide whether to tell you where we are *when* you decide."

The door opened. Jack and Snowflake had returned. Jack's nose looked red and runny. Well, it was colder than a witch's you-know-what out there. His eyes looked bright, though, and he had a bounce to his step. Snowflake ran to greet me and I leaned down and petted her.

I pointed at the phone and mouthed, "I'm on a call," to Jack.

He unclipped Snowflake and mouthed, "I kind of guessed that," smiled, and walked toward his office.

"Are you still there?" Greg asked, and his voice had lost its strident edge. It sounded scared, desperate. It hurt my heart.

"I am. But I have to go now. I'm sorry."

"When will you decide?"

"Call me at five. I'll let you know then what I'm able to do. And you can let me know whether you guys have changed your minds."

"Okay, but we won't." He hung up.

Betsy. I had dodged one bullet with the bogus arrest. I couldn't let anything jeopardize an adoption. Could I? I sat with the phone in my hands, paralyzed with uncertainty and a growing dread.

CHAPTER 10

At lunchtime, Nadine and I dined on green veggie curry at My Thai courtesy of her employee discount. Our food came, Nadine chatted, yet all I could think about was the predicament Greg's call had put me in. My mind flitted from Betsy's smiling face to horrible images of Greg and Farrah in a succession of dire circumstances: running from a barreling eighteen-wheeler with TUCK69 plates, crouched inside a closet while an enormous man pounded on the door, shivering and hungry under a snow-covered overpass. I had barely said "boo" to Nadine the entire meal, and I smiled and nodded when she talked, without really hearing her.

I had to do better.

I shook myself mentally and forced words out of my mouth. "What're you doing this afternoon?" I scooped up a bite from my dwindling plate of curry.

She swallowed and wiped her mouth with a paper napkin. "I'm putting in a few hours at the Rainbow Room."

I held the fork poised in front of me. "I don't know how you do it. I really don't. Two jobs, single mom, and you volunteer, too? You're my hero."

A petite Asian waiter stopped at our table and filled our water glasses. She looked at us with a thumbs up, and we nodded. She reached into her apron and pulled out a faux leather bill holder and set it in the center of our table. She stepped back, cocked her head, then scooted it with one finger an imperceptible distance to the left and moved away behind a sparse plastic fichus tree to another table.

Nadine said, "People have always helped me out. I owe it back."

"Still." I shoveled a bite in and chewed. The tastes and textures registered, a little. Sweet coconut milk, spicy curry, an al dente bell pepper.

She lifted her eyebrows and lowered her fork to the mauve plastic placemat. "When I was sixteen, my mother's bad-news boyfriend Bill moved in. He started visiting me in the middle of the night, and Mama didn't want to hear it. Things got pretty wild from there. Drugs. Staying out all night. Older guys, just not as old as Bill. Anything to keep away from him and forget. You know?"

"Yes. I'm so sorry," I said, nodding. Not that I had personal experience with any of what she'd gone through—my high school days were Sandra Dee compared to hers—but I knew what she meant, and I couldn't imagine how hard it must have been for her. I set my fork down, too. She had my full attention now.

"I ran away a few times, and the police threatened to refer me to a CPS group home or put me in a detention center. Then Mama discovered crack cocaine."

"Nadine, that's so awful." My words felt like dust on my tongue. Dry, insubstantial, useless.

"Yeah. It was. So I showed up on the doorstep of one of my teachers from Fannin Middle School—Ms. Davidson; she was retired—and she said I could move in with her if it was our secret. I stayed with her and her longtime girlfriend for months."

"You're kidding!" I wanted to squirm in my seat. Well, Ms. Davidson wasn't trying to adopt a sweet little girl. There was no comparison between our situations.

Nadine smiled, her eyes soft and sad. "I would have stayed forever, but she died suddenly, and Bill had left, so I went home."

"Oh no!"

"I still miss her every day. But Ms. Davidson wasn't the only one to take a chance helping me. A few years ago my first son's dad left me. My mother was in the gutter, literally. Homeless, showing up at my doorstep. Stealing from me. Buying drugs right outside my house. Screaming so loud the neighbors could hear." She wiped a tear away with a rough backhand motion. "Someone called CPS. And instead of taking my son away, the Rainbow Room ladies helped me. They gave me a car seat and diapers and formula and some clothes, which was great. But they went way beyond that." Her voice grew thicker. "Referred me to a state-funded rehab facility for Mom. Helped me get on a list for a subsidized daycare place. Encouraged me. Followed up with me. Never judged me."

My throat tightened and my eyes stung. I'd never imagined Nadine had had it so bad. "Nadine." I tried to say more, but I couldn't find the words. I reached out and grabbed her hand and squeezed it tight, then held on.

"So, that's why I make time to work in the Rainbow Room, and to take flowers to Ms. Davidson's grave. Because without either of them, I wouldn't be here today."

The enormity of what Ms. Davidson had done, of what she had risked to prevent harm to Nadine, came crashing down on me.

I spoke, but my words came out broken and raspy. "I understand." I cleared my throat.

Why, why, why was I being tested like this, with Greg and Farrah and their problems? Betsy needed me, too. But as soon as I thought it, I was hit with a deep sadness. That wasn't really true, was it? She was clean, fed, in school, with new siblings, and had a safe place to sleep at night. I'd seen her. She was playful, confident, and happy. A far cry from Greg and Farrah. My resistance wasn't because Betsy *truly* needed me, not like the teens did. It was because I truly *wanted* Betsy. Ouch. Forced to choose between the teens' needs and my desires, I felt cornered, like the feral dog that I'd found sleeping in our barn one winter morning long ago, snappy and snarly and untrusting.

I took a deep breath. I was surely more rational than a wild dog. What did Greg and Farrah really need me to do, after all, that was so huge? Come get them, let them stay for the night, then take them somewhere safe and far away? Those weren't big things, not really, and no one had to know. I would just have to put the fear of God in them about never, ever, ever telling a living soul I was the one who had helped them. And if worse came to worst, I could turn them over to Wallace. I didn't want to, but I could. Whichever way it went, I would be careful, and I could still adopt Betsy.

"Cat got your tongue?" Nadine asked.

I smiled at her, not really feeling it yet, but closer. "Sorry. Got lost in my thoughts there for a moment. Your story is powerful."

She nodded. "But all that is in the past. Are you ready to go?" she asked, yanking me the rest of the way out of my head.

"Sure." I fished a twenty and ten from my wallet and stuck them in with the bill, then slid it to overhang two inches past the edge of the table, but centered precisely.

"Wait, you can't get that." Nadine grabbed her purse.

The waiter appeared out of nowhere and took the folder like a trout taking a fly.

"I already did." I smiled and stood up. "Want to come with me to see the duplex I'm hoping to lease?"

She got to her feet, towering over me in high-heeled boots. "My kids are in school, and I've got nowhere to be for a few hours. Why not?"

Nadine drove her Harley, following me south on Soncy Road toward a new neighborhood on the outskirts of town. After a mile or two of stoplights, I veered left onto Hollywood, through former prairie on both sides of the road. Other than a few real estate signs, there were no marked improvements to the land I'd known since childhood, until we came to a cluster of houses on the left. Even once we'd turned into that neighborhood, I couldn't see much change to the land's former condition, other than houses plopped down onto square plots of snow-speckled brown grass. The houses themselves were nondescript: brick flanked on each side by mirror-image driveways and entrances. The vehicles out front were mostly midrange hybrids and electrics, a far cry from what you'd find in old Amarillo. I pulled in behind a Ford Focus and got out. Nadine rumbled to a stop behind me and parked at an angle to the curb.

A pregnant woman stood in the doorway on the right side of the house in a flannel empire-waist maxi dress and a heavy gray shawl.

"Hello," she called out and waved.

I raised a hand in greeting, waiting for Nadine to dismount and join me. We walked up the sidewalk together.

"I'm Emily," I said, holding out a hand, which the woman took. "This is Nadine."

"Nadine, Emily, I'm Sara Edwards, one of the homeowners. Nice to meet you."

"You, too." Nadine shook Sara's hand.

Sara tucked her chin-length brown curls behind one ear. "Shall we go inside?"

"Absolutely," I replied.

The three of us walked to the far side of a tiny entryway with earth-toned ceramic tile floors. The tile ended at each edge of the entrance and gave way to neutral tan carpet. We stood on the edge of the large space that held the living room, dining area, and kitchen, with windows all across it to a barren backyard.

As I admired the maple kitchen cabinets in a natural finish, the light granite countertops, and the stainless steel appliances, I thought I saw something out of the corner of my eye. A little girl flew high in a swing, kicking her feet, being pushed by a teenage boy. Another girl about his age sat in another swing, twisting side to side with her toes on the ground. They looked familiar but were too far away to recognize for sure out of my peripheral vision. I glanced away from the kitchen and looked for them, and they were no longer in the yard—if they were ever there. I sidestepped and put my hand out, suddenly feeling dizzy.

Movement in the kitchen caught my peripheral attention again. Three dark heads in stairstep height, six hands busy washing and drying dishes. I switched my gaze quickly from the backyard to the kitchen. No kids.

What was wrong with me? A psychotic break? Normal people didn't see imaginary kids in strangers' houses. I put my fingers to my cheek to refocus myself and studied the interior décor.

The walls in the kitchen and the other two rooms were a tasteful-if-nondescript almond with crisp white trim. My Dallas condo had been white, black, and silver to suit Rich's taste, so this would be a refreshing change for me. I lowered my hand and swiveled to look in either direction off the foyer. Hallways jutted toward doorways beyond.

The faint laughter of children bounced toward me down one hall. I wanted to clap my hands over my ears; that, or see if Sara had any Valium.

Sara's voice pulled me back into the real world. "My husband and I are moving into a bigger house." She put her hand on her enormous belly. "Number four. We need more space. But he's always wanted to own rental properties, so here we go, right?" She beamed, revealing perfect white teeth.

"Congratulations," I said, as I tried to peer down the hallway without drawing attention to myself. Maybe there really were people down there. Sara's kids, perhaps? But why did I think it had sounded like Betsy's laugh?

"Thank you," Sara said.

Nadine shot me a "gag me" look with her index finger jabbing into her mouth behind Sara's head, but I barely noticed, my mind on the tricks my imagination was playing on me. Seeing people that weren't there? Hearing sounds that weren't real? Maybe it wasn't a psychotic break; maybe the curry was spoiled, and this was food poisoning.

Sara put her hand on my arm. "Is it just the two of you that would plan on living here? Not that we have anything against lesbians, of course."

Nadine set down the framed picture she had lifted from a low table in the entryway. "Good to know." She took a deep breath, raising her shoulders an inch.

I hurried to prevent Nadine from going any further. "Us either. But, it's only me. Nadine's providing me with moral support today."

"Ah. Well, it's a lot of house for one person."

The sound of Betsy's voice broke through for a moment, and I fought not startling and widening my eyes in reaction. "Can I have the bedroom with the purple butterflies?" her little voice asked. "Farrah can share with me until she moves away."

Just like that I was certain, as certain as I ever could be. I would get this house and adopt Betsy and help Greg and Farrah and have it all, dang it, because I could pull this off and everybody would be the better for it.

"No," I said to Sara. "It's the perfect amount of space. I'll take it."

Nadine raised her eyebrows, and I flashed her a weak smile.

CHAPTER 11

Hours later—per Greg's instructions—I pulled my Mustang flush along-side an unremarkable apartment complex in the center of town. I eased forward until I was as near as I could get to the stairs on its north side. Twilight had fallen, and the meager lighting cast an eerie glow on the hulking brick building and asphalt lot around it. Red, green, yellow, blue, and orange lights blinked from a lone window on the upper floor. Some-where behind me, an engine revved. Glasspacks, loud enough to wake the neighborhood.

Greg and Farrah had taken refuge here with a young man who had aged out of the foster system, a guy Greg had lived with in a previous foster family. It was a decent enough solution to their desperate situation the night before, but obviously their problems had morphed from those of mere runaways in the dead of winter into those of a much more dangerous kind.

The passenger-side back door opened suddenly, and I squeaked. I whipped my head around in time to see Farrah's tiny figure scoot across the backseat and Greg's bigger but still-too-thin body follow her. Each teenager wore black, head to toe. Greg shut the door softly, and Farrah laid her head on Greg's legs. He lowered his to her back, which put them well below the bottom of the windows. They were hidden, unless someone walked right up to my car.

"You scared me to death. I never even saw you guys out there," I said.

"Sorry," Greg said.

"Thank you," Farrah added.

"You're welcome." I hadn't even put my car in park yet, so I eased off the brake and made a wide left back to the parking lot exit. "Do you need anything in town before we drive out to Heaven?"

"Heaven?" Farrah's voice rose in pitch.

"Sorry. Bushland. Where I live. Heaven is my boss's nickname for it."

"Why?"

"It's west of town, and he says that makes it halfway to the Heaven that is New Mexico."

"Is New Mexico Heaven?"

I laughed, turning left on Paramount toward I-40. "Parts of it are quite lovely."

"We need to get where we're going, quick, before someone sees us," she said.

Her words made my skin prickle. I checked my rearview mirror, getting a fix on the cars behind me. Black Ford F-150. White minivan of some type. Silver Camry. "Greg said the shooter saw you guys. Do you think he knows who you are? Or followed you?"

"Yes."

"How do you know—did he call you by name?"

Neither kid answered. I let the silence linger as I merged onto I-40 going west. "Have you seen him before?" I scanned the rearview for cars again. The minivan was still behind me. I cut my eyes back to the road, then stretched upward to catch the kids in the rearview. It didn't work, so I adjusted the mirror until I could see their faces. They were both staring back at me. "Well?"

Farrah answered. "We can't talk about it."

"Why?" Silence met my question again, like a brick wall. Then it hit me. "You guys don't trust me."

"Nothing personal."

"Then why'd you call me?"

"We trust you more than anyone else."

"How come?"

"Remember that time when we met you?"

"Yeah. What about it?"

"We could hear you out there, you know, talking to that CPS guy. Walter or whatever."

"Wallace."

"Yeah. Anyway, he didn't want to come in the house, because he wouldn't break the rules, even though you guys were looking for a lost little girl, and she could have been in there."

"Right, so?"

"So, you were. You were brave enough to go in by yourself, too. So, we trust you, mostly."

I laughed. "Most people would reach the opposite conclusion from that story."

Greg's deeper voice— not by much—said, "Not us. And it's not just about trust. If we tell you, then you could be in trouble."

I met his eyes in the rearview mirror. "Greg, if you're being watched, whoever it is assumed you've already told me, as soon as he saw you get in this car. Don't kid yourself."

I looked away to check the road and then back at him again. He stared at me and nodded, his head sideways over Farrah's shoulders, but he didn't say anything else. They looked so young and vulnerable. Remembering that they'd been seeking a ride out of town at the Love's the night before, I recalled that the newspaper article I'd read that morning mentioned public indecency issues at the truck stop. I cringed. They'd probably come closer than they'd known to a lot more than witnessing a murder.

I watched the road again. "So, at my house, there's one other person. My mother. But it's cool. You guys can stay in my room, and she'll never know you're there."

"No one else can know about us," Greg reminded me.

I chose my words carefully, not wanting to overcommit. "I understand."

As we exited Amarillo proper, we passed the iconic Cadillac Ranch on our left, or at least we passed where I knew it to be. It was too dark to see the ten angled Cadillacs planted in the dirt, every square inch of each covered in a rainbow of spray-painted graffiti that would be partially obscured by snow right now. I saw them every day, sometimes more than once, and I knew them by heart.

I checked behind us again. No white minivan. No nothing, no nobody, as far as I could see. If the murderer had been watching them, he or she didn't seem to be following us now. And if CPS or the police had been onto their whereabouts, they would have been doing more than watching. Maybe the kids were being paranoid that they'd been recognized, that the murderer was searching for them, even following them. Or maybe they weren't.

Acid churned in my gut. I was out on a limb here, transporting known runaways from the same state system I was trying to get permission from to foster and adopt, on the heels of getting myself arrested on charges of inappropriate behavior with a child, however bogus. Going behind Wallace's back, too, and smack dab in the commission of a crime, maybe even a felony if harboring underage runaways was as illegal as it felt.

Risking Betsy's adoption. Putting myself squarely in the sights of the same killer that was after Greg and Farrah. Yeah, I was way out on this limb, to its very tip with the bough bending toward the ground as far as it would go, and the loud crack of it snapping in two only a heartbeat away.

But my heart told me I had no choice, and I would have to have faith that it wouldn't break.

I parked a few minutes later in front of the little white house on fifteen acres where I lived with the maternal half of my gene pool. Once again, I checked the side-view mirror. No headlights. I scanned the street ahead of me. No chatty neighbors out braving the cold temperatures. Our porch light had burned out the week before, and I meant to replace it, but kept forgetting. Now I was glad I'd procrastinated. Under cover of darkness, we ran to the house. I put a finger to my lips, and two heads nodded.

"Mother?" I leaned my head in the front door and listened for a reply. I knew she'd made it home before me. Her Civic was out front, and I smelled pot roast cooking.

"In the kitchen." Her perky voice ended on two descending singsong high notes.

I motioned Greg and Farrah in ahead of me. I whispered to the two young people. "Down this hall, first door on the right." I used a half shout for my mother. "I'll be in there in a second. Gotta run to the bathroom first."

"Okey dokey," she sang.

I scurried ahead of the kids to my room, the kitchen noise and hall carpeting muffling what little sound we made. My feet were like raindrops; theirs were as silent as dew. I may have trained to be Sacajawea, but they'd had a lot more real-world experience at becoming invisible and soundless. We entered my Western-themed room and I pulled the door shut behind us, turning the knob so that the latch wouldn't click as I eased it closed. I flipped on the bedside table lamp, and low light bathed my childhood bedroom. Green and brown-clad cowgirls rode horseback across every fabric surface—the wall included—twirling their lassos against a red background.

Greg made a prune face, like he'd gotten a snoot of vinegar. "Holy shit, this room is—"

"Really cool." Farrah smiled for the first time since I'd known her.

My mother kept the house a sweltering eighty degrees in the winter, yet neither Greg nor Farrah removed their black knit caps. The ends of her pixie hair curled around the edges of hers. Her smile sparkled from her eyes like onyx.

Greg shook his head. "That wasn't what I was going to say." The boy's hair, lighter than Farrah's, showed below the edges of his cap, and it was longer and stringier, like a young Kurt Cobain. So was his body. I'd have to feed him while he was here—a lot.

Farrah turned to me. "I love horses."

"Me, too. As you probably guessed, this was my room when I was a lot younger." And now, for the time being, anyway. My divorce had left me essentially destitute. I planned to move out when I had enough cash, which I hoped would be soon. "We can make spots for you to sleep on the floor in here with me for tonight, and figure out a better plan for tomorrow."

"Thank you." Pink spotted Farrah's cheeks, the only color besides her lips on her entire body. "We know you could get in a lot of trouble for this. We won't let it happen."

"Yeah, thanks." Greg lowered his voice. He couldn't be more than fifteen, and Farrah younger than that, and the affectation made him sound even younger.

"Yep. We just have to keep you guys a secret from everyone." Especially Wallace. He would be fired or even arrested if he didn't report the runaways back to the authorities. "Okay, I'm going to see my mother so she doesn't come looking for me. There are blankets and pillows in the closets, the password's taped to the monitor for the desktop, and there are books down there." I pointed to the bottom shelf on my nightstand. "Lock the doorknob, and I'll be back soon, with food."

They nodded, and I slipped out the door, shutting it quietly behind me. On the other side, I leaned against it and drew in a huge breath and held it, counting to five-one-thousand, then let it out. I pasted a smile on my face. It felt wrong, and I tried again. Better. I walked to the kitchen.

The kitchen décor made my bedroom seem blah. Red cedar paneling competed with gold Formica countertops and wallpaper of blue and purple flowers and twirling green vines. The chrome-legged table had a Formica top, too, but green. It could drive a woman to drink, which sounded like a good idea about now. I opened the refrigerator and pulled out the box wine.

"How was your day, Mother?"

"You'll never believe it, but Pastor Robb announced today that he's leaving. Only this must have been in the works for a while, because we'll have a new pastor by Sunday. And it's a woman! I've never worked for a woman before."

Mother doubled as the secretary and most fervent worshipper at the Panhandle Believers Church, with a belief system older than she was by several decades. She wiped her hands on a frilly white-skirted apron longer than her skirt. Even with the homespun apron, she looked like an aging Vegas showgirl. Mother had a penchant for stilettos, and she didn't like to cover too much of her long legs if she could help it. She never went in public without a full face of Mary Kay and half a bottle of Aqua Net—White Rain would do in a pinch—holding her baby-fine blonde hair perfectly in place.

I pulled a glass tumbler from the red cedar cabinet. "Want one?"

"A smidge." She indicated about a sixteenth of an inch with her finger and thumb.

"So, that's pretty big news. How are the Believers taking it?" I grabbed a second glass and poured her smidge and my own full up.

"People were quite devoted to Pastor Robb, and I'm not sure everyone accepts that God intended women to lead the church." My eyes fluttered up into their sockets, but she didn't seem to notice. "I'll be surprised if we don't lose members over this. That big church outside of town, Mighty is the Word or whatever they call it, is recruiting new members, and I do mean recruiting." She shrugged, a hopeless gesture. "They have a male pastor."

Ah, Mother and the Believers. I love the woman and I look like her, but I don't think like her. And Mother didn't know everything about her soon-to-be-former boss and worship leader. My friend Nadine counted Pastor Robb as one of her top customers at the Polo Club, quick with a fat tip and always paying in cash. Was it a coincidence that most people left cash in the collection plate each Sunday? I didn't think so. Anyway, Nadine would hate to see him go. I handed Mother her glass, then clinked mine to hers. "Well, I'm sure you'll grow to love the new pastor, too."

Mother harrumphed. "How was your day, dear?"

I took a tiny swallow of the white zinfandel. I shuddered. The first sip was always the worst. "Same old."

This was my standard answer. Mother had an insatiable urge to feed the gossip gristmill of her Sunday school class at Believers, and they'd ground up my personal life a few too many times, talking to the Lord and whoever else would listen. I'd learned to keep the interesting things to myself. For instance, I had neglected to tell Mother about wrecking Jack's Jeep two nights before or the murder we'd almost stumbled upon at Love's, and I sure hadn't told her I'd spent half the day cooling my heels in lockup yesterday.

"Anything new with Ja-ack?" Her voice trilled his name.

For someone upset that her boss and worship leader was leaving her, she sure sounded happy. Actually, she'd sounded downright perky for a week or two now. Could she have met someone? I looked closer at her. I'd never seen the snug skirt she was wearing or the soft pink sweater. Hmmm, something to keep an eye on.

"We're working on Betsy's case and a few others." I pretended not to understand her meaning about Jack. She had finally given up on reuniting Rich and me, although I wasn't sure she'd accepted that he couldn't be re-established as a red-blooded heterosexual. She now pinned her hopes for my happily-ever-after and her grandbabies on Jack. Which brought up another subject I'd neglected to update her on: my very iffy reproductive potential. It could *definitely* wait.

"I got her something little for Christmas. To go in the backpack you got her."

"About that." I slugged down half my wine in one swallow, skipping most of the too-sweet taste experience. "Her foster parents aren't allowing her to accept gifts. Or visitors."

"What? Whyever would they not?"

"On account of it's Jesus's birthday." The rest of the white zin slid down my hatch.

Mother set her unsipped-from glass down on the counter. "Well, I never. I daresay I'm as well-versed as almost anyone, and I don't see anything in the Bible that *prohibits* exchanging gifts, at Christmas or any time." She picked her glass back up to salute with it. "Tasteful ones, and not in excess. All things to the glory of God."

I refilled my wine.

"Do you have plans for your Friday night, dear?"

"I'm going to take some roast and vegetables back to my room for now. I'm really tired," I ladled an enormous bowl.

"You don't want to watch *Murder, She Wrote* with me?"

We'd seen every episode at least three times. I smiled at her. "You tell me whodunit at breakfast tomorrow." I kissed her on the cheek. "Thanks for making dinner." What I left out telling her was that I needed to get in touch with Jack. He didn't know it yet, but he was going to have passengers on the way to New Mexico tomorrow.

CHAPTER 12

Early the next morning outside the Maxor Building, Jack dropped his bag and Snowflake's collapsible kennel into the trunk of my Mustang, then opened the passenger door. Snowflake hopped in and he followed her. She adjusted herself into his lap.

Jack swiveled in his seat. "Morning."

I'd texted Jack late the night before, asking to hitch a ride to his ranch for me and two, which he'd agreed to if I'd pick him up on my way to the airport, since his Jeep was still in the shop. The kids accepted that he would believe our cover story that they were two family friends who I was dropping in Alamogordo. I knew the chances of him buying it were slim to none, but a) I trusted him with the secret and b) I was still going to give it my best shot.

"Jack, these are the two family friends of mine I was telling you about, George and Frannie." I used the cover names we'd picked together. "Guys, this is my boss, Jack." I paused, then added the nickname I occasionally used for him on a whim. "Short for Jack Ass."

Greg and Farrah stared at me for a split second.

Greg—who I had to remember to start thinking of and calling George—laughed first. "Nice to meet you, Mr. Ass."

"Jack, please." Jack rolled his eyes. "She doesn't show me a lot of respect."

"Who, me?" I winked toward the teens.

We drove out of downtown, passing several of the older, more established churches on the way. At the First Baptist Church's sign, I read

POTLUCK SUPPER SUNDAY AT 5:00 PM—PRAYER AND MEDICATION TO FOLLOW. I laughed.

"What's so funny?" Jack asked.

I pointed at the sign and he chuckled. "I can just picture some little blue-haired lady carefully writing that in her shaky handwriting for one of the youth group members to put up." Remembering the one from the night before, I decided that I really needed to start writing them down. I could write a hilarious little book, and surely authors made more money than paralegals.

Jack's left dimple appeared. "Church bulletin typos made Sundays worth it for me as a kid."

I merged onto I-40, keeping a sharp eye on the rearview mirror, as I had the entire way from Heaven in to pick up Jack. No followers that I could tell. Jack chatted with the kids as I exited and made a few quick turns to get us to the nearby Tradewind Airport. I parked as close as I could to the edge of the surface lot nearest Jack's hangar—on the opposite side of the facility from the airport's small terminal building—and checked the mirrors one last time. Still no suspicious vehicles.

Jack grabbed Snowflake's kennel and his suitcase, and she walked beside him on a leash. I followed with my one rolling bag, and the kids fell in beside me, each of them carrying mostly empty plastic grocery bags. We passed a pole crowded with painted arrows pointing in different directions and denoting mileage to a multitude of destinations. It looked like an old-school Rolodex in mid twirl. Jack unlocked the door and we entered his pitch-dark shared private hangar. He flicked a switch. Fluorescents crackled, hummed, and then flooded the interior, revealing eight small planes. It was barely warmer inside than outside.

"Wow," Greg/George said. His voice echoed in the cavernous space. "Cool!"

"Do you like to fly?" Jack asked him.

"I think so, but I never have."

"I did when I was a baby," Farrah/Frannie said, but her voice was less enthusiastic.

"If either of you want to learn more, you can help me get ready."

"I do!" Greg said.

"I'll stay with Emily," Farrah said, moving so close to me that her side pressed against mine.

Jack spent the next ten minutes prepping the plane, under a watchful teenage eye. We girls visited the hangar bathrooms, then we all loaded up. Five minutes later, we were under way to Wrong Turn Ranch.

Cabin conditions in the Cessna 172 were not ideal. For starters, I still hadn't fallen in love with small planes and the concept of amateur pilots. I trusted Jack, and his Skyhawk seemed airworthy, but I'm of the belief that humans are creatures of the earth rather than the sky. I'm not overly fond of big planes and professional pilots, either. Not only that, but before today I had my own spot in the backseat. Today, Greg and Farrah had bumped me into shotgun, where I held Snowflake's kennel, with Snowflake in it. Even a tiny dog in a tiny kennel gets old fast when it's on your lap for three-plus hours, buckled in the seatbelt with you. It reminded me of the times Dad had me ride in the stock trailer with the horses as a kid, something probably akin to forcing your unhelmeted, unbelted children into the back of a pickup truck these days. I'd always considered it a badge of honor to shepherd the animals back then. Now? Not so much.

Other than Snowflake in my lap, though, the front seat was better than the back. Up here, I could wear headphones that allowed me to talk to Jack during the flight. It was much too noisy without them to hear each other even from less than two feet away. In general, I'd found that, in the two months I'd known him, Jack didn't talk much. Today was a different story. His voice crackled in my headphones, surprisingly loud and clear. He looked straight ahead as he spoke, although I noticed that he couldn't see much of anything but his instrument panel in front of him while in flight. That was something I would have to try not to think about.

"I'm an officer of the court. You realize I could get disbarred for this, right?"

I knew he was talking about the kids, and I did know how much trouble this could bring down on him. It bothered me. A lot. "If, hypothetically speaking, you knew you were doing something wrong, then, yes, you could get disbarred. You've got plausible deniability, though, and I'd like to keep it that way." My heart clenched like a fist as I said it. I would never forgive myself if I got Jack in trouble, so I would have to make sure I didn't.

"So that confirms my pretty good guess about who those two are." Now he glanced at me, and I saw his chest rise and fall. "You do keep it interesting, Emily." His lips pulled tight as he looked away, and my heart did its normal little flip-flop when I had earned one of his lopsided smiles.

I nodded. "Friends of the family, like I said."

"Ha. The same ones that called you at the office yesterday, I suppose."

I licked my lips. "That was Katie."

"She never calls you on the office phone."

I guess I hadn't fooled him after all. I turned to check on the teenagers, shooting them an okay sign with my thumb and forefinger in question. Greg's arm was slung around Farrah, and her head was tucked in the V his underarm made with his chest and shoulder. Her face looked pale, but they both gave me thumbs skyward.

"Hypothetically, my two friends tell me they may have seen a murder take place at a certain truck stop Wednesday night."

Jack's head whipped toward me for a second. "No shit?"

"None." He shook his head, eyes wide, and I continued. "I gave them my card when I saw them in the field the other night. They said I'm the only one they can trust, but they haven't trusted me enough to tell me who it is. They're plenty scared though, and they're convinced the shooter saw them and is coming after them."

Jack's thumbs danced on the yoke. "That's why they were running away from Love's."

I nodded. "Yep. They've had such a rough time. Losing their families. Sexual abuse at the foster home where they met, at least Farrah. On the run from the group home CPS put them in after that. Honestly, it doesn't sound like the group home was all that bad, but they've lost faith in the system and are just young enough to believe they're invincible together."

"Young and stupid."

"Young and, sadly, experienced. And idealistic."

"Did you tell Wallace?"

"No, no one else. I can't put him or the kids in that position."

His lips twitched. "But you can put me in it."

I decided it was best to pretend I hadn't heard his last remark, even though my gut tightened with guilt. I looked out the side window at the ground far below us, like the surface of a Life game board without its color. Treeless, wrinkled, brown dotted with white. Ribbons of black asphalt wound through the landscape, vehicles crawling along them at the pace of snails compared to us. Here and there, small clusters of roofs gave evidence of community. We'd long since crossed the border into New Mexico and I tried to identify the towns. Clovis? Portales? Or were they even on our route?

Jack's voice crackled in my ear again. "So, what now?"

I stuck a finger in Snowflake's kennel and was rewarded with a tiny, rough tongue. Snowflake didn't hold back her affection, or her constant search for a crumb or tiny dried remnant of whatever I'd last eaten.

"I was hoping we could let them lay low in Tularosa for a while. At least for the weekend with me. Maybe longer if I figure something out." Jack's family ranch was between the tiny towns of Bent and Tularosa, New Mexico, but closer to Tularosa.

"Such as?"

Snowflake's tongue bath over, I used my fingertip to scratch behind her fluffy white ears. I couldn't hear her, but I knew from the many times I'd scratched there that she was humming her special happy noise.

"Maybe someone at the ranch could take them in for a while. It'd be good for them." I braced myself for Jack's response, expecting a verbal wallop.

Instead, he nodded again. "That might work. We can ask Mickey and Laura what they think." Jack turned and met my eyes, looking deep into them. "No promises."

"Of course not."

"You sure do seem to have a knack for finding the lost souls." He reached over and chucked his knuckles gently against my cheek.

My heart jackhammered in response to his touch.

Jack taxied to the barnlike hangar from the rough dirt runway at Wrong Turn Ranch. He pivoted the plane, and turned off the propeller. Two minutes later, Greg and Farrah hopped out of the plane, jaws hanging open.

"That was the coolest thing ever," Greg said, his voice almost a shout.

"You're a better flier than me," I told him.

I patted Farrah. She still looked a little green around the gills, but she hadn't used the barf bag, which was more than I could say for myself on my first trip out here. The kids loitered and watched as I helped Jack. He opened the hangar and I got in the awaiting old blue Suburban. The keys stayed in the ignition, so I pulled it out and around the side of the building. Jack retrieved a tow bar and hooked it to the plane's front strut, and together we started to push it over to a spindly-legged silver fuel tank—with Greg scrambling to help on my side when he saw what we were doing—then the boys maneuvered it backwards into the hangar when Jack had finished fueling it up. Greg shut the hangar for Jack, then we all piled in the land vehicle with the dog and the bags.

Jack drove us down a dirt road away from the private airport, through high-desert pastureland and toward the foothills of white-topped mountains beyond. A light layer of snow covered the ground and bushes around us, enough to look like icing on an Italian cream cake, but not enough to make driving—or landing a plane—difficult. I could still see the outline of yucca stalks and blades, but the snow rendered most of the other flora unrecognizable.

"Where are we?" Farrah asked.

Jack put one hand on my seat back as he turned himself toward Farrah. Even with him facing away, the Suburban stayed on course, practically steering itself through the rutted dirt track. With his hand almost touching me, I could feel his nearness in every cell of my body, and I wished it didn't make me tingle all over. Or that he'd lower that hand to my shoulder. Or my leg.

"We're a little more than a hundred miles from the southern border of

New Mexico. Of the United States, for that matter. Less than two hours that way"—he pointed to his right—"is Mexico."

"How far are we from Amarillo?"

"About five hundred miles."

I turned toward her in my seat, my mouth now close enough to Jack's hand to kiss it, if I'd wanted to, which I did. I lowered my voice. "Far enough away that no one will follow."

Greg said to Jack, "Is this all yours?"

Jack lifted and dropped his shoulders. He moved his hand away from my seat and back to the steering wheel, causing a twinge in my chest. "Most of it, although it belongs to my parents, not me."

"Will it be yours someday?"

"I guess so. Unless I go before them."

"You must be really rich."

Jack laughed. "You'd be surprised. It costs a lot of money to run this ranch. But we do okay. Plus, I have a job."

"You're Emily's boss, right? A lawyer?"

"Yep."

I smiled and looked from one kid to the other. "The house is really nice here, and they have lots and lots of horses. Racehorses."

Farrah leaned forward, eyes round. "Can we see them?"

Jack turned the Suburban to the left at a **T** intersection in the dirt road. "Absolutely. In fact, if you'd like, we could take a ride this afternoon."

"That would be awesome." Farrah bounced in the seat, regressing a few years in her excitement, then stopped. "But I've never ridden a horse."

"Me either." Greg's voice sounded tight and worried.

"Nothing to it. We'll put you on some gentle ones that will do whatever mine and Emily's do. It will be as easy as riding in this old Suburban." Jack patted the dashboard.

The two kids looked at me, Greg clearly still uneasy with the arrangements, Farrah as clearly thrilled.

Jack continued. "Did you know Emily was a rodeo star in college?"

Farrah's brows rose and scrunched together. "Really?"

I smiled. "I went to college on a rodeo scholarship, and my dad was a professional rodeo cowboy. I rode horses before I could walk. And Jack's right. This will be a piece of cake."

CHAPTER 13

Greg and Farrah were riding along with us through the snow-dusted coniferous trees of the foothills only two hours after Jack had landed the plane. Every now and then, a branch would dump its snow in a cascading plop surrounded by a shower of powder. The scent of pine and sap tickled my nose and I wanted to throw my arms in the air and shout with joy. Even though it was snowy, Tularosa air was even drier than Amarillo, so the cold didn't feel as painful, and the trees shielded us somewhat from the wind that whistled through their highest branches. The kids didn't have clothes for this type of weather and activity, but Jack had loaned Greg a long leather duster. It hung on him and flapped around his legs. Farrah had on one of Laura's puffy down jackets and it fit just right.

Farrah had gotten the hang of the rudimentaries of horseback riding in five minutes, and she was keeping up a steady stream of chatter to her mount, Lilac, a fifteen-year-old brood mare with a white star in the middle of her red forehead. I had clipped the lead line from Lilac to my saddle on Jarhead, the former racer whose special treasures had ended up at ABC Half-Price Resale in Amarillo.

Pink splotches brightened Farrah's cheeks, and she was far more talkative than she'd been since I'd known her. "I like your—" She pointed toward her teeth, lips bared.

I knew what she meant: my gap. I had a love-hate relationship with it. "Thanks. It's because I didn't wear my retainer after I got my braces off, but it's not bad."

"I think it's cute." She lowered her voice, and motioned her head toward Jack ahead of us. "Does he like it?"

"Jack?" I laughed, remembering my orthodontist's lecture and Jack calling me Snaggletooth. "I don't know."

Jack didn't react, so maybe he hadn't heard the question. I wondered what he thought about it. I hadn't had much of a gap when I met my soon-to-be-ex-husband, Rich, but over the years it had widened back to the size it had been pre-braces. Rich hadn't liked it.

Louder, she asked, "Are you guys married?"

My mouth worked a little, searching for words, and Jack's head turned back toward Farrah. Then his eyes locked on mine, and I could feel the heat rushing to my cheeks.

He said, "Huh. No, we're not."

Greg didn't give any sign that he was keeping up with our conversation. He had a two-handed death grip on the saddle horn in front of him, his knuckles strained and white. His tall horse, Buzz, had a rolling gait that seemed to be giving Greg the willies. Jack had clipped Buzz to the saddle on Hopper, the tall black thoroughbred who was Jack's normal ride.

Farrah nodded. "Is that why she calls you Jack Ass?"

I broke in quickly. "It's a term of endearment."

She cocked her head. "What's a term of endearment?"

I stuttered a little. "I-i-it's a nickname for someone you like."

"You call people you like Jack Ass?"

Jack said, "The girl has a point, Emily."

I couldn't think of an answer before Farrah thought of her next question. "Are you married to anyone else?"

"No," Jack and I said, almost at the same time.

"Have you ever been married to anyone before?"

"Yes," we said, again in tandem.

"Do you have kids?"

I shook my head.

Jack cleared his throat. "A boy and a girl."

I drew in a breath as quietly as I could and held it for several seconds. Jack had never mentioned his kids in front of me.

"Do they live here?"

Jack drummed the fingers of his left hand on his saddle horn. "Follow me."

He clucked to Hopper, who moved off, tugging Buzz behind him. I worried about Greg for a moment, but he didn't panic. His eyes were the size of silver dollars, and not the Susan B. Anthony kind.

I squeezed my ankles against Jarhead and he broke into a slow lope before I pulled him up beside Hopper, Lilac following suit, and Farrah giggling like a kid on a carousel.

I leaned into Jack and whispered. "Where are we going?"

Jack didn't answer.

Silence fell over us, save for the soft plop of the horses' hooves on the snowy ground. The tall trees muffled even that noise, creating a cathedral-like atmosphere. The air grew colder as the horses climbed. Heat and the smell of sweat and leather clung to the animals. I marveled at the moment, these kids—orphans, runaways, witnesses to a murder, victims of abuse— here, in these pristine conditions. It was like the forest was giving them back their innocence. I could feel the tension easing in them, *and* me.

After ten minutes, we reached a partially cleared hilltop. The ground fell away over a pond on its far side. A large coyote was drinking and his head shot up at our approach. He sniffed with his nose in the air. His enormous ears twitched our way and he lifted one front paw, preparing to bolt. He froze, statue-still, for long seconds, then bounded into the forest. I wondered what he was doing out in broad daylight, but guessed he was hungry. The ranchers hated the coyotes. The clever animals preyed on livestock when their natural food sources dwindled, especially in the dead of winter, like now. Their reputation had been tarnished of late, too, by the poorly named coyotes that crossed the border with contraband of various kinds, usually drugs. But I admired the animals. They were survivors, often relying on their wits and bravery to stay alive when other animals perished in dwindling habitat and harsh conditions.

I shivered, remembering the mask of the Clown, the Apache Mountain Spirit Dancer that I had seen on my last visit to New Mexico, as Betsy and I ducked into Jack's plane and her kidnappers bore down on us with guns. The Clown had worn the snout of an animal on his face, and the ears of an animal in his headdress. I had thought it was a wolf, then, but maybe it was a coyote. This creature today reminded me of the Clown, and brought some of the magic of New Mexico back to my conscious thought.

Jack stopped his horse. I felt his eyes on me, and I looked over at him. We held each other's gaze for a moment. I barely breathed.

Then, with his eyes still locked on mine, Jack pointed to his left, to the edge of the clearing, at a collection of about a dozen headstones of varying ages, sizes, and angles. A low, rusted iron fence surrounded the plot. A cemetery.

"A few years ago, I had a case against a very bad person, a man who made teenage runaways work for him as prostitutes."

I snuck a glance at the kids, wondering if they saw the parallel to their precarious situation. They didn't react.

Jack was still telling his story. "I started getting death threats, but I ignored them. One day after my wife picked our kids up from school, she came to my building to borrow my car. She called me, but I didn't pick up. She parked and loaded the kids and my son's yellow Lab puppy into my car. When she turned it on, a bomb exploded. I heard it—everyone for miles around heard it. I realized when I got outside that it was my car, but I hadn't checked my messages. I didn't know my family had come, and I didn't know they were in it. I stood there watching it, not knowing. I couldn't have saved them, but still, I didn't know."

A warm wetness worked its way down my cheeks. I'd known what had happened to Jack's family from his secretary, Judith, but the version she'd told me was from her perspective. It had been sad, but nothing like his. My mouth fell open but no words came out. Still, Jack's eyes held mine.

"Someone was trying to kill you?" Greg asked.

"Yes. And got my family instead." Jack swallowed and his Adam's apple worked hard to get it down.

"Did he go to jail?"

"Not for that."

My hand covered my mouth. "Oh God. I'm so sorry, Jack."

He inclined his head to me, acknowledging my words. "There wasn't much left when the firefighters were done. But there was enough to give them a place here, to be remembered, at the family cemetery"—he pointed —"facing the sacred White Mountain."

His words drew my eyes upward, and I realized that the cemetery had a perfect view of Sierra Blanca Peak to the north, the jewel of the Sierra Blanca range. I swiveled my head around, searching, but the clouds blocked my other views. Thanks to Jack's cousin Mickey, I knew that to the southwest was the Three Sisters Mountains, to the northwest the Oscura Peak, and to the southeast the Guadalupe Mountains. The mountains provided a frame of reference for directions within the Mescalero Apache territory and were embodied in their sacred Mountain Spirits. I understood the placement of the cemetery now, and I was glad his family had found a resting place there.

"See the dark spot against that hillside?" I looked up and saw Jack was staring in the same direction as me, and that he was talking to me.

I peered again at the next hillside up the range. I did see a dark spot. "Yes."

"That's the old Sacramento Silver Mine. My family's occupation before my grandfather got us into horses."

"Like the photograph in your office?" He kept a black and white of an entrance to an old mine on his wall of fame back in Amarillo.

"Yep."

"That your wife took."

He turned to me, nodding. "The summer before she was killed."

"She was very talented."

He smiled with sad eyes. "Yes, she was."

Jack dismounted, stepping over to help Greg off of Buzz while still holding on to Hopper's reins. I hit the ground ready to give Farrah a hand, but she'd already slipped off Lilac's back on her own.

"What do I say to Jack?" she asked me, quietly.

I wiped my pooled tears and squeezed her arm. "Nothing." I shook my head. "There's nothing you can say, except you're sorry."

She walked toward the cemetery, as did Greg, but she paused to whisper something to Jack, who nodded and hugged her around the shoulders with one arm before she moved on. I watched as hers and Greg's paths converged. Greg opened the creaky little gate and they stopped in front of a headstone. Farrah knelt and rubbed snow from its face.

Jack turned, meeting me as I moved toward him, Jarhead following me. My arms wound around Jack of their own accord. He looped his around my waist, and I laid my head against his chest. "I am so sorry about your family."

He squeezed hard.

"I was wondering if you were ever going to tell me about them."

I felt his head nod. "I'm a little slow, but I get where I'm headed, eventually."

Jarhead's muzzle pressed into the back of my head.

"The horse is getting jealous," Jack said.

I laughed, softly, and rubbed my tears off on Jack's coat then held perfectly still, afraid of breaking the spell, of Jack's arms pulling away from me. I watched the two teenagers in the graveyard and listened to his heartbeat.

Greg called out, "There's an Indian name on this one."

Against my ear, Jack's voice rumbled in his chest. "My family is part Apache."

"Was your wife Apache?"

"No."

Farrah wiped another headstone. "Some people think I'm Indian, but not like your Indians here. Like from the country of India. I'm not, though. My family is mostly Syrian. Sometimes I think it would be easier if I *were* from India."

Greg's fists balled. "People blame her when they do bad things to her. They tell her it's because she's a Muslim, and that she and her family should go home."

Jack squeezed me tight again.

"Only I have no family. Not anymore. They were Muslim, but I've never even been to a mosque. Not that I remember, anyway. I've always been in 'Christian' foster care." She made quotes in the air around her head. "I want to learn more about the Koran someday. I think it would help me understand my family."

"So you don't have any family here in the U.S.?" I asked.

"No. My mother died in a car crash in Amarillo when I was little. My dad and brothers disappeared back home before I was born."

"I'm so sorry."

Jack turned toward the kids, one arm still around me. "Family makes us who we are, even after they're gone. If it were easy, we would be less."

My mind flitted to the father I took after, the one who had run away, and the mother I loved but was nothing like, the one who had stayed. To the family Jack had lost that still shaped him. To the fact that all of us here had lost the people closest to us.

Farrah nodded. "It's hard sometimes, but I wouldn't want to be someone else."

She stood up and walked through the plot, her hands trailing on the tops of the stones, her champion beside her.

Jack turned to me again, and this time he leaned down and pressed his lips against mine. They were warmer than I'd have expected out there, and so, so soft. Mine clung to his for long seconds. When the kiss ended, he pulled me to him again. I tried to swallow, but I couldn't get past the lump in my throat as I hung on to him for as long as I could.

Mickey and Laura leaned against the gold, rusty brown, blue-gray, and tan granite island countertop in Jack's kitchen. Or his parents' kitchen, rather, although they now traveled the states in an RV and only came home every year or three. Mickey had one arm around his dark wife's tiny waist, and he was nodding as Jack spoke. Snowflake gobbled down kibble from her silver bowl to their left, by the hallway to the garage. The kids were upstairs getting cleaned up, Farrah in my room, and Greg in Jack's.

"Emily took in some more lost children. These two are teenagers. A boy, George, who's fifteen, and a girl, Frannie, who's fourteen." It felt odd to hear their cover names from Jack's mouth. "They're runaways, and they're witnesses to a murder. We shouldn't have them, but we didn't know what else to do."

"Shouldn't have them like 'could go to jail for it,'" I said.

Jack nodded. "We'll have them here for the weekend, until we can figure out a plan for them."

Laura looked from Jack to me and back to Jack. "What about their families?"

I answered, stirring boiling pasta as I did. "Both of them said their parents are dead. No other family in the picture. They've had a terrible time of it."

She sucked her lips in and spoke in a softer voice. "Have they been in any trouble with the law?"

"Only for running away from abusive living situations." I lowered my voice, too. "Don't get me wrong. They're tough and savvy. There's probably not much Gr—George wouldn't do to protect Frannie."

My timer started ringing. I turned it and the gas off and grabbed a strainer.

Mickey and Laura looked at each other, and she nodded at him, shaking her sleek, brown bobbed hair.

He spoke. "Are they . . . intimate?"

I poured the pasta into the strainer over the sink, then turned on the cold water to rinse the noodles. "I don't know. They don't act like it, but then again, all they have is each other, and they're human."

Jack had on an apron with a cowboy Santa on it, and he slipped on a matching oven mitt. "I wondered if you guys wanted to shepherd them for a week or two, before I asked anyone else, because, well—" He stood there, his mouth open but no more words coming out.

"It's okay to say it, Jack." Mickey put his other arm around Laura, and he squeezed her to him. "Because you know we want kids but haven't been able to have any of our own."

"Yet," Laura said in a fierce voice from inside his bear hug. "I'm retiring, and the doctor is hopeful that when I gain weight I'll have better luck." Sinewy muscle defined Laura's body, and there wasn't an ounce of fat on her anywhere.

"And because I couldn't think of anyone I'd trust more with kids we aren't supposed to have that need protection." Jack opened the oven door and peeked in. "The garlic bread needs a few more minutes." He shut the door. "Plus you've already had the foster training, haven't you?"

"No." Laura extricated herself from her bear.

Mickey looked down. "I jumped the gun on that. We weren't ready."

Laura's stiff body language and crossed arms left little doubt as to who wasn't ready of the two of them, then or now.

Jack didn't seem to notice the dissonance in the room. Back when I was an active horsewoman, I'd known this vibe well. It was the feeling I'd get when saddle breaking a young horse, like once when I was forcing a filly to accept a saddle cinch. She was scared, and her eyes were wide and white rimmed. It was a sign to step back, to let things progress at a speed she was more comfortable with, so that she learned to give in instead of fight. I'd praised her and given her time to think about the saddle cinch loose around her belly, and an hour later, she'd let me tighten it without a fuss while she chewed the apple treats she'd taken out of my hand.

"No need to make any decisions now," I said, as I poured the pasta back into the pot and dumped half a jar of pesto into it. I stirred it briskly with a wooden spoon, shaking a blend of Romano and Parmesan cheese in as I did, trying not to look like I was desperate to hear them say they'd host the kids. Snowflake showed up at my ankles, hopeful that I would spill a little cheese near her mouth. I pinched some and dropped it to the floor. She scarfed it up.

I saw Laura's chest heave, and she moved an inch back toward Mickey. "It's really bad timing for us."

I could hear the wind outside and icy individual snowflakes pelting the window, the heater cycling on, and the dishwasher running with the load of lunch dishes. I'd forgotten to turn it on until we started cooking dinner. Jack and Mickey didn't make a sound.

"I understand." I did, even if I didn't like it and prayed she'd change her mind.

Footsteps thumped down the stairs. Greg appeared, looking both ways at the bottom. To his right was the great room.

I hailed him from his left. "In here."

He grinned and ducked his head. Water glistened in his hair, and I realized he didn't have on his grimy cap. He shuffled into the kitchen, hands deep in the pockets of Jack's too-large maroon New Mexico State University sweat pants. Snowflake pranced to meet him, and he bent down to ruffle her ears. "Where's Far—"

I hurried to cover his slip. "Frannie's still upstairs. George, this is Jack's cousin Mickey and his wife, Laura."

Greg stood up. "Whoa, now I can see what you meant about part of your family is Apache."

We laughed. Mickey had long black hair that he wore tied back low in a leather thong accented with silver and turquoise. He couldn't have looked more Native American if he'd had on a full-feathered headdress.

Greg blushed. "Nice to meet you, sir." He held out his hand, and Mickey shook it. He nodded his head at Laura. "And you, too, ma'am."

"Nice to meet you," Mickey replied.

Laura smiled weakly at Greg.

I walked the pot of pasta to the table and set it down. "We're having pasta, garlic bread, and a salad. I put some plates and silverware here on the table. Could you set them out in six places?"

"Okay. I mean, yes, ma'am." Greg's sudden company manners were endearing.

"Thanks. There are napkins out for each place setting, too."

Jack pulled two bottles of salad dressing out of the refrigerator. As he walked toward the table with them he said, "Well, there she is."

We all looked up to see the diminutive Farrah in the kitchen entry, nearest Laura. The girl could have been her twin, twenty years before.

Farrah lifted her hand in a wave. "Hi."

Laura whipped her head toward Mickey, her eyes welling with tears.

CHAPTER 14

The six of us shared cleanup duties after dinner. Afterwards, Jack showed the teens how to operate the electronics in the living room, and soon the sounds of a horror movie's overly dramatic soundtrack echoed off the walls and ceiling. Amused, I walked to the staircase to take a look into the great room. Jack's mother had plastered family photographs over the entire far wall. In the corner nearest the floor-to-ceiling windows looking out on the Sierra Blanca and Sacramento Mountains stood an enormous Christmas tree. I'd gotten a close-up of it earlier, and someone had strung it with popcorn and barbed wire, burlap ribbons, apples, and metal ornaments in the shape of the Wrong Turn Ranch "WTR" brand. Gold twinkled from it, the only illumination in the high-ceilinged room now, other than ambient light from the kitchen and the TV screen. Shadows loomed off the ceiling beams, and darkness hugged the corners like a blanket around the shoulders of the room. From the reflected glow of the screen, I saw one dark head, a small dark body, and one slightly lighter head and slightly larger white body, plus a white blob where Snowflake had opted to hold the couch down between the two of them.

I couldn't help but compare it to my own childhood Christmases, and it made me miss my dad. I remembered the year I found a bridle under the tree with instructions to go look in the little barn in the pasture behind our house. My first pony awaited me there. He was feisty, white, and just right. Dad had given me a leg up to his bare back, and I'd thrown my arms around his neck, my face buried in his scratchy mane.

"Well, what are you going to name him?" Dad had asked.

I had known his name from the moment I'd laid eyes on him. "Cotton," I said reverently.

More than twenty years later, my eyes teared up at the memory. I had outgrown Cotton, and the pony had moved on to another home and another child long before my father left. I shook myself and wiped my eyes. It wouldn't do to sully the present with memories of a past I couldn't change.

Jack walked up to me.

"They look contented," I said.

"Yep." He put his hand on my shoulder, which made me want to kiss him again, but Jack gave me a slight tug, then released my shoulder. We returned to the kitchen together. He went behind the breakfast bar and I stayed on its near side.

"Coffee, anyone?" Jack asked.

Mickey, Laura, and I raised our hands.

He laughed. "I'll leave the Tylenol PM out on the counter."

He added water to the coffee maker and opened the bag of cinnamon roasted beans that I loved. He filled the well of his coffee grinder and pulsed the on button. The machine whirred and grred and whined. He turned it over and tapped the side until the soft ground coffee fell into the removable clear lid, which he in turn dumped into the gold filter in the swing arm of the coffee maker. He popped the arm shut and hit the start button. Seconds later the gurgling and drizzling started, and the wonderful toasty aroma filled the kitchen.

I sat down at one of the cowhide-covered stools at the breakfast bar, feeling only a little bit guilty as Jack retrieved four tan WTR-branded porcelain mugs from the cabinet. "Do you need help?"

"Nope. I'm about done."

I watched, transfixed as he grabbed a carton of Half & Half from the refrigerator and set it beside the antiqued wooden tray that remained permanently on the granite counter. It held a tub of sugar cubes in white and golden brown, honey, cinnamon, a crock of stirring sticks, and a bowl with yellow and pink fake sugar packets in it.

He caught the direction of my gaze. "My mother's setup."

"It's great."

Mickey came around for two mugs. "Yeah, good ole Aunt Nell has never done coffee halfway, Standing Hair." He winked at me, teasing me with the "Apache name" he'd christened me with on my last visit, in reference to my bangs.

Mickey poured two coffees and added cream, brown sugar cubes, and cinnamon, then stirred them. He walked one mug over to Laura and kept the other for himself.

"Thanks, hon," Laura said.

I filled the spot Mickey had vacated by the pot and prepared my cup. A generous splash of cream went in first, then a shake of cinnamon and two packets of pink stuff. I topped it with coffee, not bothering to stir. I sunk my face in the mouth of the mug and inhaled. Deep, dark, wonderful scents flooded my olfactory system and I sighed. Better than red wine. Or at least as good as.

As if he'd read my mind, Jack said, "I'm getting old—or rude. Beer or wine?"

Mickey and Laura looked at each other and shook their heads. He said, "None for us tonight."

I remembered the last time I'd been here, how much we'd all had to drink, how the company had cheered me up, and how well the night had gone—despite the fact that I was recovering from surgery post-miscarriage and tube rupture—until my friend Collin got too drunk and made a pass at me and a donkey's fanny out of himself. And then? After a wonderful night with Jack, how poorly the next day went. Jack had gotten the wrong idea about Collin and me. Mickey and Laura had barely spoken to me that day, and it had marked the beginning and the end of Jack's and my fledgling relationship, until the flickers of the last few days. I sure as shootin' wasn't messing things up with him again.

I shook my head, holding in a sigh. "I'll pass, too."

"Mickey, do you mind looking at a few things with me in the office?" Jack sounded casual, but my radar went up. I'd seen the office on the far side of the great room—with its shelves of books and big desk and high-backed leather chair—on my last visit, but no one had used it in my previous two visits.

Mickey kissed Laura on the lips. "No problem. Let me top off my cup, first."

The men left and my ears followed them. I didn't want to be left alone in the kitchen with Laura, with this awkwardness. We hadn't seen each other in the two months since that very bad day. Our last conversation hadn't gone well, and she was partly responsible for the bad information Jack got about Collin. I didn't blame her, though. Most of the fault was mine—well, Collin's, really—and Jack was her family. I had just been some new employee of his that no one really knew. She was at the table behind me, and I stayed facing the kitchen, sipping my coffee, trying to decide how to handle our sudden pairing.

"Hey, what are you guys watching?" I heard Mickey saying, in the living room.

Farrah answered. *The Fourth Kind.*"

"Well, I gotta warn you, that's some seriously bad medicine."

"What is?" Her voice sounded worried.

"That owl there, with his head rotating all the way around." I knew what he was talking about. I hated horror movies, but I'd watched *The Fourth Kind* with Rich, and that scene with the owl's head rotating around freaked me out. "You're in Mescalero Apache country, and around here, owls are like ogres. They carry off little children. I wouldn't be watching a movie about owls if I were you."

Farrah laughed, sounding relieved. "It's not about an owl. It's about alien abductions in Alaska. You should talk to Gr—George, though, because he used to play this game called Owlman." She made an ooooooo-ooooooooo sound.

"Shut up," Greg said. I smiled into my coffee cup.

"Well, all I know is that in our legends, the Coyote is the only one ever to defeat the Owl."

Farrah laughed. "Yeah, George never won when he played Owlman either."

Sounds of scuffling in the great room broke out.

Laura spoke, tearing my attention away from their shenanigans. "You'll never guess who I ran into in Alamogordo last week."

The universe of southern New Mexico residents we both knew was small. I could count the ones I was acquainted with on one hand, and most of them were present tonight. But I rotated my barstool to face her and pretended to be stumped. "Who?"

"Tamara." Collin's fiancée, or ex-fiancée, rather. An army pilot. She'd dumped him after he cornered and kissed me, right upstairs.

"How is she?"

"She's great. She said she's been dating a UFC fighter."

"Not Collin?" Collin had vowed to win her back last time I'd talked to him.

"Nope. She said she doesn't believe he'll ever change, and she doesn't want to be the woman he resented for trying to make him into someone he isn't. I would have thought you'd have known." She looked down at her hands around her mug.

"No, I haven't talked to either of them since—well, since the last time I talked to you."

She ran her bottom teeth over her upper lip. "You and Collin didn't date?"

"Heavens no. Never. We've been close family friends for years, but after that weekend, I haven't even talked to him. He knows I am none too happy with him."

Laura frowned, her black eyes dark and deep. "I'm sorry about what happened with you and Jack, and any part I had in it. Mickey and I are a bit protective when it comes to him."

I nodded once. "A bit" was an understatement, but I couldn't pretend I didn't long for family bonds like theirs. "What matters is that I found Betsy and got her back safely that weekend. I try to forget the rest."

Laura smiled. "How is Betsy?"

"Good, I think. I don't get to see her. She lives with an ultrareligious foster family who has weird rules. But when I talk to her, she always mentions how she misses that horse we rode in our getaway. Thunder."

"He's here, you know."

"What? Where?"

"In the stable, actually. No one ever asked for him, and we couldn't stomach the idea of sending him back over there to Paul's place. The police had arrested everything that moved over there, and the future of the animals was so uncertain. We think of it as a rescue."

"I'm so glad. What happened to Paul's daughter?" His teenager had facilitated our rescue by breaking us out and giving us Thunder. She hated her father, and it turned out she was right to feel as she did about him. He was a monster, trafficking, enslaving, and selling off Mexicans desperate to live in the U.S.

"She went to live with her grandmother in Alamogordo, I hear. Her mother's mother." Laura nodded. "If I thought that it would have helped her in any way, I would have given Thunder back, but the girl was in the same fix the animals were."

I wrapped my fingers around my mug. It was still warm. "Betsy's going to be happy to hear Thunder was rescued. It was amazing how she fell in love with him that night. She was scared of him at first, of course, but within minutes he had this mesmerizing effect on her. She was calmer and more confident."

Laura finished a sip of coffee, then smiled. "That happens. We've sold some of our older horses to an equitherapy group."

"Equitherapy?"

"Equine therapy, for humans. It's basically pairing damaged souls with gentle horses, and letting the magic you're describing happen."

"Lilac had a similar impact on . . . Frannie. The girl's been physically and mentally abused, really suffered from the bad things people have done."

Laura peered closely at me. "Sexual abuse?"

"Apparently so."

"Geez. Poor thing."

"Yeah.

Laura closed her eyes for several seconds, then sighed as she reopened them. "Well, enough of that serious stuff." She stood. "Little girl's room. Back in a flash."

I was alone in the kitchen, and I felt it. I wandered into the great room. Greg and Farrah were asleep in front of the movie, her head on his shoulder, his head on her head, and the sleeping Snowflake evenly distributed between their laps. I grabbed an afghan from the arm of a giant club chair and draped it across their legs, then moved on toward the office. I'd never entered it before, and I stood to the side of the door now. I could hear Jack talking inside.

"Besides the saddle, there was a box of our stuff. I'm not sure I got it all. If I can get an inventory, I'll go back and see."

I inched closer and heard Mickey.

"No problem. Any ideas where he got it?"

"Not yet."

"So, have you told Emily about—"

I stepped in. "Hi, guys. Has Jack told me what?"

Both men stared at me like I was Medusa. Jack stood beside a desk whose top appeared to be made of reclaimed lumber. He rubbed at something on its bare surface with his thumb, eyes downcast. "Uh, I was telling Mickey about what we found at Alan's shop."

Jack's cheeks puckered, and his eyes shifted around the room, landing everywhere but on my face. To the grandfather clock by the French doors, to the black iron stove by the window, to the plaid wing chairs facing the desk.

"Why do you look like that?" I said, and then realized how loud my voice was. Like yelling loud. Whoops.

"Like what? I don't look like anything."

But he did.

Mickey said, "Jack told me that your client ended up with our Wrong Turn Ranch things, and that, um, he's basically being forced to sell stolen merchandise."

I slitted my eyes back and forth between them. They looked and sounded skittish, like two colts before a thunderstorm. I leaned against the built-in bookshelves and crossed my arms over my chest.

"So Mickey and I were discussing the robbery here, and how we'd thought it was an inside job. And we still think it probably was. But now it seems maybe it's connected to something bigger."

"Hey, guys, what's going on?" Greg walked in, rubbing his eyes, with Farrah stumbling along behind him. She was holding a yawning Snowflake in her arms.

"I heard loud voices. Did the party move down the hall?" Laura slipped in behind them and walked across to Mickey, who was standing by the stove. She moved slightly in front of him, facing me, and it registered on me how wan she looked. Mickey pulled her closer against his chest.

I recapped quickly. "Mickey and Jack were talking about how our client, who is being forced to sell stolen goods, was coincidentally selling stuff that was stolen from here."

"Whoa," Greg said.

To Jack, I said, "So, someone that works here is involved, you think?"

"Possibly."

"Do you know who it is?"

Mickey said, "We think so, but he bolted."

"What do the police think?"

"We didn't report it." Mickey released Laura and shoved his hands in his back pockets, swaying from foot to foot.

"Why not?"

He huffed out a tense breath. "It's possible we're wrong, and we don't want to get a good guy in trouble if we are." He shook his head, opened his mouth, then shook his head again.

Jack stepped over to me and put a hand on my upper arm. "It's complicated. You're going to have to trust me on this. Okay?"

I looked around me. Usually I loved it when Jack touched me, but every eye was on me, and I felt conspicuous. Why should I trust Jack, I wondered, when it seemed he and Mickey—and probably Laura—all knew something I didn't? But it was his ranch, and his law firm, and, honestly, while he wasn't very open with me about his personal life, he wasn't untrustworthy, per se. His family trusted him. His secretary, Judith, trusted him. In fact, everyone in his life seemed almost fanatically loyal to him. I sighed, and as I did, I felt a little vertigo, like I was on the back of a horse that had spooked out from under me.

"Okay," I said. "I'll trust you." I turned and walked out.

CHAPTER 15

The next morning, the kids were still wearing the same clothes we'd found for them the evening before. They sat side by side at the big plank table in the kitchen. Greg's eyes drooped and Farrah's were closed completely. Snowflake snuggled in Farrah's lap. Jack was in the kitchen, leaning toward them across the breakfast bar. I grabbed a mug of coffee and joined the kids. Even though they were right in front of them, neither appeared to have noticed the names carved into the table: JACKSON. JULIA. The names of Jack's children. I could hardly look at the etching without getting emotional, myself, especially after Jack's story yesterday.

I cleared my throat, and four eyes opened, a little, and looked in my direction. "Jack and I are joining Mickey and Laura for church this morning. We'd love for you to come, too, if you're willing."

Neither kid reacted, and I took one sip, then two. "After our talk yesterday, I didn't want to force it on you, um, Frannie."

She blinked. "No one has ever asked me if it was okay before."

I smiled at her.

"Yeah, it's cool. I figure there's one God and he probably would rather me do something instead of nothing."

I laughed. "Me, too. I've been trying to find the right place for myself to do something back home."

"How long have you been looking?"

Since I was twenty-one. I did the math. "Nine years."

Jack's voice came from behind me. "Where all have you tried in Amarillo?" I heard a pop from the toaster.

"Well, Believers, of course, because of my mother. I've given it several tries actually, but I'm too different. Then Unitarian with Wallace, but there, I don't think I'm different enough."

Greg snorted. "You want different? Our last foster family made us go with them to Mighty is His Word. That new place halfway to Oklahoma. Weird as shit."

"I think I can pass on 'weird as shit.'" I laughed. "What do you mean by weird, though, like what kind of stuff?"

"They hate everybody. They make you sign pledges to go to war— that's what they call it—against other religions, anyone they think are sinners, people from other countries, which sucks, because Far—"

"Frannie?" I interrupted.

"Yeah, because Frannie was right there."

"That does suck. And suddenly my mother's Believers sound pretty normal after all."

Jack brought a plate stacked with cinnamon-raisin bread in one hand and a tub of butter with a knife in the other. Two young hands snagged toast almost before the plate hit the table. I grabbed a piece, too.

"I can promise you the church we're going to today is nothing like that." Jack returned to the kitchen. "Orange juice in a pitcher and some glasses on the counter. We leave in half an hour."

No one answered him. We were already chewing. Jack brought a mug of coffee and glass of orange juice to the table and joined us. I had so hoped that Laura and Mickey would change their minds about the kids, but the time had come to address the fact that the plane was heading back to Amarillo after church, and that the kids needed to be on it.

"Listen, guys, Jack and I are flying back to Amarillo after church," I said.

I heard a door open and close in the front of the house. Footsteps approached.

"Morning," Jack shouted.

Laura turned toward us down the hall from the entryway. "Morning." She had a little color in her cheeks.

"Good morning," the kids and I chofrom.

Farrah immediately redirected us to the topic we'd been discussing. "What are we going to do when you go back to Amarillo?" She held her toast poised in the air, but she didn't take a bite.

Laura took a seat at a barstool behind us. I turned to look at Jack beside me at the table, but he kept his eyes on the plated toast in front of him. I kicked his ankle and he jerked upward. When he looked at me, though, his eyes were so soft and helpless that I let him off the hook.

I chose my words carefully. "Well, I think the best thing to do is keep you with me, so you can ride back with us."

In a rush, Greg said, "Wait, what about—"

Laura spoke over him, to Jack, and Greg yielded to her. "Aren't you coming back here for Christmas?"

Ever verbose, Jack said, "Yep."

She nodded. "If it's okay with Emily, the kids could stay here and help us a little around the ranch. We don't pay a lot, but it's a good Winter Break job." She got up and walked around to the coffee setup. "Probably best if they stay at Mickey's and my house, though."

A moment of stunned silence followed her words. I had given up on her too soon. Not that Laura was a filly, but I couldn't help but think she'd taken to the cinch after all.

"Emily, please?" Farrah said. Her dark eyes bored into me.

"It would be so awesome," Greg added.

I wrinkled my face, pretending to think about it, and their wide eyes stayed on me like I was Santa Claus deciding if they'd been naughty or nice. "Well, I suppose so."

Happy noises erupted in the kitchen. Young arms grabbed me and hugged me, and my heart took flight.

Snowy fields flashed by on either side of the highway as we crossed onto the reservation. Jack, the kids, and I were following in the Suburban behind Mickey and Laura's Silverado. A steepled stone building about half a mile away rose out of the blanket of white, a hill tufted with snow-topped desert bushes behind it. ST. JOSEPH'S APACHE MISSION PARISH, the sign read. An announcement bulletin with crooked letters spelled out DON'T LET WORRY KILL YOU OFF—LET THE CHURCH HELP. I wanted to giggle, but worried that it would be rude. I giggled anyway.

Farrah touched my shoulder. "What's so funny?" She was so pretty in a red dress Laura had loaned her.

I pointed to the announcement. She laughed, too, and her normally evasive eyes looked clear and happy. We pulled into the parking lot.

"You Catholic?" I asked Jack.

"I come here when I'm in town." He turned off the ignition.

Which didn't exactly answer my question. "Where do you go in Amarillo? St. Mary's?"

"No."

He opened his door and got out. So did I. Four doors slammed. Jack started walking toward the building with Greg beside him in jeans and a button-down shirt that would fit him in about ten years. Maybe. Laura and Mickey had parked closer in than we had, and we caught up with them.

"Good morning, Mickey," I said.

Mickey smiled. "Hey, everyone. We're only going to be five minutes late. That's good for us."

Laura's olive cheeks had a rosy glow at the cheekbone, the kind from fresh air and improving spirits. Mickey had his hand on her shoulder.

A new voice interrupted us, from my left. "Begays. Holden. Good to see you this morning."

All heads swiveled toward the voice. It was from a man, Apache, best I could tell, and tall. Maybe six foot two? He had a large, bony frame with broad shoulders and huge hands. Pits covered his cheeks. Teenage acne, it looked like. The pits were so big they made me think of smallpox, but I didn't think that was a possibility in the states anymore.

Mickey stuck out a hand. "Here for work or worship, Brown?"

They shook.

"Worship, although you never know." He pecked Laura's cheek and shook Jack's hand next. "Who are your friends?"

Mickey nodded his head at me. "Emily." Then at Greg and Farrah. "George and Frannie." He then nodded at the man. "Edward Brown, Alamogordo Police."

Out of the corner of my eye, I saw Farrah slip her hand into Greg's.

I smiled to hide the nerves that shot through me. A cop, when I was smack in the middle of the commission of felony runaway harboring. "Nice to meet you."

"Likewise."

The kids didn't speak. I rubbed my hands against the cold. I hadn't worn gloves, since we would be going straight from the vehicle to church, just my heaviest shawl over a sweater and pants. The wind was picking up, tossing the hair I had worn down. Luckily the skies were clear for our flight.

Jack started walking again, so we all did. "Let's get inside before it's over," he said.

Brown fell in beside him and kept his eyes on Jack's profile. "Haven't found any more dead Mexicans on your place lately, have you?"

I bristled. If I wasn't mistaken, so did Mickey, Jack, and Laura. I assumed Brown was referring, however rudely, to Betsy's father, who died a few months ago on Jack's land, after he was beaten and escaped from Johnson's place.

"All's quiet." If Brown's comment had bothered him, Jack's voice didn't give any feelings away, but, then, it rarely did.

"Hadn't seen you in, what, fifteen years before that?"

"Something like that."

Brown turned to Mickey. "I'll never forget it. Got a call about shots fired in a residence in town from a concerned neighbor. When we showed up, we found one dead, one injured." He grinned at Laura and me. "The refrigerator dead, ADA Holden injured."

"It was an accident," Jack said, his voice tight.

Brown laughed out loud. "People still tell that story. Drunken Assistant District Attorney, a local boy who should know better, shoots himself through the hand and takes out his wife's brand new refrigerator."

The scar, I realized. This was what caused the scar on his palm that I'd noticed a few days ago at the police station. Jack's tension was now palpable. None of us laughed. I itched to shake my finger at Brown for humiliating Jack, and my right fist clenched and unclenched.

"My gun had jammed. I was cleaning it."

"Shoulda charged you for shooting an unarmed refrigerator." Brown winked, and I cringed. "Let you see how your defendants felt."

Jack's anger was like a blast of heat from a furnace. I wanted to do something, anything, but I didn't want to make it worse. Before I could decide on a course of action, Mickey dropped back, letting Brown, Jack, and Laura lead on.

He lowered his voice, speaking to the kids, although I could hear as well. "You guys ready to learn how to do a little work on a horse ranch?"

I smiled at how naturally he had solved half the problem, distracting the teenagers from the unfriendly interaction ahead of them. My eyes followed Jack, hoping Laura managed to change the subject.

Farrah's eyes lit up like someone had struck a match inside them. "I can't wait."

Greg swallowed. "Yeah, sure."

Watching Jack the whole time, I said, "George will probably like the horses a lot better with both his own feet on the ground for a while."

Mickey clapped him on the back. "That can be arranged."

Farrah fell in step beside me as we climbed the front steps to the church door. "When will you be back?"

"Within a week. You'll be so tired and busy you probably won't even notice I'm gone." I dropped my voice to a whisper. "And hopefully the police will catch the shooter by then, and we can bring you guys back to Amarillo."

Greg caught the door from Jack. He and Farrah shared a look as she walked past him. They didn't have to say a word for me to realize they'd agreed "not over our dead bodies."

CHAPTER 16

I got to Williams & Associates the next morning a little later than usual. An enormous fruit basket sat on my desk. Oranges, grapefruits, and apples surrounded a pineapple in a nest of crinkly paper shavings. There wasn't just fruit, though. I touched a wedge of cheddar in red wax and Monterey Jack in green. Walnuts and pecans in-the-shell filled the empty spaces between the pieces of fruit and cheese. A huge red and green bow graced the handle of the basket and a card in an envelope protruded from the display on a plastic stick. I pulled it out and read quickly.

Merry Christmas. Present under the fruit. Your ex, Rich.

I raised an eyebrow. I hadn't gotten him anything, but what was the appropriate gift for the husband who had spent all the money in your joint accounts on his new love? Coal? Still, this was nice. I lined the contents of the basket up on my desk piece by piece then shoveled out paper shavings into the garbage until I came to a flat manila envelope at the bottom. I shook a few last nuts off, then extracted the stapled papers from inside.

Our divorce papers. I flipped to the end. He had signed. So had the judge. A yellow sticky beside his name read: *Congratulations. You have managed to get rid of me. RB.* More like he was rid of me, although he had tried to halt the divorce when he'd learned I was pregnant. After I'd lost the baby and cut off contact with him, he hadn't bothered me again, until now. And I didn't mind this kind of bothering at all.

"Merry Christmas, me," I said aloud.

Belatedly, Snowflake appeared, trotting over to the desk. She put her front paws up on its sides, attempting to get a look at the bounty on top.

"So, girl, you're falling down on the job, not even meeting me at the door today." I ruffled her fur and she sniffed the air, searching for foods dogs like to eat. "Don't bother. Dogs aren't into fruits and nuts." I'd have to hide the cheese from her. Dogs were way into cheese. I pulled her crusts from a napkin in my purse. "Sit." Her bottom hovered a millimeter above the ground, wiggling. I tossed her the toast.

Jack came down the hall, whistling "Jingle Bells."

"Morning," I said, before I saw him.

"More like good afternoon." He walked barefooted to the couch in his worn jeans and untucked red and blue flannel snap-front shirt, holding his briefcase. He sunk to the couch, put down his case, and pulled on his ancient boots, which I hadn't noticed sitting there before. Then he stepped over to my desk with his briefcase, set it down, and whisked an apple into one of his loose shirttails. He polished the fruit, flashing a little olive-toned ab as he did.

My throat closed. I fought to swallow. "I must not be too late since you're still half-naked." It sounded like I was talking through a wad of cotton. I cleared my throat. "That came out wrong. What I meant was ten percent naked." I shook my head, heat flaring into my face. "Not that I mind." I groaned.

He laughed and took a bite of apple. Juice dripped onto his chin. My throat closed up again.

I shook my head. "I need coffee."

He waved the apple at the basket. "What'd'ya get?"

"Signed divorce papers."

He nodded, his lower lip pushed out in a contemplative expression. "Cause for celebration."

I picked up a Redrope accordion file and straightened the papers inside. "It *is* a time for me to celebrate."

He didn't seem to get my drift. "Have you heard from your 'family friends' in New Mexico?"

I kept myself from pouting by sheer force of will. "No. I'll text Laura later and see how they're doing." And then I remembered. "Well, I can email her I guess, since I have no phone."

Jack frowned at me, creasing his forehead tight. "You haven't taken care of your phone yet?"

"Um, no, I was going to do it Friday, and then with Greg and Farrah—"

"You mean George and Frannie?"

"Yes, right, George and Frannie." I put my hands out to my sides, palms up. "I forgot about the phone."

"If the cops still have your phone, they can read anything new you get."

"I thought you said a police officer would have known to take out the SIM card and deactivate it?"

"I don't *know* what they did with it. They *could* have deactivated it. Or they *could* be turning it on occasionally to check your new messages."

He was right, and I'd missed it. "Ugh. I'll take care of it."

"Okay. On that topic, I'm heading out to file the complaint against Burrows and Samson. You need anything?"

I licked my lips. Um, yeah, a kiss would be nice. But I wasn't going to tell him about it if he couldn't figure it out himself. "I think I'm good."

"We'll talk when I get back."

"About?"

He looked at the ground. "A few things." With one hand, he tucked his shirt in. "I shouldn't be long." He took a few steps backwards toward the front door. "Oh, and thanks for getting yourself arrested. This is the highlight of my week."

I raised my eyes to the ceiling, shaking my head. "Glad to provide the entertainment."

He nodded. "You do that." He waved and was gone.

I fanned myself with my hand. The electricity between Jack and me had recharged considerably in the last week, and I was beginning to think he believed in second chances after all. We'd made progress in New Mexico. Now I had to figure out how to nudge him along further, especially since I was a free woman.

I had made a to-do list over toast and coffee with Mother that morning, while she read the paper. It read:

1) Work on discovery requests for Betsy's survivor action

2) Call orthodontist

3) Continue work on Freeman trial notebook

4) Work on discovery responses for Escalante

Escalante was a client with an armed-robbery trial coming up in a few months. In fact, I was expecting him to drop by and help me with his responses sometime today. I jotted a number five:

5) Report phone missing and get new one

The door swept open, and Nadine waltzed in. The first thing I noticed was she'd ditched her nose ring. Her black hair was tied back in a brilliant red scarf, its long ends hanging, but most of it had come loose. The baby pieces around her head were electrified. Static electricity in the cold, dry Panhandle winters was not a thing to trifle with.

I pulled a can of Static Guard out of my desk drawer and held it out. "Look what blew in."

She grabbed it. "Literally. Have you been out there in the last hour? It's practically a tornado." She sprayed liberally and handed it back to me.

"Two words: Aqua Net." I put the can back in the drawer.

She snorted and plopped down on the couch. Nadine stood about five foot ten—six feet in the black biker boots she had on with her jeans today —and most people would describe her as voluptuous. Very voluptuous. On top of that, she could probably kick my butt with one hand tied behind her back. I loved that about her, that and every one of her thirteen tattoos.

She tilted her head and stared at me. "Hey, you're blushing."

More heat suffused my cheeks. "Too heavy-handed with the makeup this morning, I guess."

She patted her chest. "No, I'm pretty sure it's all the way down to your rack."

My hand grabbed the V-neck of my lavender pullover sweater.

She laughed. "Where's your hot boss?"

"He just left."

"Ah, well, there you go."

I shrugged, noncommittal, but her smirk told me I wasn't fooling her.

The door opened slowly. Counting the fruit delivery this morning, this was our third visitor today. That tripled our daily average, and it was only nine a.m. An ancient man struggled to create an opening wide enough for his skeletal frame.

"Clyde!" I jumped to my feet and rushed over. "How are you?"

The name partner of Williams & Associates righted himself, stretching to reach his full five foot two inches. He raised a tremulous hand. "Merry Christmas, my dear."

"Merry Christmas." I let the door shut behind him then followed him across the lobby/office. "Clyde, have you met my friend Nadine? She's here about one of our clients." I crossed my fingers behind my back, although in truth she might be. I just didn't know yet.

Nadine jumped to her feet, all her best parts jostling each other as they rearranged themselves.

Clyde stopped, his rheumy eyes wide as he studied her. "Well, aren't you a fine-looking woman." He inclined his head at her, his version of a courtly bow—I knew from experience.

"Nadine, Clyde is the founder of Williams and Associates."

She smiled wide. Nadine had an incredible smile, with sparkly teeth from here to Dallas and back. "Thank you. So pleased to meet you, sir."

Clyde waved at her to sit, and she did, which he took the time to watch and appreciate before he resumed his walk. All told, he made it from the door to the chair in front of my desk in three minutes flat, a record for him. I suspected he was trying to impress Nadine. He put his hand on the back of the chair.

"What can I do for you, Clyde?"

"Jack called me for a consult. Is he around?"

"No, but he won't be long. Do you want to wait? If so, I'll let him know you're here."

"If you don't mind, dear." He hung his cane on the arm of the chair and positioned himself in front of it in tiny sidesteps. He put both hands behind him to catch the arms and began to lower himself, slowly, slowly. I couldn't breathe during this process. Jack wouldn't let me help Clyde, but that didn't mean I didn't worry and wish I could. I'd hate for him to break a hip on my watch. Clyde's hands gripped the chair's arms on his descent, arresting his fall. He settled in, and I resumed normal respiration.

Clyde turned to Nadine to flirt and I returned to my desk and typed an email to my boss:

Clyde here!!! Says you called for consult. He's waiting for you in front of my desk. Hurry?

J

The front door to the office whooshed open for visitor number four. If this kept up, I'd have to start charging admission. Or lock the door and hide in Jack's office, so I could get something done. I hit send and looked up. Phil Escalante, one of our clients, was taking off his jacket by the doorway.

"Phil! Come on in. We're having a pre-Christmas get-together."

Phil grinned. "I forgot my fruitcake. You sure I'm welcome?" Phil wasn't a tall guy, but he made up for size in big personality and a lot of muscle. Not that there wasn't a goodly layer of insulation to his bulk, too, thanks to the fact that he approached everything in his life with gusto. Food, laughter, women, and booze. In fact, his trouble with the law related back to his enthusiasms. He ran a private swingers' club. It had attracted the ire of a militant religious group who'd started harassing them outside their events. Phil had broken into the home of the group's leader, looking for information to help fend them off, but he'd been caught, and charged with B&E and attempted burglary.

I gestured at my fruit basket. "I've got you covered."

Nadine stood again, and something about the way she moved caught my eye. She rubbed her lips together, then they fell apart slightly. She rolled her shoulders back, which did something magical to her chest, apparently, because Clyde nearly fell out of his chair, and Phil's attention moved from me to her in a flash of lightning. He froze for a full five seconds without breathing.

I broke the spell. "Phil, this is Nadine. Nadine, our client, Phil."

Phil moved to Nadine. She towered over him, although he was a good half a foot taller than Clyde. "So that's your name. Nadine." He took her hand, not like a handshake, like a caress. His hand dwarfed hers. My mouth fell open, and I gawked.

She smiled, but didn't. Like Mona Lisa. "Hello, Phil."

Clyde gaped at the pair, too, eyes narrowed. I got the sense he was a little jealous. I felt a little dirty, like a voyeur.

"Um, Phil, if I could make one more introduction?"

Phil didn't relinquish Nadine's hand or gaze. "Yes?"

"This is Clyde Williams. He founded our law firm. So he's like Jack's boss. A very important figure in Texas civil rights and criminal defense."

Clyde straightened in his chair.

Phil got the hint. He swung fully toward the old man, and stuck out his hand. "So it's you I have to thank, sir. Jack is representing me, and I know I'm in the best of hands. Thank you, thank you so much."

Clyde shook. "It's our honor. To facilitate you exercising your right to due process and a speedy trial by a jury of your peers. We couldn't ask for anything more noble."

Clyde had a way of making me want to salute the flag. Only there wasn't one in there. I settled for beaming with pride at him.

"So, Phil, are you here to work on the discovery responses with me?" I asked.

"I am." He shot a suggestive glance at Nadine. "Then I have a lunch date."

She tittered, and if I'd have been holding a drink, it would have hit the floor.

Glancing back and forth between the two of them, I said to Phil, "Well, if you can give me a few minutes, there seems to be a line forming at my desk."

He moved over to the couch and stood by Nadine. "I think I could bear the wait if you could spare a seat on this couch beside you, Nadine?"

The two looked at each other in a way that made me really, really hungry for chocolate.

I waved at him. "Have a seat, Phil."

Phil bowed to Nadine, and she sat first, and he followed suit, very, very close beside her.

Time to get control of the room. "So, Nadine, you want to go first?"

She rubbed her lips together to moisten them, a coquettish move if I'd ever seen one. "I wanted to tell you how it went with Betsy this weekend."

To Clyde, I explained, "Betsy is the daughter of our deceased client Sofia Perez, who was murdered while incarcerated at Potter County Detention Center. We're filing a survivor action against the county on Betsy's behalf."

Clyde nodded. "Sofia. Betsy. Yes, good, good." He turned toward

Nadine again, holding on to the armrest to keep himself facing her. "We're all ears, Nadine." More like all eyeballs—eyeballs to Nadine's cleavage. Nadine was holding her girls up high, so I was guessing she didn't mind all the male admiration.

"I made the Rainbow Room visit to her at the Hodges' place this weekend, like we'd discussed. I told them we were clearing out some items that we had to have off the books in 2014. Never mind that it didn't make any sense. They bought it." She smoothed one side of her wispy flyaways behind an ear. "I gave Betsy the backpack, but it didn't go all that well."

My stomach clenched. "No? What happened?"

"She started crying. She said she already had a backpack, that she lost it in "Mexico," and that her mama made her promise she'd never lose it, so her friend Emily was going to find it for her."

"Oh no."

"Oh yeah."

"I haven't the slightest clue where to find that backpack."

"Sounds like you'd better start looking anyway."

"For real."

"It got worse."

"Oh?"

"The Hodges. They are some weird-ass people. Their place is like the Stepford wives, Branch Davidian version."

Phil lunged forward in his seat. "Trevon and Mary Alice Hodges?"

Nadine turned to him. "Yes."

"They go to that Mighty is His Word church, the ones where the assholes that harassed me go."

My fists clenched in my lap. "We've got to figure out a reason to get her away from them."

Clyde shook his head. "Freedom of religion is an important right, too."

I lifted my shoulders and dropped them. "I wouldn't disagree with you, Clyde, but in this case, it's more like they're inflicting their religion on others. Which can have the effect of depriving others of *their* right to freedom of religion."

"Not to mention freedom of association," Phil added. "And freedom to make a legal buck."

I was impressed. Not all of our clients became so knowledgeable about the law, but Phil seemed to have it down. That, and a healthy capitalist spirit.

Clyde opened his mouth, but at that moment Jack burst in. I glanced at my computer screen. I'd missed his email reply, but it was there: *Tell him I'm on my way.*

"Hello, all. Clyde, good of you to drop by," Jack said.

The notion that Clyde could spontaneously drop by tickled me. Clyde had a home nurse, a housekeeper, and a driver, all of whom worked full time to keep him moving at all. He thrived on the law, though, and I knew that his continued involvement with the practice he loved kept him one foot out of the grave.

"How'd it go?" I let my eyes drink in the beautiful sight of Jack Holden as he answered.

"Crooked cop complaint filed. Red flag waved at bull. Or bulls, as the case may be." He held up a plastic bag. "And one missing mobile phone returned."

"What? They found my phone?"

He tossed it to me. "Surprise, surprise."

"I'm so glad I hadn't replaced it yet." I pulled it out of the bag and turned it on.

Nadine snorted. "What is it about the cops in this town? We've got one Asian cop that practically lives up at the Polo Club, and he's not there working security. He's a lousy tipper, too. And one of our dancers is so freaked out about a bad cop she won't even come to work."

I had certainly had my fill of bad cops this week, but the others I'd encountered here were fine. "The one I met when I got conked over the head last fall was good enough." The conking had occurred when I'd stumbled across a murder in progress, while I was trying to find Betsy. That cop—Wilson, maybe?—had a horrible mustache, but other than that he seemed nice. "Hopefully it's a minority of them."

"I'm not the one to vouch for that." Phil shook his head. "I can't get any help with those fanatics harassing me."

Clyde raised a fist in the air at least six inches above his lap. "There's a thin line between police and police state, and it's our job to guard that line." And with that, he collapsed in a heap in front of his chair.

CHAPTER 17

"How're you doing, Clyde?" I lifted the gnome-like hand from the bed and squeezed it.

We were at the Southwest Hospital Emergency Room, three hours after he'd bit the dust at our offices. I glanced around the curtained space and shuddered. I'd logged more time here than I'd cared to last fall, and I didn't love being back.

Clyde waved his other hand at me. "A bunch of fuss about nothing. I've told these quacks I have to be home before dinner."

Jack and I shared a smile, and Clyde's regular home nurse, Betty, clucked. "Slow down, Mr. Williams. We're gonna see what the quacks have to say before we go making any plans."

If Betty ever left nursing, the beefy woman had a future in sumo wrestling. She certainly threw her weight around when it came to Clyde. She'd met us here minutes after we'd arrived and immediately taken charge. Clyde's driver was out in the waiting room. The two doted on Clyde. We all did, really.

"Low blood sugar. That's all it was. Low blood sugar."

"Maybe. Maybe not. Whatever it was, you can't go running off by yourself like that anymore, you hear me? You're lucky you didn't break a hip in that fall."

As Clyde started to wind up, Jack stepped between the two of them. "See you later, Clyde. Merry Christmas."

I saluted him. "Merry Christmas, sir."

Clyde's face softened. "Merry Christmas, you two." He motioned me over to him and I leaned close. "Tell Nadine I'm fine."

I nodded gravely.

Jack held the door to the room open and I exited. As soon as it shut, Clyde's voice resumed, arguing with Betty. I felt bad for the old guy, but I sided with her on this one. Thank God I'd had help around when Clyde fell. Getting old sucked, although it did beat the alternative.

Jack and I walked down the hall without speaking. I was hyperaware of his nearness, in a good way. When we reached the door to the parking lot, I slipped on my jacket, and he took my arm. We exited together, walking to my car. The cold hadn't eased up, and the wind whipped against my face. I pulled the collar of my coat closed higher on my neck.

"The shop called. My Jeep is ready. Can you drop me by to get it?" he asked.

"Sure."

"After that, can you hold down the fort by yourself for a few hours?"

"Don't I always?"

He squeezed my arm. "You're taking Wednesday off, right?"

"It's Christmas Eve. I had planned to. Do you need something?" We approached my car and I pulled my keys from my pocket and clicked to unlock the doors.

"No, no. It's just, well, in case we don't get around to it before then, I thought maybe we could talk Wednesday night."

"Christmas Eve night?"

"Well, if you don't have plans."

"Other than it being Christmas Eve, you mean?"

"Maybe you could come to services at my church with me. And then we could talk."

I stood at the driver's side, hand on the door handle, Jack beside me. My heart stopped beating in my chest. After a slow count of three it exploded into a chaotic rhythm. Was Jack asking me out?

Jack shuffled his feet. "If you aren't already committed—"

"No, no. I'm not. I mean, yes, I'll go with you."

"Good. I'll pick you up at five thirty." He opened the door to my car.

I stood there beside him, smiling, floating, not sure if it was real yet. "Sounds perfect."

I sat in an examination chair in Dr. Parks's orthodontic office half an hour after dropping Jack at the mechanic. Large mauve flowers floating in a sea of green ivy assaulted me from walls in three directions. Apparently, Dr. Parks had consulted my mother for decorating tips.

The orthodontist probed inside my mouth and shook his head. "Well, can't say I didn't warn you. Oh, your poor mother. All that money, wasted." He removed his hands from my mouth, then pulled off his gloves finger by finger, snapping the rubber as he did so. "I can have a treatment plan together for you after Christmas. Martha will take all your X-rays now."

"Treatment plan? Can't I get another retainer?"

He shuddered. "Goodness no. What's there to retain? Your teeth are nowhere near alignment. But these days we can do wonders with products like Invisalign that work as well as traditional braces and are less obvious, in less time, too. No one will even notice you're wearing them."

"How long would I have to have them?"

"Well I haven't seen your films, but maybe six months."

"And the cost?"

"A few thousand. My office would get you the exact figures." He pushed his stool away and rolled across the floor.

I nearly gasped. I wanted to ask him why I needed to do this, but before I could he said, "Martha will be here shortly," and was gone.

"Thank you," I whispered to the empty room.

My head reeled. My bank account couldn't take that kind of hit. Every cent I had was accounted for in the adoption process and with the duplex. Even after Dr. Parks's dire predictions—and presumptions—a few days ago, I wasn't sure whether I wanted to do this. So what was I doing here? The X-rays would have to wait. I ripped the bib from my neck and got to my feet. I retrieved my purse and headed for the reception and billing area. I stopped at the window for checkout.

"Hello. My name is Emily Bernal. What is the charge for my exam today?"

The woman behind the counter had gray curls that lay flat against her skull like they'd been painted on. She peered up at me through half-glasses perched at the end of her nose. "Emily Phelps? It's me, Mrs. Parks. How are you?"

Of course. The orthodontist's wife had always worked with him. "Hello, I'm good. And you?"

"Dealing with the insurance companies gets harder every year, but, other than that, fairly well, thank you." Her eyes swept the desk in front of her. "I'm afraid I don't have your file."

"Well, Dr. Parks examined me, and Martha was going to do X-rays, but my office called, so I'm going to have to run." I held up my cell phone. "An emergency."

"We'll take care of the billing by mail then. Are you still at the same address?"

"Yes," I said through gritted teeth. That question was almost as bad as when the host at a restaurant said, "Just one, ma'am?"

"Would you like to reschedule your X-rays?"

"I'll call. Thank you and good-bye."

She waggled her fingers at me.

I turned to go, and as I did, I almost ran headlong into a man coming in through the exit door. "Excuse me," I said.

"Pardon me." Police uniform. Red hair. Full face. He kept walking.

I called after him, "Officer Burrows?"

He looked back at me, eyes narrowed. "Yes?"

Steam built up in my ears. "You don't even remember me, after what you did?"

"Hmmmm." He pulled a small flip notepad and pen from his pocket.

Hissssssssss went the steam. "You arrested me and took my phone?"

"I guess." Burrows scribbled something in his notepad.

"Officer Burrows?"

He looked up and snapped the notepad shut. "Take care, now." He walked briskly down the hall, away from me.

What the H-E-double-hockey-sticks was up with him?

CHAPTER 18

After I left the orthodontist, I returned to the office. I unlocked the door and let myself in. Snowflake didn't run out to greet me, which was odd.

"Snowflake?"

No jingle of bells and dog tags. I was still a lot unsettled by my encounter with Burrows, and my heart pounded in my ears. I pulled the baby Glock from my purse. I knew Jack had said he wouldn't be here, but he hadn't said a word about the dog. I tiptoed down the hallway, moving cautiously up to and around the kitchen door, checking for intruders within. Nothing but the normal white refrigerator, white cabinets, and wooden-topped table and white chairs. I did the same at the door to Jack's office, dropping into a shooting stance on the far side of the doorway as I peered in. No one. I bent over and checked for feet under his massive desk.

Clear.

I put my gun away. I felt a little silly wielding it, but better safe than sorry. This is why I practiced at the gun range, every month since my father gave me the gun. If the situation called for it, I knew how to handle my weapon. "You got no business owning a gun if you can't use it properly," he'd said. I'd just never needed to use it, and I hoped I never did.

I made a mental note to remind Jack to tell me anytime Snowflake wouldn't be here, so I could skip the whole heart failure thing. I walked normally down the hall to my work area as the booming in my ears subsided to a thumping and then to nothing. When I got to my desk, my cell phone rang, its harsh sound making me jump. It wasn't my normal ringtone.

"Geez!" I fumbled in my purse for it. Another note to self: change the annoying ringtone. As I answered I saw the caller was UNKNOWN. "Hello?"

Someone cleared his throat, at least I thought it was a he from the sound of it, but honestly, I didn't have much to go on.

"Hello??"

The call dropped. Greg again? Surely not. The kids were safe on the Wrong Turn Ranch with Mickey and Laura. To be sure, I texted Laura: *How are things going?*

Her reply was almost instantaneous: *We're having fun! Been out riding with them, and now they're exploring on their own.*

Okay, so probably not the kids. My phone made another unfamiliar noise. I fumbled with it and saw that I had four voice mails. Scratch "change ringtone." I needed to reset all my notifications and sounds. I hadn't known I had messages. I played them, one by one. Two calls last week from an 806 number. That was probably the kids. Two calls today from an unknown number, one of which I had just experienced. Weird.

I put my purse away under the desk and booted up my computer. The background screen loaded Betsy's sweet face and a pang shot through my heart. It was time to tell Mother I was moving out. That wasn't a conversation I looked forward to having, although she'd understand why. I pulled up the network and clicked on the folder for Elizabet "Betsy" Perez and opened the draft complaint.

The office phone rang.

"Williams and Associates, Emily speaking."

"Emily, give me Jack."

I recognized the voice, but no way was I giving this woman the satisfaction of admitting it. In my slowest Amarillo accent, I said, "May I ask who's calling?"

A withering sigh rattled the phone line. "Assistant District Attorney Melinda Stafford. You may remember me. Now give me Jack."

I hadn't talked to my childhood nemesis Melinda since I socked her in the jaw for telling me my miscarriage of Rich's baby was "for the best." She had threatened to sue me, but Jack had paid her off, and had a little too much fun doing it. Melinda was one of the ADAs, so I had to play nice, though. At least a little bit.

"I'm sorry, Jack isn't available at the moment. May I take a message or assist you in any way?" The words and saccharin-sweet tone puckered my mouth.

"You can tell him to get control of his client, for one thing."

"I'm sorry, I don't know what you're talking about. Perhaps if you give me a client name and a brief description of the incident I can relay it to him?"

"Cut the crap, Emily. Alan Freeman was up here demanding to meet with me so he could make a plea bargain." She huffed. "He chose to work with your firm, so I'm not about to meet with him without Jack present. I had the receptionist send him packing."

I paused, long enough that I could have written a message, if I were so inclined. I wasn't. "Got it. Anything else?"

"Yeah. Tell him if he wants to get a plea bargain done, I'm off for the Christmas holidays as of six p.m. sharp today. Otherwise, he's gonna get his ass kicked in court after the New Year." She hung up.

"Merry frickin' Christmas to you, too, Melinda." I slammed the phone down in the cradle, and enjoyed it.

Jack was going to want to know this, stat. I picked the phone back up and pushed speed dial for his mobile. It went to voice mail. I ended the call and sent him a text message instead: *Call me ASAP. Alan went to Stafford asking for a plea bargain?? She's off for holidays after 6 today.*

What in God's name had gotten into Alan? When we'd talked to him the week before, he seemed antsy about having his fate still up in the air. He hadn't mentioned second thoughts, though. His case wasn't rock solid, but neither was the city's, and they had the burden of proving his guilt beyond a reasonable doubt. Assaulting Wu and resisting arrest were serious charges, and we trusted a jury of Freeman's peers to treat them as such, especially in the wake of Ferguson: Freeman was black, Wu was a half-white Asian, and they told two completely different stories, with no witnesses to the alleged assault. Freeman had no priors, and he was no thug. I had faith the jury wouldn't swallow Wu's version of events. Freeman had faith, too, as far as I'd known up until five minutes ago.

With difficulty, I wrenched my attention back to the complaint for Betsy. The beginning of a case really didn't reveal anything shocking or sexy. We were alleging wrongful death, that PCDC had caused Sofia's by not providing adequate supervision to prevent her murder by other inmates, and that their violent actions were foreseeable. The upfront process was formulaic and had to do with establishing the county's responsibility. Honestly, I'd never worked on one of these cases before and neither had Jack, so I spent a lot of time researching forms online. I had to keep reminding myself how important this lawsuit was to Betsy's future to keep myself awake long enough to finish the draft.

I worked steadily for all of two minutes when the door whispered open. Without Snowflake to alert me to company and because I was concentrating on what I was doing, the visitor didn't even register in my consciousness until Alan Freeman was standing right in front of my desk.

"Emily, is Jack here?"

"Oh!" Alan had dressed to the nines today. He wore a black suit and shiny cobalt blue tie over a white shirt. His scalp shined. I'd never seen him like this, and it took me a moment to answer. "Alan, wow, you look sharp. Jack's not here, but the ADA called and spoke to me."

He looked up and then down furtively, but he said nothing.

"Let's go sit in Jack's office. I'll get you something to drink. Water? Soft drink? Coffee or tea?"

"Water. Thank you."

I grabbed my cell phone, a pen, and a yellow pad, and Alan followed me down the long wainscoted hall with its Western paintings, past the kitchen on the right, and down to Jack's office on the left. Really, it was Clyde's office first, but Jack had inherited it with the practice and it was magnificent. Richly stained built-ins dominated the farthest wall. His desk consumed most of the central space, and a conference table and leather chairs on rollers sat nearest the door. Behind it was a *real* Remington painting, a huge splurge by Clyde back in the day. I put Alan at the near side of the table. He could enjoy the long wall of windows or the facing wall of photographs, art, and diplomas from there.

"I'll be right back with your water."

"Thanks."

As I walked to the kitchen, I typed Jack another frantic message: *Alan here. Looking for you. Help.* Jack hadn't answered my earlier message, but it had only been twenty minutes since I sent it. I wouldn't panic yet.

I grabbed two glass tumblers from the cabinet and filled them with ice cubes and filtered water from the door of the refrigerator. I would have to talk to Alan, see what I could do to steady him, and stall like crazy until I heard from Jack. I walked back into the office.

Alan was standing at Jack's wall of fame, looking at an arresting black-and-white photograph of an old, abandoned mine. Above its entrance hung a lopsided sign: SACRAMENTO SILVER MINE. The photo even had a name: *Old Dreams at the Wrong Turn Ranch.* I knew it by heart. It was the one Jack had mentioned when we visited the cemetery with the kids on Saturday. It was a beautiful piece, but I preferred the charcoal drawing beside it of a little girl and a spotted pony. The artist? Jack. The subject? His daughter.

Alan heard me and returned to his seat. He had placed coasters from the holder in the center of the table in front of his chair and one across from him where I'd left my pen and yellow pad. I set the glasses on the coasters, and sunk into buttery leather.

"The ADA said you tried to meet with her about a plea deal," I said.

"Yeah." He looked down.

"So, tell me what's going on."

He shook his head. "I can't do this."

"Can't do what?"

"The trial."

"I don't understand. You didn't seem to have reservations before. Have you and Jack talked about you taking a deal?"

"No. Well, at the beginning."

"So, has something changed?"

He looked up at me. A single tear glistened in the corner of one of his eyes.

I put my hand over his. "What is it?"

His voice broke. "I can't do this to my wife and daughters."

"I know you're worried about them. But if you plead guilty, you'll be a convicted felon. That will impact them forever."

"I know. But if I don't it will be much worse."

I licked my lips. I wished Jack would hurry up and get here. "What was the plea offer before, do you remember?"

"If I'd plead guilty to assault, they'd drop the aggravated part, and I'd do two years and be eligible for parole in six months."

"So you want to be in prison for six months—or more? You think that will be better for your family?"

I heard the sound of the front door. Jack. I jumped to my feet.

A deep voice bellowed down the hall. "Anybody in here?"

Not Jack. But a voice that sounded familiar. Across from me, Alan's face had frozen in a look of terror. I walked over to Alan and put my hands on his shoulders.

I whispered, "What is it?"

He didn't answer, and I gave him a little shake.

He croaked out, "I need to go," and jumped to his feet.

Samson's uniformed bulk filled the doorway to Jack's office, and, worse, Burrows appeared behind him.

I took a step toward them, between the two officers and our rattled client. "If you gentlemen can take a seat in the lobby, someone will be with you in a moment."

Burrows ignored my words and pushed around Samson and inside, taking a visual inventory as he did. "I thought I heard voices. Where's Mr. Holden?"

Alan sunk back into his chair.

I didn't back up. "Sir, we're in the middle of a private meeting. I will see you in the lobby in a moment."

He lowered his voice. "I asked you where Jack Holden is."

He frightened me, but I was determined not to show it. "He's not here right now. I'm going to—"

From the doorway, Samson said, "Well, hello, Freeman."

Alan was looking down again. "Officer Samson."

I ignored the pleasantries. "Unless the two of you have an official reason to be in Jack's office, like a warrant to serve, I am telling you in front of a witness that you are not invited to be in here and need to go to our lobby."

"Not a problem. We'll wait out there." Samson held his hands up and gestured with his head for Burrows to follow him. To Alan, he said, "See you around, Freeman."

Burrows joined him and the two men walked out.

"I'll be right back, Alan." I hurried after them. "Jack may be awhile. May I help you with something, Officers?"

Samson entered the lobby and Burrows walked over to my desk. Between the two of them, they blocked access to both my desk and the exit. Burrows blatantly read my computer screen, shuffled my papers, then grabbed one of my business cards from their holder.

I jabbed at the off button on my monitor. "If you don't need something, then I need to ask you to leave, for the privacy of our clients and their information."

Burrows slapped my card against the thumb of his left hand several times then made a show of reading it.

Samson said, "We came by to see if you or your boss have heard from those two teenage runaways."

"What?"

Samson crossed his arms. "I spoke to you last Wednesday night about the two teenagers that had run away from their group home, Greg Easley and the Arab girl. I'm following up. Have they called you or come by? It sounded like you developed a rapport with them. And I hear you have a thing for strays."

"No." My head spun. Could he know they had, somehow? Surely not.

"And you'd tell me if they had?"

"Actually I'd call Byron first. They aren't accused of any crime that I've been made aware of. He's their caseworker. But I haven't had my phone, so if they contacted me on it, I wouldn't have known."

Burrows pocketed my card and cut in. "So sorry to hear that. But you've got it back now, right?" He didn't wait for me to answer. "I don't know what kind of magic you're expecting to happen by filing a complaint against Samson and me, though." He pantomimed magic hands in front of his chest, his fingers doing a poof and his hands moving away from each other, down, and around back to his waist.

Samson laughed, a short bark.

"I think filing a complaint against you will do a lot of things. It already made my phone reappear."

Burrows stepped closer to me. "Maybe other things will start reappearing now, too."

Burrows turned and the two men took their sweet time walking out.

Five minutes later Jack crashed in through the office door. "Sorry. I was Christmas shopping. Left my phone in the car."

"Please tell me you have Snowflake."

He mumbled something.

"What?"

"She's fine."

"Does that mean you have her?"

He mumbled again.

"Jack, where's the dog?"

"At a doggie daycare and spa, okay? It was her Christmas present."

Laughter burbled from deep inside me. "That's . . . unexpected."

He growled. "How'd it go with Alan?"

"Not great at first, then Burrows and Samson showed up, and it got much worse."

"What?"

"Yeah, they asked for you, but never really said what they wanted with you. They asked me questions about Greg and Farrah and left."

"Hmm."

"Alan seems adamant on that plea deal. Says he can't do this to his wife and kids."

"Huh."

"Are you even listening to me?"

"Thinking."

My leg started to bounce. "Okayyyyy." When he still didn't speak, I sighed and started working on my complaint document again.

"How'd you leave it with Alan?"

"I didn't. He's in your office, waiting for you."

He glanced at the wall clock. "It's already four o'clock. You said Melinda leaves at six?" I nodded and he continued. "We have to do something."

"Yet only one of us has a license to practice law."

"Come with me?"

I sighed and followed him down the long hall.

Jack and Alan shook hands. Within moments of joining him at the conference table in Jack's office, we picked up the conversation pretty much where I'd left it with Alan, with his insistence that a plea bargain was the right thing to do for his family.

"There has to be a better reason than that for me to participate in putting you in jail before Christmas." Jack leaned back in his chair, his arms crossed.

Alan hung his head. "There's no better reason than a man's family."

"If you're dead set on it, take the holiday with them, and we'll do it after."

He shook his head without looking up. "My mind is made up, but I understand if you can't do this for me. I can fire you, if you need me to, so I can work directly with the DA's office."

"I still don't understand," I blurted. "How does this make things better for your family?"

Alan looked up at me with the saddest eyes I'd ever seen. "You don't have to understand. I need y'all's help is all."

Jack leaned toward him, elbows and forearms on the table. "You understand, if we make this deal, you could be put in jail tomorrow?"

"I expected as much."

"Two days before Christmas."

"So my calendar tells me."

Jack frowned, but he picked up his phone. Fifteen minutes later, he had convinced ADA Stafford to honor the original plea offer. He looked pale when he hung up. "She'll meet us in court tomorrow morning."

"But her vacation—" I said.

"She said her flight doesn't leave until noon."

Alan shook our hands and thanked us profusely as he left. He seemed relieved, like an enormous weight had been taken off him. Not me, though. I was shaken and confused. Today had just about leveled me. I went back to my desk to try to work, but my brain was fried and my heart too heavy. I checked the time. Nearly five.

I hit intercom on the office phone. "Jack, do you mind if I leave a little early? I'm wiped."

"Okay."

Objection! I wanted to shout. *Nonresponsive!* But I wasn't up for it. I grabbed my handbag and slipped out.

CHAPTER 19

The jingling bell on the door announced my arrival at ABC Half-Price Resale. A tall, slim black woman stood behind the counter ringing up a customer, a short woman with graying pin curls and French-roast skin tone, decked out in red and green sweats with flashing lights on the Christmas tree across her chest.

The customer turned and called out to a skeletal old man sitting in a folding chair near where I stood by the front door. "Herbert? I told you we'd find it cheaper here. Twenty-two ninety-five."

The man beside me grunted. His skin was so loose it looked like wrinkled fabric.

I went straight to the toys, looking for Betsy's horse, figuring someone had probably snapped it up by then. It was a fine toy. But no, it was there, still perfect. I grabbed the box and pulled it to my chest. To hell with the Hodges and their rules. I'd find a way to give it to her.

I kept browsing, looking for gifts for Greg and Farrah. I hardly knew them, but I would be with them over Christmas. They had so little, I hoped I could find something they'd like. I ended up with a multi-item hair-dryer set with brushes to straighten, curl, or diffuse, for Farrah, and a Swiss Army knife for Greg. I picked several ornaments from the tree display for Laura, Mickey, and Jack's secretary, Judith.

Jack would be harder. Or so I thought, until I ran across a collector's set of hardback, signed Tony Hillerman books. I stacked the small knife package on top of the books, which went on top of the hair-dryer box, which was itself stacked on top of the horse box. I gripped the ornaments in one hand and lifted the tower of boxes. I walked behind it, my head craned around to see where I was going, and set it on the glass display case beside the register, dropping the ornaments there as well. I prayed fervently as I did: *Dear Heavenly Father, please don't let me inadvertently purchase stolen goods. Or at least not regift to anyone things stolen from their own place. Amen.*

The tall woman rang me up, which gave me time to study her. She was attractive, her shoulder-length hair worn in natural-looking curls. She wore a small diamond ring and gold band on her left hand. She didn't smile, though, and she seemed distracted. She had to enter several of my items into the register more than once.

Her hands shook, and when she spoke, her voice was tight. "One ninety-nine thirty-two. Will that be cash or check, ma'am?"

"Check, please."

"I'll need to see some ID."

"Of course." I handed her my driver's license and started writing a check. "Is Alan here?"

"He's in back."

"I'm a friend of his, would it be okay if I ran back and said hello to him? Let him know I did my shopping here?" I gave her my most winning smile.

"That wouldn't be a good idea."

I looked up at her. Enormous tears threatened to spill. I pulled my eyes down quickly and finished filling in my check. In the memo line, I wrote *If you need help, call me,* and added my phone number. I handed it to her. "Thank you, ma'am, and Merry Christmas."

"Thank you, Merry Christmas to you, too, and God bless you."

I exited, and the bell jingled again behind me. I moved fast, depositing the presents and my purse in the trunk of my Mustang. I dropped my keys and phone into my deep skirt pocket and slammed the trunk. "Not a good idea," the woman had said when I asked to visit Alan. Which made it sound like a really good idea to go see if he was in trouble. Like maybe the delivery guy was here with stolen merchandise again. If he was, I could get a picture of the license plate this time, which would make a great photo to stick in Jack's Christmas present.

Dusk had fallen over Amarillo, as had lower temperatures, even while I was in the store. I walked quickly along the front sidewalk. I hadn't exactly dressed for running around outside. I didn't have anything but a light jacket that ended at the waist, over a thin black blouse and tank top. I pulled my jacket tighter around me. My high-heeled black boots and black maxi skirt looked great for impressing my boss, but now the wind whipped my skirt around my thighs as it distributed a dumpster's worth of trash around the parking lot. At least in the all-black clothes I had on the bad guys wouldn't see me as easily, I thought. I rounded the corner to the side of the strip mall, and the sidewalk ended. My heels teetered as I stepped off the concrete. Gravel, glass, and bottle caps littered the pavement. I kept a close eye on the ground, squinting in the near-dark.

I came to the back edge of the building. The alley extended to my left behind another strip center and to the right behind Alan's. Dumpsters lined the alley behind each business. An eighteen-wheeler was parked halfway down to my right. I was pretty sure it was behind Alan's store. Its headlights were on and pointed in my direction, limiting my vision, but it didn't look like there were any humans out between it and me. I decided to move fast from dumpster to dumpster until I was close enough to get a good shot of the truck's plates.

Keeping tight to the backs of the buildings, I hurried down the alley. My boots crunched glass and squished foreign substances I didn't want to identify. Nausea rolled over me in a wave, but I couldn't let myself think about it. I came to the first dumpster, panting, and I took a moment to catch my breath and peer around the trash can. Still no humans in my path.

Three dumpsters to go. I dashed around the next one and back to the building, tripping over something when I was a foot away from the wall. My toe smashed into a hard object, with nothing between it and the obstacle but soft, supple leather. I bit my lip to keep from screaming in pain. I caught myself with one hand on the wall and held still. Stars danced before my eyes. When the fireworks and shooting pain subsided, I hobbled along, using one hand on the building to steady myself.

I reached another dumpster. Tears in the corners of my eyes made it hard to see, and I began to wonder if this was a really bad idea. I put weight on my foot and winced, taking it back off again immediately. A door flew open beside me. A huge black woman in a tent-like red wool dress stepped out, holding a stuffed black trash bag.

She studied me for a moment. "Child, you look a fright. You be needing a hand?"

I shook my head, half-smiling. "No, I was just walking down to visit with Alan, you know, at ABC Half-Price Resale, and I stubbed my toe."

She clucked. "It's dark as Satan's heart out already. Here, I'll turn my light on so you can see where you're going, hon."

She leaned in and messed with something I couldn't see and the light was on before I could scream, "No."

"You're so sweet." I pasted on a big smile. "Well, I'll be heading toward Alan's now."

I shot a glance down the last ten well-lit yards. So well lit that I could have taken a picture of the license plate on the truck, if it weren't for the fact that the woman was watching me.

"You be careful now." She tossed her garbage in the bin. "I'll wait here until you make it safe and sound 'fore I turn out the light."

There was no way I was walking out into the alley when it was lit up like an operating room. I wracked my brain for a way to get the light out and the woman inside. Inspired, I pulled out my phone and turned on its flashlight.

"Silly me, I forgot about this. I'll be fine. I don't want to keep you out in this cold."

"You sure?"

"Oh yes, this is great." I shined the flashlight all about to demonstrate how great it was, like an epileptic radio operator sending Morse code.

"All right."

"Merry Christmas, and thank you."

"God bless you and yours."

I waved, and she shut the door behind her. The light went off. I heaved a relieved breath. Last dumpster to reach, then I could lean out and get my shot. I turned off the flashlight, tested my wonky foot—it was better—and ran, in what passed for a sprint in my current footwear and injured state, along the building. It was almost anticlimactic to have made it. I crouched at the edge of the trash bin and leaned around. I snapped the picture, checked the focus, and took another for good measure.

I smiled. Jack would be so surprised. And then I heard the voices.

"What have we here, Freeman?" a man asked.

I couldn't hear well enough to recognize it, but the tone wasn't a nice one.

Alan's voice replied, "You're getting what you want."

"I never thought I wouldn't."

"Then, please, can't you leave me alone?"

A third man spoke. "Hey. How ya doing?"

The sound of skin slapping against skin was unmistakable.

"I can't complain. And you?" first man said.

"I could use less hours and more money, but it could be worse," third man said.

"*Feliz Navidad.*" First.

"Yeah, Merry Christmas to you, too." Third.

A short, skinny silhouette sauntered around the rear delivery door and toward me. I slunk back around the dumpster, out of sight. I had barely seen the guy, but I was sure I hadn't recognized him. My heart hammered so loudly I wanted to clap my hands over my ears, but I knew it wouldn't do any good. The tractor-trailer roared to life, and I crouched and ran back to the building. I managed to wedge myself between the dumpster and the wall before the big rig rolled by.

Holy cow, that was close. With the noise of the eighteen-wheeler gone, I could hear Alan and the first man talking again. I moved out to peek around the dumpster. I couldn't see Alan or anyone else. I decided that they must be standing inside the delivery bay.

"Are you here to rub it in?" Alan said.

A car engine revved somewhere nearby and drowned out the other man's answer.

What the fudge were they talking about? Alan spoke again, but I couldn't understand him either. The engine noise stopped but Alan's voice moved away from me. I needed to get closer, but I had to find a better place to hide. There looked to be a door well on the building, about fifteen feet away from me. I wasn't sure if it would provide enough cover. I leaned out to get a better view, but saw nothing. The men had disappeared, and so had their voices. I crouched down behind the dumpster again. I'd just send Jack a text with the picture. I pulled it up and putzed with the lighting and contrast for a few minutes until the license plate was clearly visible.

A hand clamped over my mouth, and an arm wound around my body. The arm jerked me into an unyielding chest. My heart seized and felt like it would explode.

A man's voice said, "Not a sound, understand?"

I nodded, the movement of my head restricted by the hand pressing into my mouth.

"We need to talk. I'm going to remove my hand, but if you scream, things will get worse before they get better."

I nodded again.

The hand slipped away, and the arm loosened around me. I whirled to find myself in the grasp of Officer John Burrows.

Burrows hustled me out of the alley and to the front of the strip center by my car. He let go of my arm. I bent over, hands on knees, trying to catch my breath. He wasn't even winded. His eyes roamed the parking lot and street. For the first time, I noticed he was in plain clothes, dressed for stealth. Dark jeans. Black hoodie. Black baseball cap. His exposed white face glowed in the low light like a beacon, though.

"What"—pant, pant—"was"—pant, pant—"that"—pant, pant—"all about?"

"Trying to keep you from interfering in police business and getting your damn self killed. Now, get out of here."

"I thought you"—pant—"wanted to talk to me?"

"Not here."

"Where?"

"Later. Right now, we both need to leave before someone sees us together. Or at all."

Before I could respond, Burrows disappeared into the parking lot. I heard an engine rev, but with the interference from Amarillo Boulevard traffic noise in the background, I couldn't fix on the location. I stood up, searching for interested faces. No one was looking at me. I pulled out my keys and got in the Mustang.

I put my head on the steering wheel, still breathing hard. The car beside me started and pulled out of its parking space, but I didn't even glance up. What had just happened? Clearly, Burrows was keeping tabs on someone. It could be Alan. Or it could be me. He had shown up at my orthodontist's office that morning, after all, and he didn't wear braces. The thought of a police officer tailing me all over town made me sick to my stomach.

I reviewed what I'd seen and heard before Burrows interrupted me. The conversation made no sense. And what about the driver? Was he the one who delivered the hot goods? Or was he only a normal old delivery driver making his rounds? If normal, I'd peeved off a cop for nothing more than a hard working driver's license plate. The circuits in my brain shorted. I put the Mustang in reverse, then noticed Burrows had pulled into the emptied spot beside me in a silver sedan, passenger-side window down. I lowered mine, too. A woman sat beside him in the passenger seat, a skanky-looking woman not wearing enough clothing for the weather. She chewed rhythmically, like she had a big wad of gum in her mouth. She didn't look at me. Burrows didn't either.

He said, "You got a place we could meet where no one would see us?"

Last week this man had arrested me when Mary Alice Hodges had called on the wrath of God, just because I was watching Betsy. He wasn't any too nice about it, either. Then my phone had disappeared for days. I'd filed a complaint against him. He'd shown up at my orthodontist's and my office, then grabbed me behind Alan's store. Burrows scared me, and now he wanted me to meet him somewhere private? *Whoa, big fellow.*

"I don't think that's a good idea."

"Would you rather I take you in to the station again?"

"For what?"

"Criminal trespass for starters. I could think of a few more things if I needed to."

He looked away from me, holding up one hand and inspecting the back of it. The woman blew a bubble and it popped. She reached up and peeled it away from her face, put it in her mouth, and resumed chewing.

My ears and cheeks burned. "Fine," I snapped.

I didn't like the idea of meeting him somewhere secluded, but I sure didn't want to be arrested again. I ran through the best possibilities I could think of. Jack was at the office. My gossipy mother would be home by now on a Monday evening. Then I had an idea.

"What about the parking garage for the Maxor Building? Most everyone's left for the day by now. The Downtown Athletic Club's there, but people park on the first floor for it. I could meet you on the third."

Jack frequented the DAC daily, for the workout and the shower facilities. So far, I hadn't caught the workout bug.

"Wait. Isn't there a restaurant in the building, too?"

"It's only open at lunch."

He nodded. "Okay. Pull in nose first by an empty space. Stay in your car. I'll find you."

He threw his car in reverse and backed out quickly.

"You're welcome," I called after him.

I cruised down Amarillo Boulevard slowly, getting honked at twice by impatient drivers. The worsening weather seemed to have everyone on edge. I pulled off the Boulevard back into downtown on Polk and came upon the Maxor courtyard seconds later. White Christmas lights sparkled from the iron fencing and trees. Someone had decorated the Center City's buckskin horse sculpture with a wreath around its neck. I turned on Fourth Avenue, then into the garage, winding my way up the darkened ramp.

The third story was empty, and I picked a space far from the lighted elevator. When I'd parked, nose in, a car rolled behind me. Too late, it occurred to me that I should have told someone where I was and with whom before meeting a scary man I barely knew alone in a deserted parking garage. Well, it wasn't like I didn't know how to protect myself. I pulled out my Glock for the second time that day.

The rear end of the silver sedan eased to the wall, its white backing lights illuminating the space for a moment. The engine noise ceased. A door slammed with an echoey sound. A tap sounded on the passenger-side glass, sharp and sudden. I jumped, instinctively half-raising my gun hand.

"Put that thing away." The window muffled Burrows's voice, but I could hear him well enough to know he was irritated.

I lowered the gun.

"Not down. Away."

I tucked the gun back into my handbag, but I left the purse in my lap. I hit the unlock button, and Burrows got in.

"You know how many people are killed each year with their own guns?"

I didn't answer him. He didn't know me and had no way of knowing the hours I logged in gun-safety courses and at the shooting range, or that my best memories with my father involved either horses or guns. Sometimes both.

So I changed the subject. "Who's the woman in your car?"

"Doesn't matter."

It did to me. His evasive answer worried me even more. While Burrows wasn't a large man, the interior walls of my car still seemed too close with him in it. I could feel the weight of the filed complaint against him in the air. I wanted this over with as fast as I could make it happen.

"This"—I waved my hand around the front seat in the air between us— "feels wrong." I breathed through my nose slowly. One one thousand. Two one thousand. Deep breath in. Deep breath out. "Am I under arrest?"

Burrows readjusted in his seat to face me. "Not yet."

I turned and looked him dead in the eye. "So I have no legal obligation to talk to you?"

"None." He held my gaze without blinking. "But you need to keep your damn nose out of police business."

"I don't have my nose in police business."

"Then what do you call tonight?"

If that was police business, were they onto Alan's part in the smuggling ring? If so, Alan needed help, and I had some of the evidence to help him here on my phone camera, possibly. Alan didn't belong behind bars like a criminal, not for the assault charge, and not for getting bullied and intimidated into this. I held my breath and prayed for our client and his family.

Finally, I answered Burrows. "Looking out for a client. I do work for a law firm, you know."

He shook his head and his voice dripped acid. "Don't give me that crap. You were spying, and we both know it."

Louder than I'd intended, I said, "You have no idea what you're talking about," and smacked the steering wheel with the palm of one hand.

The silence after my mini-explosion was oppressive. A car drove up the ramps behind us. I heard the thrump-thrump of its wheels and felt the slight vibration of the structure. The tires squealed as it turned and moments later the thrumps moved back in our direction. The car slowed as it came to us, and Burrows turned to watch it. I did, too. The driver rubbernecked at us then drove on.

Burrows looked around the garage, like he expected someone to be there, and lowered his voice. "I hope we don't have to have this conversation again."

A sharp knock on my window nearly sent me through the roof. Someone shined a spotlight-strength flashlight in at us.

A man's voice, high-pitched, asked, "Ma'am, are you okay?"

Burrows said, "Roll down your window. It's a security guard."

I turned my key to power the car and hit the down button. "Good evening, sir." Good, now someone besides Burrows and the mystery woman knew I was here.

Burrows leaned over and held a badge in front of me. "Is there a problem?"

The security guard, peg toothed and skinny, lowered his light from our eyes. "Just doing my job." He nodded at us and backed away. He put his free hand on his hip, where I saw a can of mace. I hoped he didn't run into real problems. He didn't look like he was strong enough to wrest the can from its holster.

Burrows tracked the security guard with his eyes.

I powered the window back up. "Were you following me, earlier?"

Burrows grinned, showing teeth so perfect they were like whitewashed pickets in a fence. "I needed a new retainer."

He opened the door and got out, then leaned back down. "Quit making trouble with cops. Especially when you go around waving a fucking gun. It's a good way to get shot, yourself."

He disappeared into his car.

CHAPTER 20

Jack and I met Alan and his wife in one of the tiny attorney-client conference rooms off the foyer to the 499th District Court in the Potter County
Courts Building at eight a.m. the next morning. As I had guessed, Alan's
wife, Janelle, was the stressed-out woman who had rung up my purchases
the night before at their resale shop. She recognized me, too, and we had a
nice enough exchange, but really, how friendly can a woman be when
she's in court to say good-bye to her husband two days before Christmas
as he heads to jail for a crime she doesn't believe he committed? I didn't
want to be overly familiar with her, but I patted her arm, trying to transfer
a little positive energy. Jack went over the morning's schedule and strategy, and Alan didn't say much, mostly just looked at the tabletop. When
we were done, we exited into the foyer.

"Do we have to go through another?" Janelle asked, pointing at an
oddly placed metal detector against the wall.

"Nope." Jack held open the courtroom door. "This way."

He led us to the front row of the gallery behind the wooden bar that
separated the public seating from the courtroom proper. We squeezed
down the row and took seats. The hard plastic fold-up seats barely held
my tush, and across the aisle sat a woman three times my size. Hers spilled
over the metal seat arms on either side of her. It looked incredibly painful.
Under my feet was scrubby carpet in a color I'd have to call government
neutral. It blended with the walls and the leather counsel and jury chairs.
The room itself was an odd shape, like a quarter of a circle. The jury box
was tucked into the curved section of the wall. The judge, court reporter,

and witness box faced it at an angle that also encompassed the counsel tables and public seating.

The double doors behind us burst open. I turned in time to see Melinda Stafford breeze in. Her navy pencil skirt was as tight as usual, and she'd slung her matching jacket over her shoulder so that she could give us all a better view of her tailored white blouse. I hadn't seen her since I'd punched her in the jaw, and, to my great disappointment, it didn't appear I'd done any lasting damage. She took a seat on the front row, opposite from us.

"All rise for the Honorable R. Charleston Herring," the bailiff commanded, moments later. She snapped the words out like a drill sergeant. "All rise, all rise."

Everyone stood. In my peripheral vision I saw that the heavy woman had a lot of trouble extricating herself from the seat. What had the courtroom designers been thinking? One third of America was her size or more.

Judge Herring pulled my attention away from her predicament as he swept into the courtroom from his private entrance. The man cut an imposing figure. Well over six feet before he donned his boots and ascended to the bench, he wore his head shaved and his gray mustache neat. He was a legend in the District Attorney's office before he became a judge, and most defense attorneys didn't relish appearing in his court.

"Be seated." He lowered himself to his chair. "Pretty big crowd for the day before Christmas Eve."

I looked around. Half the gallery was filled.

He donned some half-glasses and then slid them down his nose while drawing a piece of paper toward himself. He adjusted it in the air a few times, then nodded. "Anyone here to pitch a plea agreement?"

Judge Herring entertained plea agreements before starting court each day, either by advance appointment, or because, like us, you came early and got in line.

Jack and Melinda stood at the same time. Jack inclined his head and waited for her to speak first.

A squatty man with jet-black hair sped through the batwing gate in the bar and to the defense table on the right. "Your Honor," he said, in a voice with a New England accent, which sounded like Yowuh Ahnuh, "if I may, just a quick matter to discuss with you first."

The judge didn't look happy. "Counsel, return to the gallery until you have been called."

In a strident voice, the man said, "But Your Honor, I drove in from Lubbock this morning and I have an appearance in the 457th at eleven and the roads are—"

Judge Herring rapped his gavel. "Out of order." He pointed the gavel at the door. "You get one more chance to return to the gallery, and if you blow that one, you get no more chances."

"But—"

"Bailiff, can you please encourage our unnamed counselor to remove himself."

The man raised two thick hands. "I'm going, I'm going." He walked to the gate, and flung it open. There was a resounding crack as the split doors hit the front row seats. He kept going, doing roughly the same thing with the double door exit. The courtroom grew deathly quiet.

Judge Herring raised an eyebrow at the bailiff. "Bring that one back."

"Yes, Your Honor." The bailiff scurried after the attorney, and the doors, opened and closed more softly this time, were the only sound.

Seconds later, the two returned through the bar doors.

"Your name?" the judge said.

"Stanley Perkins," the attorney said, his voice belligerent.

"Ah yes, I recognize your name, Mr. Perkins. Since this is your first time in my courtroom, I'm going to give you a chance to avoid time in a holding cell for contempt of court. Do you have anything you'd like to say?"

Perkins shot a glance back at the gallery, his eyes searching for a clue as to his next move. Beside me, Jack kept his eyes down.

I whispered to him. "What's going on?"

Without moving his lips, Jack spoke so softly I could barely hear him. "Herring wants an apology."

Judge Herring's voice boomed. "Mr. Perkins?"

"What?" the man barked.

Judge Herring smiled. "You're not from around here, are you, Mr. Perkins? Boston, if I recall correctly."

"No, sir. Yes, Boston."

"Well, welcome to Amarillo, then. Bailiff, escort Mr. Perkins to the holding area. He will be allowed a phone call to reschedule his time in the 457th."

Sputtering, Perkins backed up a step.

"Oh, I wouldn't do that if I were you," Judge Herring said, and he smiled.

Perkins froze, then submitted and walked through the large metal door to the right of the defense table with the bailiff. Jack looked at me with one brow raised. Apparently, the rumors about Judge Herring's toughness weren't exaggerated.

"Now, where were we?" The judge looked at his watch then down at something on his desk. "Ah yes." He looked up again. "Does anyone have a plea agreement to pitch?"

"Yes, Judge Herring," Melinda said as she and Jack stood. "Melinda Stafford for the DA's office."

"Yes, Your Honor," Jack said. "Jack Holden for defendant Alan Freeman."

"Is the defendant present?"

Jack turned to Alan and nodded at him.

Alan stood, in the same suit he'd worn the previous day. "Present, Your Honor."

Judge Herring beckoned them with four fingers, palm up. "Come forward, please."

Jack, Alan, and Melinda went through the batwing gates in the bar, single file. Melinda moved to stand behind the table to the left, Jack and Alan to the right, next to the metal door through which Perkins had just disappeared.

The Judge waited for them to get situated then said, "ADA Stafford, you may begin." He frowned down at her.

Melinda beamed. "Thank you, Your Honor. We have aggravated assault against a police officer, and resisting arrest. We've reached an agreement, subject to your approval, of course, sir, to plead down to ordinary assault for a two-year sentence, with eligibility for parole at six months."

"Counselor Holden?" The judge smiled at Jack.

"Yes, sir. Judge Herring, this is Alan Freeman. Mr. Freeman is a tradesman by experience—does fine tile work, I highly recommend him—and recently came to inherit his parents' business upon their deaths. ABC Half-Price Resale. Mr. Freeman is married to Janelle Freeman"—Jack gestured back toward Mrs. Freeman, and she stood and half-curtsied—"and they have three young daughters. Mr. Freeman wishes to plead guilty, Your Honor, to expedite the resolution of his case and ensure his speedy return to his position in the community and, most especially, in his home, so that he can care for his family."

Judge Herring peered over his glasses at Alan. "Mr. Freeman, you understand that by pleading guilty you will wear the mantle of a convicted felon for the rest of your days?"

Alan cleared his throat. "Yes, sir."

"You understand that it is two days before your wife and children celebrate Christmas—that you are showing up here less than one month before your trial, but before the holiday, and while you are still legally out on bail, when you could have, if nothing else, waited until after Christmas to come in—and that all of this is *highly* irregular?"

Judge Herring took his glasses off as much by turning his head away from them as by pulling them away from his face.

Alan's mouth opened and shut.

The Judge continued, his voice deepening. "And, yes, I know who you are, Mr. Freeman. I know who all of my defendants are."

Sweat trickled between my breasts. I wished that Janelle and I were sitting with Alan.

Alan glanced back at his wife, then back at the judge. "Yes, sir," he said, but his voice was softer than before.

"This is all so irregular, in fact, that I have to ask myself what could possibly motivate you to do such an irregular thing. You understand?"

"Yes, sir," Alan whispered.

Beside me, Mrs. Freeman made an anguished noise and put her hand to her chest.

The judge's delivery sped up. "So, Mr. Freeman, are you here of your own free will?"

"Yes, sir."

"Has anyone threatened you, explicitly or implicitly, to obtain your agreement?"

Melinda jumped to her feet. "Your Honor, may we approach the bench?"

He glared at her. "No."

"But—"

"Did I not make myself clear?"

"Yes, sir, I'd—"

"Enough."

She sat.

The Judge grumbled to himself for a moment, then said, "Mr. Freeman, let me ask you again. Has anyone threatened you, explicitly or implicitly, to obtain your agreement?"

"Yes, sir."

Melinda leapt up again, but Judge Herring held his hand high in warning. She stood with her mouth hanging open.

"What, Mr. Freeman?" he asked.

"I mean no, sir."

Again, Melinda sat.

"Are you receiving anything in addition to this reduced sentence in return for your agreement today?"

"I don't understand what you mean, sir."

The Judge shot new daggers, first at Melinda and then at something in the back of the room. I turned to see who it was, and saw a pasty, redheaded man and a tall Asian guy. I did a double take. I'd seen the Asian guy in pictures: Jason Wu, the former cop who said Alan assaulted him, and Burrows. At Burrows's side was a woman who looked much like the one I'd caught a glimpse of in his car the night before. Maybe she was even the same one.

"I mean, has anyone paid you or offered you anything of value to enter this agreement?"

"Oh. No, sir."

"You understand that you will be sentenced to two years, to commence immediately upon my approval of this agreement, if I choose to do so, at the Potter County Detention Center—which, by the way, is a highly disagreeable place, if I do say so myself—and that you will serve a minimum of six months of that sentence, away from the pleasures of hearth and home, with people I trust you will find to be of a most unsavory nature?"

"Yes, sir."

The judge shook his head. "Mr. Holden, is there anything else I should be asking your client that could help us get to the bottom of this?"

"I wish I could think of something, sir, but I cannot. As far as I can tell, this is what he wants, and he understands what he's doing, even if I don't like it."

"Nor do I," Judge Herring intoned. He put his glasses back on. "With the greatest of reluctance, this plea is approved. Bailiff, remand Mr. Freeman into custody, please."

Alan looked back at his wife and mouthed, "I love you. I'm sorry." A choked cry escaped from Janelle Freeman beside me, and I put my arm around her shoulders as the bailiff slipped handcuffs onto Alan's wrists and led him through the metal door to the prisoner holding area beyond it.

CHAPTER 21

"Pecan pancakes, please." I handed my menu to the waiter the next morning at the Pancake House, where Wallace, Nadine, and I were celebrating Christmas Eve. We weren't the only ones with the idea, apparently. The restaurant was normally lean on décor, but candy canes hung from rope draped nail to nail in swoops around the walls of the restaurant. It echoed with booming wishes of Merry Christmas, and the whole place smelled like cinnamon rolls and coffee. The only negative was the crowded space felt like a sauna, with too much heater and too many bodies compensating for the weather outside.

The waitress didn't look up from the pad on which she was scribbling my order. "Bacon or sausage?"

"Neither."

Now she looked at me, and her eyebrows descended and pinched together. "What?"

"I'm a—"

Wallace leaned between us, hand out as if to block me. "She'll have fruit on the side, please."

The woman nodded, jiggling her chins, and recited our entire order back to us. Slowly. She had it right, so Nadine, Wallace, and I all made affirmative noises. She walked toward the kitchen, studying the notepad again, and crossing something out.

"Merry Christmas, you guys." I set two small gifts in the center of the table. I had wrapped them myself the night before in shiny gold paper with silver bows and a tiny ornament tied to each. Wallace got bicycle Santa and Nadine motorcycle Santa.

Wallace put two envelopes with them. "Happy Hanukkah."

"You're not Jewish." Nadine frowned. "And breakfast is on me, because nothing says Happy Kwanzaa like the Pancake House."

Wallace's voice sounded droll. "How do you know what they eat for Kwanzaa in Africa?"

"Kiss my ass, Wallace."

"Sorry, honey, but you're not my type."

"So early in the morning . . ." I picked up my envelope. "Can I open it?"

"Sure."

"Me, too?" Nadine asked.

"Of course."

Nadine and I tore into the flaps.

Wallace said, "I got us a pedicure party at Top Ten. All three of us! I have to get my dogs in shape." He winked. "New man in my life."

"Awesome!" I hadn't had a pedicure in months. "When do we get to meet him?"

"Soon, I think."

Nadine stuck her envelope in her purse. "I've never had a pedicure before. I'm kinda picky about who touches my feet, and for what purpose."

Wallace waggled his eyebrows. "Do tell."

"Don't!" I cut in. They laughed. "But I do want to hear all about you and Phil."

"Who's Phil?" Wallace asked.

She held up a hand. "There is no me and Phil. Phil's a regular at the Polo Club. He's been hitting on me for months. I *never* give the douchebags my name." She pointed at me with her raised hand. "Yesterday he got it from her."

"He's a client. You were in the office. How was I to know introductions weren't in order?"

"I didn't say they weren't in order. Now that we've been properly introduced, I wouldn't mind letting him have a go at my feet."

"Stop!"

Wallace laughed. "Emily, you're such a prude."

"I'm not a prude. I just don't want to hear the details."

"So you wouldn't let Jack suck your toes, then, or put them—"

"That's not up for discussion!"

Now they both laughed. Nadine put her hand on my arm. "Since I'm in the holiday spirit, I'll quit terrorizing you." She pulled her hand back and snapped her fingers. "Which reminds me. You filed a complaint on a dirty cop, right?"

"Well, two cops that I think were acting improperly, anyway."

"Potato, Poh-tah-toe. One of the dancers called in sick last night because she's afraid to leave her house. She thinks some cop is after her for something she saw, a murder, she claims. After one of the dancers disappeared last summer, all the girls have been much more skittish. I told her about you, and I gave her your number. In case she needs to talk to someone."

I lifted my shoulders, about to say, "Sure, no problem," when something else popped out instead. "What's her name?" I'd met a dancer the week before at Love's. Irina? Sasha? Something European. Ivanka. That was it.

"Beth."

Our plump waitress appeared with three plates on each arm. She put them down on the table, one by one, all in the wrong places. "Anything else?"

Wallace held up a finger. "More coffee."

I waited for her to turn her back then pushed Nadine's bacon and sausage sides over to her. I tried to convince myself that the flesh on the plate grossed me out, but my stomach growled at the aroma, greedy and animalistic. I grabbed my pancakes and fruit and snatched the butter and syrup before anyone else could get to them. Staving off meat cravings constituted an emergency.

I started slathering butter. "Y'all didn't even open my gifts."

Wallace had ordered biscuits with sausage gravy and a side of hash browns in addition to his pancakes. There was a benefit to maleness and triathlon, for sure. I'd blow up like a whale if I mixed all that fat with all those carbs. I scraped some of the butter off my pancakes, then a little more.

"Shit, honey, I'm sorry. Let's do it when she clears the food." Wallace stuffed a giant bite of biscuit and gravy in his mouth.

I eyed the syrup I'd chosen. Maple. There were a few more in a wooden rack. I read the labels and saw "sugar-free." I sighed and poured a lake of it on my plate.

One of our cell phones rang. I still hadn't reset my ringtone and sounds, and I glanced at mine. Nope.

Wallace pulled his from his pocket and answered in a robotic voice. "You've reached the voice mail of Wallace Gray. I'm celebrating Christmas with my friends and can't come to the phone right now. Don't bother leaving a message, because I won't call you back until—"

He stopped speaking and listened, his face growing dark. "You're absolutely sure of this?"

He looked at me, and it was a look of such incredible pity that I knew immediately something had happened to Betsy. I made a strangled noise. It must have been louder than I'd realized, because heads turned.

"What is it?" Nadine whispered.

"Betsy?" I croaked.

Wallace put his phone down and reached for my hand. "I'm sorry, Emily. Immigration is coming for Betsy."

Our breakfast abandoned, Wallace and I huddled in his pristine car and I called Jack. Tiny crystals pelted the windshield and roof of the car. Snow? It looked more like ice. I hated ice storms. I turned the heater to high.

Wallace said, "It won't get any warmer until the engine warms up."

I ignored him.

Jack's voice spoke into my ear. "Jack Holden speaking."

I touched "speaker" on my phone screen. "Jack, you're on speaker with Wallace and me."

"What's up?"

"Wallace got a tip from a friend with Immigration that they're coming for Betsy after Christmas."

"Shit. I was afraid this would happen. She's not a secret to the feds because of the kidnapping and trafficking case against Johnson."

I couldn't hold my anger and fear in, and I shouted. "Don't they have enough criminals here illegally that they can leave one poor little girl alone?"

Wallace hit the steering wheel with one hand. "It's ridiculous. She's not a danger to anyone."

Jack sighed. "They do cast the net pretty wide."

My voice came out shrill. "We have to do something, Jack. We can't let this happen."

Wallace held a finger up. "I can spend the day Monday in the Mexican consulate. We may not know where she was born, but maybe I can find someone who is willing to help me search for birth records for her anyway."

I shook my head. "But you don't have a picture ID for her."

"I'll take her picture and a notarized letter from CPS attesting to her identity."

"Will they accept that?"

"I don't know, but it's better than nothing."

Jack's voice broke in and out. "I'll"—crackle, crackle—"Monday"—kercrackle—"birth"—cracklety-crackle—"enough." Bad cell reception.

Wallace said, "Can you repeat that?"

Jack tried again. "I'll go ahead and file for Special Immigrant Juvenile status on Monday as well. They'll return it to us asking for her birth certificate, but maybe the fact that we've attempted to file will be enough to forestall federal custody."

My voice broke. "But they could still take her, and then she'd be in prison, basically, waiting." I took a deep breath. "I can't let that happen. Maybe she just needs to run away. She might end up with a nice place to stay and then not get found until we've got this all sorted out."

Wallace shot me a killer look. "I'm going to pretend I didn't even hear you make that terrible joke."

I averted my eyes.

"And on the subject of runaways while I have you together, I'm sorry to pass along more bad news, but we still haven't found Greg or Farrah."

I squirmed inwardly, but said, "Oh no."

"Yeah, I wanted you both to know." When neither of us spoke again, Wallace added, "Jack, anything else you need me doing in the meantime?"

"No. I think this is all we can do, Wallace."

"Okay. Well, Merry Christmas, and thanks."

"Yep, you, too. Emily, the weather's supposed to keep getting worse. Dress warm tonight." He ended the call.

Wallace smacked me in the shoulder. "Emily Bernal, what haven't you told me about tonight?"

Worry about Betsy weighed me down, but a flicker of happiness still made it through. "Jack's taking me to Christmas Eve services with him."

"Shut the front door."

"It's not that big a deal."

"The hell it's not. This is a date. A bona fide D-A-T-E."

"Do you think so?"

"I know so."

"Okay, then I need your help."

"I'm glad you've finally realized that."

I punched his arm. "I need an outfit that says 'I'm the one,' but in a Catholic-church-appropriate way. Any ideas?"

Wallace threw his head back and laughed.

"What?"

"Have you ever been to a Catholic church before?"

"Once."

"How did they dress?"

"Normal, I guess."

"There you go. Dress like you would normally, except wear a garter and fishnets underneath."

"Wallace!" He had a point. Everyday lingerie wouldn't do. I had a pair of lavender tap pants and matching bra that would work, just in case.

"You're gorgeous. It will be fine."

My phone rang. Expecting Jack, I hit accept. "Yes?"

"Hi, my name is Beth. Nadine from the Polo Club suggested I call for Emily?"

Beth. Beth who was having a problem with a bad cop. "Yes, this is Emily. I'm with Jack Holden of Williams and Associates. How can I help you?"

"I'm sorry to call over the holidays. I work with Nadine, and I've got a problem. She said you've had a similar one: a bad cop messing with you?"

"Yes, two of them, unfortunately."

"Yeah, well, that's my problem, too."

"Would you like to get together?"

"If it's not too much trouble for you."

"Not at all. But I'm leaving town tomorrow. Can you get together today, say about noon?"

"Yes. Can I text you an address?"

"Sure."

The call ended and seconds later a text came through: *This is Beth. 1000 Shasta, noon today. Thank you for meeting with me. I didn't know where else to turn, and I'm scared to leave my house in case he sees me.*

I replied: *See you then.*

Wallace had unwrapped his present while I talked to Beth. He held up the gift certificate to Sun Adventure Sports, the store he favored for triathlon gear. "You're a peach."

"I feel like I'm contributing to the delinquency of a misogynist."

"A what?"

"A misogynist. You know, a person who enjoys pain."

Wallace groaned, laughing. "Masochist, Emily. Masochist. A misogynist is someone prejudiced against women."

"Oh. Well. Yeah, masochist then. I'm contributing to the delinquency of a masochist."

"Nah. I'm much more into—"

I stuck my fingers in my ears. "La la la la la la."

I spent the rest of the morning with Mother decorating sugar cookies for her Sunday school classmates. She was blasting Christmas music through the house and singing along at the top of her lungs. I usually couldn't resist joining her, but I was really preoccupied with worries about Betsy. If I dwelled on it too long, I started to think about the Freeman family, too, so I tried not to dwell. Tonight I had a date with Jack. No matter how grim things seemed, I couldn't lose sight of that, and I certainly couldn't let anything mess it up.

I squirted from a miniature tube of white icing to create snow on a Christmas tree. "You sure you're going to be all right without me tonight and this weekend?"

"Why, of course. I'm so glad you and Jack are spending time together."

I put the top on the tube and licked my fingers. I'd finished my last cookie. "I'm worried you're going to be lonely."

Mother didn't look up from the cookies she was arranging in a red basket. "What, why would you say that?"

"Um, because I won't be here."

"Oh. Yes, well, I'll be fine, dear."

Mother wasn't an unhappy person, per se—although she harbored some bitterness about how hard her life had turned out, especially in comparison to people she felt got more help than she did—but she was especially cheerful today. That was good, I guessed. Better than the alternative: making me feel guilty for deserting her over Christmas. It was the second time in a week, though, that she'd seemed much more jolly than usual.

I scrutinized her more closely. "Is that a new dress?"

"This?" She ran the back of her hand over a black suit-dress with a Peter Pan collar and gorgeous square black buttons. "Oh, well, hmm, I can't remember if you've seen it before." She giggled.

If I didn't know better I'd suspect she'd been into the box wine, or had a boyfriend. Neither was plausible for her, though. I had planned to tell her about Betsy while we did the cookies, but I didn't have the heart to weigh her down with something that heavy when she was in such high spirits. Besides, I needed to be optimistic about Betsy and positive in general. And optimistic meant that I had to plan for Betsy to remain in the U.S., and for me to adopt her. Which meant I needed to tell Mother I was moving out.

I turned on the sink water and rubbed my hands together under it. "You know how I'm applying to adopt Betsy?"

"Yes, dear. How's it coming along?" She started on a new cookie basket.

"Well, fine, except I have to live on my own. And I've found a place." I shook my hands to get the excess water off.

She froze with a cookie in each hand. "Really?"

"Yes." There was a dish towel hanging by the sink, and I used it to blot the last of the water off my hands.

She resumed putting cookies in the basket. "And?"

I turned to her. "It's a duplex off Soncy Road."

"That's close." She smiled at me.

I exhaled. A smile was a good sign. "My lease could start after New Year's. I need to sign it and take the security deposit and first and last month's rent over."

She nodded. "Good for you."

I nearly fainted. That had gone so much easier than I'd expected. Who was this woman, and what had she done with my needy, dependent mother? Battle won—or rather, battle conceded by the opposing side—I didn't linger on the subject.

I leaned back against the counter. "So, what are you going to do this afternoon?"

"My friend Josie is opening her salon for me, and she's doing a complete Christmas makeover on me, including manicure and pedicure."

"That'll set you back a pretty penny." I was a little bit jealous that she hadn't invited me, but I was glad she was doing something fun.

"She's giving me a huge discount as a Christmas present."

"Do you want me to drop you off and pick you up? The roads are getting bad."

"No, that's okay." She finished up Bing Crosby's big number with him, wishing for a white Christmas, which she'd definitely have this year.

I looked at the time on my phone: eleven thirty. "Mother, I've got to go meet a client. I can help you with the dishes later."

She waved her hand at me, and joined in with the next tune. Dionne Warwick: "O Holy Night."

I threw my apron in the dirty clothes, smiling at my mother's off-key voice. I hadn't forgotten about my problems, or Betsy's, but I was keeping them in perspective and looking forward to an evening with Jack. Before I realized what was happening, I heard my own voice belt out, "A thrill of hope, the weary world rejoices."

Mother had broken me down. In a good way, because I was no help to anyone if I didn't stay upbeat. It didn't mean I didn't wish Betsy was here with us so we could teach her all the words to our favorite carols and how to decorate cookies with the perfect swoosh of snow icing. I wiped a tear from my eye, happy mixed with sad, and pulled open the front door, singing, "O ni-ight divine."

CHAPTER 22

Siri directed me through the slippery white streets of Amarillo. I took Washington south from I-40, driving slowly and carefully. The pellets earlier had definitely been ice, and they'd stuck. Nothing I hadn't driven on every year since getting my license, but what I'd learned from Dad years ago still applied: heavy sliding objects don't stop or turn well, but they crunch real good. I had stomped my brakes and turned too late one winter day, sliding my car right into one of Tech's new stock trailers, and I still winced as I remembered waiting for the inevitable sound of crumpling metal. Lesson learned: The best way to stop or change direction on ice was to coast.

So I rolled along like a turtle, creeping through intersections, passing other vehicles planted against each other, curbs, and light poles. I saw a tree seller in a parking lot on my right. He had nothing but a few scrubs left, and he was ringing a large handbell. He'd have a heck of a time selling the rest of them in weather like this, but I was impressed that he was trying. I hoped those fuddy-duddy Hodges at least had a Christmas tree at their house.

I made a right on Shasta without losing traction, stopping in front of 1000 without even applying the brakes. The house was at the end of a cul-de-sac, with an oversized square of yard on one side of the front sidewalk and a smaller square of one on the other. It looked like most of the other houses on the street. Small one-story ranch houses circa 1970, brick mostly in shades of tan to match the landscape, what there was of it. The house had no driveway or garage in front, nor any car at the curb. No lights shone from inside, either.

My phone made a random noise. I sighed. I really had to fix the notification sounds. I turned it over. A call, but I'd lost my darn contacts so iPhone couldn't tell me the name of the caller. It was a 340 area-code number, though, and that meant Katie, or someone else from the Virgin Islands.

I accepted. "Hello?"

"Merry Christmas!" Katie's pretty voice sang out.

"And to you, Katie Kovacs! Did you get my card?"

"I did. Ours will be late. But that's not why I called."

"Oh? What's up?"

"You know Ava is in Amarillo?"

"I knew she would be in the area sometime soon, but not when."

"She had a big Christmas Eve shindig there tonight, but it's been weathered out."

How weird to be doing a show on Christmas Eve, in Amarillo no less, I thought. But I said, "Poor Ava."

I got out of the car, slamming the door. The cold and wind and ice pellets attacked my exposed nose. I'd worn a scarf, but now I wound it higher, over my nose, muffling my mouth. I started for the front door.

"Yeah. Her phone battery was on fumes, so I said I'd call you to see if she could crash at your place tonight."

Oh. Oh my. I love Ava, but she is, well, a *handful*. I pressed the button for the doorbell. "Mother and I have a guest room she can stay in, but I'm heading to New Mexico tomorrow with Jack—"

"*With* Jack or 'with Jack'?"

She sounded like Wallace. "I'll let you know when we get back." I rang the bell again and peered through the opaque glass in the front door. I couldn't see any movement inside. I knocked on the glass, hard enough to hurt my gloved knuckles.

"Sounds promising."

I couldn't text Beth while I was on the phone with Katie, so I decided to walk around back and see if I could get her attention from there. I tramped over icy ground cover in the yard. "Anyway, she's welcome, but I won't be here after tonight."

"I'll tell her."

I opened the side gate, leaving it ajar behind me. "And you guys, is everyone doing all right?"

"Oh my gosh, the girls are about to start walking, and Taylor is so hyper. Thank God for my in-laws. And Nick. Nick is a dream."

As I emerged from the narrow strip of brown and white patchy lawn between the six-foot wooden fence and the house, I came around the back corner straight onto a concrete porch, placing my feet carefully so I wouldn't slip on the ice that was thicker there from the gutter downspout. I looked up after I was on the porch and stopped short. One more step and I would have planted my foot in the midsection of a woman, a woman lying facedown and unmoving.

I screamed, once, long and loud, and dropped my phone to my side. Even from that distance I could hear Katie.

"Emily, what's wrong? Are you all right?"

I put the phone back to my ear. "I . . . I, yes, I just found someone who's not. I've got to go. Have Ava contact me."

I hung up and crouched beside the prone woman. She had on gray sweat pants and a matching hoodie with zebra-print house slippers. I rolled her toward me. Her face was ghoulishly pale, but still I recognized her. Ivanka, the woman I'd met at the Love's truck stop. The makeup that had camouflaged her a week ago was absent now, and she looked closer to my mother's age than mine. She was even smaller than I remembered her, almost like a young girl.

I jerked my glove off and tossed it aside, then put two fingers against the cool skin at her carotid. No pulse. I readjusted my fingers to try again. They were already as cold as her neck. I'd never seen a dead person up close, but I'd seen plenty of dead animals closer than I'd liked. Despite my love of target shooting, it didn't translate to hunting. Dad took me one time, and I'll never forget the young pronghorn antelope's eyes as the light faded from them. It had chilled me to the bone. They'd looked like Ivanka's did, and hers were having the same effect on me now.

Suddenly I felt very exposed, and I jumped up, looking around me. The blinds on the back windows were closed. I still didn't see any lights on. I could see in the kitchen through the glass half of the door, but when I pressed my face to the glass for a better look, I couldn't see anyone inside. I tried the back door. Unlocked. I hesitated. I had no business in there, and there was a woman out here I might be able to save. I released the knob. Quickly, I scanned the backyard. It was covered in a blanket of crisp unbroken white. No trees. No shrubs. No furniture. Just weathered boards jutting up to a puffy gray sky. I didn't see anyone, not even any tracks save my own, but that didn't make the vulnerable, watched feeling go away.

I dialed my phone. It went to Jack's voice mail. "Call me. I went to visit a friend of Nadine's, and she's dead in her backyard. Oh, and it's Ivanka from Love's last week, the dancer."

I hung up and dialed 911.

A woman answered in a drawl. "9-1-1, what's your emergency?"

"I've found a woman in her backyard at 1000 Shasta. She's not breathing. Please send help." I dropped the phone and kneeled beside Ivanka. At close range, her cheap perfume nearly knocked me over, and I breathed through my mouth to avoid it. I tilted her head back, listened for the breath I knew wasn't there and started CPR.

A bundled-up female police officer arrived five minutes later. I was still doing chest compressions and life breaths with Ivanka, and I didn't catch the woman's name. I didn't even get much of a look at her before she took over the CPR. By the time the ambulance arrived, five minutes after the officer, it was clear nothing would help Ivanka, or Beth, or whatever her real name was. In the meantime, I had slowly but surely nearly frozen to death. I moved as close as I could to the house, out of the howling wind and pelting ice, and wrapped my arms around myself.

A second officer arrived, this one male but equally bundled. He conferred with the female officer for a moment out of my earshot. Her back was to me, but I saw her motion my way.

He walked over to me. "I'm Officer Jones. I'd like to ask you a few questions. We could talk here, or we could sit in my car where it's warmer."

My teeth chattered. "Emily Bernal. C-c-c-car."

As we walked around to the front of the house, my phone rang.

"Do you need to get that?" the officer asked.

Probably. "No." I let it go to voice mail.

We reached the squad car. Officer Jones, who looked roughly my age somewhere peeking out from all the winter clothing on his face, head, neck, hands, and body, opened the rear door for me, giving me an unwelcome surge of déjà vu. I frowned. To think I'd gone my whole life without getting in a cop car and was now being put in the backseat of one for the second time in a week.

He must have understood the look on my face, because he said, "Would you rather sit in front?"

"I would, thank you, if that's all right."

He shut the back door and opened the driver's door, got in, and then opened the passenger door for me from the inside. I slipped in, too. He pulled off all his outerwear except his coat, and underneath I saw that not only was he about my age, but he looked like Channing Tatum. Definitely the hottest police officer I'd seen in Amarillo. Scratch that. That I'd seen, ever, anywhere.

He picked up a clipboard that was between us on the seat and clicked a ballpoint pen. "Just a few questions."

"Absolutely."

"Your full name, address, and birthdate?"

I told him.

"How did you know the deceased?"

"I didn't."

He glanced up from his paper. "How did you come to be in her backyard?"

Lately I'd had far too much need to use the coaching I'd heard Jack give his clients. He always stressed to volunteer as little information as possible to the cops, so I spoke judiciously. "One of her coworkers introduced us virtually, and she asked me to come by."

"You'd never met her?"

My mind flashed to Ivanka's face under the fluorescent lights in the Love's parking lot, snow falling around us, her sashay as she took Wallace's arm. Had she introduced herself to me? She had not. So I answered truthfully, if incompletely. "No."

"Do you know what she wanted with you?"

I'd thought about this question long and hard while I gave Ivanka the breath of life. No way was I telling a random cop that Ivanka and I both held low opinions of some of their brethren. "Um, I work for a criminal attorney. My understanding was that she had run into some trouble and needed advice."

He nodded. "You mentioned her coworker. Where did they work?"

"The Polo Club."

"Ah." He looked up at me, like he was trying to figure out if I was hiding a secret life as a dancer, too.

"I don't work there."

He pinned his eyes back to his clipboard. "Did you see anybody else when you got here?"

"No."

"How'd you end up in the backyard?"

"I knocked on the front door but there was no answer. I knew she expected me, so I went around back in case she hadn't heard me."

He looked at me sideways without turning his head, his eyes narrowed to slits. "Do you always go into people's backyards if they don't answer the front door?"

Truthfully? Usually. "No," I said.

He stopped writing. "And this time you did, because why?"

"It was freezing outside. I didn't want to leave unless I'd tried every way I could think of to keep our appointment, but if she wasn't there, I wanted to get back in the car with the heater on. And not have to come back later."

He twirled the pen through his fingers, appearing to be lost in thought.

My phone rang again. I ignored it.

"Was there anything at all that you saw that led you to form an opinion as to how"—he glanced at and tapped a display screen mounted on his dashboard and facing him—"Beth McIntosh died?"

Other than ice? A hard concrete patio? Again, I stuck to the minimum responsive answer to his question. "No."

"All right, we're nearly done here, Ms. Bernal, if you'll give me a few more minutes."

"Sure."

He began typing into the keypad of the device on his dashboard; I checked my voice mail. Two messages. The first was from Jack. Returning my call. Did I need him to come? Was I okay? I texted my response: *No. Yes. But thanks.*

The second one was Ava. Her phone was dead. She was calling from a pay phone at the bus station for a ride, and, from the sound of her voice, she was extremely cold. If my phone rang again, I would have to answer it. No fair leaving her standing out there dialing me over and over.

Officer Jones said, "So, this isn't the first dead body you've found for us?"

"What?"

"It says here that we responded to a 911 call over the murder of Maria—"

"I didn't make that call, and I never saw a dead body. I was unconscious on the floor. The person that murdered her almost got me, too."

"Hmm. And last week you were brought in—"

"As a form of harassment."

He read some more, and his lips moved.

"Listen, I have a friend who is expecting me to pick her up at the bus station. Hence my ringing phone. She's waiting for me out in the cold. I hadn't really anticipated finding a dead person today. I want to help, I really do, but if we're done, I do need to go."

His eyes moved back and forth as he stared at the display. Acting as if he didn't hear me, he said, almost fearfully, "You filed a complaint against Samson and Burrows?"

"I did, but it doesn't have anything to do with"—I waved my hand in the general direction of Ivanka's backyard—"this."

He pursed his lips, nodding slowly, staring again at the screen. "Yeah, you're probably right." He pressed a button and the slight glow from his screen disappeared. "Someone will call you if we have any more questions, but this case looks like a pretty simple slip and fall. We get those in this kind of weather. Thank you, Ms. Bernal."

"You're welcome."

I opened the door and got out, then leaned back in. "Merry Christmas, Officer Jones."

"Merry Christmas to you, too."

I walked to the Mustang, which was now frigid inside. I turned it on, with heater and defrost on full icy blast, Wallace's comment to me earlier be damned. Only an hour or so had passed, yet a layer of ice covered my windshield. My phone made one of its inexplicable noises. I turned it over.

Laura: *We are ALL looking forward to seeing you tomorrow.* She ended with a smiley face.

I typed one-thumbed, keeping my other hand deep in my pocket as the temperature in the Mustang rose a nanodegree at a time. *Me too!*

I grabbed my ice scraper and hopped out again. I held my hand up and caught some precipitation. It was snow. *Hallelujah.* Winter driving in Amarillo and Lubbock, and some in Dallas, taught me to fear ice and respect snow. The weather forecast on the radio during the drive over here promised snow and freezing temps. Snow would improve the icy roads. Soon, anyway. Right now, I still had to contend with the exposed ice.

When I finished scraping, I did some shoulder shrugs and rolled my neck. The creepiness of finding Ivanka's dead body was slowly dissipating, enough that I remembered my date with Jack and felt a flare of excitement. Then it hit me. I was picking up a houseguest for the evening. A handful of a houseguest. And then I was leaving for New Mexico in the morning. Ava and I would barely even get to talk. She'd think I was an incredibly rude and terrible hostess.

I couldn't—I wouldn't—cancel my first real date with Jack Holden. I supposed I could invite her to go with Jack and me tonight, but hopefully she'd be exhausted from traveling and want nothing but a soft bed and long winter's night sleep. Ava liked men, liked them a whole lot, and they liked her back. I didn't need that kind of pressure on my fledgling relationship. I sighed with a rising note of exasperation. I was being unfair. I'd cast Ava in a role, and she hadn't even stepped onstage yet. I needed to chill. I would chill. Starting right now, I was chill.

I got back in the Mustang and put it in drive.

CHAPTER 23

I rolled well below the speed limit down Fourth toward Tyler and the Greyhound Bus Station. The station was only four blocks past the Maxor Building, where Jack and Snowflake would be doing whatever it was they did when the office functioned as their condo instead of workplace. The bus station itself occupied part of a block on the edge of Amarillo's small downtown. It stood about two and a half stories high and had an art deco-ish feel, with rounded corners and square blue tiles three-high around the bottom, sort of in the style of the restored Paramount Theater sign on Polk Street.

I turned right on Tyler. The bus station was just ahead, and I spotted Ava outside the front door but inside the recessed overhang. She wore an electric-blue jumpsuit and black leather coat, and she was stamping her feet in spike-heeled black boots. She didn't exactly blend into the background, even if her outfit did match it. I coasted to a stop, threw the Mustang in park, and popped the trunk.

I climbed out and ran carefully to her. "Ava! What a fun surprise! Get in, you must be freezing." I hugged her and grabbed her two suitcases, practically in the same motion.

"Yah, I freezing my bana, for true," she said, her island lilt an odd sound here, like a scene from *Cool Runnings*. It took me a moment to remember "bana" was the West Indian word for "bottom," too. "Thank you for coming for me." In her accent, "thank" came out as "tank."

"No problem." I threw her bags in and slammed the trunk. I was back in my seat as fast as she was, but, then again, I was wearing retro moon boots I'd appropriated from my mom's closet, not stilettos.

My phone made a weird noise from its perch on the console. A message from Nadine: *How'd it go with Beth?*

Oh God. She didn't know about her friend yet. I typed: *Call me.*

Ava shut her door. "So, how you entertain an island girl in this town on Christmas Eve?"

As I groaned inwardly at Ava asking precisely the wrong question, the phone rang. It was Nadine, way faster than I'd hoped. I didn't know which I dreaded more: telling Nadine about Beth, or telling Ava about my plans that evening. I decided to let Nadine go to voice mail. I'd call her back later.

Ava kept talking, leaving her first question behind us. "The weather here terrible," she said. "How you stand it?"

"Most of the population isn't familiar with the alternatives."

"But you?"

I put the car in gear and coasted into motion on Tyler, then slowed at the corner. There was no traffic. I turned right onto Seventh Avenue. "I have no excuse, other than I'm broke."

"Yah, Katie tell me your husband an anti-man."

I opened my mouth then shut it.

"You got no idea what I talking about, do you?"

I turned right onto Taylor. Suddenly, the connection occurred to me, and the translation of the island slang made perfect sense. Katie had told her Rich was gay. I laughed.

"It took me a minute, but I got it. Yes, Rich likes men, and his guy has expensive taste, so they ran through our cash before I even caught on. But my divorce is final, and I'm pretty much back on my feet."

"You living with your mother?"

"I am." And not wanting to talk about it. "Are you still living with Rashidi?" I referred to the gorgeous UVI professor she sometimes dated who was a mutual friend of Katie's, but not the father of Ava's daughter.

She waffled her hand. "Roommates still. For now."

Rats. I had hoped she was in a serious relationship. "So, your gig got weathered out tonight, huh?"

"Yah, the organizer, Phil, he cool, though. He reschedule me, and he pay me half."

"What kind of group has a Christmas Eve party anyway? Most of Amarillo will be at church."

She laughed. "Phil see me when he visit St. Marcos, and he know everybody. Got me booked for two weeks at parties in three states. He tell me they all private. That they, uh, swingers."

"Swingers?"

"Yah, you know, people who trade partners."

"Yeah, I know, but we have a client named Phil who runs a swingers group."

"Sound like the same guy."

Phil, Phil, Phil. I wondered if Nadine had any idea what she was getting into, or if it would even matter to her. "What I really want to know is how are you, and how is your baby?"

"She good, I good, my mother—she save my life. Don't even think about having a baby without a grandmother near you house, I tell you."

The loss of my baby had left a cold, empty space in my heart, and my fear of losing Betsy tugged the edges wider and wider. I'd love to have a baby anywhere, anytime, now that I knew I couldn't. Or most likely couldn't. But maybe I could have a big girl, maybe I could have Betsy. If I could help Jack and Wallace keep her in the states long enough for it to happen, and keep the whereabouts of Greg and Farrah a secret.

But I kept all of that inside and instead said, "Good advice. I'll remember that. Are you and the father, um—"

I merged onto 287 and quickly veered onto the I-40 entrance ramp, then negotiated another careful merge. These icy flyways were tricky today.

"Lord no. He worthless. So if you know a man need a woman who look good on his arm when he out spending his cash, I the one for the job."

My stomach lurched. That was exactly what I was afraid she'd say. We drove in silence for a few minutes. A dinging noise from my dashboard panel grabbed my attention. I glanced down. Low-gas light. I switched on my right turn signal to exit at Bell for gas.

At the station, Ava ran inside. I huddled in the car for warmth while the gas pumped. A huge army-green panel van backed to the pump station catty-corner in front of my car. It was the kind of van that construction crews use. Them, and serial killers. A man who looked vaguely familiar exited and worked at the pump. Of course, just about everyone in Amarillo looked familiar to me. I either went to elementary school with them or knew them from their kids or I'd seen them at United Supermarket a couple of thousand times or they were Jack's clients or family or, God forbid, victims of Jack's clients.

This guy looked a little older than me. He had a square face with a lot of graying facial hair and wore a cap with wool-lined ear flaps over his head. He took a few drags off a cigarette then crushed it under the toe of his boot. He went to the back of the van and opened one side of the doors —like the batwing gates in Judge Herring's courtroom—and I couldn't help watching, even if it was impolite. His body blocked most of my line of sight, so I leaned to the right for a better view.

"Ho ho ho, Merry Christmas, boys and girls," a deep voice slurred, so loud I could hear him through my car window. A tall Santa lurched in front of my car, toward the back of the van. He was a little on the slim side for Santa, and even more on the drunk side, it appeared. He steadied himself with a hand on the open van door but still managed to knock the driver to the side and, from the looks of it, slosh half a bottle of something all over him, too. The bottle dropped to the ground and rolled away. Santa's eyes tracked it, and he moaned. The driver righted himself and brushed liquid off his body, flicking his hands in exaggerated motions as he did.

"Shorry," Santa shouted, or tried to. "How about shome candy canes for the kiddos?"

The pump clicked and I saw it had shut off. I opened the door to go put the nozzle up and get my receipt. Alcohol fumes hit me as I took the long way around the back of my car to the pump. I pulled the nozzle from my car. As I screwed on my gas cap, I saw the van driver grab Santa by his fuzzy red jacket fronts. I backed into the pump, gaping as he shoved him against the closed side of the rear door to the van. For the first time, I got a good view of the interior. It was filled with kids. *Filled* with them. Long, dark braids and a sweet face caught my attention. I stood frozen, nozzle in midair.

"Betsy?" I called out, but my words were muffled by the roar of the van driver, who I now realized was Trevon Hodges, Betsy's foster father.

"Stay away from those kids with your drunken idolatry."

"But shir, I din mean nothing by—"

"Sinner!" He pushed the man away.

Santa stumbled to his knees, then stood. "Sh'okay." He held up one hand. "I may be a shinner, but Jesus died for my shins, sho I'll be okay." He stumbled toward the van again.

Trevon Hodges reached into the back of the van and pulled out a tire iron, and I heard screams from inside. I shoved the nozzle back in place on the pump. A voice I knew well screamed, "Mama!"

I started to run toward Betsy, but saw she was facing away from me, holding her arms out toward the front of the van. Just barely, I recognized Mary Alice Hodges, a few rows up.

Hodges pointed the tire iron at Santa. He dropped his voice so low I could barely hear him. "That won't save you from the wrath of God, sinner. Now, go, before it catches up with you in the here and now."

Santa turned and staggered away, mumbling. He picked up his bottle and disappeared around the corner of the gas station. I remained inert, my mouth open. Hodges tossed the tire iron back into the rear of the van and seemed to notice me for the first time. He nodded, then slammed the back door, blocking my view of Betsy. A low whimper caught in my throat. Hodges went around the side of the van. I heard the pump click and the sound of the nozzle inserted into its home station. He didn't appear again. I heard his door slam and the engine start, then the van pulled away, dragging my heart along with it.

On wooden legs, I took the three steps back to the door of my car. Somehow, I got it open and lowered myself inside. Betsy. Betsy had called out for her mama and that scary Mary Alice Hodges was the only one there. I was still months away from being able to try to adopt her, and she needed a mama now.

Ava yanked the door open and dove inside, her teeth chattering. She slammed it and looked at me. "Damn, girl, you look like you seen a jumbie." She used the island word for ghost or spirit, which I knew from my time there with Katie.

"Something like that," I said. I bit my lip, holding back tears, and pointed the Mustang toward Heaven.

At five twenty-five, I poofed my bangs a little and shellacked them into place. If the sky was still spitting snow, my hair needed the support. Heck, I needed support as much as my hair did. I'd ended an emotional call with Nadine a few minutes before. She was understandably shaken about the death of her coworker/friend. Finding Ivanka and all that came after hadn't been the highlight of my day, either, but it was the sight of Betsy and the sound of her voice calling out to her mama that I couldn't shake. I had to, though. I took a deep breath. Obsessing about it wouldn't do me a bit of good. I turned sideways in front of the bathroom mirror, checking myself from all angles. Peach flocked wallpaper provided the backdrop, and a Phelps family tree cross-stitch sampler framed my head. The lavender lingerie set was hidden, but I smoothed my hand over the waist of my black flowing skirt. No one would have ever guessed I was pregnant less than three months ago from my flat belly now.

The doorbell rang at five thirty, exactly as Jack had promised it would.

Mother's voice chirped, "I'll get it."

"Thanks, Mother."

A few taps sounded on the bathroom door.

I opened it. "All yours," I said.

Ava stepped toward me, her hands splayed at hip level on either side of her. She smacked a kiss in the air five inches from my cheek. "I won't be but a minute."

I couldn't imagine what additional primping she needed for a Christmas Eve service, although it wouldn't hurt my feelings if she changed clothes entirely. The curve-hugging black dress with the peek-aboo chest and crisscross back straps might have worked for her canceled gig, but it was bound to raise a few eyebrows at a church. Not to mention her four-inch black pumps with little bows on the heels that accented the back seams in her pantyhose.

We exchanged places in the bathroom. She leaned into the mirror, pursing her plum-colored lips and pushing her breasts farther up and out of her dress. Her perfect, café au lait skin glistened above her neckline, sparkled even, and I suspected she'd dusted her décolletage with something. A lot of something. My mouth went dry watching her, and I wasn't even attracted to women. I cringed to think the impact she could have on Jack. Sure, I was pretty, but Ava was sex on two legs.

I heard my mother greeting him, and the rumble of his hello back to her.

I swallowed and said to Ava, "Meet us in the living room." I turned to go, then added, "The roads are bad, so we need to get moving as quick as we can."

She winked at me. "No problem, mon."

I walked down the dark hallway from the bathroom to the strains of "What Child Is This" playing. My low-heeled riding boots were almost soundless against the carpet. They had seemed a smart, attractive choice half an hour ago but now hopelessly bland. I straightened my red cashmere sweater. The soft wool was luxurious to the touch, but was it too "school marm" beside Ava?

"Enough of this bull hockey," I whispered to myself. "Woman up."

I'd already had a more-than-full day, but this evening was important to me. I wasn't going to let insecurity or anything else spoil it. I pasted on a smile, and walked to the door of the bright living room.

Jack and my mother stood in front of the hearth before a roaring fire. She had pressed a rosy-cheeked Santa mug in his hand, and steam rose from its mouth as the aroma of spiced tea wafted my way.

"I just can't thank you enough, Jack. For everything."

I stayed rooted in the doorway. What did she have to thank Jack for? Hackles rose on my arms. Surely she wasn't talking about him giving me a job?

"Yep." But of course the man of few words—and those usually off topic —wasn't going to expound on her remarks. "Can I entice you to Downtown Methodist with us tonight?"

Mother beamed. "Maybe next year. I helped with the stage set for the children's program this year at Believers, and I can't miss the pageant." She put her hand on his non-mug arm. "I'm thrilled Emily's going with you."

Since the conversation seemed poised to take an embarrassing direction without any further illumination on what my mother had to be thankful to Jack for, I broke in. "Merry Christmas Eve."

Mother clapped her hands together. "There she is."

Jack's improbably topaz eyes met mine. "Merry Christmas Eve to you." His left-sided smile warmed me inside.

I crossed the room to join them. Mother went all out for Christmas, and the living room was overflowing with jolliness. Hand-knitted Christmas stockings hung from the mantel over the fireplace. Mother had made them herself. There were three, of course: mine, hers, and my father's, despite the fact that the last Christmas he'd spent with us was fifteen years before. Her snow globes decorated the coffee table. A nativity scene of embroidered figurines graced an end table. The tree commanded wholly a third of the room from its spot in front of the window, and wrapped gifts spilled over the dark green velvet tree skirt below it. Homemade ornaments— mostly Mother's crafts, but some I recognized from my school days— covered the tree branches. A construction-paper chain in faded red and green. A picture of me glued in a plastic coffee can lid. A Popsicle-stick reindeer with a cotton-ball tail and red puffy nose. I loved it all.

When I reached them, Jack put his hand under my elbow, and butterflies exploded in flight in my tummy.

Fighting to cover my nerves, I asked, "Have you heard anything from Clyde?"

"They kept the old codger overnight, but he's home now, and driving Betty up a tree."

"That's great."

"Unless you're Betty. Are you ready?"

"Well, nearly." The butterflies crash-landed. "I have a favor to ask."

"What's that?"

My mother raised her eyebrows, pulling her thin skin thinner below them.

I put my hand up toward her and shot her a warning glance. To Jack I said, "A friend of mine from the Virgin Islands needed a place to stay tonight, and she wants to join us. Is that okay?"

Jack took one sip of tea, then another. The logs crackled and popped in the fireplace. I looked at Mother and she at me. My chest grew tight and then tighter as Jack remained silent without answering my question.

And then Ava appeared in the doorway. Or shot in like a Roman candle, rather. She had thrown a red shawl over her dress, and I couldn't help but wither as I compared my black skirt and red sweater to her black and red ensemble.

She tossed her thick mane of sun-bronzed black hair behind her shoulder and said as only she could, "Emily, introduce me to this fine boss of yours."

If Ava had an effect on Jack, he hid it well. He raised one brow at me, though.

The frog in my throat made my voice thin. "Jack, this is my friend, Ava Butler, from St. Marcos. Ava, this is Jack Holden."

Ava walked to him and held out one hand.

He took it and bowed his head to her. "Ms. Butler, a pleasure."

Her accent was a musical purr. "Call me Ava. And the pleasure be all mine, meh son." She held on to his hand a little longer than I thought was really necessary, her glistening eyes locked onto his. "Thank you for letting me crash your party with Emily. Christmas a lonely time for me this year, far from my daughter and the island I call home."

"Okay," I said. My voice, meant to break her spell, came out almost a shriek. But it worked. Ava dropped Jack's hand. "I think we're ready. Mother, please drive carefully."

"You know I will."

Ava hugged my mother. "Thanks for having me. I know Emily come from good people, first time I meet her."

Mother was always a sucker for flattery. She hugged Ava back. "Of course. Stay as long as you'd like." She turned to Jack. "Is the weather going to be good enough for you and Emily to fly out tomorrow?"

I wanted to jump up and down and wave my arms "no," but Ava's phone made a noise, and she pulled it from her handbag to check it.

Jack said, "We'll have to see."

"See what?" Ava asked.

I grabbed Ava's arm. "You're going to fall on your bana in those shoes. Let me help you out to Jack's car."

As the service drew to a close, the organist and choir burst into the recessional, "Hark the Herald Angels Sing." I stood up between Jack and Ava and continued singing as the front pews filed out. We had sat near the back, so we had a long time before we would be exiting.

I flipped the program to the back cover. Jack had surprised me again. I had assumed we were going to a Catholic mass, and it turned out he was a member of Downtown Methodist, a church up the street from our offices. I kept singing as I read over it: Announcements. Singles. Ladies Bible Study. Youth Group. Choir practice. A potluck—THE CHURCH WILL HOST AN EVENING OF FINE DINING, SUPER ENTERTAINMENT, AND GRACIOUS HOSTILITY. I smiled. Another gem for my collection.

Our row emptied into the center aisle and we began a slow walk toward the sanctuary exit. Jack led and Ava and I followed, side by side. Inside the nave, the carol sounded exultant, glorious. As we neared the propped-open doors, the sound changed to a happy jangle of music mixed with chattering voices. By the time we exited, the chatter was dominant and the music the background.

Without the aid of the choir, people in the foyer sang out of rhythm and off-key all around me—except for Ava, who sang at full voice and perfectly, which drew as many eyes as did her va-va and her voom. On my left, two openly gay men held hands as they talked to a heterosexual couple with twin boys. Three blue-haired women leaned against each other for support and spoke in slow, tremulous voices to my right. Someone grabbed my arm from behind, stopping me short.

I called out, "Jack," but my voice didn't begin to cut through the din.

Jack kept going, Ava behind him. I turned to my accoster. Officer Samson's towering frame loomed behind me, recognizable even when he wore a sport coat, sweater, and button down over navy pants, instead of a police officer's uniform. He continued pulling me from the crowd, and I considered resisting, but decided that probably wasn't something one did with cops, even when the object of one's affection was walking off with the sexiest woman within a five-hundred-mile radius. I acquiesced, letting Samson lead me to the side of the room, out of the flow of human traffic.

He put his head close to mine without letting go of my arm and shouted, "I heard you reported a murder today."

I scowled, processing his words. Officer Jones told me he thought it was a slip and fall. I had wanted to believe it, but I remembered the eerie feeling I'd had in her backyard, like someone was watching me. I'd shaken it off, but I'd wondered about foul play, especially since she'd been scared to leave her home.

"Murder?"

"Yes, and I'm starting to worry about you."

My fist clenched. Was he trying to intimidate me like that jerk Burrows? "Oh really?"

He released my arm. "You keep showing up where people are dying. That's high risk. You should take up a nonhazardous hobby and spend some time away from crime scenes."

His voice hadn't sounded hostile. In fact, he sounded grandfatherly, even warm. I relaxed. "I'll think about it. What are you doing here?"

"Christmas Eve service with my family."

"Huh." I looked around for a wife giving him the stink eye for talking to me, but I didn't see any likely candidates.

"Anyway, since we're here, about the other day, and your phone." He cleared his throat. "I'm sorry."

His sudden change in subject stalled my brain like the swamped engine of my dad's truck once when he drove through a high-water crossing in Palo Duro Canyon. "Huh?"

He shook his head quickly, in small motions. "There's a lot I can't say. I'm a member of the APD. You've filed a complaint. But I regret that it happened."

I stared at him a moment then shook my head.

"What?"

"You're absolutely sure it was murder today?"

"So they say. I haven't seen the final report."

People streamed past us toward the exits. Cold air blew in from the street, and the arctic gusts blew snow all the way to where we stood. I wrapped my arms around myself. Jack and Ava were probably going steady by now. I couldn't stand here freezing my tail off letting that happen.

As I was about to make my getaway, Samson broke his silence. "How'd you know her? I don't picture you as running in the same circles."

I stuck with the story I'd given Officer Jones earlier. "Friend of a friend."

"And you were there because why?"

"That's all going to be in Officer Jones's report, I'm sure. Listen, my friends have—"

"It said she needed a criminal attorney."

"Yep."

"She dated a cop, you know."

The people around me blurred and their voices squelched like feedback. The crowd seemed to collapse in. All the warm bodies in the overheated space made it humid, close, and claustrophobic. I wanted to rip off my jacket and run but meanwhile my brain slowed to the speed of a slug.

"No, I didn't. Which one?"

Before he could answer, I heard Jack's voice in my ear. "Emily, there you are."

Samson released me, saluting as he disappeared with a few sidesteps into the crowd.

I whirled, catching Jack by both arms. "I was just on my way."

He peered more closely at me, then at Samson's retreating figure, but I ignored the question on his face. I'd tell him about Samson. About my whole day, my whole last few days.

Later.

Jack parked his Jeep at an angle at Mother's house, with his headlights illuminating the icy walkway. Ava got out of the backseat on his side and lurched, nearly falling. No shocker. She'd been having trouble on the ice in her heels all night. Jack put his hand under her elbow and guided her around the front of the Jeep, where I joined them and took his other arm. I glanced at the pristine new bumper and silver bodywork—yet another shade in the rainbow of colors on the Jeep. He still refused to take my money for the repairs. Slowly, we walked toward the house on the ice-rink walkway and stepped carefully onto the slippery porch.

I said to Jack, "Would you like to come in? Maybe we could talk about whatever it is you wanted to talk about?" I hoped to give him his present tonight, too.

His eyes darted to Ava, then back to me.

Ava eyed him like a Grade A steak. "Yah, Jack, come in. It so cold out here, and there two women inside to warm you up."

Jack's eyes looked as terrified as a calf in the chute before a roping competition. I didn't blame him a bit. Possibly I should have warned him about Ava. Possibly I should have warned Ava I had dibs on Jack. If I had, then maybe I wouldn't be imagining strangling her sparkly throat right now.

He said, "Uh, well, we can talk in New Mexico."

I was disappointed, but I smiled at him.

Ava smiled, too. "New Mexico! When? That where I gig next."

"Tomorrow," Jack replied.

"You two driving?"

"Flying in my plane."

"Sweet! Carry me with you?"

"Uh . . . I guess we could . . ."

"Perfect. I take a bus to Albuquerque from there."

Jack looked at me. "Okay, then?"

Not okay. But what could I say, really? She was my friend, she was stranded, and if Jack didn't object, then how could I?

"Okay, then," I said, and hard as I'd tried to sound enthusiastic, my voice rang a false note to my ear, but neither Jack nor Ava reacted.

"I'll get a report on conditions and text you when I know more in the morning," Jack said to me.

"Sounds good."

I stood my ground in the cold, trying to wait Ava out. I opened the door. "Better get in before you freeze to death, Ava."

She put her arms around Jack and tilted her head back. "I falling in love with Texas, Jack." She kissed him, on the mouth. "See you tomorrow." She walked in the door, then cocked her hip and put a hand on it. "You coming, Emily?"

"I-I-I . . ." I licked my lips, my eyes darting between Ava and Jack. I wanted to give him a chance to kiss me. This was supposed to have been a date. But there was no way the ultra-private Jack would put his lips anywhere near mine with Ava staring at us, if he'd even been considering it at all.

"Ava, give us a moment?" Jack smiled at her and gestured toward the inside of the house.

My breath caught in my throat.

"Ohhhh yah." Ava disappeared from the open doorway, but not before shooting me a lascivious grin.

When she was gone, Jack closed the distance between us. "I thought we'd never get rid of her."

"Me either." My heart pounded harder, and I was afraid he could feel it through his chest.

He took off one glove then slid his hand under my hair at the base of my neck. I closed my eyes and his warm lips covered mine. They were soft and full, and they clung to mine like I realized I was now clinging to him with both my hands. He nudged my lips apart and took my top lip into his, sucking gently. I groaned, and I reached up to grasp the back of his head. Within seconds, we'd drifted away from the porch light and Jack's hands had worked their way inside my wrap, my top, and the silky bra I was suddenly oh-so-glad I'd worn. The man had lightning hands, but mine found his butt just as fast and I squeezed and pulled him close. As cold as it was outside, suddenly, I had an urge to rip a few layers off. Jack turned my back to the wall of the house and leaned into me, harder and harder. His lips broke from mine and he kissed his way down my neck, his lips rough against my cold skin.

"Ooooh," I gasped.

He didn't answer, which was good, because I didn't want him to stop what he was doing. I grasped his hair with both hands and laid my head against the wall.

"Emily, I making hot tea. You want some?" Ava said, her voice shattering the silence only inches from my eardrum.

I yelped, and Jack's face shot back from my chest.

Ava grinned. "Oh, sorry." She turned away. "Um, um, um," she said, shutting the door behind her.

"Awkward," I said to Jack. But she'd probably arrived in the nick of time to save us from a citizen's arrest for public indecency from the nosy neighbor lady across the street who used to bang on the window when I made out with my high school boyfriend in his car. That wouldn't have looked good after my bogus bust by Burrows and Samson last week.

Jack didn't answer. He pushed me back against the wall, and his mouth claimed mine.

To hell with the neighbor lady, I thought, and ripped his shirt hem out of his jeans.

CHAPTER 24

Luckily, the runway was clear and the temperature in the thirties the next morning. In the plane it was a nippy forty-five degrees, but as much as I hated the cold, I couldn't have been happier. Jack put Snowflake's kennel in the backseat, and when Ava suggested that she ride up front as a first-timer in a Skyhawk, he told her that he was putting me in shotgun so he could hold my hand. Which he did, off and on, for most of the three-and-a-half-hour flight. My arm actually got tired from holding it up to reach his, but I didn't care. I wouldn't have cared if I had to flap my arms to get us there. I was that happy.

White blanketed the landscape below us most of the way, but the sky was clear and a vivid blue, like the Caribbean Sea around Ava's home island, St. Marcos. It matched my buoyant mood. As we began our descent over the Sierra Blancas toward the tiny strip on Wrong Turn Ranch, however, the clouds grew thicker. Soon we were cruising along above an endless blanket of gray cotton balls. Jack had to let go of my hand, and his face was intense, his eyes locked onto the instrument panel. My head started to ache.

The pitch of the engine changed and we started descending. In seconds, we'd bumped and bounced into the pit of gray cotton balls, and they clung to us, obscuring our vision. The ground could be coming up on us fast, or a mountain peak could be right in front of us. Despite the temperature in the plane, a cold sweat ran down my back. I snuck a look at Jack, and saw he was sweating, too. The gray cottony clouds seemed to go on forever, but finally we slipped out the bottom of them. Then I saw a mountaintop poking through another layer of gray cotton below. These were ominous, darker, more like mounds of ash. I put my head down and started whispering a prayer: "Dear God, if you could help us land safely, I promise to be nicer to my mother."

Before I got to *amen*, a hand tapping my shoulder startled me. I whipped around. It was Ava. I leaned toward her as far as I could, as she leaned toward me. Her dark skin seemed to have a gray-green undertone. I couldn't hear her, but I read her lips.

"Is everything okay?" she asked.

I gave her a thumbs-up sign. Just then, everything around us went dark. The Skyhawk bounced as it hurtled across the sky and toward the earth. I turned back around and clutched the armrests. The turbulence shook us so hard that I lost my sensation of up and down and sideways, with the only light coming from the instrument panel inside the plane. I could barely see Jack, only enough to know he was keeping his eyes on the dashboard controls. Nausea came over me, and my mouth went dry. The plane bucked violently, and my seatbelt cut into my lap as we dropped straight down. I felt my mouth stretch open and my ears pop. If I was screaming, I couldn't hear myself.

But as suddenly as we'd started shaking and dropping, we stopped falling and floated out of the clouds. The ground was below us, maybe five hundred feet, and I could see the orange windsock that marked the runway at the ranch ahead. I wiped sweat from my forehead and noticed my hands were shaking as hard as the Skyhawk had moments ago. I felt a nervous vibration in my throat.

I studied the ground and took deep, calming breaths. The snow here was only patchy, and it looked like someone had plowed the runway, because it was completely clear. Those were good things. Everything would be all right.

The plane's wheels hit the dirt. Fifteen minutes later, we had loaded an unsteady Ava along with Snowflake and our bags into the Suburban—which took twice as long as usual since we'd brought presents for half of Tularosa—had fueled and hangared the plane and were on our way to the ranch house. I turned my phone on and it searched for a signal. When it found it, it made a series of burps and whistles I'd never heard before. Today. Today I was resetting all the dang tones into something recognizable. I read the screen. Three voice mails. Six text messages. Twelve emails. I viewed the list of numbers from which I had voice mails first. All three calls were from an unknown number. I didn't play the unknown-number game. Telemarketers, probably. I put my phone down, then, worried about Betsy being snatched by Immigration, I picked it back up and pressed play anyway, then put it to my ear.

A man said, "Emily, Merry Christmas."

I pressed my fist to my mouth, hard. A gravelly voice from the past. A voice I hadn't heard in nearly a decade from a person I hadn't seen in fifteen years. But I would recognize this voice until the day I died, even though it sounded older. It was a voice that turned me into a child who'd been left, again, in a split second. My father, Johnny Phelps.

His message kept playing. "I know you're probably surprised to hear from me. I would really like to talk to you and explain what happened. I've missed you more than I can say, and I love you."

The voice mail ended. Swallowing down bile, I pressed play for the next one.

"Uh, I forgot to tell you how to get hold of me. Please call me as soon as you can. There's some things you need to know, not just for me, but because they're important for you." He recited a phone number.

The voice mail ended. I put my phone in my lap and breathed in and out a few times. I wanted to get the last one over with, so I looked down, and fat teardrops rained on the iPhone screen. I had to wipe them away with my sweater before I could play the last voice mail. I felt Jack's eyes on me, and he reached out and took my left hand.

"Emily, one more thing. If you could please talk to Jack, tell him it wasn't me that took that stuff, I would appreciate it. I've made my mistakes, but I don't take another fellow's things. Thank you, Sweet Pea. I love you."

Sweet Pea? He had the nerve to call me Sweet Pea when I hadn't heard from him in years? And what was this about Jack? My Jack?

I jerked my hand away from My Jack and pressed play again. Listened again. Pressed play again. Listened again. There was no denying what I'd heard. My father knew Jack. Jack knew Dad.

Well, Merry frickin' Christmas to me.

I dropped the phone in my lap then my face in my hands and sobbed.

CHAPTER 25

Jack stood on the other side of the door to my bathroom. "I'm sorry. Your dad made me promise to let him tell you. I shouldn't have waited this long."

I was mad enough to kill him, possibly madder than I'd ever been at anyone in my whole life. I sunk into the bubble bath up to my eyeballs, wanting to tune him out, but wanting even more to hear what he had to say. I would have to wait and kill him when he was done.

I eased my ears and mouth out of the water and hollered. "You should have told me the first second you knew!"

Jack's voice grew frustrated. "Looking at a picture of you and your dad in a family album while sitting in the living room with your mother, you want me to say, 'Hey, isn't that Johnny Phelps? I put him in the slammer'?"

"I didn't even know he was alive, much less that he was in prison!"

"How was I supposed to know that?"

"You found out soon enough. You could have told me then."

"I needed to figure some things out first."

"What?"

"Things."

He kept talking, but I sunk beneath the water again where I didn't have to hear him. He could have all the good reasons in the world but the fact remained that I deserved to know my father was alive. I deserved to know where he was. Jack could have found a way to tell me, but he didn't. I came back up for air.

Jack said, "Are you even listening?"

"I'm not sure. What did you say?"

There was a thrump against the door, and when he spoke his voice sounded different, farther away. I pictured him, leaning against the door, arms probably crossed, eyes on the ground twelve inches in front of his boots. My heart tugged a little, and I smacked it away without mercy.

"I said I've been trying to tell you for a week. Things kept getting in the way."

"A week? Seven twenty-four-hour days? And you couldn't find any time in them?"

"It's not like you tell me everything, like who that guy was you were talking to at church last night."

I submerged again. The things I ran out of time to tell him and the things he couldn't find time to tell me were so different they weren't even events in the same rodeo. They were different like bull riding from ballet. The silence of the water thrummed in my ears. I felt my long hair floating, touching my arms. I came up for a breath.

"So tell me now."

"This would be easier if you'd let me in."

"I'm in the bathtub."

"I won't look. I can't talk to you through a closed door."

"In a minute."

"Okay." Something started scratching against the door. "Snowflake, no," he said in an alpha voice. The scratching stopped. "I met your father ten years ago. In Alamogordo. After he was arrested for murder."

"Murder? My dad is a murderer?" I jumped to my feet, and water sloshed over the sides. I didn't care.

"He's a good guy that got caught up in a bad situation."

"What kind of bad situation?" I sank slowly back into the tub. More water sloshed out.

"He should be the one to tell you." Jack paused, waiting for me to let him off the hook, I assumed, but I didn't. "He got injured and couldn't rodeo, had money trouble, picked up odd jobs. Got crossways with someone he worked with."

Oh no. I squeezed my hands into fists.

"They got in a fight. He killed the guy with a broken beer bottle. Your dad said it was self-defense, but it didn't look good."

I became aware that I was rocking back and forth in the water, arms wrapped around myself, keening softly.

Jack whispered, his voice sounding agonized, too. "Are you okay?"

I made myself stop the noise. I hated that he heard me. I hated being this weak, this vulnerable. I snapped, "Just finish."

Again, I heard a noise like he turned, and then his voice was louder. "I was the prosecutor. He had a shit court-appointed attorney, but no priors, so I took a plea for involuntary manslaughter. He got out in November."

"So where's he been since he got out?"

"Here."

"Here where?"

"Wrong Turn Ranch."

"He was here at Wrong Turn Ranch?"

"Up until two weeks ago, yes. Working for Mickey for a month."

Mickey knew, too. And Laura. Half of Otero County probably knew. My head pounded, boom, boom, boom, like a mallet against a drum. My father, who I hadn't seen in fifteen years, had been working for Mickey. But that meant he worked for Jack, since it was Jack's family that owned Wrong Turn Ranch. *My father worked for Jack. Until two weeks ago.* And now Dad was calling me, wanting me to make peace between Jack and him.

My lips felt numb when I spoke. "Jack, why did he leave?"

The water had grown cold in the tub. I twisted the left spigot. As hot water poured in, I heard Ava's voice. I moved to the end of the tub nearest the door, careful to avoid scalding myself, but trying to catch what she said. She didn't whisper, so it wasn't too hard.

"Good evening, Jack. Emily okay?" Again, her island accent seemed so strange to me, first in Texas, then in New Mexico.

"She's upset with me. She'll be out soon."

"I put dinner on, all right? Take your time. You two taking care of me, let me do something for you."

"We have a big group tonight. It's too much."

"How many?" Ava's voice said.

"Nine."

I added up names in my head. Jack, Ava, Emily, Mickey and Laura, Greg, Farrah, Judith, and me. That was eight.

"Who's number nine?" I blurted.

"Uh, Collin."

I shouted, unable to contain myself, and turned off the water at the same time. "What? Collin is coming to dinner? All the way from Taos, on Christmas? I thought you hated Collin?"

"I got over it. I asked him for help on this smuggling thing."

"Oh. My. God."

"He had to be down to Las Cruces Monday anyway. He's stopping by."

I heard Ava's voice again. "Collin? My girl Katie's brother Collin live in New Mexico. That Collin?"

"The same."

"Nine people then. Can I cook anything I find in your kitchen?"

"Uh, yeah, and there's several very well-stocked freezers in the garage."

"I on it."

This was perfect. Collin, who had messed up my life last time I saw him, coming tonight, when my life had gotten back on track only to tank again. The competing scents of bath products—vanilla soap, coconut shampoo, cinnamon-apple bubble bath, freesia conditioner—suddenly made me feel nauseous. I lifted the tub drain and dried myself off in fast, rough strokes. I donned a robe from a hook on the back of the door. I wrapped the tie around my waist and knotted it. I pulled open the door, and Jack fell into me, pulling my robe open a few inches as he caught himself. Snowflake jumped in the air and put her front paws on my shin.

"Jack!" I jerked it closed.

"Sorry."

"I'm getting dressed now. I'll talk to you later."

He looked at the ground and his posture was so hangdog it was almost comical, except that this wasn't funny, and I wasn't laughing. He turned and left, with a dejected Snowflake behind him.

The downside of throwing Jack out of my room, I discovered later, was that he went straight to the kitchen to cook with Ava. Her lilt and flirty laugh rang through the house. I pictured her displaying her assets to their greatest advantage for him, and it raised my hackles. It wasn't like me to be so insecure and jealous, and I hated it in myself, but there it was, green-eyed, shrewlike, and on the rampage, even though Ava was only being kind and thoughtful. Well, I could do penance later. Right now I *hated* that I'd gotten my hair wet and that I had to waste the time drying it when Jack had her fun-loving nature and sexy smile as a contrast to my anger and harsh words. Which didn't change the fact that I was mad at him—very, very mad—and that I wasn't sure if I could ever trust him. He had a disturbing habit of withholding important information, and this time it wasn't his secrets he kept from me, but mine. I jerked a wide-toothed comb through my tangles. It hurt. *Good.*

I went into the bedroom and pulled warm clothes out of my suitcase. More voices had joined Jack and Ava. Young voices. Greg and Farrah? I tried to muster up a smile, but my mouth wouldn't do it yet. Still, it would be great to see them. I slipped into Levi's and a purple mock turtleneck, then shoved my feet into fur-lined Crocs my mother had given me for Christmas. I'd never owned—or wanted—anything like them. But they were mine now, so I was going to give them a try. I grabbed my phone and headed back into the bathroom. I flipped my hair upside down and aimed the blow-dryer at it with one hand and scrolled through my missed texts and emails with the other.

The first few were from a 575 area-code number I didn't recognize.

The first: *Mickey and Laura got us smartphones for Christmas!* I wasn't sure if it came from Greg or Farrah, but the text included a selfie of the two of them in front of the Wrong Turn Ranch sign out by the highway. IF YOU'RE HERE, YOU'VE MADE A WRONG TURN. HIGHWAY 70 IS BEHIND YOU. I loved that sign. I loved those kids.

And a second text from an unfamiliar 575 number: *Laura said she can teach me how to be a jockey.* Ah, Farrah. So the other number had to be Greg. I had another from Farrah, too: *A colt was born in a manger this morning so we named it Jesus. But pronounced in Spanish, so it's not sacrilegious: Hay-SEUSS.* I couldn't help but smile at that. My mother would be appalled.

I typed one-handed, very slowly. I texted back to Greg: *Looking good. Merry Christmas. C U soon!* To Farrah, I sent: *Amazing, she's great. Cool re colt!* Unfortunately, I knew it was doubtful that Farrah would spend enough time at Wrong Turn Ranch to make the jockey dream happen, but maybe if the seed was planted, she could pursue it somehow, wherever she ended up. It made my heart ache to think about it. I'd never imagined adoption before Betsy, and I'd never considered older kids even since then. These two needed a home, though. I could continue to give Farrah access to this life, and to Laura. I felt disloyal to Betsy even thinking it, but I knew in my heart of hearts that getting her was a long shot. Even if I did, it didn't mean I couldn't adopt other kids, too. It was a lot to take on by myself, though. I chewed on a hangnail and scrolled.

The other four texts were in a group string with Wallace and Nadine. The topic was Betsy. I chomped harder and lower on the hangnail.

Boss won't let me take the day to go to the consulate 'for a wild goose chase.' SHIT. Wallace.

Let me see if I can get time off. Nadine.

DOUBLE SHIT. Polo Club short staffed because of holidays. They won't let me go. Nadine again.

And a new text, in the last half hour: *Emily, could you go? I can't promise they'll work with you, but I could get a notarized power of attorney for you to act on my behalf. Or something. Ask Jack what he thinks.* Wallace.

I turned off the blow-dryer and set it on the corner of the countertop, flipping my head and hair into an upright posture as I doused it with hairspray, the first of my usual two applications—one at half-dry, one at full-dry. I typed fast, and my iPhone autocorrected me into nonsense. I erased the nonsense and tried again, slower, breathing deeply to calm myself: *I'll be back from NM on Sunday and can go to the consulate, no problem. Hate this! Are we absolutely sure they won't come for her sooner?*

I stared at the phone, willing a response from Wallace. Nothing from him, but another from Nadine: *Another one of our dancers is being hassled by some cops.*

That made three: the woman who disappeared last summer, Ivanka, and now this woman. I texted back: *Oh no! Did she say who they are?*

Nadine: *I heard it's that Asian cop Wu and some redheaded guy.*

Some redheaded guy. Burrows. My hands shook, and I clasped them in my lap and stared into my own eyes in the mirror. *Get a grip. Do* some-thing, *something constructive, something distracting, something positive.* But what? Betsy's face flashed in my mind, as it so often did. I wanted so badly to make it better for her. I couldn't stop the Immigration Customs and Enforcement folks, but I was here in New Mexico, and I could look for her backpack. I had all day tomorrow, and Saturday, too, so that was what I was going to do. That, and ask Jack about my dad's last voice mail, which somehow I had forgotten about in our last conversation. Two sharp raps at my door tore my attention away from the phone and my thoughts.

Expecting Jack, I was terse. "I'll be down when I'm ready."

Farrah's voice answered me, meek and chastened, and I regretted my harpy tone immediately. "Okay, I just wanted to say hi."

"Wait!" I trotted to the door and threw it open.

The girl before me in a green Christmas sweater looked like the midnight version of Cathy Rigby as Peter Pan. She smiled and I opened my arms for a hug. She stepped into them, barely enough to fill them up. The waif couldn't weigh more than ninety pounds. I released her but held on to her upper arms as Snowflake whirled in happy circles at her feet.

"How have things been?"

She lit up like a sparkler. "Awesome."

"I knew they would be." I let go of her and pointed at my hair. "I'm almost done. Tell everyone I'll be down in five?"

"Okay."

I closed the door and went back to the bathroom. The first thing I did was check my phone. Still no answer from Wallace about Immigration. Ugh. I flipped my hair over. I turned the dryer on and tried to turn my brain off.

CHAPTER 26

"We having a good, old-fashion St. Marcos Christmas dinner, New Mexico style." Ava lifted a serving dish over her head, which hiked her fitted black top up nearly to the bottom of her breasts. "Johnnycakes."

I watched from where I sat at one of the kitchen table's chairs as Ava slunk toward me, carving a path through the small crowd gathered in the kitchen with the sway of her hips in a short black skirt that matched her top. She set it on the table in front of me. Snowflake put her paws on one of the chairs, trying to get a closer sniff—or a bite—from the serving dish. The fried West Indian bread smelled delicious, but, then again, anything fried smelled good to me.

Collin crossed his arms over his chest, which emphasized that he'd had a lot of time to work out since Tamara had broken off their engagement. "I'll have whatever you're cooking, Ava."

His blue eyes glittered and his serious expression didn't quite hide his trademark grin. I was relieved his eyes were glittering over someone besides me this visit. His short-cropped *Top Gun* hair had grown out some, and for the first time I saw streaks of gray in it. Even Tom Cruise had to grow older some time.

Ava chuptzed him, long and loud, a teeth-sucking act of derision perfected by those in the West Indies. She sauntered back into the kitchen, where Jack was stirring something in a tall pot. Collin, no stranger to the chuptz from his time on St. Marcos, laughed.

"You want some of what I cooking, you best get in the kitchen and help," she said.

Now everyone laughed, and Collin ran the few steps to join her.

She swatted him with a towel, then picked up a knife and pointed it at several chickens, fried whole. "Carve."

He bowed, took the knife, and set to work. I had planned to offer help, but there was no way I was entering that kitchen with Jack and Collin in it. I'd set the table earlier. That would have to be my contribution.

Judith had arrived after I came downstairs, and she walked to the counter and poured a glass of Pinot Gris from the Wines of the San Juan. From behind her, it struck me how much of her long black hair was shot with steel gray. Today she wore it at the base of her neck in a silver clasp with turquoise, red, and black stones. It was a formal look, in fitting with her old-fashioned straight brown suede skirt and its matching beaded blouse.

She turned to me. "You want some wine?"

"A small one, thank you." I joined her at the counter and took the glass she offered. "How are things at the home office?" I asked, referring to Jack's adobe office in Tularosa, where she had worked since she followed him there from the DA's office in Alamogordo.

She took a sip of wine so small that she appeared to absorb it into her tongue instead of swallowing it. Shades of my mother. "Busy. It's a good thing Jack couldn't represent anyone in the indictments from the Paul Johnson mess, because that tied up all the other local attorneys. Everything else is coming to us."

Although Johnson had—briefly, and under false pretenses—retained Jack, Johnson's men had kidnapped me and assaulted Betsy's father, who died on Jack's land when he was attempting to escape. That made Jack and me both witnesses and conflicted our firm out. The conflict didn't only extend to Johnson, who Jack wouldn't have defended anyway, but to anyone involved in the sordid affairs.

Judith added, "Plus with the work coming out of Amarillo, it's a lot. I told him I might need help if this keeps up."

Without discussing it, Judith and I moved away from the counter and out to the great room. The sky still loomed gray and low, but even dreary it looked spectacular viewed through the east-facing floor-to-high-ceiling windows that stretched across one entire side of the room. I took a sip of the Pinot Gris and savored it. It tasted of pear and some kind of citrus.

"I can't believe you'd let someone else handle anything." I was teasing, sort of. Judith hadn't taken kindly to Jack sharing their load with me, at first.

She nodded, her black eyes grave. "It would be a last resort."

I put a hand over my mouth and cleared my throat to cover a laugh.

Remembering that Judith's brother once worked at Johnson's Ranch as an electrician, I asked, "Say, does your brother still do any work out at Johnson's place?"

She absorbed another few drops of her wine and then shook her head. "It's deserted. They froze all Johnson's assets, you know, and the judge didn't allow bail."

"I was afraid of that. I'm looking for something of Betsy's, and I need to see if it's out there."

"They have big padlocks on everything. At least that's what people say."

It wouldn't hurt to swing by and check. Jarhead would enjoy the exercise. I mentally scheduled it for first thing the next day. But I kept those thoughts to myself. Judith and I chatted some about pending cases until Jack ushered everyone into the kitchen for dinner.

We had all gathered noisily—Judith and me, Mickey and Laura, the kids, Ava, and Collin—but quieted at once when Jack held a finger in the air.

"Thanks everyone for celebrating with us. Mickey, will you bless the food?" Jack said.

Mickey cleared his throat. "Join hands, please." He closed his eyes and bowed his head. As he prayed aloud, I snuck a peek at Jack. His eyes were on me. *Cheater*, I thought, then realized my eyes were as open as his. I closed them. Mickey finished, and together we all said, "Amen."

"And thank you for bringing these two very special young people into our lives," Mickey added.

Laura stood between Greg and Farrah, holding one hand of each. The two kids looked embarrassed, like they couldn't believe Mickey had singled them out. Laura's eyes watered and she laughed and made a show of wiping her eyes. Mickey walked over and hugged her, then patted each teen on the back.

Voices quickly covered the silence following Mickey's blessing, and I heaped my plate with beans and rice, sweet-potato casserole, and johnny-cake. I took the plate into the living room and perched on the couch with my plate balanced on my knees. Jack sat down next to me. His knees, boots, and long legs created a higher, more angled tabletop for his plate, and he struggled with it, then gave up and put his plate on the coffee table. I tried not to look at him, but it was hard when he was all my heart could see, and it made me mad at myself and him.

The living room continued to fill. Ava sat on my other side, Collin took a seat catty-cornered from her, and Mickey put his plate on the stone hearth in front of us. The chimney extended to the ceiling behind him, the enormous rocks appearing as if they would tumble onto his head at any moment. The voices of Laura, Judith, and the kids still rang out from the kitchen, but I could barely hear them over the Christmas music someone had turned on. Mariah Carey: "All I Want For Christmas Is You." My very favorite Christmas song. Sadness welled inside me that my dad, Jack, and their big, fat secrets had tarnished this day. I sucked in a deep breath of air through my nose. I didn't need to let it impact anyone else's night, though.

Jack set his silverware on the table. Snowflake eyed him hopefully, then moved on to me. I pinched a small piece of johnnycake and held it out. She took it from my fingers in a lunge, like a trout to a fly, and gulped it down.

Jack said, "Collin, we're hoping to enlist your help with a problem we've been having here."

Collin had just taken a giant bite of rice and beans. He chewed with wide eyes and circled his hand by his mouth to show he was hurrying. Everyone but me laughed. When he'd swallowed, he said, "Of course, buddy. I owe you a big one, for, ahem, taking advantage of your hospitality last time."

"Actually, the problem seems bigger than Wrong Turn Ranch."

Mickey stood and paced. "I feel responsible, and stupid. A few weeks ago, someone made off with a load of our stuff. Someone who had a good idea of what was valuable and enough about us to know when to get to it, where, and how to get it out fast." He looked at Jack, then stopped talking.

Jack nodded. "She knows."

I bristled. *Yes, finally, she knows.*

Mickey took a deep breath. "At first we thought it was an inside job. We'd brought on an ex-con—"

"My father." Everyone's heads whipped around at me, and I realized I'd cut Mickey off. Loudly.

Mickey sighed. "Yes. Johnny Phelps. Emily's dad. I all but accused him, and, later that night, he disappeared."

Jack put his hand on my knee, and I flinched. His warm eyes met my cold ones, and he removed it. "Then Emily and I ran across some of the stolen Wrong Turn Ranch items at ABC Half-Price Resale in Amarillo. Our client is the owner. He admitted he's been selling stolen merchandise."

Collin rubbed his chin. "Somebody's been a bad boy, smuggling stolen goods across state lines."

"Yesterday Phelps called me," Mickey said. "Told me he didn't do it, gave me the license plate number of a blue sedan out here the day of the robbery, and hinted at a connection to some dangerous people. Said he had to figure out a way for it not to come back on him before he'd tell me more."

I shoved my plate onto the coffee table and turned to glare at Jack.

He threw his hands up. "I tried to tell you earlier."

"Define *earlier*." I realized I had something to tell him, too, though, and

I changed gears. "Wait a sec. I have the license plate number of a truck that dropped off a shipment at ABC Half-Price Resale." Snowflake slunk to Jack's feet and curled up, trembling. The poor thing hated conflict.

It was Jack's turn to glare at me, left eyebrow arched. "When did you get that?"

My head bobbed sideways a little. "When I bought your Christmas present, Jack Ass," I said, with a tad too much emphasis on the Ass part. The room went so quiet I could hear the ringing in my ears. I didn't dare look around, for fear of what I'd see in people's eyes. I closed my own for a split second to steady my frayed nerves. "Then Burrows showed up and dragged me away."

Jack's olive face turned a crimson hue. He spit out his words like fish bones stuck in his throat. "Do tell."

"Whoa, whoa, whoa, whoa." Collin shook his head. "Slow down here. You've got the license plate of a vehicle being used in the smuggling?"

I opened my mouth, shut it, then opened it again to speak. "I don't know. Maybe." I pulled up the photo and handed it to him.

"New Mexico plates." Collin typed keystrokes on my phone. "I'm texting it to myself."

I felt silly. I hadn't noticed the plates in the dark, and I hadn't even looked at the picture since I'd taken it, what with everything that had been going on, until now.

"Send it to me, Collin." Jack clenched his jaw. "Since Emily didn't." Snowflake huddled closer to her master, her eyes wide and fixed on him.

I put my plate back in my lap. Under its cover, I flexed the fingers of my left hand, then clenched them closed, then did it again, and again, and again.

Collin nodded and typed some more. He handed me back my phone. "Done. Emily, tell us the rest."

Everyone stared at me, rapt. Great. How to tell everything that had happened in the last few days without giving up the moral high ground with Jack? I told myself that it was different. He kept secrets from me that should have been mine. The secrets I kept from him weren't really his. Or were only kinda sorta his. Some of them. Ugh. This wasn't going to go well.

"The night before we entered Alan's plea—"

Jack interrupted. "Monday night."

"Yes. Monday night I went to do some last-minute Christmas shopping at ABC Half-Price Resale, Alan's store. The woman at the register—"

He interrupted again. "Alan's wife?"

"I didn't know that at the time, but yes. Anyway, I asked the woman I later learned was Alan's wife, Janelle, whether Alan was there, and she said he was out back, and she looked upset. So I thought I'd get a picture of the truck's plates for *you*, in case it was the smuggler, and I went around back and took one."

"Just like that."

"There might have been a little more to it than that, but nothing relevant."

"Okay."

"Then, I was hiding behind a dumpster, when—"

"Reckless."

I jumped up. "If you don't stop interrupting me, we're all going to die of old age before I finish telling you the story." I looked around. This time all the eyes on me shifted away from mine. Ava's were gleaming. Collin's were twinkling. Judith's looked uncomfortable. And Mickey's told me he felt guilty. Good. He should.

"Fine." Jack threw his hand out at me in a "go on" sort of way.

"Fine." I huffed a deep breath in and out. "Alan was back there. He was talking to the driver and someone else." I looked around the room. "Alan is our client in Amarillo, who supposedly assaulted a cop but says he didn't. He took a plea bargain, so we aren't sure. Anyway, I couldn't see him, and then the driver walked out in the alley. The driver was short and kind of skinny but I didn't get a good look at him. He drove off. Alan and the other guy disappeared, and Officer Burrows showed up and made me leave."

"Made you leave?"

"Yeah."

"Why?"

"He told me to butt out of police business and that I was going to get myself killed."

Jack snorted.

Collin said, "He sounds like an intelligent guy."

"Ha ha," I said. "Except that he told me to meet him somewhere private. When I got there—"

Jack shouted, "When you *what?*"

"When I got there."

"Why didn't you call me?"

I turned away from him. "As I was trying to say, when I got there, he was weird. He all but admitted he'd been following me."

Jack made another loud noise, but I didn't stop. Snowflake had buried her head under her paws and looked like she needed a Valium.

"Because earlier that day, when I was at the orthodontist's office, he showed up there, too. And of course he showed up to arrest me when Mary Alice Hodges called on the wrath of God."

"Arrested you?" Collin asked. The corners of his lips curved up millimeters short of a grin.

"Long story." One I didn't want to relive. "It was all very mysterious, and then a security guard banged on the car, and Burrows left." I paused to take a drink of water.

Jack crossed his arms. "Is that all?"

"Almost."

Jack threw his hands in the air. He wasn't usually this open and *dramatic*, except around Mickey, but then they went back to childhood as cousins and best friends. Well, I'd asked Jack to communicate better, so I guess I was getting what I asked for. Sort of.

My eyelids fluttered a smidge as I answered him. "On Christmas Eve, Nadine told me a friend of hers was scared of a bad cop. She had the friend call me. The friend said her name was Beth, and we agreed to meet at her place at noon. When I got there, she was on her back patio. Dead."

"That, I knew about."

Ava put her hand over her heart. "Yesterday, when I got there?"

I pursed my lips and nodded. "Right before, actually." I looked at Jack. "Here's the part I haven't talked to you about. When we were leaving church last night, Samson pulled me aside."

"Now you get around to telling me." Jack said.

This time I didn't spar with him. "Yes. He was pretty okay, actually, and apologized about my arrest and the phone, but he did ask me how I ended up at the scene of the murder of a dancer from the Polo Club. That's a strip bar," I explained to the group. "Nadine knew her as Beth, but she'd introduced herself to Jack and me as Ivanka when we met her at a truck stop the night of another murder."

A gasp from the doorway cut me off. It was Greg, looking extremely young with the black knit cap gone, his hair shiny and straight, and clean clothes on his lanky frame. Farrah stood beside him. I wondered how long they'd been standing there, but knew they could have heard us from anywhere in the house.

Farrah whispered, "Oh my God," into the sudden silence, and buried her face in Greg's shoulder.

Laura had already reached the kids before I got my first word out.

"What is it?" I asked them. But I was sure I knew. They'd heard me say that someone who'd been at the truck stop was murdered. Whether there was a connection to what they saw or not, it had to be terrifying. I'd be scared if I were them, too.

Laura patted Greg, then went to the other side of Farrah and slipped an arm around the girl's waist. The two were almost exactly the same height, although Farrah was even slighter than Laura. Greg shook his head at me.

Laura whispered to him, and the three of them left the room. Snowflake sprinted to catch up to them.

Jack put his hand on my knee again, and this time I didn't object. We looked at each other, and he shook his head, just barely perceptibly. "Anything else, Emily?"

That I love you even if I want to string you up by your heels right now? That I wish I hadn't yelled at you in front of everyone? That I want you to put your arms around me and make this all better? When I opened my mouth, a whisper came out: "No."

Jack squeezed my knee.

"Luckily I've got all weekend with nothing to do," Collin said. He stood up. "But right now, I'm going for seconds."

Jack said, "Me, too." He let go of my knee and followed Collin.

I snapped out of my daze and shifted to go after him, but Ava stopped me by wrapping a hand around my arm, her long fingernails clicking together as she did.

She leaned in. "I so lost. What *up* with this place, these people?"

"It's never like this."

She chuptzed me, and I almost laughed. "You lie, I think. But that okay. I used to the melee from Katie and Nick."

"They're in another league."

"More important question: are you and your boss an item, or not?"

"I wish I knew." Maybe. Sometimes. "Right now I'm having trouble trusting him."

"About your daddy?"

"Yeah. About him."

"Seem like Jack have good intent."

I sighed. "He probably does. But he almost never tells me what's going on."

"He look good though."

Now I laughed and stood. "Yes, he does."

"And it appear from last night you like he tongue down your throat or wherever it was I see it."

I squawked.

Ava laughed. "That better."

Collin came back into the great room and held his hand out to Ava. "Madame, your manservant awaits his next instruction." He bowed.

She fanned herself. "I like the sound of that."

The two of them walked ahead of me into the kitchen. Laura and the kids had disappeared. Judith was placing a giant CorningWare serving dish out on the counter, full of something with a bubbling top that smelled like cinnamon and spice and everything nice. There was a tub of Blue Bell

Vanilla Bean ice cream beside it, along with a stack of dessert bowls and a bunch of spoons. I decided to skip seconds and go straight for the good stuff. I dug a serving spoon into the virgin surface of the as-yet-to-be-identified dessert. I ladled out a large chunk. Bread pudding. I put my hand on the side of the serving dish. Still warm. I added two scoops of vanilla ice cream. I looked around the once-again crowded room. No one seemed to be watching me.

As quietly as I could, I walked to the stairs, still keeping one eye on everyone in the kitchen. I tiptoed up each tread unnoticed. When I came to my room, I turned the handle and ducked in the door. I closed it softly, releasing the knob only when the tongue was positioned over the recess in the latch.

Peace. I sat down, taking a moment to breathe. Then I set the bowl on the side table along with my phone. A moment of guilt gave me pause. I'd snuck out before we'd even opened presents. But Laura had left with the kids, so I was off the hook. I flopped backward onto the fluffy white comforter and landed with my head in the mountain of pillows. What a day. What a long and difficult day.

I reached out for my phone. I was relieved to see a text from Wallace, although it wasn't in the group string with Nadine. And I had another from an 806 number I didn't recognize. A sense of dread crept into my chest. Betsy.

I pulled Wallace's text up first: *Please oh please oh please God let Emily not have done something incredibly stupid that will reflect poorly on me and keep her from being approved to adopt.*

It didn't sound like anything had happened to Betsy. More like I'd done something. *What in Hades are you talking about?* I hit send.

Then I opened the other text: *This is Byron from CPS. Wallace gave me your number. He said you communicate best by text. Please call me at your earliest convenience.*

Oh geez. Iciness flowed over my face. Byron was the CPS investigator working on Greg's and Farrah's cases.

Wallace responded: *Tell me you aren't with them. Please.*

If push came to shove, I could answer that one truthfully, but it wasn't time to show my hand yet. *With WHOM? Please give me a little to go on.*

I chewed the ragged edge of my now swollen hangnail. Could Byron have any other reason to call me except about Greg and Farrah? Maybe, but probably not. Could Wallace possibly be referring to anyone other than the two teenagers? Maybe, but probably not. Put the two together, and the answer to the first changed to "not likely."

Wallace: *G & F.*

Just because I expected it didn't mean I didn't throw up a little in my mouth when I read it. I couldn't honestly say I wasn't with them. But I could pretend to misinterpret the question. Then I could be truthful. *No, I don't have them. Has there been news?* Send.

Wallace: *Anonymous phone tip to Byron.*

Oh no, oh God, no, no, no. Who knew the kids contacted me? Jack was the only one who knew everything. I closed my eyes and pictured every move I'd made with the kids in Amarillo. I hadn't seen anyone following us. My mother had never known there were teenagers in our house. So how, how could someone have seen me with them in Amarillo? They couldn't have. They just couldn't have.

That left Jack. What if Jack had told someone? Even one person in passing would have been enough. It had to have been him, even if it was only an accident, it had to have been him. Because it sure wasn't me.

I answered: *Crazy! I'll call him.*

I stared at the phone. I had no idea what to say to Byron. In a text, I could evade his questions. A call was harder. Voice mail would be ideal, but he had to be expecting my call; he'd called on Christmas day. He'd be watching for my number.

My number. Not a random number. *That* was the answer. I'd call from a house phone. I looked around the room. No phone. Jack's bedroom down the hall might have one. There might be one in the kitchen or the office, but I didn't want to go back downstairs.

Spit.

I put my phone's ringer on silent and turned out the light. I slipped out the door and crept down the hall away from the staircase. Jack's door was closed, but his light was out. Holding my breath, I turned the handle even more carefully than I'd turned my own a few minutes before. I eased the door open a generous crack and ducked in, then repeated the silent shutting of the door and latch.

I exhaled. Using the flashlight on my phone, I searched the room. There, on the bedside table on the far side of the room was a phone. Tiptoeing, I reached it in seconds. I lifted it from its base, still using my phone as a light. I pressed the button to turn the house phone on and got a dial tone. I typed in the number from Byron's text and the phone started dialing, then ringing, although I could barely hear it over the pounding in my ears and my labored breaths. I hated lying. I was no good at it. If he answered, I'd hang up.

I heard the tone change in my ear as the two phones connected. I closed my eyes.

"You've reached my voice mail. Leave a message." Byron's voice. Short, uninformative.

I chose my words carefully, with my fingers crossed for good measure.

"Um, hi, this is Emily Bernal calling for Byron. Byron, I spoke to Wallace earlier. I wanted to assure you I don't have Greg and Farrah, and I can't imagine who would think I did, or why they'd call anonymously. I guess I have an enemy out there." I was babbling. I hated it when I babbled. It made me sound defensive, and ding-y. "I'm in New Mexico for Christmas. If you find them, please let me know, even through Wallace. I've been so worried about them. Thank you."

I pressed "off." I put the house phone back in the cradle, then I dropped my phone on the bed, where it landed flashlight up, and I lowered my face into my hands.

"That didn't sound good," a man's voice said from across the room.

I screamed and jumped back a good three feet. An eerie face watched me from a doorway across the room. The bathroom doorway, I realized. The man stepped forward, but I already knew who the voice belonged to. Jack. Which made sense, since I was in his bedroom.

I was in *his* bedroom. I flew over to the bed and snatched up my phone. "I'm sorry, I shouldn't be in here uninvited." I rushed around the bed for the door.

He intercepted me, catching me by the shoulders. "What's the matter?"

"Someone told Byron at CPS that I had Greg and Farrah, and only two people in Amarillo knew. You, and me. And it wasn't me."

"Huh."

That's all he had to say? My brain shorted out, and a blank white screen appeared where logical thought should be. I jerked away from his grasp. "Huh? I could lose my ability to adopt Betsy, and maybe even be charged with a crime. That's more than a 'huh.' At a minimum, it's an 'I'm sorry,' and then maybe you could throw in whether or not you may have caused it, and if you did, it would be nice to hear how it happened, too."

"Uh . . ." He looked at the floor between us.

Tears spilled, and I realized I was losing it, overreacting. Too much. It was all too much. "I'm sorry, I can't talk anymore. I need to be alone." I whirled and fled for my room.

CHAPTER 27

The next morning I was on my way to the stables by six o'clock, sleepy but determined, having left a heartbroken Snowflake in the kitchen instead of bringing her with me. The sun wouldn't rise for quite a while yet, but I doubted that I would be the first person out there. Sure enough, the doors were unlocked, and a light shone into the open space between the stalls on either side, emanating from Mickey's office. It was frigid outside and still really cold in the stable. I'd worn gloves, a wool cap, a scarf, and a heavy jacket, but I knew I'd still be freezing my tushy off for the next few hours. I exhaled, admiring my frosty breath, then knocked on the glass in Mickey's office door. Steam rose from a Purina coffee mug beside him. He looked up, his wide eyes registering surprise, and motioned me in.

"Good morning," I said.

"You're up early."

"And still not as early as you."

He laughed. "It's a holiday. I slept in."

I knew well the demands of rising early to care for animals. I missed a lot about my rodeo days, and sometimes I even missed this part: working alone before dawn, waking the animals, feeding them, being the one they relied on to care for them. I imagined it was a lot like having a baby. My "babies" had just weighed in over a thousand pounds each. A special bond forms in the dark, when you are the only one there, when they need you.

"I was hoping to take Jarhead or one of his friends out for a ride this morning. Would that be all right?"

"Jarhead would love it." He got to his feet. "Is Jack coming?"

"No, just me."

He stopped for a split second, his eyes raking my face, but I didn't let a flicker of emotion cross it. "Let me get you a saddle."

We walked together to the tack room next door. It smelled of leather and saddle soap, and I inhaled it greedily. "If you can point out what you're comfortable with me using, I can take it from there. I don't want to be a bother."

He hefted the saddle I'd ridden on during my last few rides from a wall peg, along with the Navajo blanket underneath it. He added a bridle. "Gives me a chance to talk to you. Grab that brush, will you?"

I picked up the soft-bristled brush he had indicated and followed him out. "So how have the kids done?" I asked.

Mickey set the gear on the ground outside a stall, and Jarhead stuck his nose out, snorting. Mickey put both his hands on the beautiful animal's bobbing face. "They've done well. Laura's the one I'm worried about."

"Laura? Why?"

He opened the stall door and slipped the bridle over Jarhead's ears, then the bit into his mouth. "She's getting attached. The kids need somebody, and she needs to be needed."

"Yeah. Those phones she gave them for Christmas—they seem like a long-term sort of gift." I rubbed the wood-handled brush over Jarhead's back with my right hand and ran my left over his supple flanks. His muscles quivered, and he turned to watch me.

Mickey patted Jarhead's neck. "She's taken Farrah under her wing. The girl loves horses."

I smiled. I could relate. "Anything special about this big fella today?" I kept brushing, working my way around to Jarhead's other side.

"Nah. He's had breakfast, but he's always fine after he eats, as long as you aren't planning on riding him to Alamogordo and back. You know he's a handful, of course."

"That's what I love about him."

Mickey positioned the blanket on Jarhead, swinging the saddle up to land perfectly in place. He pulled the strap through the cinch and tightened it, then pulled the whole rig back a little so it wasn't too close to Jarhead's elbow. Then he tightened the cinch again, a full inch more, and Jarhead snorted and tossed his head.

"He puffs out a little on the first go-round."

"Poor boy. But you don't want me hanging upside down under your belly, do you?" I let him sniff my hand and feel it with the sensitive whiskers on his muzzle. He nodded his head up and down. "Oh, you do? Fine." I laughed.

"Where you thinking about taking him?"

I stuck with mostly true. "Out to the highway and east. I want to expunge the demons from my wild midnight ride on Thunder."

Mickey puckered his lips up and nodded. "All right. Well, the weather is supposed to be fine. The snow cover isn't deep. Everyone is pastured on the west side right now, so I think you'll find most of the gates open and you can leave them that way. If any are closed, they're gonna be hard to manage in this cold, the wires tight. Do you have a phone in case of trouble?"

I patted his shoulder. "Yes, Mom."

"I'm not worried about you, Standing Hair, I'm talking about the moneymaker here."

We both laughed. Jarhead's stud fees were a large part of Wrong Turn Ranch's income. I led the moneymaker from the stall, and he started prancing.

Mickey pointed across the aisle. "You know who that is?"

A black horse stuck his entire neck out the window of his stall. If it was the horse I thought it was, I'd only seen him in the dark before. I walked Jarhead closer to him. The two horses protested at each other's nearness, and Mickey held out his hand. I gave him Jarhead's reins and walked the rest of the way to the black horse on my own.

"Thunder?" I asked.

"Yep."

"Hey, Thunder, remember me?" I rubbed his neck briskly as he sniffed to catch my scent. "Good to see you. You landed in high cotton here, didn't you?" I reached in my jacket pocket for my phone and snapped a selfie with him. For Betsy, later. I stroked his face one last time then moved on. I poked my head through the window of the next stall. A black mare and her knobby-kneed foal. "Is this little Hay-SEUSS?" I asked, pronouncing Jesus in my best Spanish.

The mare moved between the foal and me, blocking my view and pointing her hindquarters in my direction.

Mickey shook his head. "Yeah, and I'm afraid we're going to Hell over that one. But he sure is cute, and it made the kids happy to name him."

He was probably right about the Hell part. Mickey walked Jarhead and me to the door, and I grabbed the horn and reins in my left hand, put my left foot in the stirrup, and swung up and over, settling into the cold, hard saddle. It was a good fit.

"Thanks, Mickey. See you in two hours or so."

He shook his head. "One more thing. Do you have a weapon? The big coyotes get pretty crafty and hungry this time of year."

Under my jacket, I had worn a long purse strap across my chest for exactly this reason. I had money, ID, and my baby Glock tucked inside the little bag at the end of the strap. I even had coffee in the interior pocket of my coat, in a flask I'd found in Jack's kitchen.

I patted my stomach. "My father taught me well."

"About your dad."

I shook my head. "It's okay."

It was, even though *I* wasn't, and I sure didn't want to talk about it. I spent most of the night before tossing and turning, my thoughts back and forth between Dad, Betsy, Jack, Greg, and Farrah, with disturbing memories of Ivanka's bloodless face and the bloodied figure of the truck driver at Love's for good measure. I fretted over good cops and bad and how to know the difference. I obsessed about the potential trouble I was facing with CPS. And I worried about Alan spending Christmas in prison, when I was pretty sure he hadn't done what he was accused of doing. It had been easy to rise early for the ride, because I'd never really gone to sleep.

Jarhead hotfooted in place, eager to be off.

"Your father's a good guy. He talked about you a lot. I hope . . ." Mickey trailed off.

"Really, it's okay."

He nodded and lifted his hand in salute.

I held Jarhead to a walk through the grounds and first gate, then let him warm up in a fretful trot. Patience wasn't his strong suit. By the second gate, he was loping. And by the fourth gate, I gave him his head and let him race his imaginary opponents all the way to the highway.

We crossed over the pavement and onto Johnson's Ranch. As Judith had said, the gate was padlocked. I trotted Jarhead along the front fence line to the east. In about 150 yards, we found a wire loop gate like the ones we'd ridden through on Jack's place. Mickey was right, these things were tight in the cold. But I managed to work the loop up and over the post, and we were in. From there it wasn't that long a ride up to the house and the outbuildings. By the time we reached them, I needed to walk Jarhead for a cool down and find him some water, which I found in an automatic watering tub by the barn. A pump ran continuously, circulating the water, so there was no ice. Jarhead slurped noisily, and water dripped from his muzzle to the cold ground, melting the snow. My phone made a noise so I pulled it out.

There was a text from Nadine to Wallace and me: *The dancer who was being harassed is MISSING. Everyone freaked.*

I replied to my friend: *Oh no, be careful, Nadine. Scary!*

Another dancer, after cops harassed her. Missing. Maybe dead. What was happening to my safe, sleepy hometown? I had worried Ivanka's death was connected to Love's, but was it something else, something worse?

I put the phone away. "Now what?" I asked Jarhead.

"I guess you could start by explaining what the hell you're doing here," a man's voice answered.

I slipped my hand into my jacket and into my open purse, closing my fingers around the Glock's grip, then swiveled my head to see who was speaking. A tall, unsmiling man with pock-marked brown skin faced me. He was dressed in jeans with a heavy brown work jacket and cowboy boots. Like Mickey had been wearing that morning. Like practically every man in this part of the world.

His expression changed when he saw my face. "Ma'am." He dipped his head at me. "Nice horse. Sorry if I startled you."

"Thank you. I didn't think anyone was here."

I took my fingers off the gun and slid my hand out. The feel of the baby Glock's grip had grown mighty familiar in the last week. It made me think of my dad, and I didn't want to think about him.

"Only me. Edward Brown, Alamogordo Police. And you are?"

I shook off the thoughts of my father. I'd met this man, although at the time he was dressed in his Sunday best.

"Emily Bernal. Did I meet you at St. Joseph's last weekend? I was there with the Begays and Jack Holden."

He smiled. "Yes, I recognize you now. You look a little different." He pointed at his head.

My head and hair were entirely covered by my cap. My purple scarf obscured my chin. "It's pretty chilly out."

He raised his eyebrows, stretching and flattening the pits in his face. "It is. And early, on the day after Christmas. What brings you out here?"

"Mostly trying to shake demons. I had a bad experience here."

His gaze didn't flicker. "I'm aware of that, of course. I'm sorry about what you went through."

"It's okay. I'm recovering. And a lot of good has come from that night."

"It certainly has. You will be forever revered as a merciful angel by the people Johnson held here."

I swallowed. I hadn't ever really thought of it that way. "I hope you guys find them all. The women and children, I mean." The authorities surmised that Johnson had sold them to the highest bidders, to the kind of people that liked their play things disposable and anonymous. I shivered. Thank God Betsy had avoided that fate.

Brown shook his head. "Me, too."

Brown seemed nice, and helpful, and I decided to take a chance on him with the truth. "The little girl who escaped with me, Betsy—"

"Elizabet Perez."

It warmed me that he knew the case so well. And with so many victims, he remembered Betsy's name. That was good. "Yes. She lost her backpack, and she's been quite upset about it. The last place she saw it was here. I was hoping that I could look in some windows, see if I can find it."

"I'd be happy to take you through the place, but don't get your hopes up."

"Why?"

"Most of the stuff here ended up in evidence or with Johnson's daughter."

"Stella?"

"Yes. And then some of it disappeared."

"What do you mean, disappeared?" I rubbed my arms. Now that neither Jarhead nor I were exerting ourselves, it really *was* getting cold. The horse snorted and stamped, and I knew he felt it, too.

"I mean it looks like the place got picked over. It's been empty for the last six weeks, and sometimes that happens. I like to drop by occasionally for that reason. Keep an eye on things, keep away the thieves, vandals, or squatters."

Like Wrong Turn Ranch across the road. So the thieves had hit more than one ranch in the area. Mickey and Jack hadn't reported it, though, so I kept it to myself. "That's awful."

"It is. So, you want to look around?"

"If you honestly don't mind, I would. And maybe I could let my horse warm up inside while we do it?"

He nodded and pulled out a ring of keys. I followed him into the barn. I'd been inside it once before, unfortunately. We passed the open door to the room where I'd been held against my will, where I first met Betsy. In my memory it was a dark room filled with clutter. Today it was bare except for the swath of dim light across the floor from the high, narrow window. Chill bumps rose on my arms under my layers of clothing.

"You can tie him up here," Brown said, indicating a fat post in the center of the open area that extended all the way to the roof.

All I had on Jarhead was a bridle. Flat leather reins didn't tie well, and they tied short at that. I had on a stylin' web belt though, with a double ring in lieu of a buckle. I looped the belt around the post, then tied the reins to the end of it. That gave Jarhead enough room to move his head.

I patted his flanks. "Back soon, boy."

Brown gestured around the barn. "Do you want to look in here?"

I surveyed the mostly empty space. The only things left in the room were rejects: a flat tire, half a long-handled rake, a pile of mulch, a broken syringe. Whoever had burglarized this place had done a very thorough job. It was disheartening, in light of my search, and more than a little eerie. But I was accompanied by a police officer, one who went way back with Jack and Mickey, and I would be fine. I couldn't give up before I'd even started. I owed it to Betsy.

"Lead the way," I said.

CHAPTER 28

Four hours later, I was showered, safe, warm, and piloting Jack's Suburban toward Alamogordo in sunlight made twice as bright by its reflection off the snow. Jack and Collin had vanished, so I had left Jack a note back at the house.

I borrowed the Suburban. Ava's with me. I'm showing her around and taking her to eat. We'll be back by midafternoon, unless I hear from you that you need us or the vehicle sooner. ~ E

Ava had stayed glued to my side since my return from Johnson's Ranch, pumping me for information on the intrigue going on around her. Over donuts and coffee at Yum-Yum's in Tularosa, I had finally gotten her up-to-date on almost everything: Betsy, Alan, the hush-hush situation with Greg and Farrah, dead people, my arrest, and even my now-ex-husband and Jack. Ava actively participated in stories, so it took a long time, even the short version. I had made it all the way in my narrative to my early morning excursion across the highway, which I was telling her about as I drove and she drank her second cup of coffee.

"Turn left to merge onto US 70 South," Siri's robotic voice commanded.

I obeyed. "Okay, so you know I went for a ride this morning?"

"Yah mon."

I smiled over at Ava. A wide zebra-print headband held her hair back from her lovely face. She'd tamed her curls into long waves, but it still had the volume of lion's mane, and she hadn't skimped on the eyeliner and lipstick. She dressed in her version of conservative wear for our excursion, which meant fabric covered all her skin, even if it was still fuchsia Lycra.

Her spike-heeled, zippered black leather boots were the final detail to an ensemble that guaranteed she would not blend in the crowd today.

"I love hearing that accent," I said.

"Well, we don't want to Yank and sound flat and nasal like everyone else, do we?" she said, in a perfect parody of a Midwestern accent. The Virgin Islanders called stateside accents "Yank" talk, and Ava could switch in and out of her accents in mid-sentence.

"Even my Texas accent sounds foreign in these parts," I drawled.

She switched back to her normal speaking voice. "So, lady, tell me 'bout you ride this morning."

"I took Jarhead across the road to the ranch where Betsy was held hostage. I wanted to see if I could find a backpack that means a lot to her. The place was locked up, but one of the Alamogordo cops that's working the case was out there."

"At god-awful early in the morning? Why?"

"Checking up on the place, I think. Anyway, he took me through all the buildings to search for it."

I set the cruise to seventy-five miles per hour and glanced in the rearview mirror at the lonely road behind me. Almost lonely. A big, dark blue sedan of some type had kept pace a few hundred yards back since we turned onto 70. It was still there. Odd. Would anyone have reason to follow us? And then I remembered Byron's call. It wasn't out of the question.

"You go in a deserted house with a strange man? Girl, you crazy."

"He was a police officer." Which didn't necessarily mean much. "He was nice."

"Nice? He probably looking at your bana then."

"No! He wasn't like that."

She chuptzed. "All men like that. Some just more sneaky."

I laughed.

"Hey, what that thing rolling by the side of the road?" She pointed at a tumbling mass of leafless bush.

"That's a tumbleweed."

"Those things real? And it moving fast. Even in the winter?"

"Year round. The wind out here is fierce."

I hadn't even noticed the tumbleweed until she mentioned it. Some things became part of the landscape after a while. Ava did have a way of making me smile.

She stared out the window, shaking her head. "This a strange place." She looked back at me. "Go on with you story."

"Okay, so where was I? Oh yeah, the cop let me search, but the place—the ranch house and outbuildings—had been picked clean."

"Thieves like rob Jack's place?"

"Just like. Although I'm sure some things went with the daughter and others into evidence first."

Her accent thickened and her voice rose in pitch. "You tell Collin and he 'bout robbers dem across the way?" Dem after a noun was a form of island pluralization, although redundant in some cases, like this one.

"They were gone when I got back."

"You best call."

She was right. "When we stop."

"Where we going, anyway?"

"The police say they don't have Betsy's backpack. I couldn't find it at the ranch. And since I can't ask the robbers, that leaves the daughter, Stella, as the next person to ask about it." I turned to her. "So that's where we're headed. To visit Stella."

"She know we coming?"

"She does. I found her on Facebook and messaged her."

Ava drained her coffee and set the empty cup in the holder in the console. She dug in her purse and came out with a lipstick, then applied fresh fuchsia and pressed her lips together several times.

"I ready," she announced.

Siri directed us the rest of the way to Stella's new abode, with me checking the rearview frequently for a tail. I saw the blue sedan behind me a few more times, but when we made the last turn toward Stella's, it went straight, and I breathed a sigh of relief. It felt safer to be in a residential neighborhood, with people all around. Not that it was the best neighborhood in town. It was mostly inexpensive apartments, although a few complexes were fairly new.

I parked at the curb and texted Jack: *I ran into Edward Brown this morning.* I left out the details. *He said Paul Johnson's ranch got robbed. Thought you should know.*

As if texting him had summoned messages from the heavens, another came in. Byron.

I turned my phone over as if the sight of it would blind me. "Spit."

Ava looked up from her own phone, where her fingers had been flying. "Did you just say 'spit'?"

I ignored the question. "That CPS investigator that thinks I took the teenage kids is texting me again."

She arched her brows. "Well, you did, right?"

I ignored her again and read the text aloud. "Thanks for your voice mail. I would still like to talk. Please call when you can." Well, I couldn't possibly until Monday at the earliest, could I? That would be my story, anyway, and I'd stick to it. "Doesn't sound like they're sending the po-po after me yet. Ready?"

"Born that way."

We got out of the car and headed up the sidewalk. Stella had lived the high life with her father, but her maternal grandmother, it appeared, didn't provide the same standard of living. These apartments were okay—nice for the neighborhood, anyway—but still low rent compared to Stella's old lifestyle. We walked through rock and cactus landscaping to the security panel. I pressed the buzzer for Unit 1222, which Stella had sent me via text. Someone buzzed us in without checking to see who we were. We scurried through the gate. No surprise, stucco covered the walls of the complex for an adobe look, here and on the outside, too. Inside, the apartments ringed an oval pool, which had a winter cover and a layer of snow on it. It looked barren with the large apron of concrete around it empty. Stella's unit faced one of the narrow ends of the pool.

I rang the doorbell.

From inside, a female voice answered. "It's open."

Stella was prone on a leather sofa in front of the boob tube and didn't rise to greet us. The length of her body and the way it draped across the couch hinted at her height. The scent of patchouli hinted at weed, but I didn't notice any other evidence of pot. She wore a gray hoodie and drawstring sweat pants that had stains across the front, and her hip bones jutted above the fabric. She'd tucked her hair inside the hoodie, which held it away from her head, but it still poked out the sides of the front, covering some of her blanket of freckles. I remembered that hair, that improbable and amazing afro of hair.

"Sit anywhere," she said.

"Hi, Stella. Is your grandmother here?"

"No. She's addicted to bingo." Her eyes cut to Ava then back to me. "Who's she?"

"This is Ava, my friend from the Virgin Islands."

Stella's eyes narrowed. "For real? The Virgin Islands?"

"Yah mon. I visiting New Mexico. Albuquerque next week. Hoping to make it up to Santa Fe and Taos after that." Santa Fe and Taos were news to me.

Stella nodded. "That's pretty cool."

My jaw nearly dropped. This was the fourth time I'd been in Stella's presence and she'd never said so much as "boo" to me before, but apparently Ava was pretty cool. Well, maybe I could use her approval of Ava to my advantage in this conversation. I started by upping Ava's coolness quotient even further.

"Ava's a singer. She's here doing shows."

Stella sat up. "That's *really* cool."

"Well, I away from my baby too long gigging, and the money shit, but I guess it cool."

I noticed her accent had thickened. I wanted to hug her. *Go, Ava.*

"Oh, you have a baby, too?" Stella's voice took on a longing tone. How old was she, anyway, that she had baby fever? Seventeen? Far too young.

"Yah, she a beauty. Hard work, though."

"I play guitar. And sing a little. I'm auditioning for a band after New Year's. An all chicks kind of thing."

I jumped in. "Good luck. You'd look amazing on a stage. Exotic."

Another hungry look toward Ava. "You think so?"

Ava, the professional, nodded. "For true."

Stella's features softened. Maybe she was younger than I'd thought. "Thank you."

I smiled at her. "You're welcome. And I'm really sorry about all this with your dad."

A frown pinched her face. "I hate that douchebag. I hope he rots in prison the rest of his life."

I couldn't argue with her about what a horrible person her dad was, but Mother taught me that if you can't say anything nice, you shouldn't say anything at all, so I didn't. "I want you to know that you probably saved my life, and Betsy's, and I appreciate it."

Stella had played guardian angel to the immigrant children in the families her father had trafficked, dressing up like the Clown from the Apache Mountain Spirit Dancers. It had added some magic to their hard lives.

I added, "You make an awesome Mountain Spirit Dancer."

"They're real, you know. The Mountain Spirits." Stella looked at me with narrowed, defensive eyes.

"Oh?"

"Yeah. I've seen them."

I'd seen one myself, on the runway as Jack came for Betsy and me in the Skyhawk. The Apache spirit had saluted me, and I him.

Softly, my back to Ava, I said, "Me, too."

Stella nodded gravely.

"Betsy said to tell you hello."

Stella's face lit up, and she was beautiful, without warning. "Tell her hello for me. She's cute."

"Yes, she is. I hope to adopt her."

Again, the hungry look. "That would be awesome for her."

"She deserves some awesome. Losing her mom and her dad, being alone in a strange place."

Stella's eyes clouded. "Yeah."

I knew she could relate. I didn't know why her mother wasn't in the picture, but she hadn't been as long as I'd known the girl. Stella was one grandmother away from Greg and Farrah's circumstances, from what I could tell.

Out of the corner of my eye, I noticed that Ava was texting and smiling, oblivious to our conversation. That was okay. I knew I could pull her back in if I needed her. Right now, Stella and I were rolling.

"Betsy lost something important to her at the ranch. A pink backpack. She never went anywhere without it," I said to Stella.

"I remember it."

"Do you remember seeing it after everything went down? After you helped me rescue her?"

Ava giggled, and we both looked at her. She noticed and said, "Oh, sorry. Message." She held up her phone then lowered it and started typing again.

Stella raised her brows toward Ava but continued. "Yeah. I saw it in Dad's barn office, you know, when that police guy let me go through and take all the stuff that was mine or special."

My heart leapt. Hope. The backpack had been there after Johnson was arrested. "Do you know what happened to it?"

"Nah. I left it there. I'm sorry. I was getting my stuff."

I allowed myself a moment of intense frustration. Jack and I had made multiple requests for the backpack through the task force, and we'd left messages for individual officers working the case. We'd called and left a voice mail on the phone out at the ranch. The task force said they didn't have it, which I now believed, since Stella had seen it after the evidence collection was finished. But why hadn't the officers called us back? It was there. All they would have had to do was tell us and someone from Wrong Turn Ranch could have run across the street and picked it up. And now? It could be anywhere, with anyone, or nowhere at all. I wouldn't think that it had any value except to Betsy, but who knew what drove some people to take things that weren't theirs? Once my backpack had been stolen when thieves broke into my car at Tech. All they'd gotten was spiral notebooks, loose change, a few pens, and a chicken salad sandwich I'd forgotten to eat that day. I hope they got food poisoning from it, I really do.

I covered my frustration with a smile. "Hey, you didn't know we were looking for it. No problem."

The doorbell rang again. Stella frowned. "Who's there?"

"Manny." The voice from outside the door sounded guttural and demanding, even in only that one word.

"Just a minute." Her eyes flew wide and she whispered, "Oh shit. I look awful."

"Who's Manny?"

"This guy . . ." She jumped up. "I've got to go change."

Ava put a hand on her hip. "Hold up."

"Yes?"

"Did you know that boy coming?"

"Uh, no, uh—"

"Don't you go jumping to please him when he not even man enough to call first. Tell him you got plans. Make him work a little. You worth it."

Stella looked at me. I nodded.

"But, what if he doesn't come back?" she said.

Ava chuptzed. "Then he garbage." The way she said GAHR-bahj and drew out the second syllable made her pronouncement gospel.

Stella went to the door. She looked back at Ava. "That's what you'd do?"

"Yah mon. For true."

Stella opened the door to the end of the security chain. A guy too old for her with greasy hair and a hooked scar on his cheek pushed at the door. "Let me in, Stell."

She licked her lips. "Sorry, Manny, I have some girls over. Friends of my father. Call me later?"

His face darkened. "What's that shit? I'm busy later."

She sucked in a wavery breath, shot another look at Ava, who threw her hands in the air with an exaggerated roll of her eyes and head shake. I wasn't sure how Ava managed to do everything she did at once, but it worked.

"Sorry, Manny. Another time." Stella closed the door, over his "What the fuck?" protestation.

"Good." Ava marched over to the girl and hugged her. Stella towered over Ava by a good six inches. "Now, Emily and I taking you to lunch. You way too skinny."

CHAPTER 29

After we dropped off a chattering, smiley Stella—whose head was now crammed with advice on men, music, and motherhood from her new idol Ava—I parked to check my phone. I noticed Ava's flying fingers and that telltale grin again.

"Okay, who has you lit up like a firecracker? I asked.

Ava didn't raise her head. "Some guy."

"Does he have a name?"

She stopped and peered at me. "Emily, I your friend, right?"

I caught my breath. "Yes, of course."

"Friends don't let friends wear that hair. We fixing you up once we back at the ranch."

"What?"

Ava pointed at the crown of her forehead. "That. We fixing that, and you can thank me later."

I liked my bangs. I touched them with my fingertips. I hated when they hugged my head like a greasy cap. I wanted them light and fluffy off my forehead. I looked at my friend in her tight, loud outfit.

"The only way you're touching my hair is if you let me make over your wardrobe," I retorted.

Ava snorted and went back to her texting. I realized too late she'd probably been trying to distract me. At least I hoped that was it. A dark blue sedan drove by, and I did a double take. I tried to decide if it was the same one from earlier, but I couldn't tell for sure. I'd completely forgotten to look for it on the way to and from lunch.

Smarting and jumpy, I scrolled my own notifications. Jack, from an hour and a half before: *Interesting. Helpful. Collin working on this today, w/license plate photo.*

I answered him: *Good. Ava & I took Stella to lunch. She saw Betsy's backpack in barn office after evidence collected!! Gone now though.* I added a little frowny face.

Almost as soon as I'd hit send, my phone rang. I jumped. *Please don't be Byron, please don't be Byron, please don't be Byron.* And it wasn't.

"Hello?"

"It's me." Which my phone had already told me.

"Hi, Jack."

"Good news."

"What's that?"

"Collin has tied the license plate from your photo to a driver who lives outside Alamogordo."

"Why am I not surprised?"

"He wants to drop in on the guy."

"Are we invited?"

Collin's voice boomed, and I realized we were on speaker. I hit speaker, too. "Not officially, but I've been told I'm not very observant, so if other people are there when I drop by, I might not even notice them. Besides, Emily, you might be able to help identify him."

Jack said, "We called the guy's house and he's home. We're on our way there now."

"Text me the address and we'll meet you."

"See you there."

I hung up. "Heck yeah!"

"That the best you can cuss?" Ava shook her head. "Girl, you got no game."

"I got plenty of game. We're about to get to watch Collin roust a smuggler, all because of *my* game."

"Forget your game and get back to the rousting part. Actual sexy cop shit like on TV, that kind of rousting?"

"Exactly like that."

She grabbed her lipstick and brandished it like a sword. "Better move this bucket of bolts before I get out and push."

I threw the Suburban into park ten minutes later in the bare front yard/parking lot next to the front steps of a glorified mobile home. Almost simultaneously, a vintage green and white Ford Bronco on jacked-up wheels backed in beside us. I recognized the heads in it. Collin was at the wheel, and Jack on the passenger side.

"Whose car that?" Ava breathed.

"It looks like maybe it's Collin's."

"That so fine." She gave her lipstick another swipe and her girls a boost.

I laughed, because the classic SUV was fine, but I'd have never expected Ava to think so. We got out and the guys came around and met us. I hadn't forgotten I was upset with Jack, but he caught my gaze and smiled at me and a little ice in my heart melted. He was trying. It didn't make it any easier to stay mad at him that he had on my favorite blue plaid flannel shirt with his lived-in Wranglers and boots as old as the Bronco in front of us. His hair had gotten a little on the long side—dark, curling at the tips—and his skin had darkened since yesterday. Why did he have to look so good when he'd been so wrong?

Collin grinned. "Yo, ladies, you ready to play good cop?"

Ava wriggled a little and made some funny noise that I tried to block out. I was immune to Collin with his full swagger on.

"What's the plan?" I asked, without rolling my eyes.

"I'll tell him I've received a complaint of a hit-and-run with his license plate number. You three are my witnesses, but you need to wait in the Suburban. Be seen and not heard, unless I ask you a question. Then go with a simple headshake or nod. At most an 'uh-uh' or an 'uh-huh.' Got it?"

The glare off the snow reflected into my eyes, even through my sunglasses. I added a hand shield. "How will we hear?"

"Roll down your window. Hopefully he'll come outside." He winked at Ava. "I can be very persuasive."

Ava purred. "I sure you can."

"All right, enough of that," I said. "I'm feeling like I stumbled into the back booths in an adult video shop."

Collin laughed. He pointed at the Suburban and the three of us went back to it. I deferred to Jack for the driver's seat since it was his vehicle and sat behind him, window down.

The white house in front of us sat on a barren piece of land, three acres or so, with a fenced area behind it. To call it a house upgraded it a little more than it deserved, although someone had added a small wooden front porch and steps and skirted the entire unit with lattice. Whoever it was needed to come back with a hammer and some paint. A corner of the lattice flapped in the wind. Pieces of trash had woven their way into the lattice itself.

Collin walked up the steps. Despite the sun, temperatures still hung below twenty-five degrees, according to the Suburban's display. The wind blew at roughly tornado speed in a straight line instead of a circle. In the lee of the house the Suburban was sheltered from it a little. Still, the lattice vibrated in the wind, and the whole house shuddered. How it hadn't blown away in the wind already was anybody's guess.

Collin knocked on the storm door three times, hard enough to rattle the glass.

Seconds later, the door opened. An Asian-looking woman in a sweater of peacock colors poked her upper body out, her movements jerky. Barely five feet, she looked like a little hummingbird, and I was afraid the wind would grab her if she stepped any farther out the door.

"What do you want?" Her accent made her English hard to understand.

"Hello, ma'am. My name is Collin Connell and I'm here to see Ricky Brewer. Is he your husband?"

She nodded.

"I see his truck is home, Mrs. Brewer." Collin pointed at the tractor rig I hadn't even noticed earlier protruding in front of the far side of the house. "Would you ask him to come out and speak to me, please?"

"Why?"

Collin pulled out his wallet and flipped it open to his New Mexico State Police badge. "State Police business, ma'am, but nothing to worry about. I need to ask him a few questions."

Her eyes drilled over to the Suburban and into each of us in rapid succession, sharp and hostile. "Wait here." She shut the storm door and the inner door behind her. Thirty seconds passed. I heard a car driving by and glanced out at the road. Blue sedan. Too far away to confirm whether it was one I'd seen earlier, but the coincidence was becoming too big to ignore. I prayed Byron hadn't notified the local CPS to have me tailed. It was unlikely they'd follow me onto the private roads on Jack's property, though, so—while nerve-wracking—the kids would remain hidden and safe. I hoped.

The door reopened. My adrenaline surged. A man stepped out. Short. Skinny. Dark-skinned with jet-black hair standing up on one side. He rubbed his swollen eyes.

Collin flipped his wallet open again. "Collin Connell, NMSP. Are you Ricky Brewer?"

The man grunted.

"I'll take that as a yes. We've had a complaint against your tractor for a hit-and-run, and I need to ask to see your logbook, sir."

Brewer crossed his arms. "Not me. I didn't do no hit-and-run."

"Well, the reason I'm here, sir, is that the citizens who reported it gave me your license plate number." Collin's demeanor suddenly shifted. "So, you can show me the log here, or I can arrest you and we can talk about this at the district offices."

"Arrest me? What's my offense when I ain't done nothing?"

Collin crossed his arms. His upper body looked forbidding, and his heavy winter coat added to his bulk. "It's whatever I say it is. Sir."

Brewer stared at him, rotated glances over at us like his wife had, then stared at Collin again. The wind howled around the house. Beside me, Ava shivered.

"All right. Wait here."

Brewer disappeared.

Ava leaned toward the backseat and whispered to me. "I gettin' hot."

"Take off your jacket."

She gave a mini-chuptz. "Not that kind of hot."

I half-groaned. "You're the most overtaxed person I've ever met."

Without turning his head, Jack said, "Don't you mean oversexed?"

"That's what I said," I lied.

Ava shrugged. "Everybody gotta be best at something."

Jack made a choking noise, then coughed. I looked at him in the rearview mirror and saw he was laughing.

The door opened and Ava sucked in her breath.

Brewer had donned a coat, and he carried a ledger. He shut the doors behind him this time. Right in front of us, I saw the blinds part, and the eyes and nose of his wife appear in the gap, like a beak.

"Here," Brewer said, thrusting the ledger at Collin.

Collin took the book from him and flipped pages. "Hmm." He flipped more slowly. "Umm." He stopped, turned the book toward Brewer. "This here says you carried a load to"—he rotated it back to himself, then to Brewer—"Amarillo. Construction materials, I guess, because right here you wrote 'Top Hat Construction.' Who'd you carry it for?"

Brewer grunted, pointing.

"Ah, Allied Distributing. Down in Las Cruces." Collin turned the book around, studied it. "Did you backhaul?"

Brewer grunted again, pointed again.

"Contracted a load from Owens Corning back here. Gotcha."

Brewer cleared his throat. "What's this got to do with a hit-and-run, and them folks there?" This time he gestured with his head instead of his finger.

"I'll ask the questions." Collin slammed the book shut. "Does this book represent all your jobs, all your driving, all your pickups, all your drop-offs?"

"Yup."

"Let me show you something." Collin pulled his phone out of his jeans pocket. He typed in something, scrolled through screens, then turned the phone to face Brewer. "Is that your rig?"

Brewer frowned and leaned toward the phone. Leaned back. "Yup."

"Do you recognize where this picture was taken?"

He leaned in again, his forehead lines scrunched. He licked his lips. "Can't say."

"Do you know when it was taken?"

Brewer's chin jutted out. "If I don't know where, how am I s'posed to know when?"

"So you 'can't say'?"

Brewer nodded. "Can't say."

"I can. That picture was taken in an alley behind ABC Half-Price Resale in Amarillo where the photographer had watched you unload stolen goods, Monday, December twenty-first, at about five thirty in the afternoon. I got the shop owner can testify to that, and the person behind the camera that took this picture. Two witnesses, against you. Does that help you say?"

Brewer didn't answer.

"Your log on the twenty-first doesn't mention ABC Half-Price Resale. That alone is a nice-sized fine, isn't it? Falsifying a log?" Collin handed the book back to Brewer. "But honestly, I don't give a shit about your log. I don't even necessarily give a shit about *you* trafficking stolen goods. I could probably convince the DA not to give a shit either."

Brewer stared at Collin, who remained silent. Ava reached for my hand. I gave it to her, and she squeezed it, hard. As the seconds dragged on, I wiggled my toes, hoping for feeling in them and a quick resolution to Brewer's dilemma.

Finally, Brewer broke. "How?"

"By giving the DA something better than one pissant shipment."

"But that's all I got. I only did that one."

Collin coughed into his hand as he said, "Bullshit. Give me the address where you picked up the stuff you dropped at ABC Half-Price Resale, and the name of your contact, and I'll plead your case to the DA."

Brewer wiped his forehead. "You wouldn't tell who said? Because snitching's likely to get a man killed."

"Nobody that wouldn't need to know."

"When do I have to decide?"

"Five fucking minutes ago, padnuh." Collin pulled out his cuffs. "Time to read you your Miranda rights." He snapped the cuffs onto one of Brewer's wrists. "Ricky Brewer, you are under arrest for smuggling stolen property. You have the right to—"

"Wait." Brewer's eyes were wide and darting toward the window where his wife still took in the whole scene. "Wait."

Collin finished the Miranda warning and pulled Brewer around and pushed his face against his front door, snapping the cuff around the other wrist behind his back as he did. "I'm not feeling it, Mr. Brewer. I'm just not feeling it."

"We can work something out."

Collin gave the cuffs a tug, pulling Brewer upright. "Let's take a ride." As they walked down the steps, he called out, "Jack, can you drive so I can sit in the back and chat with Mr. Brewer?"

Jack exited the Suburban and held his hand out. Collin dropped his keys in them. Texas Rangers key ring. I smiled. You can take the boy out of Texas and all that.

My eyes followed the three men toward the Bronco. From the backseat, I was even with the bumper and for the first time registered the macabre sight at the front end. A scream came out of my mouth before I could clap my gloved hand over it.

Jack turned in a circle, looking for the source of my vocal horror. "What is it?"

I pointed at the Bronco. A large bird was impaled on its front grille, stretched out in full run, beak open, wings out. It was grisly. Ava jumped out to see for herself, and she screamed, too.

Without cracking a smile, Jack said, "Score one for Wile E. Coyote."

Collin kept a straight face and tight grip on Brewer, but he turned his head toward the Suburban. "Anybody hungry?"

Jack and I laughed. Ava didn't.

"What is that horrible thing?" she asked.

Jack answered her. "Roadrunner."

"Fast little fuckers," Collin said. "I don't remember us hitting anything."

"You could've been driving around with a hood ornament for days," I suggested.

Ava laughed as she backed up to the passenger door of the Suburban and climbed back in. Collin pushed Brewer's head down and loaded him in the Bronco, then climbed in the other side. Seconds later, Jack saluted me as he pulled the vehicle away toward Alamogordo.

CHAPTER 30

When I'd finished checking to be sure that I hadn't heard from Byron or Wallace, I put my keys in the ignition. "Well, that was something you don't get to see every day."

Ava gathered her hair in one hand off her neck and fanned with the other. "Wouldn't mind if I did."

She was dramatic. Incorrigible. And she cheered me up, distracting me from all the screwed-up things going on.

I backed out, then put the Suburban in drive. "You're the guest. Do you want to explore, shop, go back to the ranch, or what?"

Before Ava could answer, a dirty Monte Carlo hurtled around us. Mrs. Brewer peered over the steering wheel—barely. She veered onto the shoulder on the left, spewing snow and gravel from her wheels as she did. Ava and I swiveled our heads in tandem to watch her. Mrs. Brewer corrected the vehicle and pulled in front of us, accelerating.

"She in a hurry."

"Like maybe she's going for help?"

"Or to tattle." Ava chuptzed.

We grinned at each other.

"Wanna see which?" I asked.

"Heck yeah," Ava drawled, with a smirk, and I laughed. She impersonated me perfectly.

I pulled within a hundred yards of Mrs. Brewer's car. Its exhaust alone made it easy to follow, even though the white car blended against the snow-covered terrain on either side of the road. Soon, though, we were passing through Alamogordo on the highway. She wove in and out of traffic with no blinker, ten miles faster than the flow. I bit my lip as I changed lanes repeatedly, trying to keep up with her, yet keeping my eye out for a disturbing blue sedan behind me. Our path reminded me of pole bending, a rodeo event I competed in as a kid where you race a horse through a series of six poles in a serpentine pattern, then back again. It was a lot like slalom skiing. And like following Mrs. Brewer.

"She getting away."

I gripped the steering wheel harder. "Not if I can help it."

On the south side of town, the Monte Carlo accelerated. I pressed the gas to pace her. Eighty. Eight-five. Almost ninety. Ava held on to the armrest and the door grip like they were anchors. The Suburban's frame shook. I scanned the dash. We were in four-wheel drive. The snow had disappeared south of town, as if we'd passed a line of demarcation, so I wasn't worried about traction, but I couldn't remember if it was okay to change out of all-wheel on the fly, only that it wasn't recommended for high-speed driving. Hopefully I wouldn't wreck the transmission. I kept my foot pressed down hard. I didn't smell anything burning or see any smoke, and those were good signs.

We passed a highway sign that said LAS CRUCES, 50, EL PASO, 102, CIUDAD JUAREZ, 110.

"We almost to Mexico?" Ava shrieked. "Where she going, anyway?"

"Hopefully not there."

Suddenly, the Monte Carlo turned off the highway into the parking lot of a cluster of flat-roofed warehouse-like buildings. Faded signage out front indicated the property was for sale, although I couldn't tell if it referred to the whole group, or only to one of the buildings. A handful of cars were parked without any regard to linear spacing. We were far enough behind the Monte Carlo to see it pull in at an angle in front of the nearest building. Mrs. Brewer got out, and then we were past her.

Ava's head did a *Fourth Kind* owl move, nearly. "She went in," Ava said. "What now?"

"Let's drive for a few minutes, then we can turn around and see if she's still there when we make it back. Keep doing it until she leaves. Then maybe we can check it out."

Ava nodded. "We make good cops."

"Jack doesn't think so. He hates it when I investigate things on my own."

She chuptzed. "He just jealous of real talent."

I laughed. "And there's no law against it." Well, there were laws against some of the things I'd done in the course of checking things out. Like letting myself into a few homes where I wasn't technically invited.

But I only did that when there were extenuating circumstances, like people's lives at risk. Even if that wasn't a defense in court, it sure helped me sleep better at night.

I took the next exit and we reversed course back toward Alamogordo.

When the warehouse was in sight, Ava said, "She still there."

"Yeah, let's make another loop."

As we passed the cluster of warehouses from the south, I noticed a cross in the window of the last one and in plain block letters above the door, CHURCH. A sign in one window read EXORCISE DAILY. RUN FROM THE DEVIL. And in the next window: SEXUAL EXPLOITATION WORKSHOP THIS SUNDAY. My eyes widened.

"That woman need to hurry. I gotta pee."

I shook off the oddly disturbing church signs. "How are you going to be a cop if you can't hold it on a stakeout, or when you're following someone?"

"Where I come from, if you drive as far as we have, you reach the end of the island and stop for rum and Coke."

I mimicked Ava's accent, badly. "For true."

She shook her head and drawled, "Not even close, cowgirl," nailing mine again.

We stopped at a Love's on the outskirts of town, which got me to thinking about Greg and Farrah. Which made me think about Byron. Which made me think of Ivanka. Which made me think of the missing dancer. *Stop it,* I told myself. *Just stop it.*

I decided to take a pit stop, and, afterwards, I bought a sweet tea. While waiting to pay, I stared at my phone. My anger from the night before had nearly gone away. I didn't want to be crossways with Jack. I wanted things to be like they had been on Christmas Eve. I worried my swollen hangnail with my teeth then typed a message to him: *I'm sorry I got so upset last night. Maybe we can talk later and I can give you your Christmas present.*

Ava read over my shoulder. "Ah, you getting soft."

I hit send and handed the clerk my money. "I may have overreacted, but I'm still not completely okay with him hiding my father from me." A father I hadn't called back. I'd decided to block it out until I returned to Amarillo. I'd decide whether to call him then.

We walked out together.

"That ain't gonna keep you warm at night, is it?"

I pointed my drink at a white Monte Carlo at a pump on our far right, ignoring her last question. "That's Mrs. Brewer."

We sprinted the rest of the way to the Suburban—or, rather, trotted as fast as Ava's heels and my sloshing drink allowed—and jumped in.

I craned to see the Monte Carlo. "I don't think she's in it. Maybe she's in the store."

Ava looked, too. "Don't see her."

"Let's get out of here."

I exited the Love's lot on the side farthest from Mrs. Brewer's car and turned back onto the access road, whipping a U-turn under the overpass, then accelerating up an entrance ramp into the southbound lanes. In less than ten minutes we were the sole vehicle parked in front of the ware-house where we'd seen the Monte Carlo earlier. I pulled a scrunchie from my purse and gathered my hair in a high ponytail.

"You want to wait here?" I asked Ava.

"You soft in the head?"

"Come on, then. Follow my lead."

"Why, you got a plan?"

We got out. I always hated that question and found it best not to dignify it with an answer, since the answer was usually no. My footsteps clonked on the pavement and Ava's clicked sharply as we walked up to the glass front door. I grasped the handle and pulled it open, planless.

We stepped onto commercial-grade white speckled linoleum in a small lobby area, which was really nothing more than a tall reception desk in front of a closed metal door. No pictures graced the walls, no clock ticked out the time. There weren't even any chairs for visitors to sit on. A powdery odor like dust dried my sinuses while fluorescent lights flickered over our heads, making buzzing and popping noises like a bug zapper, and casting disco lighting onto the water-stained ceiling tiles.

"Hello?" I called. My voice frogged.

Ava put her hand in front of my arm against my wrist. "You scared?"

"Nah."

"Liar."

We both laughed, but our voices sounded hollow.

"Hello?" I called again.

No answer.

I said, "Well, let's poke our heads in that door, take a quick look."

A quick look was like dipping a toe in the water. No commitment. We could always shut the door and leave after our quick look, if the water was too cold. She nodded, and I grasped the knob and tried to turn it. Nothing happened. I pulled, then fell back as the door gave way. Ava had started breathing harder. So had I.

"You first," Ava said.

From a safe distance back from the opening, I called, "Hello?"

No answer. No sound. I leaned all the way in. The lighting in the inte-rior bordered on darkness and seemed to come mostly from high windows

434 PAMELA FAGAN HUTCHINS

near the ceiling. Still, even in the shadows, I got a sense of the inside. Tall racks lined up along the length of the space, leading away from us. It reminded me of the ceiling-high shelves in discount centers and home improvement stores. From where we stood, these looked maybe half-full. What I couldn't tell from this vantage point was what the racks held.

I whispered to Ava. "Can you watch the door? I want to get a closer look."

She peered inside, then looked at me, her eyes dubious. "Maybe old lady Brewer drop something off. Or she work here. What you gonna learn in there you can't tell from out here?"

"Won't know until I look."

But that wasn't true. Seeing a deserted warehouse full of stuff made me wonder where it all came from, and whether I'd find anything from Wrong Turn Ranch.

I put my hand on her upper arm. "I'll be fine. You stand here and hold the door open so I'll have more light, and if someone comes in, shout hello at them loud, like you're hard of hearing. Tell them your friend is looking for a bathroom."

Her brows knitted, but she slid her short frame along the door and backed it all the way open. Fear made her look much younger, like she was a little girl playing dress-up in her mother's clothes and makeup.

"I'm glad you showed up in Amarillo, Ava Butler."

"I let you know if I agree when we outta here."

I held up the five fingers of my right hand. "No more than five minutes."

I backed up. The gloom swallowed me, like I was falling down and backwards into a black, bottomless pit. I fought off the sensation and flipped my phone over to turn on its flashlight and got a bad surprise. Low battery warning: ten percent. I could have had it charging in the Suburban for the last hour, but it hadn't occurred to me it would be on fumes. I'd cried myself to sleep the night before, and now, looking back, I couldn't remember plugging it in. I wanted to groan in frustration, but I kept quiet, thinking. I only needed light for five minutes, and ten percent might be enough. I activated the flashlight, shining it ahead of me, illuminating floating dust particles in its beams. On impulse I turned it back around and turned the ringer off, then resumed scanning ahead of me.

Even though no one had answered our hello, I put each foot down slowly, carefully, and whisper-soft. It was the kind of place that called for it. Plus, someone had left that front door unlocked. They probably hadn't left for the day. Maybe whoever it was had run out for a late lunch, or was in a bathroom, but surely they would be back.

I walked to the far side of the first rack and trained the flashlight beam on its shelves, moving the light and my eyes slowly, methodically across the space, from top to bottom. It was an odd assortment with no discernible organization. Some things were boxed up like new—microwaves, computers, a rifle, mobile phones—and others looked used. A big screen TV on its back. An opened jewelry box. A walkie-talkie set without a box. I came upon bag after bag of feed and fertilizer and bolts of fabric. Some stuff even looked past its useful life. Old shoes. Cracked and stained kitchen appliances. My nerves tightened and twanged like a piano wire. Given the connection of Mrs. Brewer and her husband to trafficking stolen merchandise, this had to be one of the storage facilities.

I scanned both sides of the second aisle as I walked quickly back toward Ava, then the third heading toward the back wall again, practically holding my breath to stay quiet. Halfway down the third, my light flashed across something bright pink. I stopped and pointed the beam back to where I'd seen it, but at that moment, my phone died and the flashlight with it.

"Mother Goose," I whispered.

When I pressed the on button, the phone and light came on like a flash-bulb, lasting only long enough for me to see two things. The battery indi-cator reading one percent and that I had two texts from Jack showing on the lock screen. The first one said: *Collin checked the plate number your dad gave us. It's a cop. Brewer confirmed.* Before I could read the other, the bulb had popped and the screen was dead.

My father was helping catch the Wrong Turn Ranch thieves. Something flickered in my gut, and it wasn't a bad flicker. It was almost a prideful one, vindication on behalf of him. Or maybe I was just happy the case was breaking open. I needed to finish and get out of here, plug my phone in the car charger, and call Jack and tell him what I'd found and get the scoop from him.

I stood rooted in place, giving my eyes time to adjust to the sudden absence of light. Within seconds I could see well enough to make out the shapes on the shelf in front of me, but most of the colors looked like varying shades of gray. I moved to where I thought I'd seen pink. It had been farther back on the shelf, and possibly behind a sander and a Skilsaw I'd seen on the front edge. I reached out to nearest items and ran my hands over them gently. The first one was rounded and smooth. Possibly the cover of the Skilsaw.

I walked my hands farther backward. My eyes continued to adjust and colors slowly seeped back into my field of vision, like the time my ex-husband and I went scuba diving on our honeymoon trip to Aruba. Down at fifty feet everything looked drab. As we ascended, stopping for decom-pression breaks, the colors returned, more with every passing foot. It was like watching the animation of a black and white movie become colorized.

A brightly colored object caught my eye. I couldn't tell if it was orange, red, or pink, but given its location, I was putting my money on pink. A loud buzz of excitement started ringing in my ears. My fingers walked my hands to it and I put my palms on its surface. Canvas, with slick waterproofing. I inched my hands along the material and came to a long strip of puffy fabric. I followed that to hard plastic with a skinny strap out of its other end. I smiled. A strap. A strap on a pink backpack.

Mindful of the razor-sharp objects between my treasure and me, I hefted the bag high. It was light. I heard noises from the front of the warehouse, but I ignored them as I concentrated, using one arm to anchor the saw, and bumped the backpack over to me. As I got it to the edge of the shelf, it knocked into an item I hadn't seen, sending it crashing to the floor. There was a loud crack, and a shattering of glass. I held myself perfectly still, holding my breath. I strained to hear sounds, any sounds around me.

Nothing. Whatever the noise had been up front, it was silent now.

I exhaled and laughed. Turning toward the door, I raised my voice a little over a conversational tone and a little below a shout. "Ava, I found Betsy's backpack."

A whimper came from behind me, followed by a man's voice. "Ava's indisposed at the moment, but I'm sure she's quite happy for you."

Time slowed, seconds seeming to pass between each beat of my heart. Whatever I did next affected Ava more than me, and as much as I wanted to go on the attack, I had to be cautious for her sake. The voice had sounded close. Ten feet? Fifteen? Five? Probably ten, I decided. My hand still held the backpack perched on the edge of the shelf. I released it, hoping it looked like I had only been using the shelf for balance. My baby Glock was nestled in my purse near my stomach. The man didn't have a light on me, so with minimal movement I slipped my hand between the open sides of my jacket and into my purse. I felt the cold, hard grip and wrapped my hand around it. Using mostly my wrist, I tucked it into the front of my pants, just behind one side of my coat.

I turned toward the voice. All I could see of him and Ava was a shadowy outline, large and ominous. Regardless, I curled my lips into the biggest smile I could muster.

"Sorry." I stalled by coughing in my hand. "I was looking for the bathroom in here when I dropped my phone." I held it up. "I found it!"

The shadow advanced on me, and Ava materialized out of the darkness. Blood dripped from her busted lip, and an arm circled her neck. A pistol pressed into her temple. The top of a man's head appeared, his face mostly hidden by Ava's head, as was his body. *Coward.*

I held up a hand. "Wow, hey, there must be a big misunderstanding here. Look, I'm so sorry I trespassed. I've had this really embarrassing stomach problem, and I was desperate, and the front door was unlocked, and—"

"Shut the fuck up."

I raised my other hand. "Okay, okay."

"We're going for a walk."

"Yeah, no problem."

He took the gun off Ava's temple and waved it at me. "Move!"

Just then, Jack's voice shouted, from what sounded like the reception area. "Emily? Ava? Are you guys in here?"

The man jerked his head toward Jack's voice and his arm slipped and loosened. Ava and I made eye contact and I shouted, "Go!" as I grabbed my gun and waved my left arm to the side, hoping she would jump in the direction I was signaling.

Ava donkey-kicked as she wrenched herself down and away from her captor. She dove under his arm and rolled to her right. He grunted and bent forward for a second, firing wildly as he did. I heard the bullet ricochet off shelving to my left. My gun was in front of me in my right hand, and I sighted it just like my daddy had taught me, like I'd practiced for the last fifteen years at shooting ranges in Lubbock, Dallas, and Amarillo. By the time my left hand reached its steadying position, I was crouched and firing.

My first shot missed to the right but the second hit the man's hand. I heard the lovely sound of his gun skittering across the floor. He groaned and staggered to his right. I adjusted my aim, and my third and fourth shots struck their target. He clutched his thigh, screaming as he fell to the floor. Out of my peripheral vision, I saw Ava scoop up his gun as I assessed our situation. My magazine held ten rounds, plus one in the chamber for a total of eleven, so I had seven bullets left. Hopefully I wouldn't have to use them. I kept my gun trained on him and advanced until I was a yard away.

"You're messing with the wrong girl," I said.

I resisted the urge to blow pretend smoke from the barrel of my Glock. I'd never shot at a person before—never wanted to have to—but I'd always wanted to say the words my father had inscribed around the barrel for me. The man groaned and writhed, cursing in general and at me in particular. As he rolled I got my first good look at his face.

"Son of a biscuit!" I yelled. It was Edward Brown. Suddenly I knew what Jack's second text would have told me. "Well, Officer Brown, you had me fooled. Checking up on Johnson's place. More like seeing if there was anything else left out there you could steal."

"Fuck you," he spat.

"No, thank you," I said.

Running footsteps approached. "Emily?" The warehouse reverberated with Jack's cry.

"Over here. We're fine," I yelled back.

Looking at Ava, I said, "I don't suppose you have any idea how Jack knew where to find us, do you?"

She stood—holding Brown's gun by its trigger guard with two hooked fingertips—and grinned, blood dripping from her temple like she was the bride of Frankenstein. "Collin and I conversating some via text today." She tossed her hair. "And I might have mentioned what our bad asses up to."

I groaned. "There's probably a lot there I don't want to know, but thank God for whatever it was the two of you were up to last night that saved our bad asses from ending up dead today."

"What the hell, Emily?" It was an angry Jack, closing in on me fast. "Do you have a death wish? What the hell's the matter with you, anyway?"

I shoved my gun into the back of my waistband and raised my hands in the air. "Don't shoot," I said.

He shook his head, and I closed the rest of the distance between us in one giant step, landing with my head against his chest and both his arms around me.

CHAPTER 31

I snuck Betsy's backpack out to the Suburban after we called the cops, past Jack, who shook his head and put his hands over his eyes. Yes, I knew I shouldn't tamper with evidence, but there was no way I was letting it get tied up in a multiyear court case. The Alamogordo police had plenty left in the warehouse without this backpack, worthless to anyone except one very special little girl.

When the cops did arrive, things got real in a hurry. It's a sobering time when good cops are forced to process a bad one. Part of me wanted to apologize. Part of me wanted to ask them all politely how the heck the jerkface could get away with this stuff under their noses. I didn't do either, just answered their questions the best I could.

Ava and I drove back toward Wrong Turn Ranch after the police had finished with us, and Jack left in Collin's Bronco at the same time, promising to see us after he'd picked Collin up at the NMSP district offices on the way home. I plugged my phone in to the charger the second we got into the vehicle.

Ava was rubbing her neck. She already had a large fingerprint bruise.

"Do we need to stop and have someone take a look at that?" I asked.

"Nah. It good." She rolled her head. "Things always this exciting round you?"

"No," I said, then realized that wasn't true. "Well, yeah, sometimes."

"Still water run deep."

I laughed.

A few minutes later, Ava said, "I feeling a little shaky all of a sudden. I call my daughter and mom real quick. Say I love dem, hear their voices."

The gravity of the danger we'd escaped was starting to hit me, too, now that the adrenaline had worn off. Brown had shot at me. He'd held a gun to Ava's head. Ava and I had each come a slim whisker from dying. My lips quivered and I pressed them together.

Ava pressed a button on her phone. She spoke to her mother for a moment, then her accent thickened and her voice softened into baby talk. "Mama miss you, baby girl."

I knew her daughter wasn't even a year old. I imagined the tiny girl cooing on the other end of the line, and a lump formed in my throat. I wanted that. I wanted a child of my own—I wanted *Betsy*. Somehow, I had to find a way to keep her in the U.S., to resolve the Greg and Farrah situation, and to prevail on my adoption application.

Beside me, Ava blew kisses into the phone to her daughter, then said good-bye to her mother.

She slipped her mobile back into her purse. "I miss her. Home in two weeks, though."

"I can't imagine. Time will go quickly, though."

I turned on the radio and scanned for stations. Christian pop. Talk radio. 70s rock. Mexican pop. Country. Nothing grabbed me. I switched it back off and we rode in silence. As I drove, I thought ahead to our evening at the ranch.

I said, "Hey, I imagine Jack and I will do a gift exchange with Mickey and Laura and the kids after dinner, since we didn't get to that last night."

Ava readjusted her headband in the mirror. "Sound fun."

"You coming back to Amarillo with us in the morning, or heading on to Albuquerque?"

"Oh, I heading on."

I shot her a look and she avoided eye contact. "Heading on to Albuquerque?"

"Soon. In time for my gig."

"Do you need a ride anywhere?"

"Nope." I caught a smile teasing at the corner of her mouth. I had a pretty good idea how she would be getting to Albuquerque, but if she wanted to be cagey, I could play along.

I stopped for gas in Tularosa. While it pumped, I got back in the Suburban with Ava to stay warm and to call Laura about plans for the evening. I pressed Laura's name in my contacts and my speaker phone connected.

"Hello?" Mickey's deep voice answered instead of his wife's.

"Hi, Mickey. It's Emily. We're all on our way back to the ranch, and, boy, do we have a lot to tell you about today. But first I wanted to see if we could bring gifts over to you guys and the kids tonight."

I heard Laura's voice in the background. It was high-pitched, and she sounded upset. Mickey spoke, but he'd muffled the phone. I caught "It's Emily." Then, louder, unmuffled, he said, "We let the kids go out riding by themselves for the first time this afternoon, and they were supposed to be back by now. We're getting worried. You haven't heard from them, have you?"

Dusk was falling outside, and my stomach started gnawing on itself. "I haven't."

"You don't think they would have run off, do you?" Mickey's voice sounded tight, stressed.

Would they? I knew they didn't want to go back to Amarillo, but the time hadn't come for that yet. "I don't. They love it there. They love you guys. They feel safe."

Anxiety started gnawing at my gut. If the kids hadn't run off, where were they? Sure, they could just be running late, like normal kids. Or a horse could have gone lame. Or one of them was sick or hurt. And there were worse things. Things I didn't want to imagine. I shuddered.

I spoke fast. "Mickey, I need you to know something. Last night I got a call that someone thought I had the kids and reported it anonymously to CPS. I don't want to overreact but—"

Ava gasped and put her hand over her mouth.

He finished my thought. "But we have to find them, now."

"Exactly. I'll be there in ten minutes."

"And Jack?"

"Longer than that, I'm afraid, but he's on his way. Collin, too."

Mickey grunted. "I'll start getting the horses ready."

"Wouldn't four-wheelers be faster?" I knew they had a platoon of them.

"A little, but they're too noisy. We need to be able to hear if they call out, especially since it's dark. They could be injured." *Or worse,* I thought.

"We'll meet you at the stables."

My heart triple-timed as I called Jack.

Twenty minutes later, I'd dropped Ava at Jack's and was assembling lights, energy bars, first-aid kits, and canteens of hot chocolate in saddlebags. Packing the bars made me realize it was dinnertime, and I hadn't eaten. Jack and Collin probably hadn't either. Nor would we. Laura and Mickey were saddling up four horses for our search party. They had saved Jarhead for last. The horse was amped up. He could probably sense our own tension.

Mickey threw the blanket and saddle onto Jarhead's back, then said, "Laura's gonna stand by in my office."

Laura said, "You guys can stay in touch with me by walkie-talkie, and if the kids come back, I'll call you off."

I had noticed that they'd placed a walkie-talkie by each bag. "Why walkie-talkies? Why not our phones?"

Laura shifted from saddling horses to helping me with assembly. "Lot of dead zones up there."

Bouncing lights on the stable walls announced the approach of a vehicle. Doors slammed and Jack and Collin came trotting in.

"We're about ready," Mickey said.

"What's your plan?" Jack asked.

"We've saddled horses for each of us, and we put together supplies." He pulled out a map of the ranch and tapped a circled area. "They took off in this direction. They like to go up by the cemetery. I was thinking we'd go in twos for safety—Emily with me, Collin with you, Jack, since you and I both know how to track—and that we'd take these two routes." He traced lines equidistant from the middle of the circled area and its outer edges. One was highlighted in yellow, the other in green. "Emily and I will take the green route. I told the kids the first day that if they heard this call" —he demonstrated the ca-caw of a raven—"to come on back, we were looking for them."

Jack nodded. "Like the parents used to use with us."

"Yeah, it carries a lot better than shouting."

"And just in case of bad guys, doesn't give us away," I said.

"Yes." Mickey looked at Collin and me. "Is everybody dressed warm enough? I've got more gear in the tack room."

"I'm set." I'd already grabbed heavy gloves, a hat, and a scarf to go with my jacket, since most of my things were at Jack's house. Luckily, I had on good cowboy boots that I'd re-waterproofed this winter, with jeans and a sweater.

"Me, too," Collin said. "But I think it's time to call for backup."

Mickey stuffed his map inside his coat and zipped it up.

"I'll call now," Laura said, her face pale and pinched. She walked toward Mickey's office, then ran back and threw her arms around Mickey and kissed him. She turned to all of us. "You guys be safe."

"We will, babe," Mickey said.

Laura disappeared into his office.

Jack walked over to me and touched my shoulder. I turned, and he caught my chin in one hand and kissed me.

"Be careful," he said.

"You, too."

He shook his head. "You're reckless. Please."

I reached for his gloved hand with mine and squeezed it. "I promise."

I led Jarhead out of the stable and mounted up, along with the guys. Jarhead snorted puffs of steam as he trotted in place. All the horses seemed especially eager, actually. Mickey swung a leg over his big roan horse and allowed the animal to take off at the same time. Without another word between us, I squeezed Jarhead with my heels. He squealed with excitement and I held him to a frothing lope as we followed Mickey into the deepening twilight. Behind me and to our left, I heard the hooves of Collin's and Jack's horses as they peeled off toward their route.

Mickey led the way through the same open series of gates I'd ridden through with Jack and the kids last weekend. The moon was shining so bright that we didn't turn on our tracking lights, not that we'd be able to track them yet anyway. The area we were traversing was too well and recently traveled by many others. Slowly we increased speed, but not enough to satisfy Jarhead, who nodded his head emphatically in rhythm to his lope.

I leaned forward and whispered to him. "It's okay, boy. This isn't a race."

He shook his head, rattling the rings on the edges of the bit in his mouth.

Emotionally, horses and people often operate on the same wavelength. I thought of the way Jarhead and his pals had picked up on our stress back at the stable, and of how Thunder's calm had soothed Betsy when we'd escaped from Johnson's Ranch. Whenever Jib—my college barrel-racing horse—had sensed a race coming up, she'd become so high-strung I was afraid she'd injure herself. I'd learned that singing in her ear and rubbing her neck helped her settle down, sort of like how a snake charmer hypnotizes a cobra with pungi music.

So I tried it with Jarhead, patting his neck and singing "O Holy Night," a little off-key like my mother, my voice cracking on the high notes. After only a few minutes, he had stopped his snorts and head bobs. His ears twitched as he vacillated between his urgent need to sprint and reluctant attention to my song. It distracted me, too, from thinking about why Greg and Farrah hadn't come home.

I stopped singing and spoke aloud. "Maybe one of their horses got hurt."

Jarhead nickered.

"I'm not talking about a permanent injury, here, and I know it's not ideal, but it's better than any of the alternatives."

He snorted softly.

"Okay, how about they were lost but now they've found their way home, and we'll see them any second?"

This time Jarhead blew softly out his nose. I patted him again and resumed singing.

We started up the incline into the treed foothills. The sky grew darker, and the snow less disturbed. I kept Jarhead tight on Mickey's roan. I had only been up here once—to the cemetery with Jack, Greg, and Farrah—and in the dark I had no idea if we were still headed in that direction. We didn't need me getting lost tonight, too. The trees and the wind absorbed the noises around us, and in the relative silence, the hoofbeats of the horses sounded like muted thunder. The air smelled clean, and when I breathed it in and licked my lips, I could taste the earthiness of melting snowflakes, even though I couldn't see the snow falling. The sky looked crystal clear, in fact, and if it hadn't been for the trees and darkness lit only by moonglow, I imagined I would have seen Amarillo in the distance. As it was, I only saw the snowy forest floor, the trunks of aspens and ever-greens, and the rump of the horse in front of us.

Mickey slowed his horse and dismounted as it stopped. He held the reins in one hand and switched on his handheld spotlight in the other, pointing it at the ground. He swept his beam across the snowy forest floor, studying the area, then knelt and touched the compressed snow in the imprint of several hooves and brushed powder out of another. It made my heart ache for my father, the one I used to know, the one who had taught me that a real scout gets close to the ground and puts his hands on the earth.

Mickey said, "Looks like two horses came this way today." He pointed ahead of us, but to where I wasn't sure.

I stared at the ground and saw only a mass of hoofprints, despite my dad's coaching. I'd have to take Mickey's word for it. He trained the light on the ground around us in expanding sweeps. He stopped and reswept an area. I clucked to Jarhead. He followed Mickey and his horse, calmly walking instead of bouncing like a pogo stick.

"Four-wheeler." Mickey turned to me. "Also today."

The four-wheeler tracks were obvious, even to me. "Is that good or bad?"

"I'm not sure. Could have been one of the hands. Nobody else has any business up here. The tracks run parallel to the horses. We'll follow the horses and keep an eye on the four-wheeler. I've got enough light without the spot, so I'm going to turn it off for now."

"Okay."

He switched off his light and spoke into the walkie-talkie. "Found two sets of horse tracks and one set of four-wheeler tracks, all recent. We're following them."

Our handsets crackled and I heard Jack's voice. "We've got nothing. Assume you want us to stick to the plan?"

"Roger."

Laura's voice cracked. "Please find them, Mickey."

He whispered something in a language I recognized as Apache from my visits to this area, although I didn't know a word of it, then stuffed the walkie-talkie back into a holster on his saddle. He mounted, leaning back in his saddle, and ca-cawed long and loud. Jarhead snorted. Even I was startled at how realistic Mickey sounded. Wild. Dangerous.

We waited and I listened with every bone in my body but heard no answering ca-caw.

He motioned ahead. "Let's ride, but we need to be extra quiet now."

"Like an Indian scout," I said, then immediately felt like an idiot for saying it aloud. Sure, I had idolized Sacajawea as a kid whose father taught her his white-man version of the ways of Indian scouts. I still channeled her on occasion. But to say it to Mickey, who really was a Native American? My face flamed in the dark.

He nodded, though. "Like that. But tonight we are hunters."

Mickey's horse took off, and I gave Jarhead his cue and he lunged after him.

As we raced silently through the woods, the tracks of horse hooves and a four-wheeler slowly converged until the four-wheeler crushed the hoofprints underneath. A shadow flashed over us, and a screech owl shattered the forest silence with his nerve-wracking cry. My heart slammed into my throat and Mickey pulled his horse up short and whirled to me.

He whispered. "Emily, someone followed them up here, I'm sure of it. Are you armed?"

I shook my head, whispering in return. "Cops have my gun. I shot one today."

"Shot one what?"

I shook my head. "I'll tell you about it later."

Mickey nodded once. "Okay, well, I have a gun, so stay behind me like you've been doing." He shifted like he was going to take off, but instead he said, "Listen, this isn't exactly scientific evidence, but that screech owl—it's a very bad omen. The Owl is evil personified in Apache lore, like an ogre or a bogeyman. It steals souls, especially those of children. Seeing an owl or hearing one, its presence in the woods . . . trust me, this seals the deal for me."

I remembered Mickey telling Greg and Farrah about the Owl. Maybe six months ago I would have dismissed his words as nonsense, but not anymore. I'd seen the powerful magic of the Apaches firsthand. If he told me that the owl meant someone bad had the kids, I believed him.

Mickey ca-cawed again. I held my breath while we waited for a reply, but the only answer was another screech from the owl flying above us.

"The tracks have veered away from the path to the cemetery. I think they're headed toward the old mine." Mickey held a finger over his lips, and we moved on.

But his words lingered in my head, chilling me. The mine? I'd never been there. I'd only seen it in a picture and from a distance. It sounded dangerous. Not a place for kids to hang out in the dark, even teenage kids. Especially not if someone was following them. I tried not to panic, but adrenaline surged through me, the scared kind, and all I wanted to do was get to them, wherever they were, as fast as we could.

We followed the tracks another half mile, the only sound besides the wind was the snow-muffled hooves of the horses and their panting breaths. Suddenly, the forest cleared. Mickey reined his horse in, and I did the same. From the cover of the trees, I saw a black square in the side of the rapidly rising hillside in front of us. It was the entrance to the mine. The snow ended outside its mouth, and the tracks led to its edge, horses and four-wheeler both.

Mickey dismounted and walked his horse away from the mine entrance, along the edge of the clearing. "Oh no." He crouched low. "See this?" He pointed at tracks and gestured back down the hill. "It's the horses. But they're different than before." He looked up at me. "Riderless."

I slipped off Jarhead and bent down beside him.

Mickey pointed back to the entrance. "The tracks come from there. And there's more. Something is blocking the entrance."

I'd never seen the mine before, so I hadn't known what to expect. But I peered closer now, trying to figure out what he saw in the darkness. Slowly, quietly, we moved a little closer, at an angle. Mickey drew his gun and carried it in his right hand. The object in the center of the entrance took shape.

"It's the four-wheeler," I said.

"They're inside," Mickey whispered. "Someone is with them, and they're inside."

The radios squawked. "The horses are back at the barn, Mickey. The kids aren't with them."

Mickey grabbed his radio and keyed his mike. The console light turned red. "It's okay, Laura, we've found them. Jack, Collin—"

A gunshot cracked. Mickey let out an oomph and fell, spinning to the right and down, and purple exploded from his shoulder. His horse bolted, disappearing into the blackness of the woods like a ghost after the horses that had gone before.

Jarhead leapt straight sideways away from the mine entrance before the second shot. The bullet whizzed past us, so close I could hear the zing as the bullet displaced the air against my cheek. I jumped off of Jarhead, holding tight to his reins, and ran with him behind me to a tree. I couldn't risk him running off, too. I needed him for Mickey, at least, and maybe the kids. I repeated my belt trick from that morning to tie his reins to the slim tree trunk. Then I hit the dirt and bear-crawled uphill back to Mickey, praying I was too low to be seen. I crawled past him to his feet, which positioned my body outside of the mine entrance on the opposite side from where I'd tied Jarhead. The horse snorted and pawed, then whinnied and jerked at the reins. If he pulled with any of his strength at all, he'd snap them and be back at the ranch in minutes. *Dear God, please help Jarhead find his zen place without me there to sing him Christmas carols.* A huge gust of wind rustled through the treetops. It whined, the trees moaned, a coyote howled. It was like a chorus, and, surprisingly, Jarhead quit pulling. He still snorted and shifted his hooves, but he stayed in place. God had come through.

I had to hope I'd judged the angle right and that the shooter couldn't get a bead on me anymore. I counted to three for courage, then I stood and rolled Mickey over on his back using torque from his legs. I tried to be gentle, but he groaned. I winced. I hated hurting him. And this would be worse. Grasping hold of one of his ankles in each hand, I dragged him backwards down the slick hill until he was well out of the line of fire. He didn't make a peep.

"Mickey, can you hear me?" I patted his cheeks. "Can you hear me?" My breaths came in quick, quiet pants.

He rolled his head to the right, toward his injured side. "Yeah, I . . . hear you." His voice was low, but he could speak, and that was good enough for me.

"Okay, I'm going to take a look at the bullet wound."

I peeled the edges of his disintegrated clothing away from it. In the moonlit clearing, I could see it was bleeding fast, but not gushing. It was on the right shoulder, so, by definition, that made it less dangerous than if it had been on his left, by his heart. At least I hoped it did. I took off one of my gloves and gathered a handful of snow. I closed my eyes and pushed the snow into the center of the wound, then followed it with the glove.

Mickey grunted.

I grabbed his left hand and put it on the glove, forcing his fingers to grasp it. "Hold this here, tight. You hear me?"

"Yeah, hold it tight. Got it."

I needed his gun. I felt a little squeamish about hunting for it but I didn't have time to pussyfoot around, as my dad would say. I patted Mickey's hips under his jacket. My fingers found the hard metal of the weapon where he had tucked it into his waistband, and I removed it carefully. It was a full-size Glock 9mm, which was lucky for me. It operated like my baby Glock, only bigger, heavier, and with more bullets.

Mickey lifted his head. "What're ya doin'?"

"I'm borrowing this, so I can go get the kids."

His voice grew stronger. "Wait for Jack and Collin."

I'd forgotten all about the guys. I grabbed my walkie-talkie. I prayed the unit wouldn't feedback and keyed it to life, hoping the wind would cover the sound of my voice. I covered the console with my hand, too, to hide its light. "Don't answer me, just come to the mine. We've found them and we need help. Mickey's been shot. Repeat, do not answer. Use caution and be quiet. They know we're here, but not you. Hurry." I stared at it, afraid it would squawk to life. I added, "Over and out," then turned it off quickly, grabbing Mickey's and switching it off, too.

I checked the glove on his shoulder. He was doing a good job with the pressure. He would be fine. He had to be fine.

"I'm sorry, but I can't sit here with those kids possibly in there with a person who shot you. I have to do something."

He shook his head. "You heard the Owl. He's an omen of death. Don't do something stupid and make it yours."

I checked that I had my spotlight and stuck the gun in the front of my jeans. "That's exactly why I can't wait. If somebody is going to die, I can't let it be one of those kids. And I know you said the owl is an omen, but you also said the coyote can outsmart him, and did you hear what I heard a minute ago, after you were shot?"

Mickey grimaced. "That doesn't mean anything."

"So you heard the coyote, too. And it means every bit as much as hearing an owl. So make some covering noise out here, Mickey, so they can't hear me."

Mickey sucked in a breath then shook his head as he released it. "Gotcha covered, Standing Hair."

I checked his pressure hand on the glove one more time, then crouched down, belly to the ground again. I took the gun from my waistband and held it in my right hand. I began an awkward bear-crawl back up the slope toward the entrance.

Behind me, Mickey screamed like a screech owl. The hairs stood up on the back of my neck as he serenaded the entire forest with his cry. I entered the dark hole in the hill, moving cautiously around the four-wheeler. The stillness was immediate. So was the change in temperature.

It was warmer. A stale smell wafted toward me, the opposite of the clean, crisp air of the forest. I went slowly at first, careful not to make a sound, but then I grew in confidence as I mastered the slinking motion. I was ten feet in when I heard approaching hoofbeats. They were louder in here. Good. Backup. I kept going, moving like a salamander through the dark. One of the horses whinnied outside. I crawled faster, their noises and Mickey's continued cries providing the cover I'd hoped for. Fifteen feet. Twenty. Thirty. Fifty.

A male voice spoke, close by, maybe another twenty feet away, but facing away from me. He sounded like he was muttering to himself. "Little bastards. I'm going to go kill your fucking friends first, and then I'm going to come back and kill you, too. Hiding from me won't do you a damn bit of good."

Even at its low volume, the voice echoed off the sides of the tunnel: good, ood, ood, ood, ood. I wanted to shoot at the voice, fire all fifteen shots in the magazine until I heard the man scream in pain, but I couldn't. Not with the kids in there somewhere. Did I recognize him? Was it someone I knew? The tunnel warped the sounds, and I just couldn't tell. At least the kids had gotten away from him. Maybe they'd found a safe hiding place. I hated the thought of them running blind in the darkness, stumbling upon some old mine shaft, and I forced my mind away from it. Action. I needed to act, not let worry cripple me. But first, I had to get a fix on this guy.

My eyes had adjusted some to the darkness, enough that I could see roughly to the end of my nose, where before I had seen only pitch black. I wasn't going to be able to do this by sight. Outside the mine, I heard the mournful howl of the coyote again, and it galvanized me. I could outsmart this guy. It was my only chance.

He had said he was coming this way, and I was running out of time. I reached toward the sides of the tunnel in both directions, but neither hand connected. I had to believe he couldn't see much better in here than I could, so if he was walking out holding a gun, he'd probably be touching the wall with the non-gun hand. Odds were he was right-handed, so that would be his most likely gun hand. He'd be on the left, using his left hand on the wall. So I needed to be to his right, which was my left since I was facing inward.

I rolled to the left, three full revolutions until I hit the side of the tunnel. Footsteps moved toward me, and I realized that as soon as he passed me, he'd be slightly silhouetted by the light from the tunnel entrance. I'd have a shot. Heck, even if he ran into me, I'd have a shot, away from the kids. But if I missed, I could hit Collin. Or Jack. The thought of hurting Jack, of accidentally killing Jack, made my stomach lurch. But if I didn't take the shot, this man was headed out there to shoot them. To kill them. I had to stop him.

I faced my prone body on my side toward the center of the tunnel, the gun in my hands. I held my breath as the footsteps came closer and closer.

A man's foot stepped on my left foot and a huge body toppled forward and on top of me, his feet at my feet, my face under his chest.

"Goddammit," the man's voice growled.

I heard a clatter on the rocky floor of the tunnel, a sound I hoped was his gun. If so, he would gather himself and go after it before I could draw another breath. I closed my eyes against who knows what in the utter darkness, twisted the Glock hard to get the mouth of the barrel aligned toward the body before it moved away from me, and fired up at an angle into it.

"Ugh, pfft . . ." the man said, and his body jerked. Then nothing. He lay completely still on top of me. A warm wetness oozed onto my hands.

"Jack?" I called. I raised my voice to nearly a shriek. "Jack?"

"Emily!" Jack's voice shouted into the mine's opening.

"Emily!" Greg and Farrah screamed my name almost simultaneously from the other direction.

"All clear," I shouted, or tried to under dead weight that felt as heavy as a pony. "I got him."

A light shone from the entrance and footsteps pounded like buffalo toward me from all directions. My head was turned to the side and I saw four feet in boots, and then the body rolled off of me.

Collin aimed the light down on me. "Are you hit?"

Jack fell to his knees at my side. He grabbed my hand in his and smoothed my hair back from my forehead. Lighter footsteps pounded toward us from the interior.

"I'm fine. It's his blood, not mine."

Greg and Farrah careened up to us and both of them threw themselves on top of me, pulling my hand away from Jack.

"I'm so sorry," Farrah sobbed.

I put both arms around her and squeezed. Someone grabbed one of my hands. "I'm just glad you guys are all right."

Greg stood, and by the pull on my arm, I knew it was him that held my hand. He let it go. "I knew he'd come for us."

Collin had crouched by the unmoving figure. I watched him, in a sort of daze as I continued to hug Farrah.

"He's got a pulse," Collin said.

Collin rolled the man to the side, pulling his hands behind his back, and cuffed him. Then he took off his own jacket and shirt and ripped the shirt into strips. He started tying them around the man's abdomen.

I released Farrah and stood. Jack had, meanwhile, pulled out the guy's wallet and pawed through it. He shone a light on its contents. Farrah rose and nestled into Greg's shoulder, clinging to him. Greg rubbed her back in circular motions.

Jack clutched my left hand. "Take a look at this."

He pointed the illuminated wallet at me. A man's Texas driver's license. It was hard to see in the low light, but I read the name.

"Samson." I said it as a statement of fact. He'd tried to pretend he was the good cop, but I was beginning to wonder if there even were any besides Collin.

Greg snorted. "Yeah, Officer Samson. We saw it all. That poor truck driver told him he was done hauling stolen shit for him, and Samson pulled out a gun and blew him away, right in front of us."

Farrah said, "But you got him, Emily. You saved us."

"It pains me to admit that not all my brethren are as principled or as good-looking as I am, but it's actually pretty rare that we find a dirty cop, per se." Collin looked up. "I think he'll live, but we've got to get him out of here. Mickey, too."

I'd almost killed a cop for the second time in a day. Zero for two was something to be thankful for. Jack squeezed my hand, and I smiled weakly.

CHAPTER 32

The first thing I insisted on doing when we made it back to Amarillo Sunday afternoon was take Betsy her backpack. The poor girl missed her mama, and she deserved to get this treasure back as soon as possible, before Immigration showed up. I'd texted ahead to Wallace before we left the hospital in Alamogordo. We'd camped out there with Laura until we got a glimpse of a groggy Mickey postsurgery. The bullet missed everything vital, and the doctors dug it out and patched him up. They didn't like his loss of blood, but, other than that, they gave him a good prognosis.

Mickey wasn't the only victim of our escapades who was in the hospital. Brown was recovering down the hall. I'd heard his wounds were really fairly minor. Samson wasn't as lucky. Somehow, I'd shot down through his gut, where the bullet plowed through his abdomen and out his groin. He was still in surgery when we left. Collin said the cops were renaming the surgical ward the "Annie Oakley Police Convalescence Center." Everyone laughed but me. Shooting people was even worse than shooting antelope, it turned out, even when they deserved it.

Wallace was waiting for us when we pulled up to the hangar. He had on a huge black bomber jacket and a plaid scarf wound over and over around his neck, its fringed end fluttering by his shoulder. He looked top heavy on his long slim legs in his get-up, huddling inside the door away from the frigid temperatures and gusting wind. Watching him made me realize what a seasoned flier I had become, because we'd landed in that wind, and I hadn't given it a second thought. I had a lot of other things on my mind, too. As we drew closer to him, I saw another man behind him, a shadow across his face. I craned for a better look but couldn't get one.

We taxied in and Jack hustled out to pull the hangar door closed. I jumped out, too, and the temperature hit me like a sledgehammer. It was even colder than in Tularosa.

Wallace met me as my feet touched the ground. His words were tough, but his face was smiling. "I should kick your ass. I should get your adoption application rejected. I should refuse to do another thing to help you with Betsy."

"I'm sure I have no idea what you're so huffy about." I batted my eyes but kept them averted from his.

"Greg and Farrah. I'm supposed to believe they got to New Mexico on their own, happened upon Jack's ranch, coincidentally hit it off with his cousins, and convinced them to take them in, all without you knowing about it until thirty-five seconds before you contacted me?"

"You left out the part about Samson tracking them there and trying to kill them." I heaved out my purse and suitcase. Snowflake yipped at me from the backseat. "Hold on, girl. You're next." I set my bags beside the plane and launched into the explanation we had agreed upon with Greg and Farrah before we left the hospital. "I was as shocked as you were. It turns out they found Jack's place in New Mexico from the business card I gave them, you know, when I saw them in the field outside Love's?"

"I don't follow."

"The card gives his office address in Tularosa, and his name."

"That's pretty thin."

I pretended he'd bought my answer. "What a blessing that they're safe, and that they've found a family who wants them."

Wallace pulled me to him and hugged me so tight I made a little "woof" noise. "What, are you out to save them all now, too?" He rocked me back and forth.

I pulled my head back. He had tears in his eyes, and so did I. "There's so many of them. But two more are going to be okay." I smiled, and the water in my eyes made him appear glisteny and angelic.

Jack put a hand on each of our shoulders. "Are we all set to go see Betsy?"

Wallace released me, then said, "Oh, my manners. Emily, Jack, this is Ethan. Ethan, Emily and Jack."

The man who had stayed in the shadows stepped out of them now, hand extended to me to shake, then to Jack. I got my first good look at him. He had pitch-black skin, a shaved head, and was nearly Jack's height, but Jack outweighed him by "a sack of feed," in Phelps's household terminology. Ethan was whippet thin.

"Nice to meet you." I shook.

"Likewise." Jack shook, too.

"I've heard a lot about you both. So glad to finally meet you," he replied, his voice like cognac.

"Ethan's a gate agent for Southwest." Wallace turned to me and wagged a finger. "We're dating, don't make a fuss."

"Who, me?" I winked at Ethan.

He laughed. "I met Nadine and Phil last night. Maybe all six of us can go out together soon."

"That would be great," I said. I put my hand up to shield my lips and said loudly, "Wallace, he's so hot."

Ethan laughed again, and Wallace beamed.

Jack let Snowflake out and clipped on her leash. Then he picked up a bag in each hand. I grabbed the kennel and collapsed it.

"Follow me," Jack said.

Half an hour later, Wallace, Jack, and I stood at the dark brown door to the Hodges' tan brick ranch house on the south side of Amarillo, while Snowflake and Ethan waited in the car, engine running, heater at its max. The snow had stopped, but you could hardly tell because the wind still whipped it through the air. The Hodges' home had a shroud of white over its roof, treeless yard, and flower beds. Wallace rang the bell and we waited.

I heard footsteps in the house, and a man's voice, loud and commanding. "Mary Alice. The door."

It opened, and there stood the woman I'd last seen in the front seat of a paneled van on Christmas Eve.

"Hello, Mrs. Hodges," Wallace said.

Her eyes landed briefly on each of us, and her face pinched. "You didn't tell me she was coming."

Wallace smiled. "I'm sure I did. She's the one who found Betsy's belongings in New Mexico. And she works for Jack, the attorney who is handling all of Betsy's legal matters, pro bono. Jack, this is Mary Alice Hodges. Mary Alice, Jack Holden."

Mary Alice gave a brief nod. Jack inclined his head slowly, then raised it. Watching him made me warmer, and proud.

Wallace stepped over the threshold. "May we? It's far too cold to be outside."

Mary Alice stepped aside for him, and Jack followed. I slipped in behind them. Trevon Hodges rose. I recognized the graying facial hair and round face. He was burly but less heavy than I'd imagined when I saw him bundled up outside the Hodges' van.

"What's this?" he asked, his tone like the serrated edge of a hunting knife.

Mary Alice wrung her hands. "Betsy's CPS caseworker has brought some of her belongings. They were recovered in New Mexico, where she came from." She gestured at Wallace, then Jack. "This is Betsy's attorney."

I stepped slightly forward. "And I'm his paralegal." I held up the dirty pink backpack. "Is Betsy here?"

Trevon stared me in the eye. "The children are all busy with chores."

Wallace cleared his throat. "I need to fill out an assessment after our visit. This will only take a minute, if you'd get her for us, please."

Trevon glowered and returned to his seat.

"Betsy," Mary Alice called. "To the living room, please."

Running footsteps moved toward us, and then my little angel appeared, slowing to a walk as she entered the room. Her eyes sought Trevon first, in a way that hurt my heart. Then to Mary Alice, gauging her situation. The woman nodded her head sideways at Wallace.

Betsy turned to him. "Hello, Mr. Wallace."

When she saw him, she caught sight of Jack and me. She gasped, and launched herself in my direction.

"Betsy," Trevon thundered.

She stopped, looked at him. He shook his head, his face dark.

She said, "Yes, sir," and curtsied to me. "Hi, Emily."

I bridged the gap between us, holding out her backpack. "Hello, sweetie. Recognize this?"

"Oh," she squealed and reached both hands out.

"What do you say?" Mary Alice asked.

Betsy grasped the backpack and hugged it to her body. "Thank you."

She unzipped it, and when she saw what was inside, she looked up at me. I glanced quickly at Trevon and Mary Alice. The woman had moved over beside her husband's chair and was looking down at him. His attention was on the silent TV, which flickered a news show. I put one finger to my lips, briefly, and Betsy gave a tiny nod. She set the pack on the floor and reached in with both hands, pulling out the picture of me with Thunder and the beautiful horse from Alan's store. She swallowed and ran her hand over the horse's mane. "Thunder. I missed him."

"Yes." We smiled at each other.

She dug her hands in again, and came out with worn brushes for her hair and her teeth, some scrunchies, and a tattered set of Barbie pj's. Then she pulled hard on something from the bottom of the inside, and I heard a tearing sound.

My mouth fell open a little, and I looked at Jack. He shrugged his shoulders.

Betsy tossed aside a dirty pink panel rimmed with Velcro. Then she fished a plastic baggy from her backpack and handed it to me. "Mama said I could never lose my backpack, because of the paper inside."

Paper? I took the gallon ziplock baggy from her. "What kind of paper?"

Betsy lifted her shoulders. "Something important, she said."

I examined the ziplock. There was one sheet of paper inside. I pulled the edges of the bag apart and turned it upside down. The single piece of paper fell out. My Spanish minor at Texas Tech came in handy in moments like these.

I read the words aloud. *"Certificado de Nacimiento."*

Wallace came to stand beside me. "What is it?"

I smiled so hard I thought my face would split. "It's Betsy's birth certificate."

CHAPTER 33

An hour later, I sat at my desk in the Williams & Associates offices and sealed the FedEx envelope containing Betsy's filing packet for Special Immigrant Juvenile status and adjustment to permanent residency. Jack felt sure that once we had proof of filing, DHS would let her stay in foster care pending a decision. And USCIS would owe that decision to Betsy within six months, not much longer than it should take for me to get a yay or nay on my own status as a prospective adoptive parent. That was a long time, but it wasn't forever. The wheels were turning now, and there was every reason to be hopeful.

"You'll drop it in the morning?" Jack asked.

"I'll be waiting when they open."

He smiled at me, one side only, and retreated back down the hall to his office, Snowflake trotting behind him. I wiggled my mouse, and my screen woke up to the picture of Betsy. I was back on track to becoming her mother. Adoption. Parenthood. Heavy stuff. A lifetime commitment. Or it was supposed to be, anyway. I wondered for the umpteenth time why my father had chosen not to keep his commitment to me for the last decade. I still couldn't make up my mind whether to call him back and find out. I picked up my phone and held it in my hand, staring at it, not dialing his number. Instead, I called Laura for an update on Mickey. He was resting well, and she said he had more nursemaids than he knew what to do with, in her and the teenagers formerly known to her as George and Frannie and now going by their real names of Greg and Farrah.

I ended the call and picked up a page I'd printed from the USCIS website on the Special Immigrant Juvenile status decision process. Almost instantaneously, I heard a knock at the door to the offices. Snowflake tore down the hall, yapping and spinning. Thinking it couldn't be anyone other than Wallace coming to check on Betsy's application, I kept reading my printout as I walked across the room. At the last second, I looked up and through the window.

Officer Burrows waved at me through the glass. I unlocked the door and opened it, but didn't move aside. Snowflake lunged at his ankles, dodging, feinting, and sniffing.

"I hope I'm not bothering you." His tone was one I'd never heard from him before. Friendly. Conciliatory.

"What are you doing here? My boss, Jack, is just down the hall."

"Good. I came to thank the two of you."

"Really?"

"Really. I have some things to tell you that I think will help you understand what's going on."

I stood aside to let him in and put my desk between us. He shifted back and forth beside the couch.

Jack's heavy boots on tile gave away his approach before he appeared beside me. Snowflake ran a few laps around Jack then went back to inspecting Burrows.

"John Burrows." The officer stuck out his hand.

Jack shook it. "Jack Holden. Thank us for what?"

"I moved from the Plainview PD here to work undercover for the last few months, trying to bust the smuggling operation. I couldn't have wrapped it up so quickly without all that you guys did."

My mouth dropped. "But I thought you were a rookie. That you were training with Samson."

Snowflake jumped onto the couch and put her head on her paws.

He smiled. "So did he."

"So you were investigating *him*?"

"Pretty much. Samson managed to do most of his dirty work when I wasn't with him, but we've suspected he was involved for some time now. I was certain of it when he hacked and monitored your phone—"

"He *hacked* it?"

"Yeah."

Jack folded his arms across his chest and rocked back on his heels, a smug grin teasing up the left corner of his mouth.

No wonder Samson figured out I had the kids. And he had to have been the one who called Byron. Found the kids in New Mexico. The blood drained from my face. Got to Ivanka before I did. I put a hand to each cheek and shook my head. It hurt me to think that talking to me had led to a woman's death.

"Wait—do you know anything about the missing dancer?"

He rubbed his lips together like they were chapped. "Yeah, someone reported it Friday. She turned up at a wedding chapel in Vegas." He shook his head. "I met her a few days before that. Busted her for drug possession. She seemed like she was heading down a bad path. I hope the nuptials are a good sign, but somehow I don't think so."

"But at least she's alive, that's good. Better than Ivanka, or the dancer still missing from last summer." I was relieved, especially for Nadine, who had been understandably concerned about the average life span of employees of the Polo Club, such as herself. I lowered my hands and made a rolling motion with one.

"Oh, she's not missing."

"What?"

"She's dead. Wu killed her."

"Who, whoa, whoa, back up. None of this is making sense."

Burrows grinned. "Wu was Samson's enforcer. Samson had Wu in his pocket because he knew Wu had 'accidentally' killed his dancer girlfriend, supposedly a rough-sex thing. He's still working for Samson, or he was until we busted him this morning. Anyway, when Freeman threatened to rat Samson and Wu out, Wu tried to strong-arm him, and Freeman fought back. Wu and Samson slapped assault charges on him to discredit him."

"Oh my God."

"I'll bet you'll never guess who Samson's little sister is, either."

"I have no clue."

"Mary Alice Hodges."

"Oh my God," I shouted. "That's how she sicced you guys on me so fast."

"Yep. And I had to go along with it, with all of it. Samson was always wary of me. The big stuff, like running the smuggling operation in Amarillo, murdering the guy at Love's and then 'Ivanka,' framing your client to get his cooperation—those he did when I wasn't around. I did my best to shadow him, but it was hard to do without tipping him off, especially once Emily started poking around."

"Hey, I think I did some good."

Burrows clapped me on the shoulder. "Without even getting yourself killed. You guys managed to bust this whole thing open from the other end."

Jack put his arm around my shoulders. "That was all Emily."

I looked at him, locking eyes at close range. This was the guy who hadn't called the cops on my father, even when he suspected him of the robbery at Wrong Turn Ranch. He'd given him a first chance, and a second. Like he'd given me. The knot of tension inside me eased further.

"No, it took all of us to figure it out," I said. My father, Alan, Greg, and Farrah. And Ivanka, may she rest in peace. Stella, Ava, Mickey, Collin. "And barely soon enough for Greg and Farrah."

Jack tightened his grip on me, and I relaxed into him.

"So anyway, Samson will be charged when he's coherent. When he's well enough, he's looking at the rest of his life in prison, where things aren't very pleasant for cops."

"Good. He deserves it."

"I hope you don't think all cops are like him and that guy in New Mexico, Brown, who's already been charged, I understand. You've seen the bad side of things, but by and large, we're good people."

Jack added, "Doing a hard job."

"You could have fooled me the last few times I've run into you," I said, but I smiled.

"I was trying to keep you safe and protect the operation without blowing my cover. You'll see the real John Burrows from here on out."

"That's good to hear." I smiled, then frowned again quickly. "We've got to talk to Alan, Jack. This may change everything. Wu is dirty. He has no credibility."

Jack said, "Yep. Might not happen overnight, but we'll fix it."

"I hope so." To Burrows, I said, "So, are you going back to Plainview now?"

"Nope. I'm a full-fledged member of the APD."

"Good. I feel a lot better with you around."

Jack returned to his office while I chatted a little longer with Burrows. After he left, I stomped around the office, making as much noise as I could. Jack and I had gone straight from the airport to see Betsy and back to the office. I didn't have my car, and I was counting on Jack for a ride home. He didn't seem to notice my hints. After another fifteen minutes of waiting around, my stomach growled.

I leaned against Jack's doorframe. "Are you planning on taking me home any time soon? If not, I can call my mother."

He jumped to his feet. "Sorry. Clyde emailed me for a status report. He saw the news."

"Clyde emails?"

Jack's dimple did its thing. "He dictates them to Betty."

I shook my head. "That woman is a saint."

Jack grabbed his coat off the back of one of his conference table chairs. He stuck his hand in one of his pockets and rooted around. He nodded, then shrugged on the jacket. "Let's go."

The drive out to Heaven was a quiet one except for the wind whistling as it buffeted the Jeep back and forth. White powder blew in almost a straight line across the road, except during the deep gasps between gusts. The heater struggled to keep up with the cold outside. The interior was warmish, but the pockets of air near the windows stayed below freezing, and the side windows frosted over.

We pulled up to my mother's house.

"Thanks. I'll see you tomorrow, I guess. If the weather doesn't get worse."

Jack turned off the Jeep. "I want to pay my respects to Agatha."

"It's freezing. You don't have to do that. I'll pass the message."

He grinned at me, and the left side of his face came alive, jumpstarting me with it. "I'll race you inside," he said.

I shook my head, but when he bolted out the door, I scrambled after him, laughing. I slipped and slid up the walkway in my ancient moon boots. I reached the porch first, but only because Jack stopped to grab my suitcase from the backseat before taking off for the house.

I knocked the snow off my feet. "I win."

The door opened before I could turn the knob, revealing the figure behind it.

Johnny Phelps. My father.

I STILL COULDN'T BELIEVE the couple sitting on the couch holding hands was my parents. They looked much the same as my child's eye remembered them from last time they'd sat with me, although Dad had aged far more in fifteen years than my mother. His strong, broad frame had withered to half its size. He'd kept his hair, but it was nearly white. Deep furrows creased his face and age spots covered the backs of his hands. Still, he held his head high and his shoulders squared. His light blue eyes sparkled as he looked from Mother to where I sat on the hearth with Jack and back again, like he was surrounded by Cracker Jack prizes and couldn't believe his luck.

Mother was trying to explain it all to me. "Your dad called me a few weeks ago. When he got out."

"You knew he was 'in'?"

"Yes." She smiled at the man beside her. "About a year after he, um, took up residence there, he wrote to me. And to you."

I jumped to my feet. "He wrote to me?"

"He did."

My dad nodded. "Once a week ever since the second year."

Mother smiled, but it was a shaky one. "I kept them for you, dear."

My voice came out as a screech. "Why didn't you give them to me before?"

She frowned. "Your father left us, he humiliated us, and his being in jail only made it worse. He was in jail because he *killed* someone. What would Rich have thought? His family? Your friends? Your employers? I didn't want you hurt. I didn't want anyone to know."

"More like your friends. Your church. Your employer." I turned to my father. "And you were okay with that?"

He shook his head. "I didn't know. I thought you weren't answering. I didn't blame you."

I paced back and forth in front of them. I whirled on my mother. "I was a grown woman. You deciding for me? That's not okay. Not okay!"

She hung her head. "I understand that now. I'm sorry."

Dad put his other hand over their clasped ones. He looked at me. "Sweet Pea, I was pretty angry at your mother, too. But I've thrown away a lot of my life, spent it apart from the ones I love. I don't have time to be angry anymore. I forgave her, and she forgave me."

I sank back to the hearth and put my head in my hands. Jack slipped an arm around my waist. I couldn't wrap my head around this. The father who had deserted me really hadn't. The mother who didn't leave me had kept him from me, out of supposed misguided intentions, or, more likely, bitterness. And now they'd kissed and made up like the last decade didn't matter? Maybe it didn't to them, but it did to me.

I lifted my head, glaring at both of them. "So this"—I pointed at their clasped hands—"came about how and when?"

Dad lifted their hands. "Well, she started writing me back a few years ago. Then, when I got out, I called her. Asked if I could come see her."

Mother beamed. "He got here Christmas."

I made a growling noise. "And, just like that, you forgave him, after all these years angry at him, all those years keeping me angry at him, too?"

She cocked her head at me. "He's my husband. Your father. I love him."

They looked at each other like two teenagers. Mother giggled. She *giggled*.

My father touched their hands to his chest, one, two, three times. "And we won't waste another second."

"Amen." She put her head on his shoulder.

I scraped my teeth over my bottom lip. "So I'm supposed to forget how you struggled, Mother? Or that I couldn't understand why my father didn't want to see me win Southwest Region Champs my senior year at Tech? Or give me away at my wedding?"

"Well, that didn't work out so well, dear."

I glared at my mother. "That's not the point. The point is how do you propose we forget all of this?"

Her blue eyes made big **O**s. "We don't. We just move forward."

Dad stared at his knees or his feet or something on the floor away from my face. He cleared his throat. "I'm sorry, Emily. For everything. I've got so many regrets."

"Well, at least you're sorry."

"Emily—" Jack said.

I turned on him, reclaiming a bit of my earlier anger. "What about you, Jack? Are you sorry? Sorry for hiding things from me and lying to me?"

His face lost color. "Uh—"

I jumped to my feet again. "How come you all think I'm so fragile, that I can't handle the truth?"

Dad's wrinkles deepened and sagged. Jack stood beside me, but it was Mother who spoke. "Oh, honey, it's not about you being fragile. It's about you being loved."

I looked at the three of them, wanting to pounce, but it stopped me mid-leap. Love. Love stopped me. All that love, imperfect and painful and real and waiting. I didn't want to waste any more time either. I took three big steps toward my father, and he stood in time to catch me in his arms as my tears fell.

I saw Jack motion to my mother and the two of them slipped from the room. Dad patted my back and rocked me until I quieted and my tears dried up.

Dad held me away from him. "Once your mom came around, she started sending me pictures, keeping me up-to-date on you. I'm so proud of you."

I wiped my eyes, shaking my head. "I've made such a mess of everything."

"Oh, Sweet Pea, I'm an expert at making a mess, and I can promise you, you are a minor-league mess."

I laughed.

"About the time I found out about you being back here with your mother, Jack got in touch with me. I'm sorry if the way I decided to handle things upset you. I wanted to come home and talk to you face-to-face myself."

"I understand. I don't like it, but you're the dad I've known and loved all my life, and I understand."

His big hands squeezed my shoulder. "I hear you're the big hero once again. I swear, Emily, after hearing what you did to save that little girl and all those people in New Mexico in the fall, and now how you saved those kids and Mickey, I'm two inches taller again."

I fell back into his chest, unable to stop the tears again. "Oh, Daddy, it was all you. Everything I did, it was all what you taught me."

He laughed against my hair. "They just didn't know they were messing with the wrong girl."

HALF AN HOUR LATER, Jack sat at the kitchen table talking with my dad, while Mother chopped vegetables for a salad and I stuck the steaks in the oven on broil.

"I'm having a glass of wine. Anyone else want one?" I opened the refrigerator door.

Jack stopped. "Not me. But I need to talk to you before dinner."

"Oh my gosh, I'm so talked out." I groaned as I unscrewed the cap from the white zin. "What do we have left to talk about?" I pulled a glass down from the cabinet and began to fill it.

"Betsy."

I stopped mid-pour. "Did we forget to do something for her?"

"It's not that. But maybe we could step out back for a moment?"

"Are you crazy? It's"—I looked at the thermometer in the window—"seventeen degrees outside. Colder with wind chill."

"So wrap up. It's important, and last time I told you we needed to talk and then we didn't, you got pretty darn mad at me."

"Honey, don't be difficult with Jack." Mother, taking Jack's side, his biggest fan as always.

"Okay." I capped the wine box. "Where's my ski suit?"

Twelve layers later, Jack and I stepped onto the back patio. It was a hair past seven thirty and dark outside. The porch lights shed enough illumination that I could see the shadowy outline of our dilapidated little barn at the back end of our property, looking abandoned. Well, now that Dad was back, that would change. A lot of things would change.

I realized Jack was speaking. "What?"

"The state of Texas isn't going to move you to the front of the line to adopt, not with the way things stand now."

"What do you mean?"

"Well, you live with your mom for one thing. And dad now, too, I guess."

"I'm putting my money down on a duplex this week."

He shook his head. "That won't get you past the unmarried issue."

The skin prickled on the back of my neck. "That's not as big a deal as it used to be."

"Why give them any more red flags than you have to?"

"You're depressing me. I'm trying my best, Jack. This is me, trying."

"I know it is. And you're doing good."

I shivered. "It's freezing. If you're done busting my chops, can we go back inside?"

He crouched on one knee on the snowy concrete. He pulled a small box out of his jacket pocket. "I'm trying, too. Here."

"What the heck are you trying to do?"

"Just open it, please."

"Why are you down on the ground?"

"I'm beginning to wonder that, myself."

I pulled the wrapping paper off the box. Inside was a jeweler's box. A small one. My heart and breath froze, and time stood still. I opened the lid. In it was a piece of paper folded over and over and over.

"Cute. I almost fell for it." I snapped the box shut.

"Open it. And please be very careful when you do."

I reopened the box and unfolded the edges of paper. Inside it was another piece of paper, folded up like the other.

"You know, some people think the whole psych-out gift thing is funny."

"This was supposed to be easier." He stood up, brushed snow from his knees, and straightened the paper out in front of me. "Look at it." He shifted the partially shadowed real-estate flyer. "Gorgeous new 4 BR/3 BA family home on 5 acres w/fencing/stables in Bushland, TX." There was a cross-out mark through Bushland. Above it HEAVEN was written in block capitals. Jack's handwriting.

"You're buying a new house?"

He sighed and kneeled again. "Open the other paper."

Out of the corner of my eye, I saw movement in the kitchen window. Two heads together, watching us. I examined the white paper and felt something hard sliding around inside it. My irritation gave way to confusion. I unfolded it, and poured its contents into my hand.

A ring. A gold band with a big fat shiny teardrop diamond.

Jack took it from me, grasped my left hand, and held the ring toward it. "Emily, will you please marry me and move into this house with me and let me adopt Betsy with you?"

A million thoughts flashed through my mind. The first time I'd seen Jack's face. My palms sweating when he offered me a job. Jack at the emergency room with me when I lost the baby. Our first kiss. Jack, angry and hurt and remote. Learning about his wife and kids. Jack at their graves.

That I hadn't told him about my own pitiful reproductive situation and needed to, soon. Realizing I was in love with him, that of all the men on Earth, he was the man who did it for me.

I opened my mouth to answer, but nothing came out. Instead I gave his shoulders a shove. He toppled off the patio, and I followed him. Down, down, down to a drift of snow, where I landed on him with a windblown, icy-nosed kiss.

HELL TO PAY (EMILY BERNAL #3)

A WHAT DOESN'T KILL YOU TEXAS-TO-NEW MEXICO ROMANTIC MYSTERY

ONE

Disco lights whirled around me, or was it the room? My inner party animal had atrophied, not that I'd ever been a real heavyweight. If it wasn't for the fantastic people-watching—and the fact that this was the celebration party for the burglary acquittal of our firm's client Phil Escalante the day before, and his engagement to Nadine, one of my best friends in Amarillo—I'd've bagged this shindig. Instead, there I was with tendrils of fake smoke floating past my face, ten feet from a DJ dressed in a black latex fetish costume and spiked dog collar and spinning 70s tunes.

A tall woman maybe ten years older than me appeared out of the low lights and sidled up to me, engulfing me in the odor of cigarettes. Her vanilla hair sported a generous dollop of dark chocolate roots, which was pretty funny to me since she had a body shaped like a cone. A waffle cone. A waffle cone with sparkly sprinkles from the spinning ball overhead. Behind her trailed a paunchy man of roughly her height. His eyes had locked on me in a way that made my skin crawl with leeches that weren't there.

Rick James's "*Super Freak*" ended. The silence in the cavernous L-shaped room was immediate and complete, but short-lived. A clamor of voices from the one-hundred-or-so guests resumed, their voices echoing off the bare walls and drop ceiling.

"Hey, Foxy Loxy," the man mouthed at me. Or did he? Surely not. It was hard to tell with the lights playing tricks on my eyes.

The woman spoke past me. "You and your wife got any plans later?"

Her bellow seemed to fill the room to its farthest corners, even with all the other voices. I winced and shrank under the eyes that shifted our way.

Not Jack, though. The horse rancher cum criminal attorney was nothing if not unflappable. His topaz eyes twinkled. "Emily's not my wife."

The man surged toward Jack. "You're not together?"

"I'm his fiancée," I said through my recently tightened braces and painfully rubber-banded teeth, leaving out "and he's my boss." I waved my big, fat teardrop-shaped diamond at him to accentuate my point, then I pinched Jack's arm where my hand was looped through its crook. I'd capitulated to the mouth gear when my childhood orthodontist saw the gap between my front teeth and insisted I needed Invisalign, then filled my mouth with metal instead. Payback for never wearing my retainer, I guess.

The man and woman looked at each other and nodded. She asked, "Care to join us? We've got a room at a no-tell hotel nearby."

Jack's whole body shook and I didn't dare look at him. I was a sucker for his laugh. In fact, I was a sucker for everything about him, from his lived-in boots to his permanent tan to his Apache cheekbones. Before either of us could think of an appropriate response, Phil interrupted.

"Millie, Pete, leave my poor friends alone." He clapped a hand on my shoulder and gently pushed me aside to clap his other onto Jack's. "They're not swingers. And this isn't a swingers social. I'm out of the business."

The space between Millie's eyebrows narrowed and puckered as drops of light rained down on her face. "It's a free country, ain't it?"

"Well, sure—"

"We're not intewested." Ugh. Between my braces and the booze, I sounded like a toddler with a lisp. "But thank you."

The man shrugged. "Didn't know you blew spit bubbles when we made the invite. I think I'll pass."

My lower jaw unhinged. I straightened my powder-blue spring-weight top. I sputtered but nothing came out. This time Jack's laugh was audible, and he squeezed me past Phil and over to him.

Millie leaned toward Phil, her voice derisive. "Those Mighty is His Word folks got you running scared."

Jack and I looked at each other, and his raised brows mirrored mine. The Mighty is His Word congregation was the self-appointed sin police in these parts, and they had harassed Phil's swingers club and its patrons relentlessly. Phil swore the group had a mole, since the dates of the events and identities of the members weren't public information. He'd decided to find out, so he let himself into the pastor's personal quarters to investigate.

That would have gotten him two to twenty if the jury hadn't latched onto his excuse that he'd entered the unlocked rooms thinking he was still in the church and only looking for a restroom. That, and if he hadn't picked Jack as his attorney. Jack was good in the courtroom. Very, very good.

Beside Phil, Nadine appeared, a combo of Amazon warrior and Macbethian witch. Her long black hair was pulled back in a jet-hued scarf, kohl liner rimmed her eyes, and a long-sleeved black dress held her in place, somewhat. A shiny pair of black biker boots completed her ensemble, and it looked like she'd dressed Phil to match. He put both his arms around her ample waist and grinned into her even more ample cleavage, located conveniently at his eye level. The music restarted: Rod Stewart crooning "Hot Legs."

Phil chuckled. "The Mighty is His Word fuckers? Nah. They don't scare me. I've just gone straight. Love's made a changed man of me."

Not that Phil had changed much. He and Nadine had recently opened Get Your Kicks, an adult novelty store, in the same downtown building we were celebrating in, that used to house his swingers club. Not like in the same room we were standing in now, but in the corner of the L where they had carved off and re-created retail space. But sexual mores aside, I didn't know a kinder, more generous soul than Phil. In the four months they'd been dating, he'd become the father Nadine's sons had never had and the defender of her honor from every lech that assumed she was slinging more than drinks at the Polo Club.

"My hero," Nadine said. Her voice teased, but her eyes shone like she meant it, and I knew she did.

Phil released Nadine and pulled his cell from a belt-loop holster. I could just barely hear it ringing. Staring at the screen, he held up a finger. "Business calls, my sweet." He turned slightly away from the three of us and starting talking into his phone.

From where I stood, I couldn't hear Phil, but I saw the tightness in Nadine's face and the hunch of her shoulders. Just as things were getting awkward with all of us standing around staring at each other while Phil yakked, his call ended.

He turned back to us, his face dark. Then he grinned so fast I wondered if I'd even seen the unhappy expression. He tilted his face to kiss Nadine. "I've gotta hit the head. Bring you a drink when I come back?"

"Crown and Coke." She watched his retreating figure with a look on her face I hadn't seen her direct at Phil before. Distrust? Concern? Doubt?

My eyes shifted to Phil, too. What struck me as odd about him was that he didn't have an empty drink in his hand. Phil never went drinkless. I'd never seen him sloshed, but he was always well lubed, as my Dad liked to call it.

Millie whispered to her friend and they left without further comment, heading in the same direction as Phil.

I leaned in to Nadine. "Everything okay?"

She nodded, still watching Phil, but the look on her face didn't agree. Then she turned to me and smiled. "I can't believe you got those braces. You look fourteen. Hardly old enough to be the mother of a six-year-old."

Thirty-one was closing in on me, fast. "If Betsy's adoption gets approved." Which wasn't a sure thing, even though it was one of the most important things in my life. I looked for wood to knock on, but there was none. I rapped lightly with my knuckles on Jack's noggin instead.

"Hey, what's that for?" He rubbed his head.

"Superstition."

His left eyebrow shot up.

Months had passed since I'd applied to adopt Betsy. We'd overcome her kidnapping and the death of her parents. We'd found her missing Mexican birth certificate and applied for a Special Juvenile Immigrant status visa, which would give her permanent resident status if granted. We hoped to hear back on approval in the next two months. I'd endured the home study and done pretty well, I thought. Still, the state of Texas, in its infinite wisdom, hadn't approved me yet, and I was getting anxious. Meanwhile, Betsy languished in a foster family with eleven other kids. A Mighty is His Word family at that. I believe in God, and I go to church, but there's religion and then there's full-on daffy, and the Mighty is His Word group struck me as the latter.

Nadine turned to my fiancé. "What do you think of her braces, Jack?"

His gaze heated my cheeks. As my oh-so-classy, tactful mother had said to me the week before, Jack had me hot to trot. Smiling, he put a palm to my flaming cheek then tapped my lips with his index finger. "I'm kind of partial to her gap, second only to her bangs." I opened my mouth to object—he gave me unending heck about the volume of my bangs—then closed it. "But I like Emily no matter what she has on." He put his lips to my ear and his words were a nibble. "Or not on."

I inhaled him slow and deep. Leather, sunshine, furniture polish, and the lingering scent of our afternoon romp brought back our conversation from earlier. *Now that I've moved out of the office into a real house, this Murphy bed isn't getting any use,* he'd said as he opened the cabinet and put his hand on the mattress. *Poor neglected Murphy bed,* I'd purred while untucking his shirt. The memory of it coupled with his ear nibbles did yummy, squirmy things to me now.

"Oh, for Pete's sake, get a room," a voice gayer than RuPaul's broke in. I didn't have to turn to know it was Wallace Gray. Wallace downplayed his sexual orientation by day, but vamped it up off hours. I didn't blame him for his daytime subterfuge. Amarillo was not a blue city, and Texas was not a blue state.

I blinked away my bedroom eyes as Nadine exchanged cheek kisses with Wallace. Jack and I got to pay our homage.

"Something's different with you." Wallace took me by the shoulders and cocked his head. "Did you have a stroke?"

I said, "Orthodontia isn't a laughing matter." Or tried to. I shook my head and spat out, "Chihuahua," accentuating the first syllable with a *sh* instead of a *ch* sound.

"Say it, don't spray it, Bugs Bunny." He cocked his head at me. "Hey, wait. Was that a new non-curse word? SHE-wah-wah. Like SHE-yutt?"

I nodded.

"I like it. Way to liven up your game there, wild thing."

I socked his wiry bicep. "Kiss my grits, Wallace."

He winced and rubbed it even though I'd barely tapped him. "Hey, Nadine, where's the man of the hour?"

A shadow crossed Nadine's face. She peered around the open space, through the revelers who had come out in force for the Thursday night celebration. "Bathroom? Bar?" She pursed her lips sideways like a semicolon. "He should be back by now."

"I'm gonna head that way myself. I'll let you know if I see him." Jack patted my behind twice and set off toward the bathrooms.

"Have you guys set a date?" Wallace asked.

Nadine and I said, "No," both at once. I smiled and shrugged at her.

"We were waiting for the verdict." Nadine looked toward the bar, then the bathrooms again. "I know Jack was confident all along, but that bitchy ADA was so aggressive and sure of herself, I didn't want to take any chances." The ADA in question—Melinda Stafford—had been my mortal enemy since childhood, and I thought Nadine was being too charitable about her.

"Sounds reasonable. And what's your excuse, rodeo queen?" Wallace said, referring to my cowgirl and pageant past. "Because we know Jack's not the holdup." He crossed his arms over his chest.

The music had stopped again, and the background hum of conversation seemed to halt with it, as if the whole room was awaiting my answer. The disco ball shot beams that danced on Wallace's head like spotlights. Two sets of eyes bored into me, as I shifted from foot to foot. Wallace was right. Jack would have married me months ago if I'd agreed, but I'd been dragging my feet. It was hard to explain why, especially since he was successful, handsome, kind, and great in the sack. My cheeks heated again. Yeah, *really* great in the sack. It was just that he'd lost his wife and kids a few years ago. Then he'd proposed marriage to me to help me adopt Betsy, so I wasn't sure whether he wanted me or just wanted to help me or even just wanted to replace his family. Especially because the L-word hadn't been part of the deal. And I wanted the L-word. I wanted him to want me for me. I hadn't admitted that to anyone, though, and now didn't seem the time or place.

I pointed to my mouth. "I'm waiting to get these ugly braces—"

A hand tugged my wrist. I wheeled toward the pressure to find a pale, wiry man I'd never seen before. He stepped into me, into my space and eyeball-to-eyeball, his deep-socketed ones black and intense. "Tell Jack I didn't do it."

He released me and jogged off, punching the front door open. He stepped aside to let Phil in, then dashed out. Phil's voice boomed over every other sound in the room. "Help! We need a doctor outside—and an ambulance!" I caught a flash of wild eyes under dark hair, and then he was gone.

Despite the fact that it was statistically unlikely that everyone in the room was a doctor, the crowd moved as one toward the door, with me in it. My mind reeled from the double whammy of the disquieting interruption by the pale man and Phil's frantic announcement. Nadine broke to the front of the pack, with Wallace and me right behind her. We burst out into the parking lot. Cool air and the stink of cattle feed lots hit me. The smell wasn't surprising as Amarillo is the cattle-feeding capital of the world, or at least Texas. The parking lot was unlit, except for a street lamp on the corner and the sparkling stars in the clear April sky, not unlike the lights from the disco ball inside. I stopped, searching for Phil, and so did Wallace, but Nadine kept running.

Wallace pointed past her. "There's Phil."

"What's going on?" Jack asked, appearing out of nowhere and catching up to us.

We took off running again, Jack with us this time, in Nadine's wake.

"Phil came in yelling for a doctor and ambulance," I said, but I was starting to huff and puff so it didn't come out all in one piece. "That's all we know."

We wove through the parked cars to the farthest, darkest edge of the lot, where it bordered an abandoned-looking building. Phil was kneeling over someone or something, his body blocking our view. Sirens wailed in the distance, moving closer. Nadine crouched beside her fiancé. We came to a stop behind them.

A tall woman in fishnet hose, garters, satin panties, and a pink satin baby-doll top lay facedown on the pavement, a pair of bunny ears on a headband askew. For a moment I thought, *Ah, like Playboy*, but then I realized there was no bustier or tail; it was almost Easter, and the ears were white, at least where they weren't splashed with an explosion of something mushy and red. My stomach bucked. Phil and Nadine gently rolled the woman to her back. As they did, I realized that the mushy mess was an enormous sheet cake decorated with what looked like . . . I stared harder, not believing what I was seeing at first. The entire intact left side was covered by a red icing penis. Above the penis were the words "Congrats, Phil &—" but I couldn't read the rest, because the right-hand side of the cake had been obliterated by the woman's face.

Phil wiped cake from the woman's nose and mouth and leaned down to begin CPR breaths. Nadine's hand clutched at the back of Phil's black shirt. I stepped closer. Now I could see blood dripping across the woman's gashed temple and onto the pavement. I re-examined the cake and shuddered. Its top edge abutted a concrete parking stanchion, covered in dripping red liquid that couldn't be icing. I shuddered, and Jack slipped an arm around my waist. The wiry man's words echoed in my head: *Tell Jack I didn't do it.*

The scream of the sirens was very near, growing louder. When it held steady, I peered down the street. A police car had parked ten yards away. Two cops approached, hands on their guns.

"Amarillo Police Department," one of them shouted. "Put your hands where we can see them, everyone." I knew the voice. Officer John Burrows, a good cop and a good friend.

I held my hands up, waving one, then pointing. "John, it's Emily and Jack. There's a woman over there hurt bad."

John's red head drew closer until I could see his face. He nodded at me and said something to the short, muscular female cop striding beside him. An ambulance drew to a stop at the curb behind the cruiser, and paramedics hopped out.

"Over here. Bring the gurney," John yelled back to them.

A throng of people had gathered behind us. I glanced at them, their faces blurring together. Jack pulled me closer. John and the female officer started moving people back from the woman on the ground. The paramedics rushed over with their rolling stretcher through the space the officers had cleared. Phil stopped CPR to make room for them. He turned toward us, and my hand covered my mouth.

Phil's face was covered in blood and icing. Red, cornflower blue, yellow, and black smeared together in a macabre mask. He sat on his haunches, unmoving, seemingly oblivious to it. Nadine lifted the corner of the skirt of her dress and wiped at his face, but he pushed her hand away. He lowered his head into his hands and rolled forward on his feet until his forehead rested on the pavement.

A woman's voice shrieked, "Oh my God, that's a man!"

My eyes shot back toward the woman on the ground. Her panties were askew, revealing indisputable evidence that she was in fact genetically a he.

Jack and I stood beside Phil in the open doorway of Get Your Kicks as John and the female cop—who had introduced herself as Alicia Nurse—questioned him. We'd already given our statements, so they allowed us to be present as his counsel, on the condition that I meet with a sketch artist later to capture my memory of the strange man that had appeared and disappeared so quickly, with a suspicious message at a suspicious time.

John said, "Do you know the deceased?"

"His name's Dennis Welch." Phil pointed to a black F-250. "That's his truck."

The cops shared a look. "How do you know him?" John asked.

Phil shook his head, his eyes closed. "We've been best friends since middle school." He flicked on the light to the room, and I squinted as my eyes adjusted.

This was my first time in Get Your Kicks. I'd expected something très trashy, given the merchandise they planned to carry, the reference to Route 66 in the name, and the customer base I'd imagined for them, since Nadine worked in a strip bar and Phil had run a swingers club. But it was actually more sexy than tacky. The light was soft and rosy. The walls were painted a boudoir red, and curtains of dark lace were draped over black lights, casting moody shadows on the ceiling. They had a big space to work with, and they'd partitioned the center of the room with standing screens. One section featured an iron four-poster bed on which bondage merchandise was displayed in leather, metal spikes, synthetic rubber, and latex. Another one contained an old dance cage from an 80s club. One made me shudder, given what I'd just seen in the parking lot. It held a female mannequin in a sexy red-and-black bunny costume, holding an Easter basket full of fake green grass topped off with a dildo and flavored lubricating oil. The display I liked best had a swing hanging from the ceiling by colorful silk scarves tied one to another.

The gently divided sections faced different types of toys on shelves and racks. Men's wear. Women's wear. Bondage. Media. Intimate items to enhance, ahem, pleasure. My mouth grew moist and I itched to slide my hands over some of the silky goodies in the women's section, to slither them onto my body, and to try the swing. I looked back at Jack, and his amber eyes were as hazy as mine felt.

He cocked his sexy left brow, and my stomach tightened as his lopsided half smile drove his dimple into his left cheek. "Later," he mouthed at me, and the rest of me suddenly felt moist as well. Yes, Mother was right. He had me hot to trot.

While I was lusting after my fiancé, John kept talking. "Where did you meet him?"

"Boys Ranch."

That got my attention. I hadn't realized Phil was a Boys Rancher. I was pretty sure I'd heard Nadine complain about his mother, so I hadn't thought he was an orphan, but I knew that Cal Farley's Boys Ranch for many years had taken in boys—and girls these days—who were in trouble, either themselves or because of their family situations. I'd been out to their facilities northwest of Amarillo for one of their rodeos. You wouldn't realize Boys Ranch was anything but a small Texas town from looking at it. Modest but normal homes with house parents and kids living in them, a church, a medical facility, a school. It was completely self-contained, and everyone that lived there pitched in. They had a fantastic track record for saving kids, and Wallace had once told me that CPS referred as many kids their way as they could.

"Did he, uh, always dress like that?" John asked.

"No. It was a joke. He told me he couldn't afford a stripper. For my engagement. That's what the party was for. My engagement, and some, uh, recent good news."

"Did you know he was going to be here?"

"Yeah. I invited him." He held his phone aloft. It was smudged with blood and icing. "He called me from a few blocks away. I went outside to meet him."

"Meet him for what?"

Phil looked at Jack. *Not the look*, I thought. Nothing good came after a client looked at his attorney like that. Jack kept his face impassive.

Phil finally answered. "He asked me to help him carry stuff in."

This time it was Officer Nurse who spoke. "Did you talk to him in the parking lot?"

"No. I found him. Like that." Phil's voice broke.

"Did you see anyone else?"

He shook his head. "No." He scrubbed his eyes and then his head angled forward into his hands and his back shook.

I patted Phil's back, feeling inadequate for the task, wishing Nadine was there in my place, but she was outside per police instructions. The cops didn't let witnesses listen to each other, and they hadn't talked to her yet.

"Is there any other way we could verify where you were at the time?"

Phil pointed toward the office. "We just installed surveillance cameras, but the farthest one out just gets the perimeter of the building, not the parking lot."

"My guy," I said, and four heads swiveled toward me. "The one that came up to me inside right before Phil found his friend. He'll be on the video."

Officer Nurse wrote something down. "We'll need to view and take a copy of that video, Mr. Escalante."

"Of course."

"Do you know anyone who would want to hurt Mr., uh—"

"Welch. Dennis Welch."

"Mr. Welch."

Jack had been staring at the ground, lips compressed, but he looked up at Officer Nurse. "Do you guys know yet whether this was foul play or an accident?"

"We're just covering all the bases."

I swallowed, my throat dry. A possible murder right outside the party where a strange man who knew Jack had accosted me, and they were treating us all like suspects, especially Phil. It was all sobering. Amarillo seemed like a safe place, but bad things happened here just like everywhere there were humans.

Phil was shaking his head. "He doesn't even live here. He lives in Borger. And Denver."

"Is this your place?"

"Yes."

"Any trouble with break-ins, muggings, or whatnot?"

Phil waffled his hand. "Harassment. I used to run a swingers club here, and that goddamn church, Mighty is His Word—they'd stand in the way of cars, take pictures, hold up signs. Intimidate and humiliate people."

"Were they ever physical?"

Phil shook his head. "Not that I know of."

The two officers shared a look and Nurse sighed.

Jack jumped in. "Officers, is that all for now? We'd like to take care of our friend. He's had a horrible shock."

Nurse shook her head. "We're going to need him to show us the video first. Stick around, though, please, in case we have more questions."

"Can we come see the video? Emily might be able to ID the man she saw."

Nurse and John looked at each other and shook their heads. John crossed his arms. "Jack, no offense, but we only have your word on where you were when this happened, and Emily is your fiancée. Let's sit her down with the sketch artist, then we'll show her the video."

"And me?"

John shook his head.

"But it's my client's evidence."

"And your client can choose whoever he wants for an attorney, even someone who hasn't been cleared in an investigation, but we won't compromise our investigation because of it."

"Fine." Jack put his hand on my back, easing me toward the exit.

I took off and he followed.

"We'll be in the office area." John took Phil by the arm and started walking toward the back of Get Your Kicks to the office.

I stopped. Jack veered around me and kept going. "John?" I said.

He turned to me and cocked his head, and his partner waited beside him.

"Do you guys know how Dennis died? Was it from hitting his head on the concrete?" I stammered a little, feeling awkward with Nurse there, even though she seemed okay.

He shook his head. "We'll have to wait on the autopsy. Could be anything. A heart attack. Drugs. Or hitting his head."

I nodded. "Okay."

He smiled at me, the first time his guard had lowered since he arrived. Nurse started to walk away, and he leaned toward me and spoke softly. "Stay safe, Calamity Jane. The cavalry is only a few digits away."

I saluted him. "Good night."

As his comment sunk in, I got a funny feeling about it. Was John flirting with me? I knew he was going through a divorce, but surely he wouldn't flirt when he knew I was engaged to Jack, and with Jack so close by. Well, whatever he was doing, it was nice he had my back. When John and I met a few months before, he'd accused me of being reckless and too quick to pull the gun my father had given me a lifetime ago. He was wrong, of course. My daddy had raised me to be self-reliant. But then, Dad *had* ended up in jail for killing a guy with a broken bottle—in self-defense, although that didn't do much to lessen the way it made me feel. Or the taint on our collective reputations. But I wasn't going down that path. Yes, I am self-reliant. I found Betsy and rescued her from kidnappers when the police hadn't, and I saved two teen runaways from a bad cop all by myself, too.

Maybe I didn't need John or anyone else coming to my rescue, but I'd keep him on speed dial just in case.

TWO

My head was at the wrong end of the bed and my body entwined in covers after an athletic night stimulated by the sight of all those silk scarves, swings, and pleasure toys. We'd gotten home late from the police station, where I'd worked with the sketch artist—which had really keyed Jack up for some reason. Not that I was complaining. Who needed sleep anyway? Jack's face was pressed against my hair. Ah, the beautiful after-glow. My whole body tingled and I rubbed my legs against his, luxuriating in the sensation of his skin. I touched my kiss-swollen lips and smiled.

"I love you," I cooed, sleepily.

Silence.

My throat constricted, wanting to pull the words back in. I hadn't meant to say them. I'd promised myself that I'd make Jack go first. He was the one who had proposed, after all. It was just I was all mushy with the intimacy and half-asleep to boot.

Brrrring!

Jack groaned in my ear. "Whose is it?"

Brrrring!

"Mine." My heart hurt. Maybe Jack had been saved by the bell, but how could he just ignore my declaration like I hadn't spoken? I reached for the bedside table, disentangling myself from my boss/fiancé as I did.

Brrrring!

I swiped my phone screen to silence the persistent noise. My scrunched morning eyes were too bleary to read the screen to see who it was, but these days I always answered it. It could be Betsy. Or good news about the adoption. "This is Emily."

"Hi, Emily. This is Michele." The warm voice on the other end made me smile despite the interruption, the early hour, and the fact that it wasn't good news about Betsy.

I grabbed the lavender sheets in one hand and pulled them over my torso as I sat up. "Hi! I can't wait to see you." Michele Lopez Hanson was the Baylor law school roomie of my best friend and former boss, Katie. We met when I tagged along to a reunion as Katie's plus one back before she got married, so she wouldn't have to face alone all her married classmates talking about their perfect kids and spouses.

Beside me, Jack shucked the covers and levered his naked body off the tall four-poster iron bed. He was ten years older than me, but in far better shape for his age, even though I'd taken up hot yoga recently in an effort to keep up. He disappeared into the sage-green bathroom, shutting the door behind him. A little of my hurt dissipated.

"That's why I'm calling. I'm going to email you my itinerary, but I wanted you to know I'm coming in Tuesday evening. Is that okay?"

Wallace had booked Michele next Wednesday to speak to Tri AMATX, Amarillo's triathlon club. Michele had just completed an Ironman triathlon as a tribute to her deceased husband, a professional triathlete. The two had coauthored a successful triathlon training book, too, before he died, so she was a hot commodity in the endurance athletics world. Wallace loved the sport, so he was over the moon about her coming. I admired it, but I got tired just watching it on TV. Seriously. When Wallace made me sit through the TiVoed World Championship race, I'd fallen asleep way before Michele ever crossed the finish line.

"Absolutely. Wallace and I will pick you up."

"And I thought I'd go home Saturday, if you don't mind me staying that long. I've scheduled workouts with some of the local triathletes on Thursday and Friday."

Better her than me. "You go, girl."

The doorbell rang. I pulled my phone away from my ear and squinted at the tiny characters in the upper right-hand corner of the screen. 7:49 a.m. "Holy mother of pearl. Michele, someone's at the door."

"What did you say?"

"Someone's at the door."

"No, before that."

"Oh, mother of pearl?"

"Yeah. That. Oh, you were cussing. Wow. Okay."

"Got it," Jack yelled from the bathroom.

I never understood why it was such a shock to people that I didn't take the Lord's name in vain or say the F-word. "Well, I really do have to go."

"I'll email you. And see you soon. Bye," Michele said.

"Bye." I put the phone down.

Jack flashed by toward a pile of yesterday's clothes on the chintz armchair.

I was still smarting a little from his dissing my "I love you," but he was too cute to stay upset. I sang, "Oh yes, they call him the street. Boogiedad boogiedad."

He stopped. "Huh?"

"You know, that old song about a guy who runs around naked in public."

He laughed and grabbed his jeans. "The Streak. They call him the *Streak*. Because he was streaking."

I crossed my fingers under the sheets. "I know that. My braces just make me hard to understand."

Jack grinned at me like he knew I was lying and hopped into his jeans, commando, and pulled on a T-shirt. He was out the bedroom door and trotting toward the front door before I was out of bed.

I rose and stretched. What kind of person showed up before eight o'clock, anyway? Maybe it was a neighbor bringing Snowflake back, if she'd escaped again. Jack had let the little Pomeranian out to do her business before we got down to ours, so to speak. We'd installed a nanny cam so we could monitor her from our phones and computers—which was usually only footage of the little red fox who'd staked a claim to our yard —but I hadn't checked on her yet.

I heard the front door open and shut and voices talking as I walked to my closet through the bathroom. I loved my closet there at the house we'd dubbed Shangri-La, a nod to Jack calling our community west of Amarillo "Heaven" because it was closer to his beloved New Mexico. Before Jack bought Shangri-La, I'd lived in my childhood room in my parents' smallish three-bedroom house. And before that, I'd lived with my ex-husband in a Dallas condo that was fancy but compact. At this house, I had a walk-in closet of my very own with pegs for all my boots and floor-to-ceiling shoe racks. I twirled as I entered, then threw on some clean underclothes with a fresh pair of leggings and a soft tunic with deep, low pockets.

I walked into the great room. Jack was sitting with Margaret Fletcher, the woman who had conducted the home study for our adoption application. My hand flew to my hair, but it was too late to do anything about my bed head. Or my unbrushed teeth. Jack could have warned me. Margaret looked poised and put together in tan pants and a tan jacket with a pink shell top. She was a small woman, and Jack's brown leather chair dwarfed her; her black ballet flats didn't quite touch the ground.

I managed to glare at my fiancé and smile at Margaret at the same time. "Good morning. I wasn't expecting you, but welcome." Ruff. Ruff. Wham! Ruff. I glanced at the French doors leading out into the backyard. Snowflake was standing on the brick pavers, alternately barking and launching her white fluffy body at the glass. All five pounds of her. "Excuse me one second." I opened the door and let her in.

Snowflake danced around me on her hind legs like a circus monkey, then sprinted to Jack to do the same. She finished up by dashing quick circuits around the living room. I didn't try to stop her. We'd gone through doggy obedience school together the month before, and one of the things I'd learned was that I had to let her work off her joy before her brain re-engaged with her body.

Margaret furrowed her brow and her thin, high eyebrows came together to form an almost invisible blonde line across her forehead. "But I got a message that you requested a follow-up today. That's why I'm here."

I'm sure my mouth hung open to my shoulders—I was that surprised. "I'm sorry. I didn't contact you."

I sank into the couch beside Jack. Snowflake jumped into his lap. On the wall, the cuckoo clock that had belonged to Jack's grandparents chimed eight o'clock. It nested against bamboo weave wallpaper that I hadn't had time to strip and replace with a good coat of paint yet.

"How odd. It was a voice mail from a woman. She said she was you." Margaret clutched a small brown purse in her lap with both hands, a clipboard under it on her legs. "Well, do you have any questions for me, since I'm here?"

My insides burned. Someone impersonating me? The only woman who had a reason to do so and make me look bad in the process was Betsy's foster mother, Mary Alice Hodges. I shook my head. "I'd love a status report, although I don't want to keep you. I'm sure you have to get to work, and I know we do." I put my hand on Jack's knee. Snowflake licked it. "But we do keep hoping to hear we've got a court date to approve an adoption soon." Some of my hair was sticking to the corner of my mouth. I smiled and pushed it behind my ear, casual-like, trying to give the impression I was a woman who would have been up and had breakfast on the table an hour ago for a six-year-old before taking her to school. I hoped Margaret noticed I was at least the woman who'd decorated for Easter with cheery eggs, chick and bunny figurines, and a "He is Risen" framed needlepoint my mother made and foisted on me, insisting we hang it together.

"No news." She set her purse on the arm of the chair. "I'm sure you know that there is active *opposition* to your application from the foster parents, Trevon and Mary Alice Hodges." She glanced down at her clipboard and continued almost under her breath, "Wonderful people. So devout. Such giving foster parents."

I took a deep breath. Jack's hand lowered onto mine and Snowflake nuzzled them both. "Yes, we're aware. We had agreed with the caseworker from CPS that we could have biweekly visits with Betsy, but they've managed to prevent that three visits running, and they won't even make up for them with a Skype visit."

She pulled a pen loose from the clip holding her papers, and started tapping it on the board. "I had an email from them just this morning saying you were at a party last night at a swingers club." Her lips pressed thin and white.

I jumped to my feet, dislodging Jack's hand and our canine ball of fluff. "What? We were at an engagement party for a client of the law firm where we work. It was held at a building downtown. Not a swingers club. Not a swingers party." Margaret was staring at me, a little wide-eyed, so I smiled and sat down. Snowflake moved to safety on the far side of Jack's lap. "No swingers."

"Was that the party in the news this morning where a hooker was murdered in the parking lot?"

I started to jump up again, but Jack squeezed my knee and pressed down.

He spoke in his best imitation Amarillo accent, persuasive and reassuring. "Ms. Fletcher"—(Fletch-uh)—"I don't know where you get your information, but it seems to be from a very biased source. There were no hookers at this party. A man did fall and was found deceased there, but the police didn't say he was murdered."

She sniffed and patted her sandy-haired bun. "An engagement party. That reminds me of one little item I needed to follow up on. Have the two of you gotten married?"

Jack gave her his lopsided grin. His left dimple pulled up the corner of his mouth. Snowflake cocked her head and sat up straighter. "Not yet, but soon."

"Can I have a date for my notes?"

I started to protest. "Bu—"

"Ms. Fletcher, you're going to make me spoil the surprise for Emily." I turned to Jack, and his left eyebrow rose in a perfect arch. The right one stayed straight and dignified. He patted my knee. "No use begging, Emily. You'll thank me later."

Margaret looked back and forth between the two of us, and I pasted on the appropriate smile for a woman learning that her fiancé was planning a secret wedding. "Please do let me know when you've made it official," she said.

"Of course," Jack drawled.

"And in the meantime, I take it from your"—she wrinkled her nose—"state of undress that you are cohabiting in the home?"

Jack drew back as if in shock. "I just came over for breakfast. I live in my office downtown, like I have for the last five years."

Margaret nodded. "Uh-huh. And that's the office where Ms. Bernal works for you?"

"Mm," he grunted.

Margaret turned to me. "I don't think we've talked about your father yet, Ms. Bernal. What role would you anticipate letting him have in Betsy's life, given his—"

Jack's phone rang and Snowflake broke into a frenzy of barks. Out of the blue the month before she had decided that ringing phones were advance warning of alien invasion. Jack glanced at his screen. "My apologies, ladies. It's the office." He moved the yapping Snowflake aside, stood and walked out. His voice rang out from the hallway, and I heard him say, "Jack Holden speaking." Snowflake whined and ran across me to the far side of the couch, nearest where he'd gone, but close enough to provide assistance to me should another cell phone commence an attack.

Margaret strained to hear Jack on the phone, her whole body leaning toward where he had gone, giving me the opportunity to ignore her previous question, even though my blood was boiling. She'd hit a nerve. I tried to pretend I didn't have my own worries about my dad. He'd never been violent around me as a child, but what was inside him that he could kill somebody with a beer bottle? For that matter, what had prison done to the man I'd known? If he hadn't been a true killer before, didn't being around all those other violent criminals do something to a person? And that was on top of my pain from not hearing from him for nearly ten years —even if the hidden letters from him were my mother's doing—or dealing with what other people thought about him. Emotional baggage. I was still carrying more of its weight than I liked with regard to him.

In a raised voice, I said, "Well, if there's nothing else, I need to finish cleaning up our breakfast dishes so I can get to the office." I rose and reached toward her, offering my hand to shake.

"Search warrant? What for?" I heard Jack say. He sounded tense, and my stomach clenched.

Margaret gathered herself up, but I could tell she'd heard it, too.

"Jack has a very interesting job." I gestured toward our glass-paneled front door and walked to it, opening it for her. Just then, I heard my phone ringing in the bedroom, which I'd left open. Snowflake's yips pierced the air and nearly my eardrums as she flew down the hall toward the intruding sound, her feet barely touching the carpet. My pulse pounded in my ears now, between Margaret and her questions, Snowflake's racket, Jack ignoring my ill-advised love talk, and too many early morning phone calls.

"I'm on my way," Jack said into his phone, and he jogged past us to the bedroom. When he got to the door, he turned back. "Emily, we need to be out of here in five minutes."

"Aye, aye." Margaret hadn't moved, but I needed to. "Have a blessed day," I said to her. I trotted off after Jack.

"Well, alrighty, then," she said, and slammed the door behind her.

Jack rocketed at thirty-two miles per hour past a speed limit sign that said 30 on the way out of our neighborhood to Phil's place, which is how I knew he was worried. Jack usually navigated like he was driving Miss Daisy, and he never broke the law, on the theory that police officers and judges lie in wait for defense attorneys to screw up. I'm hoping they don't feel that way about paralegals who work for defense attorneys, too, or I'm toast.

Our normal route was blocked by a wreck, and Jack swore, and backtracked, making several turns before swinging his Jeep Wrangler onto a street I had never driven, in all my years in Amarillo. There weren't even street signs, at least not at the corners we'd passed. A wooden church loomed on the right.

"Not a good omen," Jack muttered.

"What isn't?"

He pointed at an enormous Jesus painted on the front of the church, his beating heart outside his chest, his arms outstretched with palms down and fingers extended like claws. Jesus only had one eye, which seemed to track us as we passed him. He was strangely terrifying, in a kitschy way that was obviously a custom paint job, albeit one peeling with age.

"We came to visit Clyde when I was nine. We drove past this, and I had nightmares for weeks." Clyde Williams was the name partner of Williams & Associates, Jack's law firm, and a dear friend of Jack's father. He'd provided Jack a safe place to hide and lick his wounds when he was fleeing the pain of losing his wife and kids.

I put my hand over my giggle. "Sounds scarring."

"I thought he was chasing after little kids. That night I saw him coming after me. Fell and broke my arm. Everyone said it was just a shadow." His hairline lifted on his forehead. "Maybe."

I looked back at Scary Jesus. He was still watching us, but now it looked like he was chasing the human-sized white Easter Bunny balloon tethered to the sign of a used car lot we'd just passed.

"Every time I've driven past it, something bad has happened. Once I had a wreck. Another time I lost a trial."

"Maybe we should sacrifice a fatted calf."

Jack's eyes darted over to me; his lips curved into a grin.

"What?"

"Lamb."

"What about it?"

"The fatted calf was killed to welcome home the prodigal son."

I sighed. "Close enough."

He turned back to the right at the next corner, and in two minutes we'd found our way to Phil's.

Phil actually lived in a suite of rooms that ran from front to back on the far side from the Get Your Kicks store. From the outside of the red brick one-story building, you would never know there was an apartment in it at all. On the far right, a snazzy new Get Your Kicks sign had just been installed earlier that week. There was a center entrance to the main open space in the building—the area the party the night before had been in. And then there was the entrance to Phil's living quarters, all the way around the left side of the building, nearly to the back. The building itself dated back to the 1940s. The building and the neighborhood were pretty industrial and busy by day, but the side-entrance apartment was isolated and a little scary at night.

We parked in front next to a line of police cars and got out. Phil was standing outside waiting for us in a ripped and stained, red Cheap Trick T-shirt that said *Live at Budokan* over jeans with frayed hems and a pair of flip-flop sandals. Thick stubble covered his chin and climbed partway up each of his cheeks. Dark shadows sagged under his dilated eyes. He looked like a man coming off a serious bender.

He stepped toward us. "Thanks for coming." His voice jittered in a two-pots-of-coffee sort of way.

"Of course." Jack shook his hand. "Who's in charge?"

"That guy from last night. What's-his-name, the redhead."

"John Burrows." I hugged Phil, who was at least two inches shorter than me. It was like hugging a fire hydrant. Thick, unyielding, with hard, protruding edges of elbows and knees and hips.

"Right here," John said, coming around the corner. He nodded at us but didn't smile at me. Cop friends are always cops first when something's going down.

Jack's phone rang. He glanced at it and handed it to me, then herded John off a few steps, all business, leaving me with Phil. "Can you show me the warrant, please?" I heard him say. The phone rang again.

John had tucked the folded paper inside his waistband, and he pulled the warrant out and handed it over to Jack. Jack's phone continued to ring. Jack read, lips moving silently, and John turned so that Phil and I were included, if we wanted.

I hurried to answer the call before it quit ringing, without looking at the caller ID. "Emily Bernal for Jack Holden. May I help you?"

Phil leaned back against the building. I walked away a few steps.

In my ear, a crotchety old voice barked, "Where's Jack?"

"Good morning, Clyde. Jack's with a client. We're onsite for a search. Can I help you?"

"Betty forgot my keys." Betty was his beleaguered personal nurse, and somehow I didn't imagine it was Betty's oversight at all, but I wasn't dumb enough to say so. "Can't get in the office."

"I'm so sorry. You know, your name's on the lease. The Maxor Building management office will probably let you in."

"Never mind."

It wasn't like Clyde to be so grouchy. "Are you okay, Clyde?"

"Family problems, and now this. Will you be in Monday?"

"Unless a client needs us. How about we call you if something comes up that prevents us from being in the office?"

"Or Betty can just bring my keys next time."

I watched Phil as he lowered his face into his hands. "Tell Betty hello. Have a nice day, Clyde."

"Not that nice so far. Good-bye, Emily." He ended the call.

I joined Phil against the building. He looked awful. "Where's Nadine?"

"Home with the boys."

"Want me to call her?"

He shook his head so hard his lips flapped. "No, no, no. No Nadine. I don't want her to know about this."

"Phil, she's going to want to—"

"She just finished going through this with me, Emily. I don't want to humiliate her or drag her through it again. Promise me you won't tell her."

My mind conjured a picture of my own father, and I got a jolt of the humiliation I tried to pretend I didn't feel about his jail stint. I put my hand on Phil's shoulder and gentled my voice. "I promise, but if it goes any further, you know you can't keep her from finding out."

"I know that, but it won't. I didn't do anything wrong."

Well, that and sixteen quarters would buy him a small coffee at Starbucks, but the Lord knows things don't always go the way we want them to, even when we haven't messed up. Before I could think of a way to explain that to him and coax him into calling Nadine, a painfully thin brunette rounded the corner and nearly ran into Phil and me.

"Excuse m—" she started to say, then bit her words off. "Emily. Mr. Escalante."

Phil's eyes flashed like a lightning storm. "What the hell is this bitch doing here?" His chest rose and he seemed to swell toward her.

I put an arm in front of his body. "Melinda." To Phil I said, "Just ignore her."

"How's that adoption going, Emily?" she asked. "Probably not impressive that your ex-con dad is back in town to play grandpappy."

Melinda Stafford—Assistant District Attorney and chopper of my ponytail when we were eight years old—wrinkled her nose and picked her way around us on four-inch heels like she was stepping through a field of cow patties. I'd socked her in the jaw once, and for a brief, irrational moment, I wanted to do it again. Instead, I took my own advice, for once, and ignored her.

"But what is she *doing* here?" Phil growled again.

Melinda spun back around, flaring the bells of her pants legs but not a hair on her chestnut head moved. *Too much product*, I thought.

"My case, Mr. Escalante. I can be here if I choose to." She whirled and marched to a silver Jaguar parked at the curb.

Great. Melinda was the ADA assigned to the case. I was only slightly less unhappy about it than Phil.

His eyes shot death rays at her back. She lowered herself into the car, and as she started it, she shot a glance back in my direction. Her face didn't look as haughty as it had moments before. More like something was eating her. Maybe literally, as skinny as she'd gotten.

I kept a just-in-case hand on Phil's arm but turned my ears back to John. He'd started talking again. Jack looked up from the search warrant. Melinda's Jaguar pulled away from the curb.

"We're about done. Everyone is packing up to leave now." John pointed at a cruiser as the driver's side door slammed shut and it roared to life.

Jack handed the paper back to him. "So I don't get it. How'd Stafford get the judge to probable cause on this one? I got the impression last night this was going to be ruled an accident."

John shrugged. "A witness places Phil with Dennis in the parking lot before the murder, arguing and scuffling."

"That's not true," Phil shouted, leaping toward John.

"Whoa." John put his hands up as if to fend Phil off.

Phil stopped but balled his fists. "I never talked to Dennis out here. There was no argument. The witness is lying."

"Why would a witness lie to me?"

Jack stepped between them. "Phil, if they'd found what they were looking for, you'd be under arrest. You're not."

I said, "Plus, there's the guy that the sketch artist drew for us last night. He's a real suspect." I wished I had remembered to bring a copy of the sketch with me so I could show it to Phil, but we'd left in such a hurry that morning I'd forgotten it on the kitchen counter.

"But what are they looking for? I don't get it." Phil's face was redder than I'd ever seen it, even in the worst days of his burglary charge and trial.

"Reading between the lines on the warrant, I think they're looking for a weapon."

John didn't flinch, just watched Phil.

"A weapon? That still doesn't make sense. Dennis hit his head."

"They think Dennis was struck on the back of his head before he fell."

Phil's jaw fell. "Oh God. Poor Dennis." His shoulders slumped, and he put a hand over his face.

My eyes searched John's face, hoping he could see Phil's sincerity, but if he had any favorable thoughts about Phil, his stone face didn't give them away.

THREE

An hour later, Jack and I pulled away from the curb, leaving a caffeinated but still morose and mourning client with a trashed apartment. I'd begged Phil one last time to open up to Nadine. He'd refused. On the bright side, the police hadn't found their smoking gun. Jack advised Phil to carry on normally and to hope for the best, so he'd bid us good-bye and opened Get Your Kicks.

Jack sped down I-40 back to Shangri-La. Our home was only twenty minutes from Phil's place—and our downtown offices—and the commute boasted a drive-by view of Cadillac Ranch. Even better, if you grew up horsey like me, our lot was five acres with an empty stable—which we planned to fill someday—in our backyard. The house itself was a farm-style white "clapboard" nee HardiePlank two-story with a wraparound porch. I loved it second only to the giant log cabin on Jack's family's southern New Mexico horse ranch. That's where we were headed as soon as we picked up our bags and my parents, to meet his for the first time. Nell and Gordon Holden hadn't been at Wrong Turn Ranch on any of my previous trips since they'd spent most of their time on the road in their RV in the last few years.

As we pulled into the garage, I groaned.

"What?" Jack turned off the engine.

"I promised my mother I'd pick up a flock of roaster chickens. She's cooking them for a church event on Monday." No hot yoga for me today. I'd hoped to squeeze it in before we left.

"Can't you buy them when we get back?"

I raised an eyebrow at him, then opened the door and sidled out of the car. "Have you met my mother? It's all she'll talk about this weekend if I don't do this one simple little thing like she asked." I walked to the other side of the garage to my Mustang.

Jack tapped his wrist.

"I know. I'll be back in twenty minutes."

I hustled at the grocery store, then wrestled a dozen frozen birds into the trunk. They were heavier than they looked, and my hands were like ice afterwards on the steering wheel. I blew on them as I whipped the car out of the United Supermarket parking lot.

I pulled back into the garage twenty-five minutes after I'd left it, feeling pressure to make up time I'd lost against my estimate to Jack. I lifted the lid on our chest-style garage freezer. We'd thrown groceries in randomly so it was full without being full. I leaned in and frantically rearranged, then popped the car's trunk and started chunking the birds into storage. I banged my head on the trunk as I came out with number eleven.

"Ow," I yelled, rubbing my crown. I slammed the offending lid shut and offloaded the chicken. I shut the freezer and trotted inside. "I'm home," I called.

Jack was in the office. I stepped into the doorway and with great relish tapped a finger to my wrist. He made a noise somewhere between acknowledgement and raspberry and held up one finger on his left hand while his right continued typing.

"What are you doing?" I asked.

"Judith." His secretary in New Mexico. "One sec."

"I'm going to pack, then."

I grabbed a small rolling suitcase from the hall closet and threw it on our unmade bed. Before I had it half-filled, Jack appeared with a duffel bag. Five minutes later, we were both ready. Jack's cell phone rang. Snowflake lost her mind, growling and snapping at the air.

"Jack Holden," he said, grabbing his bag and walking toward the kitchen.

I followed with mine, Snowflake between us, still fired up.

He stopped inside the door to the garage. "Uh-huh." Pause. "Okay." Pause. "All right." Pause. "Yep." He hung up.

"What was that about?" I asked.

He tucked his phone back in his front pocket. "Potter County accepted our second settlement offer." We'd filed suit on Betsy's behalf for the wrongful death of her mother Sofia, who'd been killed while she was incarcerated at Potter County Detention Center. We'd been negotiating with the county for the last week.

I clapped my hands together. "That's wonderful news." Betsy now had the money she'd need to secure her future. "And so fast."

"Yep." He grabbed a bag in each hand and headed for the garage.

"Anything interesting from Judith?"

It sounded like he mumbled something before the door slammed shut behind him and Snowflake, but it was unintelligible.

"Grrr," I breathed. Well, I'd ask him again later. "I forgot my purse," I said, louder. I dashed back to our bedroom for it. Finally, we departed, only fifteen minutes behind schedule.

By noon, we were tucked with my parents into Jack's Cessna 172. The little SkyHawk sat four comfortably, or four-plus-one-Pomeranian-in-her-carrying-kennel uncomfortably. I yielded my normal spot in the shotgun seat to Dad, who insisted on holding Snowflake. His tall frame more than filled the front seat, and his gray felt cowboy hat grazed the ceiling. Jack was over six feet tall, but my daddy was a good six four. He seemed only half the size he was in his heyday as a muscle-bound steer wrestler on the pro rodeo circuit. That's what a decade in jail does to a man, I guess. He looked good, though, and Johnny Phelps clearly wasn't a man to hold grudges; Jack was the prosecutor who had put him away, but Dad was grinning ear to ear at Jack as we taxied to the runway.

My mother leaned so close to me in the backseat that her head was on my shoulder. "I know you trust Jack as a pilot, Emily, but this is my first time in one of these tiny planes."

I reached over the Easter basket mother was bringing as a thank-you gift to Jack's parents. I sure hoped they liked needlepoint, religious tomes, and Easter decorations. "You'll be fine. Say a prayer and don't think about it. I made sure there are lots of barf bags in the seat-back pocket in front of you." I patted her exposed knee. Mother's knees were always exposed. She'd never admitted that she'd been a Vegas showgirl when she met my dad there years ago, but I'd bet my life on it. If she had been, she'd more than made up for it since, working as a church secretary for various congregations as far back as I could remember, currently the Panhandle Believers Church. Her breathing sounded shallow so I smoothed her baby-fine blonde hair behind one of her ears and then pulled her hand into both of mine. "So do you want to go shopping for a mother-of-the-bride dress when we get back to Amarillo?"

A wide smile lifted almost to the corners of her pale blue eyes. "Oh yes! And for a dress for you, and bridesmaids, and a certain flower girl."

Launching into her favorite topic proved to be sufficiently distracting to keep her mind off the tiny plane and the giant sky around us. After an hour, she fell asleep. Dad and Jack kept up a steady conversation in front of me. The noise of the plane drowned out their voices, and I was alone in the backseat, watching them like a silent movie.

It was amazing to me, really, that Jack could just forget that my father had killed a man in cold blood and befriend him like he was doing, although he'd had far more interaction with him than I had in the last ten years. It's funny, because I had forgiven my mother for hiding his letters, now that he was back, as long as I didn't let myself think about it. But I hadn't really forgiven him. I couldn't forget what he'd done, either—me and everybody else, if people like Margaret and Melinda were any indication. I indulged my urge to worry it over in my mind now. I'd shot a man in self-defense—well, two men, really, but neither of them died, so who was counting? Maybe I wasn't in a position to judge, but the shame of my father's actions stuck with me like skunk spray, no matter how hard I tried to scrub it off. And who wanted to smell like a skunk when she met her future in-laws for the first time?

I sighed and rubbed my eyes. My dad's transgressions weren't something to obsess about right before I took him to meet Jack's parents, so of course that was what I was doing. It was slightly better than obsessing about adopting Betsy or about Jack not responding to me when I told him I loved him that morning, but only very slightly.

The jolt of our touchdown on the high desert runway at Wrong Turn Ranch broke me out of my destructive train of thought and woke my mother.

"Oh!" she squeaked. She lifted her head from the side of the plane where she'd rested it. Red creases marked her face and her eyes were unfocused. She shook her head a little and sat up straighter.

I smiled at her. "Look at the view, Mother." I squeezed her hand as I drank in the vista. The yuccas were in bloom—bell-shaped white blossoms on long stalks—as were the red-flowering cacti and some yellow stunners I wasn't familiar with. Behind and above the desert floor rose the Sacramento Mountains, and in the distance the Sierra Blancas towered. Between them and us lay the ranch as well as the Mescalero Apache Reservation. Behind us was the road to Tularosa, New Mexico, where Judith manned the Western front of Jack's law practice.

We bounced and hopped over the semi-smooth taxiway of dirt and grass to the tan metal hangar. Mother and I trundled her basket, our bags, and Snowflake to the Suburban garaged there, then I moved it so that Jack and my dad could park the plane after they'd refueled it. When we were all in the car and headed toward the Wrong Turn Ranch headquarters, bumblebees took flight in my tummy. Jack's parents were waiting for us at the ranch house. I wondered what Jack had told them about me, about my dad's shady past, about us. An image of a rodent with black hair and a thick white stripe lodged in my brain.

"You're right, Johnny. It's just beautiful here," my mother was saying.

Again I'd deferred to my dad on the front seat, and I sat behind Jack. Dad turned to Mother and beamed. "I love the wide open spaces."

The skunk raised its tail at me again as I automatically responded to Dad in my head. *Of course you do since you've been locked in a prison cell for ten years.* I closed my eyes for a moment and told my inner voice to buzz off.

Jack steered the Suburban left at a fork in the road. "You guys are welcome here anytime. With my parents on the road and me working mostly in Amarillo, the house sits empty. You'd have the run of the place. Although Mickey's likely to put you back to work, Johnny."

Jack's first cousin, Mickey Begay, was the Wrong Turn Ranch manager. When my father first got out of jail, Jack got him a job with Mickey.

"How about it, Agatha? Think you could get some vacation time from that new boss of yours and come out here with me?" Dad asked.

Mother snorted. "Don't get me started about her again. She's got me doing the socialist medium for the church now."

"What?" I stared at her.

"Like mother like daughter," Jack said to my dad.

Dad nodded.

Mother waved a hand in the air. "You know. Twittering and all that."

I shook my head. "Social media, Mother."

"Your father's helping me."

I laughed out loud. "Let me know how it goes."

Dad turned to me. "You'd be surprised. I learned all about technology and email and stuff last year in . . . last year."

I winced.

"Just feel free to visit," Jack broke in, drumming his thumbs on the steering wheel. "Anytime."

"There's the house." Grateful for the redirect, I pointed in the distance for my mother's benefit.

She drew a sharp breath. "Oh my."

Oh my was right. The log house was an old beauty, weathered-enough looking for its surroundings yet perfectly preserved. It held court over white-railed pastures of glossy, thick-muscled quarter horses and an array of outbuildings anchored by a large tan metal stable that almost blended into the landscape. I'd dreamed of places like this all my life and pinched myself that the ranch came with Jack as a package deal.

By the time Jack parked the ancient Suburban in front of the house, a man and a woman stood on the deep front porch, her just in front of him waving at us, him with his hand on her shoulder. I recognized them from the wall of family pictures I'd seen in the house: Jack's Apache father and his Anglo mother. They looked like they were the same age as my parents, and she was blonde like Mother and he was dark like Dad, but the similarities ended there; her legs were covered, and he didn't look like he'd ever spent a day in the slammer. Beside them wiggled the dog of my dreams, a blue heeler.

"Oh," I gasped.

"What?" Jack asked.

"The dog."

He grinned, then took his sweet time unfolding his lanky body from the Suburban. I fumbled with my door, stalling to take longer than him. Jack's mother—Nell—gave up on Jack and ran toward the vehicle.

"Jack!" She careened around the front of the Suburban and threw her arms around him, nearly knocking him over.

"Whoa, Mom." Jack laughed and twirled his mother in a circle.

I had exited the car and stood behind them. The dog came up to greet me and I let him sniff me, then gave him a vigorous ear rub. When Jack set his mother down, I got my first really good look at her. She was beautiful. About my height, she had graying dark blonde hair and magnificent golden eyes, like her son. And dimples. Dimples that put a double exclamation point at the end of her smile.

"Emily?" she said, with the smile attached.

Trying not to blind her with a full-on flash of the metal on my teeth, I stuck my hand out toward her. "Mrs. Holden?" Ugh, did my voice sound as quavery as I thought it did?

"Call me Nell," she said, and moved past my outstretched hand to pull me into a hug. "You're family." She rocked me back and forth. "So good to have you here."

"So good to be here."

"This is Bruiser," she said as the blue heeler leaped in the air around Jack. "Down, Bruiser."

"Nice to meet you, Bruiser."

Jack took me by the hand and led me toward his father, who had descended the porch steps by the time we reached him. Behind us, I heard Nell and my parents greeting each other. "An Easter basket of goodies, oh, you shouldn't have," Nell said. "And Johnny, I've heard so much about you. Nice to meet you." The skunk image loomed large in my mind, and I tried to shoo it away.

"Son," Mr. Holden said. His deep voice seemed to vibrate the air around him.

Jack grabbed his father's upper arm and pulled him in. The two were spitting images of one another, save for twenty-five years and the golden eyes and dimple Jack got from Nell. Dark heads of hair, skin toasty golden brown and weathered by the outdoors, broad shoulders and lean, muscular bodies. They clapped each other's backs, then Jack released his father and put his hand on the small of my back, gently pulling me forward.

"Dad, this is my fiancée, Emily Bernal."

"Hello, Mr. Holden." My lips barely moved as I spoke. He stared at me for a moment, and, without planning to, I curtsied, like Jack was presenting me to royalty or something. Heat surged to my cheeks. I hadn't curtsied like that since the Junior Miss Rodeo Amarillo pageant when I was nine years old.

"Welcome, Emily." He looked deep into my eyes with Jack-like intensity, the moment so solemn and earnest it felt ceremonial, like I'd made a commitment before the Holy Trinity or something, making my curtsy seem appropriate after all.

After we had settled Snowflake and changed, we all walked to the stables together for a midafternoon get-to-know-each-other ride, Bruiser running in circles ahead of us.

Jack's father said, "Jack's the better guide for us today, I'm afraid. I'm out of touch with what's going on here at the ranch."

Nell slipped her arm through his, her eyes a-twinkle. "For a good cause, right, Gordon?"

His olive cheeks creased. "Of course—the best." He spoke to the rest of us without turning his head. "The horses and the land tied us here for years. I promised Nell we'd see the world when we first agreed to marry. I've had some making up to do."

"We're starting with the Americas, and then we'll just have to see where our travels take us," she said.

My phone buzzed and I snuck a look. A text from Nadine: *A friend told me the police went to Phil's this morning. I can't get him to return my calls, and I'm at the Polo Club or I'd head over there. Do you know anything?*

I closed my eyes for a moment, aching for my friend. I didn't want to have to lie to her now or break my promise to Phil yet, and I'd have to do one or the other if I answered her text. I decided when I got back to Amarillo, I would tell her about the search at Phil's, promise to him or not. Even though Jack would remind me that we had a duty to our clients, she was my friend first. But for now, well, I couldn't be rude to the people I was with and text her, could I? I relaxed a bit at the thought. Thank the Lord for the excuse of good manners. Jack met my eyes as I slipped my phone into my jeans at the small of my back. He raised one brow, and I mouthed, "Nadine." He nodded without saying anything and looked thoughtful—

his normal response.

"Sounds wonderful," my mother was saying. "I'd love to be able to travel."

Dad's eyes moistened and dropped. *Good*, my inner voice said. *You should feel guilty that she hasn't and may never get to.*

We reached the large stable and found several stable hands waiting by the tie-down rack with our mounts, thanks to Jack calling ahead while I changed clothes. I looked around for Mickey, but no dice. I did see my favorite horse in the world, though: Jarhead. A champion racer, real quarter horse royalty. I rode him whenever I came to Wrong Turn Ranch, but I held back to see if one of Jack's parents planned to ride him instead.

Nell said, "Bruiser, go to place." The blue heeler trotted to a horse blanket on the ground next to a hay bale and dropped himself onto it.

"Where's Mickey?" I asked Jack.

Jack swung a leg over Hopper, the thoroughbred he normally rode. Hopper had been his wife Lena's horse. "He texted me a little while ago. Greg had a track meet today. We'll see them later."

Mickey and his wife Laura, a former jockey, had two teenage foster kids they were trying to adopt. Runaways who'd turned to me for help in Amarillo after witnessing a murder, and who I'd delivered to Mickey and Laura, with Jack's help. Greg had just turned sixteen and Farrah wasn't quite fifteen yet.

Jack wheeled Hopper and noticed me still flat-footed on the ground. "What are you waiting for?"

I saw that his mother and father had chosen their horses. "Jarhead's for me?" I said, trying not to sound like a schoolgirl with a crush.

Jack grinned. "I told my parents you guys have a special relationship. They respect that. Plus, he's a little much for Mom, and Dad has an old favorite." He pointed, and I saw that Gordon sat astride a tall, gray-muzzled roan.

I ruffled Jarhead's ears, and he nickered. "Hey, boy." I vaulted to the saddle and Jarhead was off before I'd settled in and grabbed the reins. I laughed as I checked him in a little. "So that's the way it's going to be, is it, fella?" My fears started slipping away behind us with his every step.

Jack struck out toward the far northern edge of the property where it dropped off into an arroyo, and we rode in a staggered line behind him, me holding Jarhead to an exaggerated, barely restrained lope. We single-filed down the arroyo's steep banks at a bend. Jack had told me once that the wash only filled with water a few times a year, and today a small stream trickled through the wide, flat bed. Rocks jutted from between the scraggly trees and the cactus clinging to the interior walls and reaching up for the sun. I leaned back slightly as Jarhead waddled and hopped his way to the bottom.

A scream rang out from behind me, quickly followed by Nell's laugh.

"Sorry, I've been out of the country too long. I let a little rattlesnake startle me." She pointed at the ground at the bottom of the arroyo, to the right of the trail.

Her words drew me back for a closer look. A rattler lay stretched out in the sun. I looked around for Jack. He was backing Hopper away from it. I cocked my head at him, my brows up.

"I hate snakes," he said.

My dad rode up beside my mother. "Me, too, but not my Agatha. Aggie, show them what you can do with that thing."

I groaned. When I was eleven, Mother impressed upon me the urgent need to pass along the legacy of my recently dearly departed grandfather. Gramps, it seemed, had been a pastor in a church with some rather extreme beliefs and practices back in the day. One of them was that the righteous man could handle and even be bitten by a rattler and survive it unscathed. It was bull hockey, of course. They milked the venom from the snakes before services, and handled them knowing full well that the nasty animals were no more harmful than a tomcat, at least temporarily. The worshippers ate it up. My sweet mother learned to catch and milk rattlesnakes at her father's knee as a young child, with her bare hands. So guess what skill she lovingly passed on to her only child? Yeah. Whether I wanted to learn it or not. Which I sort of did, back then, but it still wasn't something I bragged about to the other kids at school.

"Oh, Daddy, let's not make a spectacle—" I said.

Mother interrupted me. The woman could cut diamonds with that voice if she had a mind to. "I'm too old and slow, but Emily can. She was always a better snake handler than me anyway."

Heat burned the tips of my ears. This isn't exactly what I had wanted the Holdens to learn about me. In my mind, a circus ringmaster crowed to cheers and hoots, "Hey, Nell and Gordon, step right up and witness your daughter-in-law-to-be coming from a long line of crazy that she'll pass down to any grandchildren she might give you."

I shuddered. Probably lucky for them that the chances of me getting pregnant were slim to none with only 1/1000th of an ovary left in my baby oven.

"What?" Jack asked, his eyes wide.

"Don't," I said to my dad.

He ignored me. "Emily can catch a rattler with her bare hands. Want to see?"

"No!" Jack and I said at the same time as my mother shouted, "Yes!" and clapped her hands.

"Really?" Gordon asked.

"Are you sure it's safe?" Nell didn't look convinced.

My dad grinned. "It is the way she does it. Come on, Sweet Pea."

"We've got antivenom back at the stables," Gordon said, his eyebrows rising as he became more enamored of the idea.

I looked around me and even Jack's face was expectant. My parents were right. I was good at this, even if it made me feel like a freak show almost equal to my crazy grandfather and my nearly crazy mother. And I already felt trailer parky compared to Jack's family. So, I thought, if I'm going to be low rent, I should kick some booty at it.

"Fine." I tossed my hair over my shoulder. "It's really not that big a deal." I hopped off Jarhead. "The trick is to find the right stick. Without it, or a special tool, I won't touch a snake." I walked back up the side of the ravine, looking at the stunted trees. I found a four-foot branch with a tight fork in it. I snapped it off and stomped the forks off to nubs. I tested it on the ground to make sure it was solid, then held it up to the Holdens and my parents. "Like this one. Now, I need a helper. I'm going to walk up behind the snake, and I need my helper to distract it so it doesn't focus on me coming."

"I gotcha, Sweet Pea." Dad slipped off his horse and handed his reins to Mother.

As I positioned myself behind the snake outside its line of sight, Dad walked back and forth in front of it waving his arms and hollering, "Yah!" I took a deep breath and jammed the fork of my stick right behind the snake's head. The Holdens gasped. My mother drew in a happy breath. The snake's tail whipped but his head stayed planted to the ground under my stick.

"Now I walk my hands down a little until I'm in close enough to grasp its neck, but first I secure the tail with my foot." Which I did. The snake's body still struggled and I felt it pressing up under my foot, but the tail no longer whipped around. "They've got a lot of strength back there, so you've got to keep the snake's back end still."

"I think I'm going to be sick," Jack said under his breath.

Adrenaline pulsed through my veins. "Now, I grasp the neck, and when I'm sure I have it good, I use my other hand to set the stick where I can get to it again in a moment." I fitted my hand around the snake's neck, near enough to the head that it wouldn't be able to turn on me. The powdery cool texture of snakeskin against my own always set my teeth on edge. I gripped it tight and felt the muscles in its neck fight against my hold, but I didn't budge, holding it firmly against the dirt. Then I set the stick on the ground leaning against a rock. "While I'm still holding the head on the ground, I get ahold of its tail and I slowly remove my foot." I did it, and the body writhed between my hands on the ground.

Nell gasped. "Oh my God, Jack, she's holding a rattlesnake. Get a picture."

Jack pulled out his phone and pointed it at me. "Smile for some socialist medium."

He was funny—especially since from Mother's smile it seemed his witticism had blown right over her—but I was extremely occupied. I shot him a sour look and continued my narration. "You can lift the snake into the air, if you want." As it left the ground, I absorbed its undulations, and I never took my eyes off its fangs. "And then I reverse the process to release it. Unless anyone wants to pet it first?" From a safe distance, I pointed the business end of the snake around the group to a chorus of "no thank yous" as it rattled its tail at us. Then I set the snake on the ground, put my foot on the tail, grabbed my stick and replaced it firmly on the snake's neck, and released it with my other hand. Sweat dripped into my eyes and down the side of my nose. "When I let this snake go, it's not going to be real happy, so why don't y'all back up a few steps?"

Everyone took my advice.

"I'm going to move away very quickly and trust him to be a self preservationist and do the same thing in the other direction." I took my foot off the tail, then checked behind me one last time to be sure the coast was clear. I backed up to the extent of the length of the stick, then I released it and sprinted away, stick still in my hand in case I needed to ward the snake off.

The angry snake first rose up to see what it could strike, but when it found itself alone, it slithered away to cover, rattling and hissing as it went.

Around me, everyone clapped.

"Well, I never," Nell breathed. "How did you learn to do that?"

I laughed. "On garden snakes first, with big snake-handling gloves. Then I graduated to rat snakes. And finally Mother trained me on the real thing."

"Way to go, Sweet Pea," my proud father said. He turned to Gordon. "First time I saw her mama do that, I told myself right then, 'That's the woman I'm going to marry.'"

Gordon cracked his first real smile, and Nell laughed aloud. I sensed a little skunk spray in the air, but I laughed, too.

I walked up to my fiancé and said, "What did you think?"

"I think I'm going to have nightmares about this for a very long time," he said, but he flashed me a killer lopsided smile.

FOUR

After my one-woman Wild West act, our parents were positively jovial with each other. They chatted amiably as we rode up the wash for an hour and then headed back to the ranch house. When we'd finished with the horses and cleaned ourselves up, Jack kissed me on the nose and told me he was running to his office.

"Is it about Phil?" I called after him, into the closing door. I hadn't answered Nadine, and the couple and their woes were on my mind.

He didn't answer.

I swallowed the urge to shout after him. Jack's communications were limited, at best. I figured he would be back quickly, though, since he was leaving me here alone with the parents. He might even just be running downstairs to the home office instead of into Tularosa. I blow-dried my hair, thinking about Nadine and my promise to Phil and still not texting her back. No Jack. I examined my braces. Nothing I could do about them, so I put on makeup, and went back over the visit from the caseworker. No Jack. I changed into a three-quarter-length sleeve empire-waist dress with accordion pleats in the skirt, added silver and turquoise drop earrings, and fluffed my hair. I prayed that no one had told Jack's parents my dad was a broken-beer-bottle-wielding bar fighter who'd killed a man and been in the New Mexico State Pen for ten years. No Jack. Twenty-five minutes had passed. Finally, I let myself think about the thing bothering me the most: why hadn't Jack responded to my accidental "I love you"? And why the heck had he run out without telling me what he was up to? I flipped my hair and sprayed Aqua Net, then stood and decided I'd done all I could and I would do nothing but fret if I didn't get out of there. Snowflake met me at the bathroom door, both paws on my shins.

"Hello, princess. I don't suppose you know what Jack is up to, do you?" I leaned down and ruffled her ears but she didn't cough up any information. I was suddenly feeling quite blue, and I closed my eyes and took a deep breath, knowing I had to bring my A game anyway. "Let's see what smells so good, girl."

We began walking down the stairs together. Nell's voice reached me from the breakfast area. "Well, Lena was very different from Emily. Feminine. Reserved. She was from a hoity-toity family in Santa Fe. The only thing she liked doing out here was taking pictures."

I froze on the stairs, out of their line of sight, mentally translating: Lena was Caroline Kennedy. I was Honey Boo Boo. Snowflake stopped and looked up at me, her head tilted. My eyes left her face and traveled upward. A poignant charcoal drawing Jack had done of his son, Jackson, hung on the wall. It hadn't been there the last time I visited.

My mother answered. "Yes, that would be very different from my daughter." She lowered her voice and I couldn't hear the rest of what she said.

"I'm not sure he'll ever be completely over the loss. Those babies." She paused, and I wiped my eyes and imagined she was, too. "I am glad to see him living again. He's really found himself, in a way that he never had before."

I waited several beats but neither continued. I flung myself the rest of the way down the stairs and through the entryway to the kitchen, Snowflake running past me and all the way to Nell. "Hello!" I said in a cheerful voice.

They stood on opposite sides of the gold, rusty brown, blue-gray, and tan granite-topped kitchen island, leaning on their elbows. Both looked at me intently, but I was determined not to reveal that I'd heard their conversation. Nell reached down and gave Snowflake a quick pat.

"Hello," they each said.

With a cheek-burning smile, I marched to the breakfast bar. Immediately I noticed the open picture album. The page facing me showed a picture of a very young Jack standing in front of a small plane, holding a hand-lettered, torn piece of fabric—T-shirt material, it looked like. I picked the album up. *May 13, 1991*, the picture read.

"What's this?" I asked, pointing at the picture of the young Jack.

Nell turned and peered under the lid of a simmering pot. "Jack, the day of his first solo flight."

"That's great." I flipped a few pages. Jack in a football uniform, with a wavy mullet. Mickey and Jack in cap and gown. And then suddenly, Jack with his wife and two children, standing in front of the plane we'd flown in today. His *deceased* wife, Lena, and children, Julia and Jackson, the ones blown up in a car bomb meant for Jack, back when he worked as an ADA at the Alamogordo, New Mexico, District Attorney's office. My heart froze in my chest. Lena really was beautiful. Maybe she was the reason he couldn't love me. Because he had loved her and still did.

"Is that the plane we flew in today?" Mother asked.

"Yes. That was taken the day he got it. Lena wasn't a good sport about it like you, Emily." Nell reached over and patted my hand, then gently closed the album. "Anyway, I got this out to show your mama when she asked how Jack learned to fly airplanes."

"A little late for that now, isn't it, Mother?" I smiled to let her know I was sort of kidding.

"He's a fine pilot. Didn't I sleep like a baby the whole way here?"

I swung around the breakfast bar and into the kitchen interior, put an arm around her, and squeezed, as much for my benefit as hers. "You did good."

Nell leaned back on the island, this time on both palms. "Jack got his pilot's license before he got his driver's license. He wanted to be a military pilot, but he was medically disqualified. A concussion when he was fifteen and thrown from a horse."

I reopened the album to the picture of Jack when he first soloed and studied my fiancé/boss. "A concussion can keep you from becoming a military pilot?"

"It can. He was devastated." Nell returned to her pot and turned the burner down. "He's kept up with his pilot training and certifications all this time, the most advanced a private pilot can get." She turned to me and winked. "I think it was to prove they were wrong to turn him away."

I could vouch that Jack read a lot of flight books and magazines. "Yeah, he was off a day last month to re-up on one of his licenses or certifications or something." I held up my empty hands. "Can I help? Set the table or something?"

Nell set me to work arranging bowls of chips, dips, and veggies on a wooden tray with aged iron handles. I had almost worked up my courage to ask how Jack and Lena met, when I heard a clanking noise out back, and then the door from the patio to the kitchen burst open, followed by Dad and Gordon. Seconds later, the door from the garage exploded inward and I heard the voices of Mickey, Laura, Greg, and Farrah in the hall.

The only person unaccounted for was Jack. I moved to the mouth of the hallway, swallowing my words and forcing a smile.

"Emily!" Farrah shouted. The dark-haired pixie flung herself at me, and I staggered back in a compound hug from her and the less vocal Greg.

"Oomph. Hi, guys." I stood back to take them in.

I couldn't believe it had been only four months since they came to New Mexico from bad foster situations in Amarillo, after they'd witnessed a murder. We'd nearly lost them and Mickey, too, because of what they'd seen, and they had a special hold on my heart. A tall young woman stood behind them, her eyes downcast, her pale face framed by an enormous volume of hair. She looked up, and my heart soared.

"Stella!" I said. I'd met Stella when she helped Betsy and me escape from her father, Paul Johnson. He was now in jail, and she lived with her grandmother.

Her smile was shy, almost apologetic. "Hey, Emily." Last time I'd seen her, she was a half step away from heading in the wrong direction. That girl was sullen and rebellious. This one was clear-eyed and fresh-faced.

Farrah looped her arm through Stella's. "Stell's my best friend, Emily. We're in school together."

"That's awesome. Stella can show you every cool thing around here."

"She does and she's awesome."

Stella beamed, and I couldn't help but return it times two. By loving Greg and Farrah, Mickey and Laura might just be saving Stella, too.

"Whatever, losers," Greg said, and swung his hip into Farrah, knocking her into Stella.

Farrah pushed the taller, fairer young man playfully. "Greg says I'm not old enough to be a bridesmaid at your wedding, that I have to be a flower girl. That's not true is it?"

I wound my arm around Greg's neck in a faux chokehold. The boy was taller than me now. "I'm not sure if I'm having bridesmaids or flower girls, but if I do, you are definitely bridesmaid material, and Betsy would be right for flower girl." I continued in baby talk. "Greg, on the other hand, would look great carrying a wittle bitty piwwow with a wittle bitty wing on it." I let him go.

The smiles on the faces of the three teenagers made my heart zing.

"Hey, Standing Hair," Mickey said, using the nickname he'd christened me with when we first met.

I smiled wide at him. "Hey, Mickey."

"Whoa." He pointed at his teeth. "I think we're going to have to come up with a new name for you."

Reflexively, I covered my braces and rubber bands with my hand.

"How about Metal Mouth?" Greg said.

Mickey clapped his hand on the boy's shoulder. "Not bad."

"Ignore those two. You look great. How are those wedding plans coming?" Laura asked as she hugged me.

"Um, fine?" I said. "Alk-tay ater-lay?" Not so long ago our relationship had been tense at best, back when she worried I was going to mess up Jack's life. How far we'd come.

She stepped back and side-eyed me. "You okay?"

I nodded. "I want to hear how the process is going with those two." I pointed to the backs of Greg and Farrah, who had moved into the kitchen and were sampling food.

She held a finger to her lips. "And I have a proposition for you later."

From the kitchen, Nell shouted, "Where's Jack? It's almost time to eat."

Good question. "He said he'd be back soon," I said.

"And I am." Jack's hand suddenly landed on my neck, gently kneading it.

I leaned backward into him, turned my head to his face and whispered, "Where have you been?"

He raised his left eyebrow and waggled it, a special skill of his that always flipped a switch in me. I tried to look stern, but he just kissed my nose and nudged me back upright. "Hey, what's to eat around here?"

"Barbecue." Gordon held up a pair of tongs and a large metal roasting pan. "Going to bring it in now."

"But Emily's a vegetarian. What's she going to eat?" Farrah chirped.

Silence fell, except for the hiss of my escaping breath.

"Vege—"—and here Gordon made a noise like a cat hacking a hairball—"—tarian?"

I looked at Jack, begging with my eyes, but he crossed his arms and grinned. "Emily, did I ever tell you my father won the New Mexico State Fair barbecue contest three years running?"

"They made him an honorary lifetime member of the New Mexico Cattle Feeders Association for his contribution to the industry," Nell chimed in.

"Oh." I swallowed. "That's fantastic."

"Do you mean to tell us you don't eat *meat*?" Gordon asked.

"Um, no, sir, I don't."

"What's wrong with your girl?" Gordon bellowed, turning to my father.

"Must be her mother's influence," he said.

"She didn't get it from me," Mother declared.

Everyone but Farrah, Stella, and me laughed.

"I think we can all agree that it's my father who's had the influence on me. Look at this." I reached for my purse hanging from a peg on the wall, pulled out my baby Glock and handed it to my dad.

He checked to make sure it was unloaded then passed it, handle first, to Gordon. "Got her this for her fifteenth birthday. Read the barrel inscription."

Gordon pointed the barrel at his face. "Wrong Girl," he read. He turned to Jack. "Wrong girl, son? She don't even eat meat." And he laughed.

Farrah grabbed my hand. "She may not eat meat, but she shot the man that was trying to kill Greg and me. The guy that shot Mickey." Her voice was shrill, and everyone turned to look at her. Her eyes widened. She cleared her throat and in a softer voice added, "So there."

I hugged her.

"Thank you for that, Emily." Nell smiled at me and I smiled back, a little wobbly. "And on the subject of blessings like Emily, who will ask for the Lord's blessings on our food tonight?" Nell demanded, hands on hips.

Gordon gave thanks, and we adjourned to the enormous wooden picnic table under the small stand of aspen trees in the backyard, everyone carrying a dish or platter with them. Bruiser did his best to help, and Nell sent him to another horse blanket, this one beside the door to the house. Bruiser minded her, but he moved slowly, in a hangdog slouch. I loaded up on potato salad and filled my iced tea glass with white wine. Jack sat down beside me and raised his left eyebrow at me. I ignored how jauntily it framed his amazing eyes and the way they looked in his handsome face and stuck out my tongue at him instead.

I eyed my potato salad hungrily. Eating was no cakewalk these days, with the constant ache, the protruding metal, and the interference of the bands. I reached my lips out to claim a bite and hoovered it in, chewing as gently as I could.

"I've got Emily's new name," Mickey announced. "Seabiscuit."

"That's it," Greg shouted. "She looks like a horse when she eats." He puckered his lips.

"Not very nice, guys," I muttered, pushing my plate away. Jack squeezed my shoulder.

"Jack," Gordon called from the head of one of the picnic tables.

Jack swiveled his head toward his father, who was brandishing his Bud Light. "Yes, sir?"

"In honor of this occasion, I want to make a toast."

Clanks and rustles sounded as everyone lifted up their glasses.

Gordon stood. "To my son. My only child. May you and your lovely Emily be as happy as your mother and I have been, for as many wonderful years."

"Cheers," Nell said, and everyone repeated her and drank.

Gordon held up his hand.

"Oh no," Jack said, but only loud enough for me to hear.

"I want to share a story about my son."

Several people chuckled.

"Now, you all know I'm proud of Jack. He's a handsome fellow"—this got lots of laughs, since they looked so much alike—"a fair enough pilot, decent with a horse, and he'll work hard when he has to. Course, he screwed that all up when he became a lawyer." More laughs. "But for all that, Jack makes some fairly rash decisions."

Jack reached over and took my fingers in his under the table.

"Take for instance back when he was with the District Attorney's office in Alamogordo. One day Jack was parked in a lot that didn't take anything but cash, which he had none of." Gordon pulled out his wallet and flipped it open. "He offered his credit card"—Gordon held one out toward my dad, who reached for it, but Gordon held onto it—"but the attendant said no." My father shook his head and pulled his hand back. "He offered a check." Gordon put his wallet back in his pocket and pulled out a check-book. He stuck one in my dad's direction. Dad knew the game now, and he shook his head. Gordon nodded. "But the attendant said no. So Jack told this woman he worked for the ADA, that he was a public servant." Gordon smiled. "She said lucky she wasn't charging him extra for that." He raised his beer bottle to acknowledge audience appreciation. "She refused to let him go through. Jack said, 'but it's just five dollars.' She said, 'I don't care how much it is.' Jack asked her, 'What the heck do you expect me to do? I'm no magician. I can't make cash appear. And there's a line of cars behind me.' She said, 'Sorry, sir, you can't pass through this gate without paying.' So Jack said, 'Oh yes, I can,' and he drove right through the arm blocking his way. Boom! Tore it right off."

Jack was shaking his head, and I noticed his neck was a little red near the V of his shirt.

"The next morning he gets to work, and his boss walks down the hall from his corner office—the DA himself—and says, 'Know anything about an arrest warrant out on an ADA for destruction of property and theft?' Jack stares at him like a deer in the headlights. The DA said, 'I think a check to repair the property and pay for the parking might clear things up.' So that is how my son, Jack, ended up paying a thousand and five dollars for parking that day."

Gordon bowed, and everyone clapped.

Jack shook his head. "I was young and impetuous, like my father." As Gordon sat, Jack stood, and Mickey hooted. "What Dad didn't tell you is that when he was the age I was at the time of the alleged parking lot inci-dent, he ordered a steak well done at Doc Martin's in Taos."

"Who'd ruin a perfectly good piece of meat?" Mickey asked.

"Regardless of whether he should have, that is what he did. He and his buddies put away a few before their food came. When it did, Dad swears the steak they served him was still mooing. He motioned for their waiter. Poor fellow came back and Dad drew his revolver, threw his steak over his

509 (EMILY BERNAL #3) 509

head, and shot a hole through it, right into the ceiling. Dust and little pieces of the ceiling came down on all their heads. Steak landed on the table. Dad stuck his pistol into the back of his pants, put the steak back on the plate and handed it to the waiter. Said, 'Now that I've killed it for 'em, could you send this back to the kitchen so they can cook it?"

I laughed so hard I had tears in the corners of my eyes.

"Bet that steak cost about what my parking did." He raised his own Bud Light. "Cheers to my father. Guess I'm just a chip off the old block."

"Cheers," we all echoed.

My phone vibrated under my thigh where I'd stashed it. I snuck a peek and saw that it was an incoming Skype video call from Betsy. I rarely got to see her or talk to her, and we hadn't scheduled a video call. Longing coursed through me, and I pressed to accept the call as I scrambled out of my seat and walked a few feet away from the table.

"Hi, Betsy!" I tried to keep my voice down, but I heard rustling behind me and knew everyone was watching me.

Her sweet voice chirped, "Hi, Emily. Your screen is dark. I can barely see you."

"I'm at Jack's ranch and we're in the backyard. The sun is going down."

"I wish I was there. Why can't I live with you now?"

Behind her, Mary Alice's face appeared. Her stern voice broke in. "Betsy, you don't have permission to be doing this." She grabbed the mouse and clicked. The last thing I saw was Betsy's sad, startled eyes and round mouth, then the image disappeared. All that was left was her icon photo by her name. Two low ponytails, sparkling eyes, and a giant smile with a missing front tooth. My eyes burned, and I put my hand to my mouth to hold back the sob that wanted to burst out. Instead, I put my phone into my pocket and gazed up at the sky. The sun was setting in a flame of orange, pink, and yellow on the horizon. Something else in that direction caught my attention: the silhouette of a small animal running across the pasture.

"Hello, fox." I turned back toward the table.

This brought my own father to his feet, and I wished I hadn't drawn attention to myself. I slunk back into my seat.

"When Emily was little, she was convinced she was an Indian. I guess it started with some books Agatha gave her, but she also loved to hear stories about her Hopi great-grandmother. I guess she was about four or five when she announced to us one day that she was going on a vision quest."

I looked at my mother, and my throat closed. She was gazing up at my father in pure adoration. I had some reservations when she took him back, fifteen years after he left her, and just after he got out of prison. But she loved him. She really, really loved him, and I almost lost track of his words watching her. It made me feel small, worrying like I did about his criminal record. And it made me feel desperate to have someone love me like she loved him. My heart seized up. I wanted it so bad tears stung my eyes and my mouth went dry. I looked at Jack, but his gaze was locked on my father. I swallowed and fought my way back into the moment. He was telling a story about me, and I couldn't flake out now. Maybe later, but not now.

"She went out into our unfenced backyard with nothing but a cookie and a sippy cup of milk. She wandered around for a good long while, then she came barreling through the door. 'Daddy, Daddy, my spirit animal is a fox. I saw it. I saw my spirit animal.' Sure enough, I looked out back, and there was a red fox in the field. It stared at us for a minute, then ran off. After that, you couldn't convince her of anything else." He took a sip of his beer while people chuckled. "I don't know, maybe she was right. She's always been a clever girl. So raise a glass to my Emily and her spirit fox."

Funny, I had forgotten that story, but it resonated with me, partly because of the little fox who liked to visit our Shangri-La backyard, and partly because my dad was right, I needed to use my brain and quit letting my heart jerk me around. *Needed* to. I wasn't sure if I was going to be able to, though.

Cheers and clinking glasses rang out.

Jack stood again. "I've got something that needs taking care of." He knelt before me like he had when he proposed on my parents' back porch. What was he doing now? I felt my eyebrows burrow into my forehead. "Emily, will you please do me the honor of actually marrying me here at Wrong Turn Ranch, one month from today?"

Farrah shouted, "Yes, she will!"

I batted my eyelashes a little, trying to seem to my future in-laws like I was appealing and feminine and sweet, and not like a snake-handling vegetarian who was irrationally opposed to setting a wedding date. "Mmm," I said, trying to smile while wobbling my head side to side, like I was in a Bollywood movie.

Everyone seemed to take my response as a choked-up yes, and I put my arms around Jack's neck and pulled him down to me. I buried my face in his chest, but his warmth and familiar musky scent didn't soothe me like it usually did.

While our family buzzed around us, he said, "That wasn't a yes, was it?"

I pretended not to hear him.

FIVE

After we helped clean up from dinner, Laura and I snagged bowls of peach cobbler and homemade ice cream and snuck outside to chat under the stars. Part of the back porch was covered, but it led out onto a large wooden deck open to the sky, looking out on the picnic table where we'd eaten our meal. I chose a cushioned sun chair with its back up in a seated position. I snuggled my dessert into my lap and lifted my face on an inhale.

Then my phone rang.

Laura raised her spoon to her mouth but spoke first. "Do you need to get that?"

I pulled the offender from my pocket and read the screen. Nadine, and a picture of her looking like a much more curvaceous version of Dita Von Teese, the burlesque star who was once married to Goth rocker Marilyn Manson. Only Nadine was prettier.

I still wasn't ready to pretend I didn't know the police had searched and trashed Phil's house, though. "No, it's okay." I declined the call, switched the phone to silent, and put it in my pocket, where it couldn't taunt me. "Tell me about the kids."

Laura licked her lips and dug her spoon in again. "The kids, great. The adoptions, *mezzo e mezzo.*"

I had a mouthful but I didn't let that stop me from asking, "What's wrong?"

"Nothing, on the Farrah front. It's been less than four months since we started the process, and it looks like it could go through any day now. I'm told that's miraculous."

My gut clenched and I saw green. "Yeah. It's been over six months now with Betsy."

She patted my hand. "I know, and I feel guilty that it's going so well."

"Don't. Farrah deserves it. She's a great kid."

Laura set her bowl between us on a small round black metal table. She drew her knees up to her chest and wrapped her arms around them, setting her chin on her knees. "She is. She's great. They both are. It just turns out that something Greg told us wasn't quite true, and it was something big."

I scraped the last of my peach cobbler from my bowl. All the ice cream had melted, but I made sure to get some of the liquefied cream in my spoon, too. "Uh-oh. What about?"

"He's not eligible for adoption."

"What?" I set my spoon and bowl beside hers and swung my legs to sit sideways on the chaise and face her.

"Yeah. He's not an orphan. He's just"—she scraped her teeth over her top lip—"embarrassed, I think."

"Why?"

"His mom is in and out of residential treatment for mental illness. She's schizophrenic."

"Oh no. Poor Greg."

"Yeah. But she's in touch with reality some of the time and she doesn't want to give up parental rights. She *had* been visiting him. Now he's too far away and she's demanding time."

I leaned toward her. "And?"

"He clams up when I raise the issue."

I thought about all the years I'd missed with my father. Learning he'd killed a man and had been in prison. The shame I carried now. Would I have felt like Greg, embarrassed and not wanting to see him, if I'd known he wanted me to visit him in jail? Maybe. Probably. But, oh, I had missed him so. I wished I could have had the chance to at least decide whether to write to him. Wouldn't Greg feel that way someday, maybe even now? "Could he write to her? Talk to her on the phone?"

"Maybe. Or maybe . . ."

"What?"

She looked down at her bare toes and wiggled them. "Maybe he should move back to be near her again."

"Oh."

"Yeah. Oh." She let go of her legs and kept them bent but leaned against her seat back. "I just think about what if I were his real mother, how would I feel, and, well, Mickey says he'll do whatever I think is best, so I'll just have to sit on it a little longer. We'll figure it out."

"You're awesome, to be able to see it from her perspective."

She flapped a hand. "I don't know about that. But it's somewhat related to an idea I have for me, for maybe you and me."

There was a lot more to say about Greg, but I let it go for the time being. "What is it?" Beetles had started gathering at the lights by the back door. They buzzed, clicked, scrabbled, and—some, at least—sizzled.

Laura recaptured my wandering thoughts with my favorite subject. "Remember a few months ago you told me about the effect that Thunder had on Betsy?"

Thunder was the horse Betsy and I had ridden when I rescued her from Paul Johnson and the human traffickers that had brought her and her family over the border from Mexico and killed both her parents. When things were at their scariest, Thunder had calmed her and given her confidence. Unbelievably, unexpectedly, but undeniably.

"I remember. Horses have had a similar effect on Farrah, right?"

"They have." Laughter erupted from inside the house, and we both turned toward it for a moment before she continued. "I told you that we'd donated some of our retired horses for equine therapy, where they help disabled or emotionally traumatized kids, right? I've seen them used for speech therapy, too."

"Yeah, it sounds amazing."

I watched her profile, backlit by the lights from the house. She nodded. "I'm enjoying having the kids, but honestly, they're occupied with school and activities so much of the time that I find myself at loose ends." Laura had retired from two decades as a jockey only three months before.

"I can only imagine."

"Sooo," she turned to me with a big grin. "I want to do it. I want to get certified and do equine therapy here. For kids like Betsy and Farrah and Greg." She started talking faster. "And I've seen you with Jarhead. We could do summer camps. School holiday camps. We could remodel one of the buildings into a bunkhouse. You could do it with me, or just help me talk Mickey and Jack into it."

"Wow!"

"So what do you think?"

I was smiling so hard my face hurt. "I think it's the coolest thing I've ever heard and I want to help."

She jumped off her chair and both her arms shot in the air. "Yay!"

I did it, too. "Yay!"

She laughed and threw her arms around me. "I'm so excited. You have no idea."

"Me, too."

She stepped back but held onto my upper arms. "Just one thing."

"What's that?"

"You have to come clean with me about what's eating you, because I know something is."

To the wife of Jack's cousin and closest friend? Somehow that really didn't seem like a good idea. As I stared at her, trying to think of a response, the back door onto the patio opened.

Jack stuck his head out. "Sorry to interrupt, you two, but I've got some news for Emily."

"Good or bad?" I asked.

He shook his head.

I took three running steps toward him, panic rising in my throat. Betsy —had something happened to Betsy? "What is it?"

My phone vibrated in my pocket. I stopped and pulled it out, afraid to look at it, to guess what Jack's news was. Wallace. Oh God, Wallace—just as I'd feared. "Betsy?" I said to Jack.

"No, no, Betsy's okay. It's Phil. They've arrested him for murder."

"Of Dennis?"

"Yes."

"That's crazy. I don't understand why they aren't looking harder at the weird guy that I IDed for them. Poor Phil. Poor Nadine." I exhaled the breath I didn't know I'd been holding and saw that I'd accidentally hit Answer on my phone.

"Emily? Are you there?" It was Wallace. The connection stretched his voice thin by the time it met my ear.

I held up one finger to Jack. "Hey, Wallace. Gosh, I feel terrible. I saw Nadine had called earlier and I didn't call her back."

"What?"

"I heard."

"You did?"

"Yeah, it's terrible."

"Um, yes, it is. Are you okay?"

"Oh, sure, just sad for Nadine that she's going to have to go through this again."

"Nadine? What are you talking about?"

"Phil being arrested. What are *you* talking about?"

"Oh, honey, I hate to be the one to tell you this, but the Hodges put in an application to adopt Betsy this afternoon."

"What?" I shrieked. I shook my head and kept shaking it. "Those, those, those . . ."

"Bastards?"

I wracked my brain for the biggest gun in my cursing arsenal. "Mother truckers," I yelled. "Well, I'm not going to let the Hodges have her. I'm not. I applied first."

The connection ended in a series of shrill tones that sent me jerking my head away from the receiver. I put one hand over my ear for a moment then turned back to Jack and burst into tears just as it hit me that the Hodges had filed on the same day we'd settled the wrongful death suit that would result in Betsy receiving hundreds of thousands of dollars.

Mother truckers indeed.

SIX

"All rise for the Honorable R. Charleston Herring," the bailiff called out. She sounded listless, which was unusual for her. Usually she was like the flipping Gestapo. "All rise, all rise."

Chairs rolled and squeaked over carpet behind the counsel tables, clothing rustled, and an "achoo" rang out. The bailiff grabbed a tissue from her pocket and covered her nose. Judge Herring's private entrance door swung open. He paused in the doorway as he surveyed his domain, his tall, thick figure drawing every eye in the courtroom. He had stern eyes, a wide squared gray mustache, and a shaved head. I imagined the smell of cigar smoke every time I saw him, ever since I'd once accompanied Jack to meet the judge in chambers and found him puffing away. Herring thundered to his bench over his wood floor, an earthquake atop two boots. The rest of the courtroom was carpeted in a drab "government neutral" grayish-greenish-tan, and I suspected he used the hardwoods to up his intimidation factor, although he didn't really need to. Herring was a former District Attorney, a terrifyingly good one, according to local legend. As a judge, he was fair to the attorneys that appeared before him, but tough as the hide of a feral boar on the defendants. You didn't want to be found guilty before Judge Herring.

I had a good view of the back of Jack's brown hair from my leather seat behind the defense table. There were a few curls at his hairline, and my fingers itched to fuss with them. Time for a haircut. Phil sat beside him, sweat running down his neck, his hand shaking on the back of Jack's chair. He turned to catch Nadine's eye behind me every few seconds, alternately looking plaintively at her and glowering at everyone else. He worried me. His skin had an odd cast to it. Like he hadn't slept or had eaten something bad. Or was scared out of his pants.

The judge was directly in front of Jack and Phil, his court reporter between them, but offset. To the left of the judge along a curved wall was a witness stand and empty jury box. The room itself was an odd shape, like a quarter of a circle, with the judge and his retinue on the straight vertical line; the counsel tables and the public gallery behind them were on the horizontal.

Judge Herring took a seat, as did the bailiff to his right, and I sank back into my chair, too, in the front row, right behind the wooden bar separating the spectators from the business end of the courtroom. The plastic fold-up seats in the gallery were barely big enough for someone my size, and Nadine was squinched into hers between the unforgiving metal armrests in the row behind me.

She tapped me on the shoulder. I turned my ear toward her.

"I have to leave. I just got a message that Eric is vomiting at school," she said, referring to the older of her two boys, who was in kindergarten. "Text me as soon as you can." Her whisper barely stirred the air, and I could only *just* make out her words. She'd logged many an hour in this courtroom during Phil's burglary trial, and she knew better than to draw Judge Herring's ire.

My guilty conscience over ignoring Nadine's messages all weekend was like needles pricking my skin. Yes, I would keep her updated. I would probably repave her driveway by hand if she needed it done in the next year, too. I'd been a terrible, selfish friend. I nodded slowly, carefully. I heard Nadine stand and her soft "'Scuse mes" as she worked her way down the row.

The judge picked up a stack of papers and files and tapped the bottom of them against his large desk, shuffling the edges until the stack was neat and tidy. "Mondays. I hate the damn things. And I hate repeat visits in my courtroom." He glared at Jack and Phil. "But I get them both today as we consider the charges against Mr. Phil Escalante and his possible bail." He set the stack of papers down, hard. "ADA Stafford, are you ready?"

Across the aisle to Jack's left, the hated, skeletal form of Melinda Stafford shot to its feet. "Uh, prosecution is ready, Your Honor." She was dressed in steel gray, chin to toes, and buttoned up tight. She looked like she would blow away in the wind. *Dear God, if we have a natural disaster in the next five minutes, please let it be a tornado.*

I realized I was humming the chorus to Carrie Underwood's "Blown Away" when the woman next to me cleared her throat and I stopped.

The judge nodded. Melinda sat. No buttons popped, to my disappointment, but she almost fell from her platform pumps on her way down. I pictured the tornado steamrolling through the courtroom, and all that remained of the Wicked Witch of West Texas was her high heels protruding from under the fallen roof.

"Counselor Holden, I don't have to ask if the defendant is present." Jack stood, pushing his chair back and putting both hands in front of him at his waist. Judge Herring shook his head, and turned the full intensity of his gaze on Phil. "Mr. Escalante." His voice boomed as he said Phil's name, and I jumped a little in my chair. "I can't say I'm pleased to see you again so soon. Not here, not under these circumstances." He shook his head. "Counselor Holden, are you ready?"

Jack dipped his head. "Yes, sir, Your Honor."

Judge Herring's eyes caught Jack in a withering gaze for several beats. Jack remained standing, chin up, until the judge released him with his eyes. As Jack stood there, our previous visits together to this courtroom flashed through my mind like a slide show. A happy image with Alan Freeman when his assault against a police officer charge had been dropped. A tense picture of Phil's trial as the judge sent the case to the jury for deliberations, mainly because it was clear to anyone with half a brain that Phil had done exactly what he was accused of. Still the judge had allowed the jury to proceed to a not guilty verdict, though I wasn't completely sure how Jack had pulled it off.

From the looks Judge Herring was throwing Jack's way now, it appeared his patience had worn thin with Jack and Phil. "Mr. Escalante, the charge against you by the state of Texas is first-degree murder. You have several important rights, which you may recall from your *last* trial."

I winced.

"But duty and the law require me to repeat myself anyway." His head tilted to the left. "If you'll be so kind as to rise, I will remind you of them."

Phil stood, knocking into the table in front of him, and his shoulders heaved and bowed. His fists balled at the end of his sports jacket, but they were hidden from the judge by the wooden defense table.

The judge cleared his throat and donned half-glasses. He waved a paper in front of himself then looked down to read from it. "Mr. Escalante, you have been accused of murdering Dennis Welch in the first degree. You have the right to retain counsel, which you have done, and you have the right to remain silent. You have the right to have your attorney present during any interview with peace officers and to terminate any of those interviews at any time." He directed his gaze at Phil. "You're not indigent or unable to pay for counsel, are you Mr. Escalante?"

"No, Your Honor." Phil's voice sounded weaker than usual. Normally he was a bit of a loudmouth, to tell the truth.

"Well, if you were, you'd have the right to request appointment of counsel. If you become so, you need to let me know so that we can see about getting counsel for you. Mr. Holden isn't going to work for free, in my experience."

Jack's head twitched just a little. Judge Herring seemed to be trying to get under his skin. He knew Jack worked plenty of cases pro bono or for services in kind. Our office flooring had been changed out twice in the last year alone in lieu of fees. Phil, aware of this fact, had offered us a truckload of "adult novelty items" in payment for his defense. Jack was holding out for cash, at least in part, but I saw that amazing swing from Get Your Kicks in my future, and I liked it.

Judge Herring was still intoning Phil's rights. "You're not required to make a statement, but if you do, it can be used against you. You have the right to a hearing on bail, which I will conduct during our time together today." Herring ripped off his glasses and tossed the paper aside. "I know these damn things by heart. You'll have the presumption of innocence beyond a reasonable doubt through these proceedings as well as the right not to self-incriminate. And, unless you waive it, you can't be prosecuted for the felony crime of murder in the first degree without a true bill indictment by a grand jury. Do you wish to waive your right to a grand jury?"

Phil looked at Jack and nodded his head. Jack shook his. Phil looked around, searching for something or someone, and I realized he didn't know Nadine had left. His eyes drifted over to me, and they seemed unfocused, confused. He turned back to Jack and shrugged.

Jack said, "He does not, Your Honor."

"Very well, then. We should have your case before the grand jury tomorrow or Wednesday at the latest, Mr. Escalante. We'll meet again for an arraignment if the grand jury returns a true bill for your indictment, and you can enter a plea at that time." He cleared his throat. "You have the right to a copy of the accusation against you. Should you be indicted, you have the right to a speedy trial by an impartial jury, the right to confront the witnesses against you and to have compulsory process for obtaining witnesses on your own behalf, and the right of appeal." He sighed and his shoulders lifted and fell. "Do you understand these rights as I have *once again* explained them to you?"

His heavy emphasis on "once again" was a whomp over the heads of Jack and Phil with a big stick.

"Yes, sir, Judge Herring," Phil said. His voice was steady, not beaten down, but he leaned on one hand on the table, and his other still quivered. Phil was a stiff backbone, chin up kind of guy; something was wrong with him. "Thank you," he added. Even though his voice wasn't strong, I could hear the tiniest tinge of sarcasm to it, which was more in character.

"So, on to bail." Judge Herring leaned forward, toward Melinda. "Go ahead, Ms. Stafford."

Phil sank back into his chair.

Melinda wobbled up from hers. "Uh, um, the state asks for the defendant to be held without bail, Your Honor. He's, um, a repeat defendant, and this is a serious crime. He's known to consort with a bad element, and we believe he is a danger to the community."

I stared at her. Melinda was always pale, but the teeter-tottering on her heels, the way she was speaking like a novice debater instead of a seasoned ADA, these things weren't like her. She was off her game. As I watched her, she bit her pinky nail.

The judge seemed to notice as well. His brows furrowed like accordion doors across his forehead before he turned to Jack. "Mr. Holden?"

"Ridiculous, Your Honor. Mr. Escalante owns a business in the community, he has a fiancée here, and two young boys that think of him as a stepfather. He's not going anywhere, and he was already exonerated in this court one time."

"I'm inclined to agree, although I wouldn't hang my hat on that last point. Give me a number, Ms. Stafford."

She threw up one hand. "Two million."

Jack snorted. "That's the same as no number at all. My client doesn't have that kind of money. We propose that he be released under his own recognizance."

"Neither of you is any help." The judge rolled his eyes. "One million." He stood. "Ms. Stafford, you should get some Emergen-C from the bailiff. You don't look well."

Melinda's mouth fell open, and she worked her jaw. But for once in her life nothing came out.

"Dismissed." With a swirl of black robes and a clomping of boots, Judge Herring disappeared back into his chambers.

Phil slumped over with his head on the table.

SEVEN

The ambulance that came for Phil took him to the Southwest Hospital Emergency Room. Jack and I raced after it in his Jeep Wrangler. People turned to watch as we went by and I wasn't sure if it was the ambulance or the chartreuse back quarter panel that swiveled heads.

I hit Nadine's name on my favorites list to call her. Voice mail picked up.

"Nadine, this is Emily. Please meet us at Southwest Hospital. I am sure everything will be fine, but Phil is being transported there now. He collapsed in the courtroom."

Jack glanced over at me, his eyes soft and concerned. "Maybe we should go pick her up."

"Yeah, if we can find her." A half wail escaped my lips. "Oh, Jack. This is nuts. Everything. Everything has just fallen apart. Poor Phil and Nadine. And Betsy, the Hodges . . ." I put my fist to my mouth.

Jack's hand crawled over to mine for a quick squeeze before he had to make another turn.

I sat up. "I know. I can send Wallace for her."

I was already hitting speed dial by the time Jack nodded approvingly.

Wallace picked up on the first ring. "How did court go?"

"Awful! Phil collapsed and hasn't woken up."

"Oh my God!"

"He's in an ambulance to Southwest. Nadine had left to pick up Eric because he was barfing at school. I can't get ahold of her. I left her a voice mail, and I'm worried about her."

"Oh my God," Wallace repeated.

"I'm with Jack. We're following the ambulance."

"How can I help?"

"Can you find Nadine and bring her to the hospital?"

"Absolutely. Ethan and I are on our way." Ethan was Wallace's significant other. Possibly more significant than I'd realized.

"Oh, thank you, and thank him, too. I feel like I let her down so badly this weekend, and I just, well, I just want someone to be with her."

"Before we go, anything else about the proceedings?"

"They're sending it to the grand jury. Bail's a million."

"A million? Jesus, Mary, and Joseph."

"I know."

We said our somber good-byes.

Jack pulled into a parking space outside the emergency room. "Won't be a need for bail any time soon, the way this is going."

I stared at him openmouthed. Then I shuddered. He was right.

Three hours later, we stood inside Phil's room in the Intensive Care Unit. Monitors beeped and lights blinked. A strong antiseptic scent competed with something metallic and earthy. I held Nadine to me in a humid embrace, her hot tears sliding down my face, her head on top of mine. Jack stood staring out the window into the blue nothing. Phil lay on the hospital bed with wires, tubes, and an IV running from him to the bank of machines behind him that were keeping him alive, and a handcuff securing his wrist to the guardrail on the side of the bed. He was pale and clammy, and in a diabetic coma.

"I didn't even know," Nadine kept repeating. It had been her mantra since the doctors left. "I didn't even know."

"I understand. We didn't either." I swayed gently side to side, guiding her with me.

Jack's voice sounded muffled against the window. "He always took food breaks when we were preparing for his trial. I didn't think anything of it."

Nadine sniffed. "Yeah, same with me."

Jack turned toward us. "The doctors said he had a couple of medications in his system. That he had to have them with him or at the jail before court. Have you seen him taking any meds, Nadine?"

"He takes vitamins. He keeps them in pill cases, you know, like Monday morning, Monday noon, Monday night, for each day of the week. I tease him about it." She slowly released me. "I guess they could have been diabetes medications. I never looked that closely." A sob caught in her throat. "I trusted him."

Jack nodded slowly, like his head was keeping rhythm to a slow, sad song.

I looked from Jack to Nadine. "Well, the best news is that they think they can manage this and get him out of the coma."

Nadine flopped into the chair next to Phil's bed. "But they don't know how long it will take. It could be days." She grabbed his hand and pressed it to her cheek. In a whisper she said, "Or never."

I couldn't let her go down that path. "What can I do, Nadine? For you, for your boys? For Phil?"

"Me, too," Jack said. "I've got my Jeep."

Nadine didn't raise her head. "Wallace has the boys, but I imagine I'm going to need help with them tomorrow if Phil's not better."

I made a command decision. "Can you run get us some food, Jack?"

Nadine shook her head. "I can't eat."

"I can. And you will later."

"Where and what?" Jack asked.

"Curries from My Thai."

Nadine's head rose enough that her eyes showed. "Make them give you my employee discount."

Jack and I smiled at each other. "I'm on it," he said. He walked up to me, put his mouth to my ear, and whispered, "See if she knows anything about Phil and Dennis."

I pulled my head back to see if he was joking. His eyes were serious. I leaned in and whispered furiously, "You're deluded if you think I'll pump her for information while Phil lays here near death!"

He kissed my temple. "When he wakes up, he goes back to jail and faces a murder charge. *Phil* is our client."

Anger coursed through my veins like mercury to the top of a thermometer. *Phil is our client.* Anything ending in "our client" were words I least liked to hear coming out of Jack's mouth, because they always meant he was telling me to do something that felt wrong.

Jack winked at me like he didn't know I was furious. "Hang in there, ladies. I'll be right back."

My brain trapped Jack's cold words inside my head, and they froze in place. Phil is our client. Phil is our client. Phil is our client. *But Nadine is our friend!* I wanted to shout. How had I managed to betroth myself to a man so callous that he wanted me to take advantage of my friend's emotional distress to get her to spill her guts? Who couldn't even spit out the words "I love you" to the woman he wanted to marry in one month? Who didn't find it necessary to tell me what he was working on, when we were supposed to be partners on all of his cases? I wanted to scream and stomp my foot like a child, but my eyes darted to Nadine, bowed over Phil, to the bank of flashing monitors behind them, and I held it in.

Now, that was love—the look on Nadine's face, the tenderness in her eyes. She was one of the best friends I'd ever had. If I could help her get what she wanted most in the world by doing something in my power, then I should do it, and Jack could take a long walk off a short plank. So I just had to figure out what it was that she would want. I watched her gently kiss Phil's forehead, and a tear from her cheek slipped onto his.

When the realization hit me, I wracked my brain for a fresh, satisfying curse word that didn't violate my mother's rules. Her old standby, "spit in a well bucket"? Something foul and hospital worthy, like "pusbuckets"?

"Fudge!" I said, drawing out the *F* much louder than the whisper I'd intended.

Nadine straightened up. "Fudge?" She wiped her eyes, then her nose.

"Nothing."

She flopped down into the chair beside Phil.

I perched on the window seat. A quick glance toward the hall revealed no one was lingering outside. I gut-checked my epiphany from a moment ago. Would Nadine want to have Phil out of the hospital and out of jail, so they could be together, more than anything else in the world? Of course she would. I couldn't help with the hospital part, but since Phil was our client, I could help with the other. Which meant . . . Jack was right—an annoying habit of his. And I loved him—an irritating susceptibility of mine. Insensitive or not, I loved him.

Besides, I wasn't exactly Miss Sensitive myself, now, was I? I was the one who hid from Nadine all day Friday without answering her questions about Phil, knowing she was troubled.

I picked at my too-dark plum fingernail polish, which gave me somewhere to look besides into Nadine's eyes. "I'm sorry I didn't call you back Friday."

"I understand. You were meeting Jack's parents." She said the right thing in the wrong tone of voice, the tone that said she would have called me back in my place.

"Yes, but still."

"Plus, you aren't a good liar. And I know you were going to lie to me about the search at Phil's."

"I—"

"Phil told me he made you guys promise. Pulled the client card on you."

"Um, yeah, but I'd already told Jack I was going to tell you Monday. It's just that, well, things went bad before then." I had tucked the sketch artist's rendering into my purse that morning, planning to show it to Phil that day. I pulled it out. "Do you know this guy?"

She took it from me, studied it. "I saw you talking to him at the party, but that was the first time I'd ever laid eyes on him." She handed it back to me. "Why?"

"He wanted me to tell Jack 'He didn't do it.' That's why he came up and talked to me."

"Didn't do what? Kill Dennis?"

"Maybe, but I have no idea. I told the police and they had an artist do this picture, and then they went ahead and searched Phil's place Friday morning."

"What could they have possibly been looking for?"

"Besides a murder weapon—which they didn't find—I was hoping you might know."

"Me? Why?"

I flicked the last of the plum nail polish to the floor and scooched it under a chair with my foot. "Because you knew Phil and Dennis, their relationship."

Nadine took a deep breath and started to speak. "There is—"

A young blonde nurse in flowered scrubs poked her head in. "Pardon me, ladies. Time to get some vitals."

Nadine sighed and waved her flattened hand back and forth in a noncommittal gesture. The young woman switched out an IV bag, checked Phil's pulse manually, and wrote on a chart. She looked super fit, in a triathlete kind of way. "Are you two, um, family?"

Nadine glared at her.

The nurse backed up. "I only ask because we have very strict visiting rules in Intensive Care."

I pointed at Nadine. "My sister is his wife."

She nodded briskly. "Excellent, carry on, then." Her fancy running shoes made squelchy noises as she left.

"Who says I'm not a good liar?" I wriggled my eyebrows at Nadine.

"I take it all back."

"You were saying?"

"What?"

"Before we were interrupted?"

"Huh?" She tucked sheets under Phil's legs with her back to me. "I don't remember."

This time she was the one making up stories. Nadine was usually a straight shooter. So I decided to play it her way. "Yes, you do."

She whirled. "Are you calling me a liar now?"

In my softest voice I said, "I'm on your side, Nadine. If there's something you want to say, I'm the right one to say it to."

A few short breaths through her nose later, Nadine's face crumpled. "But what if what I have to say is bad for Phil?"

I got up and took both her hands. "That's the most important kind of thing to tell me. To let Jack and me know, so we know what to look for, what to anticipate, what to protect Phil from."

She pulled away from me and turned to Phil again. Her words were barely audible. "I heard him. At the party, I heard him on the phone with Dennis."

"That's good."

Her long jet-black hair swayed as she shook her head. "No, it isn't." She put her hands on the side rail to Phil's bed and her body rocked forward and backward. "And I didn't even ask him about it. I should have trusted him enough to ask him instead of hiding it away and stewing over it."

I put my fingers lightly on her shoulder and waited.

She threw her voice lower, like a man. "Why did it have to be her, you dumbass? I got your forward. Meet me outside. We need to talk."

I rubbed her back in small circles. "Are you sure it was Dennis?"

"Yeah. I saw it come up on caller ID."

"Forward, like forwarded email?"

"That's what I assumed."

"Any idea what Phil was talking about?"

"None. But he was really pissed."

My brain sorted through all that I knew about the case so far. It didn't take long, because it wasn't much, if you discounted the man I'd seen and focused in on Phil instead. John had said a witness saw Phil and Dennis arguing in the parking lot. Nadine heard Phil and Dennis talking, and Phil was angry. So she was right. What she had to tell me sure didn't help. I needed to know more if I was going to help him.

"Do you have Phil's phone?"

"No."

"Do you know where it is?"

"It could be at his house, if it's not with his things at the jail." Phil had spent three nights there after his arrest, and I knew what Nadine meant. All his personal belongings would have been confiscated.

"Well, we've got to find it so I can see the call log between them and read his texts and emails." A small frisson of excitement shot through me. I had a new lead. A tiny one, but still a lead that might take me to the information we needed to exonerate Phil. "It sounds like there's something going on between Dennis and Phil that we need to get our eyes on."

EIGHT

The next morning as I got in the shower, I heard Jack's phone ringing in the bathroom and Snowflake exploding into cell phone attack mode.

"Hello?" Jack said over Snowflake's hysteria, then his boot steps faded as he walked away from the bathroom.

Two minutes later, Jack poked his head into the bathroom. "I've got to get in early today."

I opened the glass shower door, eucalyptus mint shampoo tingling on my scalp. "I need fifteen minutes."

He shook his head. "Gotta leave now."

"Okay," I said, drawing the second syllable into a third. I cocked one hip, but his eyes weren't even on my body.

"See you later."

I puckered my lips and leaned out for a good-bye kiss, but too late. Jack was gone. I stood there with soap running in my eyes and my mouth open. What was up with him? He seemed tense and distracted, unlike the sweet if not very talkative man I'd come to know kinda-sorta well.

I took my time getting ready, nursing my bruised feelings in the deathly quiet house. Jack must have taken Snowflake. I missed the jangle of the tags on her collar and her cold, wet nose against my skin. I finally dragged myself to the garage half an hour later. I opened the outer door and felt the unseasonably warm air in the garage escape. It was barely April and already we'd had temperatures in the 90s over the weekend. I opened the door to the Mustang and plopped down into the driver's seat, immediately gagging. A noxious odor enveloped me. My eyes stung and I jumped back out with the acidic taste of bile in my mouth from my two-coffee, no-breakfast morning.

"What in Hades?" I slammed the car door. My first thought was a skunk. I peered through the closed window. The car looked tidy and rodent-free. Had someone planted a stink bomb in it? Or a true enemy could have poisoned me with mustard gas. Both seemed highly unlikely. I didn't want to open the car to test the smell again, but I knew I was going to have to get in it eventually. I cracked the door and took a cautious sniff. Nausea roiled my belly again, but my brain still whirred, searching for the stink in my memory files. I got a hit almost immediately: we'd had an old hound dog when I was in elementary school, and he liked to chase birds. In fact, he was quite successful in his chasing and often caught them, which ended badly for the birds. He'd bring his prizes home and put them in his doghouse. During the winter, it was a disturbing habit, but in the summer it was a disgusting one. The worst stench he ever wrought on our backyard was the neighborhood rooster, four days after the last time I'd heard it crow.

Chicken. I smelled rotten chicken.

I lifted my knit shirt over my face and ducked into the car, searching for an errant chicken nugget or finger or patty from some fast food meal of Jack's hidden away under a seat but came up empty-handed. I popped the trunk and went behind the car. When I was still three steps away, the odor intensified, and suddenly I knew what I would find.

My eyes watered as I peeked into the rear compartment and saw the swollen-to-almost-bursting plastic-wrapped roasting chicken that I had forgotten in the trunk. Mother had dropped by Sunday night to pick up the chickens from the freezer, and I'd never thought about them again. I groaned. Besides smelling to high heavens, the darn thing looked like it would explode if I touched it. I did a pirouette, looking for something to use to lift it out. I saw a newspaper in the yard. That would do. I rolled the rubber band off of it and grabbed a foldout sheet in both hands. Gingerly, I scooped the pages under the chicken and lifted. I race-walked around and through our side yard to our alley where the city maintained a dumpster. I hefted the chicken in and heard a pop and hiss. I ran for dear life.

With a wet rag over my face and all the windows down, I drove the car in to The Works car wash. I walked to the counter.

"Can I he'p you, ma'am?" Warm brown eyes regarded me.

"I pray that you can. I accidentally left a chicken in my trunk and it rotted."

The warmth was replaced with mirth. The man pushed an intercom. "Thelma, to the front please, Thelma to the front, please. We've got another customer with a rotted chicken in a vehicle." He grinned. "How aggressive would you like us to be, ma'am? And by that I mean, what's your budget?"

My beautiful Mustang, with years of kick left in her. I groaned and pulled out my credit card.

It turned out that The Works was more than happy to offer me a ride to the car rental lot after I told them that price was no object, and they suggested I might want to leave my car with them for a few days. I picked out a red Mustang convertible with a black cloth roof, and the rental staff helped me sync my iPhone to its hands-free system. I roared up to the Maxor Building with the top off and trudged into the office an hour and a half later than I'd planned. Yet another day where life intruded on what was supposed to be a hot-yoga routine. I guess that was all I could expect when my life was such a hot mess.

The light on the office phone told me Jack was on a call, so I dug into preparing a discovery request for information from the DA's office on Phil's case. Snowflake jingled her way from Jack's office to my desk and flopped onto the bed I kept for her under it.

"I don't suppose you want to tell me what's going on back there, do you, girl?" I scratched her behind both ears, but she didn't say a word. "Fine."

I turned my attention back to my computer screen and evidence for Phil's case. We couldn't get the DA's witness statements, but we could find out who they had talked to and get out there and talk to them ourselves. Not to mention that we could learn what they'd found, if anything, in the search at Phil's place. I'd made these types of requests many times in the months since I switched from civil litigation to criminal law with Jack, and I worked quickly from a template on my desktop. I had a draft for Jack's review fifteen minutes later, about the time the light went off on the phone.

I grabbed a small handbell from my drawer and started ringing it as I walked the draft back to his office, Snowflake strutting at my heels. We tromped down the narrow hall that connected my work area (aka the lobby) with the rest of our space. Horses and a buffalo or two galloped by on my left in Western paintings, and I passed the very white and very functional kitchen on my right before I came to Jack's office door.

Back when I first came to work for him, Jack gave me the bell and made me promise never to walk down the hall without ringing it first. I had assumed he was up to something perverted, or at the very least, tawdry and inappropriate. When I refused to use the bell one day, I burst in on his big secret: he lived a solitary life in his office where he kept a virtual shrine to the family he'd lost. And that day? He was painting a portrait of his daughter. I'd felt two inches tall. Since then, he'd told me to ditch the bell. I still rang it, though, out of lingering guilt for barging in on him. I gave it one last ring as I came to his doorway.

I knocked on the doorframe. Snowflake ran to sit at the edge of Jack's desk. Ever since her training classes, he kept freeze-dried liver treats in his top drawer, and she knew it.

Jack had inherited an amazing office from Clyde. There was a running dispute between the two as to Clyde's role in the firm now that he was pushing ninety. He reclaimed his desk as often as he could. I'd revisit my office if it was as nice as this one, too. It wouldn't appeal to anyone who didn't like natural wood, but I wasn't one of those people. A whole wall of windows, a wall of bookshelves and built-ins, and a wall of diplomas, certificates, and art that included an original Remington painting? Yes, please, and may I have another? In fact, the only thing that I would change, if I could, were all the photographs by Lena Holden interspersed in the artwork. There were even more of them in Jack's Tularosa office. They were lovely. She was talented. And I was a shrew, jealous of a dead woman.

Jack grunted, but he didn't look up from his laptop screen. Snowflake whined to no avail.

"Can I get you to review this discovery request so I can get it over to Melinda today?"

His fingers typed fast and furious.

"Jack *Ass*." I used dulcet tones for this term of endearment. "Your hair is on fire."

He looked up, his topaz eyes glazed and irritable. He'd been in a hurry that morning even before his surprise announcement while I was in the shower, too much of a hurry to notice my snuggling him, naked and hopeful. I was trying not to get a complex about it, but he wasn't making it easy. "Huh?" He shook his head, and the normal Jack returned. "I'm sorry, what did you say?"

I walked in and set the pages in front of him. "Review these so I can get them out ASAP. Please."

He flipped, scanned, and scratched his physician-worthy signature at the end.

I put the back of my hand to his forehead. "Are you ill? Where's the red pen that's normally attached to your right hand?"

Snowflake cocked her head at him like she was befuddled, too.

He smiled, but it wasn't lopsided and left-dimpled and wonderful like usual. "I trust you."

I plopped down in the chair in front of his desk. "Jack Holden, what is the matter with you?"

He rubbed his forehead. "I'm sorry. A lot on my mind. Phil's condition." Which was unchanged, I knew from Nadine's group text an hour before. "A couple of new DWI cases in New Mexico. And they're already going to the grand jury with Phil's case, so we should have an indictment —or not—today."

And Betsy, I mentally added to his list, and the Hodges' application to adopt her. Or maybe it was just on my mind and not his. "Okay."

He tapped his pen on his desk once, hard. "John said they located me on the video at the time Dennis died, so I'm off the suspicious person list."

"That's good."

"He let me drop by to see it."

"See what?"

"The surveillance video."

I leaned forward. "And?"

He looked over my left shoulder up at his wall of fame. "Nothing helpful."

I tried to catch his gaze, but his eyes didn't come back to me. "Was my guy on it?"

"Can't be sure."

I could have. My fists clenched. I couldn't believe he'd gone to see the video without me. Was that where he was called to so early this morning? "So has anyone identified him?"

He shook his head. "Oh, I almost forgot. This came in." He looked down and shoved a paper across the desk to me.

"What is it?" I asked, not picking it up.

"Betsy's permanent visa was approved."

"That's wonderful news!"

He smiled, but it was so watered down that the edges were balanced and no dimple appeared. Where was the left-centric grin that I loved?

My excitement slowly fizzled. "So what do you want me focusing on?"

"Phil. We embarrassed Melinda in the burglary trial. We need to know more than her—yesterday."

"Any ideas?"

He shook his head, and his eyes went someplace else. "You know what to do." Which didn't normally stop him from telling me anyway. "I'm going to be out most of the day."

I stayed silent, waiting for him to elaborate.

He rose, stuffing keys in the pocket of his threadbare blue jeans and grabbing an unlabeled file from his desk. He put his gray cowboy hat on, leaned down and kissed me on the lips in a quick and distracted way, and walked out. His weathered boots clomped down the hall.

As the door shut, I said, "Well, alrighty, then," realizing that he hadn't asked me anything about my day and that I hadn't even told him about the chicken. What kind of relationship did we have if we didn't watch surveillance videos together and I couldn't even tell him about rotten chicken stink in my car?

Snowflake whined and licked my hand.

I returned to my desk dejected. Jack had sucked all the life out of the office. I tried to refocus on the boring but necessary early stages of information gathering, but not very successfully. Partly because of Jack and partly because I kept thinking of Betsy, which led me to thoughts of the Hodges, which got me nowhere. I needed action. I needed—

The door to the offices opened, revealing the stooped figure of Clyde Williams. His normally dapper attire was askew. His tweed jacket hung lopsided off one shoulder. His bow tie was crooked. His oxford shirt was untucked on one side. His pants cuff was stuck in the top of one sagging plaid knee sock.

I stood. Clyde waved me off. "No, no, don't get up. I'm just here dropping off some documents I signed for Jack."

His nurse, Betty, stood holding the door. Her ample frame barely fit through it behind him. Jack had urged Clyde to hire her originally, in part because she was big and strong enough to keep Clyde in hand. He was wily and had repeatedly escaped his former nurse, a slight young man who lacked the necessary self-confidence to go toe-to-toe with Clyde.

I came out from behind my desk and waited for him. "How are you today, Clyde?"

"Can't complain too much." Clyde scooted his walker forward an inch then shuffled after it. He repeated this process one hundred and thirty-seven times or so and positioned himself in front of my desk, Betty behind him, her eyes sparkling but her face stern. I winked at her when Clyde was looking down. "Betty, can you get the papers for her out of my briefcase, please?"

"Certainly." Betty already clutched the papers but she didn't tell Clyde that. She handed them to me and winked back.

"Thanks, Betty." I glanced at the top line: *Last Will and Testament of Clyde Joseph Williams*. "Oh my. You've redone your will?"

Clyde coughed, long and deep. His back heaved and his face turned red. He let go of his walker with one hand to cover his mouth and Betty stepped closer, but he recovered and straightened. When he spoke, his voice was thinner than before. "Yes. My only surviving child has decided I'm an antichrist who represents evil people who deserve to be punished. He's disowned me."

"Oh no!"

"Joined some damn church that makes him the judge of everyone. Changed his name and everything. I don't know how many more trips around the sun I've got in me, so I figured I'd better make sure I don't offend him by leaving him any of my tainted money."

Not to mention the law firm. I was never sure whether to believe Clyde's claim of ownership or Jack's that he bought the practice. If Clyde's version was true, then having a disapproving owner like his son would certainly throw a monkey wrench in things for us. I knew how important it was to Clyde that we carry on his life's work preserving civil rights and human dignity through defense work. "Well, I'm sorry you had to do this, Clyde. I hope he comes to his senses."

"He won't. Stubborn like his mother was." Clyde spoke to Betty from the side of his mouth, his version of turning around, "Can you get the door for me?"

"Bye, y'all," I said. I blew Clyde a kiss. "Be nice to Betty, now."

Clyde shifted his body to the right, dragging the walker this time.

Brrrring! The office phone rang. Jack's line.

I wriggled my fingers at Clyde and Betty. "Williams and Associates. This is Emily Bernal speaking."

"Good morning, Emily. May I speak to Jack, please?" The familiar, soothing voice in my ear made me smile, partly out of affection, and partly because I could always count on Jack's secretary, Judith, to be keeping tabs on him.

"You could if he was here. Or if he'd taken his cell phone with him. I've been hearing it ring back in his office." I looked at the clock above the couch. It was already eleven. I glanced back at Clyde. He'd made it halfway to the door when he stumbled. Betty was there and caught him by the shoulder before he went down. She put her hand at the small of his back and he resumed his journey.

"Okay. Can you tell him I pulled the old files he asked for when we met Friday night? I need to know whether to scan them and email them, or to put them in an envelope and send them to him, or what."

I typed an email to Jack rapidly, seething. Why couldn't he have just told me he met with Judith? "Got it. And this is on which case, again?"

"Oh, he didn't tell you? Huh. Well, it's not my place."

Betty turned and saluted me as she closed the door behind Clyde. Her eyes were troubled.

"Judith, he's acting weird. I'm worried. What's going on?"

"Uh, just an old case. I'm sure he'll tell you in good time."

I made sure she got the full impact of my enormous sigh, pausing for effect, but she didn't elaborate further. Her loyalty was to Jack, even if she and I had become friendly. "I don't like it, but I'll give him the message." I bit down hard before I continued. "Everything good with you?"

"I can't complain. My brother visited me last weekend, and the wild-flowers are starting to bloom."

"That's great."

"Oh, and Nell said your wedding is coming up soon. I'm looking forward to it."

My stomach clenched. "Uh-huh. Well, I'll see you soon, then. Buh-bye." I clicked send on the email to Jack as I ended the call.

I shoved my laptop into its bag and grabbed my purse and Snowflake's leash. "Come on, girl. Let's go cause some trouble."

NINE

Snowflake's toenails clicked on the concrete floor of the parking garage as she trotted beside me to the rental Mustang. I opened the door to the backseat and she leapt in gracefully. I pulled the spare doggie seatbelt/harness I carried from my purse and buckled her in.

"Where to?" I asked her, as we pulled out of the parking garage onto the wet street. The sun was shining, though, so the shower must've been short-lived.

She thought about it for a few moments, then barked.

"Drive by Betsy's school and wave to her? Great idea!" I was relieved the dog hadn't guilted me into yoga.

The wind in my hair and the lingering fresh smell in the air did wonders for my attitude by the time I parked beside the playground at Windsor Elementary. I was a little early for lunch recess, so I booted up my laptop and tethered it to my iPhone's connection. I could work as well here as in the stuffy, lonely old office. Before I could start, the phone rang, setting Snowflake off into a tizzy. I seriously needed to pull my dog training videos back out and refresh myself on how to allay Snowflake's phone phobia. The caller ID on the dash said KATIE, but I couldn't remember how to answer it hands-free. I snatched the phone up before Snowflake could get to it.

"Katie!"

"Emily! I just got through talking to Michele, and she said she's staying with you next week. I'm so jealous." The beautiful voice of my former boss and longtime best friend sang across the line.

"You should be. We're going to have fun. And it's so good to hear your voice."

"What's the matter? You sound a little poopy."

In the background, I heard a young boy. "Mommy, you said a bad word."

Something muffled their voices a little, but I could still hear them. "No, I didn't. Taylor, Mommy's on the phone. Can you please go play with your sisters?"

"They're too little."

"Oh, look, there's Oso," she said, referring to their enormous German shepherd.

"Oso," the boy's voice screamed, fading as the word dragged out.

Katie's voice came back full volume. "Okay, I'm back. I swear, they don't give me a moment of peace, ever. If it's not one of them crying, it's another whining, and the third one has a dirty diaper, or worse yet, dirty training pants."

"It sounds wonderful," I told her, meaning it.

"Oh, it is. I know I shouldn't bitch about it. Plus, I've got my in-laws, who help a ton. And business is really good, which keeps Nick hopping, and he's letting me play detective, too, sometimes." She had gone from practicing law to singing in clubs and in the last year she'd started working with her husband, Nick, in his private investigations business. "Hey, have you heard from my brother?"

Her brother, Collin, was also a good friend of mine. He worked in the Taos area with the New Mexico State Police. "Not in months, why?"

"I think he has a girlfriend. That's the rumor circulating with our high school friends, anyway."

My brain froze. Last time I'd seen Collin, he was making eyes at Ava, Katie's friend and former singing partner from St. Marcos. Ava'd been in the states on a string of gigs. I hadn't told Katie about her and Collin, because I wasn't sure there *was* a her and Collin. Knowing Collin, though, he might be dating someone completely different by now. He was a notorious womanizer. He'd even tried his moves on me, which ended his engagement and nearly put the kibosh on my relationship with Jack before it started. It seemed like years ago, even though it was only months.

But I kept that all to myself and went with, "Huh. Wow. Wouldn't that be something?"

"If you get any scoop, call me."

"Of course."

"So, why do you sound poopy?"

I sighed. "Betsy's foster parents have applied to adopt her."

"Wait, hadn't you already been picked?"

"I wish. No. Her foster parents are nuts, and they have a bajillion foster kids already. They'd never love her like I do."

"Of course not! That's awful. I'm so sorry."

"Yeah."

"Is that all that's wrong?"

"Well, Jack's pushing me to set a date."

"I fail to see how it's a problem that the man you're in love with wants to marry you."

"That *is* the problem. I told him I love him, but he ignored me. And he's acting weird. I think he only wants to marry me to replace his old family with Betsy and me. His kids and the wife he loved, unlike me."

"You know that's just crazy talk, right?"

I yelled, "ARGH! I don't know. Maybe it is, maybe it isn't. I just know I don't want to marry another man unless he adores me."

"Emily."

"I'm serious."

Her voice was gentle. "I know you are. So just take a deep breath. And do what makes you happy."

I heard an enormous crash through the phone line.

"Oh no, Taylor and Oso knocked the steaks I was marinating off the counter. Broken glass and raw meat everywhere. Well, broken glass, anyway. No, Oso!" she yelled.

The phone went dead.

"Bye, Katie," I said into the silence. I held my phone in my lap, imagining myself thousands of miles away on the U.S. Virgin Island of St. Marcos, watching her herd a dark-headed little boy and a black and tan beast out of bloody glass. I missed her. I was happy for her, but I missed her. She loved a man who loved her back, and she had gorgeous one-year-old twin girls in addition to Taylor. I pounded my fist on the steering wheel. Now I was jealous of my best friend. This was getting ridiculous. I didn't have time for a pity party. I needed to do something, to chase all this crazy out of my head or it would suck me down into a deep, dark place. Snowflake whined.

I turned. "Hey, girl, how you doing back there?"

She wagged her tail.

"Sit."

She placed her behind daintily on the seat. I got a dog treat from my purse and gave it to her.

"Good."

She chomped noisily then smacked her lips.

"That's it. Down."

She dropped to her belly and settled her head between her paws.

"Good girl."

I gave her another treat.

I put my phone on the passenger seat and swished my index finger on the mouse pad of my laptop. The screen came to life, and my fingers hovered over the keys. Phil or Betsy? Phil or Betsy? Which to work on first? My heart made the decision for me.

I pulled up Google and typed in Trevon and Mary Alice Hodges. "Let's see more of what I'm up against," I muttered.

I knew the basics about the Hodges. Heck, I knew a little more than that from kinda-sorta stalking them when Betsy first went to live with them. They had a modest house on the edge of town. They were very active in the Mighty is His Word church. They fostered eleven kids that qualified as "special needs" either because of their mental or physical conditions, their race or ethnic background, their age, or some combination. Betsy, a six-year-old Mexican, fit their profile. They also had one birth child.

I pulled up social media to see what they'd been up to. They didn't let their kids use Facebook, but Mary Alice lived on it. I scrolled. Church stuff, religious quotes, recipes, survivalist tips, crafting, a post congratulating her husband for winning an archery competition, more church stuff. Nothing interesting. I couldn't find Trevon on Facebook. Googling their names hadn't yielded a whole lot more, not even their property record. I had their address memorized, so I searched for the house itself.

The result was odd. The Mighty is His Word church owned the property. I wrinkled my nose. Did they work for the church? Had they tithed their home?

A hand knocked on the car door beside me and I jumped.

Peering down at me from behind mirrored sunglasses was Officer John Burrows.

I turned to look at Snowflake in the backseat. "You're not a very diligent watchdog." She wagged her tail. To John, I said, "Déjà vu." He'd arrested me in this very spot before Christmas, back when he was pretending to *be* a bad cop to *catch* a bad cop. He hadn't made my day then, but he did now. "How are you?"

He grinned. "I'm good. New wheels?"

"What? Oh, no." I told him the story, realizing as I did that he was the first person I'd shared it with, other than the employees at The Works.

He laughed a lot longer than I thought my sad tale merited and wiped the corner of his eye. "Only you, Emily Bernal."

"And apparently one woman in the early stages of Alzheimer's, according to the people cleaning it. So what are you doing here?"

"One of my kids goes to school here now. I just got through doing a little 'my daddy the police officer' presentation to his first-grade class."

"Betsy's in first grade. Is he in her class?"

"I'll have to ask him."

It felt funny sitting down while he was standing up talking to me, so I got out and we both leaned against the side of the Mustang. The metal was hot. I put my hand against it, then to my cheek. "Global warming."

"A crock. Hey, I heard about Escalante. Man, that's rough."

"It sucks." I ground the ball of one of my leather sandals into the pavement. "Kinda hard preparing a defense when the victim is dead and the client is comatose."

"I'd imagine."

I felt his eyes watching the side of my face and I remembered him flirting with me a few days before. Heat crept up my neck. Maybe I shouldn't have gotten out of the car. I made my tone businesslike and scooched away from him just a smidge. "I sent our discovery request over to Stafford today. So what's the deal—why do you guys think he did this?" I held up my hand. "Just the stuff I'm going find out anyway. I'm not trying to get you to spill state secrets."

He laughed through his nose. "Yes you are." He took his sunglasses off and untucked a tail of his shirt and began to wipe them. I averted my eyes. "You remember I told you that a witness placed him and the vic fighting in the parking lot, right?"

"Yes."

"She—her name is Millie Todd and she's a longtime member of the swingers club he used to run—said they were arguing about Dennis sleeping with Phil's wife."

All thoughts of whether John was flirting left me, and my mouth fell open so far it nearly hit me in the Adam's apple. "Shut up. No."

"Yeah, that's what she said."

"But Phil doesn't have a wife. He has an ex-wife and he has a fiancée."

"There's that."

"Emily," a high-pitched voice squealed.

I turned to see a tiny brown dynamo with flying black braids kicking her legs as she swung high in the swings. Snowflake stood up and barked frantically. I waved. "Betsyyyyy!"

"I love you," she shouted.

I gulped and smiled. "I love you, too, baby." I stayed turned watching her and said to John, "So which one was it?"

"Millie didn't know."

"And?"

"And what?"

"Did he?" I rolled my hand to signal I needed him to hurry up and get with my program, still keeping my eyes on Betsy. "Did Dennis sleep with Phil's ex or"—I shuddered, literally shuddered at the horrible thought of it —"Nadine?"

"Who knows? Doesn't really matter to us."

"Why not?" I glanced at him.

"What matters is that Phil had motive, opportunity, and"—John held up his two hands—"means."

"Says this Millie person."

He reached into his pocket and pulled out a pack of Stride chewing gum. He held it out to me.

I shook my head. "Is there anything but her linking him to the crime?"

He unwrapped a piece, put the trash and the pack back in his pocket, and popped the blue gum into his mouth. "Does there need to be?"

My stomach clenched, but I lifted my shoulders, tried to stand a little taller. "There would be if I was on the jury."

"Good thing you won't be." He grinned. "Gotta run. Stay safe, Calamity Jane." He patted his phone on his hip and pointed at me. "I'm only a phone call away." As he said it, it rang, and he answered it as Snowflake catapulted herself at his phone, stopped only by her doggie seatbelt.

"Wait, thanks, but one more thing." I hadn't asked him about the video and whether they'd found the guy from Phil's party on it, or identified him.

He shrugged and mouthed sorry. Into the phone he said, "Yes, boss." He walked out of my line of sight.

I watched Betsy on the playground, soaking her in, trying to keep the negative at bay a little longer. She had moved on from the swings to a game of ring-around-the-rosy with several other little girls. Their high-pitched voices sang out the words of the familiar song: "Ring around the rosy, a pocket full of posies, ashes, ashes, we all fall down." Five little girls holding hands fell to their rumps together then clambered back to their feet and joined hands again. They skipped in a circle, pulling each other along.

The bell rang and in an instant they separated and ran to form a line at the door of the brick school building. Seconds later, Betsy was high-step-ping along with a boy even shorter than her. She waved at me one last time before they disappeared through the doorway.

I buckled back into my seat in the rental Mustang and let my head sink to the steering wheel with the weight of John's information.

"You haven't told me much about your new boss, Mother." I shifted on my plastic-covered seat and my stomach growled. I glanced at my phone, hoping for a call back from Millie Todd. I'd left her a message after getting her number from Information. So far, no luck.

"She's not all bad." Mother took a sip of her iced tea, leaving a crimson smudge of lipstick on the glass. "She's given your father a job at the church. He's doing the yard and maintenance."

It wasn't exactly easy for a felon to land a decent job straight out of the pokey. The new pastor went up several notches in my estimation. A new job gave Dad respectability, and that didn't hurt me any, although I felt a little shallow thinking it. I knew in time people would forget he was a felon and what he'd done to become one—maybe faster than I would— just like they'd forgotten about all my drama from when I moved back to town pregnant and in the middle of divorcing my cheating bisexual ex-husband. But it didn't happen quickly, and it was painful while the gossip lasted.

"That's fantastic." I took a sip of sweet tea.

A waiter appeared with a tray of food. He looked about my parents' age, except for his dour face, which made him appear a decade older. He wasn't the same guy who'd taken our order. "Who had the quesadillas?"

I raised my hand. "Me."

He lifted the plate but held it in front of him, squinting at it. "These don't have any meat."

We'd already waited twenty minutes on our food and I was starving. I smiled tightly. "That's right."

He pulled it farther away from me. "You had refried black beans and rice?"

"I did."

He lowered it to the table in front of me, releasing it just a moment too soon. The plate clacked loudly. "And you have the beef soft tacos, correct, ma'am?" he asked my mother.

"I sure do."

He set her food down. "Be sure y'all save room for dessert." His voice sounded as bored as if he were reciting his multiplication tables. "We have Easter Bunny sugar cookies and Blue Bell homemade vanilla ice cream today."

Mother stared at my plate. Her mouth fell open.

"Anything else?" the waiter asked.

"It's Jesus," Mother gasped.

"I'm sorry?" the waiter tilted his head.

"It's the face of Jesus in my daughter's quesadilla."

The waiter put his hand to his chest and leaned over my food.

I groaned and looked around us. Thanks to Mother's megaphone voice, people at the next table were already peering at my food. I flicked my eyes to it, grudgingly. The browning on the side of my tortilla did bear an unfortunate resemblance to the typical rendering of Jesus, if one had a vivid imagination.

"Dear God," the waiter breathed.

My mother's hand hovered over my plate like she was praying over it. Which she was. Her lips moved rapidly.

"She's got the face of Jesus on her quesadilla," the waiter shouted. Color suffused his cheeks, and he panted in his excitement. "It's Jesus on a quesadilla!" He waved the couple breaking their necks to see from the next table toward my plate.

Only in Amarillo, I thought. The air filled with the sound of chairs pushing back from tables all around us. Clamoring voices crowded around me.

"It is. It's the face of Jesus on her quesadilla."

"It's an Easter miracle."

Voices whispered prayers around me, and I pushed my chair back. A man at the next table was ignoring the spectacle, and I muttered to him, "People in this town are freakin' nuts."

He didn't look up. I saw a hearing aid in his ear and realized he hadn't even heard me, which was probably for the best or he'd be over here, too.

My mother moved to the chair nearest me. "Emily, this is a sign." She leaned over and pulled me to her, squeezing me in her excitement.

Our waiter turned to look at her. His mouth hung open and he slowly started nodding.

"A sign of what?"

She ignored me and returned to her seat, smiling widely.

The kitchen staff had now come out for a viewing of Jesus. I tugged on the sleeve of our waiter, who was still nodding. If he didn't close his mouth, he'd soon be drooling, too. "Could I have a cheese quesadilla ASAP without any religious imagery, please?"

He turned to me, his eyes wide, and his lips moving in what looked like the Lord's Prayer.

"Never mind." I sighed. "Mother, I'm headed to the bathroom. Back in a sec."

I retreated to the refuge of the bathroom. There were two stalls, and high-heeled pumps peeped from under one. Turned around backwards. The unmistakable sound of retching followed by a splash and then a gagging throat-clearing followed. Great. I was in here with someone spewing germs.

"Are you okay in there?"

"Fine," a voice responded.

"Can I help you?"

"No."

I entered my own stall and sat. A moment later the other stall door opened and the woman walked to the sink. She was thin, like a whippet in a business suit. She leaned over and splashed water toward her face, her golden brown hair falling forward. She made a swishing sound, and then I heard her spit. She washed her hands, used a paper towel to dry them, and left. I exited my stall and did the same, tossing my towel after I used it to open the door.

I returned to a line at our table, Mother gesturing wildly and talking in an excited voice to everyone within earshot. I sat and motioned for her to join me. She did, but she didn't stop her commentary. I endured it for about thirty seconds, then decided I'd had it. I'd just make a run for it, escape this crazy train, through the enraptured crowd, concrete arches, and out-of-place faux palm trees. I got up, but my exit from Abuelo's was blocked by Melinda Stafford.

"Hello, Emily, Mrs. Phelps."

I prayed for a fire alarm so I could run into her like a blocking dummy. I pictured her golden brown hair flying up in the air as I rammed my shoulder into her Ann Taylor-clad midsection, sending her tumbling off her ridiculous stiletto heels and splitting the seam of her pants as I drove her into the ground.

I stood by my chair and mentally chanted my ABCs as a distraction from my current situation.

"Hi, Melinda. So good to see you." My mother jumped to her feet and hugged her.

That's when I realized the woman I'd heard throwing up in the bathroom was Melinda. Maybe she was sick. Or bulimic. She certainly looked nearly anorexic. Mother wasn't heavy by any stretch—her legs were downright thin and her waist had only thickened a little with middle age —but she was three times as substantial as Melinda. I felt a wave of pity toward her.

"Oh my. Mexican food and braces," Melinda said.

It was hard to feel sorry long for a woman as completely unlikeable as Melinda, especially when I was sure she only felt safe being this mouthy at me because of the crowd and public setting. I kept chanting. I was up to Q R S and going strong.

"What's all of this?" Melinda asked, pointing at the line of people ogling my quesadilla.

X Y Z. "Jesus," I said.

She snorted at me, but I didn't explain further.

As Mother returned to her seat, Melinda pressed pale lips together and looked at me in an almost cross-eyed way. "Fastest true bill from a grand jury in the history of Potter County yesterday."

I started over at *A*.

"I asked Judge Herring to proceed without the indictment."

I kept mentally reciting, but I narrowed my eyes at her.

She shrugged. "He said no. We have to wait for Phil to be able to make an appearance. So when is he getting out of the hospital?"

I gave up on the chant. "Melinda, he's in a *coma*. The doctors have no idea when he will come out. *If* he will come out."

She looked away, and as she did, I saw her hands. They were balled into fists so tightly that her knuckles strained at her flesh. Then she splayed them open, almost hyperextending her fingers, and her long acrylic nails looked like dripping blood. I know I wasn't imagining things when I saw her sway like a weeping willow. She put her hand on the edge of our table and seemed to find her balance.

My mother changed the subject, bless her heart. "Your mama has been sharing some hints with us in Sunday school about your beau. She said you think he's the one. We're all so happy for you."

Melinda's very meager color drained from her face. I hated to admit Melinda was actually pretty, but she looked like Angelina Jolie at that moment. The Angelina Jolie who needed a suntan and a month of good meals, though. "I'm not dating anyone."

Mother laughed. "So coy. Well, invite us to the wedding."

Melinda's nostrils flared. "My mother doesn't know what she's talking about."

Mother looked at me and both of us raised our brows at the same time.

"Good to see you, Mrs. Phelps. See you in court, Emily." Melinda's back was to us before Mother could answer. She weaved her way between tables toward the door. Her pants bagged off her rear, and she almost moved like she'd been tippling.

Wait a second, I thought. Did Melinda have a substance abuse problem? Was she drunk in the middle of the workday? In addition to the bulimia or instead of it? Oh my goodness, I might get the chance to rat her out to the DA's office. I hated myself and wanted to hug myself at the same time.

"Emily, what are you laughing about?" Mother stared at me, looking like she didn't know me.

I pulled my lips into a straight line, knowing that I wasn't thinking in a way that Mother would consider very Christian. "Nothing."

Luckily, our waiter interrupted. "Did I hear you talking about the murder case against Phil Escalante?"

I did a double take at him. "Um, yeah, why?"

"Are you his attorney?"

"I work for his attorney."

"Can I have one of your cards?"

I reached into my purse and fished one out for him. As I handed it over, I said, "Can I ask what this is about?"

"I know who the killer is." He ducked behind the line of Jesus gawkers and ran toward the back of the dining room and disappeared into the kitchen.

"Wait! I need to show you a picture! I need to talk to you!" I jumped up, knocking my chair over as I did, and sprinted into the kitchen. A waiter with an enormous tray was exiting as I entered, and she spun away from me. The dishes on her tray slid to the opposite side and she shouted, "Hey, watch it."

"Sorry!" A door on the far side of the grill slammed shut. I ran again. "'Scuse me. Pardon me." People flattened back against the walls to let me through. I flung the door open into the bright light of the parking lot. Sunglasses would have helped. I scanned the lot, searching for his black shirt and balding head, but saw no one resembling him. "Hello?" I shouted.

People walking toward the restaurant turned to look at me, but no one answered.

The waiter had vanished.

TEN

The next morning, I was loading the dishwasher after a cereal breakfast.

Jack put the milk back in the refrigerator. "Gotta make a call."

It was only five minutes before we were due to leave for the office together. He grabbed the cereal and took it to the walk-in pantry. I followed him in and wrapped my arms around him from behind, reaching up and placing my palms on his collarbones. I'd felt his reserve of yesterday slip away as we made love the night before. I didn't want him to withdraw again. I put my chin on his shoulder. "I can wait for you." Snowflake stepped on my bare feet, her little toenails the lightest of pin pricks on them.

He slipped away from me, toward the home office. Snowflake followed him, jingling. "Go on without me. I'd hate for neither of us to be there if Clyde shows up. I'll be in soon."

"He came by yesterday. Did you see the papers he left for you?"

"Yep, but we had to redo them so he may come again."

"Okay. Who's your call with?" I asked, but my words were swallowed by the sound of the French doors closing.

I heard the home phone ring behind the doors. Snowflake yapped, but I snatched her up and held her mouth shut. "Quiet," I said. I had to get control of this dog's phone issues. I stroked her. "Shhh, good girl, shhhh."

Jack was standing, and he pressed a button. "Jack Holden."

A woman's voice said, "New Mexico Department of—" before Jack picked up the receiver. He turned his back, and his muffled voice was unintelligible.

Suddenly I empathized with Snowflake and wanted to bark like a demon at Jack's phone, too. I put her down and walked to the kitchen for a treat. "Good girl," I told her. My heartbeat slowed and the energy and hopefulness I'd felt dissipated, leaving an empty spot inside me.

I RAISED the top on the red Mustang and drove. For five minutes I concentrated on nothing but the purr of the engine and the hum of the tires on the road. But as I drove past the neon colors of the oft spray-painted Cadillac Ranch on I-40, something changed. Anger filled my empty space. I decided to try out the hands-free again on the rental car, to call and give the DA a tip that something was wrong with Melinda, and that something might be affecting her ability to do her job. I focused on the possibility of alcohol or drugs, and tried to forget the pathetic figure in the bathroom. Even if she'd been throwing up, that didn't rule out drugs or alcohol. It might even mean they were more likely.

"I need the phone number for the District Attorney's office in Amarillo, Texas."

I clicked my nails on the steering wheel as I waited. I needed to give myself a manicure bad. It didn't seem fair to Jack's ring to wear it with fingers like these. It was like getting fancy hair from your stylist and wearing gym sweats with it. I held out my left hand, and the teardrop-shaped diamond winked at me, like Jack had Friday night. A wave of emotion snuck up on me, and I nearly burst into tears.

A robotic voice interrupted my pending meltdown. "Here's the number for the Amarillo District Attorney's office. Would you like to call the Amarillo District Attorney's office?"

"Yes."

The phone seemed to take an awfully long time to connect. It began to ring. It rang and rang and rang. I glanced at my dash clock. It read 8:35. Finally, a woman's twangy voice said, "District Attorney's office. Hold, please."

Muzak took over my phone line. "Come on," I said. Traffic was light—we'd overslept that morning, so I had missed what there was of a rush hour. Light traffic was one of the many benefits I'd rediscovered when I moved back to Amarillo. Another was that people had treated me with great kindness, albeit great familiarity and a lot of gossip. Kindness. I pictured Melinda's spiteful face yesterday, and remembered how unsteady she'd looked, how off-balance her whole personality had seemed. Her backward-facing heels in the bathroom. Suddenly, I felt small.

I was better than that. Bedsides, if I was wrong, she'd crucify me. On top of our long-standing feud, she'd had a thing for Jack before he and I got together. I sighed and pressed a button on the dash to end the call. Sometimes taking the high road wasn't much fun.

I swung the Mustang into the parking garage and snagged a good spot by the elevator. I had left Snowflake with Jack, so I was able to move fast. Clyde had taken to showing up later and later each time he came to the office, but it was pushing nine. When I got to our floor, I found not Clyde but Nadine seated with her back against the glass side light by our door.

She stood and pushed down the legs of her tight jeans. "I was about to give up on you."

I pulled keys out of my purse and threw the lock. "I didn't know you were coming. Did I?"

"I texted you a minute ago. I got your message last night. About what that Millie lady said. Made a split-second decision to drop by here before the hospital." I had left an update on Nadine's voice mail before Jack got home.

I hadn't checked my phone since before I called the DA's office. "You never called me back." I pushed open the door and held it.

"I had to think about it. I didn't sleep with Dennis. I barely knew him. But you know what I heard Phil say. 'Why did it have to be her, you dumbass?'"

I walked in after Nadine. Black metal lettering above my desk spelled *Williams & Associates* in cursive. "So you don't think it could have had anything to do with you?" I set my purse down on the desk beside the framed portrait of Geronimo Jack had given me, typeset with the quote, *"There is one God looking down on us all. We are all the children of one God."* I turned back to Nadine.

"Absolutely not." Her face was pale and drawn, the bags under her eyes dark and deep. She drop-sat on the couch and put her head on her knees.

"Do you need a glass of water?"

"No."

"Would it hurt?"

"No."

I trotted down the hall to the kitchen and put ice cubes and water in a glass tumbler. On impulse, I wetted a paper towel with cool water, too. I moved slower on the way back, the water sloshing up over the edge of the glass. "Here you go." I held the glass and towel out to her.

She took the white sheet and wiped it across her forehead, then pressed it to the back of her neck under her long ponytail.

"Any updates on how Phil's doing?" I handed her the drink.

She took several long guzzles before she answered me. "I got a message a little while ago. He hasn't gotten any worse. The doctors are optimistic."

"The boys?"

"Wallace came and got them yesterday."

"The man is a saint. Could we keep them for you tonight?"

She nodded. "Maybe. Thank you."

"Of course."

"I didn't mention this on your voice mail because it may be nothing, but a crazy waiter at Abuelo's told me he knows who really killed Dennis."

"What?" She sat up straighter.

"Some guy named Abel Stone. The restaurant wouldn't give me his number, and he's not in information. He has my card. I'm praying he calls."

She slumped, quiet for a few seconds, then asked, "Never heard of him. What if Phil and Dennis were fighting over Phil's ex-wife?"

"That's what I was wondering."

"But he hates her. Why would he be upset with Dennis about her?"

I put my hand on her knee. "Maybe Millie is wrong about what she heard."

"But what if she's not?" Nadine wailed.

I thought about what John had said, that all they cared about was what Millie heard. But Nadine cared about the truth. And if Jack was going to be able to defend Phil, we needed to know the truth. I came around and sat beside her on the nubby couch. "So tell me everything you know about Phil's ex-wife."

An hour later, Nadine had left for the hospital, and I was dialing the number she'd given me for Phil's mother in Borger. It wasn't as direct an approach as I would have liked to his ex-wife. But Nadine said she and Phil had made a pact to start their lives over with each other and leave the past in the past, so she knew nothing about the woman. Which made me think about Jack and how his past seemed to have kept pace with him. A little white dog that belonged to his daughter. A horse that belonged to his wife.

The phone started ringing, and a crusty woman's voice answered. "Yallo?"

It took me a startled second to return from my thoughts about Jack and remember I had called Manuela Escalante. "Um, yes, may I speak to Manuela, please?"

"Who wants her?"

"My name is Emily Bernal, and I work for the attorney that represents her son Phil."

"I can't understand you. You got cotton in your mouth or something?"

Or something. I hated those dang braces. I enunciated as best I could with the rubber bands cramping my style. "I said my name is Emily Bernal, and I work for the attorney that represents her son Phil."

"You got me."

"Oh, good. First, I wanted to tell you that Phil is a friend of mine. I am so sorry about his medical condition."

"I'm suing the state. I heard about a woman got a million dollars when they killed her son in jail. Don't suppose your law firm could help me?"

"Oh, well, um, it's a little early for that. Phil's condition is steady and the doctors are optimistic he'll recover."

She coughed, long and phlegmy. "Still, I'm due for my pain and suffering. It's almost unbearable, I tell you."

"Yes, I can only imagine." I rolled my eyes. "We have to operate under the assumption that Phil will recover fully and have to face this murder charge. The grand jury indicted him yesterday."

"Boy's always been a hothead."

"May I ask what you mean by that?"

"Well, he did it, didn't he?"

"No, ma'am, we don't believe he did."

"Oh. Well, he's still always had a temper."

I made a note on my yellow pad. *Must not let Phil's mother testify under any circumstances.* "I'm actually hoping you can tell me how to get in touch with his ex-wife."

"That whore, Cecilia? What do you want with her?"

"I understand she grew up with Dennis and Phil?"

"Yeah, what of it?"

"And she knew Dennis when she was married to Phil?"

"No shit."

"So, we need to talk to her about their relationship."

"Whose?"

I stabbed my pen several times into the yellow pad. I smiled in real life so I would sound nicer than I felt. "Phil's with Dennis."

"Well, I'm the one you should ask about that."

"Okay, tell me about it."

"It was good."

"Anything in particular?"

"They been best friends since sixth grade. Phil's always been a lot smarter than Dennis, but they got along all right. They were both into rodeo. Phil rode bulls."

"Really?" I nearly dropped the phone. Phil rode bulls? He'd always reminded me of a Hispanic Danny DeVito, so I had to reimagine him, in a good way. I had trained to be a clown while I was on rodeo scholarship at Texas Tech. My job as a clown wasn't to make people laugh—or give them nightmares. It was to protect the bull riders. A warmth spread through my chest, an affinity for Phil I hadn't felt before, even thought he was our client and engaged to Nadine.

"He was good. Dennis was too big, so he did something where you tackle cows." Steer wrestling, like my father, but I didn't bother to tell her that.

I wondered how much she could really know if the two had lived an hour away at Boys Ranch. "This was at Boys Ranch, I understand?"

Silence for five long seconds. "Some of it, yeah. Dennis visited here with Phil, though. They came back after high school. Dennis stayed."

"Do you know where Dennis is from, before Boys Ranch, I mean?"

"Colorado. Denver or thereabouts."

Phil had said Dennis split time between Borger and Denver, so this made sense. "Was he close to his family?"

"I didn't say that."

"He wasn't?"

"Didn't say that either."

I swallowed back an exasperated noise that almost slipped out. "So what are you saying?"

"He inherited some property from his father. His mother's in jail. Been there since I known him."

"For what?"

"Killing his father, of course. He was a real lowlife."

Of course. "Well, that's excellent. Thank you."

"You paying for that?"

"What?"

"Me being a witness for you."

I underlined my note to keep her from testifying, once, twice, three times. "Um, no, we aren't able to pay witnesses."

Jack walked in the door with Snowflake. I waved at him, and he smiled. It didn't reach his eyes. He dropped the *Amarillo Globe News* on my desk as he walked past me to his office. Snowflake wagged her tail then settled into the bed under my desk. Jack's door shut behind him. I glanced down at the paper, and did a double take. A picture of Mother and me at Abuelo's, beside my Jesus quesadilla.

"That don't seem right." She went into another coughing fit.

When she'd quieted, I said, "So, about Cecilia."

"She was out there at Boys Ranch, too."

I'd assumed that, but it was good confirmation.

"As trashy as she is, she took care of Phil's diabetes. This new one, Nancy, she didn't even do that."

"Nadine."

"Whatever. Nadine. Not a step up from what I can tell."

"Do you know how I can get in touch with Cecilia?"

"I guess I could, but it'd cost you twenty-five dollars."

I closed my eyes. "No problem."

"Mail the check to me here at my house." She recited her address.

I scribbled it down. "Mhmm, so do you have Cecilia's number?"

"No, but she works at the liquor store in Sanford most days, since she's been sleeping with the guy who owns it."

"What's the name of the store?"

"Only liquor store in town. Hell, practically the only store in town."

"Anything else?"

"My rent's due. Can you send my money FedEx?"

I pulled a bottle of Excedrin out of my desk drawer.

ELEVEN

I'd barely hung up from Manuela when the office phone rang. Snowflake scrambled out from under the desk. I held her mouth closed gently. "Quiet, girl." Her liquid eyes accused me of cruelty, and she whined, but stopped barking. I almost let the phone roll over to Judith, but I snatched it up after the third ring. "Williams and Associates, Emily Bernal speaking." I released Snowflake, who returned to her bed, pouting.

A monosyllabic male voice said, "You the lady with the braces?"

"Uh, yes, I have braces."

"We met at lunch. God spoke to me through you."

Dear Lord in heaven, thank you for sending me the nutso waiter, I mentally prayed, with fervor. "Yes, I remember you. Abel, isn't it? I'm so glad I could be of help. I wish you hadn't run off so fast, though."

"There is something I need to tell you."

"Right, about who really killed Dennis Welch. You said you saw it happen?"

"Not on the phone. Meet me at one thirty between Ross Rogers and Thompson Memorial Park."

"You mean by Wonderland?" I was referring to the somewhat rinky-dink amusement park that my parents had taken me to as a child. It was still there. No bigger, but that didn't matter when you were five years old and the double-loop roller coaster at Six Flags Over Texas was an unattainable six-hour drive away.

"Yes. One thirty."

I looked at the time on the phone display. "Could we make it—"

"One thirty."

He hung up.

"How rude," I said. "Don't you think so, Snowflake?"

She didn't answer my question, other than to emit a rattling snore against my foot.

I got to work diligently on preparing files and assembling background information for Phil's case. I kept the printer busy churning out nothing of any great consequence, but it was all work that had to be done, and I felt mildly virtuous. Jack stayed sequestered in his office the whole time, his bright red phone light making me feel like a third wheel. Occasionally his voice rumbled through the walls, but he wasn't a loud talker, so as close as I pressed my ear against the sheetrock, I couldn't make out a word he was saying.

After nearly two hours of productivity, I decided to drop Manuela's check in the FedEx box and to grab lunch on the way to meet the mysterious Abel. First though, I took Snowflake out to the Maxor courtyard for her midday constitutional and stopped for my own on the way back. When we returned to the office for the purse I'd forgotten, Jack was gone.

"He was just waiting for a chance to escape so he didn't have to talk to me." I told Snowflake.

She looked sad, so I assumed she agreed.

"Well, girl, that means you have to come with me."

I was feeling rebellious so I lowered the soft top and let Snowflake ride shotgun instead of in her usual spot in the backseat. We went through a Taco Bell drive-through together, and I ordered her a beef and bean burrito. I pulled the tortilla open to expose the good stuff inside and set it on its wrapper on the front seat with her. She gobbled it down like she'd missed a week of meals. I ate my hold-the-beef version at a more sedate pace as we drove. The weather was a mild seventy-five and the wind at one-tenth its normal near-cyclone velocity. The sky was partly cloudy, just enough to keep the sun pleasant on my face without the need for SPF 50. I pulled to a stop at a red light and tilted my face up, closing my eyes behind my aviator sunglasses.

The explosive sound of a Harley's straight pipes shattered my serenity as it rolled up beside me. A wolf whistle made my eyes flick open, but I tried to move slowly back into a normal driving posture, so as not to let the whistler know he'd bothered me.

"Hey, hot stuff, good-looking bitch you got there," a man shouted.

I turned to give him a piece of my mind and saw Wallace on the back of the Harley beside me, his boyfriend, Ethan, in front of him. They were decked out in brand new biker gear: fringed black leather chaps, black vests, and bandanas around their wrists.

"Takes one to know one," I shouted back with a straight face.

"That's not your Mustang." He pointed.

"Duh."

The light turned green and Ethan grinned and revved the bike. They burned rubber, smoke curling from under their back wheel.

"They're playing hooky from work," I explained to Snowflake, who strained against her seat belt and whined, watching them roar off. I shot a quick text to Wallace: *Ethan is f-i-n-e FINE. What's he doing slumming with you?* Seeing them—knowing Wallace had been helping Nadine with her boys—reminded me that Nadine hadn't decided whether or not she needed Jack and me to keep them for a few days. I drove on until we reached the next stoplight.

I typed a quick text to Nadine: Offer stands for your boys to stay at Shangri-La. Made progress through Manuela. That mysterious witness I told you about earlier called, too. Going to meet him.

A horn honked behind me. The light had turned green. I put my phone down and resumed driving. I parked the Mustang ten minutes later in a lot on the edge of Thompson Park. There was a green space filled with picnic tables and tall, budding leaves on one side of the blacktop and the zoo on the other. Since it was midday on a Wednesday during the school year, I didn't exactly have to fight for a space, although there were a little better than a handful of cars, mostly on the edge closest to the zoo.

I pressed a button to raise the soft top back into place, then unclipped Snowflake. "You're coming with me, girl. I need a watchdog."

She hopped down and danced in place while I attached her leash. We set off together toward the edge of the golf course with my determined little fur ball straining against the leash and panting. "Heel, Snowflake." Her eyes lifted to me, anguished, and she fell in on my left side. I took up the leash slack. She continued to put a little weight against it, but with less potential damage to her trachea. "Good girl."

I knew this park well. For about one minute in high school I ran cross-country. The only meet I participated in was held here. In fact, Abel had asked me to meet him very near where I'd crossed the finish line over a decade ago, panting and determined that I would never race again except on horseback. Snowflake and I reached a good spot on the edge of some trees, and I sat down, dropping her leash. She shot me a questioning look.

"I'll let you run around as long as you stay close and I can catch you without a fire drill." Snowflake was awfully quick for a dog with legs the length of my hands. When leashless, she could lead you on a merry chase if she had a mind to.

For several minutes, she traumatized butterflies and investigated smells. Her nose was caked with dirt immediately, and she managed to smear some dandelion yellow on her facial hair, too. We were alone in the park as far as I could see. It was incredibly peaceful. I reclined with my head cradled in my hands and watched the clouds shift from shape to shape. *If Abel doesn't show up, I just might take a nap.* To heck with work and my complicated fiancé.

Snowflake yipped. I sat up and looked around for her. Her ears were perked up and I followed her eyes. She had spotted Abel approaching before I did. He wore jeans and a black T-shirt. The wind lifted his light brown hair, and I could see how thin it was even from this distance. He looked more like a reference librarian or a life insurance actuary than a Mexican food waiter and certainly more like them than the star witness in a high-profile murder trial. He was moving fast, trotting and shooting furtive glances all around. I stood and waved but he didn't acknowledge me. He neared us and kept going, circling back and around to the opposite side of the trees I'd planted my tush in front of.

"Don't look at me," he said, just loud enough for me to hear. "Stay where you are."

His paranoia seemed almost humorous for a man so benign in appearance, but if he had really seen who murdered Dennis, he had a good reason to be nervous. So far I wasn't convinced of anything, though, except that he was odd with a capital O.

I pulled the artist sketch from my purse. "Okay, but I have a picture I'd like to show you, Abel."

Snowflake ignored his instruction and jingled her way around to him.

"Back," he said, his voice radiating stress like a bronco in a bucking chute. "Back."

"Snowflake, come—"

I felt a whoosh of air on my face, then heard a thud followed by a hard exhale, almost a grunt. Snowflake went berserko, barking and growling.

I hit the ground on my belly out of instinct, and my heart took off at a full gallop. "Hello?" I whispered.

Abel didn't answer. I closed my eyes, trying to think and straining to hear whatever was out there as best I could over Snowflake's noise. Instructions or not, I had to get to the mystery man and Snowflake. I army-crawled on my belly across the grass, around the tree and over toward her sounds. The first thing I saw was Snowflake's face covered in blood. A strangled scream came out before I could choke it back, and I winced at the sound of my own voice. The second thing I saw was Abel's supine body, the shaft of an arrow sticking out of his chest. An arrow. Dear God, someone was shooting arrows at us. That's what I had felt nearly hit me in the face as it made its way to Abel. I started shaking violently, and my hands felt icy cold, like they'd shatter from my tremors.

"Come, girl," I said, as softly as I could, trying not to telegraph our location. Snowflake had tangled herself in her leash, and she curved her body in a C-shape and took mincing sidesteps toward me. I turned on my side, and, realizing I still held the police sketch, I dropped it on the ground. Snowflake leapt into my arms, trembling violently, like me. It only took a second of probing gently with my hands to realize she wasn't hurt. I smoothed her ears back, unwound her leash, and set her on the ground.

I dragged myself the rest of the way around the trees, staying covered as best I could. Abel was flat on his back, his brown eyes wide and his mouth pale, slack, and open. Blood drooled from its corner, but he didn't make a sound. A lock of his thin hair had fallen onto his forehead. I leaned in and shook him slightly, but the light seemed to fade from his eyes right before me. I laid my fingers across the inside of his wrist. No pulse. My mind flashed back to a cold, lifeless woman in an icy backyard and my dizzying efforts at CPR a few months before. I didn't want to end up like her or this guy. If I knelt to perform life breaths and chest compressions on this man like I'd done for her, I'd make myself a target. Plus, how much good could I do for a man with an arrow through him? A wave of emotion coursed through me and my lips moved silently as I ground my face into my hands. *Please forgive me. I'll call 911, and maybe, if it's not already too late for you, someone can help you soon.*

Then I forced myself to focus inward. That moment was all I had. I was nearly hyperventilating, and I was wasting time. The man was dead. Whatever secrets he'd held, he'd never share with me. So be it. There was someone out there with a bow and the skill to use it. I needed to figure out how to keep Snowflake and myself alive and to call for help. And my brain needed oxygen to make that happen. If the last few months of hot yoga had taught me nothing else, it was how to breathe. I sucked air in deeply through my nose and pushed it out through my mouth, making a *ha* sound on my full exhale. I did it again. And again. Then, I gathered up my inner power with a lion's breath, growling and widening my eyes, feeling like a total idiot yet ten times better all at once. *Keep breathing*, I told myself.

As I breathed, my brain came alive and I patted my body, searching for my purse strap. Nothing. Still breathing, I reached around the side of the tree back along the path I'd crawled and found it. I jerked it to me, dug my hand into my bag, breathing out, slipping my fingers around the barrel of my little Glock. I drew in a deep breath, then fired three times in the air in rapid succession, hoping to at least let the shooter know I was armed, and maybe alert someone who would call the police. Six rounds left in my gun.

Time to call in the cavalry. I worked my phone out of my pocket, gun still at the ready in my right hand, and with my left dialed 911 and texted John Burrows while it connected.

The police released me from the scene two agonizing hours later. I reclaimed my wadded-up police sketch, and I drove home to wash my blood-covered dog and change my clothes. I'd texted Jack an update over an hour before, but I still hadn't heard from him. My heart was heavy with his absence. Besides nearly getting shot, I'd lost our best witness, a witness Jack didn't even know existed, since we'd barely spoken in two days.

No next of kin had been located for Abel, but I'd just have to pray that I could find someone else in his life who knew what he'd been unable to tell me: who killed Dennis. I'd tack on a prayer that the answer wasn't Phil, too, because even though I really liked Phil, if there was one thing I knew as the daughter of a murderer, it was that people could surprise you, and not always in good ways. So I could follow up at Abuelo's and try to talk to Abel's employer and coworkers, and I could run down Internet info about him, but right now that seemed daunting. Futile. Depressing. Potentially devastating. Maybe I'd feel better when Abel's blood wasn't literally on my hands.

Or maybe I'd keep feeling this bad until the police figured out what had happened in the park. They were still processing the scene when they dismissed me, but I already knew from watching and listening that there were no fingerprints on the arrow, nothing left behind except crushed grass where the archer had hidden, and no witnesses found. They didn't seem to think the information I'd given them was much help, either. I had nothing other than the word of a dead man that we were meeting for him to disclose Dennis's killer to me. The responding officers seemed more fascinated with the skill they said was required to make a kill shot with a bow from that distance than they were about what they called my "wild theories." Maybe if John had come it would have been different, but he had texted me that he was forty-five miles away.

I parked the Mustang in the garage and closed it behind me, Snowflake in my arms. Her normally white fur looked like it had been used to mop up cherry Kool-Aid. I shut us in the hall bathroom and filled the tub, then lowered her into the lukewarm water. Red suffused it in seconds. I had to run fresh water three times to turn her white again. Luckily, blood coordinated well with the red barn decorating scheme in the room, because I'd splashed everywhere. I dried Snowflake off with a towel, and she ran in circles with her behind to the ground for a few moments, but then returned to me, still shaking.

After I cleaned the tub, I changed my clothes and looked in the mirror. My damnable braces reflected light back at me, but I didn't see any more blood. I took the dirty clothes and dropped them in the washer set to cold. I grabbed wet rags and dish soap to take back to the Mustang to clean the leather where Snowflake had discolored it.

It was time to go and that meant I had to put Snowflake out. The girl was rattled, and I felt horrible about leaving her alone in the backyard. We really needed to get her a playmate. Then she wouldn't be lonely and we wouldn't have to take her everywhere. But I had to leave, and I could keep an eye on her through the nanny cam. I stopped moving for a second and realized that my entire body was vibrating, like Snowflake's. I was exhausted. Had I been shaking like this ever since that arrow had pierced Abel's chest? I clasped my hands together and willed them to stillness. It didn't work. Well, shaking wouldn't prevent me from moving on, and that's what I had to do.

The brush with death had drawn my thoughts to Dennis's body, then to Phil's medical predicament. I hadn't laid eyes on Phil since the day he was admitted, and I needed to see his chest rise and fall with his breath. Maybe I would see something that would rule him out as a killer, or maybe not.

I let Snowflake out and closed the door behind her. She pressed her button nose against the glass. When I walked away, she howled. I pushed my hands against my stomach and forced myself to walk to the garage without looking back. I got into the red Mustang and started scrubbing the seats. With each stroke, a little more of my insides tore loose until I gave in, got out of the car, and collapsed on the garage floor sobbing.

I don't know how long I lay there, but at some point I drifted off. I woke up to find my face in a muddy pool of drool and my clean clothes covered in dust. I sat up and leaned back against the car, fighting the electrical storm in my head. Why was I falling apart? I'd seen dead people before. *But I've never watched someone die.* A sob broke loose from my throat, proof of the truth in my thoughts. An image of my father—broken, bloody beer bottle in his hand—standing over something just out of my line of sight intruded, but I forced it out before I could see the dead man at his feet.

I care more about this case than most because of Nadine. Tears slid down my face. Life was much easier when I was a paralegal in Dallas for nameless, faceless corporate clients. The stakes in Jack's cases were so high. So very high. I longed for an executive employment contract or even a discrimination case. Not these life, death, or imprisonment cases. I wiped at my tears.

I'm losing Jack and Betsy like I lost Rich and the baby. A much larger sob ripped through me. *No, I am not losing them. I am not, I am not, I am not.* I wouldn't let the Hodges get Betsy, and I had to believe Jack loved me and wasn't changing his mind, even if he wouldn't say it and was forgetting to act like it some of the time lately.

And I can't help Nadine and Phil. I crawled forward and up to my feet. I could. I was going to help them, I was going to adopt Betsy, I was going to figure out what the heck was wrong with Jack, and I was going to try oh-so-very-hard to forget how Abel's face looked as life seeped from his body. I brushed the dust off my jeans and scrubbed the dirt off my face with my hands and got in the car.

When I got to Phil's room, no one else was there. I stood in the door-way, taking in the surreal sight of his motionless body and listening to the steady beep of the monitors. I walked over and took hold of his hand, the one without the tubes and needles.

"Sorry about all these machines, about your diabetes, about the murder charge, Phil. I thought I had a breakthrough witness, but someone killed him before he could talk to me. I also called your mother today." I stopped, unsure what to say next to a man who couldn't hear me. Or could he? "Hey, Phil, can you hear me? Squeeze my hand if you can." I waited a few seconds, noticing the blood on my forearm. How had I missed it? But I got no squeeze so I opened up about his mother. "Well, you're ten times nicer than I ever would have dreamed you could turn out after talking to your mom. She told me where to find your ex-wife. The cops think you killed Dennis over a woman, if you can believe it. Cecilia maybe. I don't think so, really, but they do." I waited again, but still got no squeeze, no flinch, no flicker of eyelids. I stared out the window, searching for something else to say. "This would be a lot easier if you'd just wake up and talk to me, buddy."

A nurse poked her head in the door. I recognized her. The athlete. "I need to come in and chart his vitals."

"I was just leaving." I put his hand down gently on the sheet covering his body, and I walked out of the room, my throat constricted and my eyes burning. I headed straight for the ladies room and scrubbed the last of Abel's blood off my arm.

I hurried from the medical center but I was still five minutes late to Downtown Methodist to meet Jack at our premarital couples class. We attended on Wednesdays, after work but before the hallowed hour—at least in Bible-thumping West Texas—of Wednesday night church. Jack hadn't arrived yet either, so I unbuckled my seatbelt and got comfortable, waiting for him. I piddled on Facebook on my phone. Another five minutes passed. Then another. I checked my phone for emails, texts, or voice mails from him. No dice. Did it again. Still nothing. Not a word since he left this afternoon, not in response to what had happened to me or about missing our couples class. The emptiness I had felt that morning returned. The day was ending not too differently from how it started, and I could get tired of this new Jack in a hurry. Fury bloomed inside me, pushing out through my skin in hot waves. I shot him a quick text: *I waited for you at couples class. You didn't show. I'm out of here.*

As soon as I'd pressed send, I regretted it. What if he'd had a wreck? What if he was dealing with an emergency with a client? What if he'd fallen unconscious like Phil?

I started typing again, but a text came in from him: *Shit. I tried to text you earlier, but I just saw it didn't send. I can't believe what happened today. I'm glad you're okay, but I'm worried about you, and I'm very sorry, I've been detained. Wish I could call or be there. Don't wait up, this could run long.*

I deleted the message I'd been composing—the nice, worried one—and threw the red Mustang into reverse. A horn blared, and I slammed on my brakes, throwing myself into the steering wheel. "Judas Priest," I screamed, but Wallace and Nadine weren't around to praise my game. The car that had honked cruised down the parking lot aisle, and I smashed the accelerator and lurched out of my space and out onto Polk.

I headed north, not really with a destination in mind, just wanting to escape my life. A week ago, I had an attentive fiancé and was close to adopting a little girl I love. I had a dear friend who was marrying another good friend, and celebrating a not guilty verdict and a new business. So much had changed, none of it for the better. I left town on Highway 287, deciding to just go with the flow. And it was a flow. I'd fallen into a line of light traffic, and as a few cars moved around me, I noticed a similarity between them all: Mighty is His Word and Christian fish bumper stickers.

"Well, how about a little Wednesday night worship with the holy rollers?" I muttered, and exited with the school of fish onto Reclamation Road. A few familiar turns later and I was in the parking lot on the Mighty is His Word church grounds. Here was the site of Phil's breaking and entering, or, as he explained it to the jury, his *entering*. I'd been here during the discovery phase of his trial to walk the layout and see how his "mistake" had been made, when he'd ended up in the private residence. But I'd even been here once before that. I'd come here and watched Betsy when she first moved in with the Hodges. I'd seen the line of mismatched kids of all shapes and sizes waddling behind Trevon and Mary Alice. I'd been envious and coveted what they had.

It was nothing like I felt now, though. Tonight Technicolor emotions warred inside me. I was a human torch, burning from the inside.

I parked and watched as I blazed from inside the car. People disembarked and headed for the sanctuary. One after another, families of eight, nine, ten, and more kids passed by me. It was easy at a glance to tell the families were foster or adopted, because, like with the Hodges, the kids were every color of the rainbow. I'd focused so hard on the Hodges the last time I sat in this parking lot that I'd been blind to everyone else.

Tonight, the commonality was clear. Foster families. That, and a whole lot of camo gear. I slammed my car in reverse and sped out of the lot. I needed to talk to Wallace.

TWELVE

"What can I get for you, ma'am?" the tall, skinny teenage barista asked. The poor kid had a blanket of acne over his cheeks, the purple kind that look like they hurt.

Roasters. 9:00 a.m. Jack had come home late, and I was already asleep. He'd shaken me awake and held me close. My brush with death had rattled him more than me, it seemed, and he'd peppered me with questions and pleaded with me to be more careful. I wasn't at my best, physically or emotionally. Instead of letting him worry over me, I'd chewed him out for his absence, then been awake the rest of the night, sorry for how I'd acted. I fell asleep at dawn, and when I got up, he was already gone.

I shook my head and said, "You order for me," to Wallace.

He sniffed. "You don't remember, do you?"

"I do."

To the barista, he said, "She doesn't know her own order, and she's in here once a week."

I studied my phone and pretended not to pay attention to him. I took after my father, mostly, but in some unfortunate ways I was my mother's daughter, and this was one of them. I couldn't remember phone numbers, shoe sizes, coffee orders, case cites, or birthdays. Luckily, these were all things I could look up. Or let Wallace handle.

"She'll have a large café breve with sugar-free hazelnut and I'll have a caramel macchiato, large please, with whipped cream. And a cup of extra whipped cream."

The barista took my credit card. I was treating Wallace in return for the pleasure of his company, and information on the wacky Mighty is His Word families.

"Good grief," I said, not quite under my breath.

"I ran ten miles before I met you here. I deserve it. What did you do?"

I waved my hand from head to toe, like I was my own personal Vanna White.

"I forget. The former Miss Rodeo Texas has standards to keep."

"First runner-up."

"Honestly, I think you could start a consulting business. You know, like Boots, Batons, and Bikinis: We help your little rodeo princess claim her sash." He grabbed his drink and extra cup of whipped cream from the counter. "You have to pay me a commission if you use the name, though."

I took my café breve and we claimed our usual table, the one with the direct line of sight to the pronghorn antelope head mounted on the wall. The *Amarillo Globe News* blared LOCAL MAN SLAUGHTERED BY BOW MARKSMAN from our tabletop. "I'm thinking no."

"Pageants are huge these days. What was the name of that girl that had the reality show?"

"Honey Boo Boo." Which made me think again of debutante Lena compared to me from the wrong side of the trailer park.

"And there was one just about pageant moms."

"*Toddlers & Tiaras. Here Comes Honey Boo Boo* was a spin-off."

"My God, you really watch this stuff. You're into it. You want to be a beauty pageant consultant. That's why you're straightening those teeth, even if you shouldn't be. I knew it. Girl, I'm going to help launch you. Maybe we can get you a reality show."

"You've got to stop doing meth for breakfast, Wallace."

He shushed me with a wave of his hand.

"How's Ethan?"

"Ethan is fantastic. I'm taking him home to Mama next month."

"Shut the front door."

"You know it."

"So he's not still mad at you about the whole couch fiasco?" Wallace had Ethan's couch re-covered as a birthday gift, only it turned out that his deceased grandmother had done the original upholstery for him. Ethan had cried and yelled at Wallace for two days.

"He's over it. Finally. So sensitive."

I laughed and spewed a little breve in his direction. "Look who's talking. And you chopped up his favorite grandmother."

"Not his grandmother. His grandmother's upholstery."

"Tell that to Ethan."

"Anyway—watch as our hero deftly changes the subject—we wouldn't dream of missing your wedding in New Mexico." I'd told Wallace that I hadn't been able to find the word *No*, even if I hadn't said *Yes* either, to Jack's date request. "We're working around it."

"Thanks. Now, about why I bought you the extra whipped cream with your caramel macchiato—"

"Betsy." He sighed.

"No."

"Really?"

"Well, sort of not Betsy." He grimaced. "It's about the Mighty is His Word church members. I was visiting there last night—"

"Not again."

I kept going like he hadn't interrupted me. "And I noticed that every family there has like a bazillion kids of different races and ethnicities, obviously not birth kids. Like the Hodges."

"Uh-huh."

"So, that's all you're going to say?"

"What do you want me to say?"

"That it's freakin' *weird*. That you know why they're doing it."

One side of his mouth scrunched up. "I don't know why. All I know is that they single-handedly foster fifty percent of the kids that come through our system, and nearly ninety percent of the special needs kids. You may not like them, but they are a godsend to the youth in need in this town."

I didn't have an answer for that. Wallace flipped his blond highlights off his forehead and proceeded to read me the riot act for my judgmental ways. My eyes watched his lips move, but I didn't hear another word he said.

I gave Jack the evil eye later that morning as he walked backwards in front of my desk toward the office door. Snowflake stood beside me, and she joined in staring him down. I hadn't even had time to tell him about my conversation with Wallace, and here he was running away again. I was getting downright peeved about how he was acting, whether I'd been in the wrong the night before or not, and I was tired of playing nice.

"Just a few errands to run," Jack stuttered, his eyes faltering under my glare.

My tone was sweet as pure cane sugar. Jack knew me well enough to understand that meant he was in big trouble. "Anything I can help you with, *Jack*?" The phone rang on my desk. "Quiet," I said to Snowflake, pointing at her. She barked anyway. "Williams and Associates. Emily Bernal speaking."

Jack's eyes cut to the door and I shook my head and held up my index finger.

"Yeah, I need to talk to a lawyer," a male caller said.

"What's this in regards to?"

"A murder."

Normally I screened calls like this before I handed them off to Jack or to his voice mail, or even referred them to another lawyer. This time, I held the phone out to him. "It's for you," I announced loudly, without putting the caller on hold.

Jack pulled at his shirt collar.

"Jack?"

He took three quick steps toward me and I slapped the phone into his hand.

"Jack Holden speaking."

I hit speaker. Jack's golden eyes widened, but he didn't protest.

"You the lawyer?"

"I am an attorney, yes. Who am I speaking with?"

"Good. I need one."

"Have you been arrested?"

"Let's say someone got kilt and the police were looking into it. How long before a feller's free and clear of it?"

"There's no statute of limitations on murder."

"Can you say that in plain English?"

"Never. A feller's never free of it."

I put the back of my hand over my mouth to cover my automatic smile. *I can't forget I'm mad at this man.*

"Shit. Okay, well, I need a lawyer."

"So you say. Have you been arrested?"

"I cain't afford to pay much."

"Have you been arraigned?"

"There you go talking fancy again."

"Are you out on bail?"

"What do you charge, anyway?"

Jack's nostrils flared. "More than you can afford. And I don't represent people who won't answer my questions." He slammed the receiver into its cradle on my desk.

I jumped in my seat. Jack acted this way maybe once in a blue moon. Served the guy right, but more than that it said something about Jack's state.

"Well then," I said, raising my brows.

"I have to go," he growled.

"To do what?"

"Work on a case."

"Which one?"

His mouth opened. No dimple. No lifted brow. No leftie smile. "An old one."

"That's how Judith described it to me, too."

He grunted and stomped to the door. "See you in a few hours." Then he was gone.

Snowflake flung herself to the ground, her feet in the air.

I nodded. "Exactly."

In a bad mood anyway, I decided to deal with something that had been nagging at me since the previous week. I hated these stupid braces. Everyone important to me seemed to like my smile the way it was. I was tired of spewing food and saliva every time I tried to eat. If I never heard another reference to the horsey look they gave me by pushing out on my lips when I ate, it would still be too soon. I dialed.

"Dr. Parks's office."

"Yes, I need to make an appointment to get my braces off."

"What's your name, dear?"

"Emily Bernal."

"Oh, hello, Emily, this is Mrs. Parks. You aren't due to have them removed for another six months or more."

"I know. I've changed my mind."

"Oh my. That's a little unprecedented."

She waited for me to answer. I waited longer.

Mrs. Parks's voice rose to a wheedling pitch. "I really think you should talk to my husband before you do something so rash."

"I understand. But I want them off. How soon can you work me in?"

Snowflake cocked her head at my tone. Whatever she saw made her jump into my lap and press into me. I stroked her back. My dog, my conscience. But that wasn't really true. She was Jack's dog, and his daughter's before him.

Mrs. Parks lowered her voice. "You do know we can't give you your money back, right?"

I hadn't even thought about that, but I tried to sound less pushy while still pushing. "That's okay. When can Dr. Parks do it?"

I heard some clicking, and I imagined her scrolling through the days of the calendar on her computer. "How about next Wednesday, bright and early? We come in at seven on Wednesdays and that's the only time we have."

"Perfect. See you then."

I hung up the phone. I wasn't mad at Mrs. Parks. I was peeved at Jack and growing angrier by the second even with the soothing warmth of Snowflake huddled against me. What the heck was going on with him? Even if he couldn't choke out the words "I love you," he had been a contender for world's best fiancé until a few days ago. Now? Now he was furtive and evasive and distant.

I ran through possibilities. Another woman? I doubted it. The only other women in his life were his deceased wife and daughter. The old case he mentioned? I was his right hand. I couldn't imagine him not telling me about it if that's what it really was. The list of possibilities grew worse from there. Gambling. Drugs or alcohol. Money troubles. A secret medical problem. I clutched my stomach. Oh God. I hadn't even given him the benefit of the doubt. What if his evasiveness was to protect me from bad news? What if he was going to chemo? Phil's pale face flashed through my mind. Or dialysis. Jack was a tough guy, and he never complained.

But he looked so dang healthy. And performed like an eighteen-year-old. My cheeks warmed. No, he couldn't be sick.

Well, whatever it was, while I was more than tired of it already, I still worked for him, and our clients depended on me. Nadine especially. I looked at the stack of files on the right-hand side of my desk, begging for my attention.

"Time to get down, girl." I lifted Snowflake and leaned over until my stomach touched my knees to set her gently on the floor. She whined, but after a long second of plaintive looks, she walked to her bed, circled three times, and flopped down. Her eyes closed immediately. The snores followed almost as fast.

I rifled through my client files. A DUI that came in last week. A marijuana possession charge, where the defendant was a seventy-five-year-old cancer patient. I hoped the poor guy could move to Colorado. A vehicular homicide against a young guy who'd hit a bicyclist. That hit close to home, given that Wallace was an avid road bicyclist. The list went on, and these were just the Texas cases. But there were no deadlines looming, and only one client in imminent danger: Phil. I pulled my slim file for Phil's case off the top of the stack and centered it in front of my laptop. When I opened it, the notes on top scolded me. My interview with Phil's mother, and the lead on his ex-wife. I hadn't done a thing on it since I talked to Manuela.

I Googled for liquor stores in Sanford, Texas. Manuela had been right. There was only one. Joe's Liquor and Smokes. No website. Open Monday through Saturday, 10:00 a.m. through 7:00 p.m.

I called the number.

"Joe's," a man's voice growled.

Quickly, I made a mental adjustment. Time to pull out my thickest accent and shine a light from my dimmest bulb. "Um, yeah, hi, is Cecilia there?"

"She ain't supposed to be getting personal calls at work."

"Oh, sorry." Thinking fast, I added, "I'm her cousin, and I was going to be in town this weekend. I haven't seen her since we were, like, in elementary school, and this is the only number I have."

The man sighed. "I keep telling her to get a phone but she says nobody calls her that she wants to hear from."

"I'm sorry. I sure wish I could find her."

"She'll be in tomorrow. You can call her then, but keep it short, will ya? I've got a business to run."

"Thank you so much. I promise I will. God bless, and have a nice day, sir."

"Yeah, yeah, same to ya."

He ended the call.

I wrote *Joe's, Friday after 10:00 a.m.* on a fresh sheet of paper and felt lighter as I shoved it in the file.

THIRTEEN

Snowflake whined from the backseat of the rental Mustang as we cruised north with Wallace at seventy-five miles per hour along Highway 136. The bright morning sunshine splashed over waving grass on each side of the road, near waist-high and green as a go light. Yellow and white flowers lit up the rolling fields broken only by the occasional barbed-wire fence as far as the eye could see. We'd just passed the town of Fritch, and I saw the sign ahead for FM 687, which would take us to the teensy town of Sanford. I thought it would be best to surprise Cecilia, so I hadn't called ahead. Hopefully this trip wouldn't be in vain.

I reached behind me and across the back seat to scratch Snowflake behind the ears. "Sorry, princess. Your daddy is on the lam again, so you're stuck with us." I filled Wallace in on Jack's suspicious behavior.

"If you're really concerned and he's not talking to you, then get your answers from someone else."

"Like who?"

"Well, you told me that you forgot to ask John about whether they'd found the guy you had them sketch."

"Yeah?"

"So ask him." He picked up my phone. "Geez, honey, let me do it for you." He pressed and held down the button until the beep-beep. "Text John Burrows on his cell. John, did you guys find out the name of the guy that bothered me at Phil's party? The one in the sketch?"

Siri repeated his message. "Would you like to send this message?"

"Yes." He smirked at me. "Next problem."

"Well, he said he's working on an old case."

Wallace gave a long, withering sigh. Again, he activated Siri. "Text Judith. Judith, Jack asked me to have you send me the file on the old case he's working on. He's decided he wants my help on it."

Siri repeated the message through the car sound system and asked whether we wanted to send it.

"Yes." He threw his hands in the air. "Next problem."

"Nadine hasn't let her boys stay with me. I keep offering." That came out of nowhere. I hadn't even realized it was eating at me.

Wallace put his hand on my knee. "Honey, you live in a big house with a rich lawyer. She loves you, but it's hard to send her boys to that, then bring 'em back to what she's got."

"She told you that?"

"Not word for word, but she hinted enough that I got the gist."

"I feel terrible."

"Don't feel terrible. Just get Phil off the hook. And I'll talk to Nadine. Encourage her to let you help more."

"Thank you."

"You're welcome."

"How's your training going?"

He flexed. In an Arnold Schwarzenegger impression, he said, "I am the Ironman." Then he relaxed and said, "I've got to get Ethan into it. I think he's getting jealous of the time I spend away from him."

Maybe I should take Ethan to coffee and we could commiserate with each other. "Don't make the poor guy do that."

"Well, maybe not." Wallace ran his hand over the dash of the rental car. "I can't believe you rented a car just to get the other cleaned."

Wallace was germophobic, so much so that I was afraid he'd never get back in my car if he learned the truth about the chicken. I'd told him I was getting it detailed and left it at that. I crossed my fingers on my left hand. "There were some bad stains in it." I'd driven by to check on progress that morning and found my seats and carpets out and undergoing treatment. When I asked how it was going, I'd gotten a frown and a noncommittal answer about multiple steps in an uncertain process.

"Not enough people take good care of their interiors."

I thought back to the horrific smell that had knocked me over. "I couldn't agree more."

"Now, remind me how this little thing we're doing today is a CPS matter, so it's fresh in my memory when my boss calls to chew my ass out for not coming back from lunch." Wallace had pulled a wet wipe from a mini-pack in his pocket and was disinfecting all surfaces in the rental car that he could possibly come into contact with.

"You're taking a complaint from me about the Hodges, then doing some recon. I'd leave out the trip to Sanford, if I were you."

He wrinkled his nose. "I'd have *skipped* the trip to Sanford if I'd had a choice."

I shot him a look. "You did have a choice."

"Not in the mood you're in. Somebody has to keep you from doing something stupid, and I'm the only somebody around. Plus Jack made me promise to help him keep an eye on you."

"What?"

"We're worried. You . . . get into scrapes."

"Oh, please. All I'm doing is going to interview a witness for Phil's case."

"Yeah, and what if I hadn't come? Would any laws have been broken in today's excursion?"

I squirmed a little in my seat. "Impossible to know in advance."

He snorted. "Right."

I turned left onto 687, blinkerless. Jack would have mentioned it. Wallace let it slide.

"How about you finagle Jack and me a visit with Betsy this Saturday? We'd love to take her to the park. There's an Easter egg hunt."

"Oh, honey. You know this never goes well."

I pressed my lips together and gripped the steering wheel with both hands.

Wallace shook his head. "Fine." He pulled out his phone and a minute later he was speaking. "Hello, Mary Alice. This is Wallace Gray with CPS. How are you?"

A series of sounds came from the phone, but I couldn't distinguish her words.

"I'm sure they do keep you very busy, and we appreciate all you do. Listen, I was calling to arrange a date to the park for Betsy this weekend with Jack Holden and Emily Bernal."

The sounds grew louder, and he held the phone away from his ear, his eyes closed. "Well, you canceled the last several visits without notice. I was hoping that if I chaperoned we could make it happen this time."

More sounds, shrill.

"I understand you have reservations, but let's say I pick Betsy up at ten a.m. See you then." He clicked off.

"Was that a yes?" I eased off the accelerator as we came to the Sanford city limits.

"Sort of."

Joe's Liquor and Smokes wasn't hard to find, since it was on the main thoroughfare. I hadn't been sure why a town with a population of 181 needed its own liquor store until we got there. It was desolate, despite its proximity to the popular Lake Meredith recreation area and Canadian River bottoms. Most of the buildings bore signs for businesses that had long since vacated their premises. The residential area—if you could call it that—was bleak. A few scraggly trees and scrubby lawns were the only vegetation around boxy houses that had seen better days, and sagging mobile homes that had never had any.

Sanford wasn't like most small Texas towns with their town squares anchored by imposing courthouses/municipal buildings surrounded by lawns and trees. Businesses or ghosts of businesses past usually rimmed the square facing in. The smallest of towns at least had a central business district with a strip of old brick or stone structures lining both sides of the main drag. Not Sanford, though. Sanford had a few scattered buildings, several wooden and dilapidated, two brick and crumbling, and some metal and barnlike.

Joe's building fell into the barnlike category. It was eleven o'clock and there was some meager light visible through the glass front door, so I pulled to a stop in the dirt lot in front of it.

"Wow." I put the Mustang in park.

"Ugh," Wallace said.

We got out with Snowflake on a leash with Wallace. I saw immediately why the light from the store was so dim. A heavy film of dirt and disintegrating stickers obscured the door, broken up only by a few streaks where rain or some other liquid had hit, spattered, and dripped. I scanned the offering of reading material on the door quickly. Standard liquor store fare about drinking responsibly and criminal penalties for buying for minors, interspersed with T&A beer ads.

Wallace opened the door. "After you."

I curtsied, holding out a pretend skirt over my boots and holey jeans.

The lights in the store blinded me, and I shielded my eyes. Fluorescents buzzed like bug zappers and neon flickered in a cavernous interior. A checkout stand stood to the left of the front door, and nearly empty coolers lined one-third of the wall to the right, with colorful twelve-packs of Bud Light, Coors Light, Miller Lite, and Lone Star looking lonesome except for a few boxes of wine and bottles of MD 20/20 and malt liquor knocking around. Six or seven aisles of half-filled shelves stretched down the middle of the space, with plenty of room leftover to ride a horse down the empty left side of the building. Or three Clydesdales abreast.

"Good morning," I chirped, searching for a human presence.

Wallace leaned in to my ear. "This place makes me long for my old Prozac prescription."

I elbowed him.

"Can I he'p you?" a woman's voice said. It sounded like she'd missed her morning coffee or woken up on the wrong side of the bed. Or both.

I turned toward the checkout counter, and the source of the voice. A tiny woman with waist-length white-blonde hair sat on a stool in the shadow of the wall, filing her talons, and she didn't look up at us.

I walked to the counter. An array of energy shots and herbal male enhancement remedies vied for prominence. I smiled in the woman's direction. "Hello, yes, I'm looking for Cecilia."

She rolled her eyes up to look at me without lifting her head. "Why?" She had so much eye shadow on her lids I was surprised she had the strength to hold them open. Luckily, she'd propped them up underneath with a heavy stripe of black liner.

"Because her ex-husband is in a coma, and I need to talk to her."

She slid off the stool, which made her shorter. When she moved closer, I saw creases in her pancaked makeup. "What's someone your age doing with braces, and who the hell are you?"

Not someone who'd ever buy beer from your rude butt. There was not much to like about this woman so far, and I heard Wallace cough behind me. "I'm with his attorney's office. Williams and Associates. Emily Bernal." I stuck out my hand and swung my head toward Wallace. "And this is Wallace Gray."

She put cold, limp fingers in my hand. It was like shaking a partially thawed Mrs. Paul's fish filet. "I'm Cecilia."

I tried to act mildly surprised. "Oh, that's great. Phil's mother said I could find you here."

"Yeah, well, I'm working."

I cleared my throat, dangerously close to laughing. "I understand, and please feel free to carry on with that, and of course I'll wait if you need to help the customers." I waved around the empty store, widening my eyes in an attempt to look sincere.

She backed up to the stool and worked her way on, despite her tight jeans. She resumed filing her nails, nodding at me.

"So, I don't know how much you've heard, if anything, about Phil's situation—"

"That he killed Dennis and is close to dead himself?"

My eyebrows shot up almost to my hairline, giving my forehead a good stretch. "That he was arrested and charged with Dennis's murder, but we don't believe he did it. And he's in stable condition, but still in a diabetic coma."

"Yeah, well, I always told him that the diabetes was gonna kill him. He didn't take care of himself, you know."

I pictured Phil and Nadine, and what I'd seen of his lifestyle. Maybe he'd partied in the past, but he and Nadine were like an old married couple lately, albeit an old married couple that was in the sex business. I decided to change the subject. "The DA says a witness heard Phil and Dennis arguing the night Dennis died, and that it was because Dennis slept with Phil's wife."

She pursed her lips and stopped filing. "Isn't Phil married to some heifer now?" She shook her head, rolling her eyes. "Dennis didn't have any trouble getting women. Hot women. He wasn't into big girls, if you know what I mean."

The tips of my ears burned, and I turned to Wallace. He shook his head, and I knew he was right, even if I didn't like it. I reined in my desire to defend Nadine. "Did you ever sleep with Dennis?"

She licked her teeth and her mouth smacked. "That's none of your business."

"Probably not. But Phil's fiancée didn't sleep with Dennis, and we're trying to defend Phil on a murder charge. So it would help if we knew whether they could have been fighting over you."

Her head tilted to the side. "Let me think."

Wallace, who had moved forward to stand beside me, stepped on my foot long and hard. I felt his body shake just slightly and knew he was laughing.

"Take your time," I wheezed.

Her lips moved while she concentrated. Snowflake sniffed around the base of the checkout counter. The hum and intermittent buzzing of the signs was the only sound. Finally, she shrugged. "Probably, but I can't remember. What would Phil care, anyway? We both slept with other people, and it was never a big deal. It had to be over that new woman, what'd you say her name was?"

"Nadine."

"Yeah." Her eyes glazed for a moment, then she lifted a fist in the air. "Hey, you know, I saw Dennis with some skinny bitch last month, out at Lake Meredith. He was calling her honey and baby and shit, hanging on her, acting like he was real into her. Maybe it was the other way around. Maybe Phil slept with her." She reached under the counter and pulled out a pack of Kools and a lighter.

"What was her name?"

"I dunno. We weren't introduced." She lit up her cigarette and dragged on it.

"Can you describe her?"

"Real skinny. Pale. Blondish-brown hair in a ponytail."

"Short? Tall?"

"Dunno. She was sitting."

I changed tracks. "How did Phil and Dennis get along when you were with Phil?"

"Great. They were tight. Had been since I'd known them, and we go way back, back to junior high. They always dreamed of going into business together someday. Said they were going to rise up." She blew smoke.

"Were they in business together?"

"Not when Phil and me were married, but who knows."

As she answered my last question, a potbellied man with thick hair on the sides of his head and none on top entered through the front door. He stared at us, then glanced at the counter, where no merchandise was displayed. Cecilia drew in a breath so quick it was almost a gasp. Wallace saw him, too, and we shared a glance. She stubbed out her cigarette in an ashtray she pulled from under the counter, hands trembling.

"Hey, boss, I was just telling them no dogs—"

In his best "straight" voice, Wallace said, "I think I'll stick with Miller Lite." He walked to the case and grabbed a twelve-pack. "Want anything else, hon?"

"No, dear, but thank you." I picked up a bottle of something labeled Horny Goat Weed. "On second thought, maybe some of this?" I said to Cecilia.

Wallace set the beer on the counter by the horny goat weed. "I'll slip out with the dog. Thank you."

Cecilia rang us up under the watchful eye of the newcomer. As I exited through the door, I heard him ask, "Who were they?"

"Out-of-towners," she answered, and then the door closed.

Wallace buckled himself in and I put Snowflake in the backseat and myself in the front.

Wallace said in his normal voice, "Nadine is one serious upgrade for Phil."

"Cecilia was a piece of work," I agreed.

I had received two texts. The first was from Judith: *I'll talk to Jack about whether I should send the file.* It took me a second to remember that Wallace had sent her a text and what it said. *Grrr.* The second was from John Burrows. All it said was *Burt Wilde.* My blood boiled. Burt Wilde was the name of the man that had talked to me at Phil's party, the one who had asked me to tell Jack he hadn't done it, whatever "it" was. Jack said that the police hadn't been able to identify them.

Was it possible Jack had lied to me?

"Check this out." I handed Wallace my phone.

"The plot thickens."

I pulled away from the curb with a little too much acceleration and drove a block to make a U-turn. As I wound the steering wheel, I hit the brakes. "Wallace, look at that!" I pointed to a sign that read MIGHTY IS HIS WORD, COME JOIN GOD'S ARMY WITH SISTER FURMAN, 3 MILES, with an arrow pointing down a side street. "Is that the same church as the one in Amarillo?"

"What the hell?" he said. "I didn't know there were more of them." He grinned at me. "Potential foster parents."

"Potential psychos, more like it," I countered. I pulled out my phone and snapped a picture, then turned back toward Amarillo, passing Cecilia's glaring boss standing outside Joe's Liquor and Smokes as I did.

FOURTEEN

Screams of joy intermingled with shouts and laughter at Southwest Park. Kids dressed in every pastel in the rainbow sprinted around the grassy apron to the playground, swinging baskets and slinging out the colorful eggs they'd worked so hard to find. Parents snapped photos, grandmas and grandpas beamed, and organizers herded small bodies that strayed from the egg-hunting area. My traitorous mouth salivated from the delicious smell of the barbecue being unloaded from a delivery van and onto a long row of tables covered in pink, green, and yellow paper tablecloths; it was so easy to forget I was a vegetarian at moments like this.

Jack and I stood on the outside looking in, together, sort of. I'd brought him mostly up-to-date that morning on all that had happened during the week, and he'd listened, asked questions, and continued to be sweet and concerned about the horrible incident at Thompson Park, apologizing again about missing our class and being so distracted. But what he hadn't been was forthcoming. I was stewing on it, and we'd stopped talking, which Jack treated like companionable silence and which I considered at best a stalemate.

A tall black woman with shoulder-length hair crouched to help a little girl with a spilled basket. Beside them, a dark-skinned man with a shaved head held the hand of a slightly older girl, while a bored tween fiddled with a phone behind him.

"Alan, Janelle," I called out.

The man and woman looked around and caught sight of me. She

smiled and he waved. Beside me, Jack grunted. "Let's go say hello," I said to him.

"Okay." Jack shouted, "Hey," to the Freemans.

We walked over to the family. Alan shook Jack's hand and Janelle hugged us both. Their tween didn't show any sign she realized other humans inhabited her air space, but the two younger girls grinned and said, "Hello."

"Y'all remember my attorney, Jack, and his fiancée, Emily?" Alan asked them. Jack had represented Alan against a bogus assaulting-an-officer charge.

"Yes, Daddy," the older one said. Her huge eyes dominated her thin face.

"Hi," the littlest one said, and she kicked the ground, then ducked behind her mother's legs.

"Happy Easter, you guys," I said. "How are you?"

"Great," Janelle responded. "When'd you get braces?"

I raised my hand to hold in front of my mouth, then dropped it when I realized what I'd done. "A month or two ago."

"And when's the wedding?"

"Uh—"

Jack took over. "One month, in New Mexico. We're doing a backyard family ceremony."

"Will you have Betsy by then?"

I looked around for her. She was the reason we were there, after all, but there was still no sign of her or Wallace.

"Hope so." Jack put his arm around my shoulders.

"Mommy, it's time for the pony rides. You promised," their youngest daughter said, tugging on Janelle's skirt.

I laughed. "Pony rides? Sounds fun!" To Janelle and Alan I added, "Good to see you. Take care, you two."

After our good-byes, Jack and I stood childless in the crowd. Past the edge of the gathering was the playground. "Want to go swing while we wait?" I asked him.

The left side of his face slid upward a notch. "Let's do it."

A minute later, Jack and I were swinging side by side, but out of sync. I kicked my legs out and flew forward as he tucked his and pumped back. Back and forth we went, missing each other coming, then missing each other going.

"Whatcha thinkin' 'bout?" I said as I kicked my legs out again.

He whizzed past me. "Nothing. You?"

About what the heck is going on with you. "Betsy. She's missed the egg hunt."

"Those people."

Those people, as in the Hodges. It gave us something to have solidarity over. "Yeah, they're definitely not on my favorites list." I changed the subject. "Oh, I forgot to tell you. John gave me the name of the guy from Phil's party. Burt Wilde."

Jack dropped his feet and pushed his heels into the ground. They dragged, but he still swung forward. I caught up with him and for a short moment we were synchronized, then he dug his heels in again and stopped.

"Did you hear me?"

"Yeah. Did they talk to him?"

"I don't know. Who is he?"

"What do you mean?"

"I mean who is he to you? Why would he mention you to me?"

"Oh. A guy I put away in my old life."

"For what?"

"Kidnapping and pimping teenagers."

A shudder ran through me. "Oh. That's awful."

"Yeah. He's not a nice guy."

"What do you think he meant when he told me he didn't do it?"

Jack turned to me, and his face looked tight. "I don't know."

He was already upset, so I figured there was no harm in pushing a little harder. "Does he have anything to do with that old case you're working on?"

His voice was like a steel door slamming shut. "No." He looked at his feet, then dug a toe in the sand.

"Okay." I kept swinging, thinking. Jack had put a lot of defendants in jail during his time as an ADA. More than he'd represented as a defense attorney since. This wouldn't be the last time we'd run across one. But then I thought of something. "But you didn't recognize him in the drawing or on the video?"

"It's been a long time. People change."

"True."

On a whim and a memory, I launched myself off the front of the swing as it neared its apex on my next pass. Luckily, I wasn't too high. I stuck the landing, or, I almost did. I picked myself up off the grass and wiped the knees of my jeans.

Jack surprised me by clapping. "Nice."

I curtsied, but my ringing phone interrupted me. I'd left it in my purse beside the swing set. I trotted over and fished it out. Wallace. "Hey, where are you and Betsy?"

"Just me, I'm afraid. I waited at the Hodges' house for thirty minutes.

They weren't there. I've called every number I have for them, and I'm not getting a response. I'm sorry, Emily."

"Son of a biscuit!"

"Yeah, I'm with you on that."

"Is there nothing we can do?"

"Short of kidnapping Betsy—which I cannot stress enough is the wrong move— no. You're not Betsy's parent. I can't force them to let her interact with you. This is all voluntary on their part."

"Or not." Tears smarted in the corners of my eyes. "Thanks for trying, Wallace. Oh, and tell Ethan 'Hey' for us."

I ended the call.

Jack had moved to stand behind me. "I'm sorry." He put a hand on my shoulder.

The feelings raging inside me about Betsy were grayish green, like bruises and cyclone weather. It didn't take much for them to get tangled up with my black and blue feelings about Jack. The resulting swirl was dark and ugly. I stood in the center of the storm as happy children ran into the arms of waiting parents all around us.

My emotions simmered in me all afternoon like I was a pressure cooker on a stove, threatening to blow my lid off. My father called to see if I wanted to go shoot skeet with him. Mother invited us to dinner. Jack offered to take me to a movie. I spat a *no* out at all of them, and Jack wisely left for a workout and to run errands.

I hid in the home office for a few hours, the wood-paneled darkness of the interior room a good match for my mood as I tried to find dirt on the Hodges. I didn't dig up anything new, but I got an email from Michele: *See you in three days.*

How could I keep forgetting she was coming to Amarillo and staying with us? I looked forward to seeing her, but the timing was really, really bad. I would have to rise above. Company was company, and my mother didn't raise me to show my dirty bloomers.

There was also an email from my ex-husband:

Stormy and I went to Santa Fe last weekend and got married. Is it too much to hope for that you will wish us well?

A tear welled up in one eye and I swiped at it. Of course I wished him well, in addition to a lot of other stuff. I wished he hadn't cheated on me. I wished he hadn't found happiness faster than me. I wished I hadn't married a guy who wasn't madly in love with me, and I wished I hadn't miscarried his baby, my baby. But now that six months had passed, I harbored no grudge against him; I cared enough about him to hurt for him that he had been trapped, living a life untrue to himself.

I didn't want to do it again, though. To end up five, ten, fifteen years later looking back on a failure that I could have seen coming, because a man wanted to marry me for a reason other than the one right reason. Was I about to doom myself to that fate with Jack? A framed picture of the two of us smiling, laughing, riding out at Wrong Turn Ranch taunted me. He was everything I wanted, but only if I was everything to him.

Which reminded me what I'd learned on the swings that morning. I had another issue to look into: Burt Wilde. Unlike with the Hodges, Google served up a veritable smorgasbord of information on him. As I scanned articles and read about the crimes he'd been convicted of, my skin crawled. This man—this *thing* who preyed on disenfranchised youth, lured them into his clutches then forced them to sell their bodies and souls ten times a night, seven days a week—had stood next to me, touched my arm, spoken to me. Unfortunately, not everything he was accused of could be proved. I thought of Jack facing him in a courtroom, knowing that a decade inside was the best he was going to be able to do with the evidence he had, but knowing that at least he could get him off the streets for that long. One article called Jack "a rising star in the New Mexico legal community" and "impassioned" and "brilliant." A warmth spread through me. I wished I could have watched him as a prosecutor. I continued flipping virtually through articles, finding nothing new, nothing that would explain why Wilde would appear out of the blue in Amarillo asking me to tell Jack he didn't do *something*. I went faster and faster until I got to articles about his release from prison. They were dated just a few months ago. I perused a few, and that's when I found a new and different mention of Jack.

Former Alamogordo ADA Jack Holden appeared before the Parole Board to argue against Wilde's release when he first came up for consideration. Holden, whose wife and children died in a car bombing, has long said that he believes Wilde was involved in their deaths. Wilde denies this.

My hand flew over my mouth. Wilde killed Jack's family? I spent the next half hour reading and rereading everything I could find about the bombing and the ensuing investigation. Jack claimed Wilde had made threats against his family during the investigation, which Wilde denied, and the bombing occurred days after Wilde's verdict. Jack didn't suggest Wilde had done it himself—that would have been impossible since he was already in jail—but that he had been behind it.

My troubled mind struggled to put the pieces together. Wilde wanted me to tell Jack he didn't do it. Did he mean he didn't kill Dennis, or he didn't kill Jack's family? Both? Neither? And Jack didn't say a word about Wilde looking familiar when he saw the sketch. He denied that the old case he was looking into involved Wilde. None of it made sense, just like

Jack's recent behavior made no sense. Yes, he'd had a terrible tragedy, but that didn't give him a free pass now.

I hated to, but I had to call John.

He picked up on the first ring. "Yo, CJ, what's up?"

"CJ?"

"Calamity Jane."

"Very funny. Hey, I forgot to ask you the other day, was Wilde IDed from the sketch or the video or what?"

John was silent on the other end.

I got up and walked to look out the windows in the backyard, giving John a second. Snowflake was snoozing in the sun. I squinted, trying to determine what the brownish red thing in front of her was. Ah, Snowflake was napping with the little red fox. I couldn't help but smile at our own version of *The Fox and the Hound*.

I broke the silence. "John?"

"Do you really not know?"

"Not know what?"

"Jack told us who he was the night you worked with the sketch artist. Came in the next week and gave us an old file he had on the guy, too."

Now it was my end of the phone with no sound.

"I would've thought you knew."

"Yeah, me, too." I stuck my left thumbnail in my mouth where the edge was frayed, and I chomped down hard, taking off all the excess nail and more. It hurt, but not as bad as Jack's lies and secrets. "So, how do I get ahold of Wilde?"

"Emily . . ."

"You talked to Wilde, didn't you?"

"Yes."

"So you could make me work really hard to find him, or just give me a few hints."

Burrows made a funny noise, like he was blowing air through loose lips, vibrating them. Like a horse. "Yeah, fine, I guess I can save you a little time. But he's a convicted felon, Emily, and you've gotta treat that like it matters. Because it does."

So was my father. That made me more than qualified. "I will."

"No you won't. And I'm going to be sorry. But here's his number." John recited it for me. "I'm only telling you because Jack's the one that gave it to me."

As many hits to the gut as I'd received today, you'd think I'd be tensed and ready to absorb the blows, but I wasn't, and each revelation was another sucker punch. "All right, then. Thank you, John."

I was about to hang up when I heard him say, "Emily?"

"Yes?"

"Um, I was wondering if you might want to grab dinner with me this weekend?"

All those times I'd thought John was flirting with me, I'd been right. "Oh, I, um, well, huh. Jack and I, um, we, well, we have plans so I can't and did you know we're engaged?"

The silence yawned and creaked, then broke. "Yeah, I knew. But if things don't work out with the two of you or you change your mind, you know where to find me."

"I'm really sorry."

"No sweat. A guy's gotta try, after all. Swing for the fences."

A child's voice in the background, high and sweet, said, "Daddy, are you coming? It's time to leave."

I waited.

John's voice grew muffled. "Just a second, slugger."

"But you said."

"I know. I'm coming." His voice resumed normal volume. "Gotta go. T-ball game. Be safe, Calamity Jane. Keep me on speed dial."

"I will. Good luck in the game, and thanks again."

We ended the call.

"Jack?" I shouted. "You here?" I wanted to call Wilde, but I wasn't going to do it if Jack was standing in the kitchen listening. "Jack?"

"In the garage."

No calling Wilde now, then, since Jack was in earshot.

I grabbed my keys and bolted through the door to the garage.

Jack was digging around in a large cardboard box at the base of the pull-down ladder to the attic. I hadn't seen the box since we moved in, when he'd put a bunch of them up there. He jumped when I shut the door.

"What are you doing?" I stood on the other side of the boxes from him and tried to read the contents notations he'd made in Sharpie.

He put his hand on the box, closing one of the flaps and moving his hand over the writing, but not quickly enough to keep me from seeing the word *Lena*. It was probably a box of information on his secret investigation that he'd lied to me about six ways to Sunday. "Nothing."

I pointed at the box. "What kind of nothing?"

"Organization project."

I made a *hrmph* noise as I clicked the fob to unlock the Mustang.

"Where are you headed?"

"Nowhere."

His hands rose to his hips, fisted there. "Doing what?"

"Nothing."

I slammed the door to the Mustang and peeled out in reverse.

FIFTEEN

As I raced down our road, I pounded the steering wheel. I knew I was making things worse, but I didn't know how not to be upset at Jack about his lies, and about the fact that I'd been right all along. He was still obsessed with what happened to Lena and their kids, and maybe rightly so, but that didn't leave much room for me. I wanted Jack to love me, for me to be the one he had chosen, not the sensible partner after he'd lost what he wanted, not the woman he lied to while he chased down ghosts.

I burned with need to be "the one" for him, like he was for me. Because he was that for me—the one. My high school boyfriend, Scott—now, there was a catch; married repeatedly and right now with a too-young wife and a brand new baby—had been the good-looking jock type. He was just someone to date. Rich? I had loved Rich, but never crazily, never with passion. He was security and affection and friendship. And now a deep sadness and regret.

Then there was Jack. There was the drumbeat of desire that throbbed in me when my eyes caught sight of him, when I heard his voice, caught scent of him, thought of him. The aching to be near him that never went away. The way he stirred me up, brought out the entire range of my emotions, from peaks to valleys. How he made me laugh. How I loved watching him in court, his mind in motion. On a horse. In a car. Over breakfast. In our bed.

But then there was the jealousy and distrust, yes, my stupid, destructive jealousy and distrust that was ripping me apart.

I realized I had driven to my parents' house, and I laughed aloud at my not-so-subtle subconscious.

I knocked before I entered—it wasn't my house anymore—but opened the door before I got a response. I stuck my head in to hear Fox News blaring. "Hello, anyone here?"

"Sweet Pea." My dad's voice came from the kitchen.

I followed it. "Hi, Pops," I said, feeling punchy and edgy and different.

He laughed, setting down the want ads section of the paper. "Pops, huh?"

"Would you prefer Daddy-o?"

"I think I'll stick with Pops."

Mother came through the laundry room door, wiping her hands on one of her frilly white June Cleaver aprons. "Where's Jack?"

I crossed my fingers behind my back. "Working in the garage."

She nodded. "Is he getting things ready?"

"Ready for what?"

She and Dad shared a look of panic. She said, "Oh, nothing."

"What is it?"

"Um, I was just thinking about the wedding, and whether he was doing anything related to that."

"In the garage?"

Dad pulled my attention to him. "Thought you didn't want to go shoot."

"I don't." On a whim, I said, "I wanted to see if you'd take a drive with me instead."

Without hesitation, he stood, pushing down on his pant legs. He might be nearing sixty, but he still wore his close-fitting, straight-legged jeans and the high-heeled riding boots of a cowboy every day. He didn't bother answering me, just beelined for the front door.

"Dinner's at six," Mother called after him.

"I'll have him back before then." I turned and followed him to my car.

"Where are we going?"

I clicked the key fob and the rental Mustang beep-beeped at us. "Just driving."

"Yours is a different color, ain't it?"

"In the shop. This one's temporary."

He folded his body into the Mustang's passenger seat, his knees jutting up, his head sticking out over where the soft roof would have been. He moved the seat back as far as it would go, his long legs extending into something more comfortable as he did. "Looks good to me."

I pulled away from the curb and pointed the car toward Amarillo.

"You'll feel better if you talk about it, Sweet Pea."

Maybe about some things. My ponytail had collapsed. I pushed back a strand of hair that was blowing around in my face. Words came out before I thought them. "Why'd you leave Mother? The real reason."

He shifted in his seat, readjusted, looked at his hands. I took in the view. The panhandle countryside had sprung into spring. Most of the year the prairie was brown, but now it was alive with green grass, flowering cactus in yellow, fuchsia, and white, and tall stems of red yucca blossoms. Today they stood relatively straight in the absence of our usually ferocious wind.

When he spoke, he didn't turn his head to look at me. "Some men gotta lose something to know its value. Your mother is—"

"Annoying?"

"No?"

"Irritating?"

"Not that."

"Smothering?"

He chuckled. "Well, maybe a little of that. But you better watch what you say; you're a lot like her."

"I'm nothing like her! I'm like the reincarnation of you." Except that I'd never killed anyone.

He smiled. "Anyway, I married young, even younger than she did—"

"What?"

He scowled. "You didn't know your mother and I had each been married before?"

I exited Soncy and turned north onto Loop 335. "No. No one ever told me."

"Well, I was. So was she."

"Oh my dog." After all the trouble she'd given me about divorcing Rich, she'd been married before. How I wished I'd known this six months earlier.

"He was an older fella. I guess you could say it was an arranged marriage. By her parents. They were a little—"

"Nuts?"

"Zealous."

I sighed. "So how'd she get rid of him?"

"He died of a heart attack when she was eighteen."

"Holy mackerel, I'm sorry. I was being catty. Go on."

"I was divorced. My first wife left me when I wouldn't stay home and work for her daddy. In Dalhart, where we grew up."

"But you wanted to rodeo."

"Yup. And I was good at it. Made the National Finals when I was twenty-three. That's where I met your mother."

"Where she was . . . ?" I said, hopefully.

"Pretty as a picture and sweet as sugar. We got married a week later."

I couldn't imagine my parents that young and impetuous, but I had to have gotten it from somewhere. "And then?"

"She traveled with me for a couple of years. Then we had you and set up base camp here."

"So I ended the fun."

"Oh no, Sweet Pea, you started it. I wanted to be here with you guys more than I wanted to be on the road. We made it work, for a long time. And then one day, I just couldn't imagine why anyone that would want me that much was worth wanting."

"Daddy!"

He shrugged. "Jilly—that was my first wife's name—really messed with my head. I guess I loved her. And when she didn't love me, it burrowed in deep. Like a bomb with a timer, just waitin' to go off and blow my life to bits."

"Wow. I don't know what to say. I guess just I'm sorry. That sounds awful."

"It was worse for your mother. She didn't do anything wrong. Didn't see it comin'."

We passed the Wildcat Bluff Nature Center as we made the curve to the east.

I pictured my mother, back then. Red-rimmed, puffy eyes. Too bright smile. Chin high, shoulders back. "Yeah, it was hard on her."

"After a while, I went to Dalhart. Looked up Jilly."

I darted my eyes toward him. "You did?"

"Yup. I'm not gonna lie. She was beautiful. Divorced again. Making herself available."

"Did you guys get back together?" It hurt me to even say it.

"Nah. That's the moment I realized that while I'd loved Jilly, it was a long time ago. I loved your mother."

"And then what happened?"

"Nothing. Too much time had passed, and I decided I needed to make some money so I could go back and buy your mother somethin' nice, so she'd forgive me. I went to the next rodeo, then the next. Won big. Stashed my money in a safety-deposit box in Calgary." He stopped. "This next part I ain't proud of."

"It's okay, Dad, go on."

"Some men offered to pay me big to lose. So I did."

We crossed Amarillo Creek and I sucked in a deep breath. My eyes cut to him. "Oh man, that must have been hard."

"It was, the first time. I decided to go do just one more before I went home. I lost, all right, but I got hurt, hurt bad, and I couldn't rodeo. Those same guys paid me to do some little jobs. My money was still in Calgary, but I was following the circuit and before you know it we were down in New Mexico. They told me I needed to lame a horse to make sure an event came out like they needed it to. I said no."

"I'm so glad."

"One of 'em threatened you and your mother, made it clear they knew how to find you."

I turned north on 287, sneaking glances at Dad as I watched the traffic. "Oh no!"

"That's the one I got with the beer bottle."

"Wait, I thought, but Jack said, um—"

"That it was self-defense?"

"Yes."

"Well, now you know the truth." My head felt funny, light and dizzy. Dad hadn't killed in self-defense? He'd *murdered* a man outright? His voice sounded a million miles away. "Then I found myself in a six-by-six cell in New Mexico with a lot of time on my hands to think." He snorted. "I've never been much of a thinker, Sweet Pea. Even then, it didn't come to me fast or easy."

We drove in silence. My brain struggled to wrap itself around what my father had just told me. He'd admitted to cold-blooded murder. I couldn't swallow, I could hardly breathe. This made things so, so much worse, and I didn't even want to look at him or be in the car with him. Searching for a place to stop so I could get out and try to get myself together, I took an exit off 287. At the bottom of the exit ramp, we splashed through a lake-sized puddle, and when I glanced right, I saw water pouring out of an overflow pipe leading to God knew where. The route I'd escaped on was a familiar route. It led to the Mighty is His Word church and pretty much nothing else. Rather than make a U-turn, I wheeled the Mustang onto the long dirt road leading up to the church and lurched into a parking space adjacent to the sanctuary.

The church itself was a cavernous metal building. From the outside, it was just a giant red square with a silver roof. You expected to see cows spilling out the side doors and roosters in the yard. But instead there was a big white cross over the entrance and the MIGHTY IS HIS WORD logo on the side, ten feet across and nearly as high. And today, a giant banner strung from one end of the building to the other that read Are you prepared to die for God like Jesus did?

"You taking me to church?" Dad asked. "Seems like I just confessed all my sins."

"Did you ever."

He frowned at my tone of voice. "What?"

"I believed the self-defense thing. This is a lot to take in."

His mouth dropped. "But Sweet Pea, I'd do anything to protect you and your mother. Anything."

"You could have called the police."

"Well, in hindsight, that might have been an option. But in a dark parking lot when someone's threatening you and the ones you love, well, I did what I had to do."

I closed my eyes. The picture of slashing glass still loomed, much more violent and personal than, say, killing someone from a distance with a gun or poison. But I guessed I could understand him, sort of. And in a weird way I was less unhappy about him killing someone out of love for us than in a bar fight. If someone threatened Jack and Betsy, would I kill them? It depended on the circumstances, but if I was honest with myself, I might. Even now, when Jack wasn't making it easy to love him, with his lies and deceit.

I nodded, biting the inside of my lower lip. "Can I ask you a few more questions, Pops?"

"Fire away."

"Did you ever lie to Mother, hide things from her?" I knew the answer. I just wanted to get him to talk about the reason.

"Oh, gosh yes, many times over."

"Why?"

"I told myself I was protecting her, although now that I have time to reflect, I know I was mostly protecting myself. She didn't need that money in Calgary."

I nodded slowly. "She just needed you to come home."

He wiped a tear. "Yeah. But one of these days you or Jack or your Mother's going to have to make a run to Calgary for me, since I'm on parole and can't do it myself."

"Your money's still there?"

"Sure is. Enough to make fetching it worthwhile."

I grinned. "I just might could do that for you, Dad."

"Good." He smacked me on the leg. "Now, mind me asking why we're at a church?"

I turned to him, both hands up by my shoulders, and said, *"Yo no se,"* like I did incessantly when I first learned Spanish as a freshman in high school, not long before he left. Which was true, and not true. I wanted my daddy to help me figure out how not to lose Betsy, even if I wasn't yet entirely comfortable with his choices, and somehow that had brought us here.

"Well, when you do figure it out, let me know."

I grabbed my purse from the backseat and fished out my cell phone. I woke it up and opened the pictures app. The picture I'd taken in Sanford the day before came up first. I pointed it at my dad. "I think that's a match. What say you?"

He took the phone from me and held it up at arm's length, squinting, so that the logo on the side of the church and the phone screen were both in his field of vision. "Yup."

I bit my lip, pondering things before I spoke. "Jack and I had a visit scheduled with Betsy today. She was a no-show, thanks to her foster parents. This is their church." There were a handful of vehicles in the parking lot. I caught sight of their white passenger van.

"Are they here?"

"Yes." I pointed at it. I took my phone back and clicked the screen dark. As I did, motion at the entrance to the church caught my eye. "There they are." A teenage boy held the door open as Mary Alice, Trevon, and a succession of young people exited the building. I was glad I was in a rental car, because they wouldn't notice me craning and staring, which I was. The last child in line brought a quick sting to my eyes. Betsy. She was in a pink dress with white polka dots and had pink bows at the ends of her pigtails. I wanted to call out to her, but I knew better.

"Big family. Cute girl."

I wiped my eyes. "Yeah, the Hodges have eleven foster kids, plus one birth child. All of them are classified as special needs, including Betsy." I kept my eyes on Betsy, drinking her in. "Wallace told me that the Mighty is His Word families account for half the foster placements in Amarillo, and almost ninety percent of the special needs placements. Either they're do-gooders on a mission, or something else, and the cynical side of me thinks they're milking the state." I gave my head a rapid tiny shake and sighed fast and hard. Betsy was climbing into the side of the van. She hadn't smiled the whole time I watched her, or talked with her siblings, or laughed. I wanted to run to her and swing her around in a circle by her arms and hear her infectious giggle. But I couldn't. She disappeared from my view, but I kept watching.

Dad turned his head to the side, squinting at the monstrous building in front of us. "It's like a state-sponsored church. And the state ain't s'posed to be in the religion business."

The van door slammed, and the engine to the van started. "Don't ever say you're no good at thinking." I watched the van as it backed out of its parking space, Trevon at the wheel. My eyes followed it as it left the parking lot and drove away with a piece of my heart. I wiped my eyes again.

"Nah, I just had a lot of time to practice."

Since we were there, I had an urge to go in, an itch begging for a scratch. And who better to have with me if something went wrong than the man who had proven he'd do whatever it took to keep me safe? "Want me to show you the inside?"

"Why not?"

We got out and walked briskly toward the church. I left my purse in the car, so I shoved my keys and both my hands into my pockets, kicking a dirt clump as I did. Then a rock. Then a bigger rock. It zinged off my foot and onto the metal shell of the church. Clang! We turned up the sidewalk toward the entrance. It was nondescript, except for the prominent No Trespassing sign. Otherwise, just two glass front doors opening café style. I grabbed the one on the right and held it for Dad.

He tipped an imaginary hat at me, and I followed him through. We were in a fairly large vestibule. On the far end were the doors to the sanctuary. On a side was a hallway. On another side were bulletin boards. I sauntered to that one, wanting to hum the theme to *Mission: Impossible* as I did.

"Welcome to Mighty is His Word," a rich baritone voice said.

Beside me, Dad answered. "Why, thank you very much, sir."

I pretended to be reading, but I couldn't, because I knew this voice. It belonged to Pastor Will, the star witness for the prosecution against Phil in his recent burglary trial.

"We're a closed campus to visitors when services aren't in session, but I'd be happy to speak with you in my office if you would like."

"Um . . ." Dad said.

I felt bad for him. He had no way of knowing the history. "No, we'll be on our way. Sorry."

Pastor Will turned his attention to me, still pleasant until he saw my face. First he looked confounded, then angry. "You should know this is private property better than most people, and you're trespassing. I don't think the same excuse will work for you as worked for your client."

Clearly I'd worn out my welcome here. But no one knew me in Sanford, at the other location. I could continue looking into things there, maybe find something that would show why the Hodges shouldn't get Betsy. I tugged on my father's elbow. "Come on, Dad."

We walked out, and I could feel the sizzle of Pastor Will's laser-beam eyes searing my back.

"Gotta be a story there," Dad said.

"Oh, there is." We hightailed it out. I gave Dad the scoop, but in the background, my mind was putting together a plan to visit Mighty is His Word in Sanford, Texas.

SIXTEEN

From my seat in the back pew of the packed sanctuary, the female preacher looked about ten feet tall, with a thick gray braid down to her waist. The man standing behind her and to the right was about her age and even taller. They were alone on the dais, and she spoke into a wireless microphone rather than from a pulpit, pacing like a caged tiger.

"Brother Furman and I know," she said, raising both her arms in the air, then letting them fall. "We see it firsthand every day. We know the evil in our communities, the way that Satan is building his army against us. Jesus knew. He gave his life to fight against it. And on the third day he rose from the dead and ascended to the right hand of God the Father, Almighty."

The congregation unexpectedly shouted, "Amen!" as one. I jumped.

"God rewarded his sacrifice with everlasting life, like he promises us." She pointed behind her to a giant Jesus, his limp body hanging from nails on a cross.

It looked entirely too realistic to me, although I doubted that the real Jesus had limp, flabby pecs like this one, not at his age, and not with the life he led. Poor Jesus, to be memorialized as a wimp.

"You preach it, Sister Furman," someone shouted in front of me, man or woman, I couldn't tell.

The crowd started to stir in their seats, and the energy level rose.

"Brother Furman and I know something else, too, though. We know that with God with us, there's no army that can defeat us."

Now ten or more "Amens" rang out, along with some whoops.

"Look around you, brothers and sisters, look around you. These are your comrades in arms. These are the soldiers that will be fighting by your side when the Wrath of God is unleashed."

The congregation went nuts and their shouts rattled the metal roof. People leapt to their feet. "Hallelujah." "Amen." "Thank you, Jesus." "The Wrath of God." Two men beside me hugged, and a woman with long black hair lifted her face to the ceiling and cried.

It was the weirdest Easter celebration I hoped to ever see in my whole life. I noticed I was the only one still seated, so I jumped to my feet, clasping my hands in front of me. I could feel the soft, indented skin on my ring finger from my engagement ring. The one I'd left in the console of the Mustang on a whim before coming inside the church. On my right a heavy man raised both his hands to heaven and closed his eyes. He chanted, "My life for yours, God. My life for yours."

On my left a smaller man with thick facial hair threw his arms around me and lifted me in the air. "I've got your back, Sister."

He released me and I squeaked out an "Amen" in a cracking voice. I decided the lifted hands/chanting pose was safer and copied the guy on my right.

Just when I thought it would never end, Sister Furman's voice rang out over the mic.

"Our own son, Brother Richie, gave his very life to fight evil. No greater calling."

"No greater calling," the crowd echoed back.

"He died, but how many unborn children lived because he had the courage to bring the Wrath of God down upon the abortionists?"

Holy mackerel. What in the heck was she talking about? Sister Furman was scaring the bejeebers out of me. I stole a furtive glance toward the exit.

"Wrath of God," the crowd fired back at her.

"And he has been rewarded with life everlasting, I can assure you of that. I send you back out into the world, brothers and sisters, until we meet again, knowing that you will be strong in the face of evil, ready to bring the Wrath of God, for Mighty is His Word."

Every person in the church except me shouted the last four words with her, splitting my eardrums. I winced and tried to look like I was smiling. I wanted out of the church so badly I could almost cry. I wanted to run and hide like a little girl, to pretend I didn't know people this rabid existed on the planet, much less one hour from my home.

"'Scuse me," I said to the hairy guy on my left. He was the only one between me and freedom. "Bathroom. Emergency."

He pressed his legs against the pew and leaned his upper body toward the back rest, and I squeezed past him into the side aisle. My path to the exit was blocked by a wall of unmoving people. The crowd was boisterous now, pumped up by the rabble-rousing end to the sermon. The room had grown steamy from the perspiration of excited bodies. Sweat trickled between my breasts. I couldn't get enough air. Spots danced before my eyes. I swayed and saw the ground rushing toward my face.

"I said I've got your back, Sister, and I meant it," the hairy man said, just before the lights went out.

I opened my eyes to discover a ceiling. Drywall, orange-peel texture, white paint, white glass bowl over a light with one bulb out. My legs felt weighted down. I tried to sit up, and the spots came back. I groaned and fought through them.

"There she is." I didn't recognize the voice of the woman speaking.

I turned toward her and didn't recognize her face, either. "Hi, sorry, where am I?"

"You fainted. Brother Tom brought you into the Sunday school wing like a sack of potatoes. It's cooler in here, more comfortable for you to rest."

"Oh, wow." The freaky service and mob of crazy people came back to me. Mighty is His Word. Outside Sanford, aka seventh circle of Hell. I was still there.

"I'm Sister Elise, by the way." She smiled at me.

I swung my legs to the floor and a muslin blanket slipped off my legs and fell to the floor. I'd been reclined on a padded bench. The room around me seemed like an office, but it had crayon drawings and construction paper cutouts on the walls. I leaned over to pick up the blanket and held it out to her.

"We call those modesty blankets. We use them during communions and baptisms for women in skirts. Or, in your case, fainting."

"Oh."

"What's your name?" she asked, still smiling.

My dry throat felt like it was closing altogether. I willed my fuzzy brain to think. "Ce-Cecilia."

"Cecilia. Nice to meet you. Cecilia what?"

"Hodges." I regretted both names immediately, but it was too late. They were the best I could come up with in my current state.

"Hodges. Any relation to Mary Alice or Trevon in Amarillo?"

Inside I quaked. "Um, no, never heard of them." I wished I hadn't snuck out that morning, leaving Jack behind, asleep, more than I could possibly ever explain to another human. Why, oh, why had I left our safe, warm bed for this?

"Great people. True soldiers for God."

"Sounds like they are . . . fine people."

"The kind we all aspire to be."

The hairy man I'd sat next to earlier appeared in the doorway. "Good, you're back in the land of the living."

"Thanks for your help."

"No problem, sister. I'm Brother Tom."

I stood up, ready to shake his hand if he offered it, but he didn't. "Cecilia."

"Where you from, Cecilia?"

Why had I not prepared a cover story in advance? "P-P-Pampa."

"Are you married?"

I shook my head, which brought a little dizziness back.

"No? No kids?"

"None," I said, skipping the headshake.

"We always ask visitors this, so please don't feel singled out, but I'm wondering—how do you feel about contributions to the church?"

I laughed, startled. "You mean, like canned goods and hand-me-downs?"

He laughed, too. "No, no. I mean money. Like tithing. Ten percent of income."

I struggled not to telegraph my discomfort with the awkward, abrupt line of questioning. "That's what the Bible calls for, so that's what I'm good with."

"And sin? With eradication of sin from the world?"

"Pardon me?"

"How far are you willing to go as a soldier for God in carrying out his wrath against sin?"

"Wow. I guess, um, I'd have to have examples or something."

"Brother Tom," Elise chided. "Be gentle." She still wore the same smile she'd had on her face the entire time. "He's always this intense, I'm afraid. Cecilia, what brings you to Mighty is His Word today?"

I took a step and pretended to stumble. "Whoa, my blood sugar must be off-the-charts low. I have a protein bar in my car. I've really got to get out there and take care of this before I end up fainting on your floor again."

"We'll walk you out," Tom said, taking my elbow.

Elise materialized on my other side. "Be careful, sister. We've got you."

The sweat was rolling down my body again, but not because of blood sugar. "Thank you so much. I do think I've got it, though." I walked faster, pulling them along with me.

"Here's our turn," Elise said and guided me to the left.

"Oh, I see the doors now, thanks again."

Tom pushed the door open and held it, but Elise didn't relinquish my arm.

"Thank you," I said to him. I hadn't brought my purse in with me, just a key in my skirt pocket. A chill raced through me. If I had brought in my handbag, they'd have had access to my wallet with my real name. I felt pretty sure they would have looked.

"Will we see you Wednesday night?" Elise asked me.

"Um, yes, probably, maybe."

"Good. I think we're going to get along great."

"Oh yes, I think so, too."

We'd reached my car by then. I saw that its license plates were too muddy to read, and for the first time that morning, I prayed fervently and sincerely. *Thank you, God.* I got out my key and let myself into the car.

"Brother Tom, Sister Elise, thank you again. You're so kind."

"See you Wednesday night, Cecilia Hodges from Pampa."

I drove out of the dirt parking lot like a bat out of hell.

SEVENTEEN

Sitting at my office desk the next day, I still felt guilty for lying to Jack about where I'd gone on Sunday morning. He'd complimented me when I told him I'd signed on for a shift with Phil at the hospital so Nadine could take her boys to church. Then we'd spent the rest of the day together doing homey things, like planting snapdragons in the front flower beds and cleaning out the small, empty stable in the backyard, something you have to do occasionally whether anything lives there or not. Jack had grilled kabobs with steak for him and veggies for me. We'd ended up in bed early having what felt a lot like make-up sex, then eating popcorn and snuggling while we streamed back episodes of *Longmire*.

Some of my guilt over my deceit was tempered by the fact that once again Jack had things to do outside the office that he hadn't shared with me. Snowflake and I were alone there again.

My fingers took my lonely emotions out on my keyboard. If the poor thing could bruise, it would have looked like it had been in the ring with Muhammad Ali. Even though he'd been awesome the night before, I was still mad at Jack. I was frustrated that Wallace couldn't or wouldn't push harder to help me with Betsy, and I was fighting mad that I hadn't been able to see her. I'd done everything I could, with Jack and with Betsy, and if my best hadn't been good enough, then I was at a loss. So I was back on Phil's case, with a vengeance. Today I would focus on helping our client, helping my friend. Well, I would after I made a quick call to the number for Wilde. But definitely after that, I was all about helping Phil and Nadine.

I dialed and it rolled to voice mail immediately. It was one of those automated outgoing messages that just recited the number and told me to please leave a message, in a voice more robotic than Siri's. "Mr. Wilde, my name is Emily Bernal. Please call me." I gave him my number.

"Rats," I said to Snowflake. She yawned at me. I wasn't fooled by her sleepy act. She'd be a livewire the second the phone rang, so I was armed and ready with liver treats to practice the "Quiet" command.

I moved on to Phil and Nadine. Cecilia had told me that she thought Dennis and Phil planned to go into business together. It wasn't much, but it was something new to try. I typed their names into Google together and got a slew of hits, all relating to Dennis's death. Not helpful. I added the word "business" to the search. Nothing. I searched for each of them in the Texas Secretary of State records for businesses. I didn't get anything linking them together. I tried property records for Potter and Randall counties. Nada.

"Maybe Nadine knows more than she thinks," I said to Snowflake.

She opened one eye, then closed it immediately.

"I know, right? I'm full of great ideas this morning." So I called Nadine. We chatted about Phil and then I gave her an update. "I wanted you to know I met with Phil's ex-wife. Good news: she said she doesn't remember sleeping with Dennis." Since I was overstating things a smidge, I crossed my fingers.

"That's good?"

"Yes! It goes to motive, right? If she didn't sleep with him and you didn't, then that Millie woman heard them wrong."

"What does Millie say?"

"I don't know yet. She hasn't returned my call." I scribbled myself a note to stalk the woman if I had to. "Cecilia thought Dennis had a girlfriend. Skinny, pale, brownish-blonde hair. Ring any bells?"

"Not a one. Dennis was a slut. Phil said he was never with the same woman twice."

"What about business ventures? Did Dennis and Phil have anything cooking together?"

"They talked big, but I'm not sure if you could call it being in business. I know they put together holding companies and stuff and had plans. Dennis was the architect of all that. Lately, Phil was focusing on Get Your Kicks with me."

"Holding companies?"

"Yeah, you know, making companies with different names so they could do business under those names instead of their own."

I whomped my forehead with my palm. "That's why I couldn't find them paired together. They're using different names. But still, they have to have their names together somewhere. Or maybe they don't. Maybe their original deal is just a plain Jane partnership."

Nadine's voice rose. "What the hell are you talking about?"

I laughed. "Never mind. But can you get me some names of those holding companies?"

"Oh man, I have no idea what they are."

"Does he keep files?"

"He might. He doesn't keep much at the house, but we could check. He's got some boxes in one of those storage rental places, too. Not much space for that in his apartment."

The door flung back open. My heart leapt hopefully. Jack? But the appearance of an acne-speckled young face followed by a praying-mantis body dashed my hopes.

"Morning, ma'am. Where would you like this box?" The man-child gestured to the box in question on a handcart he was dragging behind him.

"Good morning." I stood. "Just put it on my desk." I gestured toward the empty corner. To Nadine I said, "Gotta go. I'll call you back later about Phil's place." We hung up.

The young man leaned down and picked the package up like it was feather light and set it on my desk. "I need you to sign for it." He pulled a folded sheaf of papers from his back pocket and smoothed them flat in front of me. He followed it with a pen from the same hip, which he clicked and handed over.

I scanned the forms. A box from the DA's office, referencing Phil Escalante. That was fast. Phil hadn't even been arraigned, due to his condition. I signed a wiggly line to confirm receipt. "Thank you."

He blinked behind thick-lensed glasses and took back the pen and papers, peeling off a duplicate page and leaving it on my desk. "Have a nice day, ma'am." He wheeled on one long leg, pivoting like a slalom skier around a ski pole.

"You, too." I grabbed scissors from my center desk drawer and cut the side tape, then cut the label from the box for our files. I slit the remaining tape between the box flaps and opened them to expose a lot of packing paper and a meager stack of documents.

I rifled through them. Phone records. Police report. A witness list. Autopsy records stating cause of death as asphyxiation. Emails to and from Dennis. I pulled those out and sat down, reading through them, trying to shed light on the recent relationship between Phil and Dennis. There were several, even one talking about Phil's acquittal and celebration party, but there was nothing to bolster the state's argument about conflict between them relating to women or anything else. For that matter, there was nothing suspicious on its face between Dennis and anyone else. Mostly, the emails were correspondence about his business. When I pulled together a file on Dennis the week before, I included in it: Wilhaul Distribution Services. No website. The phone number listed was his cell. The Dun & Bradstreet record was a nonstarter. In the emails I saw people confirming receipt, and I saw people confirming pickup, but none of the emails indicated what, exactly. They were innocuous, short on detail.

But Nadine said that Dennis had forwarded an email to Phil, so there had to be one in there somewhere. I started back at the beginning of the stack. To and from, the emails between them documented a friendship and nothing else. No forwards, not even of dirty pictures or inappropriate political jokes.

I texted Nadine: *You're sure Phil said Dennis had forwarded an email to him?*

I returned to reading emails between the two men, but almost immediately her reply came through: *100% sure.*

But there were no emails forwarded from Dennis to Phil. Either Nadine heard it wrong, or it was missing. And if it was missing, ADA Stafford had some explaining to do. "What in Hades is going on here?" I said aloud. I pondered for a few moments, then pushed speed dial for the DA's office.

"Melinda Stafford, please," I said to the monotone receptionist who answered the phone.

"Hold."

Elevator music replaced her voice.

Someone other than Melinda had recorded the message. "You've reached the voice mail of Assistant District Attorney Melinda Stafford. Please leave a message with your name, phone number, and the case to which your call regards and someone will return your call." Beep.

I decided not to show my hand on voice mail—I needed her to call me back. "Melinda, this is Emily Bernal about Phil Escalante." I left our office number. "I got the discovery documents you messengered over, and I'm calling to confirm where you obtained them from. Specifically, I am wondering if these represent computer records from Phil, Dennis, or both." I couldn't remember if they'd removed Phil's hard drive or copied it when they searched his place a week before, and Jack wasn't here to ask. "Thank you."

I hung up and smiled, but it was a grim one. Where was the forwarded email? Lost? Deleted? Withheld? If it was withheld, that would be a violation of the rules by Melinda. I filed it with my growing list of her possible misdeeds and called Nadine. I wasn't going to sit around and wait on an answer from Melinda, which might never come, and that I didn't necessarily trust if it did.

When Nadine answered I said, "Can you get me into Phil's, pronto?"

EIGHTEEN

Nadine slid her key into the lock at Phil's apartment, where I'd met her after dropping a pouty Snowflake at home in the backyard. "I haven't been in here since before Phil was arrested. He's not the world's best house-keeper." She pushed the door open.

"No worries." I preceded her in, fumbling for the switches inside the door. I found them, and the room flooded with light.

Phil's bachelor pad looked like a tornado had hit it. Papers were strewn everywhere, drawers hung half-open, closet doors were ajar. Papers and clothing obscured his furniture. About all I could see of the apartment itself was stainless steel appliances, silvery-gray cabinet doors and black granite kitchen countertops. The walls were a bright white with three large canvases on which someone—Phil? an artist?—had splashed red and black paint.

Nadine gathered an armload of papers. "This isn't right. Phil isn't this big a slob."

"Maybe it was from the search."

"No, it couldn't be. He cleaned the mess up before I came over that afternoon. Then he was arrested that night."

I held my hands up shoulder-high. "Do you think Phil has any gloves? I don't want to mess up a crime scene, in case we want to report it."

"Ski gloves, maybe." She stuffed the papers she was holding into a deep drawer in a desk alcove next to the kitchen. "But I have some dish-washing gloves. From sanitizing this place when we first started dating." She walked into the kitchen and dug in the cabinet under the sink. She straightened and popped first one, then a second bright yellow glove at me. I squished my hands into them and immediately felt like Martha Stewart.

There was a loud crash from somewhere in the apartment.

I lowered my voice. "Does Phil have any pets?"

"No." Nadine backed toward the door, and her voice was a raspy whisper.

I pulled my baby Glock from my purse and stuffed the yellow gloves in their place. "Wait here."

"Shouldn't we call the cops?"

"I don't think the cops are Phil's best friends right now."

"Okay, well, maybe we should leave, then?"

I nodded. "I'll meet you outside in just a sec."

"Emily! I meant both of us, now." She fell in behind me. "I'm not leaving you in here alone."

We crept through the living room and down the short hall. We passed a doorway to a bathroom, which was dark. Too close. The sound had come from farther down the hall. We took another step, and I wiggled my fingers to rearrange my grip on my gun. I exhaled then extended the pistol into the last doorway opening on the hall, bracing through my core.

Nothing happened. I eased my head around, just enough to see in the room. A lamp lay on the floor in a pile of broken glass. Light streamed in from the one window in the bedroom, onto the bed and its black silky comforter. A black curtain flapped in the breeze above the desk. I stepped into the room, both hands on the gun grip, knees flexed, arms straight in front of me, sighting along the short barrel. I pivoted in a 360-degree turn.

A laptop screen glowed.

"Does he ever leave his window open?" I asked Nadine.

"Never."

"Well, I think it's safe to assume he's had an uninvited guest." I shoved my gun back into my overfull handbag and pulled a thumb drive from one of its pockets. I sat down at the desk, in front of the screen. "What's Phil's password?"

Nadine leaned over my shoulder. "Nadine2014."

I typed it in and pulled up his Outlook email account. The inbox was empty. I clicked through subfolders. All empty. I opened the Deleted Items folder. Empty as well.

"I don't understand," Nadine whispered. "Why isn't there anything there?"

Blue and red lights flashed on the wall. The cops.

A sharp knock sounded at the door. A male voice shouted, "Police."

"What do we do?" Nadine asked, still whispering. Her eyes widened and her breaths were short and shallow.

"You answer the door and tell them who you are. Thank them for coming. Let them know you just got here, and that there's been a break-in."

She looked at me, shell-shocked and immobile, and I realized just how much the last week had taken out of her. The normally butt-kicking Amazon was worn to a nub.

I took her elbow and led her toward the door. "We haven't done anything wrong. They aren't here because of us." I crossed the fingers of my other hand. *I think.* I raised my voice to match the police officer's. "Coming."

When we reached the door, Nadine closed her eyes and drew a deeper breath. She opened it and her voice come out wavering a little, though it might sound normal to people who didn't know her. "Boy, am I glad you guys are here."

The two officers at the door looked like identical twins. Both were about five foot nine with brown eyes and light brown hair. Snub noses. Eyebrows darker than their matching short haircuts. Only their mouths differed. One had a broad mouth and red lips. The other a narrow mouth with thin, colorless lips. Thin Lips spoke. "This address is registered to a Mr. Phil Escalante. Both of you, hands on the wall, legs spread."

"What?" Nadine asked.

"Just do it," I said to her. Jack had coached me to comply first and ask questions later with police, and after some of the run-ins I'd had with them since I'd gone to work with him, I'd learned to take his advice. I put my hands on the wall above my head and stood with my feet apart. "My purse is on the floor, license in my wallet."

Nadine copied my stance, her breaths labored. "Mine's on the kitchen counter."

Behind us, one cop remained in position, and I heard the other grab each of our bags and paw through them.

"The baby Glock is mine. My license to carry is in my wallet."

One of them grunted.

The cop directly behind us patted me down. "Do you have any weapons on you?"

"No," Nadine said.

"Only the one in my purse," I said.

"Which one of you is Nadine?"

"Me," Nadine said.

"Who are you?"

"Nadine Piccoli. Phil Escalante's fiancée."

"You guys can turn around now, but keep your hands where I can see them."

I turned around slowly and put my hands on the sides of my thighs. Nadine again copied my actions.

"And the one with the dishwashing gloves in the purse, that's you, Emily Bernal?" he said to me.

"Housecleaning gloves. Yes. I'm with the law firm representing Mr. Escalante."

"Representing him for what?" Thin Lips said, his words seeming to seep out from the tight, straight line of his mouth.

I frowned. "You guys don't know that Mr. Escalante was arrested? Then you probably don't know he's in a diabetic coma in Southwest Hospital either, I'll bet?"

They glanced at each other. Red Lips shook his head. Thin Lips shrugged.

I said, "Anyway, there's been a break-in, if you'd like us to show you. Seems like whoever it was went out the window."

Thin Lips recovered. "We got a call about someone coming out the window about ten minutes ago."

"We heard a noise and found the open window about then."

"Was it a forced entry?"

Nadine said, "I'm not sure. The front door was closed. I used my key. But I can't remember if it was locked or unlocked."

I nodded as we walked toward Phil's bedroom with the two officers. "The window wasn't broken. There's a busted lamp in the bedroom, but that's it."

We entered the room and the uniformed men examined the window.

Red Lips said, "Lock's not forced." He pinched his upper lip then released it. "Does he keep his windows locked?"

Nadine nodded. "He's really careful. His car got broken into one time parked outside here, so he always locks everything."

He swept his hand inside the window frame, then crawled up on the desk and stuck his head out, looking up, down, and around. "No pry marks. Parking lot below the window is paved, so no footprints."

His partner walked around Phil's bedroom, surveying it. "Anything missing?"

Nadine and I shared a quick look. She said, "I'm, um, not sure. I'd have to go through everything. Even then, I wouldn't know for sure. I still have my own place, and I can't ask Phil."

"Why?"

I coughed. "Coma, remember?"

"Sorry. Right." He put his hands on his hips and turned in a circle, slowly, like I had done, but him without a gun. "Does Mr. Escalante have any relatives in town, or friends that would come by?"

"And leave through the window?" Nadine half-laughed. "No, none. Not even ones that would leave through the front door."

"Well, it's not a great neighborhood. Do you want us to file a report, send someone out to do fingerprints and the whole work-up?"

I thought about the missing emails that should have been on Phil's computer. "Yes, on behalf of Phil, yes, we do."

Three hours later, the police had come up with zilch. An hour after they left, Nadine and I hadn't done any better. I'd looked through every nook and cranny and found no clues as to business names, or whether Phil even had a business outside Get Your Kicks. For that matter, we hadn't found anything suspicious either, like notes from angry husbands or jealous lovers.

As we got ready to leave his place, I asked Nadine, "Do you have time to let me into Phil's storage unit?"

"Let me just grab his spare keys. He hides a copy of everything, even what he isn't supposed to." She walked over to the big screen TV, reached below it, and came up with a remote. She popped the back cover off and dumped a ring with two keys into her hand.

"Good hiding place."

"Phil's paranoid. He hasn't always lived or worked in the best areas."

We took my car to Phil's storage facility off of 287 on the southwest side of town. The buildings were low white concrete affairs with orange doors and flat, orange roofs. I pulled the Mustang up to a keypad a few feet in front of the imposing black gate. A maroon truck cruised to a stop perpendicular to our trunk, then sped off.

"What's the code?"

"Shit. I have no idea. Could be the same as at home." She recited the numbers 1-0-2-0 and I punched them in. "Our anniversary." Nothing happened.

"Maybe we should go to the office first." I scanned the area for something looking like an office. I didn't see one, which seemed unusual. I looked at the keypad again. I read it aloud. "Amarillo offices at," and read an address on the east side of town.

"I don't know if going to the office would do any good. He had this unit before we got together. I doubt I'm authorized to enter."

She twirled the keys in her hand, and as they spun, I saw a piece of masking tape on one of the keys. On it were numbers written in black pen.

"What's that on the keys?"

"Which one?"

"The one with the tape."

She scrutinized it. "4-6-9-3."

I punched it in. Nothing. "Any others?"

She flipped the other over, peering at it closely. "Try 1-6-1-9."

It worked. Nadine whooped and held her hand up for me to slap a high five. That was more like the woman I knew. I decided not to burst her bubble by mentioning that the other key might go to a different storage place, because maybe it didn't. She directed me to a unit on the back of the middle building. We drove down the aisle until we reached number 312. I parked and we walked to the roll-up door. Nadine selected the key with the winning code, but when she went to use it, the lock opened without it.

"That's not good." She pulled the door up. It responded with clanging metal and clackety wheels, revealing a dark space half-filled and neat as a pin, unlike Phil's place. Good. I had feared the unfastened lock meant another break-in. The bright afternoon sunlight shot into the darkness, catching slowly circulating dust in its rays. The smell was dusty, too. And dry. I sneezed.

Nadine hefted a backpack. It bulged at its seams. "This is Phil's 'go' bag, you know, in case he needs to get us out of town in a hurry to where no one can find us."

I blanched. "He needs a 'go' bag?"

She smiled. "Just wait." She pointed around the chest-high stack of boxes and items. "Generator. Well hand-pump kit. Fuel cylinders. MREs."

I knew MREs were Meals, Ready-to-Eat, and that they were singularly disgusting. She kept up her identifications, but it was clear that Phil was preparing for the second coming of Christ or *The Walking Dead*. Or both. Or maybe he'd done something really terrible, which he thought would catch up with him. Not a comforting thought with him being charged with murder. Whatever it was, if there was a zombie apocalypse, I was calling Phil.

"Does he have a place to run to?"

"He says he does." She set the backpack down again. "He said that will be my wedding present. A cabin at his hidey-hole."

"Phil's quite a romantic."

"You know it."

"So you said he keeps papers here?"

"I said he might." She kicked a stack of four boxes. "And if he does, it will be in this stack."

"Excellent." The top box was open, although I could see where tape had been ripped away before. I moved it to the right and moved the next box beside it. It too was open, with tape residue and ripped cardboard. Nadine and I each tackled a box. Mine contained file folders of old tax returns by year. Great. Interpreting IRS mumbo jumbo was not my strong suit. I pulled out the most recent year and read carefully. It appeared Phil had run the swingers club as a sole proprietorship. Continuing to read and going back over the course of five years, I concluded that his wife had disclaimed ownership of the club in their divorce. Fifteen minutes later my head hurt, but I hadn't come up with any potential business names or dealings.

"What have you found?" I asked Nadine.

Dirt smudged her nose and cheek. She kneeled over the box I'd given her. When she answered, her voice sounded funny. "Keepsakes. Albums. Mementos."

"Ohhhhh." I wished I'd had her box instead, afraid of what she might find in there. "You okay?"

"Yeah. Sad. There's a bunch of pictures of Phil and Dennis as teens." She handed me one. The two were on horseback with some other kids, riding through a river bottom.

Based on the location of Boys Ranch between Amarillo and Dalhart, I was pretty sure I knew where they were. "Canadian River." The Canadian ran all the way through the Panhandle of Texas, and eventually became Lake Meredith at a dam near Sanford, then trickled on at a reduced rate.

"I think so. That's one of his special places."

I passed the picture back to her. "They look so young."

"We all were at one point."

"Speaking of young, how are your boys?"

"They're good. We're on a more regular schedule now, and that helps." She tucked a loose wisp of hair behind her ear.

"The offer still stands for them to stay over."

"Thank you. What do you hear about Betsy?"

"That the Hodges want to adopt her. That they are saints in the eyes of CPS. That Wallace can't do anything about it, even get me a visit with her."

She slipped the picture back into an album. "I'm sorry. I've been so worried about Phil I haven't thought of anything else."

"Your priorities are in the right place. Don't worry about it."

"And you and Jack?"

I sighed and sat on my box. "He's gotten secretive, and he's always out. I've gone from distressed because he didn't love me, to depressed because I do love him and he's slipping away like Betsy."

Nadine rolled forward from her haunches to her knees. "Whoa, Emily, don't get ahead of yourself. Jack's a great guy."

"I know, but it doesn't change things."

"But he might have good reasons for things."

"Maybe." I returned to the stack of boxes. The last two were taped. "Ready for your second one?"

She nodded, so I slit one open and brought it to her and slit the other for me, which I moved a few feet away.

"More personal items." She pawed and inventoried. "Varsity letters. A baseball glove. Cleats. A Fox and Hound coaster. A clown wig."

"Let me see the wig."

She held it aloft. Orange frizzy hair over a webbed skullcap.

"I had one not much different than that. Rodeo clown gear."

She tossed it back in the box. "Other than that kind of thing—old stuff —nothing."

I dug into my box. This one also contained file folders, but each held something different. Vehicle title. Insurance documents. Deed to the building Get Your Kicks and his apartment occupied. Bank statements. Canadian River Ventures. My heart kick-started.

"Nadine?" I tossed her the folder.

She nodded, read the name, and her face fell.

"What is it?"

"There's nothing in here. But the name? That's got to be it. Him and Dennis."

"Empty?" I ran my hand over the folders in the box. "None of the rest are empty."

A shadow fell over the floor, our bodies, the boxes. A male figure stood silhouetted against the sun. From his smell, he'd doused his entire body in Axe cologne.

"Hello, ladies." His voice was a gruff drawl, but slow didn't always equal dumb and a drawl certainly didn't mean he was one of the good guys. The hair on my neck stood up under my ponytail.

"Can we help you?" I said. I eyed the red Mustang. My purse with the baby Glock was on the front seat.

He saw my glance. "Nice car."

"Thank you." Now the hair on my arms stood at attention as well. "May we help you?"

"I'm not sure. I'm looking for a guy named Phil Escalante."

I stood, and behind me Nadine did, too. She grabbed my hand. "You need to move on. You're making us uncomfortable, and I don't want to have to report you to security."

He laughed in a way that wasn't funny. "Security? You've got the wrong storage units for security. I just hopped the fence, and nobody stopped me." He moved closer to us, and I stepped around him toward the car, pulling Nadine forward with a jerk.

I whirled on him. He was younger and less muscular than I expected from the sound of his voice, but he still towered over both of us in his white T and 501s, and his gel-slicked brown hair.

"Listen, James Dean, you're messing with the wrong girls." I maneuvered Nadine in front of me and leaned into my car for my purse. I pulled out my phone and dialed 911. "Beat it."

He held up his hands. "Aren't you touchy? I was just kidding." He pointed to the next storage space. "This one's mine. I know Phil, the guy who has this unit, and you guys are standing in it. I thought you'd get the joke."

"Go," I said. I tucked my handbag under my arm, holding the phone in the same hand. I reached back into the purse.

"You can leave your piece in there, I'm going." He backed away. "Tell Phil his storage neighbor said 'hey.'" He turned and jogged down the aisle toward the fence. A maroon truck was parked outside it. He vaulted over the fence and jumped in the truck, disappearing, leaving us completely alone once again.

NINETEEN

It was hard to shake the willies off after that experience. Nadine and I returned to Phil's for her car, then parted ways, her to the hospital and me to the office.

The office door wasn't locked when I got back. Hope flickered. Maybe Jack was here. I slipped in. "Jack?"

There was no answer, which was odd. We never left the door unlocked. Maybe Jack was in the bathroom, or maybe he just forgot to lock it.

"Whatever," I yelled, at no one. I dropped my purse on the desk and booted up my laptop, standing and leaning over it. I typed the login Jack had created seven months earlier for me: Emily, RodeoQueen. It made my heart hurt. *Screw you, Jack*, I thought. I went into my settings and before I could change my mind I typed out a new password: wronggirl. *Take that.*

Quickly, I scanned my email. Nothing interesting and work related jumped out at me, but I saw one from the partner in charge of the labor and employment section at my old law firm in Dallas, Hailey & Hart. I hadn't heard from him since I quit. I opened it.

Emily: I've opened my own practice and am hiring. Could I entice you back to Dallas as lead paralegal? You'd get a 10% raise and a $5,000 signing bonus.

Move back to Dallas? There might have been a time I would have jumped at that offer, but not now. I closed it and decided to run to the bathroom. As I opened the door to the hall, I turned my head back toward the interior of the office space. Melinda Stafford was walking toward me down the hallway from Jack's office, almost like an apparition.

"What are you doing here?" I said, loudly.

"Looking for Jack." She came to a stop beside the tweed couch.

"How'd you get in?"

"It was open."

"Most visitors don't wander down our hallway and hang out in Jack's office."

"It's not like I haven't been here before, and I *know* he wouldn't mind." She shrugged. "So I sat down to wait for him. I was typing an email." She held up her phone. As she did, she swayed. She looked even more frail than the last time I'd seen her.

What did she mean about knowing Jack wouldn't mind? Had there been something more between them than a one-sided pursuit by Melinda? I smoothed loose side hairs back toward my ponytail holder. "Are you okay?"

"I'm fine."

I decided to put my fist in a velvet glove. "You know, the other day at Abuelo's, I was in the bathroom when you were. I heard you. I want you to know that, no matter our past or the cases we are working on, if you need help, you can ask me."

"What?" She gave me a withering look. "I said I'm *fine.*" She looked down her nose at me, which she was only able to do because of her shiny nude platform pumps and my flat sandals.

Well, if she was really fine, then it wouldn't hurt to see if she had alcohol on her breath.

She said, "Since I'm here, you called earlier—about the Escalante case?"

"Yes, I did." I inched closer to her. I could see the blue of veins under the skin of her face, but so far I couldn't smell booze.

She tossed her hair, and it bounced back into place. "I didn't understand what you were asking."

"About what?"

"Well, that's what I really didn't understand."

I heaved a long exhale. "I wanted to know where you got the emails that you sent over to us."

"Why?"

Her strident voice hurt my ears, and her pupils were wide. I was totally reporting her when the DA's office opened in the morning. If it wasn't alcohol or bulimia, it was something. She was trippin' with a capital T. But she'd also asked the question I didn't want to answer. Not truthfully anyway, because I had a strong suspicion she'd tampered with evidence, or withheld it, or at least produced it sloppily and incompletely. My money was on the crazy-eyed woman in front of me doing something stupid to gain an advantage in this case, so I sure as shootin' wasn't explaining to her that I couldn't find a forwarded email from Dennis to Phil.

I put one hand on my hip. "Melinda, we are going to obtain our own evidence, but I was trying to be efficient, to see if you'd already exhausted all possible sources. We are super busy, and I don't have time to run all over creation doing things that you've already done."

She stared past me, and again she swayed. "Fine. Well, it's from the hard drives of Mr. Welch's and Mr. Escalante's laptops."

"Was that so hard?"

"You're welcome."

I walked over to my desk. "Have a nice evening."

She weaved to the door, then turned for her parting shot. "Your trashy client's going to end up in the garbage this time, where he belongs."

She went for a dramatic wrenching and slamming of the door, but its air brakes foiled her, like it had me a few times in the past, and I giggled. As I thought about her nonsensical last comment, I giggled louder. And as I anticipated the call I was going to make in the morning, I started laughing out loud. From the hallway, Melinda shot me the bird.

TWENTY

A handwritten note in the half-cursive, half-print scrawl of my fiancé was on his pillow when I awoke the next morning. *Early thing, I'll be in late. Forgot to tell you. Didn't want to wake you. Jack.*

I *highly* doubted he forgot. More like didn't want me on his back, especially after a really nice night together where neither of us mentioned his "old case." He'd snuck in and surprised me by kissing the back of my neck. Then he'd laughed about my Melinda encounter and promised to match the surprising Dallas job offer I'd received. We'd cooked a mushroom risotto for me and a mahimahi fillet for Jack, and he pulled out a DVD of *Blazing Saddles*. It was hilarious even on the tenth time watching it, but I fell asleep with my head on Jack's chest and his arms around me before it was over, which I always did when we watched from bed. It was a lovely night, and it made me feel hopeful.

Now I was already late—normally Jack's phone alarm woke me. Late and out of sorts about it and Jack's note. I put Snowflake and her food in the backyard. I sprinted into the house before she could wolf it down. I didn't want her sad, accusatory eyes on me when I left without her this morning. Truth be told, I usually preferred bigger dogs, but I loved this funny little canine. She was Jack's dog, though, and lately, in his continual absences, all her care had fallen on me. So she'd survive in beautiful weather and green grass, living like 99 percent of the other dogs in the world, for a day.

I hopped into clean jeans and a soft cotton T-shirt and sandals and squirted toothpaste on my dry toothbrush. I stuffed my purse with deodorant, face tonic, and perfume, and loped out the door. I had the red Mustang on I-40 headed east three minutes later. As I drove, I brushed my teeth and took a swig from a day-before bottle of water in the console, trying not to think about the toothpaste in my empty stomach. I attacked my hair. Getting through my snarls took me until I exited into downtown. I was able to scoop my hair into yet another ponytail at a red light, with time leftover to swipe on deodorant and spray perfume before the light turned green. By the time I parked in our garage, all I had left to do was wipe the sleep from my eyes and spray my face with the rose-geranium facial tonic and pat my cheeks. I made it from the garage to our offices in two more minutes, trotting briskly, and only remembered I'd planned to tattle on Melinda after I flopped down in my desk chair. Well, something to look forward to later.

"Jack?" I shouted his name without bothering to get up. The front door had been locked. I knew he wasn't here, and there was no answer. I shook my head, closed my eyes. I wouldn't dwell on him today. I had to keep moving forward.

So that is what I would do. I called Wallace, because it was past time to tell him about the wackos out in Sanford at Mighty is His Word. I should have done it yesterday. Or Sunday. I held off only because I was so depressed about the situation with Betsy and the Hodges and, honestly, a little miffed that Wallace seemed to be handing her over to them. But those nutjobs had no business fostering kids, much less adopting them, and he needed to know, whether I got Betsy or not.

His voice mail picked up. I spoke in fast-forward mode. "Wallace, I have something I have to tell you about. Call me."

Now, pending his return call, I was going to do the research I'd postponed because of Melinda's odd visit the night before. After I finished, I'd email my old boss in Dallas to turn down his offer. I stretched my fingers and did a few neck circles, wincing at the cracks. I typed in my new password, wronggirl, and wished I had left it RodeoQueen.

Working would take my mind off my own troubles, so I opened the Secretary of State website and entered the new information: Canadian River Ventures. I pressed enter. I yawned and covered my mouth with my hand. It made my eyes close for a moment, and when I opened them, I had my results.

Nada, as in not a damn thing.

I went to property records for Potter County. Same result, or lack thereof. Randall County yielded nothing. On a lark, I tried Oldham County, the location of Boys Ranch, and still got zip. Phil's mother had said that Phil moved to Borger after school at Boys Ranch, and that he split his time between there and somewhere near Denver. *Why would he want property near Borger?* I tried Denver first. The results were getting predictable: squat. Well, it wouldn't hurt to try Borger's county, even if it seemed ludicrous to me. So I typed in Hutchinson and felt another yawn coming on. I hit enter.

And I got a hit in Borger. Well, it showed what I knew about real estate. I scrolled through the record. Canadian River Ventures owned five hundred acres outside the thriving metropolis of Sanford, Texas, where I had just wiled away my Sunday morning. Five hundred acres, which they'd acquired for the price of $500,000 and encumbered by a big fat mortgage with First National Bank of Borger. I wouldn't have paid $1,000 an acre out there, but then again, it was already clear I was no real estate mogul. I paged down farther in the record, and it took a few seconds before my brain caught up with my eyes, mainly because what I read seemed like utter nonsense. The contact person for the Sanford property owned by Canadian River Ventures was Melinda Stafford, Assistant District Attorney in Amarillo, Texas.

I sprang out of my chair calling for Snowflake. No pounding feet answered me, and it took a second to remember I'd snuck away from home, leaving her in the backyard. Who would I dance with now, to celebrate finding the name of my mortal enemy tied up with our client and the man he was accused of murdering? Well, I couldn't let the lack of a dance partner stop me. I spun in circles with my head back, laughing like a crazy woman.

Truthfully? I had no idea on the good Lord's green earth what finding Melinda's name meant, other than she had a professionally embarrassing potential conflict of interest. When I'd cleared my head from spinning, I put my thinking cap back on. I had found a Canadian River Ventures that owned property in Sanford, and I had linked it to Melinda. What I hadn't found was Phil or Dennis tied to Canadian River Ventures, the property, each other, or Melinda. That was a bummer, but my instincts told me to press on. I had the property address, a mailing address for the tax bills, and the mortgage holder. One of those was bound to lead to more information.

One minute later I was on the phone with the First National Bank of Borger, my knee bouncing under the desk. I was connected to the mortgage department.

A very bored male voice answered. "May I help you?"

"Yes, I'm with Williams and Associates law firm. Our client is one of the owners of a property in Sanford, Texas, that First National Bank of Borger holds a mortgage on. Unfortunately, my client is in a coma, and when he wakes up, he's facing a murder charge. The Sanford property is at issue in his case, so I'm trying to determine whether there is any dispute between the owners, and what the status of the mortgage is."

His voice was completely atonal. "Then ask the other owner or get a subpoena."

"I can't. The other owner is dead."

His voice perked up. "Sanford, you said? What's the property address?"

I gave it to him.

"Who did you say you represent?"

"Phil Escalante."

"I don't show a Phil Escalante associated with this property." His voice went from perky to patronizing.

I crossed my fingers under the desk. "He's the silent partner of Dennis Welch in Canadian River Ventures."

"Oh, sure, yes, Mr. Welch, the signatory for Canadian River Ventures."

"And Ms. Stafford for herself."

"Well, of course. Wait, who's dead?"

"Mr. Welch."

He grunted. "Then sounds like you need to call Ms. Stafford."

"Is there someone who can tell me about the status of the mortgage at your bank?"

Now his voice grew clipped and officious. He was certainly versatile. "With a subpoena, or with Ms. Stafford on the phone."

My own pitch came out more strident than I tried for. "My client is in a coma and is accused of murdering Mr. Welch, and I am looking for Ms. Stafford's potential motive. She's not going to cooperate. Come on, help Mr. Escalante out."

"Ma'am, I don't know Mr. Escalante from Adam. Or you. Subpoena or Ms. Stafford. Take your pick."

A low growl started in my throat.

"But if Mr. Escalante wakes up, please tell him that if he wants to pick up on the past due payments, we wouldn't argue with him about it."

Click. I didn't like being hung up on, but it went down better with a spoonful of a big hint that the mortgage was in arrears. I knew three more things than when I'd called. Phil's name wasn't on the mortgage, Dennis was involved with Canadian River Ventures, and the First National Bank of Borger wasn't getting paid.

A thought hit me. What if Canadian River Ventures was just Dennis and Melinda? If so, more the better. A mortgage in arrears held by the ADA and the deceased smelled like week old catfish on a trash heap.

I hit Jack's cell number on my phone. This news was too good not to be shared. But all I got was voice mail. I hung up when his voice instructed me to leave a message.

"Spit in well bucket." When all else fails, go with what works, and I didn't need a creative mock cuss word. I needed my fiancé.

I jumped to my feet and stomped down the hall, but my sandals barely clacked on the floors. Another disappointment. I rounded the corner into Jack's empty office and made a beeline for his desk. I dropped any pretense of respect for his privacy and rifled with abandon. Jack kept a tidy work area for the most part. Really, he kept things tidy everywhere, and usually I appreciated this quality in him. Today, it irritated me. I wanted dirt. The only items on his desk were red rope file folders for each of his active cases, fifteen of them. I read every scrap of paper in every single one. Notes from consultations, to-do lists, some draft discovery, and some news clippings. I recognized every case, and there was nothing that would tell me where he was today, nothing incriminating. I opened his center desk drawer. There was an envelope in it, a used envelope from mail that had been addressed to him by the District Attorney's office. It was empty and torn. I flipped it to the back and saw notes scribbled in his handwriting: *Paige, Thur, 8 a.m.* Underlined twice.

I spat out my words, fear and frustration overcoming me. "Paige? Jack Ass, tell me what's going on."

The phone rang, for his line. I snatched it up, dispensing with the normal pleasantries. "Jack Holden's office."

"Um, yes, is Jack there?" a woman asked in a sexy Southern drawl.

"Who is this?"

"He was supposed to be meeting me at the stables—"

"Is this Paige?"

The woman hung up. With the envelope still in my hand, I closed the desk drawer, bolted from the office, and slammed the door so hard the pictures rattled on the walls. I looked at my feet, my blood boiling and my heart aching like it was going to fall out of my chest. When I reached my desk, I glanced up. A tall, pear-shaped woman with dark roots to her platinum hair stood inside the door, her hand still on the door handle and her mouth open.

The woman stared at me. I was sure I had seen her before somewhere, and not too long ago.

"May I help you?" I rubbed my hands down the sides of my jeans. As I did, I realized I was still holding the envelope from Jack's drawer. I bent and stuffed it in my purse.

"Yes, I'm here to see Jack Holden." She held a clutch in front of her with both hands as if afraid that a mugger would dart out from under my desk and grab it from her.

"Jack's not here right now. He's been called away from the office on an emergency and I am not sure when he'll make it back. May I help you?"

She looked over her shoulder at the closed door. "And you are?"

"I'm so sorry. Where are my manners? I'm Emily Bernal, Jack's paralegal."

"I'm Millie Todd. I'm here about the night Dennis Welch was murdered."

That's where I knew this woman—I'd seen her at Phil's and Nadine's party the week before. Only there she was the brazen swinger who'd propositioned Jack and me. Here, she was carrying herself completely differently, much more timid and soft-spoken. She didn't show so much as a flicker of recognition on her face as she looked at me, though, so I didn't bring it up. "Excellent. You may not realize it, but I've been trying to get in touch with you for the last week for exactly that same reason. I'll be happy to talk to you in his place. I'm working on that case with him."

She looked down but didn't answer.

"Why don't we sit in our break area? I can make some coffee and we can talk."

She nodded, and I preceded her down the hallway. I motioned her ahead of me at the door to the kitchen, and she took a seat at the wooden table, putting her purse in a chair beside her.

I filled the water well on the Keurig. "Coffee?"

"Yes, please. Black."

I prepared my cup with Half & Half and sucralose while hers brewed. My phone rang. Wallace's name and face flashed up on the screen. "One moment please," I said to Millie.

I stepped out into the hall. "Hey."

"Hey, yourself. You called?"

"Yes. I wanted you to look into something. About the Hodges."

I heard the disapproval in his silence.

"Please?"

"What is it." A statement, not a question, in a weary voice.

"I went to that church we saw. They cornered me. Asked me a bunch of weird questions. Am I married, do I have kids, what would I be willing to contribute to the church, what are my beliefs on sin, how far would I go to save the world from sin."

"So?"

"They were quite militant. They were hinting at violence."

"Emily—"

"Can you just look into it, Wallace?"

"Okay. I'll look into it."

"Thank you."

"You're welcome. And, Em?"

"Yeah?"

"About Betsy—"

Terror filled my heart. I didn't want to hear any bad news. "I can't talk any more right now."

I ended the call, staring at the phone shaking in my hands. I slipped it in the back pocket of my jeans and walked back in. Millie was glaring at me. "Sorry."

"No problem," she said, in an icy voice.

I headed for the coffee pot. "So, were you at Phil's party on the night Dennis died?"

"Yes."

"How long have you known Phil?" I set her cup in front of her.

She crossed her arms over the chest of her light purple top. "A few years."

I went back for my cup, which wasn't ready yet. "How did you meet?"

"His club."

Which I'd believe after meeting her at the party, but would never have guessed from her daytime persona. "Did you know Dennis Welch, too?"

"No. I'd never seen him before."

"So what did you see and hear that night?" I stirred my coffee and then walked it over to the table, taking the seat directly across from Millie.

"I heard Phil out in the parking lot arguing with the man that got killed, Dennis."

"Tell me about that. What were they arguing about?"

"A woman."

"Did you hear her name?" I sipped my coffee.

"No. Phil called her his wife."

"So who was mad at who?"

She looked at the table. "Phil was mad. He said Dennis slept with his wife."

"Did either of them say when or where or why?"

"Not that I heard."

"What did Dennis say back to him?"

"That he was sorry, that he couldn't help it if women found him irresistible."

I raised my eyebrows.

"Yeah." Her lips tightened. "Pretty funny coming from a man dressed like *that*."

"What happened next?"

"Phil pushed Dennis, hard. Dennis fell and I heard this loud crack. Phil ran off."

I set my coffee cup down. "Which way did he run?"

"Toward the street."

Which would have been both an awfully strange thing for him to do, since his car was parked on the side by the door to his apartment, and an almost impossible thing, since he'd run into the club hollering for help. "Did you see him again?"

She shook her head. "Not until after the police came."

"Did either of them see you?"

She looked down again. "No. I was on the other side of some cars."

"How many cars away were you?"

"Maybe two."

I wondered if that was close enough to hear the two men, but I kept it to myself. Jack could use it for cross-examination at trial if he needed to. I made a note to check the video and see if Millie really had left the party and gone into the parking lot. "What did you do after Dennis fell?"

"I called 911."

"Did you try to help Dennis?"

She stared at me, not moving.

I waited, but when she still didn't respond, I said, "Millie? Are you okay?"

Her fingers wrapped around her crossed arms, like she was hugging herself, only they cut into her skin—more like restraining herself. She stayed that way for long seconds. Blood trickled from under one of her nails.

I stood, uncomfortable and a little uncertain what to do.

She whispered, "He was evil."

"Who was evil?" I eased myself between Millie and the door.

"That man. Dressed like that. Carrying that thing he carried."

This from a woman who had propositioned Jack and me not ten minutes before Dennis arrived? "Do you mean Dennis?"

She jumped to her feet. "I called 911. But I wasn't putting my hands on that disgusting man."

Her words ended in a shout. She grabbed her purse.

"It's okay." I used the soothing voice I usually reserved for spooked horses or injured animals.

"That's all I know. I have to go now." She pushed past me, knocking into me so hard it felt intentional, and I stumbled, catching myself on the counter.

"Millie, are you okay?" I called again.

But the door opened and shut and Millie was gone.

TWENTY-ONE

I threw the lock on the door so Millie couldn't change her mind. I wanted out of here, away from crazy people, the aura of Jack, away from Amarillo and the Hodges. But I needed to do something useful, something to help someone. Like Nadine, and Phil. I printed the property records on the Canadian River Ventures property in Sanford. For the first time, I noticed that the tax records were being mailed to Melinda at an address in Borger. Maybe this wasn't the Amarillo Melinda Stafford? But how many could there be?

I Googled Melinda Stafford in Borger, Texas. Nothing but hits on Melinda Stafford in Amarillo, Houston, Longview, and a little town called Dime Box, but no crossovers to Borger.

I grabbed my purse. I'd just go check it out myself.

I had the red Mustang headed northeast five minutes later, and I rolled down the windows, letting the wind whip through the car and through me. Five minutes into the trip, I realized I'd forgotten to email my old Dallas boss to turn him down. I jotted it down on my mental to-do list and kept driving. I took the back road, 136 up toward Lake Meredith and hooked a right in Fritch. I rolled up the windows when I'd had enough hair to eat, and turned on the air conditioner for the first time of the season.

About the time I passed through Sanford, my phone made its voice mail tone. I held down the button for Siri. "Check voice mail," I told her, and the voice mail came out at me through the stereo speakers.

"Mrs. BURR-nal, it's Trisha at The Works about your car. We treated it once, and it still has a pretty bad odor. We guarantee our work at the price we quoted you, so we are going to treat it again, at no additional cost to you. We'll call you when it's ready."

I groaned. They weren't charging me more, but the rental car company would.

The second message played. "This is Burt Wilde returning your call." Click.

I took a deep breath through my nose. Burt Wilde. Boy did I ever want to talk to him. I held down my button. "Call back." It started to ring.

Someone picked up my call, because it stopped ringing, but all I heard was loud music on the other end for a few seconds. Then, "Shit," and "Hold on," and "Dammit."

"Hello?" a man's voice said. He sounded less than happy to be taking my call.

"Burt Wilde?"

"Yeah."

"Oh, good, this is Emily Bernal. We met at a party last week, and I—"

"I know who you are. I called you back."

"Oh, that's good."

"I'm driving to work, so I don't have much time."

"Right. Where do you work?"

"Circle P Feedlot. Shoveling shit. Which I already told Jack."

"That's why I'm calling. I'm following up on some things for Jack, but he's been so busy and distracted with this other case. I apologize if I'm about to make you repeat yourself even more."

"Go on."

"When you asked me to tell Jack you didn't do it, you meant . . ."

"You sound like that stupid cop. Because I'd heard Jack was coming after me, blaming me, and I didn't need that trouble. Again. Next question."

"So how do we know you didn't do it?"

"Because when I got denied parole—thanks to Jack—a guy came up to me back in the joint and said I couldn't've done it because he knew who did."

"Who?"

"Listen, lady, no offense, but you don't sound like you're working with Jack, because I told him all this. I got no way'a knowin' if you are who you say you are, so, um, yeah, good-bye."

The call ended and I bit my thumbnail, tasting blood. My pulse pounded in my temple, threatening a major headache. I drove on, barely noticing the road, my brain in turmoil over what Wilde had told me. A red fox ran across the road in front of the car, and I swerved violently. The

Mustang squealed and ran off the road onto the gravel then into the tall grass. I let off the accelerator and concentrated on getting the car under control. The engine slowed, and I heard the swish of the grass as the car ran over it. I checked my rearview mirror. No cars. I had slowed nearly to a stop, and I could smell the sweet odor of the crushed grass. I eased back over the gravel shoulder and onto the roadway. I wiped sweat out of my eye.

I had to concentrate on what I was doing, not on Jack, or I was going to kill myself. I tried desperately to think of a way to pull myself together and came back to my yoga breathing. In through the nose to the back of the throat, out through the mouth. I tried that for a while, then breathed into my lower back. My tension eased. My pulse slowed. My brain stilled to a functional level of activity.

Somehow I made it into Borger alive. When I pulled to a stop in front of the address listed for Melinda Stafford, I checked myself in the mirror. The wind had ripped the hair around my face loose from my ponytail and sculpted it and my bangs into a helmet. I looked as crazy as Millie Todd.

I leaned down and over and looked out the passenger-side window. The address had led me to a small one-story house, 1950s vintage, with white siding and a columned front porch that was extremely deep, at least for the size of the house. The yard was low on decorative plantings, but it was green and well kept. The flag was up on the mailbox out front.

I walked up the front sidewalk—concrete edged with red brick, although I saw no other red brick from my front view—and three broad steps. The door had a black pewter knocker in addition to the doorbell. I smiled and used the knocker.

Standing back a few steps, I waited. No one answered, so I rang the doorbell. Still no answer. I took a moment to analyze the neighborhood. The lots on either side were empty, with only old foundations marking the houses that used to stand there. Across the street was a fourplex with blackout curtains inside its front windows. On either side of it were old houses that needed some attention or to be put to rest like their across-the-street neighbors. No faces watched me from windows. No curtains swayed, no doors stood ajar. I walked to the mailbox and reached in. There was an envelope addressed to the electric company, but the return address blanks weren't filled out. I put it back in, because it's not truly tampering with the mail if you don't steal it. Or it shouldn't be, in my opinion.

I walked around the side of the house along a grassed-over driveway consisting of two stripes of concrete and back to a sagging detached one-car garage. It was closed. I pressed my nose to the glass with my hand shielded. Empty. The backyard wasn't fenced, so I crossed from the garage to the door, which was on the side back. Again, I pressed nose to glass and hand over brow. From my vantage point, I was looking through the kitchen and into a hallway that led toward the front of the house and opened into a room that was probably the living room. I surveyed the kitchen. Half-full coffee cup on the far side of the sink. A bottle of Geritol liquid on the near side. A pair of earrings beside it, the kind that clip on. A plate with crumbs and a knife with butter on the countertop by the door. A clock with Roman numerals on the wall. A cat calendar stuck to the refrigerator.

I stuck my phone in my purse and discovered the pair of rubber dish-washing gloves from Phil's. Perfect. I slipped them on. Then I jiggled the doorknob. It was locked, but it was only a flimsy hand lock. I debated. From all appearances, an older woman lived here. Was I really going to violate her privacy by breaking into her home, this woman who was so innocent and trusting that she didn't have a modern door lock on her back door? I looked around again, checking out vantage points from the other yards. A German shepherd strained against a chain in the neighbor's back-yard, barking, but no one came to see why. My watch said it was noon. Most of the good people of Borger were at work. Or school. Running errands. Not watching me. I reached into my purse for a bobby pin, and thirty seconds later I shut the door gently behind me.

"Five minutes," I whispered. "No longer."

I headed into the bathroom for the medicine cabinet, the surest place I could think of to find the name of the occupant. Only there was no medi-cine cabinet. I opened the regular cabinets. No prescription bottles. I headed into the first of two bedrooms. I checked the top drawer of the dresser. Ladies underwear from three decades ago. I slipped my hands underneath them. No stashed papers or hidden treasures. Two minutes had gone by. A mirror perched on the top of the dresser. All I saw in it was me. I went to the nearest bedside table. Magazines. A book light. Lotion. A heating pad. I walked around to the other side. Finally, prescription bottles. Crestor, I read, for a Lisa Perkins. A framed picture on the table was of a woman in her sixties with a man of about the same age, but the photo looked positively ancient. Lisa? Her parents?

Perkins. Nobody related to this case had the last name Perkins. I left the bedroom and went into the other. It was nondescript. A double bed and dresser. Plaid comforter with too much hunter green in it. White ceiling fan with brass hardware. One bedside table with a brass lamp. I opened the single drawer. A pack of Marlboros and a lighter. Vicks cherry cough drops. Tissues. I went into the living room. Four minutes. I scanned the pictures on the hall wall as I passed them, looking for a man I barely knew. There were pictures of a young woman and a young man. It looked like the photo was of the woman in the picture on the bedside table, but I wasn't sure.

The back door opened. "Lisa? You home?" It was a woman's voice, high and tremulous.

My heart triple-timed. I tiptoed to the far edge of the living room. If the woman walked in there, I was a goner.

I heard the refrigerator open. "Oh, come now, what do you mean you don't have any eggs either?" The refrigerator shut, then the back door re-opened and closed.

I put my hand over the racing heartbeat in my throat. "That was close." It was time to be gone, but I saw a desk on the other side of the living room. I walked over and lifted its lid, exposing a mirrored inside face and two partitions. In the one on the right, a stack of papers. I thumbed them quickly. A page that read *Last Will and Testament of Lisa J. Perkins* caught my eye. It was a simple instrument. In it, she left everything to her nephew, Dennis. I snapped a photo with my phone, then looked for an itemization of her holdings, but didn't find one. I finished going through the stack, hopeful for a property deed or something else juicy, but I got nothing. Which I could have predicted based on my batting average on this case.

I walked to the back door, thinking about Dennis's aunt Lisa and the Canadian River Ventures mail directed to her house. How this connection to Dennis still didn't tie back to Phil yet, other than an empty file folder in a storage unit and a picture of two best friends as kids, or to Melinda except for her name in a property record and on a mortgage. I checked that all the lights were out, then twisted the back door handle. When I pulled the door, it flew in toward me, because it was being pushed from the outside.

"Oh!" a woman exclaimed in the same high-pitched voice I'd heard a minute ago. Her blue eyes were big Os under a head of soft gray curls. "I was just going to—uh, excuse me, but who are you?"

With my purse hanging from my arm against my hip and my hands behind my back, I used one hand to pull the nearly elbow-high yellow dishwashing glove off the one, then reversed the process and held both gloves in one hand behind my back. I brought my purse hand to the front, eased my purse to the other hip, then slid the gloves in, hidden from her view by the kitchen cabinets, all while smiling with all my teeth and saying, "Oh, hello. Lisa's not home. I just popped in to drop something off for her." I stepped past the woman on the back steps and scurried down the driveway. I called back to her, "Have a nice day!" but kept moving.

She leaned away from the house, watching me go, her forehead crin-kled. "Um, okay, you have a nice day, too."

I got back in the red Mustang and pointed it toward Amarillo.

TWENTY-TWO

As I cruised to a stop at a light, I checked my phone. While I'd been in Lisa Perkins's house, a text had come in from Wallace: *Where are you?*

I resumed driving and looked out my window. I was passing a tiny wooden house with what looked like Jesus framed in the enormous front picture window. I checked my rearview mirror and there were no cars behind me, so I slammed on my brakes and backed up until I was in front of the house. Or box, rather. It was really small. On closer inspection it even had wheels. And, sure enough, there was a larger-than-life Jesus nailed to a cross inside the house-shaped, glass-fronted box/trailer.

"Oh Em Gee." I pulled out my phone and took a picture.

I'd been frustrated with Wallace, but that paled in comparison to the chance to send him a picture of this. I texted it to him: *Right here.*

He called immediately. "Are you outside Fritch? I saw that Jesus in a Box on a placement trip recently."

"Must be more than one. I'm near Borger."

"You mean Fritch, don't you?"

"If Fritch were a few miles to the east and went by the name Borger then I'd mean Fritch, but it isn't, so I'm near Borger."

"Know it all."

I studied the Jesus figure, standing with his arms in a V over his head. "Hey, is it just me or does it look like Jesus just stuck the dismount on a vault?"

"Nailed it."

It took me a second, but I groaned. "That was awful."

"Hey, do you have time for a late lunch today? My treat."

My stomach growled at the thought of it. "I can meet you at one-thirty."

"Can I bring lunch to your place?"

"The office? Sure. It'll be quiet as a tomb since Jack has spent the last two weeks on the lam."

"What?"

"Never mind."

"Anyway, no, I meant your house."

"My house? Why?"

"Whoops, here comes my boss. See you soon."

Dead air.

When I got home, Wallace was already there. And by already there, I mean that he was arranging lunch on cute sea-grass placemats he must have brought with him, because he sure didn't find them at our house. His fussing was portentous.

"What are you doing?" I lifted the bag on the table. Aspen Creek Grill. New and a little more upscale than our usual lunch place.

Wallace turned to me with a smile that didn't fool me for a second. His eyes looked sad, even a little frightened. "There's my girl. I got myself the salmon. I told the waiter just to have the kitchen throw together some kind of enormous vegetarian salad for you. They swear it's edible but I can't vouch for it."

I walked to the back door and let Snowflake in. Apparently there had been a monsoon or a water main break while I was gone, because she was head-to-toe muddy, not a trace of white fur to be seen on her.

"No, girl! Back. Stop. Oh no!" In five seconds, Snowflake managed to smear mud on my jeans, track it across Wallace's loafers, and bicycle it into the carpet in the living room.

"Argh." I snatched her up and carried her to the hall bathroom.

Wallace waved a hand in the air. "I'll keep your food safe. Looks like you've got that covered."

I laughed. "I'll bet you make Ethan change the cat box, too."

He draped his hand over his sternum. "Who, me?"

Five minutes later, Snowflake was soaking wet and I wasn't much better, but her fur was white again. I set her down in the living room and she started running laps up and over the furniture and hearth. I left her to it, then checked my phone quickly, hoping to hear from Jack so I could unload the weight of all the things I hadn't had a chance to tell him, after I asked him who Paige was and what sexy-voiced woman he was late meeting today. Instead, a notification of a calendar item appeared on my screen. *Due date!!* it read. At first I was flummoxed. What was due? Huh?

And then I remembered. I'd put it on my calendar when I'd learned I was pregnant. It was my baby's due date, if I hadn't miscarried last fall.

All my energy seeped out of me, and it was a struggle not to follow it in a weightless heap on the floor. I stared out the living room window into the backyard, using the sight of the daisies I'd planted by the side fence two weeks earlier to anchor me, imagining picking one and pulling its petals one by one. He loves me, he loves me not. He loves me, he loves me not. No, I wasn't going down that unhelpful rabbit hole. I pictured myself in reverse, putting the petals back on the daisy and placing it back in the flowerbed. Don't think, I told myself. Just breathe.

"Girl, what in God's name are you doing in there staring out the window? Come eat with me." The only thing missing from Wallace's delivery was a snap at the end of his speech. The man was all about the drama.

I wasn't, yet here I was, smack in the middle of it. I needed to just maintain, though what I'd be maintaining I wasn't sure. Equilibrium? Decorum? Sanity? I walked into the kitchen. Wallace had dug into his lunch.

"Don't wait on my account." I went to the sink and washed my hands.

"I knew you wouldn't want me to let it get cold."

I took my seat, wiping my hands dry on my jeans. "So, why are you buttering me up, Wallace? I've been worried about it ever since you hung up on me."

He looked at me with the sad eyes I'd seen earlier.

"It's Betsy, isn't it? Just say it."

"I'm sorry, I fought so hard for you—"

"The Hodges are getting Betsy. Say it."

"Yes. They are."

I opened my salad, my eyes burning, my hands wooden. Wallace had laid out real silverware, and I stabbed some lettuce with my fork.

"Emily?"

I stared at my food and chewed, sending Wallace to my mental voice mail. *I'm sorry, but Emily's not available to hear this right now.* The green lettuce and bright carrots, radishes, and squash, the splash of chipotle ranch dressing, all swam together in my vision and became abstract. The islands. Katie's big yellow house, Annalise, up in the lush rainforest. *Yes, that's where Emily is.* The shimmering white sand and turquoise water on the west end. The unbelievable pink and orange bougainvillea at the Peacock Flower Resort, where I'd stayed. That was a happy place. I'd stay there for a while. Away from Wallace and his news, and this house with no Betsy, and Jack with his weird behavior, and my dad the killer, and every other blessed thing mucking things up for me.

"Emily, are you okay? Say something." Wallace reached over and took my left hand, pulling me back from the islands.

But what was there to say? Betsy would never be mine. The Hodges had won. I had failed. But why? That. That was something I could say. "What could I have done differently?"

He shook his head. "Nothing. You did great. The Hodges just have an incredibly good track record with the state. I don't know if anyone could have beat them head-to-head."

I spoke through the food still in my mouth. "They're freaking nutjobs, and I don't give a flying fig about their track record with the state." A screech came out of nowhere at the end, along with some lettuce and carrot, but I didn't care. I jumped up, ramming into the table and knocking my silverware to the floor.

"Hey, what's going on here?" Jack's voice from behind me was the final straw.

I wheeled on him with the sharp edges of my anger and disappointment. "NICE TO SEE YOU, JACK ASS!"

I burst into tears and ran into our bedroom. Belatedly, I registered that Jack had been holding a small dog with a red bow around its neck, and that Snowflake was going nuts, but I didn't falter. I heard Wallace protesting that he would leave, then explaining what had happened, but I tried to block out the sounds of their voices. I grabbed the biggest suitcase in our closet and threw things in it helter-skelter. Underwear and bras. Boots. Socks. Sandals. Nightgowns. Shirts. Jeans. Skirts. A light jacket. In the bathroom, I filled a smaller bag with toothbrush, toothpaste, hairbrush, comb, hairspray, deodorant, perfume, and my makeup bag.

Footsteps behind me, the front door closing. "Emily, I'm sorry about Betsy," Jack said, his voice soft and warm. The blue heeler puppy— because I could now see that's what it was—in his arms looked soft and warm, too. It wriggled and whined, messing up the red bow. Snowflake continued to demonstrate that the entry of a puppy into her house had fried her brain cells as she yipped crazily and jumped around Jack's feet.

Puppies would not sway me. I kept working, my eyes away from puppy cuteness and Jack's golden eyes. My face cleaner and moisturizer. A handful of scrunchies to hold back my ponytails. "Yeah, I'll bet you are. You don't get to put yourself a little family together after all. But at least you don't have to marry me."

"What?"

I turned to him, hands on my hips. "So, where have you been lately?"

"Huh?"

"Why have you been avoiding me and leaving me out of things at work?"

"I—" The puppy yelped. Snowflake echoed it.

"Who was the woman that called looking for you at the office today?"

"Uh—"

"Did you know today was the due date for the baby I lost?"

"Oh man—"

"Who's Paige, and what are you doing Thursday morning?"

He stared at me, but he didn't answer.

I grasped the teardrop-shaped diamond ring on my left hand and started to twist it off.

"No, that's yours."

I quit twisting. "I'm not marrying another man who's only marrying me to get what he wants. I was a green card and a beard. Now I'm supposed to provide a wife and child to replace the ones you lost, but I'm not doing it. You're on your own, free of me."

"That's not fair. You're wrong."

"I don't even care what's fair or right anymore." I zipped my smaller bag, threw it into my bigger one and zipped it, too. "I only care that you don't love me."

I dragged my luggage out with what little dignity I had left to muster, leaving a speechless Jack with an arm and leg full of dogs.

TWENTY-THREE

I snuck my bags into my old room at my parents' and snuck myself back out again. For the millionth time in my life, I thanked God that my mother had never installed a security system that would chime every time I came and went. I wanted to be alone, to wrestle my emotions down, to figure out which way was up and which was down. I needed to fetch Wallace so we could pick Michele up at the airport. But that left me a few hours, and I filled them by driving out to Palo Duro Canyon, down a few million years to its bottoms, over its river crossings, and back again, barely taking in the rock formations with their spectacular striations of color, the wildflowers, or the lushness of the spring vegetation. As I crested the edge of the canyon on the way up, I couldn't even remember the drive out there. I drove back to Amarillo on the smaller roads, then aimlessly coasted along residential streets in neighborhood after neighborhood on the south side of town. Finally I could stall no longer and drove to pick up Wallace at his office as he'd requested earlier. I hadn't figured anything out by then. In fact, I had come to the conclusion that I had rendered myself homeless and jobless that day when I left Jack, in addition to everything else.

"Do you want to talk?" Wallace asked, as he buckled his seat belt.

"No."

"Okay, then."

We drove in silence. My cheeks burned. Wallace was witness to my meltdown and humiliation, and he was a party—even if an unwilling one —to me losing Betsy. I loved him, but he wasn't the person I needed right now. I needed . . . Katie? Maybe . . . Jack? Sadly and definitely. I had to get over that. We parked and got out in the parking garage, still without speaking.

"Not the world's best timing." I walked beside him into the lower level of the terminal. My phone chimed with a text from Jack: *Are you okay? Where are you? I'm worried about you.* I put my phone in my purse.

"What did your parents say when you showed up at their house?"

"Nothing, because I hid from them."

"Chicken."

I tried to muster a smile, but it was as flat as my voice. "Bwock bwock."

As we arrived at baggage claim, a tiny Hispanic woman in a red tank top and jeans was hefting a shoulder bag from the conveyor. Muscles carved lines in her arms and shoulders. When she turned, her eyes met mine and she smiled and waved.

"Wallace! Emily!"

"Hey, Iron Woman," Wallace said. He grabbed her bag and kissed her cheek.

"Michele, it's great to see you." I patted her and we hugged. She was tight and muscular like a gymnast, different than when I'd last seen her.

"You're doing your teeth." She pointed at hers.

"Not for much longer." My appointment to get these darn things off was bright and early the next morning.

"Have you eaten?" Wallace asked.

We began walking to the car.

"Yes, before the flight. Pappasito's barbecue." She patted her flat stomach. "I'm stuffed."

"Are you up for a drink?" he asked her.

"I am," I interjected.

Michele laughed. "I'm game for anything."

"Don't ever say that around Wallace," I warned.

We piled into the red Mustang and swapped life updates on the way to Hummers. The sun had sunk low on the horizon by then. I skipped my lowlights so as not to be Debbie Downer, and recited highlights in a perky voice.

Wallace flipped down the passenger-side sun visor. "You can't imagine how excited everyone is for you to just be at our club meeting tomorrow night. You're a big celebrity now."

In the rearview mirror, I watched Michele as she held up both her hands and shook her head. Her fingernails were bitten to the quick. "It's hard for me to understand how a mediocre-at-best athlete could generate this recognition. I married well. We wrote a book together. That's about it."

"You're an inspiration. You showed that anyone can do an Ironman if they want to bad enough. It's about will and preparation."

"And missing six months of your life."

"Yeah, that's true. But it's not just that, and you know it. You showed people what it looks like to face tragedy, to keep your family together. Even to be a kickass magazine editor. People feel for you. I feel for you. I'm just so sorry about Adrian."

"Thank you." I glanced at her face in the rearview mirror in time to see her close her eyes and breathe in slowly. "The truth is, I didn't keep it together much, not for a long time, so if you thought I did, that's awesome. I still wake up most days and feel like a bad version of *Fifty First Dates*. I expect Adrian to be there and he's not, and the whole thing replays in my mind before I can believe that my husband is dead."

"I'm very sorry, too, Michele," I said, feeling like my words were inadequate but needed to be said.

"He was great, and I miss him every second. But at least I have the kids. Belle is off to UT next year and Sam has one last year with me before college. I don't know what I'd do without them." She exhaled, blowing air slowly through pursed lips. "Hug your loved ones every chance you get."

I ended up in the farthest possible parking space from the entrance to Hummers. Our car doors slammed, and we walked together, still chatting.

"I wish I'd met him." When I was first introduced to Michele, Adrian wasn't yet in her life.

"I only knew Michele and Adrian through triathlon club when I was still in Houston, but he was easy to like and easy on the eyes," Wallace said. "Talented, too, not just as a triathlete but as a writer. And he absolutely doted on Michele."

"Yeah," Michele said, "He had good taste."

My laugh was hollow. Listening to Michele talk about Adrian made me long for what she'd had. Jack was the closest I'd come, and I had thought we would make it there eventually. I needed to pull my head out of my butt, though, because Michele's loss dwarfed mine. If she could carry on, I had to, at least for tonight.

We entered the bar. Hummers had been the hotspot since before I was of legal drinking age. I'd come in high school to hang out with older friends. I'd order a burger since I'd been an omnivore back in the day, and pray some poor waiter would accidentally serve me alcohol. Apparently they were playing the same music as back then, because tonight Jimi Hendrix's "Foxy Lady" was blasting from the speakers. It looked much the same as circa 2000, too. The bi-level bar was decked out in sports pennants: Dallas Cowboys, Texas Rangers, West Texas A&M Buffs, Texas Tech Red Raiders—my alma mater—University of Texas Longhorns, Texas A&M Aggies, and local high school teams. They had a spacious patio for those nights when the weather was mild and the smell of cow manure was bearable. Inside, you could play shuffleboard or pool on the left, belly up to a bar in the back, or choose a table on the right. We selected an outside table. Wallace ordered a bucket of beers and I requested a flight of Jell-O shots.

"You don't expect me to help you with any of those on a school night do you?" Wallace raised his eyebrows.

"Help or don't help, I need to be numb."

"Emily, Jack bought you a puppy. You're going to—"

I couldn't let him placate me. "I lost Betsy, broke off my engagement, became homeless and jobless, and today was the due date for the baby I miscarried, the one that cost me ninety-five percent of my only ovary. Six shots won't even begin to cover it."

"Ah, shit. This is your babyversary date? I didn't know that, Em. I'm sorry as hell."

"Whoa, I thought you said you were fine?" Michele said.

Wallace translated and explained my pronouncements for her, which gave me a warmer flicker toward him again, for saving me from it.

Michele put her hand on mine. "I know all too well what it's like to put on a brave face for the crowd. But you don't need to do any of that caca for me, *comprende?*"

My Jell-O shots had come while she was talking, bright green squares in little white paper cups like the ones people use at ketchup dispensers in burger joints. I slurped one shot down, lifted another, and toasted Michele. "*Comprendo y gracias.* I should be more worried about Phil and Nadine anyway."

Michele's face rearranged itself upward. "Phil and Nadine?"

I sucked in another Jell-O shot. It went down so easily. "My friend Nadine is engaged to our client Phil who's in a diabetic coma and charged with murdering his best friend."

Michele lifted a Jell-O shot and tossed it back. "Oh my."

"Yeah." A pang of guilt stabbed me for wallowing in my own stuff. "But the doctors are optimistic about Phil's recovery."

Wallace leaned in. "Emily will break the case. She's absolutely tenacious about rescuing the underdog. Which is probably why she's been running an investigation into the family that is adopting Betsy."

I brandished my third Jell-O shot at Wallace. "Not to the detriment of my work on Phil's case. And they're religious wackos with extreme ideas. You'll see. I'm doing a public service."

Wallace conceded the point, and soon he and Michele were chatting with great enthusiasm about Ironman training and race strategy and leaving me to get serious about my remaining shots. I studied them critically and poked at my bottom lip, which I couldn't feel anymore. The shots were an unnatural green color. I had two left, since Michele had stolen one. I sucked one down. The last time I'd had Jell-O shots I was at Tech. They were cherry flavored and a deep, rich red. I remembered them as super yummy going down, but no better coming back up than anything else tasted on the return trip. These were lime, maybe, but they didn't taste like lime. What else edible came in green? Avocados. Lettuce. Zucchini. Horrible flavors for Jell-O. Oh, but there was green apple and pears. They wouldn't be too bad. Definitely edible, even if these didn't taste like apple or pear or lime. But then was Jell-O edible? It had to be, otherwise the USDA wouldn't allow it to be sold as food. Or was it the USPA? Or the FDA or the FCC or something? I wiggled the Jell-O with my finger and giggled. Some of the stuff at the grocery store was so unnatural it should never have been approved by the SPCA anyway, so what did it even mean to be approved? Jell-O didn't seem natural, that was for sure, although that had never stopped my mother from serving it at every meal, only she never served green. God didn't make green Jell-O. Martians might have, because they were green. Or these might be Martians. Baby Martians. Or Martian eggs, although maybe they didn't hatch from eggs or their eggs weren't green. It was all so confusing.

I stood up and my chair fell over behind me. "Whoopsie." I stared at it, not sure what to do. Nothing, I decided. "I have to pee," I announced, grabbing my purse.

"You're already wasted," Wallace said.

"Want me to come with you?" Michele asked.

"Nu-uh." I shook my head, then grabbed the table. I held up a finger on my other hand. "Back in a flash." I saw my one remaining Jell-O shot shiny and square in its little paper cup. "Don't eat my little Martian."

"Your what?" Wallace said, his eyebrows up to his hairline.

"Nev'uhmind."

I weaved between tables and chairs and people to the bathroom. Once inside, I splashed cool water on my face. I looked in the mirror and squeaked. Mascara had molten onto my cheeks. I looked for paper towels, but all I found were hand driers. Toilet paper would work, so I checked the stalls. All empty except one, and that one had only a little, tiny bit. Well, I did need to *go*. I went, and used the last square of TP. That was better. I rinsed my hands and wiped them on my pants and headed back out to our table.

People stared at me. Whispered. Giggled. Did they all know about my horrible day, that the man I loved didn't love me so I'd had to leave him before I could ask about the beautiful puppy? Did the puppy have a name? Was it at Jack's now? It must be so soft. But why was everyone looking at me and pointing at me?

I stopped. I hadn't checked my messages. I dug in my purse for my phone. The floor felt uneven, even crooked, and I swayed. I pulled out my phone, knocking the yellow gloves out as I did, and saw another text from Jack: *I miss you.* Ha! He missed me? He should have thought of that before he snuck off on all his secret meetings and told his fibs. I stopped to pick up the gloves, but before I could, a man stood up and caught my arm.

"Miss, are you okay?" He had on a black leather jacket and a leather bandana like a do-rag on his head. Underneath his jacket was a white T-shirt with a big cross on the front. Above the cross it said, He died for me. Below the cross it read, I ride for him.

"Baloney," I said. I knew his kind. He rode Harleys on the weekends because it was fun and cool. No way God came to him and said, "Son, I need you to quit doing stuff you like and be miserable riding a Harley, in honor of the sacrifice Jesus made for humanity." No way. He was like all those football players who seemed to think God gave a goldurn which team won on Sunday. He didn't. I was sure of it. I started to tell him so, too, then remembered he'd asked me something.

"Excuse me?" he said.

Oh yeah, he'd asked me if I was okay. Got a little side-tracked for a moment, but I was back in the saddle again. "Never better."

"Hey, were you a Sandie? I think you were in my class."

"Blow Sand Blow." Our school cheer was easily the worst in the state of Texas if not the entire United States of America.

"I'm Duane, and you're Emily Phelps, right?"

"I don't know, but I'm Emily."

His brows furrowed, then he said, "I heard about you."

"Heard what?"

"Oh, just stuff, like how your dad's a murderer and ever since he's been out on parole, you've started hanging out with a bartender from the Polo Club and a gay social worker." He patted my arm. "Some of the people we graduated with are concerned about you, you know."

"And what else?"

"That you came back to Amarillo because you were pregnant with your gay ex-husband's child—"

"He's bisexual."

"—and that you turned out like your mother, when she was younger."

"Excuse me? What's that supposed to mean?"

"Um—"

"I'll have you know that my mother has never been trashy a day in my life. And she raised me to wear a What Would Jesus Do bracelet, which was supposed to make me love him more than boys, which worked until I met Scott Walker in high school, and then even a risen Jesus was no match for the real thing." I stopped. I was confused. "What did you ask me again?"

He nodded. "You should try Jesus. He's the answer."

"That's what they said about my quesadilla."

I lifted my chin and kept plugging toward our outside table, trying to ignore all the looky-loos and gossip girls. I hoped when they had a horrible day like mine people stared at them, too. I really did. And I hoped when they were down on their luck that people made rude comments in the name of Jesus to them.

I passed the smell of Axe cologne and stopped. The guy at Phil's storage unit had worn that scent. I turned slowly and carefully toward it. A young guy with slicked-back brown hair was watching me with a half smile on his face.

"I know you." I pointed at him.

"Yep."

Suddenly my brain made a connection with his face that it had missed when I'd seen him earlier in the week. "You came to our offices last month. Wanted Jack to represent you."

His grin widened. "Yep."

"Then you plead guilty to something or other with ADA Stafford before Jack could make up his mind about your case."

"Yep."

"You're already out."

"Yep."

My thoughts were too slippery to grab hold of, but I knew this was significant somehow. I pointed at him again. "What'd you do? I know you did something."

His smile disappeared and he leaned against the back of his chair, his arms crossed over his chest. "Somebody helps me out, I help them out. I heard a friend of mine needed some things lost. So now they're lost." He winked at me and turned back to a man and woman at his table. He had on some sort of team shirt, like a baseball jersey, that read Ogletree on the back.

"Hey," I said to the back of his head.

He didn't turn around.

To heck with you, then. I made my way out the door and across the patio, then tumbled into my chair, struggling to understand what he meant. The room spun a little. Man, those Jell-O shots must have gone to my head. Only had four of them. Well, and one beer. And no dinner. Or lunch, I remembered, except for the bite I'd sprayed at Wallace.

Wallace took a break from what he was saying to Michele and glanced at me. "Oh my God," he shouted.

I jumped. "What?"

He laughed—the kind of laugh that starts in his throat and moves to his belly and then takes over his whole body—until he was bouncing his leg and pounding it with his fist while his head shook from side to side. Michele put her hand over her mouth to hide her smile, but her back was shaking so I knew she was laughing, too.

"Whah?" I said again, or tried to. Man, I was really starting to feel those shots.

"Your face. Your mascara. Oh my," Wallace said, wheezing.

Michele leaned over and dug in her purse. I just stared at her, forlorn. I had forgotten about the mascara. I remembered it from the bathroom mirror, and I knew it looked like MacArthur Park had melted in the rain and I didn't think that I could take it. Michele sat up holding a travel pack of wet wipes. I'd forgotten something else, too. Something . . . yellow.

"I love those things," Wallace said.

"He's snot kidding. He freakin' keeps 'em everywhere, and he makes me use 'em before I can touch his car."

Michele said, "Lean over here, and I'll get it off."

I did. She wiped gently, her face knit with concentration and compassion.

"That's better. No more raccoon eyes."

"Jack didn't really want to marry me," I explained to her. "He wanted to replace his dead wife and kids."

"That's baloney," Wallace interjected. "And how is what you want—replacing your ex-husband and the baby you lost—different from Jack?"

I swished my hand as if to swat a fly away. "And he's been cutting me out of his life and running around behind my back."

"You don't know that," Wallace said.

"Well, where izze spending all his time then? What's the old case he won't tell me about? Whuzzat woman who he was late to meet today? And who's Paige? Hmm? Tell me that, Wallace Wildlife Gray."

"Wallace what?"

"You heard me."

Wallace laughed again, but this time he kept himself under control. "You're crazy. And at the rate you're going, I'll be married before you."

"But you can't marry another guy in Texas."

"Which is why we plan to elope to New Mexico."

"No way."

"Way."

"You're going to be married before me," I wailed. "Just like my ex-husband and Stormy."

"Your congratulations and best wishes are noted," Wallace said, patting my hand.

Michele smiled at Wallace. "That's awesome." Then she turned to me, looking deep into my eyes. "Don't assume the worst, Emily. If you don't know, fill in the blanks with what you do know."

My wail had turned into a sniffling blubber. "I dohne understand."

Her dark brown eyes held mine, her smile hugged me. "You know a lot of good things about Jack?"

"Yes."

"Then use those to fill in the blanks, and see if you don't come up with a different conclusion. Things aren't always what they seem. People told me Adrian had cheated on me and stolen my money before he died but what I knew about him made that impossible to be true."

"Oh no. Did he do it?"

She shook her head no, making me shake my head gently back and forth along with her as she did. "No. So, take it from me: look before you leap."

Wallace snorted. "You've just told a zebra not to wear stripes."

I grabbed Michele's wrists. "Michele?"

"Yes, sweetie?"

"I think I'm going to be sick."

TWENTY-FOUR

Michele helped me slither into my own bed before she retreated to the guest room down the hall at my parents', but not before I made her pinky-promise not to tell my parents anything about Jack and me. We'd gotten home too late for my mother to meet us at the door, thank the Lord, but the first thing I heard when I woke up was her putting Michele through the third degree. What time was it anyway? I fumbled around on the bedside table for my phone. Nothing. I patted the bed and found it by my pillow. I pressed the button on the top right to wake it up. 6:15 a.m. 6:15? I groaned. But there was no going back to sleep with mother wound up, and besides, I had committed to an early appointment that morning to remove my braces—my hated, hated braces.

I checked my phone. Another Jack text: *Are you at your parents' house? Are you coming home or to work today?* I hadn't answered his first two texts yet, and I didn't answer that one either.

As quietly as I could, I gathered some clothes from my suitcase and slipped into the bathroom for a quick shower. Nausea kept sneaking up on me, gagging me, and I sipped water slowly from a tiny Dixie cup. Mother still kept a dispenser by the bathroom sink, bless her heart. I stared at my look for a moment, then took my hair down. Time for a change-up. I braided it in a low, fat tail instead and sprayed dry shampoo into my bangs. Then I slipped a flowy A-line maxi dress over my head. Soft oranges and yellows and buttons up the front would work today with my gold sandals. I powdered my nose and used some bronzer and lip balm.

The more ladylike look would take some getting used to, but I didn't hate it.

"Good morning, all," I said, joining them in the kitchen.

Dad sat at the green Formica-topped table reading the paper and drinking coffee. Mother was making pancakes, and Michele—dressed in black spandex shorts and a Triathlon World Championships T-shirt—was stretching. The muscles in her thighs made me feel guilty for skipping hot yoga the whole last week. Not that I would look like her from hot yoga alone, but it would be a start.

A chorus of hellos came back at me.

"Whatcha doin' staying over here, Sweet Pea?" Dad asked.

"Um, our house is getting fumigated, and Jack is on a business trip." I kept my eyes on the floor and prayed no one would call me out.

"Your friend Michele is a delight," Mother crowed. She flipped a pancake, then another and another. "And so accomplished."

I thought about kissing my father on the cheek like I had as a girl, but lingering uneasiness with the whole broken-bottle thing stopped me. Dad went back to his paper and coffee. *He did it for you*, I reminded myself, but it was too late.

To Mother, I said, "Yes, she is. And many other great things, besides. Are you headed for a workout, Michele?"

"I'm going with some people from the triathlon club for a run out at Palo Duro Canyon."

"Oh ho. Been there, done that, back in the day, only very poorly. But it's beautiful and should be a breeze for you."

"I'm looking forward to it."

"I have an appointment I need to run off to, but if you need a ride anywhere after that—"

"Michele and I have that all worked out," Dad said. "You and your mother run along to work, and when she needs a taxi, she knows I'm her man."

I shot them a thumbs-up. "I hope your presentation tonight is a big hit. I'll see you later." I kissed my mother. "I have something tonight, so I'll be late."

"I'll be so glad when Jack returns. I don't like you running around by yourself at night."

I winked at Michele. "I know, Mother. Bye, everyone."

"Don't you even want to take some food? I can make you a to-go coffee and some pancake-cream-cheese rolls."

My stomach lurched in horror. "I'll be fine."

By the time I made it to the front door, Mother was yakking at Michele again. "Now, sweetie, tell me about where you go to church."

I was only ten minutes late to my appointment with Dr. Parks, where Mrs. Parks hustled me into an exam room. I leaned back in the chair. The Jell-O shots and late night were still churning in my stomach and pounding in my head. What had I been thinking? I was no party animal. I closed out the loud floral wallpaper with my eyelids and breathed carefully through my mouth.

The orthodontist entered, his voice shattering my peace like a hammer to crystal. "I don't understand what we're doing here today. You want your braces off halfway through treatment?"

I didn't look at him. "Good morning. Yes, sir."

"They haven't done you much good yet. You're still at risk for all kinds of problems later. And you've already paid for them."

"I understand. Thank you, but I'd like them off, please."

He heaved an enormous sigh of immense suffering. "Can you at least explain why?"

Instead of my usual smile, I felt my teeth bear down, which hurt, thanks to the dang braces. "Just because. Now, if you'll excuse me, I need to run to the bathroom and barf before we get started."

He moved back quickly with his hands up and I bolted out. When I returned, he didn't argue with me any more.

Afterwards, my mouth ached worse than before, but when I licked my teeth they were smooth and drew no blood. I wanted out of there, and I skedaddled to my car like my tush was on fire, not even stopping to see myself in the bathroom mirror. Where to go next? I didn't want to face Jack yet, so I called the office. Judith picked up in New Mexico.

"Is Jack in? I'm not at the office."

"Let me IM him."

Tap, tap, tap. Judith was the fasted typist I had ever seen, and seconds later she said, "Yeah, he's there."

"Thank you. Have a good one." I hung up before she could question me.

Decision made, I headed toward home at nine miles per hour over the speed limit. I needed to grab a few more things, like my hot-yoga outfit, because I was totally going today, to sweat out the poisons I'd ingested the night before. The terrain changed as I neared the exit to Heaven; it grew more rugged like the West of Technicolor movies, with prickly pear cactus and mesas flat as an ironing board on multi-acre home sites, like ours. Or Jack's, rather. I opened my mouth to release a sob, but no tears fell.

I'd taken the garage-door opener with me, so I used it and pulled the red Mustang inside, where it could be hidden—where I could be hidden—behind a closed door. "Jack?" I called, as I entered the mudroom from the garage. "Anyone home?" I tiptoed in, holding my breath.

The mudroom emptied into the open-concept living space, starting with the kitchen. I looked across the island into the living room on the left. It was tidy and empty. On the right was the breakfast area. An envelope was propped against the lazy Susan in the middle of the table. EMILY, it read. My heart thumped loudly in my ears. I grabbed it and ripped it open, hoping that somehow Jack had found the words to make the last two weeks disappear. I read the note torn from a yellow legal pad.

Emily: I got this house for you. I'll be at the office tonight. There's 2 presents for you out back. They were meant to be wedding gifts, but they're yours no matter what, like the house. Take whatever time you need. I'm sorry about Betsy.

I missed you last night.

Jack

Competing emotions fought for supremacy inside me. Sadness. Anger. Disappointment. Love. Longing. Hope. Gratitude. And, yes, a flicker of excitement about presents, which I couldn't help, even in a moment when they shouldn't have mattered but did. And Jack got them for me. He hadn't told me he loved me, but he brought me gifts. It was something, and as sad as I felt right now, as much as I missed him, I needed to figure out if something was better than nothing, if something was good enough in place of "I love you." And if it wasn't, where did that leave me?

I dropped the note on the table, loose, and went to the back door. The blue heeler puppy I'd seen the day before was lying on its back in the sun, zonked out. A cattle dog. I smiled in spite of myself, stepping out onto the covered porch. The pup opened its eyes and leapt to its feet, barreling at me and planting both paws on my knees.

"No," I said, firmly returning it to the ground. I knelt and felt for tags on its collar. The first one was proof of vaccinations, and the second read CHLOE and had the address and phone number there at Shangri-La. "Chloe?" The dog wriggled on the ground, her tail sweeping the dirt. "Hi, Chloe. You're so sweet. I guess Snowflake went to work with Jack?" Chloe licked my wrists as I massaged her ears and face.

A loud nicker drew my attention toward the back of the yard and our empty stable. Only it wasn't empty. A golden face with a white-blond fore-lock hung over the closed bottom half of a stall door. The horse bobbed its head and called to me again.

"Mother butler!" I hadn't expected a horse, and I starting running. "Come on, Chloe." The dog pounced along at my heels. As I approached the horse, I said, "You gorgeous thing. You absolutely gorgeous thing." Because it was. I couldn't believe Jack had gotten me Chloe and this horse, and was insisting the house was mine. I put my hands on the sides of the horse's face and rubbed. "Wow. It's so nice to meet you." I leaned to the side to check under the horse's belly. A gelding. "Have you got a name?" He was wearing a halter, and I ran my hands along it until I found a metal plate. I peeked around his face to get a look at it. "Legolas." I laughed, and the dog barked. "Pointed ears, white-blond hair, and look at your light blue eyes. You *are* a Legolas." Jack had left him hay and water, and I saw a feed bucket that had already been licked clean.

My phone rang. Laura in New Mexico. I turned my attention reluctantly away from my beautiful, beautiful horse. "Hi, Laura."

The voice that met my ears was Laura, only barely coherent. She was crying and breathing in gasps. "It's Greg. He's in juvie lockup in Alamogordo, and I don't know what to do."

My heart lurched. "Oh no! I'm sorry, Laura. Tell me exactly what happened."

I rubbed Legolas one last time and walked back toward the house. Chloe ran circles around my legs, but I ignored her. I put a finger in one ear and listened as hard as I could with the other.

"He took a bomb to school. Oh, it wasn't a bomb, it was just a circuit board for a ham radio, but they thought it was, and when they accused him, he smarted off. So they called the police, handcuffed him, and took him to the juvenile detention center. They wouldn't even let him call us! Farrah texted me, before anyone even told us they had him."

I'd heard Jack give the juvenile rights speech many times, and I knew it by heart. "Unfortunately, minors have even fewer rights than adults. They don't have to let him make a call. I know it's horrible, and I hate it."

"He's such a good boy, he's just been angry ever since we found out about his mother. She's been trying to get him sent back to Amarillo. He wouldn't normally mouth off, but . . . he did, and they arrested him." Her sobs took over in earnest.

"How can I help you best, Laura? Do you want to talk to Jack?"

"We don't need Jack. They've decided it's not a bomb so Mickey and I are on our way to pick Greg up. What I'm worried about is his mental state. He doesn't want to leave us, but we can't adopt him or keep him from his mother. He's all messed up right now. I'm afraid he's really going to get into serious trouble. And they may expel him from school anyway."

"Okay. Let me talk to some people, get some ideas. I'll call you back."

"Thank you, Emily." Her sobs ebbed. "I was going to call you soon anyway because I got us registered for equine therapy school, but then things started spinning out of control."

"Oh . . . that's, um, great about the school," I said. How did I break it to her that I probably wasn't going to be part of their lives anymore? A chasm opened up inside of me at the thought of all that I was losing. "Okay, well, let me call you back ASAP."

I took a seat at a bench in front of the windows. The cushion was damp from the sprinklers. I knew what to do: call Wallace. After I'd explained the situation, I said, "Well? What do you think?"

"I think the worst thing that could happen is we drag him back here, but that's exactly what we're going to have to do. His mother isn't abusive. She tries, bless her heart. She's just crazier than a bessybug."

"He's going to run away again."

"You're probably right."

I remembered Phil and Dennis. "What about Boys Ranch?"

"He'd be a great fit, but it's not in Amarillo. His mother is demanding city limits."

"But it's only thirty miles away."

"And Bushland is only five miles."

"What?"

"Your place. Bushland. Heaven. You could foster him, Em. She'd agree to that."

I nearly dropped the phone as I jumped up from the bench. Would Greg go for it if Jack and I were split up? He'd want to see Farrah, and I wouldn't be heading back and forth to New Mexico, although Jack would probably be happy to take him anyway.

"Are you there?"

"I'm thinking. It's a lot to take in."

"You were going to adopt Betsy."

"Yes, and that took some getting used to as well, so just chillax." Chloe had fallen asleep in the sun with her legs in the air. I walked along the fence line, in front of the daisies. "Will it be a problem that Jack and I split up?"

"Shouldn't be. Especially if we just transfer him from the Begays straight to you and don't stop to collect two hundred. I'll talk to Laura and Mickey as soon as we hang up."

"I—"

"I'm filling out the paperwork right now. What address? Your parents or Jack's house?"

"Jack said, um, the house is mine."

"That man is a saint. Emily, what is *wrong* with you?"

I ignored him, and instead focused on chewing my thumbnail to a nub.

TWENTY-FIVE

As I was leaving Shangri-La, another text came in from Jack: *I know you were at the house. You didn't say a word about Chloe and Legolas. I get it. I'm headed to court.*

For a moment my mind reeled. How did he know I'd been here? Then I shook my head. Duh. Our security system and nanny cam. The security system would have notified him via text when I entered. Then he could have watched me on the nanny cam the whole time I was out in the back-yard. On the phone, but not calling him to say thank you. I felt small and ugly and really confused. But what to do about it? He still hadn't said he wanted me or loved me or needed me, and I had to have those things. Had to. So maybe it was better this way, with him getting frustrated and angry at me. Without him trying to make me stay, when he didn't love me. When he couldn't.

Well, I needed to go by the office for my laptop and files. I'd work from home for a while to make it less awkward. For as long as we could continue to work together, anyway. Would we be one of those couples who could go back to being friends, or at least coworkers? The job offer I hadn't responded to popped into my head. I was glad I hadn't turned it down. I needed options. Only where would Greg go if Dallas was the option I chose? My stomach tightened. A new complication, even if a welcome one. Meanwhile, I had to deactivate Jack on the security system and nanny cam soon.

I scrolled through my email on my phone to the job offer and shot off a reply:

I am so flattered you thought of me. Can you tell me more about your firm and the position? And where it's located in Dallas?

I hit send, and pain shot through my body, like I needed to take a bath in Tiger Balm. But there wasn't enough analgesic in the world to make this pain better. The pressure of all the uncertainty alone was like thumbscrews to my head. Would anything help? A solution came to me, taking me by surprise, but it shouldn't have. I dropped to my knees in the kitchen and prayed with all my might. After, I breathed in deep through my nose to the back of my throat and out through my mouth, then went to the garage and got in the car. I didn't feel all better, but there was a minute loosening of the screws.

Twenty minutes later I opened the door to the office.

"Helloooooo?" a creaky voice called from far down the hallway.

I didn't want to see other humans, but I wasn't going to get the choice. "Hi, Clyde. It's Emily."

I set my purse down on my desk and walked to Jack's office. I was surprised Clyde was here again so soon. Staying plugged in with the cases, feeling his advice was essential kept him going, though. When I reached Jack's door, Betty was waiting for me, leaning against the frame.

She smiled at me and rolled her eyes. "His royal highness is at his throne."

"I heard that, Betty Ray. Don't talk about me like I'm not here."

I stopped to hug Betty's soft body before I walked in. "Are you giving her a hard time again, Clyde? You know, she could leave you for a younger fella."

He raised a gnarled hand and smoothed back a flyaway strand of his meager white hair. "But none half so handsome."

I kissed his cheek. "Of course not."

"I'd get up, but—"

"Don't. It's just me." I took a seat in one of the leather armchairs in front of him. I glanced quickly at the built-ins that hid Jack's Murphy bed, where he'd spent the night without me.

"Your teeth," Betty exclaimed. "Your braces are off. You look great."

"Thank you." Summoning pageant mode, I flashed her a wide smile. "How are things, Clyde?"

"Seem busy enough. Jack needed a consult on this murder case he's got going, you know." He held up a finger, and his hand shook so hard it looked like he was waffling it. Behind the large desk that he used to rule from, he looked even smaller than usual, which emphasized his rather large and pointy ears. His immaculate dress shirt hung from him, and his shoulders had winnowed down to nubs. His usually jaunty bowtie—a pink, green, yellow, and blue plaid number that made him look like a wizened Easter bunny—had come untied.

"Jack really counts on you," I agreed.

"Good attorney, but there's nothing like experience when it comes to civil rights and the Constitution."

"And so few understand that's what the practice is truly about, and the nobility of it."

"Most of the time." He nodded. "Sometimes, though, it gets ugly. Like Jack's case. He thinks he's got a lead, though."

Every nerve in my body went on alert, and I pushed my hair behind my ear. "Yeah. But I haven't caught up with him today. What's the latest?"

"It's taken him in a totally new direction, but my instincts tell me he's onto something."

My hangover, emotional distress, and lack of sleep had reduced my mental capacity to a half brain cell above vegetative state. Whatever Clyde was talking about, I didn't follow. Maybe Phil's murder case?

Betty walked to Clyde's side. "Time's up, Boss."

Clyde narrowed his eyes at me. "She calls me boss when she's about to tell me what to do."

I laughed. "Hey, did you see me in the paper the other day, with my quesadilla?"

"I don't read that hogwash."

I'd forgotten that Clyde swore off the *Amarillo Globe News* when they ran a profile on him a few months back and didn't write what he told them to.

"You agreed to one hour, Clyde Williams, and it's been an hour and a half. I've got to get you back to lunch. You remember what happened last time your blood sugar dropped."

"Yeah, yeah. I'm coming." He shifted in his chair. "Oh, I fixed my will, and Betty and I got it notarized. None of my tainted money will ever damn my son's soul." He put his hand on a stack of paper-clipped papers.

Betty pulled his chair backward, so gently that if I hadn't been watching her, I'd have believed—like it seemed Clyde did—that he was pushing the chair back himself. She handed him his cane, a fancy wooden one with a brass eagle head as the grip. When he had shifted his weight forward, she gave him a little boost under his arms. He hobbled forward and Betty stayed back and to the side, watchful and ready, but letting him motor along independently. He huffed and puffed and took a rest at the exit before he started down the hall to the elevator. The process took ten minutes on a good day, and it was clear from how he was moving that today was not one. But eventually he breached the door, and I heard Betty's encouraging voice diminishing as she coaxed and encouraged him.

Time to pack up. One of my files was missing, so I went back to Jack's office where I found it on his desk. I shuffled through his papers to see if I could figure out what case Clyde had been talking about, but found nothing unexpected. I kept a special lookout for mention of Paige but struck out on her, too. I ran my fingertips across the desktop, picked up a picture he kept there of the two of us laughing in the kitchen at Wrong Turn Ranch, one that Laura had snapped. I felt a heaviness in my chest, and I put it back, then took off my engagement ring and laid it in front of the picture. I had to get out of there. I returned to my desk and gathered up my things.

Betty leaned in our door, her face bright red, and shouted, "Call 911! Clyde is down and I can't find a pulse."

TWENTY-SIX

I sat in the Maxor Building parking garage with my forehead on the steering wheel of the rented Mustang. It hadn't been low blood sugar this time. The paramedics had come and done all they could, but they'd taken Clyde away with a sheet over his face and Betty holding his hand. The man who had raised a son and created a crusading law firm and fought for the people others wouldn't touch was gone. Dead. Forever. The ink on his will barely dry, the relationship with his son unrepaired.

If he'd known today was going to be his last day, what would he have done differently, I wondered. What would I do if I knew it was mine? What was really important to me? Jack's face, left dimple punched in and pushing up the brow that lifted the corner of his mouth as if by a marionette's string. Not saying much, his eyes twinkling as they watched me. My parents: the mother who embarrassed me most of the time and the dad I hadn't learned to trust again, not completely anyway. My faraway friends like Katie and Ava. Nadine, Wallace, and Laura, the friends I'd made in my second life in Amarillo, so unlike anyone else I'd ever known before. The baby that I had lost, the ones I most likely couldn't have. Betsy. Sweet, sweet Betsy. Farrah. Greg, caught in his mother's maze of mental illness. I pulled at the steering wheel, the flesh of my forehead welcoming the bite of hard plastic, the pain that reminded me I was still here. Clyde. Oh, sweet, charming Clyde. How I would miss him.

If I truly believed the Mighty is His Word congregation was bad news, I owed it to Greg and Betsy and all the other foster kids to find out all I could and do whatever was necessary to help them. It was in the best interests of the kids and everyone that knew and loved them. I lifted my head and wiped my tears. That meant making good on my commitment to brave the Wednesday night services in Sanford. I tried to be more positive about it. Maybe I had exaggerated their creepiness in my mind Sunday. They were enthusiastic and assertive. Those weren't inherently bad qualities. Bible studies began at six, if I remembered correctly, which left me time for some puppy and horse therapy.

But first I had to find Jack and let him know about Clyde. A fresh wave of sadness washed over me. Clyde had rescued Jack when he'd lost his family, and he was far more important to Jack than a mere boss. I held my phone in both hands and stared at it in the half-light of the garage. I hated making this call. Long seconds passed, maybe minutes, before I pressed Jack's number.

It rang four times. "Leave a message for Jack," his recording said.

I clenched and unclenched my jaw. I didn't know what to say to him. The system hung up on me before I could decide.

Sister Elise in olive drab and Brother Tom in gray camo were standing outside the church door when I arrived. The parking lot was packed, and people were streaming in. Yet when I got to the door, it was as if they'd been waiting just for me.

"Sister Cecilia," Elise said. She tucked my arm through hers. "Something's different about you."

"Hi," I said, looking down then up then down, going for shy enthusiasm. "Um, I got my braces off."

"You look great."

"Where did you drive in from?" Tom asked.

"What?"

"You came from the wrong direction if you're from Pampa."

I swiveled my head from them to my car, to the road running past the church. "Oh! Yes, I came from Amarillo. Took my mother to the airport." In actuality I'd driven all over Amarillo trying to find Jack. I'd even enlisted Judith to help me, with no success. I hated leaving the news about Clyde on his voice mail, but I finally did it, as gently as I could.

Elise gave my arm a gentle tug and we began walking. "Ah. Well, we're glad you're here. It's not often that we don't get any contact information from a visitor, so we couldn't call you."

"Sorry." I licked my lips. "I've, uh, decided I'd like to apply for membership, if the church will have me."

Elise clapped her hands and Tom beamed. They looked at each other, and Tom nodded.

He said, "In that case, we have a new members class for you. Usually there's a waiting period, but we sensed you were special right away."

"Great." Lifting the corners of my mouth felt like bench pressing my body weight, but I got them to turn up, just barely.

We turned down a sparsely lit cream-colored hallway completely devoid of any artwork but teeming with people. Voices around us were subdued, so quiet that I could hear the sound of our footsteps. From somewhere not too far away I smelled burned coffee.

"Here we are," Elise announced in a bouncy voice, stopping at an open door.

Tom gestured me in ahead of him.

There were four rows of four chairs and only five people in the room, all men, each with something camo somewhere on his body. I had far too little facial hair and hunting gear for this group. I racked my brain for how to fit in. Virtue? Submissiveness? I cast my eyes down and fisted my hand into my skirt. From my side view I saw Tom watching me. I chewed my bottom lip. Looking under my lids back toward the room, I found all five men eyeing me. It didn't take advanced math skills to calculate the ratio of women to men, and I began to suspect why Tom thought I was so "special."

Another man in gray camo walked in and to a podium at the front of the room. He grunted when he saw me. "Good job, Sister Elise and Brother Tom. Welcome, Sister Cecilia. We're so glad you could join us." He pointed. "We'll begin class in five minutes."

How did he already know my name? It made me feel oogie, for sure. "Thank you." I turned in the direction he had pointed, though, and stayed my course.

A table of refreshments and snacks hugged the far wall. I sniffed. Sausage. Could the little white and red things be pigs in a blanket? I groaned on the inside. There was a short list of items that tested my vegetarian resolve, and little piggies were on it. No one else had plates or cups yet, thank goodness, so I looked away from the temptation.

Elise guided me with a light hand on my lower back to a seat nearest us at the end of the second row. I sat, eyes down, more conscious of male attention than I'd ever been in my life. So much for dressing down, my modest braid, no jewelry or makeup, and my little white Keds. It didn't seem to matter to the lookers, though. I was undeniably a relatively young woman with blonde hair, blue eyes, good skin, and no ring on my left hand. But what they didn't know was that I also had a baby Glock and years of experience with large animal control.

Elise crouched beside me and patted my knee. "I'll come back for you after class."

"Okay." If I didn't bolt before then under the ick, ick, ick weight of eyes on my body.

Elise slipped out, but Tom was rooted at the door, watching me. I glanced at his hand. No wedding ring either. He was all but drooling. *Dear Heavenly Father, please tell me I am not* The Bachelorette, *Branch Davidian version,* I prayed silently.

At the front of the room, the man at the podium raised his hands to shoulder height, palms up. "I'm Brother Edwin. Let's begin with a prayer, shall we?"

With heads bowed and eyes closed around me, I snuck better looks at my compatriots/the contestants. Age range: twenties to fifties. All in moderately decent shape, like guys that do manual labor, not marathons or yoga. The youngest-looking one had a cross tattoo and was surprisingly sinister looking, but the others were unmarked. Short hair, as short as a buzz cut on one of the two oldest men. If I'd seen any of them out in public, they wouldn't have *terrified* me, but I wouldn't have felt entirely comfortable alone with them. Buzz Cut's eyes flew open. I jerked mine away and closed them.

When the prayer ended, Elise poked her head back in the door. "Excuse me, one more new member has arrived."

Another man appeared, his tall frame filling the doorway just right. My eyes traveled up from his well-turned-out camo to his face, and I was glad that the punch cups weren't offered to us before class, otherwise I would have spewed fruity red juice all the way across the room. The dark hair and golden eyes, the left-tilting smile, the olive skin, the chiseled cheeks all belonged to Jack. My Jack.

His eyes swept across the room. If he saw me he didn't register it, but there was no way he could have avoided it. I stood out like a leper. But I realized that if he called me out, I was toast.

My cover wasn't blown. Yet.

Jack took a seat on the front row opposite me. My peripheral vision locked on him, cataloguing his every move, but I trained my eyes forward on Edwin, holding my hands gently clasped in my lap to hide their trembling. My brain picked at the new problem like a scab: what was Jack doing there? Maybe he'd come because he was worried about me. Or maybe he was trying to catch up to me to explain or apologize or beg me to reconsider. With the security camera texts and nanny cam, Jack could have followed me from the house. That had to be it. I thought back to the drive out from Amarillo. I got no visual memory of his Jeep, and it was impossible to miss with its patchwork of clashing panels. He could have rented a car—while I hadn't done it for subterfuge, it had worked for me and could have planted the seed in his mind.

Or maybe he hadn't followed me. Could someone have told him where

I'd be? That would make sense, except no one knew. I hadn't shared my plans with another living soul.

So he had to have been following me. Blood rushed to my cheeks. Maybe he didn't trust me. Maybe he thought I had moved out because I was seeing someone else. What was the old expression, the guilty dog barks first? I had seen that envelope—*Paige, Thur, 8 a.m.*—and he hadn't explained it to me when I gave him the chance. Jack *had* lied to me lately, a lot. I didn't want to believe it, but was his presence here tonight evidence of infidelity?

Then again, this was the *new members* class. It was highly unlikely they'd let him in on his first visit.

My cheeks and ears burned, and I was more confused than ever. I wished I could wipe the color away. My inner emotional state was on display to the men sneaking glances at me, every one of them in the room except Jack.

I felt Edwin staring at me. I straightened in my chair and smiled at him, letting my lashes bat down twice. My mother had always said it was a shame to leave good tools in the toolbox, even though I hated playing the vamp. It was an effective distractor, and Edwin flushed. He cleared his throat and resumed taking us through the history and mission of Mighty is His Word.

"Our soldiers are the living embodiment of the Wrath of God," he said, his voice full and proud.

Mary Alice Hodges had threatened me with that wrath of God when I met her, and the police had shown up minutes later and arrested me. To hear Edwin so matter-of-factly owning up to what I considered terrorism was chilling.

Edwin segued into our responsibilities as members. "You will be required to build a family of soldiers. Single persons marry fellow members and are allowed to have two biological children. The rest of your household is to be built through foster care with the kids in the system that no one wants, the ones for whom the state pays a premium for their care. You are to add to your army until your state income minus a 10 percent tithe to the church is sufficient for your needs. All members thus will be freed from outside employment and can dedicate themselves to God's work. Real property is to be deeded to the church, although you will of course be able to reside in your primary residence. Our members find this takes an enormous burden off their minds."

A grinding noise filled my ears. I looked around for the cause but everyone else was glaring at me accusingly. Argh, I'd ground my own teeth. I was trapped in Hell. Edwin had just confirmed the worst of my fears about the church's intentions toward the foster children. I'd known the Hodges got paid more for taking special needs kids, and that they hadn't applied to adopt Betsy until we got her a settlement with the county. But this was bigger. Mighty is His Word was institutionalizing the use of these kids as income for their army. I was ill, and I couldn't wait to tell Wallace, and to figure out our next steps. There were a lot of kids caught up in this dangerous charade, and I had to help them. I eased my hand around my phone. Moving as slowly as I could, I tried to text him, but Edwin's eyes bored into me, and I stopped. I couldn't do anything to bring the Wrath of God down on Jack or me.

After another hour of listening to Edwin, Buzz Cut raised his hand.

Edwin nodded. "Yes, Brother Chet?"

"Are there enough women to go around for this plan?"

Edwin rubbed the five-o'clock shadow on his chin. "Well, our single men do outnumber our women."

"So how's it get decided then, who gets to marry who?"

"Seniority."

"So, you mean the fella that's been here the longest marries the woman who's been here the longest?"

"No, the man chooses."

I raised my hand.

"Sister Cecilia?" Edwin said.

I lowered it. As much as I wanted to speak my mind about women getting a voice in the matter, I shouldn't. "Oh, I was just stretching. Sorry."

"So he could get her?" Chet, the man formerly known as Buzz Cut, gestured at me.

Tom spoke. "Yes, he will." And the way he looked at me turned my stomach.

Chet grimaced and shook his head.

Edwin grinned. "And I do believe Brother Tom is next up."

Young Tattoo Guy sang out, "Here comes the bride," and everyone laughed but Jack. And me.

"Any more questions?" Edwin asked us.

No one spoke.

"Well, we have a mandatory retreat for new members once a month. It runs from Thursday through Sunday service, and we hold it out at our compound." He gave us an address, and I typed it into an email to myself. "Remember, this month's retreat is tomorrow. Sign up with Brother Tom before you leave. But first we're going to go around the room so you can introduce yourself to each other before we adjourn for snacks." He pointed at Jack.

Jack started to speak but Edwin interrupted him. "Stand up, face your fellow soldiers."

Jack stood and turned toward the room. "I'm Dave."

"Good evening, Brother Dave," Edwin said.

"I'm new to the area. Work with horses. Looking for jobs, if you know of any."

"Where are you from?"

"El Paso area's where I grew up. Then it was San Angelo. Midland. Lubbock. I just keep moving on wherever the good Lord takes me."

He sat and the metal legs of his chair squeaked on the floor.

"Thanks, Brother Dave. And I apologize. I forgot my manners. Ladies first. Sister Cecilia?"

I stood and fourteen male eyes roved over my body while Jack's stayed on my feet. I wrapped my arms around my chest, comforting and protecting myself at the same time.

My heart slammed against my rib cage, and when I spoke my voice had a little vibrato to it. "I'm Cecilia. I'm living in Pampa, but I'm from Dallas. I'm hoping to work with kids." I sat, keeping my eyes chest high on Edwin and as far away from Tom and Chet as possible.

Edwin grinned at Tom, and Tom winked at him. Edwin guided the remaining men through the introductions then released us to meet and greet.

I started to bolt from the room, but Tom blocked my path. "It would be my honor to get you some refreshments, Sister."

"Oh, I'm, I, uh, need to get on the road, early day—"

"Just five minutes so we can get better acquainted." He gripped my upper arm so firmly that I had no choice but to let him guide me to the table. "Excuse us," he said to the men that were in line.

Jack wasn't one of them. Maybe he'd made it out the door, luckier than me. I wished he hadn't, though, as Tom had all but marked me like a dog at a hydrant. The men parted so Tom could make a plate for me. He dug into the pigs in a blanket.

"Oh no, I . . ."

He stopped. "What?"

If I said I was a vegetarian, they'd all think I was a tree-hugging liberal. No tree-hugging liberal would consider joining this church. I had to assimilate. "I'm watching my figure. Just two, please." I smoothed my hand down my side, and from the slight bulge of his eyes, it must have given him just enough of an idea of what was underneath to make him forget I had almost turned down God's greatest gift to cocktail parties and church socials.

When he had finished, he held the plate out to me. I took a blanket and bit into it, piggy and all. Warm grease oozed into my mouth. I tried to hold it in, but a moan escaped from my lips a la Meg Ryan in the *When Harry*

Met Sally orgasm scene. I didn't care what it did to the men around me. All I knew was that whatever else came of tonight, I'd have a hard time forgetting the taste-bud bliss of that moment. I savored both of my piggies and chased them with fruit punch.

Tom never took his eyes off of me. "Will you be attending the retreat this weekend?"

I cast my eyes down. "I have a job interview." I paused and added, "But I'll pray about it, and see what God has in store for me."

"I certainly hope he sends you. May I see you safely home this evening?"

"Oh my. We've only just met. I don't think that's appropriate."

He nodded. "I hope we get to know each other better soon, Sister Cecilia."

With my fingers crossed behind my back, I said, "That would be nice. But I'm afraid I need to go now. My mother and I promised to talk on the phone when we each got home, and I can't worry her."

Tom fussed and cajoled, but finally accepted that I couldn't stay. I bid a hasty adieu to the others and somehow managed to get out of there before Brother Tom arranged for a quickie wedding that I couldn't escape.

TWENTY-SEVEN

Taking the long way home through Pampa, I kept a sharp eye on my rearview mirror, but I was practically the only car on the dark, windy highway until I got back to I-40. I called Jack when I felt safe. Voice mail.

I left him a message: "What were you doing at Mighty is His Word? We need to talk, Jack. As soon as possible. Please."

I called Wallace next, but had to leave him a voice mail as well. I pounded the steering wheel and shouted real cuss words.

I decided to try Shangri-La before heading to my parents', in the hope that Jack would be there, even though he'd said he'd be staying at the office. All the lights were out when I got there, though, and his Jeep wasn't in the garage. I decided to pick up Chloe and check on Legolas quickly since I was there.

I went to the back door, but the puppy was gone. In a panic, I ran back into the house. "Chloe? Here, girl. Come, Chloe." I whistled and clapped my hands together. As I passed the table I saw Jack had left another note.

Didn't know your plans, so I took Chloe. Jack

A surge of disappointment coursed through me. I went back to the stable and in the light of the full moon saw Legolas lying down, asleep.

My phone rang. It was Wallace, and I answered it quickly, trotting away from the stable so as not to wake Legolas. "Hey, thanks for calling me back."

"Hey, yourself. What's got your panties in a wad tonight?"

"It's about Mighty is His Word."

"Not again, Emily. I gotta go—"

"Wait. I have something. I promise. I went to a new members meeting at their church in Sanford."

"You are relentless."

"It's one of my best qualities. Listen to this." I filled him in on what Edwin had said as I took a seat at the glass-topped patio table Jack and I had bought the month before.

When I finished, Wallace was silent.

"Well?" I demanded.

"It sounds provocative, I admit, but Emily, these kids are cared for, they have homes, food, clothes, and they go to school and stay out of trouble. So what if their church wants them to be soldiers for God? What does that really mean anyway? It's not like Charles Manson directing the Family to commit mass murder to start the Helter Skelter Armageddon."

Manson had believed that a race war would trigger the end of the world as we knew it, and I hadn't noticed any nonwhite faces in Mighty is His Word except the foster kids. But that wasn't entirely fair. I hadn't seen any evidence of racial hatred. "You know a lot about Manson. I'm impressed."

"I took a few religious studies classes in college."

So had I, to try to understand my mother's side of the family. "You?"

"Bite me. I find the ways different groups explain God to be very interesting, Missy. And Mighty is His Word is just tapping into the Second Amendment "Live Free or Die" subculture, which, if you haven't noticed, there is plenty of out here in West Texas."

I put my elbow on the table and my forehead in my palm. "They hate gays."

"I know. And they subjugate women. But they also take care of kids we can't find homes for anywhere else."

"What if I could find homes for them?" I thought of all that land in New Mexico. Jack's family's ranch. Laura. Her equine therapy dreams. We could do it. She had passion and drive, and so did I. And, well, even if Jack and I didn't work out, maybe it wouldn't be too weird and I could still help her.

"Get real."

I couldn't sit anymore. I got up and walked the length of the patio. "I'm serious. If I could find homes for them, would you listen to me?"

"Emily, we're talking about more than a hundred kids and counting. Just out of my office."

"I know," I said, pacing.

"And you're not going to be successful removing them just because the church tells its members to foster kids in need and raise them up in God's army. In fact, you'll be laughed out of court around here."

"I know."

"So?"

"So, I'll get more."

"How?"

I stopped, thinking. I wasn't sure how yet—and I hoped that the road didn't take me past Tom again—but I knew I could do it. And maybe Jack could help me, since he'd been out there now and seen it, too. Maybe he'd learned more than I had, which I would ask him, as soon as he returned my calls, which might be the twelfth of never since I'd ducked his the previous day.

"How?" Wallace repeated, pulling me back.

"It doesn't matter how. I just will."

His voice softened. "Be careful, Emily. Think about it. You're threatening their livelihood and their membership."

"I will. I promise."

We said good-bye and ended the call. I knew Wallace had the best of intentions, and I wasn't mad at *him*, not really. I was mad at the system. I was mad at bad parents who didn't care for their kids. I was mad at people who waited on perfect little white babies instead of giving homes to all the others that Mighty is His Word welcomed into their army with open arms. Blood near boiling, I returned to the stable and Legolas.

"Hey, boy." I opened the stall door, but he didn't get up. I crouched and petted his soft nose. I pressed my face against his neck. After a few minutes, he put his head down and went back to sleep, so I nestled in beside him to close my eyes for a few moments, feeling sorry for myself. No fiancé. No adopted daughter, or birth child for that matter. No puppy. Just a horse. Come to think of it, what else did I really have in Amarillo? A crazy mother, an ex-con/killer father, and friends that were misfits-bordering-on-outcasts in the community. *How my cup runneth over.* Immediately I regretted my uncharitable thoughts. These people loved me. They were good to me. *But it's true, all that other stuff is true, too.*

Sighing, I sat up and checked my email on my phone. I had a flood of messages, but one caught my attention. An answer about the job in Dallas.

We're Uptown, but not too far from Downtown. The email listed the attorneys with the firm, some of whom I was familiar with, and the other paralegal, who I knew and liked. It was very promising. So promising that a giant sob escaped from my throat.

I cried myself to sleep, but Legolas didn't seem to mind.

TWENTY-EIGHT

Legolas shook me off and got to his feet. He snorted and pawed the dirt in the dark stall. Clearly, there would be no more sleep for me in such close quarters with him.

"I'm up." I kneeled with my hands on my thighs while I got my bearings.

I pulled up the time on my phone. It was 4:00 a.m. I was due to get on the road with Michele in an hour—she was bicycling at Lake Meredith. That left time to get Legolas out of this stable for some exercise. I ran into the house and changed my rumpled, dirty dress for some jeans and a long sleeved T-shirt. Then I went back out and saddled up my new friend.

I rode by moonlight in the open fields behind our back fence. I'd always loved riding in the dark, the feeling of floating, the sensation of charging into the unknown. It forced me to concentrate on what was happening in the now, instead of worrying about the future. And Legolas was a dream. Not as high-strung as Jarhead, but just as graceful. He danced across the prairie grass and I sang "Wide Open Spaces" to him. A half hour passed quicker than a minute. By the time I had cooled him off, mucked his stall, and given him hay, feed, and fresh water, I had to hustle to stay on schedule.

But I made it, and a neon Lycra-clad Michele and I were on the road to Lake Meredith before sunrise. She was meeting a group of bicyclists that largely hailed from Amarillo and could have hitched a ride with them, but Lake Meredith was conveniently close to Sanford. I'd offered to take her so we'd have some time to chat, then I could check on the Canadian River

Ventures property. That qualified it as a work trip. It would also be near the Mighty is His Word compound, but after sleeping on it, I'd decided to gather my information some way other than the risky—for me—new members retreat.

I drank coffee while Michele talked. First she gushed over my teeth. Then we moved on to more interesting topics.

"So right now I'm trying to decide whether to build on the property Adrian left for me and move out there once Sam's out of high school." Her voice was bright but contemplative.

"Wouldn't you miss your friends?"

"Some." She smiled. "I'm not the girlfriend type, though. My boss is my best friend. I think I've won him over to the idea. Still, I'm not sure what *I* want to do."

Sadness about the boss that was my best friend tugged at me, and I had to physically shake my head to break free. "What's holding you back?"

"My tie to the area was a love for bicycling there with Adrian. It was all about us. It feels kind of pitiful to move out there alone. And if I did it and hated it, would I be stuck there? I don't know."

I thought about my ties to New Mexico. Would I feel pitiful doing equine therapy with Laura if Jack and I were no more? Probably, but it would be different if we'd been married and he'd passed away. Plus I had made friends in New Mexico and in Amarillo, and I had family to tie me to the area. But I also had a job offer weighing on me, one far away. More money. More prestige. A simpler life without all the painful complications I'd acquired here.

But that was me. This was about Michele, and me lost in reverie was not a conversation. I rolled my lips inward, trying to pick up our thread. "What about something temporary? Try it out to see how you like it?" Even as I said the words my thoughts returned to my situation, and I knew that if I left, I had to leave for good.

"You know, I was thinking about renting a travel trailer for a few months for exactly that reason. I think it would be easier to sell the land than a house if I bailed out."

"Could you stand a travel trailer?"

"I think streamlining my possessions to only what fit inside would be liberating."

I'd left all my stuff in Dallas when Rich cheated on me, and I'd moved to Amarillo with nothing. I hadn't thought about it as liberating at the time, but she was right. It was.

I checked the dashboard clock. "We're early. Do you want to run look at a property with me real quick? It's related to the murder case against my friend, the one Wallace and I were telling you about."

"Sure. I haven't almost gotten killed since last time I went sleuthing. Life's been boring." She grinned.

We passed the turn-off to Lake Meredith and continued north. Michele programmed Siri for the address to the Canadian River Ventures property, and the robotic voice spouted directions.

"What you do is so exciting. It was never like that when I worked in the law. And it's sure not like that as an editor."

"Yeah, Jack's practice is pretty interesting."

"So have you talked to him?"

"He left me a nice note and some messages, but none of them have said he loves me. I ran into him last night, too. We weren't able to talk, and he ducked my call afterwards."

"It sounds like he's hurt."

"Maybe so. Probably. Oh, who am I kidding? I know he is, and I am, too, and I'm just a mess about all of this." I turned to look at her. "I don't want to spend my life with a man that doesn't adore me. I've done that. I want the real thing." I returned my eyes to the road. "And yet I love him, and all I can think about is missing him. Until I remember the price."

"The price?"

"Being stuck again with someone without having *real* love."

"Real love." She nodded. "Adrian and I called it 'the big love.' The crazy passionate stuff that makes it impossible to live without each other. I'd never had it before. I hadn't known I wanted it or was capable of it. But now that I've had it, I'll never be the same."

"I almost have it. That's the way I feel about Jack. Sometimes I think that's the way he feels about me. Like when we're naked."

Michele laughed. "Nothing wrong with that."

"But other times, the times he refuses to say a word . . . I don't know. And the more I think about it, the more confused I am, and the more stressed I get until I'm worried I'm going crazy."

"You're not doing as bad as you think. After Adrian was murdered, Sam was in danger and no one would believe me. All the pressure just built up in me until I was convinced I was the knife-winged butterfly warrior from my grandmother's Aztec mythology. *That's* crazy from stress."

My brows rose. "I don't think I'm a knife-winged anything, but it might be pretty awesome."

She snorted. "Not as much as you'd think."

My phone chimed with a text. I held the home button down. "Check text messages."

Siri said, "You have one text message from John Phelps. Do you want me to read it to you?"

"Yes."

Siri's voice droned, "Hey, hot stuff meet me in bed at noon. I'll be the naked guy under the sheets."

"Jesus!" I yelled.

Michele's eyes were wide, then she busted out laughing.

"Do you want to reply?" Siri asked.

"No!" To Michele I said, "That will scar me for life. I think my parents have learned how to sext."

"Your parents are adorable."

I wondered if she knew about my dad. I hadn't told her, but I felt sure she did. "If you say so."

"Seriously, I love them."

Siri told me to turn right in five hundred feet. The street name rang a memory bell. Where had I heard it before? I turned right. The Mustang started to buck and pitch. The road hadn't been repaved in my lifetime, it seemed.

Siri chanted to us. "In one mile, the destination is on your left."

"Wowza, would you look at that," Michele said, pointing.

The topography changed suddenly, giving way to a jagged river bottom with high, rocky bluffs on either side. Cottonwood trees crowded the gulch to the edge of the wide, flat bed of a river. A small trickle of water coursed through the sand, and a deer leaped into the trees away from us, a spotted fawn on its heels.

"Yeah, it's gorgeous out here. These are the Canadian River bottoms."

"I never dreamed the Panhandle was so gorgeous. First, Palo Duro Canyon. Now this."

I shook my head. "It's still mostly cows, pump jacks, prairie dogs, and tumbleweeds, but even those aren't bad once you get used to them."

Michele pointed again, this time to the right, to a small sign beside a gate. "Mighty is His Word Training Facility. What's that, do you think?"

My head swiveled back to the right. That's where I'd heard the street name. The retreat for Mighty is His Word was out here. "A church. A very strange and somewhat scary church."

"Like Jim Jones and the People's Temple in Jonestown, Guyana strange or like Scientology strange?"

"I wish I knew. The couple that's getting Betsy are members."

"Betsy the little girl you were trying to adopt?"

I nodded.

"The destination is on your left," Siri announced.

I pulled the Mustang to a stop. "Want to come with me? I just want to look around for a minute."

"Try to stop me."

There was a FOR SALE sign stuck into the ground. ANGELA MARTINEZ, LAKE MEREDITH REALTY. I took a picture of the sign and her phone number. Michele and I walked to the metal swing gate in the fence. It led to a very faint pair of parallel lines. Vehicle tracks over crushed wildflowers. A road of sorts. The gate was chained but not locked, so I opened it up, and we walked through.

Michele held her blowing hair back and rotated three hundred sixty degrees, looking like an emergency beacon in all her neon. "What are we looking for?"

"I'm not sure. Get this: Dennis, the guy Phil's accused of killing, owned this property with Melinda Stafford, the ADA prosecuting the case. And Phil may have owned an interest in it, too, although that's just a hunch."

She whistled. "Sounds like a conflict of interest for the ADA."

"That's what I think."

The wheel tracks led down toward the river bottoms. I scanned the drop off and sandy expanse below us. The fence was about a quarter mile away back toward town and another half mile in the other direction.

"It sure is a gorgeous piece of property," Michele said.

My phone rang. An Amarillo number. I was surprised and happy to see I had signal. I pressed accept and said, "Hello, this is Emily."

A young woman's voice said, "This is The Works car wash. Your car is ready. You can pick it up anytime."

"Thank you. I'll be in this afternoon." Finally I could have my car back. I wondered if it would ever be the same.

Michele and I turned and walked back toward the gate. As we did, I noticed a sign that had been knocked over, inside the fence. It was lying facedown. I looked around for something to flip it with, since I didn't want to end up with a rattlesnake bite, but there was nothing. I had on boots and jeans, so I gritted my teeth and used the tip of my toe, then yanked my foot back. No snake came at me, and I relaxed. The sign was freshly painted and said FUTURE HOME OF CANADIAN RIVER VENTURES ADULT RESORT.

"Adult resort," Michele said, amusement in her voice. She put air quotes around her head. "As in sexy adventures? Nudist vacations?"

"As in those, I think." Phil's involvement suddenly seemed more likely. Mighty is His Word had to hate the resort planned across the street, if they knew about it. Not that I'd love having an adult resort in my front yard either.

"Yucky."

"Agreed." But a clue. Not only did Melinda Stafford own property with Dennis, and maybe with Phil, but she was part owner in a potential sex getaway. My brain kicked into high gear. Heavens to Murgatroyd, that wasn't all. She hadn't disclosed any of this, and it wasn't just a conflict of interest. If she was the one behind the break-in at Phil's, or hiding or destroying evidence, like the email forwarded from Dennis to Phil, then she was obstructing justice. For a fraction of a second, I remembered her frail figure hunched over the toilet in Abuelo's vomiting, her stumbling and weaving gait, and I almost felt sorry for her, until it all crystallized for me. I rubbed my palms together, my juices flowing. If she was obstructing justice, it meant she had something to hide, something big and worth putting herself at risk for.

"Hey," Michele said, pointing into the distance down nearer the bottoms. "Aren't those marijuana plants?"

We looked at each other and simultaneously broke into a run to go check it out.

I cackled with joy when we got to them. "It is. Pot. This is awesome." Shipping runs from Borger to Colorado, fields of pot? Dennis was a drug smuggler. My day—and Phil's—just kept getting better and better.

Michele slapped me a high five. I walked closer and snapped pictures with my phone from all angles.

Then I sent up a quick prayer to the big guy: *Dear God, please forgive me for wanting this to be the takedown that self-righteous witch deserves.* He didn't answer, but I wasn't struck by lightning either, so I figured he was taking my side on this one.

TWENTY-NINE

I dropped Michele off at Lake Meredith with three underfed female athletes—one of whom was lending her a bicycle—then waved good-bye to her with one hand and held down the home button on my phone with the other. Siri's tone sounded. "Call Lake Meredith Realty in Fritch, Texas." I set my phone down and put the car in drive.

The receptionist picked up on the first ring. "Lake Meredith Realty." Her voice was as old and wavery as Clyde's had been. Thinking of him sent a wave of grief through me.

"May I speak to Angela Martinez, please?"

"She'll be in any minute. May I take a message?"

"I want to drop by to discuss a property she's listing. What's your address?"

She gave a downtown Fritch street and number. "May I tell her to expect you?"

"Sure. My name is Emily."

I hung up. Fritch. Lake Meredith Realty was only ten minutes away. That still left me time to call Nadine and give her an update. She deserved some hopeful news.

After she answered, I said, "Did I catch you at an okay time?"

"Hey, Emily. Yes, and I've got great news!"

"About Phil?"

"He opened his eyes this morning!"

"Oh, Nadine, oh my gosh, that's the best news." I coasted into a turn without using my blinker. The car behind me honked. I saluted and the car raced its engine as it barreled past me.

"I told him to squeeze my hand twice if he knew who I was, and he did. They've still got his tube in, so he can't talk, but his vital signs are perfect, and the doctors and nurses are over the moon."

"Honey, I am *so* happy for you."

Nadine let out a sob. "He's going to make it."

"Yes, he is. And I have more good news for you, as long as you can keep it totally confidential."

"I'll take it to the grave."

"Well, I hope not that, but thank you. Remember Canadian River Ventures?"

"I do. Was it a good lead?"

"It was. It owns a property outside Sanford. And you'll never believe who with."

"Who?"

"Melinda Stafford."

"The ADA?" Nadine shouted.

I held the phone away from my ear. "Yes, ma'am. I still don't know if Phil was in on the deal, honestly, but I am one hundred percent sure that Dennis was. I was out there this morning, and it's up for sale. I checked with the mortgage company, and it's about to go into foreclosure. And there's a ton of marijuana growing on it and a sign kicked over on the property that says 'Future Home of Canadian River Ventures Adult Resort.'"

"Wait. Melinda is in on a sex camp and pot farm?"

"Possibly. But think about it, Nadine. She owned property with Dennis and didn't disclose it. That's a conflict of interest. And you heard Phil talking about an email from Dennis that I can't find. She was in a position to destroy or hide evidence. And if she's hiding things —"

"Then she's a suspect. As good as Phil."

"Exactly."

Nadine started sobbing again. "She might have even killed Dennis, for real."

"Maybe."

"Oh, Emily, oh my God, thank you so much."

I swallowed a sudden lump in my throat. "Of course, Nadine. I love you guys. And I'm headed to the real estate agent's office now to see what else I can find out."

"Keep me posted. And if Phil's up to it, I'll ask him about the property. He's never told me about it, which I hope means he isn't in on it. I want to believe in him, Emily."

Even though I was driving, I allowed my eyes to flick closed for a second. *Yes, Nadine, I'm right there with you.* Aloud, I said, "I'll talk to you soon, hon."

We hung up, and I cruised up to Lake Meredith Realty. It was in an old wooden house updated with fresh yellow paint and a new metal roof. The lot beside it had been paved for cars. Mine was the only vehicle in the visitor spaces, but there were three cars in the back of the building past the EMPLOYEE PARKING sign. I hustled in with a new bounce in my step. I burst through the front door and slammed on the brakes. The foyer was tiny and I'd all but vaulted over the receptionist's desk.

The little old woman jumped and gasped. "Oh my." Her hand flew to her bosom, over her large beaded cross necklace and Easter sweater set. Her entire desk was decorated in bunnies and Easter eggs. I decided not to tell her that she was a few days late.

"So sorry." I smiled at her, hoping to undo my first impression. "I'm here for Angela Martinez. Is she available?"

"Your name?"

"Emily Bernal. I called."

"Just one moment." She hit intercom. "Angela, Emily Bernal is here to talk to you about one of your listings." She cocked her head at me. "Say, aren't you the woman from the newspaper who saw the face of Jesus in her quesadilla?"

I raised my hand. "Guilty."

A fortyish Caucasian woman had come into the foyer. She was over-dressed for Fritch in the normal manner of real estate agents, with high-heeled tan sandals and an Elie Saab-like lavender outfit. Her shoulder-length blonde hair was teased into a stiff-looking, wind-resistant bouffant. Martinez had to be a married name, and I checked her left hand. A modest diamond adorned her ring finger.

"I'm Angela." She stuck out a hand and walked toward me. "And you are?"

I grasped and shook. "Emily. I saw your sign on a property and hoped to talk to you about it."

She smiled, showing teeth Crest Strips white. "It would be my pleasure. Follow me, Emily."

As I passed the receptionist I said, "Happy Easter," and she beamed.

Angela ushered me into a small conference room that had likely once been a bedroom, based on its location in the back of the house. I took a seat in a chair upholstered in jewel tones that coordinated with sparkly wallpaper with broad vertical stripes. Lake Meredith Realty was a decade behind in updating their decorating scheme.

"What property has your interest?"

I gave her the address.

"How'd you learn about it?"

"My client is part owner."

She smiled. "Melinda is your client?"

"Nope. Phil Escalante. He and Dennis Welch are Canadian River Ventures."

Her smile turned upside down. "Oh my, I haven't met a Phil. I didn't know anyone else was involved in it, to be honest with you, other than Melinda and her fiancé—former fiancé, rather. Melinda got his signature on behalf of Canadian River Ventures and that was all I needed to list it, legally."

Fiancé? I widened my eyes. "Oh, absolutely. I'm not here to dispute that. I'm here because Dennis was murdered, and Phil's in a coma." I crossed my fingers in my lap. It wasn't really a *lie*, since he had been up until a few minutes ago, as far as I knew. "I'm trying to help his family get his affairs straightened out, in case . . . you know."

"Oh my gosh! How can I help?"

"Well, Melinda was less than cooperative." I gave her my sad face.

She glared at no one in particular, then leaned toward me and lowered her voice. "Doesn't surprise me. She's, um, a—"

"Grade A bitch?" My mouth puckered a little over the word, but if anyone deserved it, I figured it was Melinda.

"Yes!" Angela hissed. "I've never had anyone talk down to me like that woman. Granted, she was pissed because she'd found out her fiancé wasn't who she thought he was. She said he was going to ruin her if she didn't"—her brow furrowed tight—"distance herself from him. That's after I sold the property to them less than a year ago, and they were gaga about each other then." She put a finger in her open mouth in a gagging motion. "Apparently they met at a lake party and it was love at first sight. Anyway, I'm not so sure Dennis was the problem. You know?"

"Oh yes, I do." I tried not to show I was nearly orgasmic. My brain coughed up a memory of gel-slicked brown hair and Axe cologne, a felon sprung from jail suspiciously quickly who said he helped a friend lose something.

"What real estate agency did you say you were with?"

I cleared my throat. "Oh, I'm not a realtor. I'm with Williams and Associates. We're Phil's legal counsel."

Her jaw bounced up and down and she licked her lips.

I went on. "I just wanted to check in with you firsthand and see how the listing is going. We're hoping for a fast sale so we never have to deal with Melinda again."

She still looked nervous, but she exhaled. "Oh, sure. I think you're about to get an offer. A local couple who already owns property across the road. They called the day the sign went up."

I kept mum, leaving her empty space to fill with words.

"His name is Furman." She fumbled through some papers and found the one she was looking for. "Lawrence, he said. He'd called a few months ago, even before I had the listing. Seems to have had his eye on it for quite some time."

Mighty is His Word the potential buyer for the property? The plot was thickening faster than the gravy I'd made with an extra cup of flour my first year out of college.

The intercom buzzed. We heard the receptionist's voice as if she were sitting outside the room. Which she was. "Angela, I've got a call for you on line one. It's the school about Michael. They said it's urgent."

Angela bit her bottom lip.

"I understand. Take it."

"Just one moment." Angela hustled out of the room. From a nearby room, I heard, "This is Angela."

I grabbed the paper on her desk and snapped an iPhone picture. My brain raced. How did the news about Furman change things, if at all? It certainly didn't take Melinda out of the picture, but if Furman had been trying to get the property, that gave us another reasonable suspect to show the jury, in addition to Melinda, for a "some other guy did it" defense for Phil. It was a good lead, and I knew where to go to chase it down. The same place I needed to be if I was going to get Wallace and CPS to do anything about all the children being forced into an army for God while the church lined its pockets.

I used my phone's camera as a mirror. My outfit today—boots, jeans, and a T-shirt—was modest enough, if a little informal. But that compound was basically a ranch, after all.

Angela bustled in. "So sorry. Kids."

I was already on my feet. "Don't I know it." I held my phone up. "Just got a call that my little Timmy is in the nurse's office. Gotta run. Thank you." By the time I finished my sentence I was halfway through the front door to the building, with Angela standing openmouthed beside the grandmotherly receptionist.

THIRTY

Jacked-up on adrenaline, my nerves and good sense didn't kick in until after I'd crossed the cattle guard into the Mighty is His Word compound. A small sign beside their dirt road said PRIVATE PROPERTY, followed by another that said VISITORS CHECK IN AT GUARD SHACK, ½ MILE. Guard shack? What kind of church retreat needed a guard shack? And me with my baby Glock in my purse. Assuming the sign wasn't a bluff, my gun wasn't going to go over too well. I steered with my knees and stashed it in my glove box.

The land rolled under the rental Mustang's wheels. The compound didn't appear to have direct river bottom access, but the topography was rugged nonetheless. I crested a rise and descended. There beside the dirt track stood a small manufactured building with GUARD SHACK written on its side.

I pulled up, and a short, muscular man with a buzz cut, an iPad, and, of course, camo clothing, met me at my window. I rolled it down.

His voice was surprisingly high. "Name and nature of visit."

"Em—um, Cecilia Hodges, and I'm here for the new member retreat."

He flicked through some screens and grunted. "You didn't confirm."

I batted my eyes. "I'm sorry, I prayed and prayed about this, and the Lord just held out on me until this morning."

He chuckled. "Driver's license."

My heart froze in my chest. The cold worked its way out to my ears, my cheeks, and the top of my head. "I'm so sorry. I lost my wallet yesterday. It was here or DPS this morning, and when God spoke, I just pointed my car this way and here I am. Brother Tom can vouch for me though, if he's here."

"Oh, he's here, all right." He tapped on his screen, and I heard a phone ringing.

"What is it, Brother Harvey?" It was Tom's voice, but gruffer than when I'd last spoken with him.

"Brother Tom, can you vouch for the identity of this guest?" He turned the iPad toward me. Tom's sweaty face filled the screen.

I waggled my fingers. "Hi, Brother Tom."

He leaned in, like he was trying to get closer to me. "Sister Cecilia. I was so afraid you weren't coming."

"I almost didn't. But the things you said, well, I couldn't forget them, and here I am."

"I'll be waiting for you at the entrance."

"See you soon."

Brother Harvey turned the screen back toward himself and tapped it. "Do you have a cell phone with you today, Sister Cecilia?"

"Yes, of course."

"Cell phones are strictly prohibited." He held out his hand. "You can pick it up on your way out."

All the saliva in my mouth dried in an instant. No one in the world knew where I was. I was here under false pretenses. Wallace had told me I was messing with the church's membership and financial livelihood. It wasn't too late to leave in a cloud of dust. But if I did, I might never find out the connection between Furman and the property Melinda owned with Dennis, and I'd blow my best chance to gather the information I needed to bust out all the Mighty is His Word foster kids from their indentured soldiertude. I'd just have to be very, very discreet and careful. And, hey, careful was my middle name, but it didn't preclude pinging the mother ship with my location.

I held up my phone and let my eyelashes flutter. "Just need to cancel my lunch plans real quick. Couldn't do it while I was driving."

He grunted.

"Thank you, Brother Harvey." I quickly shotgunned a group text to Jack, Wallace, Michele, John Burrows, Nadine, Judith, my parents. "Fumble fingers," I simpered to Harvey. I typed rapidly: *At new member retreat at the Mighty is His Word compound past Sanford and having to surrender phone. Learned today they're trying to buy the pot farm/sex camp across the road owned by Dennis and—surprise—MELINDA STAFFORD. Potential motive everywhere. If you don't hear from me by noon, send the cavalry. Michele knows exactly where it is. Wish me luck.* After I pressed send, I bit my lip. Harvey would have my phone and could reach my texts and emails and anything else he wanted. I flipped screens to Settings and continued on to set a passcode. *This one's for Phil.* I typed the passcode Nadine had told me was their anniversary: *1020.* Then I turned off my phone and handed it to Harvey.

He took it and saluted me. "Drive another half mile and park where you see the other cars."

I flashed him a smile weaker than it had been five minutes before and eased the Mustang forward. The second guesses started immediately. I shouldn't have given him my phone. I should have turned around. Even if Jack was following me again today, he probably wouldn't follow me in here. And I couldn't call him, or anyone.

Stop it. Just stop, I told myself. *You arranged for worst-case scenario backup. Get in there and get some answers and get out.* If I had to, I could fake an illness for a reason to leave early. The good Lord knew I felt sicker than a dog with fear already.

THIRTY-ONE

Half a descending mile later I came upon a cluster of multicolored manufactured houses with cars parked in two neat rows in front of them. I pulled to a stop in a grassy spot at the end of a row. Rugged prairie, blue skies, and a surreal village.

"Sister." Tom's voice, from my right as I got out of the car.

I turned toward it. He stood at the end of the row, his desert camo overalls and T-shirt blending into the background, but my eyes moved past him to a small animal peering through waving grass. I squinted. The sun was really bright, so I couldn't be sure, but it looked like a little red fox. Tom waved me over, drawing my attention back to him.

I tried to smile. "It's like a little town on the prairie."

"Just wait," he said, reaching for my arm, pulling me too close to him, and rubbing the sensitive flesh inside my elbow.

I shuddered, which made his eyes grow brighter.

Tom led me to a house with robin's egg blue siding. He opened the door and ushered me in before him. My footsteps squeaked on laminate floors in a nearly empty living room, save for a black faux-leather couch and coffee table that looked like it was made of particleboard. The only smell was bleach and lavender, and the walls were bare.

"Where is everyone?" I didn't want to be alone with Tom.

He smirked and walked through the living room and down a hall.

I stood rooted to the floor.

"Are you coming?" he asked.

"Um . . ."

He motioned me toward him and disappeared into a side room. My mouth was dry as desert sand, but I followed him, stopping at the opening of the room he'd entered. It was empty, except for him, and a trap door into the floor. He punched a code into a keypad on the wall. I couldn't see the numbers, but I heard a beep, and something in the door latch clicked. He pulled it open.

"Shall we?" he said.

No, no, no, no, no, no, no, my mind screamed. "Um, yeah, sure," I said.

I peeked inside the hatch. A bright light shone from below descending stairs. Good. At least it wasn't a ladder. I'd broken my arm when I was in elementary school when a ladder fell over onto the driveway with me on it. Ladders were not my friends.

I sucked in a breath for courage and started down them, Tom right behind me. I heard him suck in a breath as well, and regretted my body-hugging jeans. When I got to the bottom of the stairs, I was in an open room, a foyer of sorts it appeared, with white walls, no furniture or markings, and doors on three sides.

"This way," Tom said. This time his hand landed on the small of my back, then slid down a few inches lower than was appropriate.

"Brother Tom," I said, "we barely know each other." I twisted away from his hand.

"I'd like to change that."

I reddened with anger and disgust, but he seemed to take it as a blush of modesty.

He nodded. "I respect you, Sister Cecilia, and while I feel God has brought you to me for a special purpose, I will take it slower."

"Thank you."

He reached for the door on our right. "Come with me."

The door must have been soundproof because as soon as he opened it, noise exploded toward us. Laughter. Whoops. Amens.

"What's going on?" I said.

He grinned. "Something you're going to love."

He walked in front of me this time, stopping at the first door on our left. "Sister Furman, I have a happy surprise." He grasped my upper arm and pulled me in front of him. "Sister Cecilia decided to join us."

The tall female pastor rose from behind a bare desk. She swung her gray braid over her shoulder. "Well, that is a happy surprise. Welcome, Sister Cecilia. I've heard a lot about you." She smiled, but she seemed to be in another place mentally. Her eyes were glazed, and a sheen of sweat glistened on her forehead. "Brother Tom, we'll begin in a few minutes. I'll see the two of you soon."

Brother Tom backed away, pulling me with him. "Yes, Sister Furman."

He released me and began walking again. "We have time for a quick tour before we start. We have plenty of space up top, but down here is where the action is. One wing is the dormitory, for people to stay during training. It has a cafeteria and infirmary. Another wing is offices. That's where we are now. And the third wing is where the good stuff happens. There are connecting hallways between each wing, or you can access them at the entry point." He stopped. "Here's one of the connectors now."

The door he indicated was all glass, unlike the others. I peered down it, but it was curved, so I couldn't see more than a few feet. He pushed it ajar.

I smoothed some loose hair off my face. "Where's Sister Elise?"

"She's not here this weekend."

I prayed I wasn't the only woman in the building besides Sister Furman, and we walked in silence, crossing over another corridor and pushing through three more doors in quick succession before we reached the far wing. As he walked me down the silent hallway he pointed. "Women's side. The women have two bathrooms." His voice sounded almost boastful. He pointed to the other side of the hall. "Men's. We share one facility back that way." He gestured toward what I thought was the way back to the elevator. "And here's the cafeteria. It's equipped with supplies to last us six weeks, if necessary." He beamed, and I followed him in to a bunker-like room.

The walls were plastered with Bible quotes and Mighty is His Word propaganda. A giant poster of a soldier in face paint with a sniper rifle arrested my attention. Above his head it said WE ARE and below his feet, THE WRATH OF GOD.

"Amazing," I croaked. It was almost time to pull my sick routine, because that soldier poster was surely enough to get Wallace to act. I hadn't found out anything about the property across the road, but that was starting to feel like really small potatoes.

"We plan to survive no matter what happens up top."

"That's . . . great."

"You'll be back here for lunch in a bit."

From across the room I heard the clanking of utensils against metal, water running, and voices in conversation.

"I can't wait."

"We'd better hurry. Follow me."

We headed back the way we had come but this time stopped in the middle wing. Brother Tom grinned at me. "We have just enough time for you to see my favorite rooms." We turned left, away from the stairs that led to the surface, to normalcy, to the real world. Tom punched in a door code, and again I heard the click of a lock releasing. He pushed the heavy metal door open. "Our armory," Tom said, his face aglow.

When I rounded the corner into the armory, I stopped short and would've buckled if I hadn't caught myself on the doorframe. Row upon row upon row upon row of weaponry lined the room, packed in tight. Guns. Missiles. Fancy bows, which, after being shot at a few days before, gave me the willies. Bombs. Grenades. And the ammunition, arrows, and paraphernalia to go with them all. My throat filled with vomit. Their army was real. This wasn't any metaphorical Christian crusade, and it wasn't some faceless group hidden away in the mountains of the Middle East. This was David Koresh meets Timothy-freaking-McVeigh times one thousand. I put my fist to my mouth.

"What do you think?" Tom said, his mouth close to my hair.

I jumped away from him. "Scary."

He laughed. "Don't worry. I'm going to protect you."

I backed out of the room. "Th-th-thank you." As I backed up, I overshot the hall and bumped into a swinging door behind me. A hissing and rattling sound sent chills up my spine. I knew that sound all too well, and I didn't want to see the source, but I turned anyway. The room was much smaller than the armory, but twice as terrifying. I was a foot away from a snake pit that ran the length of the room. Cages of snakes filled the walls on either end. Literally, I was in a den of serpents.

I screamed, and Tom's laughter echoed louder than my cry.

"They're not going to get you." He pulled me from the room, then waved back into it. "Sister Furman grew up with snake handlers, and she keeps them for sentimental reasons."

"Snakes," I said weakly and unnecessarily. "She uses snakes."

"Only sometimes. But they milk them of their venom before they take them out."

"I don't feel so good," I whispered.

"Brother Tom, Sister." Sister Furman walked briskly past us. "We're starting now."

He snapped his fingers. "Rats. No time to show you the ceremonial room." He pointed farther down the hall. "Come on," Tom said. "There's a water fountain just ahead. You can splash cold water on your face."

I did, and then followed him into yet another room. This one was a sanctuary, a little underground church. It looked almost just like the one I'd attended above ground the Sunday before, only smaller. The men I'd met Wednesday were already inside, seated in two rows. I counted heads. Six men. When I'd entered the room Wednesday night, there'd only been five. Until Jack showed up. I counted again. Yes, six men, and one of them had the dark brown hair curling at the neck that I loved to press my face against in bed at night.

Jack.

At least there was one other sane person in this place, even if we were no match for this group and its arsenal of weaponry. But why was he here? Had he followed me again? Had he just decided to be here in case I showed up? A warmth spread through me, all the way to the tips of my toes and the top of my head. Maybe he was here for the same reason I was, because of Betsy, because he cared about her and the other kids. Maybe we were both trying to bring down Mighty is His Word to save the kids! He didn't turn around, hadn't seen me as far as I could tell, but I felt tons better anyway.

Sister Furman swept the few paces to the lectern in long strides. Brother Tom and I took a seat in the row behind Jack.

"Welcome, new members." She opened her arms to us as if to embrace the room.

I showed my teeth in something I hoped looked like a smile, holding back the bile.

Her voice rang with authority and sent shivers up my scalp. "As you are all beginning your story with Mighty is His Word, as its founder, I'm going to share mine with you."

Heads nodded in front of me, except for Jack's.

"I was called to the Lord at a young age, when I quickly learned that the people around me were far from godly. The God of my youth was fire and brimstone, wrath and judgment, but his followers were mealy-mouthed weaklings with spines of Jell-O. I made a promise to the Lord that I would be different, that I would lead a congregation of truly godly men and women. And then I met my husband. Brother Furman and I started a little church in New Mexico. We were blessed with one son, Richie, who was preaching the gospel before he was ten." She stopped to wipe a tear from her eye. "When he was just eighteen, he brought the Wrath of God down on a pit of vipers: abortionists who were killing thousands of babies every year." She stopped again, waging a battle to control her emotions.

I'd heard part of this story before, but still I was riveted.

Her jaw muscles twitched. "He was judged guilty by men, but not by God. Satan moved through that courtroom in the form of a prosecutor who had no godliness in him at all."

Suddenly, I got a really bad feeling. New Mexico. Prosecutor. A deathly coldness enveloped me.

"He asked for the death penalty for our son, our hero of God who saved unborn babies and the souls of their mothers from eternal hell. He asked for the death penalty for my *child*." Her voice rose to a howl on the last word.

A murmuring rose amongst the men in front of me, but Jack was silent.

My heart hammered. Please God, let her not be talking about Jack. Please, please, God, not Jack.

"He's here today."

Angry sounds echoed in the room.

"He's here—like Satan—under false pretenses. He thinks we don't remember him, but how could we ever forget? My son, Richie, is dead because of him."

And to my horror, Jack got to his feet. Slowly, deliberately.

His voice was calm, almost conversational. "Just as I can never forget that it's because of you, Paige Furman, that my wife, son, and daughter are dead, from the car bomb you set for me."

THIRTY-TWO

"Ah, Jack Holden, an eye for eye, no?" Paige Furman walked from the podium up the center aisle. We all watched her. I was afraid to even blink.

My brain sent me an image of the words I didn't want to remember, written on the envelope I'd found a few days before in Jack's office: *Paige, Thur, 8 a.m.* Suddenly it all made sense, and shame flooded through me, adding a pungency to my sharp terror. This woman had tried to kill Jack. She'd murdered his family. What would she do with him now, and me with no cell phone to call for help, my gun locked in my glove box fifty feet above ground? I was a horrible person, because it was pretty clear why Jack had been absent of late: he was trying to find the killer of his family. He'd told me he was on an old case. And Clyde's words came back to me. Jack was onto something, a completely new direction. New, away from his old suspicions about Burt Wilde. And how had I acted? I'd thrown a fit, moved out, and hadn't even returned Jack's calls, when all he was guilty of was honor and caring. Whether he loved me or not, he was a great man, and he didn't deserve my behavior.

Another thought crept in, guilty and unbidden. If they'd figured out Jack's identity, did they know who I really was, too? Was I next? If so, there'd be no one left to rescue the Mighty is His Word foster kids, no one to take in Greg, no one to exonerate Phil. Real nausea came back over me, and I literally gagged. My back bowed up as I did, and I clapped my hand over my mouth.

Brother Tom stared at me.

My eyes watered. I whispered, "I'm going to throw up."

"Are you always this sickly?" he hissed.

It's not me, it's y'all, I wanted to tell him. I settled for, "Never."

"Do you need more water?"

I shook my head, careful not to jostle myself. "Gonna throw up any second."

His eyes made huge Os, and I realized he was scared. "You can't interrupt her."

I heaved and gagged, but I held it in.

Paige's feverish eyes lit on me, but flitted away as fast. "Obviously, 'Brother Dave' won't be joining our membership. But I ask you, what would you *members,* as true soldiers of God, do to an enemy, Satan's own in our midst?"

I prayed Jack had a plan. Surely he hadn't come down here without one. He probably had a weapon. A connection to the outside world, beaming everything Paige said to a local TV station. He wouldn't have just come down here, would he? No one would be that foolish.

But I had been. I had come to gather information. If I'd taken this crazy risk because of love for Betsy and the other kids, for Phil and Nadine, what would Jack do to avenge his wife and children? A moan in my head turned to a shriek that blocked out all sound for a moment. My eyes darted around the room, searching for signs that the sounds in my head were escaping from my mouth, but no one looked at me.

Voices around me were answering Paige.

"Lock him up," one of my retreat mates suggested.

Paige snorted.

Young Tattoo Guy said, "Finish what you started."

Paige nodded, acting thoughtful. "It's a thought. But we're a democracy, so it comes down to a vote. Like a jury trial. With you all as the jury, unanimous and beyond a reasonable doubt, to finish his execution. Or not."

I had to get out of this vote, and I had to find a way to go for help. Instead of trying to hold back my nausea, I started contracting my throat muscles to stimulate my gag reflex. It only took a little bit to push my bile over the edge. I hurled vomit all over Brother Tom and myself.

Tom hustled me to the dormitory. I kept moaning, "Sorry, so sorry, of all the times for a stomach bug," over and over, but he didn't answer.

When we got to the dorm wing, he ducked into the female side.

"Maybe I'll feel better if I lie down for a little while."

He was brusque. "There's clothes for you to change into here," he said, pointing at drawers under one of the bottom beds among the many bunk beds in the room. "Shower's in the bathroom, and there are toiletries."

"Thank you so much. I should probably clean up and get out of here before I give the stomach flu to everyone."

He glowered at me. "Stay in here."

"But—"

"Leaving isn't possible. Once you enter the retreat, you stay through the end. No exceptions."

Tears welled in my eyes. "I think I'm going to be sick again."

He pointed to the bathroom and I ran into it, shutting the door behind me. I flung myself into a stall and stuck my finger down my throat to help things along. After, I started sobbing, as best as I could fake. "I'm so dizzy. I'm not even sure I can stand up in the shower."

From the door, Tom's voice sounded tight, almost panicked. "I've got to get changed and get back. Don't leave the room until someone comes for you."

"I don't understand."

"We have rules, Sister Cecilia. Once you enter our compound, you follow our rules."

I whined, "Okay, Brother Tom."

"Good. I'll be back in an hour or so. Please be cleaned up and do your best to be ready to rejoin the others by then."

I summoned the most pitiful voice I had, childlike and submissive. "Yes, Brother Tom."

His footsteps were loud in his jackboots. As soon as he was gone, I splashed my face with water, ripped off my boots and clothes, and ran back into the bedroom. I threw open the drawers and found blue drawstring pants and shell tops, like dental hygienists and nurses wore. I jerked them on my body, cinching the enormous pants tight, and I tugged my boots back over my feet. Meanwhile, my brain was racing. I needed to call for help. But how?

I looked both ways out the hall and saw no one. The men's dorm was across from me, and from within it I heard voices. Tom's and another man's.

"I hate to admit it, but there's something fishy about her, Brother Harvey."

The second man—Harvey the guard?—said, "I tried to check her phone but it's password protected. I could run her plates."

"Do it."

If there'd been anything left in my stomach, I would have tossed it at those words. It wouldn't take them long to find out Cecilia Hodges didn't exist. As quietly as I could manage in my boots, I sprinted to the right, throwing open doors and searching for any kind of technology to connect me to the outside world. I came upon a control room with computers jammed end to end. I scanned them. They seemed to operate all the utilities and services. No phones, though. I jiggled a mouse and a screen came to life. I clicked on the task bar to see if there was an Internet connection and opened Google Chrome. It came to life, connecting lightning fast. I thought about the fastest way to get help. I needed to text, something people would see immediately. I entered a search for texting apps, my fingers mistyping as adrenaline coursed through them, but I backed up and retyped, breathing through my nose and out my mouth until I found one. I snuck glances over my shoulder every few seconds as it loaded up. "Come on, come *on*," I whispered. Two minutes later I had an account but the only phone number I knew by heart was my father's. I'd be sending a message to a man who couldn't even sext without accidentally sending it to his daughter.

I typed as fast as I could. *Dad: Emergency. Jack is here. We're in an underground facility below the houses. I am afraid they're going to kill us. Call Officer John Burrows.Send help.*

I clicked send. No time to wait around to make sure he got it. Now, to get my gun.

Again I checked the halls both ways, then sprinted toward the stairs. I raced up them, winded. I pulled the latch for the trap door and pushed upward. Nothing happened. I did it again and again. It wouldn't budge.

"No. No, no, no!" I said.

Before me was an electronic keypad, just like the one outside the armory. I remembered Tom punching a series of keys, the door releasing with a click before he pushed it open. And that he'd done it before the hatch opened for us to come down here as well.

I couldn't get out without the code.

I needed that code, and I needed a weapon. I couldn't get past the keypad in the armory without a code either, so their guns were out. But they had a kitchen. Kitchens had knives. I broke into a run down the stairs and back down the corridor. A woman exited the dorm, and we plowed into each other. She hit the ground. I didn't.

"Sorry," I grunted, then gave her a hand up. "Are you all right?"

"Only my pride was hurt." She smiled. "I didn't know there were other women here today. My fault. Not looking where I was going," she said. "Are you a new member here for the retreat?"

"Um, yes, but I got sick all over myself. Stomach bug. Probably contagious." I backed away.

"It's going around. Can I get you anything?"

"I'm on my way to the cafeteria for a drink, while I'm feeling a bit better." I patted my stomach. "Nothing left, you know."

"I'm Sister Barb. Staying here this weekend doing some prayer warrior work while it's quiet. It was a madhouse for Easter. Nice to have most of the place to myself."

A talker. I edged away, careful not to run again since I'd just reclaimed my illness. "Thanks Barb, nice to meet you."

"Wait, what's your name?"

I ducked into the entrance to the cafeteria without answering her. From the odors wafting from the kitchen, lunch today was barbecue. The tables were all empty so I stole into the chow line. In the kitchen, vents roared like jet airplanes, sucking the odors, fumes, and smoke up from the cook surfaces into an enormous duct system. No food was displayed on the line yet, and the trays and utensils weren't out. I could see a man stirring a tall pot and a woman basting something in an oven. Between them and me was a chopping station, unmanned. Rings of onions lay on a cutting board and beside them a medium-sized serrated knife. I sidled around the food line and over to the knife. My eyes on the cooks, I palmed the handle and stuck it behind my back.

The woman looked up. Her black eyes sparked. "Hey, no one allowed back here except authorized kitchen staff."

I put the back of my hand to my cheek. With my other hand I slipped the knife into the rear waistband of my drawstring pants and puffed my stomach out to hold it in place. "I'm desperate for some Gatorade or fruit juice. I've been sick."

She shook her long-handled basting brush. "All the more reason not to spread your germs around the food."

"I called out. No one answered. I guess my voice is just weak."

The man, heavyset and grizzled with yesterday's beard, put down his spoon and went to a refrigerator. "Lighten up, Sister Grace." He took out a jug of cranberry juice and poured it into a glass. "Here you go." He brought it to me.

"Thank you so much."

"You're welcome. Now quit contaminating our kitchen, Sister." He winked.

I smiled. "God bless you." I sipped the juice as I departed. As soon as I was out of their range of vision, I stopped, stuck the knife point-up in my boot, and tossed the juice in the trash.

I had a weapon now, of sorts, and I needed to know what I was up against. I snuck through the connecting corridor to the center wing. Earlier we'd been in the sanctuary, to the right. The sounds now came from past the armory, maybe from what Tom had called the ceremonial room. I tiptoed as I made my way toward the voices. Above me was a large network of ducts of some sort. They cut through the snake room, which backed up to the kitchen. Were they pumping stuff in or out? No time to think about it now. I pressed my back against the wall outside the ceremonial room and listened intently to Sister Furman's voice while my eyes traced the ducts on the ceiling, leading to the inside of the room.

"Jack Holden, a jury of your betters has found you guilty of Satan's work beyond a reasonable doubt and unanimously sentenced you to death. As the judge, I am handing down the method of your execution, the most fitting I can imagine. We will burn him at the stake."

Chet—Buzz Cut—shouted. "Burning at the stake? Can't you just take him out back and shoot him? Seems a little extreme."

There were murmurs of agreement.

"Silence!" Paige shouted. "Could there be a greater heretic than this man who is the embodiment of Satan, who executes those carrying out our work—God's work?"

The room grew deathly quiet.

Paige spoke again in a softer voice. "Jack Holden, do you have anything you wish to say to your jury?"

Jack's voice was strong. "This is a kangaroo court and what you're doing here today is against the laws of the United States. You'll all be spending the rest of your lives in jail for even conspiring together to do it."

Paige laughed. "Counselor, you're not in the United States of America. You're under it. No one is coming to your rescue."

"A conspiracy is only as strong as its weakest member. One of you will rat the others out. If not today, then later."

There was a stir, and one of the men said, "The weak one is you." Then, "Pay, my love, God has spoken. Richie will be avenged. It's time to make it so." Brother Lawrence Furman, I realized.

I heard scuffling noises.

"What the hell?" This from Jack.

Lawrence said, "Bind Mr. Holden."

More scuffling, but from Jack, I heard nothing.

Paige's voice said, "Mr. Holden, I believe you recognize my friend here."

"I do," Jack said, from farther away.

"He's going to be given the privilege of lighting the pyre today."

A male voice spoke, one I knew and hated. Knew and feared. "Sister Furman, I'm honored."

"Of course, Brother Trevon. We can't thank you enough for carrying out the Lord's work in Amarillo, and for bringing the Wrath of God down on our enemies. Jack, you'll find this interesting, I think. Brother Trevon is the one who killed your client's friend. What was his name, Brother Trevon?"

"Abel Stone, the traitor to Mighty is His Word?"

"No, the other one."

"Dennis Welch."

"Yes, Dennis Welch. It was an accident, but it served its purpose. The real goal was putting that degenerate Phil Escalante out of business, to stop him from promoting fornication outside of marriage and selling smut. But it turned out that Mr. Welch was the co-owner of a piece of property that was going to be used as a retreat for sexual deviants right across the road from where we are here doing the Lord's bidding. God works his will in mysterious ways, doesn't he?"

I reached for the knife in my boot, ready to bust in, but as frantic as I was, I knew it was futile. There were six, seven, eight, or maybe more men in there in addition to Paige. I leaned frozen against the wall, trying desperately to think of a way to stop them. I craned my head around the opening and what I saw I'll never forget. The other five new members were binding Jack to a wooden cross. Piled up around his feet were boards and logs. Tom was sloshing a bottle of lighter fluid on him. And, as I watched, Trevon was hefting a torch dripping some liquid from its end, mercifully still unlit. Paige and Lawrence stood together, their hands clasped tightly.

Everyone's attention was focused on Jack. Could I run in and set him free, wielding only a knife? And then it finally dawned on me. I did have weapons at my disposal, right across the hall.

THIRTY-THREE

The snakes hissed and writhed in the pit.

Across the hall, Paige led the men in a prayer. I scanned the room and found exactly what I needed. Elbow-length snake gloves, which I pulled quickly over my shaking hands. A long-handle noose, a hook, and a lined bag.

I turned to the reptiles. The pit scared me almost as badly as what was happening to Jack. But the cages on the sidewalls held individual snakes. I flung the bag over my arm, stuck the hook in the side of a cage, pinning the head of a large rattler. With my other hand I slipped a noose over its head and, when it was snug, released the hook. It hissed at me and shook its rattles with force, snapping at me again and again. It was clumsy-going with the gloves on, but I opened the bag, positioned it in front of the door, unfastened the latch, and pulled the snake out with the noose into the bag. I cinched the bag shut, releasing the tension on the noose and drawing it off the snake's head and out of the bag. Working carefully, I added two more big rattlers then grabbed the bag closed by the neck and dragged it across the hall behind me at a gallop, sucking in a huge breath for courage as I ran.

"Amen," Paige said.

Tom held a lighter to Trevon's torch. Whoosh. Flames leapt from the business end and Trevon walked toward Jack. Jack's head lolled slightly, and his eyes looked glassy even from twenty feet away. I remembered his *What the hell?* They'd probably injected him with a tranquilizer. A wall of kindling formed a semicircle a few feet in front of him. Trevon stepped over the kindling and held the torch to the pile at Jack's feet. Another whoosh, and the fire sprang to life.

I stormed forward as Trevon lit the kindling line separating Jack from the others. It surged to life, a wall of fire one foot high and growing. Smoke rose from it toward the ceiling, and I barely registered it being sucked into the ducts I'd wondered about moments before. I barreled my body into his, knocking him over into the flames. I landed in them as well, but on my feet, and I danced away. Trevon screamed. So far, although the flames licked at his feet, Jack made no sound. Without a second's hesitation, I rushed Paige before she could process what I was doing. I kept my eyes only on her as I charged, screaming at the top of my lungs. She stumbled back over the kindling line, and I released the opening of the snake bag and grabbed its base, shaking the snakes out over her feet as I backed away.

"Pay!" Lawrence shouted, running toward her.

Her shriek was epic as she hit the ground. Trevon saw the snakes on her, and he stumbled to his feet and ran to her, his clothes on fire, getting to her just as Lawrence did. I ignored them all and jumped through the now two-foot-high wall of fire toward Jack. I ripped off one glove and pulled the knife from my boot. Then I shoved my gloved hand down into the flames to cut the ropes around his ankles. The heat from the fire was intense. Moving faster than I had ever moved in my goat-tying rodeo days, I slit the rope around his wrists, then his waist, then his neck, and he was free. He slumped partially over onto my shoulder. I propped an arm under his and around his back

"Let's go," I shouted, dragging a stumbling Jack with me, running clumsily through the fire and then the line of dazed men as they crowded toward Trevon and Paige, whose anguished screams pierced the air.

"Left," I said, and pulled Jack into the hall. "We need a code to get out. I don't have it." My words came between huffs.

"Stop," a man's voice shouted. "I know who you are, Emily Bernal."

I snuck a glance back. It was Harvey from the guard shack.

"She works for the attorney that had Richie killed," Harvey shouted.

Not good. I cut left down the connecting hall to the office wing, Jack dragging on me like an anchor. Bullets ricocheted in the hall we'd just exited.

"I sent messages for the cavalry," I puffed, "but I don't know if anyone got them."

"Saf yerbreath," Jack said, slurring his words.

We cut right down the office hall, and again shots pinged as they bounced from wall to wall.

"In here." I shoved Jack into an office and shut the door. I threw the lock and noticed a drop bar and hooks. I worked the bar home, barricading the door.

I looked around me, recognizing Paige's office.

Jack was shaking his head, trying to wake up. "Wha' now?"

"We look for a code. For guns. For explosives. A phone."

We both started pawing through papers and drawers, one of us faster and with more coordination than the other.

"Open up," a man's voice commanded, and someone started beating the door—bam! bam! bam! Then a shot was fired, and the same voice said, "No, you idiot, the door's bulletproof."

"Bull-a-prufe. 'S good," Jack said and slumped to a seat in Paige's desk chair.

"Yes, 's good." I shook my head. "What were you doing down here with no backup anyway? Didn't you know they'd figure out who you were? It's not like you're some schmo off the street to them, for God's sake."

He nodded, his head like a puppet on a string. "I's wearing a wire. 'Fraid 'snot working. 'Sides, I got backup." He pointed at me, then his hand flopped back to his side.

That made sense. Jack may have been emotionally invested in his mission, but he was too smart to walk in here without cover. My eyes fell on his pants and feet. He was wearing worn work boots and heavy camo pants, which was a darn good thing. The fire had burned the top few layers off his boots, exposing red skin in a few places, and it had consumed his pants and leg hair up to his knees. His shins were burned, but not nearly as bad as I had expected.

I gestured toward his legs. "Your pants."

He grunted and over-enunciated, his mouth working hard to form his words. "Fire hose pants."

I nodded, my mind already returning to the problem at hand: getting us out of here alive. I felt trapped, desperate, witless. Delirious even. I didn't have the slightest clue what to do next, and Jack wasn't going to be any help. And in that moment, I remembered my father telling everyone at Wrong Turn Ranch about my spirit animal. Yeah, well, that was no help whatsoever. I snorted, then laughed. Spirit animal. It was as good as anything else at this point. Okay, I'd go with it. Jack squinted at me.

What would my spirit animal the fox do?

A calmness stole over me like a breath of wind, and with it a surprising clarity. A fox wouldn't use brute force and run back through his pursuers. He'd sneak out through a hole in the bramble so small that no one else would notice it. So the fox would be looking for the hole now. And why not?

Paige was paranoid. She'd built an underground military training camp, for goodness' sake. She would want a back door. But was that back door far down one of the corridors, past the armed warriors for God? Maybe. I didn't think so, though. She wouldn't take a chance that she couldn't get out.

"Jack, Paige would have another way out of here. We need to find it."

He grunted. "You smart." He smacked his face hard then grinned. "You ate pigsinna blanket."

He was like a drunken child and wasn't going to be much help, but I smiled as I got to work. "I'm currently re-evaluating my dietary restrictions."

Paige had built downward once before, so maybe she had again. I got on my hands and knees and felt for seams in the floor. Jack staggered up and started doing the same around the walls, even somehow moving the bookcase off one wall so he could search behind it. The banging on the door continued and I heard Tom say, "What about an ax?"

"Or fire?" someone else asked.

I moved my search to under Paige's desk, and I heard Jack climb up on it.

"Nothing on the ceiling," he said.

My hands found a soft spot under the edge of her desk. I pushed harder and it popped up to reveal a circular handle. Keeping my voice soft so the people outside couldn't hear me as well as I could hear them, I said, "Help me move the desk."

I heard Jack hop down, and then he plopped on the floor like a sack of potatoes. I peered out. "What's wrong?"

"Sleepy," he said. "Hey, your teeth." He tried to tap his, but he missed and poked himself in the nose.

"I brought a welding torch," a young male voice yelled, and then I heard the sound of it coming to life.

Red-hot panic gripped me. We needed to get out of there, and I realized I'd be dragging or carrying Jack. He wasn't a heavy man, but at over six feet he was a lot heavier than me. I'd carried and dragged and pulled and pushed animals twice his weight, though, and I could do it now if I had to. Certainly I could move a desk.

"It's okay. I can do it." I crawled out and tried to push it. It was solid wood and didn't budge. I leaned my tush against it, knees bent, and it slid an inch. After four more tries, I'd cleared the trap door, just barely. No code needed, thank God. I opened it, and a puff of stale, musty air hit my face. The opening revealed complete darkness.

"She'll have a flashlight," I said. I scrabbled through Paige's desk and found one. I switched it on. Nothing. "Spit in a well bucket!" I cried. I reached farther into the drawer and found batteries. I changed them quickly then tried it again. Light. I nearly wept.

I didn't love darkness, and I liked small enclosures even less. It wasn't quite a phobia, but it was a healthy fear. I'd hated crawling down the mineshaft on Wrong Turn Ranch when a dirty cop had kidnapped Greg and Farrah, but that had turned out okay, and I just had to have faith it would today, too. The last order of business before descending into the darkness: *Dear God, please let this tunnel be empty and leading to the right place. I'll owe you one. Amen.* I turned and saw Jack had slumped over against the credenza, out cold.

I squatted in front of him and shook him. "Jack, come on, Jack, wake up." Outside the blowtorch cut its first slice through the door.

Jack's eyes fanned a few times and then stayed open enough to focus on me. "Clyde," he said.

"Yes, I know, and I'm sorry about him and that we haven't been able to talk about it, but we're in trouble and we have to go, Jack." I had to wake him up, so I reared back and smacked him across the face. I almost smiled. *That's for not loving me, you big dummy,* I thought.

"I'm up, I'm up."

"Can you stand?"

He started trying to push up, and I got him to his hands and knees.

"We need to go down the ladder into this hole. Can you do that?"

He nodded. He stuck his head in the hole and before I could stop him, he tumbled head first into it.

"Jack!" I screamed.

From below me, I heard an "oof!"

"Are you okay?"

"Fine."

I scrambled down the ladder and trained the flashlight on him. He was face-first on the ground, his cheek in the dirt and his butt in the air, but he gave me a sideways thumbs-up.

I shined the light around the tunnel and found an electric panel. Of course. Sister Pay Furman would have all the best for her escape route. I flipped three switches up and lights came on down the tunnel. God had come through with light, and so far he was doing pretty good on the empty part, too.

"You've got to stand, Jack. I can help you, but we don't have much time." I leaned down to him and together we got him to his feet. I slung his arm over my shoulder. The tunnel wasn't wide, but we were able to shimmy through it with me slightly in front and him at an angle leaning on me and moving his feet in a clumsy trot.

Quickly Jack's weight grew heavier and his steps less coordinated. I heard a shout above us.

"They're gone."

Then Tom. "Down there!"

I saw a ladder ahead of us. "Just a little farther, Jack. We're almost there."

He answered, but his words were nonsensical. "Hershmalanepticallen."

I lowered him into a seated position by the ladder. I dropped the flashlight in his lap and climbed. The outline of an exit hatch above me was comforting, but if it required a code, we were done for. I could hear men's feet on the ladder two hundred feet away down the tunnel. I turned the latch to open the trap door.

"God, I forgot to ask for this one last thing, but I'll bet I don't even need to tell you what it is," I told him.

The mechanism clicked and I heard air release. A hydraulic lift opened the hatch to incredible, bright sunlight and flashing red and blue lights. A quick glance around told me that we were on the back patio of one of the manufactured homes, and standing right before me was a sight for sore eyes. Fists balled and chin high, feet in a fighter's stance, my father looked ready to take on the entire Mighty is His Word army.

"Daddy! Help me get Jack!"

"Sweet Pea!" He immediately moved to descend the ladder. "Get out, run. Now."

I hustled upward and was met by dark curls around a gorgeous tan face that was splotchy, red, and sweaty. Neon bicycle clothes. Black eyes frightened and fierce. Michele. Then another face appeared beside hers, pale and round and scrutinizing me under a shock of short-cut red hair.

John Burrows said, "Did someone call for the cavalry?" He grinned. "Hey, you liberated your chompers. Good call." And he disappeared down the hole after my father, shouting, "Police, drop your weapons and come out with your hands up."

THIRTY-FOUR

"I'm riding with him," I said, diving after Jack as the EMTs loaded his gurney into the back of the ambulance.

Jack sat up, and a paramedic immediately guided him back down with a hand on the shoulder. Jack protested. "I'm fine, you go with John. Do what needs doing."

"I can go with Jack, if they'll let me," Michele said. She'd been so awesome. I still couldn't believe she'd replied all to my text to let them know she had a hunch I was in trouble, and turned back for the compound leading the peloton of riders. It was her reply that had set Dad in motion long before I texted him. The bicyclists had ridden off in a group a few minutes before, back to their cars, but Michele had stayed.

"No, I'll go." Dad said. "Jack's family."

Torn, I couldn't help but watch John as he walked to his car. He needed to hear what had happened at the compound, all of it, about how it related to Phil, and about Melinda Stafford. If she had advance warning that I was onto her, what would she do? And if the Mighty is His Word parents learned of my knowledge and intentions about their foster children, what would they do? So much had to happen quickly, or everything could go very, very wrong.

"You're sure?" I said to Jack, squeezing his hand.

"I'm sure."

He might be less sure if he'd known John had asked me out. I wanted to tell him I loved him and that I was sorry for everything. I was, and I also wanted to throw my arms around him. But I wasn't going to do it. I'd been wrong to be upset with him, but I wasn't wrong to not want to settle for loving without being loved. I had to stand up for me, even if it hurt.

"Michele, you can come with me." It was Wallace's voice. "And, Emily, next time, you don't have to go to such extreme measures to prove a point." He put an arm around my shoulders and squeezed me.

"I won't, I promise."

"Come on, Michele. Looks like I've got a lot of work to do."

"Okay." She grabbed my face in both hands. "You're amazing."

I didn't know what to say, but I smiled at her. She turned and grabbed her borrowed bicycle, which had been laying in the dirt, and rolled it along after Wallace.

I stayed rooted in place. Tom was being marched by, and he glared at me, his hands cuffed behind him, a state trooper on either side of him. Police were everywhere, literally crawling in and out of the compound below, bringing the Mighty is His Word members to the surface. Between Jack arranging for backup and my texts to Dad and the rest of the free world, law enforcement had shown up in droves. There were officers here from the sheriff's department, Amarillo, Borger, Pampa, Fritch, and God knew where else, as well as federal agents, and still barely enough handcuffs to go around.

A gurney rolled by with Paige on it, only recognizable because her long gray braid hung off its side under the sheet over her face. With a jolt, I realized that she was dead because of me, that I'd killed her to save Jack. I looked up and my father caught my gaze, and held it. He nodded at me, and I flung myself into his arms. More EMTs rolled Trevon Hodges behind Paige, his eyes wide open and his mouth releasing a stream of invectives at Satan, Jack, me, and the world in general. Two officers escorted Lawrence, who was straining to catch up to his wife.

Jack's voice called. "Emily?"

My heart soared with hope. Dad released me, and I turned to Jack, open wide.

"Thank you. For what you did in there. You saved my life. You're something else."

And just like that, my heart plummeted to the earth like a rock. "Of course." I paused, giving him one more chance.

"Go get 'em, Tiger," he said.

I locked my jaw into place, propping up a quivering lip. "John, wait up," I called and whirled.

John waved to me. I broke into a trot, then a jog, and finally a furious run until I was safely ensconced in the front seat of his cruiser. We pulled away from the compound without speaking, but I felt John's eyes on me, the way they cared just a little too much. I looked over my right shoulder and into the face of a red fox standing by the gate. *Thank you for the wisdom, spirit animal. I could use some more now.* I waited, but the fox didn't channel me any epiphanies. John's eyes still flitted from the road to me, so intense I could feel his heart. Well, the day might come when I could return John's affection but for right now, my heart belonged to the one who didn't love me back.

By the time we'd passed through Sanford, I'd regained some equilibrium and filled John in on everything I knew to be true and most of what I'd guessed or was slowly pulling together. John got on the radio and set his cohorts at the Amarillo Police Department in motion vis-à-vis the Mighty is His Word flock's foster kids and their leadership. Melinda Stafford was a sticky issue, though, since she was on the side of law enforcement and my obstruction suspicions weren't corroborated. The most I really had on her was conflict of interest, which was just an issue with the state bar association. But finally, I remembered I had a lead: the guy who'd confronted Nadine and me at the storage unit, the same one who'd admitted he was a felon recently sprung by Melinda when I'd drunkenly encountered him at Hummers. APD had been able to pull records on someone named Ogletree, which matched the name on the shirt I'd seen him wearing at Hummers. Ten minutes later they'd rounded him up and threatened him with breaking and entering, burglary, destruction of property, and obstruction of justice. He'd handed over Melinda without blinking a lash, and APD had responded quickly to John with a plan for her arrest.

With all the activity on the radio about Mighty is His Word going down across the road from her Sanford property, Melinda and the rest of the ADA staff had to be working hard assisting the smaller Hutchinson and Moore county DA's offices with what was an unprecedented area law enforcement emergency. Just the same, officers moved into place around her home while John sped downtown to meet the rest of them for the trip up to the DA's offices.

We parked, and John handed me a windbreaker that said APD on the back. "Here."

"I'm going up with you?"

He nodded once, crisply. "Just stay out of the way."

"Thank you!" I slipped the jacket on as I got out and slammed my door.

Three officers stood waiting for us. Four APD for one ADA was quite a show of force, a strong message. They put their heads together, excluding me, then broke and marched inside with me in their wake. The security officer waved us by, thanks to a call-ahead from headquarters. We rode up the elevator in silence, and entered the DA's office the same way.

"Does the DA know we're coming?" I whispered to John.

He waggled his eyebrows. "Since about thirty seconds ago."

I grinned. We were moving like a well-oiled machine.

John walked to the receptionist, a horse-loving woman I felt an affinity for although we'd never had more conversation than hello and good-bye. "The DA should be expecting us. I'm John Burrows, APD."

She stared at him. I felt pretty sure this wasn't normal protocol. She picked up the phone and pressed a button. I heard someone speaking on the other end before she got out a word.

"Yes, sir," she said, and hung up. To John, she said, "He'll be right out."

We stood in a silent huddle, waiting, but not for long. The DA, a tall Hispanic man who I'd seen only in pictures, opened the door for Melinda. She saw the four officers, then me, and her face tightened.

John said, "Ms. Stafford, could you join us out by the elevators please?"

She glanced at her boss who nodded, his face stony. "Of course," she said.

"Thank you, Ms. Stafford. And you, sir," John said to the DA.

The DA nodded again, stoic. He whirled, and went back inside. Melinda swallowed hard and followed us into the elevator lobby. John led her out of the line of sight of the DA's reception area, a courtesy to a fellow law enforcement officer.

"Melinda Stafford, you're under arrest for obstruction of justice."

Melinda looked at me, and her eyes narrowed to angry slits. A female officer cuffed Melinda's hands in front of her. Another courtesy. John read Melinda her rights.

She didn't utter a single word.

"Any questions?" John asked her.

She shook her head. I had expected her to go down fighting like the woman I'd always known. It was anticlimactic, even disappointing.

Still, as I watched her skinny frame wobbling in her ridiculous shoes down the sidewalk and into the squad car with John's hand on her head to keep her from bumping it, I did a little fist pump and shouted, "Yes!"

THIRTY-FIVE

Judge Herring rapped his gavel so hard it rattled my head. "I said order, dammit, or I'm going to start picking winners from the gallery for a free night's room and board on the state." He pointed his gavel at the big metal door to the right of the defense table. It was a shortcut to an elevator down to the holding cells, and I'd seen him send plenty of people through that same door when they crossed him.

The rumbling, grumbling gallery grew deathly quiet. It was a big group that had gathered for our motion to dismiss the murder charge against Phil. The whole town was buzzing about our evidence, and even CNN was camped outside. Heck, everybody was buzzing about our ordeal the day before. Someone at the compound had snapped pictures and sent them to the news stations and the paper. Pictures of me. Of Jack. Of snakes and fire. And of those truly responsible for murdering Dennis and Abel and Jack's family, too. I can't say I was in love with people thinking of me wielding snakes like a Pentecostal serpent handler, but I guess it was in my blood, and a girl has to do what a girl has to do. Besides, my mother was over the moon about me finally pulling from her bag of tricks in going after the bad guys, and Dad and I had re-bonded over it, with no words exchanged.

Phil was still too ill to appear in court, so Jack sat alone at the defense table. His dark hair curling against his neck still needed a trim, and I still itched to touch it as I had in court a week before, just to confirm he was alive and real and right in front of me. I restrained myself, but my heart leaned toward him until it touched what my hand could and would not.

The last twenty-four hours had been intense. Jack's parents had driven in with Judith the night before. They'd raced to the hospital—where Jack recovered from his tranquilizer and had his burns treated—and beaten me there. Jack, Judith, and I worked side by side nonstop all morning and early afternoon on Friday, preparing to get Phil's case tossed. Except for the million times Jack had slipped out to take phone calls, but he was due a break from my suspicion and mistrust. We were so busy I didn't even have time to contact Wallace to let him know I intended to resume my fight to adopt Betsy, but I would, with a vengeance, come Monday.

While we were in the office, new information continued bombarding us: Clyde's services would be Saturday, and Jack would give the eulogy. Not only that, but Clyde had left a sizeable sum to me, of all people, although Jack already owned the practice, which he bought outright five years before. I still couldn't quite wrap my head around it all. Betty had called, as well, to let us know that Clyde's son had died a few days before. It turned out that he had changed his name to Abel Stone when he joined Mighty is His Word and disowned his father, just before he took a job waiting tables at Abuelo's. But he hadn't shed his father completely. Abel had tried to do the right thing for a defendant, and had gotten killed in front of me for trying. Millie Todd was one of the Mighty is His Word folks rounded up, and she'd taken a deal immediately, confessing to being the mole in Phil's swingers club and to lying about Phil arguing with Dennis to protect Trevon Hodges. Wallace had talked to Laura and Mickey. They were enthusiastic about Greg coming to live with me, and thus remaining in their lives. Wallace almost had state approval secured. I held back from telling him there was a better than even chance I was going to take the job in Dallas, that I had already looked into boarding for Legolas and a house with a yard for Chloe and—I hoped—Betsy someday; a place where I could get over Jack without having to spend every working day tortured by his lopsided smile, sparkling topaz eyes, and perfectly worn-in boots and jeans.

With all that was going on, there'd been no chance to talk with him privately. No chance to tell him what a numskull I'd been, how wrong it was to suspect him of silly things far beneath him. That I understood his need for justice, and respected him for getting it for his family. I needed to say these things to him, to clear the air, to set the stage for us both to move on.

From my right, Judith reached over and took my hand. "It's going to be okay, Emily. You'll see."

A huge lump choked off any words. We hadn't talked about it, but it didn't take a rocket scientist to realize she'd been helping Jack track down his family's killers, and why I wasn't the one for him to reach out to for it.

A hand patted my shoulder. I turned. Nadine had somehow slid into the crowded front row of seats. I raised my brows at her. She smiled back, her eyes tired but at peace for the first time in a long time.

Judge Herring's voice boomed. "Mr. Holden, I believe you have a motion to present?"

Jack stood, not as quickly as usual, but just as straight. "Yes, Your Honor."

"My condolences on the loss of Clyde Williams. A fine attorney, a great human being."

Jack's voice cracked. "Thank you, Your Honor."

Judge Herring turned to an ADA I'd never seen before: a short, slim man dressed on the cutting edge of courtroom fashion—which was considered highly suspect and certainly metrosexual in these parts. He looked Vietnamese. "Is the state ready? I'm sorry, but I can't remember your name."

"Willis. Willis Nguyen." He stood. "We are, Your Honor."

The judge waved his hand at Jack. "Proceed."

"Your Honor, in the case of the State versus Phil Escalante, we are presenting evidence in support of our motion to dismiss."

"Call your first witness."

"The defense calls Emily Bernal."

I don't recall walking to the witness stand, just the out-of-body feeling of standing in the box behind the microphone, peering out at Jack's golden eyes locked onto me, his head nodding ever so slightly in encouragement. He was close enough that I could smell him, that tantalizing mix of earth, sunshine, and manliness, and it made my heart beat even faster. I'd never testified before, and my voice shook when I gave my oath.

"Emily, did you have occasion to hear a confession about the death of Dennis Welch?"

"Yes, I did."

"Can you tell the court where and when this occurred, and relate the incident as you recall it?"

"Yes." I proceeded to lay it out for the judge, my heart hammering and my mouth dry as I described what had happened, what I'd heard, and Jack's near-death experience. Jack just let me talk, and the attorney for the DA's office didn't interrupt at all. Looking back, it seems like it took mere seconds, but at the time, I felt like I rambled on forever. One thing I do remember: there wasn't another sound in the courtroom the entire time I spoke.

"And you're absolutely sure about the individuals you've identified and the events you've described?"

"Yes. One hundred percent, Your Honor."

Jack inclined his head at the judge. "No more questions, Your Honor."

"Mr. Nguyen, would you like to cross-examine?"

Willis Nguyen stood. "Ms. Bernal, I wanted to personally thank you for your bravery and express to you and Mr. Holden"—he swung his head for his gaze to include Jack—"how glad we all are that the two of you are with us today."

Judge Herring raised his eyebrows and pursed his lips, nodding. "Thank you, counselor. Is that all?"

"Yes, sir." Nguyen sat.

"Are you new here?"

Nguyen scrambled back to his feet. "Yes, sir."

"Replacing Ms. . . ."

"Uh, yes. Ms. Stafford."

"Who I hear I should expect to see before me soon." The judge took off his glasses and mopped his eyes with the back of his hand. He muttered but we could still hear him on the front row. "Pot farm. Obstruction of justice. Tampering with evidence. She's lucky we don't still allow hangings." He took his time replacing the glasses on his face. "Where you from, Nguyen?"

"Formerly with the DA's office in Austin. Started here last week."

"Austin? Why ever would you leave Austin?"

Nguyen grinned. "My wife grew up here, sir. You can take the girl out of Amarillo—"

"But you can't take the Amarillo out of the girl. Yes, son, I know it. That's what brought me back here, too, a coupla hundred years ago." Judge Herring lifted his hand toward the defense table. "Ms. Bernal, I echo Mr. Nguyen's sentiments. Mr. Nguyen, you may take your seat."

"Thank you, Your Honor."

I walked past Jack to my seat behind him and as I passed he whispered, "Great job." I smiled at him, but all my adrenaline had drained away, and it felt like my cheeks could barely hold up the corners of my mouth. I collapsed into my seat, and Judith reclaimed my hand.

Jack entered a few Mighty is His Word member affidavits into evidence, bolstering my testimony. When he was done, he said, "That's all we've got, sir."

Herring crossed his arms. "Nguyen?"

"The state withdraws its opposition to the motion."

Herring released his arms and grabbed his gavel. "Motion granted." Whap. He banged his gavel onto the surface of his wooden desk.

Cheers echoed in the courtroom. It was a wonderful moment, even if I hadn't doubted what the outcome would be. Judith got swept into a hug with Nadine and me, and at first she pulled back but then laughed and folded in with us.

Whap. "Did I say I was finished?" Judge Herring bellowed. Whap.

Startled silence descended.

"First of all, since Mr. Escalante is still in the hospital, Mr. Holden, would you please extend my apologies and wishes for a full and speedy recovery?"

Jack was still behind the defense table, standing at attention. "Absolutely, Your Honor."

"Now, this is a little unusual for a Friday afternoon, but it's been a highly unusual day, so why not? Emily Bernal and Jack Holden, can you come forward please?"

I whipped my head to look at Judith. She shrugged. I got up and together Jack and I walked and stood before Judge Herring's bench, close enough that the heat from Jack's body warmed my skin, but he didn't so much as glance my way.

"Mr. Gray, earlier today you asked if I'd read an order in court. Can you bring it to me, please?"

Mr. Gray? As in Wallace Gray, my Wallace? I whirled. Wallace strutted through the swinging door between the gallery and the courtroom proper. He had a sly smile on his face as he swept past us and handed a piece of paper to the judge.

The Judge lowered his glasses farther down his nose and read to himself, his lips moving. He resumed speaking to Wallace. "Judge Matthews. She's good people."

"Yes, she is, Your Honor."

"Okay, it's late and I've got a lot left today, so I'll just skip to the good part. Emily Bernal and Jack Holden, you are hereby awarded full legal custody in the fostering of the minor child Greg Easley. By order of Judge Matthews and the state of Texas and all that blah blah blah. Oh, and you're also granted custody as adoptive parents of the minor child Betsy Perez."

"Emily." Betsy's voice pierced the silence following Judge Herring's pronouncement.

I turned toward it, and Greg led Betsy toward us. She hit the swinging door at full speed and jumped into my arms. Jack put his arms around both of us and pressed his face in to kiss Betsy's head. I extended mine out to draw in Greg, who was as gawky and nervous as I'd ever seen him. Jack's arms around us felt so right, and my heart as if it had wings. Betsy was ours. Betsy was mine. And Greg would be with us, too, part of the family, and still able to see his mother. So much good. So, so much good. I laughed and wiped my tears with one hand then leaned back in.

"Can I have a big hug?" Jack asked, grinning at Betsy.

She held her arms out to him, and he took her from me.

"Can I have one?" I said to Greg.

He leaned down and wrapped his arms around me, his face finding my shoulder. I felt wetness, and I rocked him from side to side.

I touched Jack's elbow and leaned toward him, not letting go of Greg. "Thank you, Jack. For making this possible."

He smiled at me and bounced Betsy into the air.

A ripping sensation tore through my heart. That. That pain was why I couldn't stay, no matter that Jack gave me a house or that Greg couldn't go with me to Dallas. No matter how badly I wanted to, I couldn't hurt this much all the time, could I? This kind of pain did terrible things to a person. Terrible, terrible things. The room started spinning. My legs felt like they were about to buckle. "I have to go," I said to no one in particular, almost as if I was in a dream.

"What?" Jack asked.

"I have to go." A bright light shone from the doors, drawing me toward it. The ground seemed foggy, and my feet were no longer a part of my body. They turned me toward the gallery. I didn't want to, but I released a wide-eyed Greg, following the light through the swinging doors.

WHAP! The gavel rapped so hard against the surface in front of Judge Herring that it sounded like a rifle shot, startling me. I found myself in the aisle between either side of the gallery. Whap! Whap! Whap! "Ms. Bernal, I haven't dismissed anyone. Where do you think you're going?"

Honestly, I wasn't sure. But it seemed I'd peeved off the toughest judge in Potter County, wherever it was. I had to make it better, even if it meant humiliating myself in a total breakdown in front of him. I rotated back toward him, slowly, and curtsied. "I'm sorry, Your Honor."

"Return to your position and don't move again until I say you can. You've been in here enough times to know I don't take contempt of court lightly."

I literally stumbled back through the gate and back to my spot in front of him, stepping inside my prairie skirt with my boots as I did and jerking the elastic waistband below my leather hip belt and halfway to my knees in front. Mother Mary Magdalene. I was wearing nothing but a pink satin thong under my skirt. Mortified, I snatched the skirt back up, and looked at a point on the floor halfway between the bench and me. The heat in my cheeks burned. I closed my eyes and licked my lips, adjusting the lace sleeves of my satin vested top. No one in the back saw a thing. Only the judge. And he could barely see anyway, if his glasses were any indication.

I glanced up. He was grinning ear-to-ear and winked at me. I cut my eyes back to the floor. How could this be the best and the worst day of my life all at once?

"Now, for the last unusual thing of the day. Bailiff, you can let our guests in now."

My eyes followed the bailiff as she strolled to the courtroom doors, although I cut them back and forth between her and the judge a few times, just to make sure I wasn't in trouble with him again. Jack set Betsy down, and she stood between us, as did Greg. I took Betsy's hand and hoped she'd help me stay upright. She reached for Greg's, and Jack took his other one.

I leaned in front of Betsy and Greg and whispered to Jack. "What's going on?"

The bailiff threw open the door. Jack ignored me, but the left side of his face slid up as his sexy dimple sunk into his cheek. His eyebrow rose toward his hairline, and my stomach flipped.

Katie Kovacs floated in wearing a really horrible peach taffeta dress several inches too short. My dress. My senior year prom dress. In front of her she held an enormous bouquet of daisies. I laughed aloud. Nick followed her, a little girl on each hip and a little boy holding on to his pants leg. Mickey came next, in a suit and a bolo. Laura and Farrah walked behind him, Farrah dragging Stella along by the hand. The procession seemed endless. My parents. Jack's parents. Ava, Rashidi, Collin, Michele. Clyde's nurse, Betty, who waggled her fingers at me, her smile sad. Wallace and Ethan fell in with them, as did Nadine and Judith. Everyone in the gallery was standing, smiling with all their teeth.

Jack finally leaned behind the kids to answer me. "You'll see. Hey, you're crying again."

My hands flew to my face and found the tears. "Yeah," I said, and I laughed and wiped them with the back of my hand.

Katie came through the gate to stand beside me. She handed me the flowers and I hugged her.

"I can't believe you're here," I choked out.

She just smiled and didn't say a word while she peeled Betsy away and behind us, Greg attached to the little girl by the hand.

Dad slipped in between Jack and me, and Mickey came to stand on the other side of Jack.

"Did you tell her?" Mickey asked Jack, handing Betsy a pillow with a ring on it.

That got her to let go of Greg. She touched the ring with her index finger, her eyes aglow. The gate swung shut behind Mickey, and the rest of our friends and family scooched into the gallery seats.

Jack shook his head at Mickey then took a deep breath. Without taking his eyes away from the judge he said, "I only want to marry you because I love you. No other reason."

I stared at his chiseled profile, then my mouth got the better of me before my brain could catch up. "You loved your wife. You didn't stop loving her because she died."

He faced me, and I saw the tears in his eyes to match mine. "No, but she's been gone a long time, and I love you."

"But why?"

He looked upward. "Sometimes I don't know." Then he grinned at me, completely lopsided, which made a tear roll down his cheek. "Because you leap before you look and shoot better than me and can rope a man while he's running and hold live rattlesnakes in your bare hands." He shook his head. "And because you're all I think about when you're not around, and when you left the other day, all the air left with you."

My heart pounded in my ears as I kept my gaze deep in his, so deep I could see his own heart beating inside, true and strong. A smile came to my lips, and I swear I saw a halo circling Jack's head like the rings of Jupiter. Either that or I'd lost my mind, but suddenly I was so completely sure that Jack was the one that my heart nearly exploded out of my chest.

"There it is."

"There what is?"

"That little thing I love." He pointed at my teeth.

I rewarded him with an even bigger smile. Then I frowned. "But why couldn't you just tell me before?"

Jack froze, mute.

Mickey saved him, his voice gentle. "Because if he spoke it out, he was afraid the universe would take you away from him, Emily."

Not Standing Hair this time. The tears rained down my cheeks. I wiped them away and couldn't help but check my bangs.

"You look perfect," Jack said.

I shook my head, smiling. "How'd you pull this off?"

That lopsided grin and dimple nearly distracted me from his answer. "A cell phone in a hospital bed, with a lot of really eager people who wanted to make this happen no matter how difficult."

Katie nudged me in the side with her elbow. I ignored her, but she did it again, so I looked at her, then back at the judge. His lips were moving but all I could hear was the blood against my eardrums.

"I'm sorry, what, Your Honor?" I said.

"I asked whether we had a wedding to perform here or not."

"Well, what will it be?" Jack said, but in his eyes I could see he already knew.

"I do," I said, and the sounds of the laughter of my friends and family wrapped around me for a tight squeeze.

"Order in the court. We haven't gotten to that part yet," Herring protested.

"And I haven't decided whether I'm giving her away." But Dad kissed me on the cheek and put my hand in Jack's, then stole away to sit by Mother.

"I do, too." Jack pulled me to him.

I batted my eyes and he laughed.

"Contempt of court." Herring sighed. "You may kiss the woman who will soon be your bride."

And so he did, in fr ont of God, half the population of Amarillo, and everyone we loved most.

Always for Eric

BOOKS BY THE AUTHOR

Fiction from SkipJack Publishing

The *What Doesn't Kill You* Series

Act One (WDKY Ensemble Prequel Novella): Exclusive to Subscribers

Saving Grace (Katie #1)

Leaving Annalise (Katie #2)

Finding Harmony (Katie #3)

Heaven to Betsy (Emily #1)

Earth to Emily (Emily #2)

Hell to Pay (Emily #3)

Going for Kona (Michele #1)

Fighting for Anna (Michele #2)

Searching for Dime Box (Michele #3)

Buckle Bunny (Maggie Prequel Novella)

Shock Jock (Maggie Prequel Short Story)

Live Wire (Maggie #1)

Sick Puppy (Maggie #2)

Dead Pile (Maggie #3)

The Essential Guide to the What Doesn't Kill You Series

The *Ava Butler Trilogy*: A Sexy Spin-off From *What Doesn't Kill You*

Bombshell (Ava #1)

Stunner (Ava #2)

Knockout (Ava #3)

The Patrick Flint Series

Switchback (Patrick Flint #1)

Snake Oil (Patrick Flint #2)

Sawbones (Patrick Flint #3)

Scapegoat (Patrick Flint #4)

Snaggle Tooth (Patrick Flint #5)

Stag Party (Patrick Flint #6)

Spark (Patrick Flint 1.5): Exclusive to subscribers

The What Doesn't Kill You Box Sets Series (50% off individual title retail)

The Complete Katie Connell Trilogy

The Complete Emily Bernal Trilogy

The Complete Michele Lopez Hanson Trilogy

The Complete Maggie Killian Trilogy

The Complete Ava Butler Trilogy

The Patrick Flint Box Set Series

The Patrick Flint Series Books #1-3

Juvenile Fiction

Poppy Needs a Puppy (Poppy & Petey #1)

Nonfiction from SkipJack Publishing

The Clark Kent Chronicles

Hot Flashes and Half Ironmans

How to Screw Up Your Kids

How to Screw Up Your Marriage

Puppalicious and Beyond

What Kind of Loser Indie Publishes,
and How Can I Be One, Too?

Audio, e-book, and paperback versions of most titles available.

Made in the USA
Columbia, SC
16 June 2022

61798832R00391